Jane Austen, Unabridged

The Complete Unpublished works and Private Letters of Jane Austen

Edited By

Sarah Melland

RMM
RIPE MELLAND MEDIA

Table of Contents

Introduction

Jane Austen is arguably one of the best English novelists of our time, known primarily for her six major novels, which interpret, critique and comment upon the British landed gentry at the end of the 18th century. Austen's plots often explore the dependence of women on marriage in the pursuit of favorable social standing and economic security. Her works critique the novels of sensibility of the second half of the 18th century and are part of the transition to 19th-century literary realism. Her use of biting irony, along with her realism, humor, and social commentary, have long earned her acclaim among critics, scholars, and popular audiences alike.

With the publication of *Sense and Sensibility* (1811), *Pride and Prejudice* (1813), *Mansfield Park* (1814) and *Emma* (1816), she achieved success as a published writer. She wrote two other novels, *Northbnger Abbey* and *Persuasion*, both published posthumously in 1818.

Her six full-length novels have rarely been out of print, although they were published anonymously and brought her moderate success and little fame during her lifetime. A significant transition in her posthumous reputation occurred in 1833, when her novels were republished in Richard Bentley's Standard Novels series, illustrated by Ferdinand Pickering, and sold as a set. They gradually gained wider acclaim and popular readership. In 1869, fifty-two years after her death, her nephew's publication of *A Memoir of Jane Austen* introduced a compelling version of her writing career and supposedly uneventful life to an eager audience.

Austen began another, eventually titled *Sanditon*, but died before its completion. She also left behind three volumes of juvenile writings in manuscript, the short epistolary novel *Lady Susan*, and another unfinished novel, *The Watsons*. These previous unpublished works are all here for your enjoyment. This edition also includes all of her private letters to really get into the psyche of Jane Austen and delve deeper into her personal life and what made the most prolific female writer of all time.

JUVENILIA

Juvenilia are childhood writings, works produced by an author or an artist in their youth. Three of Jane Austen's notebooks survive containing early short works in a variety of genres (stories, dramatic sketches, verses, moral fragments). The earliest pieces probably date from 1786 or 1787, around the time, aged 11 or 12, that Jane Austen left the Abbey House School in Reading. The latest dated entry is 'June 3d 1793', when she was 17. Two of the notebooks, *Volume the Second* and *Volume the Third*, are among the treasures of the British Library; *Volume the First* is held in the Bodleian Library, Oxford.

All three notebooks are confidential publications; that is, they are semi-public manuscripts intended for circulation and performance among family and friends. Unlike many teenage writings (then and now), these are not secret or agonized confessions entrusted to a private journal and for the writer's eyes alone. Rather, they are stories to be shared and admired by an audience; most are accompanied by an elaborate dedication to a family member or friend, and they are filled with allusions to shared jokes and events. These are sociable texts, produced by a precocious young writer showing off her talents and expecting to be admired.

Jane Austen's earliest writings appear to have little in common with the restrained and realistic society portrayed in her adult novels. By contrast, they are exuberantly expressionistic tales of sexual misdemeanor, of female drunkenness and violence. They are characterized by exaggerated sentiment and absurd adventures. Running through them is a pronounced thread of comment on and willful misreading of the literature of her day, showing how thoroughly and how early the activity of critical reading informed her character as a writer.

Her earliest writings are comic imitations or parodies of popular novels: of the classic *Sir Charles Grandison* by her favorite author Samuel Richardson; of Oliver Goldsmith's schoolroom textbook, *The History of England* (4 vols, 1771); of the essayists Joseph Addison and Samuel Johnson; and of the anthologies of moral pieces and 'Elegant Extracts' which formed the staple of young ladies' education 'The History of England ... The spoof history is consciously modelled on Goldsmith's *History*, with its prefatory hope that 'the reader will admit my impartiality' Goldsmith too includes medallion portraits of kings.

Common to all three notebooks is their portrayal of confident, willful, even rebellious young women: heroines like Charlotte Lutterell of 'Lesley Castle' (*Volume the Second*) and Catherine or Kitty, as she is usually styled, in the longer 'Kitty, or the Bower' in *Volume the Third*. Kitty is a more naturalistic figure than the farcical adventurers of the earlier tales but, like them, she is independent and outspoken

Jane Austen did not simply outgrow her juvenile notebooks. There is ample evidence that the same critical intelligence that created these satirical depictions of the conventions and stereotypes of late 18th-century fiction, conduct books and stage farce, continued to work within the more realistic framework of her mature novels. First drafts of books eventually published as *Sense and Sensibility, Pride and Prejudice* and *Northanger Abbey* were written soon after the last of the juvenilia. It is not too fanciful to find traces of the strong-minded heroines of these early experiments in Elizabeth Bennet's unladylike energy and Emma Woodhouse's dangerously undisciplined imagination.

*All of the works in this volume, since they are unpublished, have remained intact with no changes to grammatical errors and spelling.

Chronology of Jane Austen's Life

1775 — December 16: Jane Austen is born to George and Cassandra Austen at Steventon rectory. She is the seventh child and second daughter behind brothers James, George, Francis, Henry, Edward and sister Cassandra (not to be confused with her mother, also named Cassandra.

1779 — June: Charles John Austen was born.

1782 — The first theatrical presentation is performed by the Austen family in their home. **July:** James Austen matriculated at Oxford (St. John's), where her and Cassandra are under the care of Mrs. Cawley (sister of Dr. Cooper).

1783 — Jane and elder sister Cassandra leave for Mrs. Crawley's boarding school in Oxford for their formal education. The school is then moved to Southampton where Typhoid Fever breaks out. The girls are returned home. Jane nearly died there of a fever. **October:** Mrs. Cooper (her aunt) took the infection and died.

1784 — The Austen family performs Sheridan's *The Rivals*.

1785 — Jane and Cassandra arrive at the Abbey School in Reading.

1786 — Jane and Cassandra arrive back home from school, having completed their formal education. — Cousin Eliza Comtesse de Feuillide came to England.

1787 — It is believed that at about this time, Jane begins to write short stories and poems that later are collectively referred to as the *Juvenilia* and consists of three bound notebooks of works. — Jane Austen in France.

1788 — July: Henry Austen matriculated at Oxford (St. Johns). Francis Austen went to see.

1790 — Jane pens *Love and Friendship* and dedicates the work to cousin Eliza. It is believed that at about this time, she makes the conscious decision to write-for-profit and become a professional writer.

1791 — Edward Austen married Elizabeth Bridges.

1792 — March: James Austen married Anne Mathew.

1793 — Jane begins to write and later abandons a short play entitled *Sir Charles Grandison or the Happy Man*, a six-act comedy. That same year she also pens *Lady Susan*, an epistolary novel. **Monday, June 3rd:** Jane pens the poem *"Ode to Pity"* for her Juvenilia.

1795 — It is believed that before 1796, Jane read aloud to the Austen family her story entitled *Elinor and Marianne*. The versed Austen reader would know these to be the main characters in *Sense & Sensibility*. —Cassandra gets engaged to Thomas Fowle. **May:** Mrs. James Austen (Anne Mathew) dies. **December:** Nephew of nearby neighbor's Tom Lefroy places a visit to Steventon. It is believed that Jane very much fell in love with Tom based on her letters to Cassandra, indicating that the two had been spending a lot of time in one another's company. Tom is studying in London to become a barrister.

1796 — **January:** Tom Lefroy is taken away from Steventon and Jane by his family as the marriage arrangement is deemed highly impractical as both have no money. Jane will never see Tom again in her life. **August:** Jane begins penning *First Impressions*. This work would go on to become her most famous piece known more as *Pride & Prejudice*. **December:** Jane and sister Cassandra arrive back home for good from their formal education at boarding school. — Jane subscribed to *Camilla*. *Camilla* would ultimately attract 1058 subscribers, including Jane Austen, whose father, says family tradition, bought the copy for her. This was the first occasion in her lifetime that her name appeared in print.

1797 — **January:** James Austen Marries second wife, Mary Lloyd. **February:** Thomas Fowle died of fever in the West Indies. Work is completed on the first draft of *First Impressions* **Wednesday, November 1st:** Jane's father George Austen attempts to have one of Jane's works published for the first time. It is unknown whether Jane knew of this attempt but the request is denied by the publisher Thomas Cadell (of London). **November:** Jane redirects her efforts to revise *Elinor and Marianne*. **November:** The Austen girls pay a visit to their brother James and his wife at Bath. **December:** Henry Austen marries Eliza de Feuillide.

1798 — Jane completes her revisions of *Elinor and Marianne*. This revision removed the epistolary point of view and stages the story in the more traditional 3rd person perspective. Jane begins work on *Northanger Abbey* though it is initially known by the names of *Susan* and, later, *Catherine*. **August:** Jane's cousin Lady Williams (Jane Cooper) is killed in a carriage accident. Mrs. Knight gave up Godmesham to the Edward Austen (When Edward was twelve years old, he was presented to Thomas and Catherine Knight, who were relatives of his father and were wealthy. Thomas had given George Austen the living at Steventon in 1761. They were childless and took an interest in Edward, making him their legal heir in about 1783.)

1799 — Continues working on, and eventually revises, *Northanger Abbey*. **May:** Mother and Jane visit Bath.

1800 — Jane returns to Steventon and completes her short play *Sir Charles Grandison or the Happy Man*. Work is completed on *Susan*. **December:** Jane's father - George Austen - unexpectedly announces his retirement from the ministry. He uproots the family from Steventon and heads to Bath.

1801 — **January:** Jane visits good friends Catherine and Alethea Bigg in Hampshire at Manydown Park. **May:** Mr. Austen moves the family to Bath. **October:** The Austen's return from holiday in Sidmouth, Colyton and Steventon. —One of these holidays was to the sea-town of Lyme Regis. It has also been speculated that Jane is said to have met a young man who excited her interest. The two sisters had apparently been there together and had both become acquainted with an unidentified young man. Apparently, he enquired whether they might be returning the following year and they were all planning on meeting then again. Before that time, however, the unhappy news of the young man's untimely death reached the two sisters and so was the end of the potential love story.

1802 — **September:** Charles, Jane and Cassandra leave for Godmersham. **October:** Charles, Jane and Cassandra arrive home from their trip to Godmersham. **Thursday, November 25th:** Jane and Cassandra visit friends Catherine and Alethea Bigg at Manydown Park. **Thursday, December 2nd:** Jane Austen receives her only proposal of marriage from Harris Bigg-Wither, an "unattractive" Oxford educated young man and childhood friend and heir to a large family estate. Jane accepts the proposal for practical reasons. The very next day, however, Jane withdraws her acceptance, feeling it to be a mistake. **December:** Jane works on revising *Susan*.

1803 — With Jane's permission, brother Henry submits *Susan* (*Northanger Abbey)* to publisher Benjamin Crosby of Crosby & Company in London who buys the copyright for the work for 10 pounds. Crosby promises the book will be published but never fulfills his obligation. **September:** Mr. Austen and family (mother, Jane and Cassandra) once again spend time at Godmersham. **October:** The Austen's return to Bath from Godmersham.

1804 — Jane begins work on the novel *The Watsons*. It would go unfinished. Jane and family spend the summer months in Lyme Regis. **Sunday, December 16th:** Friend and mentor, Madam Lefroy, is killed in a freak horse riding accident. This is also Jane's 29th birthday.

1805 — **Monday, January 21st:** Jane's father George Austen dies suddenly from an illness, taking the family by complete surprise. Jane consciously stops work on *The Watsons*. The Austen brothers agree to help support the mother and sisters. The Austen girls are now forced to rent living quarters. **March:** Mrs. Austen, Jane and Cassandra move to 25 Gay Street. — Jane finishes writing *Lady Susan*.

1806 — **February:** Jane and Cassandra visit Manydown Park. **Wednesday, July 2nd:** The Austen girls leave for Bath. **Friday, August 5th:** The Austen girls join Mrs. Austen's cousin in Warwickshire. **Thursday, August 14th:** The Austen women leave Warwickshire. **October:** The Austen sisters and mother, along with friend and widow Martha Lloyd, move to Southampton to live with newly married brother Frank.

1807 — **March:** The group moves within Southampton to the Castle Square house.

1808 — **January:** Yet another visit to see the Bigg family. Jane takes part in one of the family theatricals called *"School for Scandal"*. **Friday, July 8th:** Jane is in Godmersham. **October:** Mrs. Edward Austen died there after the birth of her eleventh child, John. **Monday, October 24th:** Frank offers up a six-bedroom cottage (known as Chawton House) in Chawton near his estate for the women to permanently move into as their own home.

1809 — **Wednesday, April 5th:** Jane writes an angry letter (under the pseudonym Mrs. Ashley Dennis = M.A.D.) to publisher Benjamin Crosby and offers up a revised version of the manuscript for *Susan* to force Crosby's hand in publishing the work or returning it to her possession. Crosby claims that no timeline was ever set for the book's publication and as such Ms. Austen can continue waiting or purchase back the copyright for the novel. Without the means to do so, Jane cannot purchase the copyright. — Edward has Chawton Cottage remodeled for the Austen girls. **May:** The Austen women visit Edward in Godmersham. **Friday, July 7th:** Mother Cassandra, sister cassandra and Jane move into Chawton House to a quieter and settled life. **August:** Jane tackles *Sense & Sensibility* once more.

1810 — **July:** Jane and Cassandra visit the Biggs in Manydown once more. — *Sense & Sensibility* is accepted for publishing by Thomas Egerton.

1811 — **February:** Jane works on *Mansfield Park*. **March:** Jane visits Henry and wife Eliza in London. **Wednesday, October 30th:** *Sense & Sensibility* is published by Thomas Egerton with Henry Austen acting as literary agent. The novel is greeted with favorable reviews. — The last additions to the *Juvenilia* notebooks are believed to have been made at about this time. — Extensive revisions take place on *First Impressions*.

1812 — Much of the year is spent revising *First Impressions.* **November:** The copyright to *First Impressions* is sold to Thomas Egerton for publication for the sum of 110 pounds. — Death of Mrs. T. Knight. Edward Austen took the name of 'Knight.'

1813 — **Thursday, January 28th:** *Pride & Prejudice* is published by Thomas Egerton with Henry Austen acting as literary agent. Thanks to a large amount of resources put into advertising the piece, the novel is an instant success. **Thursday, April 22nd:** Jane leaves for London to attend to an ailing Eliza. Eliza dies just three days later, leaving Austen brother Henry a widower. **Saturday, May 1st:** Jane leaves her brother's side. **June:** *Mansfield Park* is believed to have been completed around this time. **September:** Jane visits Godmersham for the last time. **October:** A second edition of *Pride & Prejudice* is printed. **Saturday, October 2nd:** *Sense & Sensibility* in first edition form sells out completely, forcing a second edition to be printed. — Egerton takes on *Mansfield Park* for publication.

1814 — **January:** Jane begins writing *Emma*. **March:** Jane, escorted by brother Henry, visit London where they catch *'The Merchant of Venice'* at the theater. **Monday, May 9th:** *Mansfield Park* is Published by Thomas Egerton. Largely ignored by professional reviewers, the novel is nonetheless another success in the public square. The first edition sells out in a short six months. — Jane writes a letter to her niece, Fanny Knight, in response to relationship advice. Jane advises not to marry if the affection is not there. **May:** On behalf of his wife, Baverstock sued Edward Knight over possession of the Chawton and Godmersham estates, a real threat to the whole Austen family's financial security. **October:** All copies of *Mansfield Park* are sold making this the most profitable work of Austen's career thus far. **November:** Marriage of Anna Austen to Ben Lefroy.

1815 — **Wednesday, March 29th:** Jane completes *Emma*. **Tuesday, August 8th:** Jane begins writing *Persuasion.* — Henry and Jane head to London to negotiate with famed publisher John Murray for the publication of *Emma*. **Monday, November 13th:** Jane is invited to admirer Prince Regent's London residence at Carolton House by his librarian, James Stanier Clarke. The Prince makes a mention that Jane should include him in the dedication of her next work despite her (private) disgust of his moral character. With little choice, she reluctantly agrees to do so. **Saturday, December 16th:** Jane returns to Chawton (on her birthday). **December:** *Emma* is published by John Murray. The book is well received and sales thrive. The novel is dedicated to the Prince.

1816 — **January:** Henry Austen purchases the copyright to *Susan* back from Benjamin Crosby. The title is changed to *Catherine*. — A second edition of *Mansfield Park* is published by John Murray. **February:** Sales of the second edition of *Mansfield Park* do not meet expectations, negating the earnings from *Emma* that same year. **Saturday, March 16th:** Henry Austen's bank venture fails, forcing the Austen family into financial uncertainty and delaying the publications of *The Elliots* and *Catherine*. In addition to this, investments in a venture by brothers Edward, James and Frank are also lost. — At some point during the year, Jane becomes ill but disregards it to continue her work, namely on *The Elliots*. **May:** Cassandra takes Jane to Cheltenham to seek medical care. **June:** Cassandra and Jane return from Cheltenham. Jane continues work on *The Elliots*. **Thursday, July 18th:** Jane completes a first draft of *The Elliots* (later to become *Persuasion*). — Jane's health declines enough for her family to begin noticing she is unwell. **Tuesday, August 6th:** Jane rewrites the concluding two chapters of *The Elliots* and finishes the work.

1817 — **January:** Jane begins work on *The Brothers* (later published under the name of *Sanditon*). **Tuesday, March 18th:** Despite completing some 12 chapters of *The Brothers*, Jane is forced to stop due to her ever-increasing illness. Walking becomes a chore and nothing can be done without great difficulty and loss of energy. **April:** Jane's illness ultimately confines the author to her bed. **Sunday, April 27th:** Jane pens a short will. **Friday, July 18th:** Jane Austen dies in Winchester during the early part of the day. **Thursday, July 24th:** Jane is buried, at her brother Henry's direction, in an aisle of the nave at Winchester Cathedral. **December:** *Northanger Abbey* and *Persuasion* are published through John Murray as a set thanks to the direction of Henry and Cassandra. Henry pens a biographical note for the piece identifying for the first time that Jane Austen is the author of these works. Sales start strong but tail off.

1820 — John Murray destroys the remaining unsold copies of *Northanger Abbey* and *Persuasion*.

1832 — Richard Bentley purchases all of the remaining copyrights to Jane Austen's works. **December:** After a 12-year hiatus of no Austen works in publication, Bentley publishes all of the works in a collection of illustrated five-volume series known as the *Standard Novels*. Jane Austen's novels would never go out of print again.

1870 — Nephew James Austen publishes his memoirs entitled *"A Memoir of the Life of Jane Austen"* and brings Jane Austen's life and works to a greater audience, solidifying her place in literary history.

Random Fun and Interesting Facts

Jane Austen is arguably one of the most well-known English authors of all time! And for good reason. If you've read some of her books, you'll know what I'm talking about. She wrote some of the best romance novels of our time, but never married. Was she too much of a hopeless romantic?

- She was raised in a family that placed a high priority on education. Jane's parents sent her and her sister to a girls' boarding school, despite the fact that it was not compulsory for them to attend school.

- Her novels were published anonymously.

- She wrote a novel devoted to someone she hated.

- She never married, but she did accept and then reject a proposal.

- In fact, neither Austen sister ever married.

- She started writing as a young girl.

- She took a decade off from writing.

- She was mainly educated by her father.

- She wrote 6 novels in total.

- *Northanger Abbey, Sense and Sensibility, Pride and Prejudice, Mansfield Park, Emma, and Persuasion* were among the six novels she wrote during her lifetime. Four of them were published before her death.

- In a letter to her sister Cassandra after receiving the first print of *Pride and Prejudice*, she referred to the novel as her own "darling child."

- In 2013, it was reported that *Pride and Prejudice* had sold over 20 million copies worldwide in its 200 years.

- She continued to imagine how the lives of her characters evolved long after she finished a novel.

- Her father wrote a letter to Thomas Cadell of the London publisher Cadell & Davies in November 1797, giving him an early version of *Pride and Prejudice*. Cadell turned it down on the spot.

- Some of her most well-known books were almost given different titles.

- Her works are translated into over 40 languages.

❖ Many of her books have been made into films, some of which have been reimagined.

❖ Cassandra Elizabeth, Jane's sister, was her biggest confidant. Throughout their lives, they were extremely close with each other.

❖ The title of her most famous book *Pride and Prejudice*, was originally *First Impressions*.

❖ The influential and powerful Wentworth family of Yorkshire — which also intersects with Austen's own family tree — bears the surnames of many Austen characters.

❖ She brewed her own beer.

❖ To supplement the family's income, her father, a clergyman, ran a school for boys in the family home and parsonage.

❖ Her mother, Cassandra Leigh Austen, came from a higher social class than her father, and she provided her with the sense of social class that runs through many of her novels. Her mother didn't seem to mind her lower social status, and she was a happy wife and mother to her family.

❖ Tom Lefroy is a name that comes up often when discussing Austen's love life. The Irishman had relatives who lived in a village near Austen's home. She described him to Cassandra as "a very gentlemanlike, good-looking, pleasant young man." Scholars argue whether their relationship was merely a fling or a true love affair.

❖ Jane Austen, according to Andrew Norman, biographer and author of Jane Austen: An Unrequited Love, may have also fallen in love with a clergyman named Samuel Blackall, whom she met while on vacation in Devon. According to Norman, Austen references this man in many letters. According to the biographer, this relationship caused a temporary conflict between Austen and her sister because they were both competing for his affection.

❖ She spent much time in a bath – a resort town in the south of England – which is often mentioned in her writing.

❖ Charlotte Brontë and Mark Twain were definitely not her fans.

❖ She was the first female author to be portrayed on British currency in 2017.

❖ She started to suffer from a crippling and painful condition around 1816, which she never received a diagnosis for. Addison's Disease, a tubercular disease of the kidneys, is now thought to be the cause. She was buried in Winchester Cathedral.

❖ She only mentioned three people in her will – her brother Henry, her sister Cassandra and strangely Madame Bigeon, the secretary of Henry's late wife.

❖ Austen's novels made her very little money, and she died with only a small estate.

Private Letters of Jane Austen.

I.

STEVENTON, Thursday (January 16, 1796).

I HAVE just received yours and Mary's letter, and I thank you both, though their contents might have been more agreeable. I do not at all expect to see you on Tuesday, since matters have fallen out so unpleasantly; and if you are not able to return till after that day, it will hardly be possible for us to send for you before Saturday, though for my own part I care so little about the ball that it would be no sacrifice to me to give it up for the sake of seeing you two days earlier. We are extremely sorry for poor Eliza's illness. I trust, however, that she has continued to recover since you wrote, and that you will none of you be the worse for your attendance on her. What a good-for-nothing fellow Charles is to bespeak the stockings! I hope he will be too hot all the rest of his life for it! I sent you a letter yesterday to Ibthorp, which I suppose you will not receive at Kintbury. It was not very long or very witty, and therefore if you never receive it, it does not much signify. I wrote principally to tell you that the Coopers were arrived and in good health. The little boy is very like Dr. Cooper, and the little girl is to resemble Jane, they say.

Our party to Ashe to-morrow night will consist of Edward Cooper, James (for a ball is nothing without him), Buller, who is now staying with us, and I. I look forward with great impatience to it, as I rather expect to receive an offer from my friend in the course of the evening. I shall refuse him, however, unless he promises to give away his white coat.

I am very much flattered by your commendation of my last letter, for I write only for fame, and without any view to pecuniary emolument.

Edward is gone to spend the day with his friend, John Lyford, and does not return till to-morrow. Anna is now here; she came up in her chaise to spend the day with her young cousins, but she does not much take to them or to anything about them, except Caroline's spinning-wheel. I am very glad to find from Mary that Mr. and Mrs. Fowle are pleased with you. I hope you will continue to give satisfaction.

How impertinent you are to write to me about Tom, as if I had not opportunities of hearing from him myself! The last letter that I received from him was dated on Friday, 8th, and he told me that if the wind should be favorable on Sunday, which it proved to be, they were to sail from Falmouth on that day. By this time, therefore, they are at Barbadoes, I suppose. The Rivers are still at Manydown, and are to be at Ashe to-morrow. I intended to call on the Miss Biggs yesterday had the weather been tolerable. Caroline, Anna, and I have just been devouring some cold souse, and it would be difficult to say which enjoyed it most.

Tell Mary that I make over Mr. Heartley and all his estate to her for her sole use and benefit in future, and not only him, but all my other admirers into the bargain wherever she can find them, even the kiss which C. Powlett wanted to give me, as I mean to confine myself in future to Mr. Tom Lefroy, for whom I don't care sixpence. Assure her also, as a last and indubitable proof of Warren's indifference to me, that he actually drew that gentleman's picture for me, and delivered it to me without a sigh.

Friday.—At length the day is come on which I am to flirt my last with Tom Lefroy, and when you receive this it will be over. My tears flow as I write at the melancholy idea. Wm. Chute called here yesterday. I wonder what he means by being so civil. There is a report that Tom is going to be married to a Lichfield lass. John Lyford and his sister bring Edward home to-day, dine with us, and we shall all go together to Ashe. I understand that we are to draw for partners. I shall be extremely impatient to hear from you again, that I may know how Eliza is, and when you are to return.

With best love, etc., I am affectionately yours,
J. AUSTEN.

Miss AUSTEN,
The Rev. Mr. Fowle's, Kintbury, Newbury

II.

CORK STREET, Tuesday morn (August, 1796).

MY DEAR CASSANDRA,—Here I am once more in this scene of dissipation and vice, and I begin already to find my morals corrupted. We reached Staines yesterday, I do not (know) when, without suffering so much from the heat as I had hoped to do. We set off again this morning at seven o'clock, and had a very pleasant drive, as the morning was cloudy and perfectly cool. I came all the way in the chaise from Hertford Bridge.

Edward[1] and Frank[2] are both gone out to seek their fortunes; the latter is to return soon and help us seek ours. The former we shall never see again. We are to be at Astley's to-night, which I am glad of. Edward has heard from Henry this morning. He has not been at the races at all, unless his driving Miss Pearson over to Rowling one day can be so called. We shall find him there on Thursday.

I hope you are all alive after our melancholy parting yesterday, and that you pursued your intended avocation with success. God bless you! I must leave off, for we are going out.

Yours very affectionately,
J. AUSTEN.

Everybody's love.

III.

ROWLING, Monday (September 5).

MY DEAR CASSANDRA,—I shall be extremely anxious to hear the event of your ball, and shall hope to receive so long and minute an account of every particular that I shall be tired of reading it. Let me know how many, besides their fourteen selves and Mr. and Mrs. Wright, Michael

---

[1] Miss Austen's second brother.
[2] Francis, afterward Sir Francis Austen, Senior Admiral of the Fleet, and K. C. B.

will contrive to place about their coach, and how many of the gentlemen, musicians, and waiters he will have persuaded to come in their shooting-jackets. I hope John Lovett's accident will not prevent his attending the ball, as you will otherwise be obliged to dance with Mr. Tincton the whole evening. Let me know how J. Harwood deports himself without the Miss Biggs, and which of the Marys will carry the day with my brother James.

We were at a ball on Saturday, I assure you. We dined at Goodnestone, and in the evening danced two country-dances and the Boulangeries. I opened the ball with Edward Bridges; the other couples were Lewis Cage and Harriet, Frank and Louisa, Fanny and George. Elizabeth played one country-dance, Lady Bridges the other, which she made Henry dance with her, and Miss Finch played the Boulangeries.

In reading over the last three or four lines, I am aware of my having expressed myself in so doubtful a manner that if I did not tell you to the contrary, you might imagine it was Lady Bridges who made Henry dance with her at the same time that she was playing, which, if not impossible, must appear a very improbable event to you. But it was Elizabeth who danced. We supped there, and walked home at night under the shade of two umbrellas.

To-day the Goodnestone party begins to disperse and spread itself abroad. Mr. and Mrs. Cage and George repair to Hythe. Lady Waltham, Miss Bridges, and Miss Mary Finch to Dover, for the health of the two former. I have never seen Marianne at all. On Thursday Mr. and Mrs. Bridges return to Danbury; Miss Harriet Hales accompanies them to London on her way to Dorsetshire.

Farmer Claringbould died this morning, and I fancy Edward means to get some of his farm, if he can cheat Sir Brook enough in the agreement.

We have just got some venison from Godmersham, which the two Mr. Harveys are to dine on to-morrow, and on Friday or Saturday the Goodnestone people are to finish their scraps. Henry went away on Friday, as he purposed, *without fayl*. You will hear from him soon, I imagine, as he talked of writing to Steventon shortly. Mr. Richard Harvey is going to be married; but as it is a great secret, and only known to half the neighborhood, you must not mention it. The lady's name is Musgrave.

I am in great distress. I cannot determine whether I shall give Richis half a guinea or only five shillings when I go away. Counsel me, amiable Miss Austen, and tell me which will be the most.

We walked Frank last night to Crixhall Ruff, and he appeared much edified. Little Edward was breeched yesterday for good and all, and was whipped into the bargain.Pray remember me to everybody who does not inquire after me; those who do, remember me without bidding. Give my love to Mary Harrison, and tell her I wish, whenever she is attached to a young man, some respectable Dr. Marchmont may keep them apart for five volumes....

IV.

ROWLING, Thursday (September 15).

MY DEAR CASSANDRA,—We have been very gay since I wrote last; dining at Nackington, returning by moonlight, and everything quite in style, not to mention Mr. Claringbould's funeral which we saw go by on Sunday. I believe I told you in a former letter that Edward had some idea of taking the name of Claringbould; but that scheme is over, though it would be a very eligible as well as a very pleasant plan, would any one advance him money enough to begin on. We rather expected Mr. Milles to have done so on Tuesday; but to our great surprise nothing was said on the subject, and unless it is in your power to assist your brother with five or six hundred pounds, he must entirely give up the idea.

At Nackington we met Lady Sondes' picture over the mantelpiece in the dining-room, and the pictures of her three children in an ante-room, besides Mr. Scott, Miss Fletcher, Mr. Toke, Mr. J. Toke, and the archdeacon Lynch. Miss Fletcher and I were very thick, but I am the thinnest of the two. She wore her purple muslin, which is pretty enough, though it does not become her complexion. There are two traits in her character which are pleasing,—namely, she admires Camilla, and drinks no cream in her tea. If you should ever see Lucy, you may tell her that I scolded Miss Fletcher for her negligence in writing, as she desired me to do, but without being able to bring her to any proper sense of shame,—that Miss Fletcher says, in her defence, that as everybody whom Lucy knew when she was in Canterbury has now left it, she has nothing at all to write to her about. By everybody, I suppose Miss Fletcher means that a new set of officers have arrived there. But this is a note of my own.

Mrs. Milles, Mr. John Toke, and in short everybody of any sensibility inquired in tender strains after you, and I took an opportunity of assuring Mr. J. T. that neither he nor his father need longer keep themselves single for you.

We went in our two carriages to Nackington; but how we divided I shall leave you to surmise, merely observing that as Elizabeth and I were without either hat or bonnet, it would not have been very convenient for us to go in the chaise. We went by Bifrons, and I contemplated with a melancholy pleasure the abode of him on whom I once fondly doated. We dine to-day at Goodnestone, to meet my aunt Fielding from Margate and a Mr. Clayton, her professed admirer—at least, so I imagine. Lady Bridges has received very good accounts of Marianne, who is already certainly the better for her bathing.

So His Royal Highness Sir Thomas Williams has at length sailed; the papers say "on a cruise." But I hope they are gone to Cork, or I shall have written in vain. Give my love to Jane, as she arrived at Steventon yesterday, I dare say.

I sent a message to Mr. Digweed from Edward in a letter to Mary Lloyd which she ought to receive to-day; but as I know that the Harwoods are not very exact as to their letters, I may as well repeat it to you. Mr. Digweed is to be informed that illness has prevented Seward's coming over to look at the repairs intended at the farm, but that he will come as soon as he can. Mr. Digweed may also be informed, if you think proper, that Mr. and Mrs. Milles are to dine here to-morrow, and that Mrs. Joan Knatchbull is to be asked to meet them. Mr. Richard Harvey's match is put off till he has got a better Christian name, of which he has great hopes.

Mr. Children's two sons are both going to be married, John and George. They are to have one wife between them, a Miss Holwell, who belongs to the Black Hole at Calcutta. I depend on hearing from James very soon; he promised me an account of the ball, and by this time he must have collected his ideas enough after the fatigue of dancing to give me one.

Edward and Fly went out yesterday very early in a couple of shooting jackets, and came home like a couple of bad shots, for they killed nothing at all. They are out again to-day, and are not yet returned. Delightful sport! They are just come home, Edward with his two brace, Frank with his two and a half. What amiable young men!

Friday.—Your letter and one from Henry are just come, and the contents of both accord with my scheme more than I had dared expect. In one particular I could wish it otherwise, for Henry is very indifferent indeed. You must not expect us quite so early, however, as Wednesday, the 20th,—on that day se'nnight, according to our present plan, we may be with you. Frank had never any idea of going away before Monday, the 26th. I shall write to Miss Mason immediately, and press her returning with us, which Henry thinks very likely, and particularly eligible.

Buy Mary Harrison's gown by all means. You shall have mine for ever so much money, though, if I am tolerably rich when I get home, I shall like it very much myself.

As to the mode of our travelling to town, I want to go in a stage-coach, but Frank will not let me. As you are likely to have the Williams and Lloyds with you next week, you would hardly find room for us then. If any one wants anything in town, they must send their commissions to Frank, as I shall merely pass through it. The tallow-chandler is Penlington, at the Crown and Beehive, Charles Street, Covent Garden.

Miss AUSTEN, Steventon, Overton, Hants.

V.

ROWLING, Sunday (September 18).

MY DEAR CASSANDRA,—This morning has been spent in doubt and deliberation, in forming plans and removing difficulties, for it ushered in the day with an event which I had not intended should take place so soon by a week. Frank has received his appointment on board the "Captain John Gore," commanded by the "Triton," and will therefore be obliged to be in town on Wednesday; and though I have every disposition in the world to accompany him on that day, I cannot go on the uncertainty of the Pearsons being at home, as I should not have a place to go to in case they were from home.

I wrote to Miss P. on Friday, and hoped to receive an answer from her this morning, which would have rendered everything smooth and easy, and would have enabled us to leave this place to-morrow, as Frank, on first receiving his appointment, intended to do. He remains till Wednesday merely to accommodate me. I have written to her again to-day, and desired her to answer it by return of post. On Tuesday, therefore, I shall positively know whether they can receive me on Wednesday. If they cannot, Edward has been so good as to promise to take me to Greenwich on the Monday following, which was the day before fixed on, if that suits them better. If I have no answer at all on Tuesday, I must suppose Mary is not at home, and must wait till I do hear, as after having invited her to go to Steventon with me, it will not quite do to go home and say no more about it.

My father will be so good as to fetch home his prodigal daughter from town, I hope, unless he wishes me to walk the hospitals, enter at the Temple, or mount guard at St. James'. It will hardly be in Frank's power to take me home,—nay, it certainly will not. I shall write again as soon as I get to Greenwich.

What dreadful hot weather we have! It keeps one in a continual state of inelegance.

If Miss Pearson should return with me, pray be careful not to expect too much beauty. I will not pretend to say that on a first view she quite answered the opinion I had formed of her. My mother, I am sure, will be disappointed if she does not take great care. From what I remember of her picture, it is no great resemblance.

I am very glad that the idea of returning with Frank occurred to me; for as to Henry's coming into Kent again, the time of its taking place is so very uncertain that I should be waiting for dead men's shoes. I had once determined to go with Frank to-morrow and take my chance, etc., but they dissuaded me from so rash a step as I really think on consideration it would have been; for if the Pearsons were not at home, I should inevitably fall a sacrifice to the arts of some fat woman who would make me drunk with small beer.

Mary is brought to bed of a boy,—both doing very well. I shall leave you to guess what Mary I mean. Adieu, with best love to all your agreeable inmates. Don't let the Lloyds go on any account before I return, unless Miss P. is of the party. How ill I have written! I begin to hate myself.

Yours ever,
J. AUSTEN.

The "Triton" is a new 32 frigate just launched at Deptford. Frank is much pleased with the prospect of having Captain Gore under his command.

Miss AUSTEN, Steventon, Overton, Hants.

VI.

"BULL AND GEORGE," DARTFORD,
Wednesday (October 24, 1798).

MY DEAR CASSANDRA,—You have already heard from Daniel, I conclude, in what excellent time we reached and quitted Sittingbourne, and how very well my mother bore her journey thither. I am now able to send you a continuation of the same good account of her. She was very little fatigued on her arrival at this place, has been refreshed by a comfortable dinner, and now seems quite stout. It wanted five minutes of twelve when we left Sittingbourne, from whence we had a famous pair of horses, which took us to Rochester in an hour and a quarter; the postboy seemed determined to show my mother that Kentish drivers were not always tedious, and really drove as fast as Cax.

Our next stage was not quite so expeditiously performed; the road was heavy, and our horses very indifferent. However, we were in such good time and my mother bore her journey so well, that expedition was of little importance to us; and as it was, we were very little more than two hours and a half coming hither, and it was scarcely past four when we stopped at the inn. My mother took some of her bitters at Ospringe, and some more at Rochester, and she ate some bread several times.

We have got apartments up two pair of stairs, as we could not be otherwise accommodated with a sitting-room and bed-chambers on the same floor which we wished to be. We have one double-bedded and one single-bedded room; in the former my mother and I are to sleep. I shall leave you to guess who is to occupy the other. We sate down to dinner a little after five, and had some beef-steaks and a boiled fowl, but no oyster sauce.

I should have begun my letter soon after our arrival, but for a little adventure which prevented me. After we had been here a quarter of an hour it was discovered that my writing and dressing boxes had been by accident put into a chaise which was just packing off as we came in, and were driven away toward Gravesend in their way to the West Indies. No part of my property could have been such a prize before, for in my writing-box was all my worldly wealth, 7*l.*, and my dear Harry's deputation. Mr. Nottley immediately despatched a man and horse after the chaise, and in half an hour's time I had the pleasure of being as rich as ever; they were got about two or three miles off.

My day's journey has been pleasanter in every respect than I expected. I have been very little crowded and by no means unhappy. Your watchfulness with regard to the weather on our accounts was very kind and very effectual. We had one heavy shower on leaving Sittingbourne, but afterwards the clouds cleared away, and we had a very bright chrystal afternoon.

My father is now reading the "Midnight Bell," which he has got from the library, and mother sitting by the fire. Our route to-morrow is not determined. We have none of us much inclination

15

for London, and if Mr. Nottley will give us leave, I think we shall go to Staines through Croydon and Kingston, which will be much pleasanter than any other way; but he is decidedly for Clapham and Battersea. God bless you all!

Yours affectionately, J. A.

I flatter myself that itty Dordy will not forget me at least under a week. Kiss him for me.

Miss AUSTEN,
Godmersham Park, Faversham.

VII.

STEVENTON, Saturday (October 27).

MY DEAR CASSANDRA,—Your letter was a most agreeable surprise to me to-day, and I have taken a long sheet of paper to show my gratitude.

We arrived here yesterday between four and five, but I cannot send you quite so triumphant an account of our last day's journey as of the first and second. Soon after I had finished my letter from Staines, my mother began to suffer from the exercise or fatigue of travelling, and she was a good deal indisposed. She had not a very good night at Staines, but bore her journey better than I had expected, and at Basingstoke, where we stopped more than half an hour, received much comfort from a mess of broth and the sight of Mr. Lyford, who recommended her to take twelve drops of laudanum when she went to bed as a composer, which she accordingly did.

James called on us just as we were going to tea, and my mother was well enough to talk very cheerfully to him before she went to bed. James seems to have taken to his old trick of coming to Steventon in spite of Mary's reproaches, for he was here before breakfast and is now paying us a second visit. They were to have dined here to-day, but the weather is too bad. I have had the pleasure of hearing that Martha is with them. James fetched her from Ibthorp on Thursday, and she will stay with them till she removes to Kintbury.

We met with no adventures at all in our journey yesterday, except that our trunk had once nearly slipped off, and we were obliged to stop at Hartley to have our wheels greased.

Whilst my mother and Mr. Lyford were together I went to Mrs. Ryder's and bought what I intended to buy, but not in much perfection. There were no narrow braces for children, and scarcely any notting silk; but Miss Wood, as usual, is going to town very soon, and will lay in a fresh stock. I gave 2*s.* 3*d.* a yard for my flannel, and I fancy it is not very good, but it is so disgraceful and contemptible an article in itself that its being comparatively good or bad is of little importance. I bought some Japan ink likewise, and next week shall begin my operations on my hat, on which you know my principal hopes of happiness depend.

I am very grand indeed; I had the dignity of dropping out my mother's laudanum last night. I carry about the keys of the wine and closet, and twice since I began this letter have had orders to give in the kitchen. Our dinner was very good yesterday, and the chicken boiled perfectly tender; therefore I shall not be obliged to dismiss Nanny on that account.

Almost everything was unpacked and put away last night. Nanny chose to do it, and I was not sorry to be busy. I have unpacked the gloves, and placed yours in your drawer. Their color is light and pretty, and I believe exactly what we fixed on.

Your letter was chaperoned here by one from Mrs. Cooke, in which she says that "Battleridge" is not to come out before January, and she is so little satisfied with Cawthorn's dilatoriness that she never means to employ him again.

Mrs. Hall, of Sherborne, was brought to bed yesterday of a dead child, some weeks before she expected, owing to a fright. I suppose she happened unawares to look at her husband.

There has been a great deal of rain here for this last fortnight, much more than in Kent, and indeed we found the roads all the way from Staines most disgracefully dirty. Steventon lane has its full share of it, and I don't know when I shall be able to get to Deane.

I hear that Martha is in better looks and spirits than she has enjoyed for a long time, and I flatter myself she will now be able to jest openly about Mr. W.

The spectacles which Molly found are my mother's, the scissors my father's. We are very glad to hear such a good account of your patients, little and great. My dear itty Dordy's remembrance of me is very pleasing to me,—foolishly pleasing, because I know it will be over so soon. My attachment to him will be more durable. I shall think with tenderness and delight on his beautiful and smiling countenance and interesting manner until a few years have turned him into an ungovernable, ungracious fellow.

The books from Winton are all unpacked and put away; the binding has compressed them most conveniently, and there is now very good room in the bookcase for all that we wish to have there. I believe the servants were very glad to see us Nanny was, I am sure. She confesses that it was very dull, and yet she had her child with her till last Sunday. I understand that there are some grapes left, but I believe not many; they must be gathered as soon as possible, or this rain will entirely rot them.

I am quite angry with myself for not writing closer; why is my alphabet so much more sprawly than yours? Dame Tilbury's daughter has lain in. Shall I give her any of your baby clothes? The laceman was here only a few days ago. How unfortunate for both of us that he came so soon! Dame Bushell washes for us only one week more, as Sukey has got a place. John Steevens' wife undertakes our purification. She does not look as if anything she touched would ever be clean, but who knows? We do not seem likely to have any other maidservant at present, but Dame Staples will supply the place of one. Mary has hired a young girl from Ashe who has never been out to service to be her scrub, but James fears her not being strong enough for the place.

Earle Harwood has been to Deane lately, as I think Mary wrote us word, and his family then told him that they would receive his wife, if she continued to behave well for another year. He was very grateful, as well he might; their behavior throughout the whole affair has been particularly kind. Earle and his wife live in the most private manner imaginable at Portsmouth, without keeping a servant of any kind. What a prodigious innate love of virtue she must have, to marry under such circumstances!

It is now Saturday evening, but I wrote the chief of this in the morning. My mother has not been down at all to-day; the laudanum made her sleep a good deal, and upon the whole I think she is better. My father and I dined by ourselves. How strange! He and John Bond are now very happy together, for I have just heard the heavy step of the latter along the passage.

James Digweed called to-day, and I gave him his brother's deputation. Charles Harwood, too, has just called to ask how we are, in his way from Dummer, whither he has been conveying Miss Garrett, who is going to return to her former residence in Kent. I will leave off, or I shall not have room to add a word to-morrow.

Sunday.—My mother has had a very good night, and feels much better to-day.

I have received my aunt's letter, and thank you for your scrap. I will write to Charles soon. Pray give Fanny and Edward a kiss from me, and ask George if he has got a new song for me.

'Tis really very kind of my aunt to ask us to Bath again; a kindness that deserves a better return than to profit by it.

Yours ever,   J. A.

Miss AUSTEN,
Godmersham Park, Faversham, Kent.

VIII.

STEVENTON, December 1.

MY DEAR CASSANDRA,—I am so good as to write to you again thus speedily, to let you know that I have just heard from Frank. He was at Cadiz, alive and well, on October 19, and had then very lately received a letter from you, written as long ago as when the "London" was at St. Helen's. But his raly latest intelligence of us was in one from me of September 1, which I sent soon after we got to Godmersham. He had written a packet full for his dearest friends in England, early in October, to go by the "Excellent;" but the "Excellent" was not sailed, nor likely to sail, when he despatched this to me. It comprehended letters for both of us, for Lord Spencer, Mr. Daysh, and the East India Directors. Lord St. Vincent had left the fleet when he wrote, and was gone to Gibraltar, it was said to superintend the fitting out of a private expedition from thence against some of the enemies' ports; Minorca or Malta were conjectured to be the objects.

Frank writes in good spirits, but says that our correspondence cannot be so easily carried on in future as it has been, as the communication between Cadiz and Lisbon is less frequent than formerly. You and my mother, therefore, must not alarm yourselves at the long intervals that may divide his letters. I address this advice to you two as being the most tender-hearted of the family.

My mother made her *entrée* into the dressing-room through crowds of admiring spectators yesterday afternoon, and we all drank tea together for the first time these five weeks. She has had a tolerable night, and bids fair for a continuance in the same brilliant course of action to-day....

Mr. Lyford was here yesterday; he came while we were at dinner, and partook of our elegant entertainment. I was not ashamed at asking him to sit down to table, for we had some pease-soup, a sparerib, and a pudding. He wants my mother to look yellow and to throw out a rash, but she will do neither.

I was at Deane yesterday morning. Mary was very well, but does not gain bodily strength very fast. When I saw her so stout on the third and sixth days, I expected to have seen her as well as ever by the end of a fortnight.

James went to Ibthorp yesterday to see his mother and child. Letty is with Mary at present, of course exceedingly happy, and in raptures with the child. Mary does not manage matters in such a way as to make me want to lay in myself. She is not tidy enough in her appearance; she has no dressing-gown to sit up in; her curtains are all too thin, and things are not in that comfort and style about her which are necessary to make such a situation an enviable one. Elizabeth was really a pretty object with her nice clean cap put on so tidily and her dress so uniformly white and orderly. We live entirely in the dressing-room now, which I like very much; I always feel so much more elegant in it than in the parlor.

No news from Kintbury yet. Eliza sports with our impatience. She was very well last Thursday. Who is Miss Maria Montresor going to marry, and what is to become of Miss Mulcaster?

I find great comfort in my stuff gown, but I hope you do not wear yours too often. I have made myself two or three caps to wear of evenings since I came home, and they save me a world of torment as to hairdressing, which at present gives me no trouble beyond washing and brushing, for my long hair is always plaited up out of sight, and my short hair curls well enough to want no papering. I have had it cut lately by Mr. Butler.

There is no reason to suppose that Miss Morgan is dead after all. Mr. Lyford gratified us very much yesterday by his praises of my father's mutton, which they all think the finest that was ever ate. John Bond begins to find himself grow old, which John Bonds ought not to do, and unequal to much hard work; a man is therefore hired to supply his place as to labor, and John himself is to have the care of the sheep. There are not more people engaged than before, I believe; only men instead of boys. I fancy so at least, but you know my stupidity as to such matters. Lizzie Bond is just apprenticed to Miss Small, so we may hope to see her able to spoil gowns in a few years.

My father has applied to Mr. May for an ale-house for Robert, at his request, and to Mr. Deane, of Winchester, likewise. This was my mother's idea, who thought he would be proud to oblige a relation of Edward in return for Edward's accepting his money. He sent a very civil answer indeed, but has no house vacant at present. May expects to have an empty one soon at Farnham, so perhaps Nanny may have the honor of drawing ale for the Bishop. I shall write to Frank to-morrow.

Charles Powlett gave a dance on Thursday, to the great disturbance of all his neighbors, of course, who, you know, take a most lively interest in the state of his finances, and live in hopes of his being soon ruined.

We are very much disposed to like our new maid; she knows nothing of a dairy, to be sure, which, in our family, is rather against her, but she is to be taught it all. In short, we have felt the inconvenience of being without a maid so long, that we are determined to like her, and she will find it a hard matter to displease us. As yet, she seems to cook very well, is uncommonly stout, and says she can work well at her needle.

Sunday.—My father is glad to hear so good an account of Edward's pigs, and desires he may be told, as encouragement to his taste for them, that Lord Bolton is particularly curious in his pigs, has had pigstyes of a most elegant construction built for them, and visits them every morning as soon as he rises.

Affectionately yours,
J. A.

Miss AUSTEN,
Godmersham Park, Faversham.

IX.

STEVENTON, Tuesday (December 18).

MY DEAR CASSANDRA,—Your letter came quite as soon as I expected, and so your letters will always do, because I have made it a rule not to expect them till they come, in which I think I consult the ease of us both.

It is a great satisfaction to us to hear that your business is in a way to be settled, and so settled as to give you as little inconvenience as possible. You are very welcome to my father's name and to his services if they are ever required in it. I shall keep my ten pounds too, to wrap myself up in next winter.

I took the liberty a few days ago of asking your black velvet bonnet to lend me its cawl, which it very readily did, and by which I have been enabled to give a considerable improvement of dignity to cap, which was before too nidgetty to please me. I shall wear it on Thursday, but I hope you will not be offended with me for following your advice as to its ornaments only in part. I still venture to retain the narrow silver round it, put twice round without any bow, and instead of the black military feather shall put in the coquelicot one as being smarter, and besides coquelicot is to be all the fashion this winter. After the ball I shall probably make it entirely black.

I am sorry that our dear Charles begins to feel the dignity of ill-usage. My father will write to Admiral Gambier. He must have already received so much satisfaction from his acquaintance and patronage of Frank, that he will be delighted, I dare say, to have another of the family introduced to him. I think it would be very right in Charles to address Sir Thomas on the occasion, though I cannot approve of your scheme of writing to him (which you communicated to me a few nights ago) to request him to come home and convey you to Steventon. To do you justice, however, you had some doubts of the propriety of such a measure yourself.

I am very much obliged to my dear little George for his message,—for his love at least; his duty, I suppose, was only in consequence of some hint of my favorable intentions towards him from his father or mother. I am sincerely rejoiced, however, that I ever was born, since it has been the means of procuring him a dish of tea. Give my best love to him....

Wednesday.—I have changed my mind, and changed the trimmings of my cap this morning; they are now such as you suggested. I felt as if I should not prosper if I strayed from your directions, and I think it makes me look more like Lady Conyngham now than it did before, which is all that one lives for now. I believe I shall make my new gown like my robe, but the back of the latter is all in a piece with the tail, and will seven yards enable me to copy it in that respect? . . .

I have just heard from Martha and Frank: his letter was written on November 12. All well and nothing particular.

J. A.

Miss AUSTEN,
Godmersham Park, Faversham.

X.

STEVENTON, Monday night (December 24).

MY DEAR CASSANDRA,—I have got some pleasant news for you which I am eager to communicate, and therefore begin my letter sooner, though I shall not send it sooner than usual.

Admiral Gambier, in reply to my father's application, writes as follows: "As it is usual to keep young officers in small vessels, it being most proper on account of their inexperience, and it being also a situation where they are more in the way of learning their duty, your son has been continued in the 'Scorpion;' but I have mentioned to the Board of Admiralty his wish to be in a frigate, and when a proper opportunity offers and it is judged that he has taken his turn in a small ship, I hope he will be removed. With regard to your son now in the 'London' I am glad I can give you the assurance that his promotion is likely to take place very soon, as Lord Spencer has been so good as to say he would include him in an arrangement that he proposes making in a short time relative to some promotions in that quarter."

There! I may now finish my letter and go and hang myself, for I am sure I can neither write nor do anything which will not appear insipid to you after this. Now I really think he will soon be made, and only wish we could communicate our foreknowledge of the event to him whom it principally concerns. My father has written to Daysh to desire that he will inform us, if he can, when the commission is sent. Your chief wish is now ready to be accomplished; and could Lord Spencer give happiness to Martha at the same time, what a joyful heart he would make of yours!

I have sent the same extract of the sweets of Gambier to Charles, who, poor fellow, though he sinks into nothing but an humble attendant on the hero of the piece, will, I hope, be contented with the prospect held out to him. By what the Admiral says, it appears as if he had been designedly kept in the "Scorpion." But I will not torment myself with conjectures and suppositions; facts shall satisfy me.

Frank had not heard from any of us for ten weeks when he wrote to me on November 12 in consequence of Lord St. Vincent being removed to Gibraltar. When his commission is sent, however, it will not be so long on its road as our letters, because all the Government despatches are forwarded by land to his lordship from Lisbon with great regularity.

I returned from Manydown this morning, and found my mother certainly in no respect worse than when I left her. She does not like the cold weather, but that we cannot help. I spent my time very quietly and very pleasantly with Catherine. Miss Blackford is agreeable enough. I do not want people to be very agreeable, as it saves me the trouble of liking them a great deal. I found only Catherine and her when I got to Manydown on Thursday. We dined together, and went together to Worting to seek the protection of Mrs. Clarke, with whom were Lady Mildmay, her eldest son, and Mr. and Mrs. Hoare.

Our ball was very thin, but by no means unpleasant. There were thirty-one people, and only eleven ladies out of the number, and but five single women in the room. Of the gentlemen present you may have some idea from the list of my partners,—Mr. Wood, G. Lefroy, Rice, a Mr. Butcher (belonging to the Temples, a sailor and not of the 11th Light Dragoons), Mr. Temple (not the horrid one of all), Mr. Wm. Orde (cousin to the Kingsclere man), Mr. John Harwood, and Mr. Calland, who appeared as usual with his hat in his hand, and stood every now and then behind Catherine and me to be talked to and abused for not dancing. We teased him, however, into it at last. I was very glad to see him again after so long a separation, and he was altogether rather the genius and flirt of the evening. He inquired after you.

There were twenty dances, and I danced them all, and without any fatigue. I was glad to find myself capable of dancing so much, and with so much satisfaction as I did; from my slender enjoyment of the Ashford balls (as assemblies for dancing) I had not thought myself equal to it, but in cold weather and with few couples I fancy I could just as well dance for a week together as for half an hour. My black cap was openly admired by Mrs. Lefroy, and secretly I imagine by everybody else in the room....

Poor Edward! It is very hard that he, who has everything else in the world that he can wish for, should not have good health too. But I hope with the assistance of stomach complaints, faintnesses, and sicknesses, he will soon be restored to that blessing likewise. If his nervous complaint proceeded from a suppression of something that ought to be thrown out, which does not seem unlikely, the first of these disorders may really be a remedy, and I sincerely wish it may, for I know no one more deserving of happiness without alloy than Edward is....

The Lords of the Admiralty will have enough of our applications at present, for I hear from Charles that he has written to Lord Spencer himself to be removed. I am afraid his Serene Highness will be in a passion, and order some of our heads to be cut off....

You deserve a longer letter than this; but it is my unhappy fate seldom to treat people so well as they deserve.... God bless you!

Yours affectionately,
JANE AUSTEN.

Wednesday.—The snow came to nothing yesterday, so I did go to Deane, and returned home at nine o'clock at night in the little carriage, and without being very cold.

Miss AUSTEN,
Godmersham Park, Faversham, Kent.

XI.

STEVENTON, Friday (December 28).

MY DEAR CASSANDRA,—Frank is made. He was yesterday raised to the rank of Commander, and appointed to the "Petterel" sloop, now at Gibraltar. A letter from Daysh has just announced this, and as it is confirmed by a very friendly one from Mr. Mathew to the same effect, transcribing one from Admiral Gambier to the General, we have no reason to suspect the truth of it.

As soon as you have cried a little for joy, you may go on, and learn further that the India House have taken Captain Austen's petition into consideration,—this comes from Daysh,—and likewise that Lieutenant Charles John Austen is removed to the "Tamar" frigate,—this comes from the Admiral. We cannot find out where the "Tamar" is, but I hope we shall now see Charles here at all events.

This letter is to be dedicated entirely to good news. If you will send my father an account of your washing and letter expenses, etc., he will send you a draft for the amount of it, as well as for your next quarter, and for Edward's rent. If you don't buy a muslin gown now on the strength of this money and Frank's promotion, I shall never forgive you.

Mrs. Lefroy has just sent me word that Lady Dorchester meant to invite me to her ball on January 8, which, though an humble blessing compared with what the last page records, I do not consider as any calamity.

I cannot write any more now, but I have written enough to make you very happy, and therefore may safely conclude.

Yours affectionately,   JANE.

Miss AUSTEN, Godmersham Park.

XII.

STEVENTON, Tuesday (January 8, 1799).

MY DEAR CASSANDRA,—You must read your letters over five times in future before you send them, and then, perhaps, you may find them as entertaining as I do. I laughed at several parts of the one which I am now answering.

Charles is not come yet, but he must come this morning, or he shall never know what I will do to him. The ball at Kempshott is this evening, and I have got him an invitation, though I have not been so considerate as to get him a partner. But the cases are different between him and Eliza Bailey, for he is not in a dying way, and may therefore be equal to getting a partner for himself. I believe I told you that Monday was to be the ball night, for which, and for all other errors into which I may ever have led you, I humbly ask your pardon.

Elizabeth is very cruel about my writing music, and, as a punishment for her, I should insist upon always writing out all hers for her in future, if I were not punishing myself at the same time.

I am tolerably glad to hear that Edward's income is so good a one,—as glad as I can be at anybody's being rich except you and me,—and I am thoroughly rejoiced to hear of his present to you.

I am not to wear my white satin cap to-night, after all; I am to wear a mamalone cap instead, which Charles Fowle sent to Mary, and which she lends me. It is all the fashion now; worn at the opera, and by Lady Mildmays at Hackwood balls. I hate describing such things, and I dare say you will be able to guess what it is like. I have got over the dreadful epocha of mantua-making much better than I expected. My gown is made very much like my blue one, which you always told me sat very well, with only these variations: the sleeves are short, the wrap fuller, the apron comes over it, and a band of the same completes the whole.

I assure you that I dread the idea of going to Brighton as much as you do, but I am not without hopes that something may happen to prevent it.

F—— has lost his election at B——, and perhaps they may not be able to see company for some time. They talk of going to Bath, too, in the spring, and perhaps they may be overturned in their way down, and all laid up for the summer.

Wednesday.—I have had a cold and weakness in one of my eyes for some days, which makes writing neither very pleasant nor very profitable, and which will probably prevent my finishing this letter myself. My mother has undertaken to do it for me, and I shall leave the Kempshott ball for her.

You express so little anxiety about my being murdered under Ash Park Copse by Mrs. Hulbert's servant, that I have a great mind not to tell you whether I was or not, and shall only say that I did not return home that night or the next, as Martha kindly made room for me in her bed, which was the shut-up one in the new nursery. Nurse and the child slept upon the floor, and there we all were in some confusion and great comfort. The bed did exceedingly well for us, both to lie awake in and talk till two o'clock, and to sleep in the rest of the night. I love Martha better than ever, and I mean to go and see her, if I can, when she gets home. We all dined at the Harwoods' on Thursday, and the party broke up the next morning.

This complaint in my eye has been a sad bore to me, for I have not been able to read or work in any comfort since Friday; but one advantage will be derived from it, for I shall be such a proficient in music by the time I have got rid of my cold, that I shall be perfectly qualified in that science at least to take Mr. Roope's office at Eastwell next summer; and I am sure of Elizabeth's recommendation, be it only on Harriet's account. Of my talent in drawing I have

23

given specimens in my letters to you, and I have nothing to do but to invent a few hard names for the stars.

Mary grows rather more reasonable about her child's beauty, and says that she does not think him really handsome; but I suspect her moderation to be something like that of W——W——'s mamma. Perhaps Mary has told you that they are going to enter more into dinner-parties; the Biggs and Mr. Holder dine there to-morrow, and I am to meet them. I shall sleep there. Catherine has the honor of giving her name to a set, which will be composed of two Withers, two Heathcotes, a Blackford, and no Bigg except herself. She congratulated me last night on Frank's promotion, as if she really felt the joy she talked of.

My sweet little George! I am delighted to hear that he has such an inventive genius as to face-making. I admired his yellow wafer very much, and hope he will choose the wafer for your next letter. I wore my green shoes last night, and took my white fan with me; I am very glad he never threw it into the river.

Mrs. Knight giving up the Godmersham estate to Edward was no such prodigious act of generosity after all, it seems, for she has reserved herself an income out of it still; this ought to be known, that her conduct may not be overrated. I rather think Edward shows the most magnanimity of the two, in accepting her resignation with such incumbrances.

The more I write, the better my eye gets; so I shall at least keep on till it is quite well, before I give up my pen to my mother.

Mrs. Bramston's little movable apartment was tolerably filled last night by herself, Mrs. H. Blackstone, her two daughters, and me. I do not like the Miss Blackstones; indeed, I was always determined not to like them, so there is the less merit in it. Mrs. Bramston was very civil, kind, and noisy. I spent a very pleasant evening, chiefly among the Manydown party. There was the same kind of supper as last year, and the same want of chairs. There were more dancers than the room could conveniently hold, which is enough to constitute a good ball at any time.

I do not think I was very much in request. People were rather apt not to ask me till they could not help it; one's consequence, you know, varies so much at times without any particular reason. There was one gentleman, an officer of the Cheshire, a very good-looking young man, who, I was told, wanted very much to be introduced to me; but as he did not want it quite enough to take much trouble in effecting it, we never could bring it about.

I danced with Mr. John Wood again, twice with a Mr. South, a lad from Winchester, who, I suppose, is as far from being related to the bishop of that diocese as it is possible to be, with G. Lefroy, and J. Harwood, who, I think, takes to me rather more than he used to do. One of my gayest actions was sitting down two dances in preference to having Lord Bolton's eldest son for my partner, who danced too ill to be endured. The Miss Charterises were there, and played the parts of the Miss Edens with great spirit. Charles never came. Naughty Charles! I suppose he could not get superseded in time.

Miss Debary has replaced your two sheets of drawing-paper with two of superior size and quality; so I do not grudge her having taken them at all now. Mr. Ludlow and Miss Pugh of Andover are lately married, and so is Mrs. Skeete of Basingstoke, and Mr. French, chemist, of Reading.

I do not wonder at your wanting to read "First Impressions" again, so seldom as you have gone through it, and that so long ago. I am much obliged to you for meaning to leave my old petticoat behind you. I have long secretly wished it might be done, but had not courage to make the request.

Pray mention the name of Maria Montresor's lover when you write next. My mother wants to know it, and I have not courage to look back into your letters to find it out.

I shall not be able to send this till to-morrow, and you will be disappointed on Friday; I am very sorry for it, but I cannot help it.

The partnership between Jeffereys, Toomer, and Legge is dissolved; the two latter are melted away into nothing, and it is to be hoped that Jeffereys will soon break, for the sake of a few heroines whose money he may have. I wish you joy of your birthday twenty times over.

I shall be able to send this to the post to-day, which exalts me to the utmost pinnacle of human felicity, and makes me bask in the sunshine of prosperity or gives me any other sensation of pleasure in studied language which you may prefer. Do not be angry with me for not filling my sheet, and believe me yours affectionately,

J. A.

Miss AUSTEN,
Godmersham Park, Faversham.

XIII.

STEVENTON, Monday (January 21).

MY DEAR CASSANDRA,—I will endeavor to make this letter more worthy your acceptance than my last, which was so shabby a one that I think Mr. Marshall could never charge you with the postage. My eyes have been very indifferent since it was written, but are now getting better once more; keeping them so many hours open on Thursday night, as well as the dust of the ballroom, injured them a good deal. I use them as little as I can, but you know, and Elizabeth knows, and everybody who ever had weak eyes knows, how delightful it is to hurt them by employment, against the advice and entreaty of all one's friends.

Charles leaves us to-night. The "Tamar" is in the Downs, and Mr. Daysh advises him to join her there directly, as there is no chance of her going to the westward. Charles does not approve of this at all, and will not be much grieved if he should be too late for her before she sails, as he may then hope to get into a better station. He attempted to go to town last night, and got as far on his road thither as Dean Gate; but both the coaches were full, and we had the pleasure of seeing him back again. He will call on Daysh to-morrow to know whether the "Tamar" has sailed or not, and if she is still at the Downs he will proceed in one of the night coaches to Deal. I want to go with him, that I may explain the country to him properly between Canterbury and Rowling, but the unpleasantness of returning by myself deters me. I should like to go as far as Ospringe with him very much indeed, that I might surprise you at Godmersham.

Martha writes me word that Charles was very much admired at Kintbury, and Mrs. Lefroy never saw any one so much improved in her life, and thinks him handsomer than Henry. He appears to far more advantage here than he did at Godmersham, not surrounded by strangers and neither oppressed by a pain in his face or powder in his hair.

James christened Elizabeth Caroline on Saturday morning, and then came home. Mary, Anna, and Edward have left us of course; before the second went I took down her answer to her cousin Fanny.

Yesterday came a letter to my mother from Edward Cooper to announce, not the birth of a child, but of a living; for Mrs. Leigh has begged his acceptance of the Rectory of Hamstall-Ridware in Staffordshire, vacant by Mr. Johnson's death. We collect from his letter that he means to reside there, in which he shows his wisdom. Staffordshire is a good way off; so we shall see nothing more of them till, some fifteen years hence, the Miss Coopers are presented to us, fine, jolly, handsome, ignorant girls. The living is valued at 140*l.* a year, but perhaps it may be improvable. How will they be able to convey the furniture of the dressing-room so far in safety?

Our first cousins seem all dropping off very fast. One is incorporated into the family, another dies, and a third goes into Staffordshire. We can learn nothing of the disposal of the other living. I have not the smallest notion of Fulwar's having it. Lord Craven has probably other connections and more intimate ones, in that line, than he now has with the Kintbury family.

Our ball on Thursday was a very poor one, only eight couple and but twenty-three people in the room; but it was not the ball's fault, for we were deprived of two or three families by the sudden illness of Mr. Wither, who was seized that morning at Winchester with a return of his former alarming complaint. An express was sent off from thence to the family; Catherine and Miss Blackford were dining with Mrs. Russell. Poor Catherine's distress must have been very great. She was prevailed on to wait till the Heathcotes could come from Wintney, and then with those two and Harris proceeded directly to Winchester. In such a disorder his danger, I suppose, must always be great; but from this attack he is now rapidly recovering, and will be well enough to return to Manydown, I fancy, in a few days.

It was a fine thing for conversation at the ball. But it deprived us not only of the Biggs, but of Mrs. Russell too, and of the Boltons and John Harwood, who were dining there likewise, and of Mr. Lane, who kept away as related to the family. Poor man!—I mean Mr. Wither—his life is so useful, his character so respectable and worthy, that I really believe there was a good deal of sincerity in the general concern expressed on his account.

Our ball was chiefly made up of Jervoises and Terrys, the former of whom were apt to be vulgar, the latter to be noisy. I had an odd set of partners: Mr. Jenkins, Mr. Street, Colonel Jervoise, James Digweed, J. Lyford, and Mr. Briggs, a friend of the latter. I had a very pleasant evening, however, though you will probably find out that there was no particular reason for it; but I do not think it worth while to wait for enjoyment until there is some real opportunity for it. Mary behaved very well, and was not at all fidgetty. For the history of her adventures at the ball I refer you to Anna's letter.

When you come home you will have some shirts to make up for Charles. Mrs. Davies frightened him into buying a piece of Irish when we were in Basingstoke. Mr. Daysh supposes that Captain Austen's commission has reached him by this time.

Tuesday.—Your letter has pleased and amused me very much. Your essay on happy fortnights is highly ingenious, and the talobert skin made me laugh a good deal. Whenever I fall into misfortune, how many jokes it ought to furnish to my acquaintance in general, or I shall die dreadfully in their debt for entertainment.

It began to occur to me before you mentioned it that I had been somewhat silent as to my mother's health for some time, but I thought you could have no difficulty in divining its exact state,—you, who have guessed so much stranger things. She is tolerably well,—better upon the whole than she was some weeks ago. She would tell you herself that she has a very dreadful cold in her head at present; but I have not much compassion for colds in the head without fever or sore throat.

Our own particular little brother got a place in the coach last night, and is now, I suppose, in town. I have no objection at all to your buying our gowns there, as your imagination has pictured to you exactly such a one as is necessary to make me happy. You quite abash me by your progress in notting, for I am still without silk. You must get me some in town or in Canterbury; it should be finer than yours.

I thought Edward would not approve of Charles being a crop, and rather wished you to conceal it from him at present, lest it might fall on his spirits and retard his recovery. My father furnishes him with a pig from Cheesedown; it is already killed and cut up, but it is not to weigh more than nine stone; the season is too far advanced to get him a larger one. My mother means to pay herself for the salt and the trouble of ordering it to be cured by the spareribs, the souse, and the lard. We have had one dead lamb.

I congratulate you on Mr. E. Hatton's good fortune. I suppose the marriage will now follow out of hand. Give my compliments to Miss Finch.

What time in March may we expect your return in? I begin to be very tired of answering people's questions on that subject, and independent of that, I shall be very glad to see you at home again, and then if we can get Martha and shirk ... who will be so happy as we?

I think of going to Ibthorp in about a fortnight. My eyes are pretty well, I thank you, if you please.

Wednesday, 23d.—I wish my dear Fanny many returns of this day, and that she may on every return enjoy as much pleasure as she is now receiving from her doll's-beds.

I have just heard from Charles, who is by this time at Deal. He is to be second lieutenant, which pleases him very well. The "Endymion" is come into the Downs, which pleases him likewise. He expects to be ordered to Sheerness shortly, as the "Tamar" has never been refitted.

My father and mother made the same match for you last night, and are very much pleased with it. He is a beauty of my mother's.

Yours affectionately,
JANE.

Miss AUSTEN,
Godmersham Park, Faversham, Kent.

XIV.

13 QUEEN'S SQUARE, Friday (May 17).

MY DEAREST CASSANDRA,—Our journey yesterday went off exceedingly well; nothing occurred to alarm or delay us. We found the roads in excellent order, had very good horses all the way, and reached Devizes with ease by four o'clock. I suppose John has told you in what manner we were divided when we left Andover, and no alteration was afterwards made. At Devizes we had comfortable rooms and a good dinner, to which we sat down about five; amongst other things we had asparagus and a lobster, which made me wish for you, and some cheesecakes, on which the children made so delightful a supper as to endear the town of Devizes to them for a long time.

Well, here we are at Bath; we got here about one o'clock, and have been arrived just long enough to go over the house, fix on our rooms, and be very well pleased with the whole of it. Poor Elizabeth has had a dismal ride of it from Devizes, for it has rained almost all the way, and our first view of Bath has been just as gloomy as it was last November twelvemonth.

I have got so many things to say, so many things equally important, that I know not on which to decide at present, and shall therefore go and eat with the children.

We stopped in Paragon as we came along, but as it was too wet and dirty for us to get out, we could only see Frank, who told us that his master was very indifferent, but had had a better night last night than usual. In Paragon we met Mrs. Foley and Mrs. Dowdeswell with her yellow shawl airing out, and at the bottom of Kingsdown Hill we met a gentleman in a buggy, who, on minute examination, turned out to be Dr. Hall—and Dr. Hall in such very deep mourning that either his mother, his wife, or himself must be dead. These are all of our acquaintance who have yet met our eyes.

I have some hopes of being plagued about my trunk; I had more a few hours ago, for it was too heavy to go by the coach which brought Thomas and Rebecca from Devizes; there was reason to suppose that it might be too heavy likewise for any other coach, and for a long time we could hear of no wagon to convey it. At last, however, we unluckily discovered that one was just on the point of setting out for this place, but at any rate the trunk cannot be here till to-morrow; so far we are safe, and who knows what may not happen to procure a further delay?

I put Mary's letter into the post-office at Andover with my own hand.

We are exceedingly pleased with the house; the rooms are quite as large as we expected. Mrs. Bromley is a fat woman in mourning, and a little black kitten runs about the staircase. Elizabeth has the apartment within the drawing-room; she wanted my mother to have it, but as there was no bed in the inner one, and the stairs are so much easier of ascent, or my mother so much stronger than in Paragon as not to regard the double flight, it is settled for us to be above, where we have two very nice-sized rooms, with dirty quilts and everything comfortable. I have the outward and larger apartment, as I ought to have; which is quite as large as our bedroom at home, and my mother's is not materially less. The beds are both as large as any at Steventon, and I have a very nice chest of drawers and a closet full of shelves,—so full indeed that there is nothing else in it, and it should therefore be called a cupboard rather than a closet, I suppose.

Tell Mary that there were some carpenters at work in the inn at Devizes this morning, but as I could not be sure of their being Mrs. W. Fowle's relations, I did not make myself known to them.

I hope it will be a tolerable afternoon. When first we came, all the umbrellas were up, but now the pavements are getting very white again.

My mother does not seem at all the worse for her journey, nor are any of us, I hope, though Edward seemed rather fagged last night, and not very brisk this morning; but I trust the bustle of sending for tea, coffee, and sugar, etc., and going out to taste a cheese himself, will do him good.

There was a very long list of arrivals here in the newspaper yesterday, so that we need not immediately dread absolute solitude; and there is a public breakfast in Sydney Gardens every morning, so that we shall not be wholly starved.

Elizabeth has just had a very good account of the three little boys. I hope you are very busy and very comfortable. I find no difficulty in closing my eyes. I like our situation very much; it is far more cheerful than Paragon, and the prospect from the drawing-room window, at which I now write, is rather picturesque, as it commands a prospective view of the left side of Brock Street, broken by three Lombardy poplars in the garden of the last house in Queen's Parade.

I am rather impatient to know the fate of my best gown, but I suppose it will be some days before Frances can get through the trunk. In the mean time I am, with many thanks for your trouble in making it, as well as marking my silk stockings,

Yours very affectionately, JANE.

A great deal of love from everybody.

Miss AUSTEN, Steventon, Overton, Hants.

XV.

MY DEAR CASSANDRA,—I am obliged to you for two letters, one from yourself and the other from Mary, for of the latter I knew nothing till on the receipt of yours yesterday, when the pigeon-basket was examined, and I received my due. As I have written to her since the time which ought to have brought me hers, I suppose she will consider herself, as I choose to consider her, still in my debt.

I will lay out all the little judgment I have in endeavoring to get such stockings for Anna as she will approve; but I do not know that I shall execute Martha's commission at all, for I am not fond of ordering shoes; and, at any rate, they shall all have flat heels.

What must I tell you of Edward? Truth or falsehood? I will try the former, and you may choose for yourself another time. He was better yesterday than he had been for two or three days before,—about as well as while he was at Steventon. He drinks at the Hetling Pump, is to bathe to-morrow, and try electricity on Tuesday. He proposed the latter himself to Dr. Fellowes, who made no objection to it, but I fancy we are all unanimous in expecting no advantage from it. At present I have no great notion of our staying here beyond the month.

I heard from Charles last week; they were to sail on Wednesday.

My mother seems remarkably well. My uncle overwalked himself at first, and can now only travel in a chair, but is otherwise very well.

My cloak is come home. I like it very much, and can now exclaim with delight, like J. Bond at hay-harvest, "This is what I have been looking for these three years." I saw some gauzes in a shop in Bath Street yesterday at only 4d. a yard, but they were not so good or so pretty as mine. Flowers are very much worn, and fruit is still more the thing. Elizabeth has a bunch of strawberries, and I have seen grapes, cherries, plums, and apricots. There are likewise almonds and raisins, French plums, and tamarinds at the grocers', but I have never seen any of them in hats. A plum or greengage would cost three shillings; cherries and grapes about five, I believe, but this is at some of the dearest shops. My aunt has told me of a very cheap one, near Walcot Church, to which I shall go in quest of something for you. I have never seen an old woman at the pump-room.

Elizabeth has given me a hat, and it is not only a pretty hat, but a pretty style of hat too. It is something like Eliza's, only, instead of being all straw, half of it is narrow purple ribbon. I flatter myself, however, that you can understand very little of it from this description. Heaven forbid that I should ever offer such encouragement to explanations as to give a clear one on any occasion myself! But I must write no more of this....

I spent Friday evening with the Mapletons, and was obliged to submit to being pleased in spite of my inclination. We took a very charming walk from six to eight up Beacon Hill, and across some fields, to the village of Charlecombe, which is sweetly situated in a little green valley, as a village with such a name ought to be. Marianne is sensible and intelligent; and even Jane, considering how fair she is, is not unpleasant. We had a Miss North and a Mr. Gould of our party; the latter walked home with me after tea. He is a very young man, just entered Oxford, wears spectacles, and has heard that "Evelina" was written by Dr. Johnson.

I am afraid I cannot undertake to carry Martha's shoes home, for, though we had plenty of room in our trunks when we came, we shall have many more things to take back, and I must allow besides for my packing.

There is to be a grand gala on Tuesday evening in Sydney Gardens, a concert, with illuminations and fireworks. To the latter Elizabeth and I look forward with pleasure, and even the concert will have more than its usual charm for me, as the gardens are large enough for me to get pretty well beyond the reach of its sound. In the morning Lady Willoughby is to present the colors to some corps, or Yeomanry, or other, in the Crescent, and that such festivities may have a proper commencement, we think of going to....

I am quite pleased with Martha and Mrs. Lefroy for wanting the pattern of our caps, but I am not so well pleased with your giving it to them. Some wish, some prevailing wish, is necessary to the animation of everybody's mind, and in gratifying this you leave them to form some other which will not probably be half so innocent. I shall not forget to write to Frank. Duty and love, etc.

Yours affectionately,   JANE.

My uncle is quite surprised at my hearing from you so often; but as long as we can keep the frequency of our correspondence from Martha's uncle, we will not fear our own. Miss AUSTEN, Steventon.

XVI.

13 QUEEN SQUARE, Tuesday (June 11).

MY DEAR CASSANDRA,—Your letter yesterday made me very happy. I am heartily glad that you have escaped any share in the impurities of Deane, and not sorry, as it turns out, that our stay here has been lengthened. I feel tolerably secure of our getting away next week, though it is certainly possible that we may remain till Thursday the 27th. I wonder what we shall do with all our intended visits this summer! I should like to make a compromise with Adlestrop, Harden, and Bookham, that Martha's spending the summer at Steventon should be considered as our respective visits to them all.

Edward has been pretty well for this last week, and as the waters have never disagreed with him in any respect, we are inclined to hope that he will derive advantage from them in the end. Everybody encourages us in this expectation, for they all say that the effect of the waters cannot be negative, and many are the instances in which their benefit is felt afterwards more than on the spot. He is more comfortable here than I thought he would be, and so is Elizabeth, though they will both, I believe, be very glad to get away—the latter especially, which one can't wonder at somehow. So much for Mrs. Piozzi. I had some thoughts of writing the whole of my letter in her style, but I believe I shall not.

Though you have given me unlimited powers concerning your sprig, I cannot determine what to do about it, and shall therefore in this and in every other future letter continue to ask your further directions. We have been to the cheap shop, and very cheap we found it, but there are only flowers made there, no fruit; and as I could get four or five very pretty sprigs of the former for the same money which would procure only one Orleans plum—in short, could get more for three or four shillings than I could have means of bringing home—I cannot decide on the fruit till I hear from you again. Besides, I cannot help thinking that it is more natural to have flowers grow out of the head than fruit. What do you think on that subject?

I would not let Martha read "First Impressions"[3] again upon any account, and am very glad that I did not leave it in your power. She is very cunning, but I saw through her design; she means to publish it from memory, and one more perusal must enable her to do it. As for "Fitzalbini," when I get home she shall have it, as soon as ever she will own that Mr. Elliott is handsomer than Mr. Lance, that fair men are preferable to black; for I mean to take every opportunity of rooting out her prejudices.

Benjamin Portal is here. How charming that is! I do not exactly know why, but the phrase followed so naturally that I could not help putting it down. My mother saw him the other day, but without making herself known to him.

I am very glad you liked my lace, and so are you, and so is Martha, and we are all glad together. I have got your cloak home, which is quite delightful,—as delightful at least as half the circumstances which are called so.

I do not know what is the matter with me to-day, but I cannot write quietly; I am always wandering away into some exclamation or other. Fortunately I have nothing very particular to say.

We walked to Weston one evening last week, and liked it very much. Liked what very much? Weston? No, walking to Weston. I have not expressed myself properly, but I hope you will understand me.

We have not been to any public place lately, nor performed anything out of the common daily routine of No. 13 Queen Square, Bath. But to-day we were to have dashed away at a very extraordinary rate, by dining out, had it not so happened that we did not go.

Edward renewed his acquaintance lately with Mr. Evelyn, who lives in the Queen's Parade, and was invited to a family dinner, which I believe at first Elizabeth was rather sorry at his accepting; but yesterday Mrs. Evelyn called on us, and her manners were so pleasing that we liked the idea of going very much. The Biggs would call her a nice woman. But Mr. Evelyn, who was indisposed yesterday, is worse to-day, and we are put off.

It is rather impertinent to suggest any household care to a housekeeper, but I just venture to say that the coffee-mill will be wanted every day while Edward is at Steventon, as he always drinks coffee for breakfast.

Fanny desires her love to you, her love to grandpapa, her love to Anna, and her love to Hannah; the latter is particularly to be remembered. Edward desires his love to you, to grandpapa, to Anna, to little Edward, to Aunt James and Uncle James, and he hopes all your turkeys and ducks and chicken and guinea fowls are very well; and he wishes you very much to send him a printed letter, and so does Fanny—and they both rather think they shall answer it....

Dr. Gardiner was married yesterday to Mrs. Percy and her three daughters.

Now I will give you the history of Mary's veil, in the purchase of which I have so considerably involved you that it is my duty to economize for you in the flowers. I had no difficulty in getting a muslin veil for half a guinea, and not much more in discovering afterwards that the muslin was thick, dirty, and ragged, and therefore would by no means do for a united gift. I changed it consequently as soon as I could, and, considering what a state my imprudence had reduced me to, I thought myself lucky in getting a black lace one for sixteen shillings. I hope the half of that sum will not greatly exceed what you had intended to offer upon the altar of sister-in-law affection.

Yours affectionately,   JANE.

---

[3] The title first chosen for "Pride and Prejudice."

They do not seem to trouble you much from Manydown. I have long wanted to quarrel with them, and I believe I shall take this opportunity. There is no denying that they are very capricious—for they like to enjoy their elder sister's company when they can.

Miss AUSTEN, Steventon, Overton, Hants.

XVII.

STEVENTON, Thursday (November 20, 1800).

MY DEAR CASSANDRA,—Your letter took me quite by surprise this morning; you are very welcome, however, and I am very much obliged to you. I believe I drank too much wine last night at Hurstbourne; I know not how else to account for the shaking of my hand to-day. You will kindly make allowance therefore for any indistinctness of writing, by attributing it to this venial error.

Naughty Charles did not come on Tuesday, but good Charles came yesterday morning. About two o'clock he walked in on a Gosport hack. His feeling equal to such a fatigue is a good sign, and his feeling no fatigue in it a still better. He walked down to Deane to dinner; he danced the whole evening, and to-day is no more tired than a gentleman ought to be.

Your desiring to hear from me on Sunday will, perhaps, bring you a more particular account of the ball than you may care for, because one is prone to think much more of such things the morning after they happen, than when time has entirely driven them out of one's recollection.

It was a pleasant evening; Charles found it remarkably so, but I cannot tell why, unless the absence of Miss Terry, towards whom his conscience reproaches him with being now perfectly indifferent, was a relief to him. There were only twelve dances, of which I danced nine, and was merely prevented from dancing the rest by the want of a partner. We began at ten, supped at one, and were at Deane before five. There were but fifty people in the room; very few families indeed from our side of the county, and not many more from the other. My partners were the two St. Johns, Hooper, Holder, and a very prodigious Mr. Mathew, with whom I called the last, and whom I liked the best of my little stock.

There were very few beauties, and such as there were were not very handsome. Miss Iremonger did not look well, and Mrs. Blount was the only one much admired. She appeared exactly as she did in September, with the same broad face, diamond bandeau, white shoes, pink husband, and fat neck. The two Miss Coxes were there; I traced in one the remains of the vulgar, broad-featured girl who danced at Enham eight years ago; the other is refined into a nice, composed-looking girl, like Catherine Bigg. I looked at Sir Thomas Champneys, and thought of poor Rosalie; I looked at his daughter, and thought her a queer animal with a white neck. Mrs. Warren I was constrained to think a very fine young woman, which I much regret. She danced away with great activity. Her husband is ugly enough, uglier even than his cousin John; but he does not look so very old. The Miss Maitlands are both prettyish, very like Anne, with brown skins, large dark eyes, and a good deal of nose. The General has got the gout, and Mrs. Maitland the jaundice. Miss Debary, Susan, and Sally, all in black, but without any statues, made their appearance, and I was as civil to them as circumstances would allow me....

Mary said that I looked very well last night. I wore my aunt's gown and handkerchief, and my hair was at least tidy, which was all my ambition. I will now have done with the ball, and I will moreover go and dress for dinner....

Farewell; Charles sends you his best love, and Edward his worst. If you think the distinction improper, you may take the worst yourself. He will write to you when he gets back to his ship, and in the mean time desires that you will consider me as

Your affectionate sister,   J. A.

Friday.—I have determined to go on Thursday, but of course not before the post comes in. Charles is in very good looks indeed. I had the comfort of finding out the other evening who all the fat girls with long noses were that disturbed me at the First H. ball. They all proved to be Miss Atkinsons of En—[*illegible*].

I rejoice to say that we have just had another letter from our dear Frank. It is to you, very short, written from Larnica in Cyprus, and so lately as October 2. He came from Alexandria, and was to return there in three or four days, knew nothing of his promotion, and does not write above twenty lines, from a doubt of the letter's ever reaching you, and an idea of all letters being opened at Vienna. He wrote a few days before to you from Alexandria by the "Mercury," sent with despatches to Lord Keith. Another letter must be owing to us besides this, one if not two; because none of these are to me. Henry comes to-morrow, for one night only.

My mother has heard from Mrs. E. Leigh. Lady Saye and Seale and her daughter are going to remove to Bath. Mrs. Estwick is married again to a Mr. Sloane, a young man under age, without the knowledge of either family. He bears a good character, however.

Miss AUSTEN,
Godmersham Park, Faversham, Kent.

XVIII.

STEVENTON, Saturday (January 3, 1801).

MY DEAR CASSANDRA,—As you have by this time received my last letter, it is fit that I should begin another; and I begin with the hope, which is at present uppermost in my mind, that you often wore a white gown in the morning at the time of all the gay parties being with you.

Our visit at Ash Park, last Wednesday, went off in a *come-cá* way. We met Mr. Lefroy and Tom Chute, played at cards, and came home again. James and Mary dined here on the following day, and at night Henry set off in the mail for London. He was as agreeable as ever during his visit, and has not lost anything in Miss Lloyd's estimation.

Yesterday we were quite alone—only our four selves; but to-day the scene is agreeably varied by Mary's driving Martha to Basingstoke, and Martha's afterwards dining at Deane.

My mother looks forward with as much certainty as you can do to our keeping two maids; my father is the only one not in the secret. We plan having a steady cook and a young giddy housemaid, with a sedate, middle-aged man, who is to undertake the double office of husband to the former and sweetheart to the latter. No children of course to be allowed on either side.

You feel more for John Bond than John Bond deserves. I am sorry to lower his character, but he is not ashamed to own himself that he has no doubt at all of getting a good place, and that he had even an offer many years ago from a Farmer Paine of taking him into his service whenever he might quit my father's.

There are three parts of Bath which we have thought of as likely to have houses in them,— Westgate Buildings, Charles Street, and some of the short streets leading from Laura Place or Pulteney Street.

Westgate Buildings, though quite in the lower part of the town, are not badly situated themselves. The street is broad, and has rather a good appearance. Charles Street, however, I think is preferable. The buildings are new, and its nearness to Kingsmead Fields would be a pleasant circumstance. Perhaps you may remember, or perhaps you may forget, that Charles Street leads from the Queen Square Chapel to the two Green Park Streets.

The houses in the streets near Laura Place I should expect to be above our price. Gay Street would be too high, except only the lower house on the left-hand side as you ascend. Towards that my mother has no disinclination; it used to be lower rented than any other house in the row, from some inferiority in the apartments. But above all others her wishes are at present fixed on the corner house in Chapel Row, which opens into Prince's Street. Her knowledge of it, however, is confined only to the outside, and therefore she is equally uncertain of its being really desirable as of its being to be had. In the mean time she assures you that she will do everything in her power to avoid Trim Street, although you have not expressed the fearful presentiment of it which was rather expected.

We know that Mrs. Perrot will want to get us into Oxford Buildings, but we all unite in particular dislike of that part of the town, and therefore hope to escape. Upon all these different situations you and Edward may confer together, and your opinion of each will be expected with eagerness.

As to our pictures, the battle-piece, Mr. Nibbs, Sir William East, and all the old heterogeneous, miscellany, manuscript, Scriptural pieces dispersed over the house, are to be given to James. Your own drawings will not cease to be your own, and the two paintings on tin will be at your disposal. My mother says that the French agricultural prints in the best bedroom were given by Edward to his two sisters. Do you or he know anything about it?

She has written to my aunt, and we are all impatient for the answer. I do not know how to give up the idea of our both going to Paragon in May. Your going I consider as indispensably necessary, and I shall not like being left behind; there is no place here or hereabouts that I shall want to be staying at, and though, to be sure, the keep of two will be more than of one, I will endeavor to make the difference less by disordering my stomach with Bath buns; and as to the trouble of accommodating us, whether there are one or two, it is much the same.

According to the first plan, my mother and our two selves are to travel down together, and my father follow us afterwards in about a fortnight or three weeks. We have promised to spend a couple of days at Ibthorp in our way. We must all meet at Bath, you know, before we set out for the sea, and, everything considered, I think the first plan as good as any.

My father and mother, wisely aware of the difficulty of finding in all Bath such a bed as their own, have resolved on taking it with them; all the beds, indeed, that we shall want are to be removed,—namely, besides theirs, our own two, the best for a spare one, and two for servants; and these necessary articles will probably be the only material ones that it would answer to send down. I do not think it will be worth while to remove any of our chests of drawers; we shall be able to get some of a much more commodious sort, made of deal, and painted to look very neat; and I flatter myself that for little comforts of all kinds our apartment will be one of the most complete things of the sort all over Bath, Bristol included.

We have thought at times of removing the sideboard, or a Pembroke table, or some other piece of furniture, but, upon the whole, it has ended in thinking that the trouble and risk of the removal would be more than the advantage of having them at a place where everything may be purchased. Pray send your opinion.

Martha has as good as promised to come to us again in March. Her spirits are better than they were....

My mother bargains for having no trouble at all in furnishing our house in Bath, and I have engaged for your willingly undertaking to do it all. I get more and more reconciled to the idea of our removal. We have lived long enough in this neighborhood: the Basingstoke balls are certainly on the decline, there is something interesting in the bustle of going away, and the prospect of spending future summers by the sea or in Wales is very delightful. For a time we shall now possess many of the advantages which I have often thought of with envy in the wives of sailors or soldiers. It must not be generally known, however, that I am not sacrificing a great deal in quitting the country, or I can expect to inspire no tenderness, no interest, in those we leave behind....

Yours affectionately,   J. A.

Miss AUSTEN,
Godmersham Park, Faversham, Kent.

XIX.

STEVENTON, Thursday (January 8).

MY DEAR CASSANDRA,—The "perhaps" which concluded my last letter being only a "perhaps," will not occasion your being overpowered with surprise, I dare say, if you should receive this before Tuesday, which, unless circumstances are very perverse, will be the case. I received yours with much general philanthropy, and still more peculiar good-will, two days ago; and I suppose I need not tell you that it was very long, being written on a foolscap sheet, and very entertaining, being written by you.

Mr. Payne has been dead long enough for Henry to be out of mourning for him before his last visit, though we knew nothing of it till about that time. Why he died, or of what complaint, or to what noblemen he bequeathed his four daughters in marriage, we have not heard.

I am glad that the Wildmans are going to give a ball, and hope you will not fail to benefit both yourself and me by laying out a few kisses in the purchase of a frank. I believe you are right in proposing to delay the cambric muslin, and I submit with a kind of voluntary reluctance.

Mr. Peter Debary has declined Deane curacy; he wishes to be settled near London. A foolish reason! as if Deane were not near London in comparison of Exeter or York. Take the whole world through, and he will find many more places at a greater distance from London than Deane than he will at a less. What does he think of Glencoe or Lake Katherine?

I feel rather indignant that any possible objection should be raised against so valuable a piece of preferment, so delightful a situation!—that Deane should not be universally allowed to be as near the metropolis as any other country villages. As this is the case, however, as Mr. Peter Debary has shown himself a Peter in the blackest sense of the word, we are obliged to look elsewhere for an heir; and my father has thought it a necessary compliment to James Digweed to offer the curacy to him, though without considering it as either a desirable or an eligible situation for him. Unless he is in love with Miss Lyford, I think he had better not be settled exactly in this neighborhood; and unless he is very much in love with her indeed, he is not likely to think a salary of 50*l.* equal in value or efficiency to one of 75*l.*

Were you indeed to be considered as one of the fixtures of the house!—but you were never actually erected in it either by Mr. Egerton Brydges or Mrs. Lloyd....

You are very kind in planning presents for me to make, and my mother has shown me exactly the same attention; but as I do not choose to have generosity dictated to me, I shall not resolve on giving my cabinet to Anna till the first thought of it has been my own.

Sidmouth is now talked of as our summer abode. Get all the information, therefore, about it that you can from Mrs. C. Cage.

My father's old ministers are already deserting him to pay their court to his son. The brown mare, which, as well as the black, was to devolve on James at our removal, has not had patience to wait for that, and has settled herself even now at Deane. The death of Hugh Capet, which, like that of Mr. Skipsey, though undesired, was not wholly unexpected, being purposely effected, has made the immediate possession of the mare very convenient, and everything else I suppose will be seized by degrees in the same manner. Martha and I work at the books every day.

Yours affectionately,   J. A.

Miss AUSTEN,
Godmersham Park, Faversham, Kent.

XX.

STEVENTON, Wednesday (January 14).

POOR Miss Austen! It appears to me that I have rather oppressed you of late by the frequency of my letters. You had hoped not to hear from me again before Tuesday, but Sunday showed you with what a merciless sister you had to deal. I cannot recall the past, but you shall not hear from me quite so often in future.

Your letter to Mary was duly received before she left Deane with Martha yesterday morning, and it gives us great pleasure to know that the Chilham ball was so agreeable, and that you danced four dances with Mr. Kemble. Desirable, however, as the latter circumstance was, I cannot help wondering at its taking place. Why did you dance four dances with so stupid a man? Why not rather dance two of them with some elegant brother officer who was struck with your appearance as soon as you entered the room?

Martha left you her best love. She will write to you herself in a short time; but trusting to my memory rather than her own, she has nevertheless desired me to ask you to purchase for her two bottles of Steele's lavender water when you are in town, provided you should go to the shop on your own account, otherwise you may be sure that she would not have you recollect the request.

James dined with us yesterday, wrote to Edward in the evening, filled three sides of paper, every line inclining too much towards the northeast, and the very first line of all scratched out, and this morning he joins his lady in the fields of Elysium and Ibthorp.

Last Friday was a very busy day with us. We were visited by Miss Lyford and Mr. Bayle. The latter began his operations in the house, but had only time to finish the four sitting-rooms; the rest is deferred till the spring is more advanced and the days longer. He took his paper of appraisement away with him, and therefore we only know the estimate he has made of one or two articles of furniture which my father particularly inquired into. I understand, however, that he was of opinion that the whole would amount to more than two hundred pounds, and it is not imagined that this will comprehend the brewhouse and many other, etc., etc.

Miss Lyford was very pleasant, and gave my mother such an account of the houses in Westgate Buildings, where Mrs. Lyford lodged four years ago, as made her think of a situation there with great pleasure, but your opposition will be without difficulty decisive, and my father, in particular, who was very well inclined towards the Row before, has now ceased to think of it entirely. At present the environs of Laura Place seem to be his choice. His views on the subject are much advanced since I came home; he grows quite ambitious, and actually requires now a comfortable and a creditable-looking house.

On Saturday Miss Lyford went to her long home,—that is to say, it was a long way off,— and soon afterwards a party of fine ladies issuing from a well-known commodious green vehicle, their heads full of Bantam cocks and Galinies, entered the house,—Mrs. Heathcote, Mrs. Harwood, Mrs. James Austen, Miss Bigg, Miss Jane Blachford.

Hardly a day passes in which we do not have some visitor or other: yesterday came Mrs. Bramstone, who is very sorry that she is to lose us, and afterwards Mr. Holder, who was shut up for an hour with my father and James in a most awful manner. John Bond *est à lui*....

XXI.

STEVENTON, Wednesday (January 21).
EXPECT a most agreeable letter, for not being overburdened with subject (having nothing at all to say), I shall have no check to my genius from beginning to end.

Well, and so Prank's letter has made you very happy, but you are afraid he would not have patience to stay for the "Haarlem," which you wish him to have done as being safer than the merchantman. Poor fellow! to wait from the middle of November to the end of December, and perhaps even longer, it must be sad work; especially in a place where the ink is so abominably pale. What a surprise to him it must have been on October 20, to be visited, collared, and thrust out of the "Petterel" by Captain Inglis. He kindly passes over the poignancy of his feelings in quitting his ship, his officers, and his men.

What a pity it is that he should not be in England at the time of this promotion, because he certainly would have had an appointment, so everybody says, and therefore it must be right for me to say it too. Had he been really here, the certainty of the appointment, I dare say, would not have been half so great, but as it could not be brought to the proof, his absence will be always a lucky source of regret.

Eliza talks of having read in a newspaper that all the first lieutenants of the frigates whose captains were to be sent into line-of-battle ships were to be promoted to the rank of commanders. If it be true, Mr. Valentine may afford himself a fine Valentine's knot, and Charles may perhaps become first of the "Endymion," though I suppose Captain Durham is too likely to bring a villain with him under that denomination....

The neighborhood have quite recovered the death of Mrs. Rider,—so much so, that I think they are rather rejoiced at it now; her things were so very dear! and Mrs. Rogers is to be all that is desirable. Not even death itself can fix the friendship of the world....

The Wylmots being robbed must be an amusing thing to their acquaintance, and I hope it is as much their pleasure as it seems their avocation to be subjects of general entertainment.

I have a great mind not to acknowledge the receipt of your letter, which I have just had the pleasure of reading, because I am so ashamed to compare the sprawling lines of this with it. But if I say all that I have to say, I hope I have no reason to hang myself....

Why did not J. D. make his proposals to you? I suppose he went to see the cathedral, that he might know how he should like to be married in it....

Miss AUSTEN,
Godmersham Park, Faversham, Kent.

XXII.

SOUTHAMPTON, Wednesday (January 7, 1807).

MY DEAR CASSANDRA,—You were mistaken in supposing I should expect your letter on Sunday; I had no idea of hearing from you before Tuesday, and my pleasure yesterday was therefore unhurt by any previous disappointment. I thank you for writing so much; you must really have sent me the value of two letters in one. We are extremely glad to hear that Elizabeth is so much better, and hope you will be sensible of still further amendment in her when you return from Canterbury.

Of your visit there I must now speak "incessantly;" it surprises, but pleases me more, and I consider it as a very just and honorable distinction of you, and not less to the credit of Mrs. Knight. I have no doubt of your spending your time with her most pleasantly in quiet and rational conversation, and am so far from thinking her expectations of you will be deceived, that my only fear is of your being so agreeable, so much to her taste, as to make her wish to keep you with her forever. If that should be the case, we must remove to Canterbury, which I should not like so well as Southampton.

When you receive this, our guests will be all gone or going; and I shall be left to the comfortable disposal of my time, to ease of mind from the torments of rice puddings and apple dumplings, and probably to regret that I did not take more pains to please them all.

Mrs. J. Austen has asked me to return with her to Steventon; I need not give my answer; and she has invited my mother to spend there the time of Mrs. F. A.'s confinement, which she seems half inclined to do.

A few days ago I had a letter from Miss Irvine, and as I was in her debt, you will guess it to be a remonstrance, not a very severe one, however; the first page is in her usual retrospective, jealous, inconsistent style, but the remainder is chatty and harmless. She supposes my silence may have proceeded from resentment of her not having written to inquire particularly after my hooping-cough, etc. She is a funny one.

I have answered her letter, and have endeavored to give something like the truth with as little incivility as I could, by placing my silence to the want of subject in the very quiet way in which we live. Phebe has repented, and stays. I have also written to Charles, and I answered Miss Buller's letter by return of post, as I intended to tell you in my last.

Two or three things I recollected when it was too late, that I might have told you; one is that the Welbys have lost their eldest son by a putrid fever at Eton, and another that Tom Chute is going to settle in Norfolk.

You have scarcely ever mentioned Lizzy since your being at Godmersham. I hope it is not because she is altered for the worse.

I cannot yet satisfy Fanny as to Mrs. Foote's baby's name, and I must not encourage her to expect a good one, as Captain Foote is a professed adversary to all but the plainest; he likes only Mary, Elizabeth, Anne, etc. Our best chance is of "Caroline," which in compliment to a sister seems the only exception.

He dined with us on Friday, and I fear will not soon venture again, for the strength of our dinner was a boiled leg of mutton, underdone even for James; and Captain Foote has a particular dislike to underdone mutton; but he was so good-humored and pleasant that I did not much mind his being starved. He gives us all the most cordial invitation to his house in the country, saying just what the Williams ought to say to make us welcome. Of them we have seen nothing since you left us, and we hear that they are just gone to Bath again, to be out of the way of further alterations at Brooklands.

Mrs. F. A. has had a very agreeable letter from Mrs. Dickson, who was delighted with the purse, and desires her not to provide herself with a christening dress, which is exactly what her young correspondent wanted; and she means to defer making any of the caps as long as she can, in hope of having Mrs. D.'s present in time to be serviceable as a pattern. She desires me to tell you that the gowns were cut out before your letter arrived, but that they are long enough for Caroline. The Beds, as I believe they are called, have fallen to Frank's share to continue, and of course are cut out to admiration.

"Alphonsine" did not do. We were disgusted in twenty pages, as, independent of a bad translation, it has indelicacies which disgrace a pen hitherto so pure; and we changed it for the "Female Quixote," which now makes our evening amusement; to me a very high one, as I find the work quite equal to what I remembered it. Mrs. F. A., to whom it is new, enjoys it as one could wish; the other Mary, I believe, has little pleasure from that or any other book.

My mother does not seem at all more disappointed than ourselves at the termination of the family treaty; she thinks less of that just now than of the comfortable state of her own finances, which she finds on closing her year's accounts beyond her expectation, as she begins the new year with a balance of 30*l.* in her favor; and when she has written her answer to my aunt, which you know always hangs a little upon her mind, she will be above the world entirely. You will have a great deal of unreserved discourse with Mrs. K., I dare say, upon this subject, as well as upon many other of our family matters. Abuse everybody but me.

Thursday.—We expected James yesterday, but he did not come; if he comes at all now, his visit will be a very short one, as he must return to-morrow, that Ajax and the chair may be sent to Winchester on Saturday. Caroline's new pelisse depended upon her mother's being able or not to come so far in the chair; how the guinea that will be saved by the same means of return is to be spent I know not. Mrs. J. A. does not talk much of poverty now, though she has no hope of my brother's being able to buy another horse next summer.

Their scheme against Warwickshire continues, but I doubt the family's being at Stoneleigh so early as James says he must go, which is May.

My mother is afraid I have not been explicit enough on the subject of her wealth; she began 1806 with 68*l.* she begins 1807 with 99*l.*, and this after 32*l.* purchase of stock. Frank too has been settling his accounts and making calculations, and each party feels quite equal to our present expenses; but much increase of house-rent would not do for either. Frank limits himself, I believe, to four hundred a year.

You will be surprised to hear that Jenny is not yet come back; we have heard nothing of her since her reaching Itchingswell, and can only suppose that she must be detained by illness in somebody or other, and that she has been each day expecting to be able to come on the morrow. I am glad I did not know beforehand that she was to be absent during the whole or almost the whole of our friends being with us, for though the inconvenience has not been nothing, I should have feared still more. Our dinners have certainly suffered not a little by having only Molly's head and Molly's hands to conduct them; she fries better than she did, but not like Jenny.

We did not take our walk on Friday, it was too dirty, nor have we yet done it; we may perhaps do something like it to-day, as after seeing Frank skate, which he hopes to do in the meadows by the beech, we are to treat ourselves with a passage over the ferry. It is one of the pleasantest frosts I ever knew, so very quiet. I hope it will last some time longer for Frank's sake, who is quite anxious to get some skating; he tried yesterday, but it would not do.

Our acquaintance increase too fast. He was recognized lately by Admiral Bertie, and a few days since arrived the Admiral and his daughter Catherine to wait upon us. There was nothing to like or dislike in either. To the Berties are to be added the Lances, with whose cards we have been endowed, and whose visit Frank and I returned yesterday. They live about a mile and three-quarters from S. to the right of the new road to Portsmouth, and I believe their house is one of those which are to be seen almost anywhere among the woods on the other side of the Itchen. It is a handsome building, stands high, and in a very beautiful situation.

We found only Mrs. Lance at home, and whether she boasts any offspring besides a grand pianoforte did not appear. She was civil and chatty enough, and offered to introduce us to some acquaintance in Southampton, which we gratefully declined.

I suppose they must be acting by the orders of Mr. Lance of Netherton in this civility, as there seems no other reason for their coming near us. They will not come often, I dare say. They live in a handsome style and are rich, and she seemed to like to be rich, and we gave her to understand that we were far from being so; she will soon feel therefore that we are not worth her acquaintance.

You must have heard from Martha by this time. We have had no accounts of Kintbury since her letter to me.

Mrs. F. A. has had one fainting fit lately; it came on as usual after eating a hearty dinner, but did not last long.

I can recollect nothing more to say. When my letter is gone, I suppose I shall.

Yours affectionately,   J. A.

I have just asked Caroline if I should send her love to her godmamma, to which she answered "Yes."

Miss AUSTEN,
Godmersham Park, Faversham, Kent.

XXIII.

SOUTHAMPTON, February 8.

... OUR garden is putting in order by a man who bears a remarkably good character, has a very fine complexion, and asks something less than the first. The shrubs which border the gravel walk, he says, are only sweetbrier and roses, and the latter of an indifferent sort; we mean to get a few of a better kind, therefore, and at my own particular desire he procures us some syringas. I could not do without a syringa, for the sake of Cowper's line. We talk also of a laburnum. The border under the terrace wall is clearing away to receive currants and gooseberry bushes, and a spot is found very proper for raspberries.

The alterations and improvements within doors, too, advance very properly, and the offices will be made very convenient indeed. Our dressing-table is constructing on the spot, out of a large kitchen table belonging to the house, for doing which we have the permission of Mr. Husket, Lord Lansdown's painter,—domestic painter, I should call him, for he lives in the castle. Domestic chaplains have given way to this more necessary office, and I suppose whenever the walls want no touching up he is employed about my lady's face.

The morning was so wet that I was afraid we should not be able to see our little visitor; but Frank, who alone could go to church, called for her after service, and she is now talking away at my side and examining the treasures of my writing-desk drawers,—very happy, I believe. Not at all shy, of course. Her name is Catherine, and her sister's Caroline. She is something like her brother, and as short for her age, but not so well-looking.

What is become of all the shyness in the world? Moral as well as natural diseases disappear in the progress of time, and new ones take their place. Shyness and the sweating sickness have given way to confidence and paralytic complaints....

Evening.—Our little visitor has just left us, and left us highly pleased with her; she is a nice, natural, open-hearted, affectionate girl, with all the ready civility which one sees in the best children in the present day; so unlike anything that I was myself at her age, that I am often all astonishment and shame. Half her time was spent at spillikins, which I consider as a very valuable part of our household furniture, and as not the least important benefaction from the family of Knight to that of Austen.

But I must tell you a story. Mary has for some time had notice from Mrs. Dickson of the intended arrival of a certain Miss Fowler in this place. Miss F. is an intimate friend of Mrs. D., and a good deal known as such to Mary. On Thursday last she called here while we were out. Mary found, on our return, her card with only her name on it, and she had left word that she would call again. The particularity of this made us talk, and, among other conjectures, Frank said in joke, "I dare say she is staying with the Pearsons." The connection of the names struck Mary, and she immediately recollected Miss Fowler's having been very intimate with persons so called, and, upon putting everything together, we have scarcely a doubt of her being actually staying with the only family in the place whom we cannot visit.

What a *contretemps!* in the language of France. What an unluckiness! in that of Madame Duval. The black gentleman has certainly employed one of his menial imps to bring about this complete, though trifling mischief. Miss F. has never called again, but we are in daily expectation of it. Miss P. has, of course, given her a proper understanding of the business. It is evident that Miss F. did not expect or wish to have the visit returned, and Frank is quite as much on his guard for his wife as we could desire for her sake or our own.

We shall rejoice in being so near Winchester when Edward belongs to it, and can never have our spare bed filled more to our satisfaction than by him. Does he leave Eltham at Easter?

We are reading "Clarentine," and are surprised to find how foolish it is. I remember liking it much less on a second reading than at the first, and it does not bear a third at all. It is full of unnatural conduct and forced difficulties, without striking merit of any kind.

Miss Harrison is going into Devonshire, to attend Mrs. Dusantoy, as usual. Miss J. is married to young Mr. G., and is to be very unhappy. He swears, drinks, is cross, jealous, selfish, and brutal. The match makes her family miserable, and has occasioned his being disinherited.

The Browns are added to our list of acquaintance. He commands the Sea Fencibles here, under Sir Thomas, and was introduced at his own desire by the latter when we saw him last week. As yet the gentlemen only have visited, as Mrs. B. is ill; but she is a nice-looking woman, and wears one of the prettiest straw bonnets in the place.

Monday.—The garret beds are made, and ours will be finished to-day. I had hoped it would be finished on Saturday, but neither Mrs. Hall nor Jenny was able to give help enough for that, and I have as yet done very little, and Mary nothing at all. This week we shall do more, and I should like to have all the five beds completed by the end of it. There will then be the window-curtains, sofa-cover, and a carpet to be altered.

I should not be surprised if we were to be visited by James again this week; he gave us reason to expect him soon, and if they go to Eversley he cannot come next week.

There, I flatter myself I have constructed you a smartish letter, considering my want of materials; but, like my dear Dr. Johnson, I believe I have dealt more in notions than facts.

I hope your cough is gone, and that you are otherwise well, and remain, with love,

Yours affectionately,   J. A.

Miss AUSTEN,
Godmersham Park, Faversham, Kent.

XXIV.

GODMERSHAM, Wednesday (June 15, 1808).

MY DEAR CASSANDRA,—Where shall I begin? Which of all my important nothings shall I tell you first? At half after seven yesterday morning Henry saw us into our own carriage, and we drove away from the Bath Hotel; which, by the by, had been found most uncomfortable quarters,—very dirty, very noisy, and very ill-provided. James began his journey by the coach at five. Our first eight miles were hot; Deptford Hill brought to my mind our hot journey into Kent fourteen years ago; but after Blackheath we suffered nothing, and as the day advanced it grew quite cool. At Dartford, which we reached within the two hours and three-quarters, we went to the Bull, the same inn at which we breakfasted in that said journey, and on the present occasion had about the same bad butter.

At half-past ten we were again off, and, travelling on without any adventure reached Sittingbourne by three. Daniel was watching for us at the door of the George, and I was acknowledged very kindly by Mr. and Mrs. Marshall, to the latter of whom I devoted my conversation, while Mary went out to buy some gloves. A few minutes, of course, did for Sittingbourne; and so off we drove, drove, drove, and by six o'clock were at Godmersham.

Our two brothers were walking before the house as we approached, as natural as life. Fanny and Lizzy met us in the Hall with a great deal of pleasant joy; we went for a few minutes into the breakfast-parlor, and then proceeded to our rooms. Mary has the Hall chamber. I am in the Yellow room—very literally—for I am writing in it at this moment. It seems odd to me to have such a great place all to myself, and to be at Godmersham without you is also odd.

You are wished for, I assure you: Fanny, who came to me as soon as she had seen her Aunt James to her room, and stayed while I dressed, was as energetic as usual in her longings for you. She is grown both in height and size since last year, but not immoderately, looks very well, and seems as to conduct and manner just what she was and what one could wish her to continue.

Elizabeth,[4] who was dressing when we arrived, came to me for a minute attended by Marianne, Charles, and Louisa, and, you will not doubt, gave me a very affectionate welcome. That I had received such from Edward also I need not mention; but I do, you see, because it is a pleasure. I never saw him look in better health, and Fanny says he is perfectly well. I cannot praise Elizabeth's looks, but they are probably affected by a cold. Her little namesake has gained in beauty in the last three years, though not all that Marianne has lost. Charles is not quite so lovely as he was. Louisa is much as I expected, and Cassandra I find handsomer than

---

[4] Mrs. Edward Austen.

I expected, though at present disguised by such a violent breaking-out that she does not come down after dinner. She has charming eyes and a nice open countenance, and seems likely to be very lovable. Her size is magnificent.

I was agreeably surprised to find Louisa Bridges still here. She looks remarkably well (legacies are very wholesome diet), and is just what she always was. John is at Sandling. You may fancy our dinner-party therefore; Fanny, of course, belonging to it, and little Edward, for that day. He was almost too happy, his happiness at least made him too talkative.

It has struck ten; I must go to breakfast.

Since breakfast I have had a *tête-à-tête* with Edward in his room; he wanted to know James's plans and mine, and from what his own now are I think it already nearly certain that I shall return when they do, though not with them. Edward will be going about the same time to Alton, where he has business with Mr. Trimmer, and where he means his son should join him; and I shall probably be his companion to that place, and get on afterwards somehow or other.

I should have preferred a rather longer stay here certainly, but there is no prospect of any later conveyance for me, as he does not mean to accompany Edward on his return to Winchester, from a very natural unwillingness to leave Elizabeth at that time. I shall at any rate be glad not to be obliged to be an incumbrance on those who have brought me here, for, as James has no horse, I must feel in their carriage that I am taking his place. We were rather crowded yesterday, though it does not become me to say so, as I and my boa were of the party, and it is not to be supposed but that a child of three years of age was fidgety.

I need scarcely beg you to keep all this to yourself, lest it should get round by Anna's means. She is very kindly inquired after by her friends here, who all regret her not coming with her father and mother.

I left Henry, I hope, free from his tiresome complaint, in other respects well, and thinking with great pleasure of Cheltenham and Stoneleigh.

The brewery scheme is quite at an end: at a meeting of the subscribers last week it was by general, and I believe very hearty, consent dissolved.

The country is very beautiful. I saw as much as ever to admire in my yesterday's journey...

XXV.

CASTLE SQUARE, October 13.

MY DEAREST CASSANDRA,—I have received your letter, and with most melancholy anxiety was it expected, for the sad news[5] reached us last night, but without any particulars. It came in a short letter to Martha from her sister, begun at Steventon and finished in Winchester.

We have felt, we do feel, for you all, as you will not need to be told,—for you, for Fanny, for Henry, for Lady Bridges, and for dearest Edward, whose loss and whose sufferings seem to make those of every other person nothing. God be praised that you can say what you do of him: that he has a religious mind to bear him up, and a disposition that will gradually lead him to comfort.

My dear, dear Fanny, I am so thankful that she has you with her! You will be everything to her; you will give her all the consolation that human aid can give. May the Almighty sustain you all, and keep you, my dearest Cassandra, well; but for the present I dare say you are equal to everything.

---

[5] The death of Mrs. Edward Austen.

You will know that the poor boys are at Steventon. Perhaps it is best for them, as they will have more means of exercise and amusement there than they could have with us, but I own myself disappointed by the arrangement. I should have loved to have them with me at such a time. I shall write to Edward by this post.

We shall, of course, hear from you again very soon, and as often as you can write. We will write as you desire, and I shall add Bookham. Hamstall, I suppose, you write to yourselves, as you do not mention it.

What a comfort that Mrs. Deedes is saved from present misery and alarm! But it will fall heavy upon poor Harriot; and as for Lady B., but that her fortitude does seem truly great, I should fear the effect of such a blow, and so unlooked for. I long to hear more of you all. Of Henry's anguish I think with grief and solicitude; but he will exert himself to be of use and comfort.

With what true sympathy our feelings are shared by Martha you need not be told; she is the friend and sister under every circumstance.

We need not enter into a panegyric on the departed, but it is sweet to think of her great worth, of her solid principles, of her true devotion, her excellence in every relation of life. It is also consolatory to reflect on the shortness of the sufferings which led her from this world to a better.

Farewell for the present, my dearest sister. Tell Edward that we feel for him and pray for him.

Yours affectionately,
J. AUSTEN.

I will write to Catherine.
Perhaps you can give me some directions about mourning.

Miss AUSTEN, EDWARD AUSTEN'S, Esq.,
Godmersham Park, Faversham, Kent.

XXVI.

CASTLE SQUARE, Saturday night (October 15).

MY DEAR CASSANDRA,—Your accounts make us as comfortable as we can expect to be at such a time. Edward's loss is terrible, and must be felt as such, and these are too early days indeed to think of moderation in grief, either in him or his afflicted daughter, but soon we may hope that our dear Fanny's sense of duty to that beloved father will rouse her to exertion. For his sake, and as the most acceptable proof of love to the spirit of her departed mother, she will try to be tranquil and resigned. Does she feel you to be a comfort to her, or is she too much overpowered for anything but solitude?

Your account of Lizzy is very interesting. Poor child! One must hope the impression will be strong, and yet one's heart aches for a dejected mind of eight years old.

I suppose you see the corpse? How does it appear? We are anxious to be assured that Edward will not attend the funeral, but when it comes to the point I think he must feel it impossible.

Your parcel shall set off on Monday, and I hope the shoes will fit; Martha and I both tried them on. I shall send you such of your mourning as I think most likely to be useful, reserving for myself your stockings and half the velvet, in which selfish arrangement I know I am doing what you wish.

I am to be in bombazeen and crape, according to what we are told is universal here, and which agrees with Martha's previous observation. My mourning, however, will not impoverish me, for by having my velvet pelisse fresh lined and made up, I am sure I shall have no occasion this winter for anything new of that sort. I take my cloak for the lining, and shall send yours on the chance of its doing something of the same for you, though I believe your pelisse is in better repair than mine. One Miss Baker makes my gown and the other my bonnet, which is to be silk covered with crape.

I have written to Edward Cooper, and hope he will not send one of his letters of cruel comfort to my poor brother: and yesterday I wrote to Alethea Bigg, in reply to a letter from her. She tells us in confidence that Catherine is to be married on Tuesday se'nnight. Mr. Hill is expected at Manydown in the course of the ensuing week.

We are desired by Mrs. Harrison and Miss Austen to say everything proper for them to yourself and Edward on this sad occasion, especially that nothing but a wish of not giving additional trouble where so much is inevitable prevents their writing themselves to express their concern. They seem truly to feel concern.

I am glad you can say what you do of Mrs. Knight and of Goodnestone in general. It is a great relief to me to know that the shock did not make any of them ill. But what a task was yours to announce it! Now I hope you are not overpowered with letter-writing, as Henry and John can ease you of many of your correspondents.

Was Mr. Scudamore in the house at the time, was any application attempted, and is the seizure at all accounted for?

Sunday.—As Edward's letter to his son is not come here, we know that you must have been informed as early as Friday of the boys being at Steventon, which I am glad of.

Upon your letter to Dr. Goddard's being forwarded to them, Mary wrote to ask whether my mother wished to have her grandsons sent to her. We decided on their remaining where they were, which I hope my brother will approve of. I am sure he will do us the justice of believing that in such a decision we sacrificed inclination to what we thought best.

I shall write by the coach to-morrow to Mrs. J. A., and to Edward, about their mourning, though this day's post will probably bring directions to them on that subject from yourselves. I shall certainly make use of the opportunity of addressing our nephew on the most serious of all concerns, as I naturally did in my letter to him before. The poor boys are, perhaps, more comfortable at Steventon than they could be here, but you will understand my feelings with respect to it.

To-morrow will be a dreadful day for you all. Mr. Whitfield's will be a severe duty.[6] Glad shall I be to hear that it is over.

That you are forever in our thoughts you will not doubt. I see your mournful party in my mind's eye under every varying circumstance of the day; and in the evening especially figure to myself its sad gloom: the efforts to talk, the frequent summons to melancholy orders and cares, and poor Edward, restless in misery, going from one room to another, and perhaps not seldom upstairs, to see all that remains of his Elizabeth. Dearest Fanny must now look upon herself as his prime source of comfort, his dearest friend; as the being who is gradually to supply to him, to the extent that is possible, what he has lost. This consideration will elevate and cheer her.

---

[6] Mr. Whitfield was the Rector of Godmersham at this time, having come there in 1778.

Adieu. You cannot write too often, as I said before. We are heartily rejoiced that the poor baby gives you no particular anxiety. Kiss dear Lizzy for us. Tell Fanny that I shall write in a day or two to Miss Sharpe.

My mother is not ill.

Yours most truly,   J. AUSTEN.

Tell Henry that a hamper of apples is gone to him from Kintbury, and that Mr. Fowle intended writing on Friday (supposing him in London) to beg that the charts, etc., may be consigned to the care of the Palmers. Mrs. Fowle has also written to Miss Palmer to beg she will send for them.

Miss AUSTEN, EDWARD AUSTEN'S, Esq.,
Godmersham Park, Faversham, Kent.

XXVII.

CASTLE SQUARE, Monday (October 24).

MY DEAR CASSANDRA,—Edward and George came to us soon after seven on Saturday, very well, but very cold, having by choice travelled on the outside, and with no greatcoat but what Mr. Wise, the coachman, good-naturedly spared them of his, as they sat by his side. They were so much chilled when they arrived, that I was afraid they must have taken cold; but it does not seem at all the case: I never saw them looking better.

They behave extremely well in every respect, showing quite as much feeling as one wishes to see, and on every occasion speaking of their father with the liveliest affection. His letter was read over by each of them yesterday, and with many tears; George sobbed aloud, Edward's tears do not flow so easily; but as far as I can judge they are both very properly impressed by what has happened. Miss Lloyd, who is a more impartial judge than I can be, is exceedingly pleased with them.

George is almost a new acquaintance to me, and I find him in a different way as engaging as Edward.

We do not want amusement: bilbocatch, at which George is indefatigable, spillikins, paper ships, riddles, conundrums, and cards, with watching the flow and ebb of the river, and now and then a stroll out, keep us well employed; and we mean to avail ourselves of our kind papa's consideration, by not returning to Winchester till quite the evening of Wednesday.

Mrs. J. A. had not time to get them more than one suit of clothes; their others are making here, and though I do not believe Southampton is famous for tailoring, I hope it will prove itself better than Basingstoke. Edward has an old black coat, which will save his having a second new one; but I find that black pantaloons are considered by them as necessary, and of course one would not have them made uncomfortable by the want of what is usual on such occasions.

Fanny's letter was received with great pleasure yesterday, and her brother sends his thanks and will answer it soon. We all saw what she wrote, and were very much pleased with it.

To-morrow I hope to hear from you, and to-morrow we must think of poor Catherine. To-day Lady Bridges is the heroine of our thoughts, and glad shall we be when we can fancy the meeting over. There will then be nothing so very bad for Edward to undergo.

The "St. Albans," I find, sailed on the very day of my letters reaching Yarmouth, so that we must not expect an answer at present; we scarcely feel, however, to be in suspense, or only enough to keep our plans to ourselves. We have been obliged to explain them to our young visitors, in consequence of Fanny's letter, but we have not yet mentioned them to Steventon. We are all quite familiarized to the idea ourselves; my mother only wants Mrs. Seward to go out at midsummer.

What sort of a kitchen garden is there? Mrs. J. A. expresses her fear of our settling in Kent, and, till this proposal was made, we began to look forward to it here; my mother was actually talking of a house at Wye. It will be best, however, as it is.

Anne has just given her mistress warning; she is going to be married; I wish she would stay her year.

On the subject of matrimony, I must notice a wedding in the Salisbury paper, which has amused me very much, Dr. Phillot to Lady Frances St. Lawrence. She wanted to have a husband, I suppose, once in her life, and he a Lady Frances.

I hope your sorrowing party were at church yesterday, and have no longer that to dread. Martha was kept at home by a cold, but I went with my two nephews, and I saw Edward was much affected by the sermon, which, indeed, I could have supposed purposely addressed to the afflicted, if the text had not naturally come in the course of Dr. Mant's observations on the Litany: 'All that are in danger, necessity, or tribulation,' was the subject of it. The weather did not allow us afterwards to get farther than the quay, where George was very happy as long as we could stay, flying about from one side to the other, and skipping on board a collier immediately.

In the evening we had the Psalms and Lessons, and a sermon at home, to which they were very attentive; but you will not expect to hear that they did not return to conundrums the moment it was over. Their aunt has written pleasantly of them, which was more than I hoped.

While I write now, George is most industriously making and naming paper ships, at which he afterwards shoots with horse-chestnuts, brought from Steventon on purpose; and Edward equally intent over the "Lake of Killarney," twisting himself about in one of our great chairs.

Tuesday.—Your close-written letter makes me quite ashamed of my wide lines; you have sent me a great deal of matter, most of it very welcome. As to your lengthened stay, it is no more than I expected, and what must be, but you cannot suppose I like it.

All that you say of Edward is truly comfortable; I began to fear that when the bustle of the first week was over, his spirits might for a time be more depressed; and perhaps one must still expect something of the kind. If you escape a bilious attack, I shall wonder almost as much as rejoice. I am glad you mentioned where Catherine goes to-day; it is a good plan, but sensible people may generally be trusted to form such.

The day began cheerfully, but it is not likely to continue what it should, for them or for us. We had a little water-party yesterday; I and my two nephews went from the Itchen Ferry up to Northam, where we landed, looked into the 74, and walked home, and it was so much enjoyed that I had intended to take them to Netley to-day; the tide is just right for our going immediately after moonshine, but I am afraid there will be rain; if we cannot get so far, however, we may perhaps go round from the ferry to the quay.

I had not proposed doing more than cross the Itchen yesterday, but it proved so pleasant, and so much to the satisfaction of all, that when we reached the middle of the stream we agreed to be rowed up the river; both the boys rowed great part of the way, and their questions and remarks, as well as their enjoyment, were very amusing; George's inquiries were endless, and his eagerness in everything reminds me often of his uncle Henry.

Our evening was equally agreeable in its way: I introduced speculation, and it was so much approved that we hardly knew how to leave off.

Your idea of an early dinner to-morrow is exactly what we propose, for, after writing the first part of this letter, it came into my head that at this time of year we have not summer evenings. We shall watch the light to-day, that we may not give them a dark drive to-morrow.

They send their best love to papa and everybody, with George's thanks for the letter brought by this post. Martha begs my brother may be assured of her interest in everything relating to him and his family, and of her sincerely partaking our pleasure in the receipt of every good account from Godmersham.

Of Chawton I think I can have nothing more to say, but that everything you say about it in the letter now before me will, I am sure, as soon as I am able to read it to her, make my mother consider the plan with more and more pleasure. We had formed the same views on H. Digweed's farm.

A very kind and feeling letter is arrived to-day from Kintbury. Mrs. Fowle's sympathy and solicitude on such an occasion you will be able to do justice to, and to express it as she wishes to my brother. Concerning you, she says: "Cassandra will, I know, excuse my writing to her; it is not to save myself but her that I omit so doing. Give my best, my kindest love to her, and tell her I feel for her as I know she would for me on the same occasion, and that I most sincerely hope her health will not suffer."

We have just had two hampers of apples from Kintbury, and the floor of our little garret is almost covered. Love to all.

Yours very affectionately, J. A.

Miss AUSTEN, EDWARD AUSTEN'S, Esq.,
Godmersham Park, Faversham, Kent.

XXVIII.

CASTLE SQUARE, Sunday (November 21).

YOUR letter, my dear Cassandra, obliges me to write immediately, that you may have the earliest notice of Frank's intending, if possible, to go to Godmersham exactly at the time now fixed for your visit to Goodnestone.

He resolved, almost directly on the receipt of your former letter, to try for an extension of his leave of absence, that he might be able to go down to you for two days, but charged me not to give you any notice of it, on account of the uncertainty of success. Now, however, I must give it, and now perhaps he may be giving it himself; for I am just in the hateful predicament of being obliged to write what I know will somehow or other be of no use.

He meant to ask for five days more, and if they were granted, to go down by Thursday night's mail, and spend Friday and Saturday with you; and he considered his chance of succeeding by no means bad. I hope it will take place as he planned, and that your arrangements with Goodnestone may admit of suitable alteration.

Your news of Edward Bridges was quite news, for I have had no letter from Wrotham. I wish him happy with all my heart, and hope his choice may turn out according to his own expectations, and beyond those of his family; and I dare say it will. Marriage is a great improver, and in a similar situation Harriet may be as amiable as Eleanor. As to money, that will come, you may be sure, because they cannot do without it. When you see him again, pray give him our congratulations and best wishes. This match will certainly set John and Lucy going.

There are six bedchambers at Chawton; Henry wrote to my mother the other day, and luckily mentioned the number, which is just what we wanted to be assured of. He speaks also of garrets for store-places, one of which she immediately planned fitting up for Edward's man-servant; and now perhaps it must be for our own; for she is already quite reconciled to our keeping one. The difficulty of doing without one had been thought of before. His name shall be Robert, if you please.

Before I can tell you of it, you will have heard that Miss Sawbridge is married. It took place, I believe, on Thursday. Mrs. Fowle has for some time been in the secret, but the neighborhood in general were quite unsuspicious. Mr. Maxwell was tutor to the young Gregorys,— consequently, they must be one of the happiest couples in the world, and either of them worthy of envy, for she must be excessively in love, and he mounts from nothing to a comfortable home. Martha has heard him very highly spoken of. They continue for the present at Speen Hill.

I have a Southampton match to return for your Kentish one, Captain G. Heathcote and Miss A. Lyell. I have it from Alethea, and like it, because I had made it before.

Yes, the Stoneleigh business is concluded, but it was not till yesterday that my mother was regularly informed of it, though the news had reached us on Monday evening by way of Steventon. My aunt says as little as may be on the subject by way of information, and nothing at all by way of satisfaction. She reflects on Mr. T. Leigh's dilatoriness, and looks about with great diligence and success for inconvenience and evil, among which she ingeniously places the danger of her new housemaids catching cold on the outside of the coach, when she goes down to Bath, for a carriage makes her sick.

John Binns has been offered their place, but declines it; as she supposes, because he will not wear a livery. Whatever be the cause, I like the effect.

In spite of all my mother's long and intimate knowledge of the writer, she was not up to the expectation of such a letter as this; the discontentedness of it shocked and surprised her—but I see nothing in it out of nature, though a sad nature.

She does not forget to wish for Chambers, you may be sure. No particulars are given, not a word of arrears mentioned, though in her letter to James they were in a general way spoken of. The amount of them is a matter of conjecture, and to my mother a most interesting one; she cannot fix any time for their beginning with any satisfaction to herself but Mrs. Leigh's death, and Henry's two thousand pounds neither agrees with that period nor any other. I did not like to own our previous information of what was intended last July, and have therefore only said that if we could see Henry we might hear many particulars, as I had understood that some confidential conversation had passed between him and Mr. T. L. at Stoneleigh.

We have been as quiet as usual since Frank and Mary left us; Mr. Criswick called on Martha that very morning on his way home again from Portsmouth, and we have had no visitor since.

We called on the Miss Lyells one day, and heard a good account of Mr. Heathcote's canvass, the success of which, of course, exceeds his expectations. Alethea in her letter hopes for my interest, which I conclude means Edward's, and I take this opportunity, therefore, of requesting that he will bring in Mr. Heathcote. Mr. Lane told us yesterday that Mr. H. had behaved very handsomely, and waited on Mr. Thistlethwaite, to say that if he (Mr. T.) would stand, he (Mr. H.) would not oppose him; but Mr. T. declined it, acknowledging himself still smarting under the payment of late electioneering costs.

The Mrs. Hulberts, we learn from Kintbury, come to Steventon this week, and bring Mary Jane Fowle with them on her way to Mrs. Nune's; she returns at Christmas with her brother.

Our brother we may perhaps see in the course of a few days, and we mean to take the opportunity of his help to go one night to the play. Martha ought to see the inside of the theatre once while she lives in Southampton, and I think she will hardly wish to take a second view.

The furniture of Bellevue is to be sold to-morrow, and we shall take it in our usual walk, if the weather be favorable.

How could you have a wet day on Thursday? With us it was a prince of days, the most delightful we have had for weeks; soft, bright, with a brisk wind from the southwest; everybody was out and talking of spring, and Martha and I did not know how to turn back. On Friday evening we had some very blowing weather,—from six to nine; I think we never heard it worse, even here. And one night we had so much rain that it forced its way again into the store-closet; and though the evil was comparatively slight and the mischief nothing, I had some employment the next day in drying parcels, etc. I have now moved still more out of the way.

Martha sends her best love, and thanks you for admitting her to the knowledge of the pros and cons about Harriet Foote; she has an interest in all such matters. I am also to say that she wants to see you. Mary Jane missed her papa and mamma a good deal at first, but now does very well without them. I am glad to hear of little John's being better, and hope your accounts of Mrs. Knight will also improve. Adieu! remember me affectionately to everybody, and believe me,

Ever yours,   J. A.

Miss AUSTEN, EDWARD AUSTEN'S, Esq.,
Godmersham Park, Faversham, Kent.

XXIX.

CASTLE SQUARE, Friday (December 9).

MANY thanks, my dear Cassandra, to you and Mr. Deedes for your joint and agreeable composition, which took me by surprise this morning. He has certainly great merit as a writer; he does ample justice to his subject, and without being diffuse is clear and correct; and though I do not mean to compare his epistolary powers with yours, or to give him the same portion of my gratitude, he certainly has a very pleasing way of winding up a whole, and speeding truth into the world.

"But all this," as my dear Mrs. Piozzi says, "is flight and fancy and nonsense, for my master has his great casks to mind and I have my little children." It is you, however, in this instance, that have the little children, and I that have the great cask, for we are brewing spruce beer again; but my meaning really is, that I am extremely foolish in writing all this unnecessary stuff when I have so many matters to write about that my paper will hardly hold it all. Little matters they are, to be sure, but highly important.

In the first place, Miss Curling is actually at Portsmouth, which I was always in hopes would not happen. I wish her no worse, however, than a long and happy abode there. Here she would probably be dull, and I am sure she would be troublesome.

The bracelets are in my possession, and everything I could wish them to be. They came with Martha's pelisse, which likewise gives great satisfaction.

Soon after I had closed my last letter to you we were visited by Mrs. Dickens and her sister-in-law, Mrs. Bertie, the wife of a lately made Admiral. Mrs. F. A.,[7] I believe, was their first object, but they put up with us very kindly, and Mrs. D., finding in Miss Lloyd a friend of Mrs. Dundas, had another motive for the acquaintance. She seems a really agreeable woman,—that is, her manners are gentle, and she knows a great many of our connections in West Kent. Mrs. Bertie lives in the Polygon, and was out when we returned her visit, which are her two virtues.

A larger circle of acquaintance, and an increase of amusement, is quite in character with our approaching removal. Yes, I mean to go to as many balls as possible, that I may have a good bargain. Everybody is very much concerned at our going away, and everybody is acquainted with Chawton, and speaks of it as a remarkably pretty village, and everybody knows the house we describe, but nobody fixes on the right.

I am very much obliged to Mrs. Knight for such a proof of the interest she takes in me, and she may depend upon it that I will marry Mr. Papillon, whatever may be his reluctance or my own. I owe her much more than such a trifling sacrifice.

Our ball was rather more amusing than I expected. Martha liked it very much, and I did not gape till the last quarter of an hour. It was past nine before we were sent for, and not twelve when we returned. The room was tolerably full, and there were, perhaps, thirty couple of dancers. The melancholy part was to see so many dozen young women standing by without partners, and each of them with two ugly naked shoulders.

It was the same room in which we danced fifteen years ago. I thought it all over, and in spite of the shame of being so much older, felt with thankfulness that I was quite as happy now as then. We paid an additional shilling for our tea, which we took as we chose in an adjoining and very comfortable room.

There were only four dances, and it went to my heart that the Miss Lances (one of them, too, named Emma) should have partners only for two. You will not expect to hear that I was asked to dance, but I was—by the gentleman whom we met that Sunday with Captain D'Auvergne. We have always kept up a bowing acquaintance since, and, being pleased with his black eyes, I spoke to him at the ball, which brought on me this civility; but I do not know his name, and he seems so little at home in the English language that I believe his black eyes may be the best of him. Captain D'Auvergne has got a ship.

Martha and I made use of the very favorable state of yesterday for walking, to pay our duty at Chiswell. We found Mrs. Lance at home and alone, and sat out three other ladies who soon came in. We went by the ferry, and returned by the bridge, and were scarcely at all fatigued.

Edward must have enjoyed the last two days. You, I presume, had a cool drive to Canterbury. Kitty Foote came on Wednesday; and her evening visit began early enough for the last part, the apple-pie, of our dinner, for we never dine now till five.

Yesterday I—or rather, you—had a letter from Nanny Hilliard, the object of which is that she would be very much obliged to us if we would get Hannah a place. I am sorry that I cannot assist her; if you can, let me know, as I shall not answer the letter immediately. Mr. Sloper is married again, not much to Nanny's, or anybody's satisfaction. The lady was governess to Sir Robert's natural children, and seems to have nothing to recommend her. I do not find, however, that Nanny is likely to lose her place in consequence. She says not a word of what service she wishes for Hannah, or what Hannah can do; but a nursery, I suppose, or something of that kind, must be the thing.

---

[7] Frank Austen.

Having now cleared away my smaller articles of news, I come to a communication of some weight; no less than that my uncle and aunt[8] are going to allow James 100*l.* a year. We hear of it through Steventon. Mary sent us the other day an extract from my aunt's letter on the subject, in which the donation is made with the greatest kindness, and intended as a compensation for his loss in the conscientious refusal of Hampstead living; 100*l.* a year being all that he had at the time called its worth, as I find it was always intended at Steventon to divide the real income with Kintbury.

Nothing can be more affectionate than my aunt's language in making the present, and likewise in expressing her hope of their being much more together in future than, to her great regret, they have of late years been. My expectations for my mother do not rise with this event. We will allow a little more time, however, before we fly out.

If not prevented by parish business, James comes to us on Monday. The Mrs. Hulberts and Miss Murden are their guests at present, and likely to continue such till Christmas. Anna comes home on the 19th. The hundred a year begins next Lady-day.

I am glad you are to have Henry with you again; with him and the boys you cannot but have a cheerful, and at times even a merry, Christmas. Martha is so [*MSS. torn*]. . . . We want to be settled at Chawton in time for Henry to come to us for some shooting in October, at least, or a little earlier, and Edward may visit us after taking his boys back to Winchester. Suppose we name the 4th of September. Will not that do?

I have but one thing more to tell you. Mrs. Hill called on my mother yesterday while we were gone to Chiswell, and in the course of the visit asked her whether she knew anything of a clergyman's family of the name of Alford, who had resided in our part of Hampshire. Mrs. Hill had been applied to as likely to give some information of them on account of their probable vicinity to Dr. Hill's living by a lady, or for a lady, who had known Mrs. and the two Miss Alfords in Bath, whither they had removed it seems from Hampshire, and who now wishes to convey to the Miss Alfords some work or trimming which she has been doing for them; but the mother and daughters have left Bath, and the lady cannot learn where they are gone to. While my mother gave us the account, the probability of its being ourselves occurred to us, and it had previously struck herself ... what makes it more likely, and even indispensably to be us, is that she mentioned Mr. Hammond as now having the living or curacy which the father had had. I cannot think who our kind lady can be, but I dare say we shall not like the work.

Distribute the affectionate love of a heart not so tired as the right hand belonging to it.

Yours ever sincerely,   J. A.

Miss Austen, Edward Austen's, Esq.,
Godmersham Park, Faversham, Kent.

XXX.

Castle Square, Tuesday (December 27).

My dear Cassandra,—I can now write at leisure and make the most of my subjects, which is lucky, as they are not numerous this week.

Our house was cleared by half-past eleven on Saturday, and we had the satisfaction of hearing yesterday that the party reached home in safety soon after five.

---

[8] Mr. and Mrs. Leigh Perrot.

I was very glad of your letter this morning; for, my mother taking medicine, Eliza keeping her bed with a cold, and Choles not coming, made us rather dull and dependent on the post. You tell me much that gives me pleasure, but I think not much to answer. I wish I could help you in your needlework. I have two hands and a new thimble that lead a very easy life.

Lady Sondes' match surprises, but does not offend me; had her first marriage been of affection, or had there been a grown-up single daughter, I should not have forgiven her; but I consider everybody as having a right to marry once in their lives for love, if they can, and provided she will now leave off having bad headaches and being pathetic, I can allow her, I can wish her, to be happy.

Do not imagine that your picture of your *tête-à-tête* with Sir B. makes any change in our expectations here; he could not be really reading, though he held the newspaper in his hand; he was making up his mind to the deed, and the manner of it. I think you will have a letter from him soon.

I heard from Portsmouth yesterday, and as I am to send them more clothes, they cannot be expecting a very early return to us. Mary's face is pretty well, but she must have suffered a great deal with it; an abscess was formed and opened.

Our evening party on Thursday produced nothing more remarkable than Miss Murden's coming too, though she had declined it absolutely in the morning, and sitting very ungracious and very silent with us from seven o'clock till half after eleven, for so late was it, owing to the chairmen, before we got rid of them.

The last hour, spent in yawning and shivering in a wide circle round the fire, was dull enough, but the tray had admirable success. The widgeon and the preserved ginger were as delicious as one could wish. But as to our black butter, do not decoy anybody to Southampton by such a lure, for it is all gone. The first pot was opened when Frank and Mary were here, and proved not at all what it ought to be; it was neither solid nor entirely sweet, and on seeing it, Eliza remembered that Miss Austen had said she did not think it had been boiled enough. It was made, you know, when we were absent. Such being the event of the first pot, I would not save the second, and we therefore ate it in unpretending privacy; and though not what it ought to be, part of it was very good.

James means to keep three horses on this increase of income; at present he has but one. Mary wishes the other two to be fit to carry women, and in the purchase of one Edward will probably be called upon to fulfil his promise to his godson. We have now pretty well ascertained James's income to be eleven hundred pounds, curate paid, which makes us very happy,—the ascertainment as well as the income.

Mary does not talk of the garden; it may well be a disagreeable subject to her, but her husband is persuaded that nothing is wanting to make the first new one good but trenching, which is to be done by his own servants and John Bond, by degrees, not at the expense which trenching the other amounted to.

I was happy to hear, chiefly for Anna's sake, that a ball at Manydown was once more in agitation; it is called a child's ball, and given by Mrs. Heathcote to Wm. Such was its beginning at least, but it will probably swell into something more. Edward was invited during his stay at Manydown, and it is to take place between this and Twelfth-day. Mrs. Hulbert has taken Anna a pair of white shoes on the occasion.

I forgot in my last to tell you that we hear, by way of Kintbury and the Palmers, that they were all well at Bermuda in the beginning of Nov.

Wednesday.—Yesterday must have been a day of sad remembrance at Gm.[9] I am glad it is over. We spent Friday evening with our friends at the boarding-house, and our curiosity was gratified by the sight of their fellow-inmates, Mrs. Drew and Miss Hook, Mr. Wynne and Mr. Fitzhugh; the latter is brother to Mrs. Lance, and very much the gentleman. He has lived in that house more than twenty years, and, poor man! is so totally deaf that they say he could not hear a cannon, were it fired close to him; having no cannon at hand to make the experiment, I took it for granted, and talked to him a little with my fingers, which was funny enough. I recommended him to read "Corinna."

Miss Hook is a well-behaved, genteelish woman; Mrs. Drew well behaved, without being at all genteel. Mr. Wynne seems a chatty and rather familiar young man. Miss Murden was quite a different creature this last evening from what she had been before, owing to her having with Martha's help found a situation in the morning, which bids very fair for comfort. When she leaves Steventon, she comes to board and lodge with Mrs. Hookey, the chemist—for there is no Mr. Hookey. I cannot say that I am in any hurry for the conclusion of her present visit, but I was truly glad to see her comfortable in mind and spirits; at her age, perhaps, one may be as friendless oneself, and in similar circumstances quite as captious.

My mother has been lately adding to her possessions in plate,—a whole tablespoon and a whole dessert-spoon, and six whole teaspoons,—which makes our sideboard border on the magnificent. They were mostly the produce of old or useless silver. I have turned the 11*s.* in the list into 12*s.*, and the card looks all the better; a silver tea-ladle is also added, which will at least answer the purpose of making us sometimes think of John Warren.

I have laid Lady Sondes' case before Martha, who does not make the least objection to it, and is particularly pleased with the name of Montresor. I do not agree with her there, but I like his rank very much, and always affix the ideas of strong sense and highly elegant manners to a general.

I must write to Charles next week. You may guess in what extravagant terms of praise Earle Harwood speaks of him. He is looked up to by everybody in all America.

I shall not tell you anything more of Wm. Digweed's china, as your silence on the subject makes you unworthy of it. Mrs. H. Digweed looks forward with great satisfaction to our being her neighbors. I would have her enjoy the idea to the utmost, as I suspect there will not be much in the reality. With equal pleasure we anticipate an intimacy with her husband's bailiff and his wife, who live close by us, and are said to be remarkably good sort of people.

Yes, yes, we will have a pianoforte, as good a one as can be got for thirty guineas, and I will practise country dances, that we may have some amusement for our nephews and nieces, when we have the pleasure of their company.

Martha sends her love to Henry, and tells him that he will soon have a bill of Miss Chaplin's, about 14*l.*, to pay on her account; but the bill shall not be sent in till his return to town. I hope he comes to you in good health, and in spirits as good as a first return to Godmersham can allow. With his nephews he will force himself to be cheerful, till he really is so. Send me some intelligence of Eliza; it is a long while since I have heard of her.

We have had snow on the ground here almost a week; it is now going, but Southampton must boast no longer. We all send our love to Edward junior and his brothers, and I hope Speculation is generally liked.

Fare you well.

Yours affectionately,
J. AUSTEN.

---

[9] Godmersham, Edward Austen's place.

My mother has not been out of doors this week, but she keeps pretty well. We have received through Bookham an indifferent account of your godmother.

Miss AUSTEN, EDWARD AUSTEN'S, Esq.,
Godmersham Park, Faversham, Kent.

XXXI.

CASTLE SQUARE, Tuesday (January 10, 1809).

I AM not surprised, my dear Cassandra, that you did not find my last letter very full of matter, and I wish this may not have the same deficiency; but we are doing nothing ourselves to write about, and I am therefore quite dependent upon the communications of our friends, or my own wits.

This post brought me two interesting letters, yours and one from Bookham, in answer to an inquiry of mine about your good godmother, of whom we had lately received a very alarming account from Paragon. Miss Arnold was the informant then, and she spoke of Mrs. E. L. having been very dangerously ill, and attended by a physician from Oxford.

Your letter to Adlestrop may perhaps bring you information from the spot, but in case it should not, I must tell you that she is better; though Dr. Bourne cannot yet call her out of danger; such was the case last Wednesday, and Mrs. Cooke's having had no later account is a favorable sign. I am to hear again from the latter next week, but not this, if everything goes on well.

Her disorder is an inflammation on the lungs, arising from a severe chill taken in church last Sunday three weeks; her mind all pious composure, as may be supposed. George Cooke was there when her illness began; his brother has now taken his place. Her age and feebleness considered, one's fears cannot but preponderate, though her amendment has already surpassed the expectation of the physician at the beginning. I am sorry to add that Becky is laid up with a complaint of the same kind.

I am very glad to have the time of your return at all fixed; we all rejoice in it, and it will not be later than I had expected. I dare not hope that Mary and Miss Curling may be detained at Portsmouth so long or half so long; but it would be worth twopence to have it so.

The "St. Albans" perhaps may soon be off to help bring home what may remain by this time of our poor army, whose state seems dreadfully critical. The "Regency" seems to have been heard of only here; my most political correspondents make no mention of it. Unlucky that I should have wasted so much reflection on the subject.

I can now answer your question to my mother more at large, and likewise more at small— with equal perspicuity and minuteness; for the very day of our leaving Southampton is fixed; and if the knowledge is of no use to Edward, I am sure it will give him pleasure. Easter Monday, April 3, is the day; we are to sleep that night at Alton, and be with our friends at Bookham the next, if they are then at home; there we remain till the following Monday, and on Tuesday, April 11, hope to be at Godmersham. If the Cookes are absent, we shall finish our journey on the 5th. These plans depend of course upon the weather, but I hope there will be no settled cold to delay us materially.

To make you amends for being at Bookham, it is in contemplation to spend a few days at Baiton Lodge in our way out of Kent. The hint of such a visit is most affectionately welcomed by Mrs. Birch, in one of her odd pleasant letters lately, in which she speaks of us with the usual distinguished kindness, declaring that she shall not be at all satisfied unless a very handsome present is made us immediately from one quarter.

Fanny's not coming with you is no more than we expected; and as we have not the hope of a bed for her, and shall see her so soon afterwards at Godmersham, we cannot wish it otherwise.

William will be quite recovered, I trust, by the time you receive this. What a comfort his cross-stitch must have been! Pray tell him that I should like to see his work very much. I hope our answers this morning have given satisfaction; we had great pleasure in Uncle Deedes' packet; and pray let Marianne know, in private, that I think she is quite right to work a rug for Uncle John's coffee urn, and that I am sure it must give great pleasure to herself now, and to him when he receives it.

The preference of Brag over Speculation does not greatly surprise me, I believe, because I feel the same myself; but it mortifies me deeply, because Speculation was under my patronage; and, after all, what is there so delightful in a pair royal of Braggers? It is but three nines or three knaves, or a mixture of them. When one comes to reason upon it, it cannot stand its ground against Speculation,—of which I hope Edward is now convinced. Give my love to him if he is.

The letter from Paragon before mentioned was much like those which had preceded it, as to the felicity of its writer. They found their house so dirty and so damp that they were obliged to be a week at an inn. John Binns had behaved most unhandsomely, and engaged himself elsewhere. They have a man, however, on the same footing, which my aunt does not like, and she finds both him and the new maid-servant very, very inferior to Robert and Martha. Whether they mean to have any other domestics does not appear, nor whether they are to have a carriage while they are in Bath.

The Holders are as usual, though I believe it is not very usual for them to be happy, which they now are at a great rate, in Hooper's marriage. The Irvines are not mentioned. The American lady improved as we went on; but still the same faults in part recurred.

We are now in Margiana, and like it very well indeed. We are just going to set off for Northumberland to be shut up in Widdrington Tower, where there must be two or three sets of victims already immured under a very fine villain.

Wednesday.—Your report of Eliza's health gives me great pleasure, and the progress of the bank is a constant source of satisfaction. With such increasing profits, tell Henry that I hope he will not work poor High-Diddle so hard as he used to do.

Has your newspaper given a sad story of a Mrs. Middleton, wife of a farmer in Yorkshire, her sister, and servant, being almost frozen to death in the late weather, her little child quite so? I hope the sister is not our friend Miss Woodd, and I rather think her brother-in-law had moved into Lincolnshire, but their name and station accord too well. Mrs. M. and the maid are said to be tolerably recovered, but the sister is likely to lose the use of her limbs.

Charles's rug will be finished to-day, and sent to-morrow to Frank, to be consigned by him to Mr. Turner's care; and I am going to send Marmion out with it,—very generous in me, I think.

As we have no letter from Adlestrop, we may suppose the good woman was alive on Monday, but I cannot help expecting bad news from thence or Bookham in a few days. Do you continue quite well?

Have you nothing to say of your little namesake? We join in love and many happy returns.

Yours affectionately,   J. AUSTEN.

The Manydown ball was a smaller thing than I expected, but it seems to have made Anna very happy. At her age it would not have done for me.

Miss AUSTEN, EDWARD AUSTEN'S, Esq.,
Godmersham Park, Faversham, Kent.

XXXII.

CASTLE SQUARE, Tuesday (January 17).

MY DEAR CASSANDRA,—I am happy to say that we had no second letter from Bookham last week. Yours has brought its usual measure of satisfaction and amusement, and I beg your acceptance of all the thanks due on the occasion. Your offer of cravats is very kind, and happens to be particularly adapted to my wants, but it was an odd thing to occur to you.

Yes, we have got another fall of snow, and are very dreadful; everything seems to turn to snow this winter.

I hope you have had no more illness among you, and that William will be soon as well as ever. His working a footstool for Chawton is a most agreeable surprise to me, and I am sure his grandmamma will value it very much as a proof of his affection and industry, but we shall never have the heart to put our feet upon it. I believe I must work a muslin cover in satin stitch to keep it from the dirt. I long to know what his colors are. I guess greens and purples.

Edward and Henry have started a difficulty respecting our journey, which, I must own with some confusion, had never been thought of by us; but if the former expected by it to prevent our travelling into Kent entirely, he will be disappointed, for we have already determined to go the Croydon road on leaving Bookham and sleep at Dartford. Will not that do? There certainly does seem no convenient resting-place on the other road.

Anna went to Clanville last Friday, and I have hopes of her new aunt's being really worth her knowing. Perhaps you may never have heard that James and Mary paid a morning visit there in form some weeks ago, and Mary, though by no means disposed to like her, was very much pleased with her indeed. Her praise, to be sure, proves nothing more than Mrs. M.'s being civil and attentive to them, but her being so is in favor of her having good sense. Mary writes of Anna as improved in person, but gives her no other commendation. I am afraid her absence now may deprive her of one pleasure, for that silly Mr. Hammond is actually to give his ball on Friday.

We had some reason to expect a visit from Earle Harwood and James this week, but they do not come. Miss Murden arrived last night at Mrs. Hookey's, as a message and a basket announced to us. You will therefore return to an enlarged and, of course, improved society here, especially as the Miss Williamses are come back.

We were agreeably surprised the other day by a visit from your beauty and mine, each in a new cloth mantle and bonnet; and I dare say you will value yourself much on the modest propriety of Miss W.'s taste, hers being purple and Miss Grace's scarlet.

I can easily suppose that your six weeks here will be fully occupied, were it only in lengthening the waists of your gowns. I have pretty well arranged my spring and summer plans of that kind, and mean to wear out my spotted muslin before I go. You will exclaim at this, but mine really has signs of feebleness, which with a little care may come to something.

Martha and Dr. Mant are as bad as ever; he runs after her in the street to apologize for having spoken to a gentleman while she was near him the day before. Poor Mrs. Mant can stand it no longer; she is retired to one of her married daughters'.

When William returns to Winchester Mary Jane is to go to Mrs. Nune's for a month, and then to Steventon for a fortnight, and it seems likely that she and her aunt Martha may travel into Berkshire together.

We shall not have a month of Martha after your return, and that month will be a very interrupted and broken one, but we shall enjoy ourselves the more when we can get a quiet half-hour together.

To set against your new novel, of which nobody ever heard before, and perhaps never may again, we have got "Ida of Athens," by Miss Owenson, which must be very clever, because it was written, as the authoress says, in three months. We have only read the preface yet, but her Irish girl does not make me expect much. If the warmth of her language could affect the body, it might be worth reading in this weather.

Adieu! I must leave off to stir the fire and call on Miss Murden.

Evening.—I have done them both, the first very often. We found our friend as comfortable as she can ever allow herself to be in cold weather. There is a very neat parlor behind the shop for her to sit in, not very light indeed, being *à la* Southampton, the middle of three deep, but very lively from the frequent sound of the pestle and mortar.

We afterwards called on the Miss Williamses, who lodge at Durantoy's. Miss Mary only was at home, and she is in very indifferent health. Dr. Hacket came in while we were there, and said that he never remembered such a severe winter as this in Southampton before. It is bad, but we do not suffer as we did last year, because the wind has been more N.E. than N.W.

For a day or two last week my mother was very poorly with a return of one of her old complaints, but it did not last long, and seems to have left nothing bad behind it. She began to talk of a serious illness, her two last having been preceded by the same symptoms, but, thank heaven! she is now quite as well as one can expect her to be in weather which deprives her of exercise.

Miss M. conveys to us a third volume of sermons, from Hamstall, just published, and which we are to like better than the two others; they are professedly practical, and for the use of country congregations. I have just received some verses in an unknown hand, and am desired to forward them to my nephew Edward at Godmersham.

> Alas! poor Brag, thou boastful game!
> What now avails thine empty name?
> Where now thy more distinguished fame?
> My day is o'er, and thine the same,
> For thou, like me, art thrown aside
> At Godmersham, this Christmastide;
> And now across the table wide
> Each game save brag or spec. is tried.
> Such is the mild ejaculation
> Of tender-hearted speculation.

Wednesday.—I expected to have a letter from somebody to-day, but I have not. Twice every day I think of a letter from Portsmouth.

Miss Murden has been sitting with us this morning. As yet she seems very well pleased with her situation. The worst part of her being in Southampton will be the necessity of one walking with her now and then, for she talks so loud that one is quite ashamed; but our dining hours are luckily very different, which we shall take all reasonable advantage of.

The Queen's birthday moves the assembly to this night instead of last, and as it is always fully attended, Martha and I expect an amusing show. We were in hopes of being independent of other companions by having the attendance of Mr. Austen and Captain Harwood; but as they fail us, we are obliged to look out for other help, and have fixed on the Wallops as least likely to be troublesome. I have called on them this morning and found them very willing, and I am sorry that you must wait a whole week for the particulars of the evening. I propose being asked to dance by our acquaintance Mr. Smith, now Captain Smith, who has lately reappeared in Southampton, but I shall decline it. He saw Charles last August.

What an alarming bride Mrs. —— must have been; such a parade is one of the most immodest pieces of modesty that one can imagine. To attract notice could have been her only wish. It augurs ill for her family; it announces not great sense, and therefore insures boundless influence.

I hope Fanny's visit is now taking place. You have said scarcely anything of her lately, but I trust you are as good friends as ever.

Martha sends her love, and hopes to have the pleasure of seeing you when you return to Southampton. You are to understand this message as being merely for the sake of a message to oblige me.

Yours affectionately,
J. AUSTEN.

Henry never sent his love to me in your last, but I send him mine.

Miss AUSTEN, EDWARD AUSTEN'S, Esq.,
Godmersham Park, Faversham, Kent.

XXXIII.

CASTLE SQUARE, Tuesday (January 24).

MY DEAR CASSANDRA,—I will give you the indulgence of a letter on Thursday this week, instead of Friday, but I do not require you to write again before Sunday, provided I may believe you and your finger going on quite well. Take care of your precious self; do not work too hard. Remember that Aunt Cassandras are quite as scarce as Miss Beverleys.[10]

I had the happiness yesterday of a letter from Charles, but I shall say as little about it as possible, because I know that excruciating Henry will have had a letter likewise, to make all my intelligence valueless. It was written at Bermuda on the 7th and 10th of December. All well, and Fanny still only in expectation of being otherwise. He had taken a small prize in his late cruise,—a French schooner, laden with sugar; but bad weather parted them, and she had not yet been heard of. His cruise ended December 1st. My September letter was the latest he had received.

This day three weeks you are to be in London, and I wish you better weather; not but that you may have worse, for we have now nothing but ceaseless snow or rain and insufferable dirt to complain of; no tempestuous winds nor severity of cold. Since I wrote last we have had something of each, but it is not genteel to rip up old grievances.

You used me scandalously by not mentioning Edward Cooper's sermons. I tell you everything, and it is unknown the mysteries you conceal from me; and, to add to the rest, you persevere in giving a final "e" to "invalid," thereby putting it out of one's power to suppose

---

[10] "Cecilia" Beverley, the heroine of Miss Burney's novel.

Mrs. E. Leigh, even for a moment, a veteran soldier. She, good woman, is, I hope, destined for some further placid enjoyment of her own excellence in this world, for her recovery advances exceedingly well.

I had this pleasant news in a letter from Bookham last Thursday; but as the letter was from Mary instead of her mother, you will guess her account was not equally good from home. Mrs. Cooke had been confined to her bed some days by illness, but was then better, and Mary wrote in confidence of her continuing to mend. I have desired to hear again soon.

You rejoice me by what you say of Fanny.[11] I hope she will not turn good-for-nothing this ever so long. We thought of and talked of her yesterday with sincere affection, and wished her a long enjoyment of all the happiness to which she seems born. While she gives happiness to those about her she is pretty sure of her own share.

I am gratified by her having pleasure in what I write, but I wish the knowledge of my being exposed to her discerning criticism may not hurt my style, by inducing too great a solicitude. I begin already to weigh my words and sentences more than I did, and am looking about for a sentiment, an illustration, or a metaphor in every corner of the room. Could my ideas flow as fast as the rain in the store-closet, it would be charming.

We have been in two or three dreadful states within the last week, from the melting of the snow, etc., and the contest between us and the closet has now ended in our defeat. I have been obliged to move almost everything out of it, and leave it to splash itself as it likes.

You have by no means raised my curiosity after Caleb. My disinclination for it before was affected, but now it is real. I do not like the evangelicals. Of course I shall be delighted when I read it, like other people; but till I do I dislike it.

I am sorry my verses did not bring any return from Edward. I was in hopes they might, but I suppose he does not rate them high enough. It might be partiality, but they seemed to me purely classical,—just like Homer and Virgil, Ovid and Propria que Maribus.

I had a nice brotherly letter from Frank the other day, which, after an interval of nearly three weeks, was very welcome. No orders were come on Friday, and none were come yesterday, or we should have heard to-day. I had supposed Miss C. would share her cousin's room here, but a message in this letter proves the contrary. I will make the garret as comfortable as I can, but the possibilities of that apartment are not great.

My mother has been talking to Eliza about our future home, and she, making no difficulty at all of the sweetheart, is perfectly disposed to continue with us, but till she has written home for mother's approbation cannot quite decide. Mother does not like to have her so far off. At Chawton she will be nine or ten miles nearer, which I hope will have its due influence.

As for Sally, she means to play John Binns with us, in her anxiety to belong to our household again. Hitherto she appears a very good servant.

You depend upon finding all your plants dead, I hope. They look very ill, I understand.

Your silence on the subject of our ball makes me suppose your curiosity too great for words. We were very well entertained, and could have stayed longer but for the arrival of my list shoes to convey me home, and I did not like to keep them waiting in the cold. The room was tolerably full, and the ball opened by Miss Glyn. The Miss Lances had partners, Captain Dauvergne's friend appeared in regimentals, Caroline Maitland had an officer to flirt with, and Mr. John Harrison was deputed by Captain Smith, being himself absent, to ask me to dance. Everything went well, you see, especially after we had tucked Mrs. Lance's neckerchief in behind and fastened it with a pin.

---

[11] Fanny Austen, afterward Lady Edward Knatchbull.

We had a very full and agreeable account of Mr. Hammond's ball from Anna last night; the same fluent pen has sent similar information, I know, into Kent. She seems to have been as happy as one could wish her, and the complacency of her mamma in doing the honors of the evening must have made her pleasure almost as great. The grandeur of the meeting was beyond my hopes. I should like to have seen Anna's looks and performance, but that sad cropped head must have injured the former.

Martha pleases herself with believing that if I had kept her counsel you would never have heard of Dr. M.'s late behavior, as if the very slight manner in which I mentioned it could have been all on which you found your judgment. I do not endeavor to undeceive her, because I wish her happy, at all events, and know how highly she prizes happiness of any kind. She is, moreover, so full of kindness for us both, and sends you in particular so many good wishes about your finger, that I am willing to overlook a venial fault, and as Dr. M. is a clergyman, their attachment, however immoral, has a decorous air. Adieu, sweet You. This is grievous news from Spain. It is well that Dr. Moore was spared the knowledge of such a son's death.

Yours affectionately,   J. AUSTEN.

Anna's hand gets better and better; it begins to be too good for any consequence.

We send best love to dear little Lizzy and Marianne in particular.

The Portsmouth paper gave a melancholy history of a poor mad woman, escaped from confinement, who said her husband and daughter, of the name of Payne, lived at Ashford, in Kent. Do you own them?

Miss AUSTEN, EDWARD AUSTEN'S, Esq.,
Godmersham Park, Faversham, Kent.

XXXIV.

CASTLE SQUARE, Monday (January 30).

MY DEAR CASSANDRA,—I was not much surprised yesterday by the agreeable surprise of your letter, and extremely glad to receive the assurance of your finger being well again.

Here is such a wet day as never was seen. I wish the poor little girls had better weather for their journey; they must amuse themselves with watching the raindrops down the windows. Sackree, I suppose, feels quite broken-hearted. I cannot have done with the weather without observing how delightfully mild it is; I am sure Fanny must enjoy it with us. Yesterday was a very blowing day; we got to church, however, which we had not been able to do for two Sundays before.

I am not at all ashamed about the name of the novel, having been guilty of no insult toward your handwriting; the diphthong I always saw, but knowing how fond you were of adding a vowel wherever you could, I attributed it to that alone, and the knowledge of the truth does the book no service; the only merit it could have was in the name of Caleb, which has an honest, unpretending sound, but in C[oe]lebs there is pedantry and affectation. Is it written only to classical scholars?

I shall now try to say only what is necessary, I am weary of meandering; so expect a vast deal of small matter, concisely told, in the next two pages.

Mrs. Cooke has been very dangerously ill, but is now, I hope, safe. I had a letter last week from George, Mary being too busy to write, and at that time the disorder was called of the typhus kind, and their alarm considerable, but yesterday brought me a much better account from Mary, the origin of the complaint being now ascertained to be bilious, and the strong medicines requisite promising to be effectual. Mrs. E. L. is so much recovered as to get into the dressing-room every day.

A letter from Hamstall gives us the history of Sir Tho. Williams's return. The Admiral, whoever he might he, took a fancy to the "Neptune," and having only a worn-out 74 to offer in lieu of it, Sir Tho. declined such a command, and is come home passenger. Lucky man! to have so fair an opportunity of escape. I hope his wife allows herself to be happy on the occasion, and does not give all her thoughts to being nervous.

A great event happens this week at Hamstall in young Edward's removal to school. He is going to Rugby, and is very happy in the idea of it; I wish his happiness may last, but it will be a great change to become a raw school-boy from being a pompous sermon-writer and a domineering brother. It will do him good, I dare say.

Caroline has had a great escape from being burnt to death lately. As her husband gives the account, we must believe it true. Miss Murden is gone,—called away by the critical state of Mrs. Pottinger who has had another severe stroke, and is without sense or speech. Miss Murden wishes to return to Southampton if circumstances suit, but it must be very doubtful.

We have been obliged to turn away Cholles, he grew so very drunken and negligent, and we have a man in his place called Thomas.

Martha desires me to communicate something concerning herself which she knows will give you pleasure, as affording her very particular satisfaction,—it is that she is to be in town this spring with Mrs. Dundas. I need not dilate on the subject. You understand enough of the whys and wherefores to enter into her feelings, and to be conscious that of all possible arrangements it is the one most acceptable to her. She goes to Barton on leaving us, and the family remove to town in April.

What you tell me of Miss Sharpe is quite new, and surprises me a little; I feel, however, as you do. She is born, poor thing! to struggle with evil, and her continuing with Miss B. is, I hope, a proof that matters are not always so very bad between them as her letters sometimes represent.

Jenny's marriage I had heard of, and supposed you would do so too from Steventon, as I knew you were corresponding with Mary at the time. I hope she will not sully the respectable name she now bears.

Your plan for Miss Curling is uncommonly considerate and friendly, and such as she must surely jump at. Edward's going round by Steventon, as I understand he promises to do, can be no reasonable objection; Mrs. J. Austen's hospitality is just of the kind to enjoy such a visitor.

We were very glad to know Aunt Fanny was in the country when we read of the fire. Pray give my best compliments to the Mrs. Finches, if they are at Gm. I am sorry to find that Sir J. Moore has a mother living, but though a very heroic son he might not be a very necessary one to her happiness. Deacon Morrell may be more to Mrs. Morrell.

I wish Sir John had united something of the Christian with the hero in his death. Thank heaven! we have had no one to care for particularly among the troops,—no one, in fact, nearer to us than Sir John himself. Col. Maitland is safe and well; his mother and sisters were of course anxious about him, but there is no entering much into the solicitudes of that family.

My mother is well, and gets out when she can with the same enjoyment, and apparently the same strength, as hitherto. She hopes you will not omit begging Mrs. Seward to get the garden cropped for us, supposing she leaves the house too early to make the garden any object to herself. We are very desirous of receiving your account of the house, for your observations will have a motive which can leave nothing to conjecture and suffer nothing from want of memory. For one's own dear self, one ascertains and remembers everything.

Lady Sondes is an impudent woman to come back into her old neighborhood again; I suppose she pretends never to have married before, and wonders how her father and mother came to have her christened Lady Sondes.

The store-closet, I hope, will never do so again, for much of the evil is proved to have proceeded from the gutter being choked up, and we have had it cleared. We had reason to rejoice in the child's absence at the time of the thaw, for the nursery was not habitable. We hear of similar disasters from almost everybody.

No news from Portsmouth. We are very patient. Mrs. Charles Fowle desires to be kindly remembered to you. She is warmly interested in my brother and his family.

Yours very affectionately,

J. AUSTEN.

Miss AUSTEN, EDWARD AUSTEN'S, Esq.,
Godmersham Park, Faversham, Kent.

XXXV.

SLOANE ST., Thursday (April 18, 1811).

MY DEAR CASSANDRA,—I have so many little matters to tell you of, that I cannot wait any longer before I begin to put them down. I spent Tuesday in Bentinck Street. The Cookes called here and took me back, and it was quite a Cooke day, for the Miss Rolles paid a visit while I was there, and Sam Arnold dropped in to tea.

The badness of the weather disconcerted an excellent plan of mine,—that of calling on Miss Beckford again; but from the middle of the day it rained incessantly. Mary and I, after disposing of her father and mother, went to the Liverpool Museum and the British Gallery, and I had some amusement at each, though my preference for men and women always inclines me to attend more to the company than the sight.

Mrs. Cooke regrets very much that she did not see you when you called; it was owing to a blunder among the servants, for she did not know of our visit till we were gone. She seems tolerably well, but the nervous part of her complaint, I fear, increases, and makes her more and more unwilling to part with Mary.

I have proposed to the latter that she should go to Chawton with me, on the supposition of my travelling the Guildford road, and she, I do believe, would be glad to do it, but perhaps it may be impossible; unless a brother can be at home at that time, it certainly must. George comes to them to-day.

I did not see Theo. till late on Tuesday; he was gone to Ilford, but he came back in time to show his usual nothing-meaning, harmless, heartless civility. Henry, who had been confined the whole day to the bank, took me in his way home, and, after putting life and wit into the party for a quarter of an hour, put himself and his sister into a hackney coach.

I bless my stars that I have done with Tuesday. But, alas! Wednesday was likewise a day of great doings, for Manon and I took our walk to Grafton House, and I have a good deal to say on that subject.

I am sorry to tell you that I am getting very extravagant, and spending all my money, and, what is worse for you, I have been spending yours too; for in a linendraper's shop to which I went for checked muslin, and for which I was obliged to give seven shillings a yard, I was tempted by a pretty-colored muslin, and bought ten yards of it on the chance of your liking it;

but at the same time, if it should not suit you, you must not think yourself at all obliged to take it; it is only 3*s*. 6*d*. per yard, and I should not in the least mind keeping the whole. In texture it is just what we prefer, but its resemblance to green crewels, I must own, is not great, for the pattern is a small red spot. And now I believe I have done all my commissions except Wedgwood.

I liked my walk very much; it was shorter than I had expected, and the weather was delightful. We set off immediately after breakfast, and must have reached Grafton House by half-past eleven; but when we entered the shop the whole counter was thronged, and we waited full half an hour before we could be attended to. When we were served, however, I was very well satisfied with my purchases,—my bugle trimming at 2*s*. 4*d*. and three pair silk stockings for a little less than 12*s*. a pair.

In my way back who should I meet but Mr. Moore, just come from Beckenham. I believe he would have passed me if I had not made him stop, but we were delighted to meet. I soon found, however, that he had nothing new to tell me, and then I let him go.

Miss Burton has made me a very pretty little bonnet, and now nothing can satisfy me but I must have a straw hat, of the riding-hat shape, like Mrs. Tilson's; and a young woman in this neighborhood is actually making me one. I am really very shocking, but it will not be dear at a guinea. Our pelisses are 17*s*. each; she charges only 8*s*. for the making, but the buttons seem expensive,—are expensive, I might have said, for the fact is plain enough.

We drank tea again yesterday with the Tilsons, and met the Smiths. I find all these little parties very pleasant. I like Mrs. S.; Miss Beaty is good-humor itself, and does not seem much besides. We spend to-morrow evening with them, and are to meet the Coln. and Mrs. Cantelo Smith you have been used to hear of, and, if she is in good humor, are likely to have excellent singing.

To-night I might have been at the play; Henry had kindly planned our going together to the Lyceum, but I have a cold which I should not like to make worse before Saturday, so I stay within all this day.

Eliza is walking out by herself. She has plenty of business on her hands just now, for the day of the party is settled, and drawing near. Above eighty people are invited for next Tuesday evening, and there is to be some very good music,—five professionals, three of them glee singers, besides amateurs. Fanny will listen to this. One of the hirelings is a Capital on the harp, from which I expect great pleasure. The foundation of the party was a dinner to Henry Egerton and Henry Walter, but the latter leaves town the day before. I am sorry, as I wished her prejudice to be done away, but should have been more sorry if there had been no invitation.

I am a wretch, to be so occupied with all these things as to seem to have no thoughts to give to people and circumstances which really supply a far more lasting interest,—the society in which you are; but I do think of you all, I assure you, and want to know all about everybody, and especially about your visit to the W. Friars; *mais le moyen* not to be occupied by one's own concerns?

Saturday.—Frank is superseded in the "Caledonia." Henry brought us this news yesterday from Mr. Daysh, and he heard at the same time that Charles may be in England in the course of a month. Sir Edward Pollen succeeds Lord Gambier in his command, and some captain of his succeeds Frank; and I believe the order is already gone out. Henry means to inquire further to-day. He wrote to Mary on the occasion. This is something to think of. Henry is convinced that he will have the offer of something else, but does not think it will be at all incumbent on him to accept it; and then follows, what will he do? and where will he live?

I hope to hear from you to-day. How are you as to health, strength, looks, etc.? I had a very comfortable account from Chawton yesterday.

If the weather permits, Eliza and I walk into London this morning. She is in want of chimney lights for Tuesday, and I of an ounce of darning-cotton. She has resolved not to venture to the play to-night. The D'Entraigues and Comte Julien cannot come to the party, which was at first a grief, but she has since supplied herself so well with performers that it is of no consequence; their not coming has produced our going to them to-morrow evening, which I like the idea of. It will be amusing to see the ways of a French circle.

I wrote to Mrs. Hill a few days ago, and have received a most kind and satisfactory answer. Any time the first week in May exactly suits her, and therefore I consider my going as tolerably fixed. I shall leave Sloane Street on the 1st or 2d, and be ready for James on the 9th, and, if his plan alters, I can take care of myself. I have explained my views here, and everything is smooth and pleasant; and Eliza talks kindly of conveying me to Streatham.

We met the Tilsons yesterday evening, but the singing Smiths sent an excuse, which put our Mrs. Smith out of humor.

We are come back, after a good dose of walking and coaching, and I have the pleasure of your letter. I wish I had James's verses, but they were left at Chawton. When I return thither, if Mrs. K. will give me leave, I will send them to her.

Our first object to-day was Henrietta St., to consult with Henry in consequence of a very unlucky change of the play for this very night,—"Hamlet" instead of "King John,"—and we are to go on Monday to "Macbeth" instead; but it is a disappointment to us both.

Love to all.

Yours affectionately,
JANE.

Miss AUSTEN, EDWARD AUSTEN'S, Esq.,
Godmersham Park, Faversham, Kent.

XXXVI.

SLOANE ST., Thursday (April 25).

MY DEAREST CASSANDRA,—I can return the compliment by thanking you for the unexpected pleasure of your letter yesterday, and as I like unexpected pleasure, it made me very happy; and, indeed, you need not apologize for your letter in any respect, for it is all very fine, but not too fine, I hope, to be written again, or something like it.
I think Edward will not suffer much longer from heat; by the look of things this morning I suspect the weather is rising into the balsamic north-east. It has been hot here, as you may suppose, since it was so hot with you, but I have not suffered from it at all, nor felt it in such a degree as to make me imagine it would be anything in the country. Everybody has talked of the heat, but I set it all down to London.

I give you joy of our new nephew, and hope if he ever comes to be hanged it will not be till we are too old to care about it. It is a great comfort to have it so safely and speedily over. The Miss Curlings must be hard worked in writing so many letters, but the novelty of it may recommend it to them; mine was from Miss Eliza, and she says that my brother may arrive to-day.

No, indeed, I am never too busy to think of S. and S.[12] I can no more forget it than a mother can forget her sucking child; and I am much obliged to you for your inquiries. I have had two sheets to correct, but the last only brings us to Willoughby's first appearance. Mrs. K. regrets

---

[12] "Sense and Sensibility."

in the most flattering manner that she must wait till May, but I have scarcely a hope of its being out in June. Henry does not neglect it; he has hurried the printer, and says he will see him again to-day. It will not stand still during his absence, it will be sent to Eliza.

The Incomes remain as they were, but I will get them altered if I can. I am very much gratified by Mrs. K.'s interest in it; and whatever may be the event of it as to my credit with her, sincerely wish her curiosity could be satisfied sooner than is now probable. I think she will like my Elinor, but cannot build on anything else.

Our party went off extremely well. There were many solicitudes, alarms, and vexations beforehand, of course, but at last everything was quite right. The rooms were dressed up with flowers, etc., and looked very pretty. A glass for the mantelpiece was lent by the man who is making their own. Mr. Egerton and Mr. Walter came at half-past five, and the festivities began with a pair of very fine soles.

Yes, Mr. Walter—for he postponed his leaving London on purpose—which did not give much pleasure at the time, any more than the circumstance from which it rose,—his calling on Sunday and being asked by Henry to take the family dinner on that day, which he did; but it is all smoothed over now, and she likes him very well.

At half-past seven arrived the musicians in two hackney coaches, and by eight the lordly company began to appear. Among the earliest were George and Mary Cooke, and I spent the greatest part of the evening very pleasantly with them. The drawing-room being soon hotter than we liked, we placed ourselves in the connecting passage, which was comparatively cool, and gave us all the advantage of the music at a pleasant distance, as well as that of the first view of every new-comer.

I was quite surrounded by acquaintance, especially gentlemen; and what with Mr. Hampson, Mr. Seymour, Mr. W. Knatchbull, Mr. Guillemarde, Mr. Cure, a Captain Simpson, brother to the Captain Simpson, besides Mr. Walter and Mr. Egerton, in addition to the Cookes, and Miss Beckford, and Miss Middleton, I had quite as much upon my hands as I could do.

Poor Miss B. has been suffering again from her old complaint, and looks thinner than ever. She certainly goes to Cheltenham the beginning of June. We were all delight and cordiality, of course. Miss M. seems very happy, but has not beauty enough to figure in London.

Including everybody we were sixty-six,—which was considerably more than Eliza had expected, and quite enough to fill the back drawing-room and leave a few to be scattered about in the other and in the passage.

The music was extremely good. It opened (tell Fanny) with "Poike de Parp pirs praise pof Prapela;" and of the other glees I remember, "In peace love tunes," "Rosabelle," "The Red Cross Knight," and "Poor Insect." Between the songs were lessons on the harp, or harp and pianoforte together; and the harp-player was Wiepart, whose name seems famous, though new to me. There was one female singer, a short Miss Davis, all in blue, bringing up for the public line, whose voice was said to be very fine indeed; and all the performers gave great satisfaction by doing what they were paid for, and giving themselves no airs. No amateur could be persuaded to do anything.

The house was not clear till after twelve. If you wish to hear more of it, you must put your questions, but I seem rather to have exhausted than spared the subject.

This said Captain Simpson told us, on the authority of some other Captain just arrived from Halifax, that Charles was bringing the "Cleopatra" home, and that she was probably by this time in the Channel; but as Captain S. was certainly in liquor, we must not quite depend on it. It must give one a sort of expectation, however, and will prevent my writing to him any more. I would rather he should not reach England till I am at home, and the Steventon party gone.

My mother and Martha both write with great satisfaction of Anna's behavior. She is quite an Anna with variations, but she cannot have reached her last, for that is always the most flourishing and showy; she is at about her third or fourth, which are generally simple and pretty.

Your lilacs are in leaf, ours are in bloom. The horse-chestnuts are quite out, and the elms almost. I had a pleasant walk in Kensington Gardens on Sunday with Henry, Mr. Smith, and Mr. Tilson; everything was fresh and beautiful.

We did go to the play, after all, on Saturday. We went to the Lyceum, and saw the "Hypocrite," an old play taken from Molière's "Tartuffe," and were well entertained. Dowton and Mathews were the good actors; Mrs. Edwin was the heroine, and her performance is just what it used to be. I have no chance of seeing Mrs. Siddons; she did act on Monday, but as Henry was told by the box-keeper that he did not think she would, the plans, and all thought of it, were given up. I should particularly have liked seeing her in "Constance," and could swear at her with little effort for disappointing me.

Henry has been to the Water-Color Exhibition, which opened on Monday, and is to meet us there again some morning. If Eliza cannot go (and she has a cold at present), Miss Beaty will be invited to be my companion. Henry leaves town on Sunday afternoon, but he means to write soon himself to Edward, and will tell his own plans.

The tea is this moment setting out.

Do not have your colored muslin unless you really want it, because I am afraid I could not send it to the coach without giving trouble here.

Eliza caught her cold on Sunday in our way to the D'Entraigues. The horses actually gibbed on this side of Hyde Park Gate: a load of fresh gravel made it a formidable hill to them, and they refused the collar; I believe there was a sore shoulder to irritate. Eliza was frightened, and we got out, and were detained in the evening air several minutes. The cold is in her chest, but she takes care of herself, and I hope it may not last long.

This engagement prevented Mr. Walter's staying late,—he had his coffee and went away. Eliza enjoyed her evening very much, and means to cultivate the acquaintance; and I see nothing to dislike in them but their taking quantities of snuff. Monsieur, the old Count, is a very fine-looking man, with quiet manners, good enough for an Englishman, and, I believe, is a man of great information and taste. He has some fine paintings, which delighted Henry as much as the son's music gratified Eliza; and among them a miniature of Philip V. of Spain, Louis XIV.'s grandson, which exactly suited my capacity. Count Julien's performance is very wonderful.

We met only Mrs. Latouche and Miss East, and we are just now engaged to spend next Sunday evening at Mrs. L.'s, and to meet the D'Entraigues, but M. le Comte must do without Henry. If he would but speak English, I would take to him.

Have you ever mentioned the leaving off tea to Mrs. K.? Eliza has just spoken of it again. The benefit she has found from it in sleeping has been very great.

I shall write soon to Catherine to fix my day, which will be Thursday. We have no engagement but for Sunday. Eliza's cold makes quiet advisable. Her party is mentioned in this morning's paper. I am sorry to hear of poor Fanny's state. From that quarter, I suppose, is to be the alloy of her happiness. I will have no more to say.

Yours affectionately,   J. A.

Give my love particularly to my goddaughter.

Miss AUSTEN, EDWARD AUSTEN'S, Esq.,
Godmersham Park, Faversham.

XXXVII.

SLOANE ST., Tuesday.

MY DEAR CASSANDRA,—I had sent off my letter yesterday before yours came, which I was sorry for; but as Eliza has been so good as to get me a frank, your questions shall be answered without much further expense to you.

The best direction to Henry at Oxford will be "The Blue Boar, Cornmarket."

I do not mean to provide another trimming for my pelisse, for I am determined to spend no more money; so I shall wear it as it is, longer than I ought, and then—I do not know.

My head-dress was a bugle-band like the border to my gown, and a flower of Mrs. Tilson's. I depended upon hearing something of the evening from Mr. W. K., and am very well satisfied with his notice of me—"A pleasing-looking young woman"—that must do; one cannot pretend to anything better now; thankful to have it continued a few years longer!

It gives me sincere pleasure to hear of Mrs. Knight's having had a tolerable night at last, but upon this occasion I wish she had another name, for the two nights jingle very much.

We have tried to get "Self-control," but in vain. I should like to know what her estimate is, but am always half afraid of finding a clever novel too clever, and of finding my own story and my own people all forestalled.

Eliza has just received a few lines from Henry to assure her of the good conduct of his mare. He slept at Uxbridge on Sunday, and wrote from Wheatfield.

We were not claimed by Hans Place yesterday, but are to dine there to-day. Mr. Tilson called in the evening, but otherwise we were quite alone all day; and after having been out a good deal, the change was very pleasant.

I like your opinion of Miss Atten much better than I expected, and have now hopes of her staying a whole twelvemonth. By this time I suppose she is hard at it, governing away. Poor creature! I pity her, though they are my nieces.

Oh! yes, I remember Miss Emma Plumbtree's local consequence perfectly.
I am in a dilemma, for want of an Emma,
Escaped from the lips of Henry Gipps.

But, really, I was never much more put to it than in continuing an answer to Fanny's former message. What is there to be said on the subject? Pery pell, or pare pey? or po; or at the most, Pi, pope, pey, pike, pit.

I congratulate Edward on the Weald of Kent Canal Bill being put off till another Session, as I have just had the pleasure of reading. There is always something to be hoped from delay.

> Between Session and Session
> The first Prepossession
> May rouse up the Nation,
> And the villanous Bill
> May be forced to lie still
> Against wicked men's will.

There is poetry for Edward and his daughter. I am afraid I shall not have any for you.

I forgot to tell you in my last that our cousin Miss Payne called in on Saturday, and was persuaded to stay dinner. She told us a great deal about her friend Lady Cath. Brecknell, who is most happily married, and Mr. Brecknell is very religious, and has got black whiskers.

I am glad to think that Edward has a tolerable day for his drive to Goodnestone, and very glad to hear of his kind promise of bringing you to town. I hope everything will arrange itself favorably. The 16th is now to be Mrs. Dundas's day.

I mean, if I can, to wait for your return before I have my new gown made up, from a notion of their making up to more advantage together; and as I find the muslin is not so wide as it used to be, some contrivance may be necessary. I expect the skirt to require one-half breadth cut in gores, besides two whole breadths.

Eliza has not yet quite resolved on inviting Anna, but I think she will.

Yours very affectionately,
JANE.

XXXVIII.

CHAWTON, Wednesday (May 29).

IT was a mistake of mine, my dear Cassandra, to talk of a tenth child at Hamstall. I had forgot there were but eight already.

Your inquiry after my uncle and aunt were most happily timed, for the very same post brought an account of them. They are again at Gloucester House enjoying fresh air, which they seem to have felt the want of in Bath, and are tolerably well, but not more than tolerable. My aunt does not enter into particulars, but she does not write in spirits, and we imagine that she has never entirely got the better of her disorder in the winter. Mrs. Welby takes her out airing in her barouche, which gives her a headache,—a comfortable proof, I suppose, of the uselessness of the new carriage when they have got it.

You certainly must have heard before I can tell you that Col. Orde has married our cousin Margt. Beckford, the Marchess. of Douglas's sister. The papers say that her father disinherits her, but I think too well of an Orde to suppose that she has not a handsome independence of her own.

The chickens are all alive and fit for the table, but we save them for something grand. Some of the flower seeds are coming up very well, but your mignonette makes a wretched appearance. Miss Benn has been equally unlucky as to hers. She had seed from four different people, and none of it comes up. Our young piony at the foot of the fir-tree has just blown and looks very handsome, and the whole of the shrubbery border will soon be very gay with pinks and sweet-williams, in addition to the columbines already in bloom. The syringas, too, are coming out. We are likely to have a great crop of Orleans plums, but not many greengages— on the standard scarcely any, three or four dozen, perhaps, against the wall. I believe I told you differently when I first came home, but I can now judge better than I could then

I have had a medley and satisfactory letter this morning from the husband and wife at Cowes; and in consequence of what is related of their plans, we have been talking over the possibility of inviting them here in their way from Steventon, which is what one should wish to do, and is, I dare say, what they expect, but, supposing Martha to be at home, it does not seem a very easy thing to accommodate so large a party. My mother offers to give up her room to Frank and Mary, but there will then be only the best for two maids and three children.

They go to Steventon about the 22d, and I guess—for it is quite a guess—will stay there from a fortnight to three weeks.

I must not venture to press Miss Sharpe's coming at present; we may hardly be at liberty before August.

Poor John Bridges! we are very sorry for his situation and for the distress of the family. Lady B., is in one way severely tried. And our own dear brother suffers a great deal, I dare say, on the occasion.

I have not much to say of ourselves. Anna is nursing a cold caught in the arbor at Faringdon, that she may be able to keep her engagement to Maria M. this evening, when I suppose she will make it worse.

She did not return from Faringdon till Sunday, when H. B. walked home with her, and drank tea here. She was with the Prowtings almost all Monday. She went to learn to make feather trimmings of Miss Anna, and they kept her to dinner, which was rather lucky, as we were called upon to meet Mrs. and Miss Terry the same evening at the Digweeds; and though Anna was of course invited too, I think it always safest to keep her away from the family, lest she should be doing too little or too much.

Mrs. Terry, Mary, and Robert, with my aunt Harding and her daughter, came from Dummer for a day and a night,—all very agreeable and very much delighted with the new house and with Chawton in general.

We sat upstairs, and had thunder and lightning as usual. I never knew such a spring for thunderstorms as it has been. Thank God! we have had no bad ones here. I thought myself in luck to have my uncomfortable feelings shared by the mistress of the house, as that procured blinds and candles. It had been excessively hot the whole day. Mrs. Harding is a good-looking woman, but not much like Mrs. Toke, inasmuch as she is very brown and has scarcely any teeth; she seems to have some of Mrs. Toke's civility. Miss H. is an elegant, pleasing, pretty-looking girl, about nineteen, I suppose, or nineteen and a half, or nineteen and a quarter, with flowers in her head and music at her finger-ends. She plays very well indeed. I have seldom heard anybody with more pleasure. They were at Godington four or five years ago. My cousin Flora Long was there last year.

My name is Diana. How does Fanny like it? What a change in the weather! We have a fire again now.

Harriet Benn sleeps at the Great House to-night, and spends to-morrow with us; and the plan is that we should all walk with her to drink tea at Faringdon, for her mother is now recovered; but the state of the weather is not very promising at present.

Miss Benn has been returned to her cottage since the beginning of last week, and has now just got another girl; she comes from Alton. For many days Miss B. had nobody with her but her niece Elizabeth, who was delighted to be her visitor and her maid. They both dined here on Saturday while Anna was at Faringdon; and last night an accidental meeting and a sudden impulse produced Miss Benn and Maria Middleton at our tea-table.

If you have not heard it is very fit you should, that Mr. Harrison has had the living of Fareham given him by the Bishop, and is going to reside there; and now it is said that Mr. Peach (beautiful wiseacre) wants to have the curacy of Overton, and if he does leave Wootton, James Digweed wishes to go there. Fare you well.

Yours affectionately,   JANE AUSTEN.

The chimneys at the Great House are done. Mr. Prowting has opened a gravel-pit, very conveniently for my mother, just at the mouth of the approach to his house; but it looks a little as if he meant to catch all his company. Tolerable gravel.

Miss AUSTEN,
Godmersham Park, Faversham, Kent.

XXXIX.

CHAWTON, Thursday (June 6).

BY this time, my dearest Cassandra, you know Martha's plans. I was rather disappointed, I confess, to find that she could not leave town till after ye 24th, as I had hoped to see you here the week before. The delay, however, is not great, and everything seems generally arranging itself for your return very comfortably.

I found Henry perfectly predisposed to bring you to London if agreeable to yourself; he has not fixed his day for going into Kent, but he must be back again before ye 20th. You may therefore think with something like certainty of the close of your Godmersham visit, and will have, I suppose, about a week for Sloane Street. He travels in his gig, and should the weather be tolerable I think you must have a delightful journey.

I have given up all idea of Miss Sharpe's travelling with you and Martha, for though you are both all compliance with my scheme, yet as you knock off a week from the end of her visit, and Martha rather more from the beginning, the thing is out of the question.

I have written to her to say that after the middle of July we shall be happy to receive her, and I have added a welcome if she could make her way hither directly, but I do not expect that she will. I have also sent our invitation to Cowes.

We are very sorry for the disappointment you have all had in Lady B.'s illness; but a division of the proposed party is with you by this time, and I hope may have brought you a better account of the rest.

Give my love and thanks to Harriot, who has written me charming things of your looks, and diverted me very much by poor Mrs. C. Milles's continued perplexity.

I had a few lines from Henry on Tuesday to prepare us for himself and his friend, and by the time that I had made the sumptuous provision of a neck of mutton on the occasion, they drove into the court; but lest you should not immediately recollect in how many hours a neck of mutton may be certainly procured, I add that they came a little after twelve,—both tall and well, and in their different degrees agreeable.

It was a visit of only twenty-four hours, but very pleasant while it lasted. Mr. Tilson took a sketch of the Great House before dinner, and after dinner we all three walked to Chawton Park, meaning to go into it, but it was too dirty, and we were obliged to keep on the outside. Mr. Tilson admired the trees very much, but grieved that they should not be turned into money.

My mother's cold is better, and I believe she only wants dry weather to be very well. It was a great distress to her that Anna should be absent during her uncle's visit, a distress which I could not share. She does not return from Faringdon till this evening, and I doubt not has had plenty of the miscellaneous, unsettled sort of happiness which seems to suit her best. We hear from Miss Benn, who was on the Common with the Prowtings, that she was very much admired by the gentlemen in general.

I like your new bonnets exceedingly; yours is a shape which always looks well, and I think Fanny's particularly becoming to her.

On Monday I had the pleasure of receiving, unpacking, and approving our Wedgwood ware. It all came very safely, and upon the whole is a good match, though I think they might have allowed us rather larger leaves, especially in such a year of fine foliage as this. One is apt to suppose that the woods about Birmingham must be blighted. There was no bill with the goods, but that shall not screen them from being paid. I mean to ask Martha to settle the account. It will be quite in her way, for she is just now sending my mother a breakfast-set from the same place.

I hope it will come by the wagon to-morrow; it is certainly what we want, and I long to know what it is like, and as I am sure Martha has great pleasure in making the present, I will not have any regret. We have considerable dealings with the wagons at present: a hamper of port and brandy from Southampton is now in the kitchen.

Your answer about the Miss Plumbtrees proves you as fine a Daniel as ever Portia was; for I maintained Emma to be the eldest.

We began pease on Sunday, but our gatherings are very small, not at all like the gathering in the "Lady of the Lake." Yesterday I had the agreeable surprise of finding several scarlet strawberries quite ripe; had you been at home, this would have been a pleasure lost. There are more gooseberries and fewer currants than I thought at first. We must buy currants for our wine.

The Digweeds are gone down to see the Stephen Terrys at Southampton, and catch the King's birthday at Portsmouth. Miss Papillon called on us yesterday, looking handsomer than ever. Maria Middleton and Miss Benn dine here to-morrow.

We are not to enclose any more letters to Abingdon Street, as perhaps Martha has told you.

I had just left off writing and put on my things for walking to Alton, when Anna and her friend Harriot called in their way thither; so we went together. Their business was to provide mourning against the King's death, and my mother has had a bombazine bought for her. I am not sorry to be back again, for the young ladies had a great deal to do, and without much method in doing it.

Anna does not come home till to-morrow morning. She has written I find to Fanny, but there does not seem to be a great deal to relate of Tuesday. I had hoped there might be dancing.

Mrs. Budd died on Sunday evening. I saw her two days before her death, and thought it must happen soon. She suffered much from weakness and restlessness almost to the last. Poor little Harriot seems truly grieved. You have never mentioned Harry; how is he?

With love to you all,

Yours affectionately,   J. A.

Miss AUSTEN, EDWARD AUSTEN'S, Esq.,
Godmersham Park, Faversham

XL.

CHAWTON, Friday (January 29, 1813).

I HOPE you received my little parcel by J. Bond on Wednesday evening, my dear Cassandra, and that you will be ready to hear from me again on Sunday, for I feel that I must write to you to-day. I want to tell you that I have got my own darling child[13] from London. On Wednesday I received one copy sent down by Falkener, with three lines from Henry to say that he had given another to Charles and sent a third by the coach to Godmersham.... The advertisement is in our paper to-day for the first time: 18s. He shall ask 1l. 1s. for my two next, and 1l. 8s. for my stupidest of all. Miss B. dined with us on the very day of the book's coming, and in the evening we fairly set at it, and read half the first vol. to her, prefacing that, having intelligence from Henry that such a work would soon appear, we had desired him to send it whenever it

---

[13] "Pride and Prejudice."

came out, and I believe it passed with her unsuspected. She was amused, poor soul! That she could not help, you know, with two such people to lead the way; but she really does seem to admire Elizabeth. I must confess that I think her as delightful a creature as ever appeared in print, and how I shall be able to tolerate those who do not like her at least, I do not know. There are a few typical errors; and a "said he," or a "said she," would sometimes make the dialogue more immediately clear; but "I do not write for such dull elves" as have not a great deal of ingenuity themselves. The second volume is shorter than I could wish, but the difference is not so much in reality as in look, there being a larger proportion of narrative in that part. I have lop't and crop't so successfully, however, that I imagine it must be rather shorter than "Sense and Sensibility" altogether. Now I will try and write of something else.

XLI.

CHAWTON, Thursday (February 4).

MY DEAR CASSANDRA,—Your letter was truly welcome, and I am much obliged to you for all your praise; it came at a right time, for I had had some fits of disgust. Our second evening's reading to Miss B. had not pleased me so well, but I believe something must be attributed to my mother's too rapid way of getting on: though she perfectly understands the characters herself, she cannot speak as they ought. Upon the whole, however, I am quite vain enough and well satisfied enough. The work is rather too light and bright and sparkling: it wants shade; it wants to be stretched out here and there with a long chapter of sense, if it could be had; if not, of solemn specious nonsense, about something unconnected with the story,—an essay on writing, a critique on Walter Scott, or the history of Buonaparte, or something that would form a contrast, and bring the reader with increased delight to the playfulness and epigrammatism of the general style.... The greatest blunder in the printing that I have met with is in page 220, v. 3, where two speeches are made into one. There might as well be no suppers at Longbourn; but I suppose it was the remains of Mrs. Bennet's old Meryton habits.

XLII.

FEBRUARY.

THIS will be a quick return for yours, my dear Cassandra. I doubt its having much else to recommend it; but there is no saying: it may turn out to be a very long and delightful letter. I am exceedingly pleased that you can say what you do, after having gone through the whole work, and Fanny's praise is very gratifying. My hopes were tolerably strong of her, but nothing like a certainty. Her liking Darcy and Elizabeth is enough. She might hate all the others, if she would. I have her opinion under her own hand this morning; but your transcript of it, which I read first, was not, and is not, the less acceptable. To me it is of course all praise, but the more exact truth which she sends you is good enough.... Our party on Wednesday was not unagreeable, though we wanted a master of the house less anxious and fidgety, and more conversable. Upon Mrs. ——'s mentioning that she had sent the rejected addresses to Mrs. H., I began talking to her a little about them, and expressed my hope of their having amused her. Her answer was, "Oh dear, yes, very much, very droll indeed, the opening of the house, and the striking up of the fiddles!" What she meant, poor woman, who shall say? I sought no farther. As soon as a whist-party was formed, and a round table threatened, I made my mother an excuse and came away, leaving just as many for their round table as there were at Mrs. Grant's.[14] I wish they might be as agreeable a set. My mother is very well, and finds great amusement in glove-knitting, and at present wants no other work. We quite run over with books. She has got Sir John Carr's "Travels in Spain," and I am reading a Society octavo, an "Essay on the Military Police and Institutions of the British Empire," by Capt. Pasley of the Engineers,—a book which I protested against at first, but which upon trial I find delightfully written and highly entertaining. I am as much in love with the author as I ever was with Clarkson or Buchanan, or even the two Mr. Smiths of the city. The first soldier I ever sighed for; but he does write with extraordinary force and spirit. Yesterday, moreover, brought us "Mrs. Grant's Letters," with Mr. White's compliments; but I have disposed of them, compliments and all, to Miss P., and amongst so many readers or retainers of books as we have in Chawton, I dare say there will be no difficulty in getting rid of them for another fortnight, if necessary. I have disposed of Mrs. Grant for the second fortnight to Mrs. ———. It can make no difference to her which of the twenty-six fortnights in the year the three vols. lie on her table. I have been applied to for information as to the oath taken in former times of Bell, Book, and Candle, but have none to give. Perhaps you may be able to learn something of its origin where you now are. Ladies who read those enormous great stupid thick quarto volumes which one always sees in the breakfast-parlor there must be acquainted with everything in the world. I detest a quarto. Captain Pasley's book is too good for their society. They will not understand a man who condenses his thoughts into an octavo. I have learned from Sir J. Carr that there is no Government House at Gibraltar. I must alter it to the Commissioner's.

XLIII.

SLOANE STREET, Thursday, May 20.

MY DEAR CASSANDRA,—Before I say anything else, I claim a paper full of halfpence on the drawing-room mantelpiece; I put them there myself, and forgot to bring them with me. I cannot say that I have yet been in any distress for money, but I choose to have my due, as well as the Devil. How lucky we were in our weather yesterday! This wet morning makes one more sensible of it. We had no rain of any consequence. The head of the curricle was put half up three or four times, but our share of the showers was very trifling, though they seemed to be heavy all round us, when we were on the Hog's-back, and I fancied it might then be raining so hard at Chawton as to make you feel for us much more than we deserved. Three hours and a quarter took us to Guildford, where we stayed barely two hours, and had only just time enough for all we had to do there; that is, eating a long and comfortable breakfast, watching the carriages, paying Mr. Harrington, and taking a little stroll afterwards. From some views which that stroll gave us, I think most highly of the situation of Guildford. We wanted all our brothers and sisters to be standing with us in the bowling-green, and looking towards Horsham. I was very lucky in my gloves,—got them at the first shop I went to, though I went into it rather because it was near than because it looked at all like a glove-shop, and gave only four shillings for them; after which everybody at Chawton will be hoping and predicting that they cannot be good for anything, and their worth certainly remains to be proved; but I think they look very well. We left Guildford at twenty minutes before twelve (I hope somebody cares for these minutiæ), and were at Esher in about two hours more. I was very much pleased with the country

___
[14] At this time, February, 1813, "Mansfield Park" was nearly finished.

in general. Between Guildford and Ripley I thought it particularly pretty, also about Painshill; and from a Mr. Spicer's grounds at Esher, which we walked into before dinner, the views were beautiful. I cannot say what we did not see, but I should think there could not be a wood, or a meadow, or palace, or remarkable spot in England that was not spread out before us on one side or other. Claremont is going to be sold: a Mr. Ellis has it now. It is a house that seems never to have prospered. After dinner we walked forward to be overtaken at the coachman's time, and before he did overtake us we were very near Kingston. I fancy it was about half-past six when we reached this house,—a twelve hours' business, and the horses did not appear more than reasonably tired. I was very tired too, and glad to get to bed early, but am quite well to-day. I am very snug in the front drawing-room all to myself, and would not say "thank you" for any company but you. The quietness of it does me good. I have contrived to pay my two visits, though the weather made me a great while about it, and left me only a few minutes to sit with Charlotte Craven.[15] She looks very well, and her hair is done up with an elegance to do credit to any education. Her manners are as unaffected and pleasing as ever. She had heard from her mother to-day. Mrs. Craven spends another fortnight at Chilton. I saw nobody but Charlotte, which pleased me best. I was shown upstairs into a drawing-room, where she came to me; and the appearance of the room, so totally unschoollike, amused me very much: it was full of modern elegances.

Yours very affectly,
J. A.

XLIV.

SLOANE STREET, Monday (May 24).

MY DEAREST CASSANDRA,—I am very much obliged to you for writing to me. You must have hated it after a worrying morning. Your letter came just in time to save my going to Remnant's, and fit me for Christian's, where I bought Fanny's dimity.

I went the day before (Friday) to Layton's as I proposed, and got my mother's gown,—seven yards at 6*s.* 6*d.* I then walked into No. 10, which is all dirt and confusion, but in a very promising way; and after being present at the opening of a new account, to my great amusement, Henry and I went to the exhibition in Spring Gardens. It is not thought a good collection, but I was very well pleased, particularly (pray tell Fanny) with a small portrait of Mrs. Bingley,[16] excessively like her.

I went in hopes of seeing one of her sister, but there was no Mrs. Darcy. Perhaps, however, I may find her in the great exhibition, which we shall go to if we have time. I have no chance of her in the collection of Sir Joshua Reynolds's paintings, which is now showing in Pall Mall, and which we are also to visit.

Mrs. Bingley's is exactly herself,—size, shaped face, features, and sweetness; there never was a greater likeness. She is dressed in a white gown, with green ornaments, which convinces me of what I had always supposed, that green was a favorite color with her. I dare say Mrs. D. will be in yellow.

Friday was our worst day as to weather. We were out in a very long and very heavy storm of hail, and there had been others before, but I heard no thunder. Saturday was a good deal better; dry and cold.

---

[15] The present Lady Pollen, of Redenham, near Andover, then at a school in London.
[16] *Vide* "Pride and Prejudice."

I gave 2*s.* 6*d.* for the dimity. I do not boast of any bargains, but think both the sarsenet and dimity good of their sort.

I have bought your locket, but was obliged to give 18*s.* for it, which must be rather more than you intended. It is neat and plain, set in gold.

We were to have gone to the Somerset House Exhibition on Saturday, but when I reached Henrietta Street Mr. Hampson was wanted there, and Mr. Tilson and I were obliged to drive about town after him, and by the time we had done it was too late for anything but home. We never found him after all.

I have been interrupted by Mrs. Tilson. Poor woman! She is in danger of not being able to attend Lady Drummond Smith's party to-night. Miss Burdett was to have taken her, and now Miss Burdett has a cough and will not go. My cousin Caroline is her sole dependence.

The events of yesterday were, our going to Belgrave Chapel in the morning, our being prevented by the rain from going to evening service at St. James, Mr. Hampson's calling, Messrs. Barlow and Phillips dining here, and Mr. and Mrs. Tilson's coming in the evening *à l'ordinaire*. She drank tea with us both Thursday and Saturday; he dined out each day, and on Friday we were with them, and they wish us to go to them to-morrow evening, to meet Miss Burdett, but I do not know how it will end. Henry talks of a drive to Hampstead, which may interfere with it.

I should like to see Miss Burdett very well, but that I am rather frightened by hearing that she wishes to be introduced to me. If I am a wild beast, I cannot help it. It is not my own fault.

There is no change in our plan of leaving London, but we shall not be with you before Tuesday. Henry thinks Monday would appear too early a day. There is no danger of our being induced to stay longer.

I have not quite determined how I shall manage about my clothes; perhaps there may be only my trunk to send by the coach, or there may be a band-box with it. I have taken your gentle hint, and written to Mrs. Hill.

The Hoblyns want us to dine with them, but we have refused. When Henry returns he will be dining out a great deal, I dare say; as he will then be alone, it will be more desirable; he will be more welcome at every table, and every invitation more welcome to him. He will not want either of us again till he is settled in Henrietta Street. This is my present persuasion. And he will not be settled there—really settled—till late in the autumn; "he will not be come to bide" till after September.

There is a gentleman in treaty for this house. Gentleman himself is in the country, but gentleman's friend came to see it the other day, and seemed pleased on the whole. Gentleman would rather prefer an increased rent to parting with five hundred guineas at once, and if that is the only difficulty it will not be minded. Henry is indifferent as to the which.

Get us the best weather you can for Wednesday, Thursday, and Friday. We are to go to Windsor in our way to Henley, which will be a great delight. We shall be leaving Sloane Street about twelve, two or three hours after Charles's party have begun their journey. You will miss them, but the comfort of getting back into your own room will be great. And then the tea and sugar!

I fear Miss Clewes is not better, or you would have mentioned it. I shall not write again unless I have any unexpected communication or opportunity to tempt me. I enclose Mr. Herington's bill and receipt.

I am very much obliged to Fanny for her letter; it made me laugh heartily, but I cannot pretend to answer it. Even had I more time, I should not feel at all sure of the sort of letter that

Miss D.[17] would write. I hope Miss Benn is got well again, and will have a comfortable dinner with you to-day.

Monday Evening.—We have been both to the exhibition and Sir J. Reynolds's, and I am disappointed, for there was nothing like Mrs. D. at either. I can only imagine that Mr. D. prizes any picture of her too much to like it should be exposed to the public eye. I can imagine he would have that sort of feeling,—that mixture of love, pride, and delicacy.

Setting aside this disappointment, I had great amusement among the pictures; and the driving about, the carriage being open, was very pleasant. I liked my solitary elegance very much, and was ready to laugh all the time at my being where I was. I could not but feel that I had naturally small right to be parading about London in a barouche.

Henry desires Edward may know that he has just bought three dozen of claret for him (cheap), and ordered it to be sent down to Chawton.

I should not wonder if we got no farther than Reading on Thursday evening, and so reach Steventon only to a reasonable dinner-hour the next day; but whatever I may write or you may imagine, we know it will be something different. I shall be quiet to-morrow morning; all my business is done, and I shall only call again upon Mrs. Hoblyn, etc.

Love to your much ... party.

Yours affectionately,
J. AUSTEN.

XLV.

HENRIETTA ST., Wednesday (Sept. 15, ½ past 8).

HERE I am, my dearest Cassandra, seated in the breakfast, dining, sitting room, beginning with all my might. Fanny will join me as soon as she is dressed, and begin her letter.

We had a very good journey, weather and roads excellent; the three first stages for 1*s.* 6*d.*, and our only misadventure the being delayed about a quarter of an hour at Kingston for horses, and being obliged to put up with a pair belonging to a hackney coach and their coachman, which left no room on the barouche box for Lizzy, who was to have gone her last stage there as she did the first; consequently we were all four within, which was a little crowded.

We arrived at a quarter-past four, and were kindly welcomed by the coachman, and then by his master, and then by William, and then by Mrs. Pengird, who all met us before we reached the foot of the stairs. Mde. Bigion was below dressing us a most comfortable dinner of soup, fish, bouillée, partridges, and an apple tart, which we sat down to soon after five, after cleaning and dressing ourselves, and feeling that we were most commodiously disposed of. The little adjoining dressing-room to our apartment makes Fanny and myself very well off indeed, and as we have poor Eliza's[18] bed our space is ample every way.

Sace arrived safely about half-past six. At seven we set off in a coach for the Lyceum; were at home again in about four hours and a half; had soup and wine and water, and then went to our holes.

Edward finds his quarters very snug and quiet. I must get a softer pen. This is harder. I am in agonies. I have not yet seen Mr. Crabbe. Martha's letter is gone to the post.

I am going to write nothing but short sentences. There shall be two full stops in every line. Layton and Shear's is Bedford House. We mean to get there before breakfast if it's possible;

---

17 Miss Darcy.
18 Eliza, Henry Austen's first wife, who had died in the earlier part of this year.

for we feel more and more how much we have to do and how little time. This house looks very nice. It seems like Sloane Street moved here. I believe Henry is just rid of Sloane Street. Fanny does not come, but I have Edward seated by me beginning a letter, which looks natural.

Henry has been suffering from the pain in the face which he has been subject to before. He caught cold at Matlock, and since his return has been paying a little for past pleasure. It is nearly removed now, but he looks thin in the face, either from the pain or the fatigues of his tour, which must have been great.

Lady Robert is delighted with P. and P.,[19] and really was so, as I understand, before she knew who wrote it, for of course she knows now. He told her with as much satisfaction as if it were my wish. He did not tell me this, but he told Fanny. And Mr. Hastings! I am quite delighted with what such a man writes about it. Henry sent him the books after his return from Daylesford, but you will hear the letter too.

Let me be rational, and return to my two full stops.

I talked to Henry at the play last night. We were in a private box,—Mr. Spencer's,—which made it much more pleasant. The box is directly on the stage. One is infinitely less fatigued than in the common way. But Henry's plans are not what one could wish. He does not mean to be at Chawton till the 29th. He must be in town again by Oct. 5. His plan is to get a couple of days of pheasant shooting and then return directly. His wish was to bring you back with him. I have told him your scruples. He wishes you to suit yourself as to time, and if you cannot come till later, will send for you at any time as far as Bagshot. He presumed you would not find difficulty in getting so far. I could not say you would. He proposed your going with him into Oxfordshire. It was his own thought at first. I could not but catch at it for you.

We have talked of it again this morning (for now we have breakfasted), and I am convinced that if you can make it suit in other respects you need not scruple on his account. If you cannot come back with him on the 3rd or 4th, therefore, I do hope you will contrive to go to Adlestrop. By not beginning your absence till about the middle of this month I think you may manage it very well. But you will think all this over. One could wish he had intended to come to you earlier, but it cannot be helped.

I said nothing to him of Mrs. H. and Miss B., that he might not suppose difficulties. Shall not you put them into our own room? This seems to me the best plan, and the maid will be most conveniently near.

Oh, dear me! when I shall ever have done. We did go to Layton and Shear's before breakfast. Very pretty English poplins at 4*s.* 3*d.*; Irish, ditto at 6*s.*; more pretty, certainly,—beautiful.

Fanny and the two little girls are gone to take places for to-night at Covent Garden; "Clandestine Marriage" and "Midas." The latter will be a fine show for L. and M.[20] They revelled last night in "Don Juan," whom we left in hell at half-past eleven. We had scaramouch and a ghost, and were delighted. I speak of them; my delight was very tranquil, and the rest of us were sober-minded. "Don Juan" was the last of three musical things. "Five Hours at Brighton," in three acts,—of which one was over before we arrived, none the worse,—and the "Beehive," rather less flat and trumpery.

I have this moment received 5*l.* from kind, beautiful Edward. Fanny has a similar gift. I shall save what I can of it for your better leisure in this place. My letter was from Miss Sharpe,—nothing particular. A letter from Fanny Cage this morning.

Four o'clock.—We are just come back from doing Mrs. Tickars, Miss Hare, and Mr. Spence. Mr. Hall is here, and while Fanny is under his hands, I will try to write a little more.

---

[19] "Pride and Prejudice."
[20] Lizzy and Marianne.

Miss Hare had some pretty caps, and is to make me one like one of them, only white satin instead of blue. It will be white satin and lace, and a little white flower perking out of the left ear, like Harriot Byron's feather. I have allowed her to go as far as 1*l.* 16*s.* My gown is to be trimmed everywhere with white ribbon plaited on somehow or other. She says it will look well. I am not sanguine. They trim with white very much.

I learnt from Mrs. Tickars's young lady, to my high amusement, that the stays now are not made to force the bosom up at all; that was a very unbecoming, unnatural fashion. I was really glad to hear that they are not to be so much off the shoulders as they were.

Going to Mr. Spence's was a sad business, and cost us many tears; unluckily we were obliged to go a second time before he could do more than just look. We went first at half-past twelve and afterwards at three; papa with us each time; and, alas! we are to go again to-morrow. Lizzy is not finished yet. There have been no teeth taken out, however, nor will be, I believe; but he finds hers in a very bad state, and seems to think particularly ill of their durableness. They have been all cleaned, hers filed, and are to be filed again. There is a very sad hole between two of her front teeth.

Thursday Morning, half-past Seven.—Up and dressed and downstairs in order to finish my letter in time for the parcel. At eight I have an appointment with Madame B., who wants to show me something downstairs. At nine we are to set off for Grafton House, and get that over before breakfast. Edward is so kind as to walk there with us. We are to be at Mr. Spence's again at 11.5: from that time shall be driving about I suppose till four o'clock at least. We are, if possible, to call on Mrs. Tilson.

Mr. Hall was very punctual yesterday, and curled me out at a great rate. I thought it looked hideous, and longed for a snug cap instead, but my companions silenced me by their admiration. I had only a bit of velvet round my head. I did not catch cold, however. The weather is all in my favor. I have had no pain in my face since I left you.

We had very good places in the box next the stage-box, front and second row; the three old ones behind, of course. I was particularly disappointed at seeing nothing of Mr. Crabbe. I felt sure of him when I saw that the boxes were fitted up with crimson velvet. The new Mr. Terry was Lord Ogleby, and Henry thinks he may do; but there was no acting more than moderate, and I was as much amused by the remembrances connected with "Midas" as with any part of it. The girls were very much delighted, but still prefer "Don Juan;" and I must say that I have seen nobody on the stage who has been a more interesting character than that compound of cruelty and lust.

It was not possible for me to get the worsteds yesterday. I heard Edward last night pressing Henry to come to you, and I think Henry engaged to go there after his November collection. Nothing has been done as to S. and S.[21] The books came to hand too late for him to have time for it before he went. Mr. Hastings never hinted at Eliza in the smallest degree. Henry knew nothing of Mr. Trimmer's death. I tell you these things that you may not have to ask them over again.

There is a new clerk sent down to Alton, a Mr. Edmund Williams, a young man whom Henry thinks most highly of, and he turns out to be a son of the luckless Williamses of Grosvenor Place.

I long to have you hear Mr. H.'s opinion of P. and P. His admiring my Elizabeth so much is particularly welcome to me.

---

[21] "Sense and Sensibility."

Instead of saving my superfluous wealth for you to spend, I am going to treat myself with spending it myself. I hope, at least, that I shall find some poplin at Layton and Shear's that will tempt me to buy it. If I do, it shall be sent to Chawton, as half will be for you; for I depend upon your being so kind as to accept it, being the main point. It will be a great pleasure to me. Don't say a word. I only wish you could choose too. I shall send twenty yards.

Now for Bath. Poor F. Cage has suffered a good deal from her accident. The noise of the White Hart was terrible to her. They will keep her quiet, I dare say. She is not so much delighted with the place as the rest of the party; probably, as she says herself, from having been less well, but she thinks she should like it better in the season. The streets are very empty now, and the shops not so gay as she expected. They are at No. 1 Henrietta Street, the corner of Laura Place, and have no acquaintance at present but the Bramstons.

Lady Bridges drinks at the Cross Bath, her son at the Hot, and Louisa is going to bathe. Dr. Parry seems to be half starving Mr. Bridges, for he is restricted to much such a diet as James's, bread, water and meat, and is never to eat so much of that as he wishes, and he is to walk a great deal,—walk till he drops, I believe,—gout or no gout. It really is to that purpose. I have not exaggerated.

Charming weather for you and us, and the travellers, and everybody. You will take your walk this afternoon, and . . .
Henrietta Street, the autumn of 1813.

Miss AUSTEN, Chawton.
By favor of Mr. Gray.

XLVI.

HENRIETTA STREET,
Thursday (Sept. 16, after dinner),

THANK you, my dearest Cassandra, for the nice long letter I sent off this morning. I hope you have had it by this time, and that it has found you all well, and my mother no more in need of leeches. Whether this will be delivered to you by Henry on Saturday evening, or by the postman on Sunday morning, I know not, as he has lately recollected something of an engagement for Saturday, which perhaps may delay his visit. He seems determined to come to you soon, however.

I hope you will receive the gown to-morrow, and may be able with tolerable honesty to say that you like the color. It was bought at Grafton House, where, by going very early, we got immediate attendance and went on very comfortably. I only forgot the one particular thing which I had always resolved to buy there,—a white silk handkerchief,—and was therefore obliged to give six shillings for one at Crook and Besford's; which reminds me to say that the worsteds ought also to be at Chawton to-morrow, and that I shall be very happy to hear they are approved. I had not much time for deliberation.

We are now all four of us young ladies sitting round the circular table in the inner room writing our letters, while the two brothers are having a comfortable coze in the room adjoining. It is to be a quiet evening, much to the satisfaction of four of the six. My eyes are quite tired of dust and lamps.

The letter you forwarded from Edward, junr., has been duly received. He has been shooting most prosperously at home, and dining at Chilham Castle and with Mr. Scudamore.

My cap is come home, and I like it very much. Fanny has one also; hers is white sarsenet and lace, of a different shape from mine, more fit for morning carriage wear, which is what it is intended for, and is in shape exceedingly like our own satin and lace of last winter; shaped round the face exactly like it, with pipes and more fulness, and a round crown inserted behind. My cap has a peak in front. Large full bows of very narrow ribbon (old twopenny) are the thing. One over the right temple, perhaps, and another at the left ear.

Henry is not quite well. His stomach is rather deranged. You must keep him in rhubarb, and give him plenty of port and water. He caught his cold farther back than I told you,—before he got to Matlock, somewhere in his journey from the North; but the ill effects of that I hope are nearly gone.

We returned from Grafton House only just in time for breakfast, and had scarcely finished breakfast when the carriage came to the door. From eleven to half-past three we were hard at it; we did contrive to get to Hans Place for ten minutes. Mrs. T. was as affectionate and pleasing as ever.

After our return Mr. Tilson walked up from the Compting House and called upon us, and these have been all our visitings.

I have rejoiced more than once that I bought my writing-paper in the country; we have not had a quarter of an hour to spare.

I enclose the eighteen-pence due to my mother. The rose color was 6*s.* and the other 4*s.* per yard. There was but two yards and a quarter of the dark slate in the shop, but the man promised to match it and send it off correctly.

Fanny bought her Irish at Newton's in Leicester Square, and I took the opportunity of thinking about your Irish, and seeing one piece of the yard wide at 4*s.*, and it seemed to me very good; good enough for your purpose. It might at least be worth your while to go there, if you have no other engagements. Fanny is very much pleased with the stockings she has bought of Remmington, silk at 12*s.*, cotton at 4*s.* 3*d.* She thinks them great bargains, but I have not seen them yet, as my hair was dressing when the man and the stockings came.

The poor girls and their teeth! I have not mentioned them yet, but we were a whole hour at Spence's, and Lizzy's were filed and lamented over again, and poor Marianne had two taken out after all, the two just beyond the eye teeth, to make room for those in front. When her doom was fixed, Fanny, Lizzy, and I walked into the next room, where we heard each of the two sharp and hasty screams.

The little girls' teeth I can suppose in a critical state, but I think he must be a lover of teeth and money and mischief, to parade about Fanny's. I would not have had him look at mine for a shilling a tooth and double it. It was a disagreeable hour.

We then went to Wedgwood's, where my brother and Fanny chose a dinner-set. I believe the pattern is a small lozenge in purple, between lines of narrow gold, and it is to have the crest.

We must have been three-quarters of an hour at Grafton House, Edward sitting by all the time with wonderful patience. There Fanny bought the net for Anna's gown, and a beautiful square veil for herself. The edging there is very cheap. I was tempted by some, and I bought some very nice plaiting lace at 3*s.* 4*d.*

Fanny desires me to tell Martha, with her kind love, that Birchall assured her there was no second set of Hook's Lessons for Beginners, and that, by my advice, she has therefore chosen her a set by another composer. I thought she would rather have something than not. It costs six shillings.

With love to you all, including Triggs, I remain,

Yours very affectionately,

J. AUSTEN.

Henrietta St., autumn of 1813.
Miss AUSTEN, Chawton.
By favor of

XLVII.

GODMERSHAM PARK, Thursday (Sept. 23).

MY DEAREST CASSANDRA,—Thank you five hundred and forty times for the exquisite piece of workmanship which was brought into the room this morning, while we were at breakfast, with some very inferior works of art in the same way, and which I read with high glee, much delighted with everything it told, whether good or bad. It is so rich in striking intelligence that I hardly know what to reply to first. I believe finery must have it.

I am extremely glad that you like the poplin. I thought it would have my mother's approbation, but was not so confident of yours. Remember that it is a present. Do not refuse me. I am very rich.

Mrs. Clement is very welcome to her little boy, and to my congratulations into the bargain, if ever you think of giving them. I hope she will do well. Her sister in Lucina, Mrs. H. Gipps, does too well, we think. Mary P. wrote on Sunday that she had been three days on the sofa. Sackree does not approve it.

Well, there is some comfort in the Mrs. Hulbart's not coming to you, and I am happy to hear of the honey. I was thinking of it the other day. Let me know when you begin the new tea and the new white wine. My present elegances have not yet made me indifferent to such matters. I am still a cat if I see a mouse.

I am glad you like our caps, but Fanny is out of conceit with hers already; she finds that she has been buying a new cap without having a new pattern, which is true enough. She is rather out of luck to like neither her gown nor her cap, but I do not much mind it, because besides that I like them both myself, I consider it as a thing of course at her time of life,—one of the sweet taxes of youth to choose in a hurry and make bad bargains.

I wrote to Charles yesterday, and Fanny has had a letter from him to-day, principally to make inquiries about the time of their visit here, to which mine was an answer beforehand; so he will probably write again soon to fix his week. I am best pleased that Cassy does not go to you.

Now, what have we been doing since I wrote last? The Mr. K.'s[22] came a little before dinner on Monday, and Edward went to the church with the two seniors, but there is no inscription yet drawn up. They are very good-natured, you know, and civil, and all that, but are not particularly superfine; however, they ate their dinner and drank their tea, and went away, leaving their lovely Wadham in our arms, and I wish you had seen Fanny and me running backwards and forwards with his breeches from the little chintz to the white room before we

---

[22] Knatchbulls

went to bed, in the greatest of frights lest he should come upon us before we had done it all. There had been a mistake in the housemaid's preparation, and they were gone to bed.

He seems a very harmless sort of young man, nothing to like or dislike in him,—goes out shooting or hunting with the two others all the morning, and plays at whist and makes queer faces in the evening....

XLVIII.

GODMERSHAM PARK, Monday (Oct. 11).

[MY DEAREST AUNT CASS.,—I have just asked Aunt Jane to let me write a little in her letter, but she does not like it, so I won't. Good-by!]

You will have Edward's letter to-morrow. He tells me that he did not send you any news to interfere with mine, but I do not think there is much for anybody to send at present.

We had our dinner-party on Wednesday, with the addition of Mrs. and Miss Milles, who were under a promise of dining here in their return from Eastwell, whenever they paid their visit of duty there, and it happened to be paid on that day. Both mother and daughter are much as I have always found them. I like the mother—first, because she reminds me of Mrs. Birch; and, secondly, because she is cheerful and grateful for what she is at the age of ninety and upwards. The day was pleasant enough. I sat by Mr. Chisholme, and we talked away at a great rate about nothing worth hearing.

It was a mistake as to the day of the Sherers going being fixed; they are ready, but are waiting for Mr. Paget's answer.

I inquired of Mrs. Milles after Jemima Brydges, and was quite grieved to hear that she was obliged to leave Canterbury some months ago on account of her debts, and is nobody knows where. What an unprosperous family!

On Saturday, soon after breakfast, Mr. J. P. left us for Norton Court. I like him very much. He gives me the idea of a very amiable young man, only too diffident to be so agreeable as he might be. He was out the chief of each morning with the other two, shooting and getting wet through. To-morrow we are to know whether he and a hundred young ladies will come here for the ball. I do not much expect any.

The Deedes cannot meet us; they have engagements at home. I will finish the Deedes by saying that they are not likely to come here till quite late in my stay,—the very last week perhaps; and I do not expect to see the Moores at all. They are not solicited till after Edward's return from Hampshire.

Monday, November 15, is the day now fixed for our setting out.

Poor Basingstoke races! There seem to have been two particularly wretched days on purpose for them; and Weyhill week does not begin much happier.

We were quite surprised by a letter from Anna at Tollard Royal, last Saturday; but perfectly approve her going, and only regret they should all go so far to stay so few days.

We had thunder and lightning here on Thursday morning, between five and seven; no very bad thunder, but a great deal of lightning. It has given the commencement of a season of wind and rain, and perhaps for the next six weeks we shall not have two dry days together.

Lizzy is very much obliged to you for your letter and will answer it soon, but has so many things to do that it may be four or five days before she can. This is quite her own message, spoken in rather a desponding tone. Your letter gave pleasure to all of us; we had all the reading of it of course,—I three times, as I undertook, to the great relief of Lizzy, to read it to Sackree, and afterwards to Louisa.

Sackree does not at all approve of Mary Doe and her nuts,—on the score of propriety rather than health. She saw some signs of going after her in George and Henry, and thinks if you could give the girl a check, by rather reproving her for taking anything seriously about nuts which they said to her, it might be of use. This, of course, is between our three discreet selves, a scene of triennial bliss.

Mrs. Breton called here on Saturday. I never saw her before. She is a large, ungenteel woman, with self-satisfied and would-be elegant manners.

We are certain of some visitors to-morrow. Edward Bridges comes for two nights in his way from Lenham to Ramsgate, and brings a friend—name unknown—but supposed to be a Mr. Harpur, a neighboring clergyman; and Mr. R. Mascall is to shoot with the young men, which it is to be supposed will end in his staying dinner.

On Thursday, Mr. Lushington, M.P. for Canterbury, and manager of the Lodge Hounds, dines here, and stays the night. He is chiefly young Edward's acquaintance. If I can I will get a frank from him, and write to you all the sooner. I suppose the Ashford ball will furnish something.

As I wrote of my nephews with a little bitterness in my last, I think it particularly incumbent on me to do them justice now, and I have great pleasure in saying that they were both at the Sacrament yesterday. After having much praised or much blamed anybody, one is generally sensible of something just the reverse soon afterwards. Now these two boys who are out with the foxhounds will come home and disgust me again by some habit of luxury or some proof of sporting mania, unless I keep it off by this prediction. They amuse themselves very comfortably in the evening by netting; they are each about a rabbit net, and sit as deedily to it, side by side, as any two Uncle Franks could do.

I am looking over "Self-Control" again, and my opinion is confirmed of its being an excellently meant, elegantly written work, without anything of nature or probability in it. I declare I do not know whether Laura's passage down the American river is not the most natural, possible, every-day thing she ever does.

Tuesday.—Dear me! what is to become of me? Such a long letter! Two-and-forty lines in the second page. Like Harriot Byron, I ask, what am I to do with my gratitude? I can do nothing but thank you and go on. A few of your inquiries, I think, are replied to *en avance*.

The name of F. Cage's drawing-master is O'Neil. We are exceedingly amused with your Shalden news, and your self-reproach on the subject of Mrs. Stockwell made me laugh heartily. I rather wondered that Johncock,[23] the only person in the room, could help laughing too. I had not heard before of her having the measles. Mrs. H. and Alethea's staying till Friday was quite new to me; a good plan, however. I could not have settled it better myself, and am glad they found so much in the house to approve, and I hope they will ask Martha to visit them. I admire the sagacity and taste of Charlotte Williams. Those large dark eyes always judge well. I will compliment her by naming a heroine after her.

Edward has had all the particulars of the building, etc., read to him twice over, and seems very well satisfied. A narrow door to the pantry is the only subject of solicitude; it is certainly just the door which should not be narrow, on account of the trays; but if a case of necessity, it must be borne.

I knew there was sugar in the tin, but had no idea of there being enough to last through your company. All the better. You ought not to think this new loaf better than the other, because that was the first of five which all came together. Something of fancy, perhaps, and something of imagination.

---

[23] The butler at Godmersham.

Dear Mrs. Digweed! I cannot bear that she should not be foolishly happy after a ball. I hope Miss Yates and her companions were all well the day after their arrival. I am thoroughly rejoiced that Miss Benn has placed herself in lodgings, though I hope they may not be long necessary.

No letter from Charles yet.

Southey's "Life of Nelson." I am tired of "Lives of Nelson," being that I never read any. I will read this, however, if Frank is mentioned in it.

Here am I in Kent, with one brother in the same county and another brother's wife, and see nothing of them, which seems unnatural. It will not last so forever, I trust. I should like to have Mrs. F. A. and her children here for a week, but not a syllable of that nature is ever breathed. I wish her last visit had not been so long a one.

I wonder whether Mrs. Tilson has ever lain-in. Mention it if it ever comes to your knowledge, and we shall hear of it by the same post from Henry.

Mr. Rob. Mascall breakfasted here; he eats a great deal of butter. I dined upon goose yesterday, which, I hope, will secure a good sale of my second edition. Have you any tomatas? Fanny and I regale on them every day.

Disastrous letters from the Plumptres and Oxendens. Refusals everywhere—a blank *partout*—and it is not quite certain whether we go or not; something may depend upon the disposition of Uncle Edward when he comes, and upon what we hear at Chilham Castle this morning, for we are going to pay visits. We are going to each house at Chilham and to Mystole. I shall like seeing the Faggs. I shall like it all, except that we are to set out so early that I have not time to write as I would wish.

Edwd. Bridges's friend is a Mr. Hawker, I find, not Harpur. I would not have you sleep in such an error for the world.

My brother desires his best love and thanks for all your information. He hopes the roots of the old beech have been dug away enough to allow a proper covering of mould and turf. He is sorry for the necessity of building the new coin, but hopes they will contrive that the doorway should be of the usual width,—if it must be contracted on one side, by widening it on the other. The appearance need not signify. And he desires me to say that your being at Chawton when he is will be quite necessary. You cannot think it more indispensable than he does. He is very much obliged to you for your attention to everything. Have you any idea of returning with him to Henrietta Street and finishing your visit then? Tell me your sweet little innocent ideas.

Everything of love and kindness, proper and improper, must now suffice.

Yours very affectionately,
J. AUSTEN.

Miss AUSTEN, Chawton, Alton, Hants.

XLIX.

GODMERSHAM PARK, Thursday (Oct. 14).

MY DEAREST CASSANDRA,—Now I will prepare for Mr. Lushington, and as it will be wisest also to prepare for his not coming, or my not getting a frank, I shall write very close from the first, and even leave room for the seal in the proper place. When I have followed up my last with this I shall feel somewhat less unworthy of you than the state of our correspondence now requires.

I left off in a great hurry to prepare for our morning visits. Of course was ready a good deal the first, and need not have hurried so much. Fanny wore her new gown and cap. I was surprised to find Mystole so pretty.

The ladies were at home. I was in luck, and saw Lady Fagg and all her five daughters, with an old Mrs. Hamilton, from Canterbury, and Mrs. and Miss Chapman, from Margate, into the bargain. I never saw so plain a family,—five sisters so very plain! They are as plain as the Foresters, or the Franfraddops, or the Seagraves, or the Rivers, excluding Sophy. Miss Sally Fagg has a pretty figure, and that comprises all the good looks of the family.

It was stupidish; Fanny did her part very well, but there was a lack of talk altogether, and the three friends in the house only sat by and looked at us. However, Miss Chapman's name is Laura, and she had a double flounce to her gown. You really must get some flounces. Are not some of your large stock of white morning gowns just in a happy state for a flounce—too short? Nobody at home at either house in Chilham.

Edward Bridges and his friend did not forget to arrive. The friend is a Mr. Wigram, one of the three-and-twenty children of a great rich mercantile, Sir Robert Wigram, an old acquaintance of the Footes, but very recently known to Edward B. The history of his coming here is, that, intending to go from Ramsgate to Brighton, Edw. B. persuaded him to take Lenham on his way, which gave him the convenience of Mr. W.'s gig, and the comfort of not being alone there; but, probably thinking a few days of Gm. would be the cheapest and pleasantest way of entertaining his friend and himself, offered a visit here, and here they stay till to-morrow.

Mr. W. is about five or six-and-twenty, not ill-looking, and not agreeable. He is certainly no addition. A sort of cool, gentlemanlike manner, but very silent. They say his name is Henry, a proof how unequally the gifts of fortune are bestowed. I have seen many a John and Thomas much more agreeable.

We have got rid of Mr. R. Mascall, however. I did not like him, either. He talks too much, and is conceited, besides having a vulgarly shaped mouth. He slept here on Tuesday, so that yesterday Fanny and I sat down to breakfast with six gentlemen to admire us.

We did not go to the ball. It was left to her to decide, and at last she determined against it. She knew that it would be a sacrifice on the part of her father and brothers if they went, and I hope it will prove that she has not sacrificed much. It is not likely that there should have been anybody there whom she would care for. I was very glad to be spared the trouble of dressing and going, and being weary before it was half over; so my gown and my cap are still unworn. It will appear at last, perhaps, that I might have done without either. I produced my brown bombazine yesterday, and it was very much admired indeed, and I like it better than ever.

You have given many particulars of the state of Chawton House, but still we want more. Edward wants to be expressly told that all the round tower, etc., is entirely down, and the door from the best room stopped up; he does not know enough of the appearance of things in that quarter.

He heard from Bath yesterday. Lady B. continues very well, and Dr. Parry's opinion is, that while the water agrees with her she ought to remain there, which throws their coming away at a greater uncertainty than we had supposed. It will end, perhaps, in a fit of the gout, which may prevent her coming away. Louisa thinks her mother's being so well may be quite as much owing to her being so much out of doors as to the water. Lady B. is going to try the hot pump, the Cross bath being about to be painted. Louisa is particularly well herself, and thinks the water has been of use to her. She mentioned our inquiries, etc., to Mr. and Mrs. Alex. Evelyn, and had their best compliments and thanks to give in return. Dr. Parry does not expect Mr. E. to last much longer.

Only think of Mrs. Holder's being dead! Poor woman, she has done the only thing in the world she could possibly do to make one cease to abuse her. Now, if you please, Hooper must have it in his power to do more by his uncle. Lucky for the little girl. An Anne Ekins can hardly be so unfit for the care of a child as a Mrs. Holder.

A letter from Wrotham yesterday offering an early visit here, and Mr. and Mrs. Moore and one child are to come on Monday for ten days. I hope Charles and Fanny may not fix the same time, but if they come at all in October they must. What is the use of hoping? The two parties of children is the chief evil.

To be sure, here we are; the very thing has happened, or rather worse,—a letter from Charles this very morning, which gives us reason to suppose they may come here to-day. It depends upon the weather, and the weather now is very fine. No difficulties are made, however, and, indeed, there will be no want of room; but I wish there were no Wigrams and Lushingtons in the way to fill up the table and make us such a motley set. I cannot spare Mr. Lushington either, because of his frank, but Mr. Wigram does no good to anybody. I cannot imagine how a man can have the impudence to come into a family party for three days, where he is quite a stranger, unless he knows himself to be agreeable on undoubted authority. He and Edw. B. are going to ride to Eastwell, and as the boys are hunting, and my brother is gone to Canty., Fanny and I have a quiet morning before us.

Edward has driven off poor Mrs. Salkeld. It was thought a good opportunity of doing something towards clearing the house. By her own desire Mrs. Fanny[24] is to be put in the room next the nursery, her baby in a little bed by her; and as Cassy is to have the closet within, and Betsey William's little hole, they will be all very snug together. I shall be most happy to see dear Charles, and he will be as happy as he can with a cross child, or some such care, pressing on him at the time. I should be very happy in the idea of seeing little Cassy again, too, did not I fear she would disappoint me by some immediate disagreeableness....

The comfort of the billiard-table here is very great; it draws all the gentlemen to it whenever they are within, especially after dinner, so that my brother, Fanny, and I have the library to ourselves in delightful quiet. There is no truth in the report of G. Hatton being to marry Miss Wemyss. He desires it may be contradicted.

Have you done anything about our present to Miss Benn? I suppose she must have a bed at my mother's whenever she dines there. How will they manage as to inviting her when you are gone? and if they invite, how will they continue to entertain her?

Let me know as many of your parting arrangements as you can, as to wine, etc. I wonder whether the ink-bottle has been filled. Does butcher's meat keep up at the same price, and is not bread lower than 2*s.* 6*d.*? Mary's blue gown! My mother must be in agonies. I have a great mind to have my blue gown dyed some time or other. I proposed it once to you, and you made some objection, I forget what. It is the fashion of flounces that gives it particular expediency.

Mrs. and Miss Wildman have just been here. Miss is very plain. I wish Lady B. may be returned before we leave Gm., that Fanny may spend the time of her father's absence at Goodnestone, which is what she would prefer.

Friday.—They came last night at about seven. We had given them up, but I still expected them to come. Dessert was nearly over; a better time for arriving than an hour and a half earlier. They were late because they did not set out earlier, and did not allow time enough. Charles did not aim at more than reaching Sittingbourne by three, which could not have brought them here by dinner-time. They had a very rough passage; he would not have ventured if he had known how bad it would be.

---

24 Mrs. Charles Austen, *née* Fanny Palmer.

However, here they are, safe and well, just like their own nice selves, Fanny looking as neat and white this morning as possible, and dear Charles all affectionate, placid, quiet, cheerful good-humor. They are both looking very well, but poor little Cassy is grown extremely thin, and looks poorly. I hope a week's country air and exercise may do her good. I am sorry to say it can be but a week. The baby does not appear so large in proportion as she was, nor quite so pretty, but I have seen very little of her. Cassy was too tired and bewildered just at first to seem to know anybody. We met them in the hall—the women and girl part of us—but before we reached the library she kissed me very affectionately, and has since seemed to recollect me in the same way.

It was quite an evening of confusion, as you may suppose. At first we were all walking about from one part of the house to the other; then came a fresh dinner in the breakfast-room for Charles and his wife, which Fanny and I attended; then we moved into the library, were joined by the dining-room people, were introduced, and so forth; and then we had tea and coffee, which was not over till past ten. Billiards again drew all the odd ones away; and Edward, Charles, the two Fannies, and I sat snugly talking. I shall be glad to have our numbers a little reduced, and by the time you receive this we shall be only a family, though a large family, party. Mr. Lushington goes to-morrow.

Now I must speak of him, and I like him very much. I am sure he is clever, and a man of taste. He got a volume of Milton last night, and spoke of it with warmth. He is quite an M. P., very smiling, with an exceeding good address and readiness of language. I am rather in love with him. I dare say he is ambitious and insincere. He puts me in mind of Mr. Dundas. He has a wide smiling mouth, and very good teeth, and something the same complexion and nose. He is a much shorter man, with Martha's leave. Does Martha never hear from Mrs. Craven? Is Mrs. Craven never at home?

We breakfasted in the dining-room to-day, and are now all pretty well dispersed and quiet. Charles and George are gone out shooting together, to Winnigates and Seaton Wood. I asked on purpose to tell Henry. Mr. Lushington and Edwd. are gone some other way. I wish Charles may kill something; but this high wind is against their sport.

Lady Williams is living at the Rose at Sittingbourne; they called upon her yesterday; she cannot live at Sheerness, and as soon as she gets to Sittingbourne is quite well. In return for all your matches, I announce that her brother William is going to marry a Miss Austen, of a Wiltshire family, who say they are related to us.

I talk to Cassy about Chawton; she remembers much, but does not volunteer on the subject. Poor little love! I wish she were not so very Palmery, but it seems stronger than ever. I never knew a wife's family features have such undue influence.

Papa and mamma have not yet made up their mind as to parting with her or not; the chief, indeed the only, difficulty with mamma is a very reasonable one, the child's being very unwilling to leave them. When it was mentioned to her she did not like the idea of it at all. At the same time she has been suffering so much lately from sea-sickness that her mamma cannot bear to have her much on board this winter. Charles is less inclined to part with her. I do not know how it will end, or what is to determine it. He desires his best love to you, and has not written because he has not been able to decide. They are both very sensible of your kindness on the occasion.

I have made Charles furnish me with something to say about young Kendall. He is going on very well. When he first joined the "Namur," my brother did not find him forward enough to be what they call put in the office, and therefore placed him under the schoolmaster; but he is very much improved, and goes into the office now every afternoon, still attending school in the morning.

This cold weather comes very fortunately for Edward's nerves, with such a house full; it suits him exactly; he is all alive and cheerful. Poor James, on the contrary, must be running his toes into the fire. I find that Mary Jane Fowle was very near returning with her brother and paying them a visit on board. I forget exactly what hindered her; I believe the Cheltenham scheme. I am glad something did. They are to go to Cheltenham on Monday se'nnight. I don't vouch for their going, you know; it only comes from one of the family.

Now I think I have written you a good-sized letter, and may deserve whatever I can get in reply. Infinities of love. I must distinguish that of Fanny, senior, who particularly desires to be remembered to you all.

Yours very affectionately,
J. AUSTEN.

FAVERSHAM, Oct. 15, 1813.
Miss AUSTEN, Chawton, Alton, Hants.
Per S. R. LUSHINGTON.

L.

GODMERSHAM PARK, Oct. 18.

MY DEAR AUNT CASSANDRA,—I am very much obliged to you for your long letter and for the nice account of Chawton. We are all very glad to hear that the Adams are gone, and hope Dame Libscombe will be more happy now with her deaffy child, as she calls it, but I am afraid there is not much chance of her remaining long sole mistress of her house.

I am sorry you had not any better news to send us of our hare, poor little thing! I thought it would not live long in that *Pondy House*; I don't wonder that Mary Doe is very sorry it is dead, because we promised her that if it was alive when we came back to Chawton, we would reward her for her trouble.

Papa is much obliged to you for ordering the scrubby firs to be cut down; I think he was rather frightened at first about the great oak. Fanny quite believed it, for she exclaimed, "Dear me, what a pity, how could they be so stupid!" I hope by this time they have put up some hurdles for the sheep, or turned out the cart-horses from the lawn.

Pray tell grandmamma that we have begun getting seeds for her; I hope we shall be able to get her a nice collection, but I am afraid this wet weather is very much against them. How glad I am to hear she has had such good success with her chickens, but I wish there had been more bantams amongst them. I am very sorry to hear of poor Lizzie's fate.

I must now tell you something about our poor people. I believe you know old Mary Croucher; she gets maderer and maderer every day. Aunt Jane has been to see her, but it was on one of her rational days. Poor Will Amos hopes your skewers are doing well; he has left his house in the poor Row, and lives in a barn at Builting. We asked him why he went away, and he said the fleas were so starved when he came back from Chawton that they all flew upon him and eenermost eat him up.

How unlucky it is that the weather is so wet! Poor Uncle Charles has come home half drowned every day.

I don't think little Fanny is quite so pretty as she was; one reason is because she wears short petticoats, I believe. I hope Cook is better; she was very unwell the day we went away. Papa has given me half-a-dozen new pencils, which are very good ones indeed; I draw every other day. I hope you go and whip Lucy Chalcraft every night.

Miss Clewes begs me to give her very best respects to you; she is very much obliged to you for your kind inquiries after her. Pray give my duty to grandmamma and love to Miss Floyd. I remain, my dear Aunt Cassandra, your very affectionate niece,

ELIZTH. KNIGHT.

Thursday.—I think Lizzy's letter will entertain you. Thank you for yours just received. To-morrow shall be fine if possible. You will be at Guildford before our party set off. They only go to Key Street, as Mr. Street the Purser lives there, and they have promised to dine and sleep with him.

Cassy's looks are much mended. She agrees pretty well with her cousins, but is not quite happy among them; they are too many and too boisterous for her. I have given her your message, but she said nothing, and did not look as if the idea of going to Chawton again was a pleasant one. They have Edward's carriage to Ospringe.

I think I have just done a good deed,—extracted Charles from his wife and children upstairs, and made him get ready to go out shooting, and not keep Mr. Moore waiting any longer.

Mr. and Mrs. Sherer and Joseph dined here yesterday very prettily. Edw. and Geo. were absent,—gone for a night to Eastling. The two Fannies went to Canty. in the morning, and took Lou. and Cass. to try on new stays. Harriet and I had a comfortable walk together. She desires her best love to you and kind remembrance to Henry. Fanny's best love also. I fancy there is to be another party to Canty. to-morrow,—Mr. and Mrs. Moore and me.

Edward thanks Henry for his letter. We are most happy to hear he is so much better. I depend upon you for letting me know what he wishes as to my staying with him or not; you will be able to find out, I dare say. I had intended to beg you would bring one of my nightcaps with you, in case of my staying, but forgot it when I wrote on Tuesday. Edward is much concerned about his pond; he cannot now doubt the fact of its running out, which he was resolved to do as long as possible.

I suppose my mother will like to have me write to her. I shall try at least.

No; I have never seen the death of Mrs. Crabbe. I have only just been making out from one of his prefaces that he probably was married. It is almost ridiculous. Poor woman! I will comfort him as well as I can, but I do not undertake to be good to her children. She had better not leave any.

Edw. and Geo. set off this day week for Oxford. Our party will then be very small, as the Moores will be going about the same time. To enliven us, Fanny proposes spending a few days soon afterwards at Fredville. It will really be a good opportunity, as her father will have a companion. We shall all three go to Wrotham, but Edwd. and I stay only a night perhaps. Love to Mr. Tilson.

Yours very affectionately,

J. A.

Miss AUSTEN,
10 Henrietta St., Covent Garden, London.

LI.

GODMERSHAM PARK, Wednesday (Nov. 3).

MY DEAREST CASSANDRA,—I will keep this celebrated birthday by writing to you; and as my pen seems inclined to write large, I will put my lines very close together. I had but just time to enjoy your letter yesterday before Edward and I set off in the chair for Canty., and I allowed him to hear the chief of it as we went along.

We rejoice sincerely in Henry's gaining ground as he does, and hope there will be weather for him to get out every day this week, as the likeliest way of making him equal to what he plans for the next. If he is tolerably well, the going into Oxfordshire will make him better, by making him happier.

Can it be that I have not given you the minutiæ of Edward's plans? See, here they are: To go to Wrotham on Saturday the 13th, spend Sunday there, and be in town on Monday to dinner, and if agreeable to Henry, spend one whole day with him, which day is likely to be Tuesday, and so go down to Chawton on Wednesday.

But now I cannot be quite easy without staying a little while with Henry, unless he wishes it otherwise; his illness and the dull time of year together make me feel that it would be horrible of me not to offer to remain with him, and therefore unless you know of any objection, I wish you would tell him with my best love that I shall be most happy to spend ten days or a fortnight in Henrietta St., if he will accept me. I do not offer more than a fortnight, because I shall then have been some time from home; but it will be a great pleasure to be with him, as it always is. I have the less regret and scruple on your account, because I shall see you for a day and a half, and because you will have Edward for at least a week. My scheme is to take Bookham in my way home for a few days, and my hope that Henry will be so good as to send me some part of the way thither. I have a most kind repetition of Mrs. Cooke's two or three dozen invitations, with the offer of meeting me anywhere in one of her airings.

Fanny's cold is much better. By dosing and keeping her room on Sunday, she got rid of the worst of it, but I am rather afraid of what this day may do for her; she is gone to Canty. with Miss Clewes, Liz., and Ma^{mne}, and it is but roughish weather for any one in a tender state. Miss Clewes has been going to Canty. ever since her return, and it is now just accomplishing.

Edward and I had a delightful morning for our drive there, I enjoyed it thoroughly; but the day turned off before we were ready, and we came home in some rain and the apprehension of a great deal. It has not done us any harm, however. He went to inspect the gaol, as a visiting magistrate, and took me with him. I was gratified, and went through all the feelings which people must go through, I think, in visiting such a building. We paid no other visits, only walked about snugly together, and shopped. I bought a concert ticket and a sprig of flowers for my old age.

To vary the subject from gay to grave with inimitable address, I shall now tell you something of the Bath party—and still a Bath party they are, for a fit of the gout came on last week. The accounts of Lady B. are as good as can be under such a circumstance; Dr. P. says it appears a good sort of gout, and her spirits are better than usual, but as to her coming away, it is of course all uncertainty. I have very little doubt of Edward's going down to Bath, if they have not left it when he is in Hampshire; if he does, he will go on from Steventon, and then return direct to London, without coming back to Chawton. This detention does not suit his feelings. It may be rather a good thing, however, that Dr. P. should see Lady B. with the gout on her. Harriot was quite wishing for it.

The day seems to improve. I wish my pen would too.

Sweet Mr. Ogle! I dare say he sees all the panoramas for nothing, has free admittance everywhere; he is so delightful! Now, you need not see anybody else.

I am glad to hear of our being likely to have a peep at Charles and Fanny at Christmas, but do not force poor Cass. to stay if she hates it. You have done very right as to Mrs. F. A. Your tidings of S. and S. give me pleasure. I have never seen it advertised.

Harriot, in a letter to Fanny to-day, inquires whether they sell cloths for pelisses at Bedford House, and, if they do, will be very much obliged to you to desire them to send her down patterns, with the width and prices; they may go from Charing Cross almost any day in the week, but if it is a ready-money house it will not do, for the bru of feu the Archbishop says she cannot pay for it immediately. Fanny and I suspect they do not deal in the article.

The Sherers, I believe, are now really going to go; Joseph has had a bed here the last two nights, and I do not know whether this is not the day of moving. Mrs. Sherer called yesterday to take leave. The weather looks worse again.

We dine at Chilham Castle to-morrow, and I expect to find some amusement, but more from the concert the next day, as I am sure of seeing several that I want to see. We are to meet a party from Goodnestone, Lady B., Miss Hawley, and Lucy Foote, and I am to meet Mrs. Harrison, and we are to talk about Ben and Anna. "My dear Mrs. Harrison," I shall say, "I am afraid the young man has some of your family madness; and though there often appears to be something of madness in Anna too, I think she inherits more of it from her mother's family than from ours." That is what I shall say, and I think she will find it difficult to answer me.

I took up your letter again to refresh me, being somewhat tired, and was struck with the prettiness of the hand: it is really a very pretty hand now and then,—so small and so neat! I wish I could get as much into a sheet of paper. Another time I will take two days to make a letter in: it is fatiguing to write a whole long one at once. I hope to hear from you again on Sunday and again on Friday, the day before we move. On Monday, I suppose, you will be going to Streatham, to see quiet Mr. Hill and eat very bad baker's bread.

A fall in bread by the by. I hope my mother's bill next week will show it. I have had a very comfortable letter from her, one of her foolscap sheets quite full of little home news. Anna was there the first of the two days. An Anna sent away and an Anna fetched are different things. This will be an excellent time for Ben to pay his visit, now that we, the formidables, are absent.

I did not mean to eat, but Mr. Johncock has brought in the tray, so I must. I am all alone. Edward is gone into his woods. At this present time I have five tables, eight-and-twenty chairs, and two fires all to myself.

Miss Clewes is to be invited to go to the concert with us; there will be my brother's place and ticket for her, as he cannot go. He and the other connections of the Cages are to meet at Milgate that very day, to consult about a proposed alteration of the Maidstone road, in which the Cages are very much interested. Sir Brook comes here in the morning, and they are to be joined by Mr. Deedes at Ashford. The loss of the concert will be no great evil to the Squire. We shall be a party of three ladies therefore, and to meet three ladies.

What a convenient carriage Henry's is, to his friends in general! Who has it next? I am glad William's going is voluntary, and on no worse grounds. An inclination for the country is a venial fault. He has more of Cowper than of Johnson in him,—fonder of tame hares and blank verse than of the full tide of human existence at Charing Cross.

Oh! I have more of such sweet flattery from Miss Sharp. She is an excellent kind friend. I am read and admired in Ireland too. There is a Mrs. Fletcher, the wife of a judge, an old lady, and very good and very clever, who is all curiosity to know about me,—what I am like, and so forth. I am not known to her by name, however. This comes through Mrs. Carrick, not through Mrs. Gore. You are quite out there.

I do not despair of having my picture in the Exhibition at last,—all white and red, with my head on one side; or perhaps I may marry young Mr. D'Arblay. I suppose in the mean time I shall owe dear Henry a great deal of money for printing, etc.

I hope Mrs. Fletcher will indulge herself with S. and S. If I am to stay in H. S., and if you should be writing home soon, I wish you would be so good as to give a hint of it, for I am not likely to write there again these ten days, having written yesterday.

Fanny has set her heart upon its being a Mr. Brett who is going to marry a Miss Dora Best, of this country. I dare say Henry has no objection. Pray, where did the boys sleep?

The Deedes come here on Monday to stay till Friday, so that we shall end with a flourish the last canto. They bring Isabella and one of the grown-ups, and will come in for a Canty. ball on Thursday. I shall be glad to see them. Mrs. Deedes and I must talk rationally together, I suppose.

Edward does not write to Henry, because of my writing so often. God bless you. I shall be so glad to see you again, and I wish you many happy returns of this day. Poor Lord Howard! How he does cry about it!

Yours very truly,

J. A.

Miss AUSTEN,
10 Henrietta Street, Covent Garden, London.

LII.

GODMERSHAM PARK, Saturday (Nov. 6).

MY DEAREST CASSANDRA,—Having half an hour before breakfast (very snug, in my own room, lovely morning, excellent fire—fancy me!) I will give you some account of the last two days. And yet, what is there to be told? I shall get foolishly minute unless I cut the matter short.

We met only the Bretons at Chilham Castle, besides a Mr. and Mrs. Osborne and a Miss Lee staying in the house, and were only fourteen altogether. My brother and Fanny thought it the pleasantest party they had ever known there, and I was very well entertained by bits and scraps. I had long wanted to see Dr. Breton, and his wife amuses me very much with her affected refinement and elegance. Miss Lee I found very conversable; she admires Crabbe as she ought. She is at an age of reason, ten years older than myself at least. She was at the famous ball at Chilham Castle, so of course you remember her.

By the by, as I must leave off being young, I find many *douceurs* in being a sort of chaperon, for I am put on the sofa near the fire, and can drink as much wine as I like. We had music in the evening: Fanny and Miss Wildman played, and Mr. James Wildman sat close by and listened, or pretended to listen.

Yesterday was a day of dissipation all through: first came Sir Brook to dissipate us before breakfast; then there was a call from Mr. Sherer, then a regular morning visit from Lady Honeywood in her way home from Eastwell; then Sir Brook and Edward set off; then we dined (five in number) at half-past four; then we had coffee; and at six Miss Clewes, Fanny, and I drove away. We had a beautiful night for our frisks. We were earlier than we need have been, but after a time Lady B. and her two companions appeared,—we had kept places for them; and there we sat, all six in a row, under a side wall, I between Lucy Foote and Miss Clewes.

Lady B. was much what I expected; I could not determine whether she was rather handsome or very plain. I liked her for being in a hurry to have the concert over and get away, and for getting away at last with a great deal of decision and promptness, not waiting to compliment and dawdle and fuss about seeing dear Fanny, who was half the evening in another part of the room with her friends the Plumptres. I am growing too minute, so I will go to breakfast.

When the concert was over, Mrs. Harrison and I found each other out, and had a very comfortable little complimentary friendly chat. She is a sweet woman,—still quite a sweet woman in herself, and so like her sister! I could almost have thought I was speaking to Mrs. Lefroy. She introduced me to her daughter, whom I think pretty, but most dutifully inferior to *la Mère Beauté*. The Faggs and the Hammonds were there,—Wm. Hammond the only young man of renown. Miss looked very handsome, but I prefer her little smiling flirting sister Julia.

I was just introduced at last to Mary Plumptre, but I should hardly know her again. She was delighted with me, however, good enthusiastic soul! And Lady B. found me handsomer than she expected, so you see I am not so very bad as you might think for.

It was twelve before we reached home. We were all dog-tired, but pretty well to-day: Miss Clewes says she has not caught cold, and Fanny's does not seem worse. I was so tired that I began to wonder how I should get through the ball next Thursday; but there will be so much more variety then in walking about, and probably so much less heat, that perhaps I may not feel it more. My china crape is still kept for the ball. Enough of the concert.

I had a letter from Mary yesterday. They travelled down to Cheltenham last Monday very safely, and are certainly to be there a month. Bath is still Bath. The H. Bridges must quit them early next week, and Louisa seems not quite to despair of their all moving together, but to those who see at a distance there appears no chance of it. Dr. Parry does not want to keep Lady B. at Bath when she can once move. That is lucky. You will see poor Mr. Evelyn's death.

Since I wrote last, my 2nd edit. has stared me in the face. Mary tells me that Eliza means to buy it. I wish she may. It can hardly depend upon any more Fyfield Estates. I cannot help hoping that many will feel themselves obliged to buy it. I shall not mind imagining it a disagreeable duty to them, so as they do it. Mary heard before she left home that it was very much admired at Cheltenham, and that it was given to Miss Hamilton. It is pleasant to have such a respectable writer named. I cannot tire you, I am sure, on this subject, or I would apologize.

What weather, and what news! We have enough to do to admire them both. I hope you derive your full share of enjoyment from each.

I have extended my lights and increased my acquaintance a good deal within these two days. Lady Honeywood you know; I did not sit near enough to be a perfect judge, but I thought her extremely pretty, and her manners have all the recommendations of ease and good-humor and unaffectedness; and going about with four horses and nicely dressed herself, she is altogether a perfect sort of woman.

Oh, and I saw Mr. Gipps last night,—the useful Mr. Gipps, whose attentions came in as acceptably to us in handing us to the carriage, for want of a better man, as they did to Emma Plumptre. I thought him rather a good-looking little man.

I long for your letter to-morrow, particularly that I may know my fate as to London. My first wish is that Henry should really choose what he likes best; I shall certainly not be sorry if he does not want me. Morning church to-morrow; I shall come back with impatient feelings.

The Sherers are gone, but the Pagets are not come: we shall therefore have Mr. S. again. Mr. Paget acts like an unsteady man. Dr. Hant, however, gives him a very good character; what is wrong is to be imputed to the lady. I dare say the house likes female government.

I have a nice long black and red letter from Charles, but not communicating much that I did not know.

There is some chance of a good ball next week, as far as females go. Lady Bridges may perhaps be there with some Knatchbulls. Mrs. Harrison perhaps, with Miss Oxenden and the Miss Papillons; and if Mrs. Harrison, then Lady Fagg will come.

The shades of evening are descending, and I resume my interesting narrative. Sir Brook and my brother came back about four, and Sir Brook almost immediately set forward again to Goodnestone. We are to have Edwd. B. to-morrow, to pay us another Sunday's visit,—the last, for more reasons than one; they all come home on the same day that we go. The Deedes do not come till Tuesday; Sophia is to be the comer. She is a disputable beauty that I want much to see. Lady Eliz. Hatton and Annamaria called here this morning. Yes, they called; but I do not think I can say anything more about them. They came, and they sat, and they went.

Sunday.—Dearest Henry! What a turn he has for being ill, and what a thing bile is! This attack has probably been brought on in part by his previous confinement and anxiety; but, however it came, I hope it is going fast, and that you will be able to send a very good account of him on Tuesday. As I hear on Wednesday, of course I shall not expect to hear again on Friday. Perhaps a letter to Wrotham would not have an ill effect.

We are to be off on Saturday before the post comes in, as Edward takes his own horses all the way. He talks of nine o'clock. We shall bait at Lenham.

Excellent sweetness of you to send me such a nice long letter; it made its appearance, with one from my mother, soon after I and my impatient feelings walked in. How glad I am that I did what I did! I was only afraid that you might think the offer superfluous, but you have set my heart at ease. Tell Henry that I will stay with him, let it be ever so disagreeable to him.

Oh, dear me! I have not time on paper for half that I want to say. There have been two letters from Oxford,—one from George yesterday. They got there very safely,—Edwd. two hours behind the coach, having lost his way in leaving London. George writes cheerfully and quietly; hopes to have Utterson's rooms soon; went to lecture on Wednesday, states some of his expenses, and concludes with saying, "I am afraid I shall be poor." I am glad he thinks about it so soon. I believe there is no private tutor yet chosen, but my brother is to hear from Edwd. on the subject shortly.

You, and Mrs. H., and Catherine, and Alethea going about together in Henry's carriage seeing sights—I am not used to the idea of it yet. All that you are to see of Streatham, seen already! Your Streatham and my Bookham may go hang. The prospect of being taken down to Chawton by Henry perfects the plan to me. I was in hopes of your seeing some illuminations, and you have seen them. "I thought you would come, and you did come." I am sorry he is not to come from the Baltic sooner. Poor Mary!

My brother has a letter from Louisa to-day of an unwelcome nature; they are to spend the winter at Bath. It was just decided on. Dr. Parry wished it, not from thinking the water necessary to Lady B., but that he might be better able to judge how far his treatment of her, which is totally different from anything she had been used to, is right; and I suppose he will not mind having a few more of her Ladyship's guineas. His system is a lowering one. He took twelve ounces of blood from her when the gout appeared, and forbids wine, etc. Hitherto the plan agrees with her. She is very well satisfied to stay, but it is a sore disappointment to Louisa and Fanny.

The H. Bridges leave them on Tuesday, and they mean to move into a smaller house; you may guess how Edward feels. There can be no doubt of his going to Bath now; I should not wonder if he brought Fanny Cage back with him.

You shall hear from me once more, some day or other.

Yours very affectionately,

J. A.

We do not like Mr. Hampson's scheme.

Miss AUSTEN,
10 Henrietta Street, Covent Garden, London.

LIII.

HENRIETTA ST., Wednesday (March 2, 1814).

We had altogether a very good journey, and everything at Cobham was comfortable. I could not pay Mr. Harrington! That was the only alas! of the business. I shall therefore return his bill, and my mother's 2*l.*, that you may try your luck. We did not begin reading till Bentley Green. Henry's approbation is hitherto even equal to my wishes. He says it is different from the other two, but does not appear to think it at all inferior. He has only married Mrs. R.[25] I am afraid he has gone through the most entertaining part. He took to Lady B. and Mrs. N.[26] most kindly, and gives great praise to the drawing of the characters. He understands them all, likes Fanny, and, I think, foresees how it will all be. I finished the "Heroine" last night, and was very much amused by it. I wonder James did not like it better. It diverted me exceedingly. We went to bed at ten. I was very tired, but slept to a miracle, and am lovely to-day, and at present Henry seems to have no complaint. We left Cobham at half-past eight, stopped to bait and breakfast at Kingston, and were in this house considerably before two. Nice smiling Mr. Barlowe met us at the door, and, in reply to inquiries after news, said that peace was generally expected. I have taken possession of my bedroom, unpacked my bandbox, sent Miss P.'s two letters to the twopenny post, been visited by M^d. B., and am now writing by myself at the new table in the front room. It is snowing. We had some snowstorms yesterday, and a smart frost at night, which gave us a hard road from Cobham to Kingston; but as it was then getting dirty and heavy, Henry had a pair of leaders put on to the bottom of Sloane St. His own horses, therefore, cannot have had hard work. I watched for veils as we drove through the streets, and had the pleasure of seeing several upon vulgar heads. And now, how do you all do?—you in particular, after the worry of yesterday and the day before. I hope Martha had a pleasant visit again, and that you and my mother could eat your beef-pudding. Depend upon my thinking of the chimney-sweeper as soon as I wake to-morrow. Places are secured at Drury Lane for Saturday, but so great is the rage for seeing Kean that only a third and fourth row could be got; as it is in a front box, however, I hope we shall do pretty well—Shylock, a good play for Fanny—she cannot be much affected, I think. Mrs. Perigord has just been here. She tells me that we owe her master for the silk-dyeing. My poor old muslin has never been dyed yet. It has been promised to be done several times. What wicked people dyers are! They begin with dipping their own souls in scarlet sin. It is evening. We have drank tea, and I have torn through the third vol. of the "Heroine." I do not think it falls off. It is a delightful burlesque, particularly on the Radcliffe style. Henry is going on with "Mansfield Park." He admires H. Crawford: I mean properly, as a clever, pleasant man. I tell you all the good I can, as I know how much you will enjoy it. We hear that Mr. Kean is more admired than ever. There are no good places to be got in Drury Lane for the next fortnight, but Henry means to secure some for Saturday fortnight, when you are reckoned upon. Give my love to little Cass. I hope she found my bed comfortable last night.

---

[25] Mrs. Rushworth in "Mansfield Park."
[26] Lady Bertram and Mrs. Norris.

I have seen nobody in London yet with such a long chin as Dr. Syntax, nor anybody quite so large as Gogmagolicus.

Yours affly,
J. AUSTEN

LIV.

HENRIETTA ST., Wednesday (March 9).

WELL, we went to the play again last night, and as we were out a great part of the morning too, shopping, and seeing the Indian jugglers, I am very glad to be quiet now till dressing-time. We are to dine at the Tilsons', and to-morrow at Mr. Spencer's.

We had not done breakfast yesterday when Mr. J. Plumptre appeared to say that he had secured a box. Henry asked him to dine here, which I fancy he was very happy to do, and so at five o'clock we four sat down to table together, while the master of the house was preparing for going out himself. The "Farmer's Wife" is a musical thing in three acts, and as Edward was steady in not staying for anything more, we were at home before ten.

Fanny and Mr. J. P. are delighted with Miss S., and her merit in singing is, I dare say, very great; that she gave me no pleasure is no reflection upon her, nor, I hope, upon myself, being what Nature made me on that article. All that I am sensible of in Miss S. is a pleasing person and no skill in acting. We had Mathews, Liston, and Emery; of course, some amusement.

Our friends were off before half-past eight this morning, and had the prospect of a heavy cold journey before them. I think they both liked their visit very much. I am sure Fanny did. Henry sees decided attachment between her and his new acquaintance.

I have a cold, too, as well as my mother and Martha. Let it be a generous emulation between us which can get rid of it first.

I wear my gauze gown to-day, long sleeves and all. I shall see how they succeed, but as yet I have no reason to suppose long sleeves are allowable. I have lowered the bosom, especially at the corners, and plaited black satin ribbon round the top. Such will be my costume of vine-leaves and paste.

Prepare for a play the very first evening, I rather think Covent Garden, to see Young in "Richard." I have answered for your little companion's being conveyed to Keppel St. immediately. I have never yet been able to get there myself, but hope I shall soon.

What cruel weather this is! and here is Lord Portsmouth married, too, to Miss Hanson.[27]

Henry has finished "Mansfield Park," and his approbation has not lessened. He found the last half of the last volume extremely interesting.

I suppose my mother recollects that she gave me no money for paying Brecknell and Twining, and my funds will not supply enough.

We are home in such good time that I can finish my letter to-night, which will be better than getting up to do it to-morrow, especially as, on account of my cold, which has been very heavy in my head this evening, I rather think of lying in bed later than usual. I would not but be well enough to go to Hertford St. on any account.

We met only Genl. Chowne to-day, who has not much to say for himself. I was ready to laugh at the remembrance of Frederick, and such a different Frederick as we chose to fancy him to the real Christopher!

---

[27] His second wife. He died in 1853, and was succeeded by his brother, the father of the present earl.

Mrs. Tilson had long sleeves, too, and she assured me that they are worn in the evening by many. I was glad to hear this. She dines here, I believe, next Tuesday.

On Friday we are to be snug with only Mr. Barlowe and an evening of business. I am so pleased that the mead is brewed. Love to all. I have written to Mrs. Hill, and care for nobody.

Yours affectionately,   J. AUSTEN.

Miss AUSTEN, Chawton.
By favor of Mr. GRAY.

LV.

CHAWTON, Tuesday (June 13).

MY DEAREST CASSANDRA,—Fanny takes my mother to Alton this morning, which gives me an opportunity of sending you a few lines without any other trouble than that of writing them.

This is a delightful day in the country, and I hope not much too hot for town. Well, you had a good journey, I trust, and all that, and not rain enough to spoil your bonnet. It appeared so likely to be a wet evening that I went up to the Gt. House between three and four, and dawdled away an hour very comfortably, though Edwd. was not very brisk. The air was clearer in the evening, and he was better. We all five walked together into the kitchen garden and along the Gosport road, and they drank tea with us.

You will be glad to hear that G. Turner has another situation, something in the cow line, near Rumsey, and he wishes to move immediately, which is not likely to be inconvenient to anybody.

The new nurseryman at Alton comes this morning to value the crops in the garden.

The only letter to-day is from Mrs. Cooke to me. They do not leave home till July, and want me to come to them, according to my promise. And, after considering everything, I have resolved on going. My companions promote it. I will not go, however, till after Edward is gone, that he may feel he has a somebody to give memorandums to, to the last. I must give up all help from his carriage, of course. And, at any rate, it must be such an excess of expense that I have quite made up my mind to it, and do not mean to care.

I have been thinking of Triggs and the chair, you may be sure, but I know it will end in posting. They will meet me at Guildford.

In addition to their standing claims on me they admire "Mansfield Park" exceedingly. Mr. Cooke says "it is the most sensible novel he ever read," and the manner in which I treat the clergy delights them very much. Altogether, I must go, and I want you to join me there when your visit in Henrietta St. is over. Put this into your capacious head.

Take care of yourself, and do not be trampled to death in running after the Emperor. The report in Alton yesterday was that they would certainly travel this road either to or from Portsmouth. I long to know what this bow of the Prince's will produce.

I saw Mrs. Andrews yesterday. Mrs. Browning had seen her before. She is very glad to send an Elizabeth.

Miss Benn continues the same. Mr. Curtis, however, saw her yesterday, and said her hand was going on as well as possible. Accept our best love.

Yours very affectionately,
J. AUSTEN.

Miss AUSTEN, 10 Henrietta Street,
By favor of Mr. GRAY.

LVI.

THURSDAY (June 23).

DEAREST CASSANDRA,—I received your pretty letter while the children were drinking tea with us, as Mr. Louch was so obliging as to walk over with it. Your good account of everybody made us very happy.

I heard yesterday from Frank. When he began his letter he hoped to be here on Monday, but before it was ended he had been told that the naval review would not take place till Friday, which would probably occasion him some delay, as he cannot get some necessary business of his own attended to while Portsmouth is in such a bustle. I hope Fanny has seen the Emperor, and then I may fairly wish them all away. I go to-morrow, and hope for some delays and adventures.

My mother's wood is brought in, but, by some mistake, no bavins. She must therefore buy some.

Henry at White's! Oh, what a Henry! I do not know what to wish as to Miss B., so I will hold my tongue and my wishes.

Sackree and the children set off yesterday, and have not been returned back upon us. They were all very well the evening before. We had handsome presents from the Gt. House yesterday,—a ham and the four leeches. Sackree has left some shirts of her master's at the school, which, finished or unfinished, she begs to have sent by Henry and Wm. Mr. Hinton is expected home soon, which is a good thing for the shirts.

We have called upon Miss Dusantoy and Miss Papillon, and been very pretty. Miss D. has a great idea of being Fanny Price,—she and her youngest sister together, who is named Fanny.

Miss Benn has drank tea with the Prowtings, and, I believe, comes to us this evening. She has still a swelling about the forefinger and a little discharge, and does not seem to be on the point of a perfect cure, but her spirits are good, and she will be most happy, I believe, to accept any invitation. The Clements are gone to Petersfield to look.

Only think of the Marquis of Granby being dead. I hope, if it please Heaven there should be another son, they will have better sponsors and less parade.

I certainly do not wish that Henry should think again of getting me to town. I would rather return straight from Bookham; but if he really does propose it, I cannot say No to what will be so kindly intended. It could be but for a few days, however, as my mother would be quite disappointed by my exceeding the fortnight which I now talk of as the outside—at least, we could not both remain longer away comfortably.

The middle of July is Martha's time, as far as she has any time. She has left it to Mrs. Craven to fix the day. I wish she could get her money paid, for I fear her going at all depends upon that.

Instead of Bath the Deans Dundases have taken a house at Clifton—Richmond Terrace—and she is as glad of the change as even you and I should be, or almost. She will now be able to go on from Berks and visit them without any fears from heat.

This post has brought me a letter from Miss Sharpe. Poor thing! she has been suffering indeed, but is now in a comparative state of comfort. She is at Sir W. P.'s, in Yorkshire, with the children, and there is no appearance of her quitting them. Of course we lose the pleasure of seeing her here. She writes highly of Sir Wm. I do so want him to marry her. There is a Dow. Lady P. presiding there to make it all right. The Man is the same; but she does not mention what

99

he is by profession or trade. She does not think Lady P. was privy to his scheme on her, but, on being in his power, yielded. Oh, Sir Wm.! Sir Wm.! how I will love you if you will love Miss Sharpe!

Mrs. Driver, etc., are off by Collier, but so near being too late that she had not time to call and leave the keys herself. I have them, however. I suppose one is the key of the linen-press, but I do not know what to guess the other.

The coach was stopped at the blacksmith's, and they came running down with Triggs and Browning, and trunks, and birdcages. Quite amusing.

My mother desires her love, and hopes to hear from you.

Yours very affectionately,
J. AUSTEN.

Frank and Mary are to have Mary Goodchild to help as Under till they can get a cook. She is delighted to go.

Best love at Streatham.

Miss AUSTEN, Henrietta St.
By favor of Mr. GRAY

LVII.

23 HANS PLACE, Tuesday morning (August, 1814).

MY DEAR CASSANDRA,—I had a very good journey, not crowded, two of the three taken up at Bentley being children, the others of a reasonable size; and they were all very quiet and civil. We were late in London, from being a great load, and from changing coaches at Farnham; it was nearly four, I believe, when we reached Sloane Street. Henry himself met me, and as soon as my trunk and basket could be routed out from all the other trunks and baskets in the world, we were on our way to Hans Place in the luxury of a nice, large, cool, dirty hackney coach.

There were four in the kitchen part of Yalden, and I was told fifteen at top, among them Percy Benn. We met in the same room at Egham, but poor Percy was not in his usual spirits. He would be more chatty, I dare say, in his way from Woolwich. We took up a young Gibson at Holybourn, and, in short, everybody either did come up by Yalden yesterday, or wanted to come up. It put me in mind of my own coach between Edinburgh and Stirling.

Henry is very well, and has given me an account of the Canterbury races, which seem to have been as pleasant as one could wish. Everything went well. Fanny had good partners, Mr. —— was her second on Thursday, but he did not dance with her any more.

This will content you for the present. I must just add, however, that there were no Lady Charlottes, they were gone off to Kirby, and that Mary Oxenden, instead of dying, is going to marry Wm. Hammond.

No James and Edward yet. Our evening yesterday was perfectly quiet; we only talked a little to Mr. Tilson across the intermediate gardens; she was gone out airing with Miss Burdett. It is a delightful place,—more than answers my expectation. Having got rid of my unreasonable ideas, I find more space and comfort in the rooms than I had supposed, and the garden is quite a love. I am in the front attic, which is the bedchamber to be preferred.

Henry wants you to see it all, and asked whether you would return with him from Hampshire; I encouraged him to think you would. He breakfasts here early, and then rides to Henrietta St. If it continues fine, John is to drive me there by and by, and we shall take an airing together; and I do not mean to take any other exercise, for I feel a little tired after my long jumble. I live in his room downstairs; it is particularly pleasant from opening upon the garden. I go and refresh myself every now and then, and then come back to solitary coolness. There is one maidservant only, a very creditable, clean-looking young woman. Richard remains for the present.

Wednesday morning.—My brother and Edwd. arrived last night. They could not get places the day before. Their business is about teeth and wigs, and they are going after breakfast to Scarman's and Tavistock St., and they are to return to go with me afterwards in the barouche. I hope to do some of my errands to-day.

I got the willow yesterday, as Henry was not quite ready when I reached Hena. St. I saw Mr. Hampson there for a moment. He dines here to-morrow, and proposed bringing his son; so I must submit to seeing George Hampson, though I had hoped to go through life without it. It was one of my vanities, like your not reading "Patronage."

After leaving H. St. we drove to Mrs. Latouche's; they are always at home, and they are to dine here on Friday. We could do no more, as it began to rain.

We dine at half-past four to-day, that our visitors may go to the play, and Henry and I are to spend the evening with the Tilsons, to meet Miss Burnett, who leaves town to-morrow. Mrs. T. called on me yesterday.

Is not this all that can have happened or been arranged? Not quite. Henry wants me to see more of his Hanwell favorite, and has written to invite her to spend a day or two here with me. His scheme is to fetch her on Saturday. I am more and more convinced that he will marry again soon, and like the idea of her better than of anybody else at hand.

Now I have breakfasted and have the room to myself again. It is likely to be a fine day. How do you all do?

Henry talks of being at Chawton about the 1st of Sept. He has once mentioned a scheme which I should rather like,—calling on the Birches and the Crutchleys in our way. It may never come to anything, but I must provide for the possibility by troubling you to send up my silk pelisse by Collier on Saturday. I feel it would be necessary on such an occasion; and be so good as to put up a clean dressing-gown which will come from the wash on Friday. You need not direct it to be left anywhere. It may take its chance.

We are to call for Henry between three and four, and I must finish this and carry it with me, as he is not always there in the morning before the parcel is made up. And before I set off, I must return Mrs. Tilson's visit. I hear nothing of the Hoblyns, and abstain from all inquiry.

I hope Mary Jane and Frank's gardens go on well. Give my love to them all—Nunna Hat's love to George. A great many people wanted to run up in the Poach as well as me. The wheat looked very well all the way, and James says the same of his road.

The same good account of Mrs. C.'s health continues, and her circumstances mend. She gets farther and farther from poverty. What a comfort! Good-by to you.

Yours very truly and affectionately,
JANE.

All well at Steventon. I hear nothing particular of Ben, except that Edward is to get him some pencils.

Miss AUSTEN, Chawton.
By favor of Mr. GRAY.

LVIII.

MY DEAR ANNA,[28]—I am very much obliged to you for sending your MS. It has entertained me extremely; indeed all of us. I read it aloud to your grandmamma and Aunt Cass, and we were all very much pleased. The spirit does not droop at all. Sir Thos., Lady Helen, and St. Julian are very well done, and Cecilia continues to be interesting in spite of her being so amiable. It was very fit you should advance her age. I like the beginning of Devereux Forester very much, a great deal better than if he had been very good or very bad. A few verbal corrections are all that I felt tempted to make; the principal of them is a speech of St. Julian to Lady Helen, which you see I have presumed to alter. As Lady H. is Cecilia's superior, it would not be correct to talk of her being introduced. It is Cecilia who must be introduced. And I do not like a lover speaking in the 3rd person; it is too much like the part of Lord Overtley, and I think it not natural. If you think differently, however, you need not mind me. I am impatient for more, and only wait for a safe conveyance to return this.

Yours affectionately,
J. A.

LIX.

AUGUST 10, 1814.

MY DEAR ANNA,—I am quite ashamed to find that I have never answered some question of yours in a former note. I kept it on purpose to refer to it at a proper time, and then forgot it. I like the name "Which is the Heroine" very well, and I dare say shall grow to like it very much in time; but "Enthusiasm" was something so very superior that my common title must appear to disadvantage. I am not sensible of any blunders about Dawlish; the library was pitiful and wretched twelve years ago, and not likely to have anybody's publications. There is no such title as Desborough, either among dukes, marquises, earls, viscounts, or barons. These were your inquiries. I will now thank you for your envelope received this morning. Your Aunt Cass is as well pleased with St. Julian as ever, and I am delighted with the idea of seeing Progillian again.

Wednesday, 17.—We have now just finished the first of the three books I had the pleasure of receiving yesterday. I read it aloud, and we are all very much amused, and like the work quite as well as ever. I depend on getting through another book before dinner, but there is really a good deal of respectable reading in your forty-eight pages. I have no doubt six would make a very good-sized volume. You must have been quite pleased to have accomplished so much. I like Lord Portman and his brother very much. I am only afraid that Lord P.'s good nature will make most people like him better than he deserves. The whole family are very good; and Lady Anne, who was your great dread, you have succeeded particularly well with. Bell Griffin is just what she should be. My corrections have not been more important than before; here and there we have thought the sense could be expressed in fewer words, and I have scratched out Sir Thos. from walking with the others to the stables, etc. the very day after breaking his arm; for though I find your papa did walk out immediately after his arm was set, I think it can be so little usual as to appear unnatural in a book. Lynn will not do. Lynn is towards forty miles from

---

[28] Miss Anna Austen, at this time engaged to Mr. Lefroy, was writing a novel which she sent to her aunt for criticism.

Dawlish and would not be talked of there. I have put Starcross instead. If you prefer Easton, that must be always safe.

I have also scratched out the introduction between Lord Portman and his brother and Mr. Griffin. A country surgeon (don't tell Mr. C. Lyford) would not be introduced to men of their rank; and when Mr. P. is first brought in, he would not be introduced as the Honorable. That distinction is never mentioned at such times; at least, I believe not. Now we have finished the second book, or rather the fifth. I do think you had better omit Lady Helena's postscript. To those that are acquainted with "Pride and Prejudice" it will seem an imitation. And your Aunt C. and I both recommend your making a little alteration in the last scene between Devereux F. and Lady Clanmurray and her daughter. We think they press him too much, more than sensible or well-bred women would do; Lady C., at least, should have discretion enough to be sooner satisfied with his determination of not going with them. I am very much pleased with Egerton as yet. I did not expect to like him, but I do, and Susan is a very nice little animated creature; but St. Julian is the delight of our lives. He is quite interesting. The whole of his break-off with Lady Helena is very well done. Yes; Russell Square is a very proper distance from Berkeley Square. We are reading the last book. They must be two days going from Dawlish to Bath. They are nearly one hundred miles apart.

Thursday.—We finished it last night after our return from drinking tea at the Great House. The last chapter does not please us quite so well; we do not thoroughly like the play, perhaps from having had too much of plays in that way lately (*vide* "Mansfield Park"), and we think you had better not leave England. Let the Portmans go to Ireland; but as you know nothing of the manners there, you had better not go with them. You will be in danger of giving false representations. Stick to Bath and the Foresters. There you will be quite at home.

Your Aunt C. does not like desultory novels, and is rather afraid yours will be too much so, that there will be too frequently a change from one set of people to another, and that circumstances will be introduced of apparent consequence which will lead to nothing. It will not be so great an objection to me if it does. I allow much more latitude than she does, and think Nature and spirit cover many sins of a wandering story, and people in general do not care so much about it for your comfort.

I should like to have had more of Devereux. I do not feel enough acquainted with him. You were afraid of meddling with him, I dare say. I like your sketch of Lord Clanmurray, and your picture of the two young girls' enjoyment is very good. I have not noticed St. Julian's serious conversation with Cecilia, but I like it exceedingly. What he says about the madness of otherwise sensible women on the subject of their daughters coming out is worth its weight in gold.

I do not perceive that the language sinks. Pray go on.

LX.

CHAWTON, Sept. 9.

MY DEAR ANNA,—We have been very much amused by your three books, but I have a good many criticisms to make, more than you will like. We are not satisfied with Mrs. Forester settling herself as tenant and near neighbor to such a man as Sir Thomas, without having some other inducement to go there. She ought to have some friend living thereabouts to tempt her. A woman going with two girls just growing up into a neighborhood where she knows nobody but one man of not very good character, is an awkwardness which so prudent a woman as Mrs.

F. would not be likely to fall into. Remember she is very prudent. You must not let her act inconsistently. Give her a friend, and let that friend be invited by Sir Thomas H. to meet her, and we shall have no objection to her dining at the Priory as she does; but otherwise a woman in her situation would hardly go there before she had been visited by other families. I like the scene itself, the Miss Leslie, Lady Anne, and the music very much. Leslie is a noble name. Sir Thomas H. you always do very well. I have only taken the liberty of expunging one phrase of his which would not be allowable,—"Bless my heart!" It is too familiar and inelegant. Your grandmother is more disturbed at Mrs. Forester's not returning the Egertons' visit sooner than by anything else. They ought to have called at the Parsonage before Sunday. You describe a sweet place, but your descriptions are often more minute than will be liked. You give too many particulars of right hand and left. Mrs. Forester is not careful enough of Susan's health. Susan ought not to be walking out so soon after heavy rains, taking long walks in the dirt. An anxious mother would not suffer it. I like your Susan very much; she is a sweet creature, her playfulness of fancy is very delightful. I like her as she is now exceedingly, but I am not quite so well satisfied with her behavior to George R. At first she seems all over attachment and feeling, and afterwards to have none at all; she is so extremely confused at the ball, and so well satisfied apparently with Mr. Morgan. She seems to have changed her character.

You are now collecting your people delightfully, getting them exactly into such a spot as is the delight of my life. Three or four families in a country village is the very thing to work on, and I hope you will do a great deal more, and make full use of them while they are so very favorably arranged.

You are but now coming to the heart and beauty of your story. Until the heroine grows up the fun must be imperfect, but I expect a great deal of entertainment from the next three or four books, and I hope you will not resent these remarks by sending me no more. We like the Egertons very well. We see no blue pantaloons or cocks or hens. There is nothing to enchant one certainly in Mr. L. L., but we make no objection to him, and his inclination to like Susan is pleasing. The sister is a good contrast, but the name of Rachel is as much as I can bear. They are not so much like the Papillons as I expected. Your last chapter is very entertaining, the conversation on genius, etc.; Mr. St. Julian and Susan both talk in character, and very well. In some former parts Cecilia is perhaps a little too solemn and good, but upon the whole her disposition is very well opposed to Susan's, her want of imagination is very natural. I wish you could make Mrs. Forester talk more; but she must be difficult to manage and make entertaining, because there is so much good sense and propriety about her that nothing can be made very broad. Her economy and her ambition must not be staring. The papers left by Mrs. Fisher are very good. Of course one guesses something. I hope when you have written a great deal more, you will be equal to scratching out some of the past. The scene with Mrs. Mellish I should condemn; it is prosy and nothing to the purpose, and indeed the more you can find in your heart to curtail between Dawlish and Newton Priors, the better I think it will be,—one does not care for girls until they are grown up. Your Aunt C. quite understands the exquisiteness of that name,—Newton Priors is really a nonpareil. Milton would have given his eyes to have thought of it. Is not the cottage taken from Tollard Royal?

[Thus far the letter was written on the 9th, but before it was finished news arrived at Chawton of the death of Mrs. Charles Austen. She died in her confinement, and the baby died also. She left three little girls,—Cassie, Harriet, and Fanny. It was not until the 18th that Jane resumed her letter as follows:[29]]

---

29 Note by Lord Brabourne.

Sunday.—I am very glad, dear Anna, that I wrote as I did before this sad event occurred. I have only to add that your grandmamma does not seem the worse now for the shock.

I shall be very happy to receive more of your work if more is ready; and you write so fast that I have great hopes Mr. Digweed will come back freighted with such a cargo as not all his hops or his sheep could equal the value of.

Your grandmamma desires me to say that she will have finished your shoes to-morrow, and thinks they will look very well. And that she depends upon seeing you, as you promise, before you quit the country, and hopes you will give her more than a day.

Yours affectionately.   J. AUSTEN.

LXI.

CHAWTON, Wednesday (Sept. 28).

MY DEAR ANNA,—I hope you do not depend on having your book again immediately. I kept it that your grandmamma may hear it, for it has not been possible yet to have any public reading. I have read it to your Aunt Cassandra, however, in our own room at night, while we undressed, and with a great deal of pleasure. We like the first chapter extremely, with only a little doubt whether Lady Helena is not almost too foolish. The matrimonial dialogue is very good certainly. I like Susan as well as ever, and begin now not to care at all about Cecilia; she may stay at Easton Court as long as she likes. Henry Mellish will be, I am afraid, too much in the common novel style,—a handsome, amiable, unexceptionable young man (such as do not much abound in real life), desperately in love and all in vain. But I have no business to judge him so early Jane Egerton is a very natural, comprehensible girl, and the whole of her acquaintance with Susan and Susan's letter to Cecilia are very pleasing and quite in character. But Miss Egerton does not entirely satisfy us. She is too formal and solemn, we think, in her advice to her brother not to fall in love; and it is hardly like a sensible woman,—it is putting it into his head. We should like a few hints from her better. We feel really obliged to you for introducing a Lady Kenrick; it will remove the greatest fault in the work, and I give you credit for considerable forbearance as an author in adopting so much of our opinion. I expect high fun about Mrs. Fisher and Sir Thomas. You have been perfectly right in telling Ben. Lefroy of your work, and I am very glad to hear how much he likes it. His encouragement and approbation must be "quite beyond everything."[30] I do not at all wonder at his not expecting to like anybody so well as Cecilia at first, but I shall be surprised if he does not become a Susanite in time. Devereux Forester's being ruined by his vanity is extremely good, but I wish you would not let him plunge into a "vortex of dissipation." I do not object to the thing, but I cannot bear the expression; it is such thorough novel slang, and so old that I dare say Adam met with it in the first novel he opened. Indeed, I did very much like to know Ben's opinion. I hope he will continue to be pleased with it, and I think he must, but I cannot flatter him with there being much incident. We have no great right to wonder at his not valuing the name of Progillian. That is a source of delight which even he can hardly be quite competent to.

Walter Scott has no business to write novels, especially good ones. It is not fair. He has fame and profit enough as a poet, and should not be taking the bread out of the mouths of other people.

I do not like him, and do not mean to like "Waverley" if I can help it, but fear I must.

---

[30] A phrase always in the mouth of one of the Chawton neighbors, Mrs. H. Digweed.

105

I am quite determined, however, not to be pleased with Mrs. West's "Alicia De Lacy," should I ever meet with it, which I hope I shall not. I think I can be stout against anything written by Mrs. West. I have made up my mind to like no novels really but Miss Edgeworth's, yours, and my own.

What can you do with Egerton to increase the interest for him? I wish you could contrive something, some family occurrence to bring out his good qualities more. Some distress among brothers and sisters to relieve by the sale of his curacy! Something to carry him mysteriously away, and then be heard of at York or Edinburgh in an old greatcoat. I would not seriously recommend anything improbable, but if you could invent something spirited for him, it would have a good effect. He might lend all his money to Captain Morris, but then he would be a great fool if he did. Cannot the Morrises quarrel and he reconcile them? Excuse the liberty I take in these suggestions.

Your Aunt Frank's nursemaid has just given her warning, but whether she is worth your having, or would take your place, I know not. She was Mrs. Webb's maid before she went to the Great House. She leaves your aunt because she cannot agree with the other servants. She is in love with the man, and her head seems rather turned. He returns her affection, but she fancies every one else is wanting him and envying her. Her previous service must have fitted her for such a place as yours, and she is very active and cleanly. The Webbs are really gone! When I saw the wagons at the door, and thought of all the trouble they must have in moving, I began to reproach myself for not having liked them better; but since the wagons have disappeared my conscience has been closed again, and I am excessively glad they are gone.

I am very fond of Sherlock's sermons, and prefer them to almost any.

Your affectionate aunt,   J. AUSTEN.

If you wish me to speak to the maid, let me know.

LXII.

To Miss Frances Austen.
CHAWTON, Friday (Nov. 18, 1814).

I FEEL quite as doubtful as you could be, my dearest Fanny, as to when my letter may be finished, for I can command very little quiet time at present; but yet I must begin, for I know you will be glad to hear as soon as possible, and I really am impatient myself to be writing something on so very interesting a subject, though I have no hope of writing anything to the purpose. I shall do very little more, I dare say, than say over again what you have said before.

I was certainly a good deal surprised at first, as I had no suspicion of any change in your feelings, and I have no scruple in saying that you cannot be in love. My dear Fanny, I am ready to laugh at the idea, and yet it is no laughing matter to have had you so mistaken as to your own feelings. And with all my heart I wish I had cautioned you on that point when first you spoke to me; but though I did not think you then much in love, I did consider you as being attached in a degree quite sufficiently for happiness, as I had no doubt it would increase with opportunity, and from the time of our being in London together I thought you really very much in love. But you certainly are not at all—there is no concealing it.

What strange creatures we are! It seems as if your being secure of him had made you indifferent. There was a little disgust, I suspect, at the races, and I do not wonder at it. His expressions then would not do for one who had rather more acuteness, penetration, and taste, than love, which was your case. And yet, after all, I am surprised that the change in your feelings should be so great. He is just what he ever was, only more evidently and uniformly devoted to you. This is all the difference. How shall we account for it?

My dearest Fanny, I am writing what will not be of the smallest use to you. I am feeling differently every moment, and shall not be able to suggest a single thing that can assist your mind. I could lament in one sentence and laugh in the next, but as to opinion or counsel I am sure that none will be extracted worth having from this letter.

I read yours through the very evening I received it, getting away by myself. I could not bear to leave off when I had once begun. I was full of curiosity and concern. Luckily your At. C. dined at the other house; therefore I had not to man[oe]uvre away from her, and as to anybody else, I do not care.

Poor dear Mr. A.! Oh, dear Fanny! your mistake has been one that thousands of women fall into. He was the first young man who attached himself to you. That was the charm, and most powerful it is. Among the multitudes, however, that make the same mistake with yourself, there can be few indeed who have so little reason to regret it; his character and his attachment leave you nothing to be ashamed of.

Upon the whole, what is to be done? You have no inclination for any other person. His situation in life, family, friends, and, above all, his character, his uncommonly amiable mind, strict principles, just notions, good habits, all that you know so well how to value, all that is really of the first importance,—everything of this nature pleads his cause most strongly. You have no doubt of his having superior abilities, he has proved it at the University; he is, I dare say, such a scholar as your agreeable, idle brothers would ill bear a comparison with.

Oh, my dear Fanny! the more I write about him the warmer my feelings become,—the more strongly I feel the sterling worth of such a young man, and the desirableness of your growing in love with him again. I recommend this most thoroughly. There are such beings in the world, perhaps one in a thousand, as the creature you and I should think perfection, where grace and spirit are united to worth, where the manners are equal to the heart and understanding; but such a person may not come in your way, or, if he does, he may not be the eldest son of a man of fortune, the near relation of your particular friend, and belonging to your own county.

Think of all this, Fanny. Mr. A. has advantages which we do not often meet in one person. His only fault, indeed, seems modesty. If he were less modest, he would be more agreeable, speak louder, and look impudenter; and is not it a fine character of which modesty is the only defect? I have no doubt he will get more lively and more like yourselves as he is more with you; he will catch your ways if he belongs to you. And as to there being any objection from his goodness, from the danger of his becoming even evangelical, I cannot admit that. I am by no means convinced that we ought not all to be evangelicals, and am at least persuaded that they who are so from reason and feeling must be happiest and safest. Do not be frightened from the connection by your brothers having most wit,—wisdom is better than wit, and in the long run will certainly have the laugh on her side; and don't be frightened by the idea of his acting more strictly up to the precepts of the New Testament than others.

And now, my dear Fanny, having written so much on one side of the question, I shall turn round and entreat you not to commit yourself farther, and not to think of accepting him unless you really do like him. Anything is to be preferred or endured rather than marrying without affection; and if his deficiencies of manner, etc., etc., strike you more than all his good qualities, if you continue to think strongly of them, give him up at once. Things are now in such a state that you must resolve upon one or the other,—either to allow him to go on as he has done, or whenever you are together behave with a coldness which may convince him that he has been deceiving himself. I have no doubt of his suffering a good deal for a time,—a great deal when he feels that he must give you up; but it is no creed of mine, as you must be well aware, that such sort of disappointments kill anybody.

Your sending the music was an admirable device, it made everything easy, and I do not know how I could have accounted for the parcel otherwise; for though your dear papa most conscientiously hunted about till he found me alone in the dining-parlor, your Aunt C. had seen that he had a parcel to deliver. As it was, however, I do not think anything was suspected.

We have heard nothing fresh from Anna. I trust she is very comfortable in her new home. Her letters have been very sensible and satisfactory, with no parade of happiness, which I liked them the better for. I have often known young married women write in a way I did not like in that respect.

You will be glad to hear that the first edition of M. P.[31] is all sold. Your Uncle Henry is rather wanting me to come to town to settle about a second edition; but as I could not very conveniently leave home now, I have written him my will and pleasure and unless he still urges it, shall not go. I am very greedy and want to make the most of it; but as you are much above caring about money, I shall not plague you with any particulars. The pleasures of vanity are more within your comprehension, and you will enter into mine at receiving the praise which every now and then comes to me through some channel or other.

Saturday.—Mr. Palmer spent yesterday with us, and is gone off with Cassy this morning. We have been expecting Miss Lloyd the last two days, and feel sure of her to-day. Mr. Knight and Mr. Edwd. Knight are to dine with us, and on Monday they are to dine with us again, accompanied by their respectable host and hostess.

Sunday.—Your papa had given me messages to you; but they are unnecessary, as he writes by this post to Aunt Louisa. We had a pleasant party yesterday; at least we found it so. It is delightful to see him so cheerful and confident. Aunt Cass. and I dine at the Great House to-day. We shall be a snug half-dozen. Miss Lloyd came, as we expected, yesterday, and desires her love. She is very happy to hear of your learning the harp. I do not mean to send you what I owe Miss Hare, because I think you would rather not be paid beforehand.

Yours very affectionately,
JANE AUSTEN.

Miss KNIGHT,
Goodnestone Farm, Wingham, Kent.

LXIII.

CHAWTON, Nov. 21, 1814.

MY DEAR ANNA,—I met Harriet Benn yesterday. She gave me her congratulations, and desired they might be forwarded to you, and there they are. The chief news from this country is the death of old Mrs. Dormer. Mrs. Clement walks about in a new black velvet pelisse lined with yellow, and a white bobbin net veil, and looks remarkably well in them.

I think I understand the country about Hendon from your description. It must be very pretty in summer. Should you know from the atmosphere that you were within a dozen miles of London? Make everybody at Hendon admire "Mansfield Park."

Your affectionate aunt,   J. A

---

[31] "Mansfield Park."

LXIV.

HANS PLACE, Nov. 28, 1814.

MY DEAR ANNA,—I assure you we all came away very much pleased with our visit. We talked of you for about a mile and a half with great satisfaction; and I have been just sending a very good report of you to Miss Benn, with a full account of your dress for Susan and Maria.

We were all at the play last night to see Miss O'Neil in "Isabella." I do not think she was quite equal to my expectations. I fancy I want something more than can be. I took two pocket-handkerchiefs, but had very little occasion for either. She is an elegant creature, however, and hugs Mr. Young delightfully. I am going this morning to see the little girls in Keppel Street. Cassy was excessively interested about your marriage when she heard of it, which was not until she was to drink your health on the wedding-day.

She asked a thousand questions in her usual manner, what he said to you and what you said to him. If your uncle were at home he would send his best love, but I will not impose any base fictitious remembrances on you; mine I can honestly give, and remain

Your affectionate aunt,
J. AUSTEN.

LXV.

HANS PLACE, Wednesday.

MY DEAR ANNA,—I have been very far from finding your book an evil, I assure you. I read it immediately and with great pleasure. I think you are going on very well. The description of Dr. Griffin and Lady Helena's unhappiness is very good, and just what was likely to be. I am curious to know what the end of them will be. The name of Newton Priors is really invaluable; I never met with anything superior to it. It is delightful, and one could live on the name of Newton Priors for a twelvemonth. Indeed, I think you get on very fast. I only wish other people of my acquaintance could compose as rapidly. I am pleased with the dog scene and with the whole of George and Susan's love, but am more particularly struck with your serious conversations. They are very good throughout. St. Julian's history was quite a surprise to me. You had not very long known it yourself, I suspect; but I have no objection to make to the circumstance, and it is very well told. His having been in love with the aunt gives Cecilia an additional interest with him. I like the idea,—a very proper compliment to an aunt! I rather imagine indeed that nieces are seldom chosen but out of compliment to some aunt or another. I dare say Ben was in love with me once, and would never have thought of you if he had not supposed me dead of scarlet fever. Yes, I was in a mistake as to the number of books. I thought I had read three before the three at Chawton, but fewer than six will not do. I want to see dear Bell Griffin again; and had you not better give some hint of St. Julian's early history in the beginning of the story?

We shall see nothing of Streatham while we are in town, as Mrs. Hill is to lie in of a daughter. Mrs. Blackstone is to be with her. Mrs. Heathcote and Miss Bigg[32] are just leaving.

---

32 Sisters to Mrs. Hall.

The latter writes me word that Miss Blackford is married, but I have never seen it in the papers, and one may as well be single if the wedding is not to be in print.

Your affectionate aunt,   J. A.

LXVI.

23 HANS PLACE, Wednesday (Nov. 30, 1814).

I AM very much obliged to you, my dear Fanny, for your letter, and I hope you will write again soon, that I may know you to be all safe and happy at home.

Our visit to Hendon will interest you, I am sure; but I need not enter into the particulars of it, as your papa will be able to answer almost every question. I certainly could describe her bedroom and her drawers and her closet better than he can, but I do not feel that I can stop to do it. I was rather sorry to hear that she is to have an instrument; it seems throwing money away. They will wish the twenty-four guineas in the shape of sheets and towels six months hence; and as to her playing, it never can be anything.

Her purple pelisse rather surprised me. I thought we had known all paraphernalia of that sort. I do not mean to blame her; it looked very well, and I dare say she wanted it. I suspect nothing worse than its being got in secret, and not owned to anybody. I received a very kind note from her yesterday, to ask me to come again and stay a night with them. I cannot do it, but I was pleased to find that she had the power of doing so right a thing. My going was to give them both pleasure very properly.

I just saw Mr. Hayter at the play, and think his face would please me on acquaintance. I was sorry he did not dine here. It seemed rather odd to me to be in the theatre with nobody to watch for. I was quite composed myself, at leisure for all the agitated Isabella could raise.

Now, my dearest Fanny, I will begin a subject which comes in very naturally. You frighten me out of my wits by your reference. Your affection gives me the highest pleasure, but indeed you must not let anything depend on my opinion; your own feelings, and none but your own, should determine such an important point. So far, however, as answering your question, I have no scruple. I am perfectly convinced that your present feelings, supposing that you were to marry now, would be sufficient for his happiness; but when I think how very, very far it is from a "now," and take everything that may be into consideration, I dare not say, "Determine to accept him;" the risk is too great for you, unless your own sentiments prompt it.

You will think me perverse, perhaps; in my last letter I was urging everything in his favor, and now I am inclining the other way, but I cannot help it; I am at present more impressed with the possible evil that may arise to you from engaging yourself to him—in word or mind—than with anything else. When I consider how few young men you have yet seen much of, how capable you are (yes, I do still think you very capable) of being really in love, and how full of temptation the next six or seven years of your life will probably be (it is the very period of life for the strongest attachments to be formed),—I cannot wish you, with your present very cool feelings, to devote yourself in honor to him. It is very true that you never may attach another man his equal altogether; but if that other man has the power of attaching you more, he will be in your eyes the most perfect.

I shall be glad if you can revive past feelings, and from your unbiassed self resolve to go on as you have done, but this I do not expect; and without it I cannot wish you to be fettered. I should not be afraid of your marrying him; with all his worth you would soon love him enough for the happiness of both; but I should dread the continuance of this sort of tacit engagement, with such an uncertainty as there is of when it may be completed. Years may pass before he is independent; you like him well enough to marry, but not well enough to wait; the unpleasantness of appearing fickle is certainly great; but if you think you want punishment for past illusions, there it is, and nothing can be compared to the misery of being bound without love,—bound to one, and preferring another; that is a punishment which you do not deserve.

I know you did not meet, or rather will not meet, to-day, as he called here yesterday; and I am glad of it. It does not seem very likely, at least, that he should be in time for a dinner visit sixty miles off. We did not see him, only found his card when we came home at four. Your Uncle H. merely observed that he was a day after "the fair." We asked your brother on Monday (when Mr. Hayter was talked of) why he did not invite him too; saying, "I know he is in town, for I met him the other day in Bond St." Edward answered that he did not know where he was to be found. "Don't you know his chambers?" "No."

I shall be most glad to hear from you again, my dearest Fanny, but it must not be later than Saturday, as we shall be off on Monday long before the letters are delivered; and write something that may do to be read or told. I am to take the Miss Moores back on Saturday, and when I return I shall hope to find your pleasant little flowing scrawl on the table. It will be a relief to me after playing at ma'ams, for though I like Miss H. M. as much as one can at my time of life after a day's acquaintance, it is uphill work to be talking to those whom one knows so little.

Only one comes back with me to-morrow, probably Miss Eliza, and I rather dread it. We shall not have two ideas in common. She is young, pretty, chattering, and thinking chiefly, I presume, of dress, company, and admiration. Mr. Sanford is to join us at dinner, which will be a comfort, and in the evening, while your uncle and Miss Eliza play chess, he shall tell me comical things and I will laugh at them, which will be a pleasure to both.

I called in Keppel Street and saw them all, including dear Uncle Charles, who is to come and dine with us quietly to-day. Little Harriot sat in my lap, and seemed as gentle and affectionate as ever, and as pretty, except not being quite well. Fanny is a fine stout girl, talking incessantly, with an interesting degree of lisp and indistinctness, and very likely may be the handsomest in time. Cassy did not show more pleasure in seeing me than her sisters, but I expected no better. She does not shine in the tender feelings. She will never be a Miss O'Neil, more in the Mrs. Siddons line.

Thank you, but it is not settled yet whether I do hazard a second edition. We are to see Egerton to-day, when it will probably be determined. People are more ready to borrow and praise than to buy, which I cannot wonder at; but though I like praise as well as anybody, I like what Edward calls "Pewter" too. I hope he continues careful of his eyes, and finds the good effect of it. I cannot suppose we differ in our ideas of the Christian religion. You have given an excellent description of it. We only affix a different meaning to the word evangelical.

Yours most affectionately,

J. AUSTEN.

Miss KNIGHT,
Godmersham Park, Faversham, Kent.

LXVII.

CHAWTON, Friday (Sept. 29).

MY DEAR ANNA,—We told Mr. B. Lefroy that if the weather did not prevent us we should certainly come and see you to-morrow and bring Cassy, trusting to your being good enough to give her a dinner about one o'clock, that we might be able to be with you the earlier and stay the longer. But on giving Cassy her choice between the Fair at Alton or Wyards, it must be confessed that she has preferred the former, which we trust will not greatly affront you; if it does, you may hope that some little Anne hereafter may revenge the insult by a similar preference of an Alton Fair to her Cousin Cassy. In the mean while we have determined to put off our visit to you until Monday, which we hope will be not less convenient. I wish the weather may not resolve on another put off. I must come to you before Wednesday if it be possible, for on that day I am going to London for a week or two with your Uncle Henry, who is expected here on Sunday. If Monday should appear too dirty for walking, and Mr. Lefroy would be so kind as to come and fetch me, I should be much obliged to him. Cassy might be of the party, and your Aunt Cassandra will take another opportunity.

Yours very affectionately, my dear Anna,
J. AUSTEN.

Note by Lord Brabourne.

But before the week or two to which she had limited her visit in Hans Place was at an end, her brother fell ill, and on October 22 he was in such danger that she wrote to Steventon to summon her father to town. The letter was two days on the road, and reached him on Sunday the 24th. Even then he did not start immediately. In the evening he and his wife rode to Chawton, and it was not until the next day that he and Cassandra arrived in Hans Place. The malady from which Henry Austen was suffering was low fever, and he was for some days at death's door: but he rallied soon after his brother and sisters arrived, and recovered so quickly that the former was able to leave him at the end of the week. The great anxiety and fatigue which Jane underwent at this time was supposed by some of her family to have broken down her health. She was in a very feeble and exhausted condition when the bank in which her brother Henry was a partner broke, and he not only lost all that he possessed, but most of his relations suffered severely also. Jane was well enough to pay several visits with her sister in the summer of 1816, including one to Steventon,—the last she ever paid to that home of her childhood. The last note which Mrs. Lefroy had preserved is dated,—

LXVIII.

JUNE 23, 1816.

MY DEAR ANNA,—Cassy desires her best thanks for the book. She was quite delighted to see it. I do not know when I have seen her so much struck by anybody's kindness as on this occasion. Her sensibility seems to be opening to the perception of great actions. These gloves having appeared on the pianoforte ever since you were here on Friday, we imagine they must be yours. Mrs. Digweed returned yesterday through all the afternoon's rain, and was of course wet through; but in speaking of it she never once said "it was beyond everything," which I am sure it must have been. Your mamma means to ride to Speen Hill to-morrow to see the Mrs. Hulberts, who are both very indifferent. By all accounts they really are breaking now,—not so stout as the old jackass.

Yours affectionately,   J. A.

CHAWTON, Sunday, June 23.
    Uncle Charles's birthday.

LXIX.

MY DEAREST CASSANDRA,—I have the pleasure of sending you a much better account of my affairs, which I know will be a great delight to you.

I wrote to Mr. Murray yesterday myself, and Henry wrote at the same time to Roworth. Before the notes were out of the house, I received three sheets and an apology from R. We sent the notes, however, and I had a most civil one in reply from Mr. M. He is so very polite, indeed, that it is quite overcoming. The printers have been waiting for paper,—the blame is thrown upon the stationer; but he gives his word that I shall have no further cause for dissatisfaction. He has lent us Miss Williams and Scott, and says that any book of his will always be at my service. In short, I am soothed and complimented into tolerable comfort.

We had a visit yesterday from Edwd. Knight, and Mr. Mascall joined him here; and this morning has brought Mr. Mascall's compliments and two pheasants. We have some hope of Edward's coming to dinner to-day; he will, if he can, I believe. He is looking extremely well.

To-morrow Mr. Haden is to dine with us. There is happiness! We really grow so fond of Mr. Haden that I do not know what to expect. He and Mr. Tilson and Mr. Philips made up our circle of wits last night. Fanny played, and he sat and listened and suggested improvements, till Richard came in to tell him that "the doctor was waiting for him at Captn. Blake's;" and then he was off with a speed that you can imagine. He never does appear in the least above his profession or out of humor with it, or I should think poor Captn. Blake, whoever he is, in a very bad way.

I must have misunderstood Henry when I told you that you were to hear from him to-day. He read me what he wrote to Edward: part of it must have amused him, I am sure one part, alas! cannot be very amusing to anybody. I wonder that with such business to worry him he can be getting better; but he certainly does gain strength, and if you and Edwd. were to see him now, I feel sure that you would think him improved since Monday.

He was out yesterday; it was a fine sunshiny day here (in the country perhaps you might have clouds and fogs. Dare I say so? I shall not deceive you, if I do, as to my estimation of the climate of London), and he ventured first on the balcony and then as far as the greenhouse. He caught no cold, and therefore has done more to-day, with great delight and self-persuasion of improvement.

He has been to see Mrs. Tilson and the Malings. By the by, you may talk to Mr. T. of his wife's being better; I saw her yesterday, and was sensible of her having gained ground in the last two days.

Evening.—We have had no Edward. Our circle is formed,—only Mr. Tilson and Mr. Haden. We are not so happy as we were. A message came this afternoon from Mrs. Latouche and Miss East, offering themselves to drink tea with us to-morrow, and, as it was accepted, here is an end of our extreme felicity in our dinner guest. I am heartily sorry they are coming; it will be an evening spoilt to Fanny and me.

Another little disappointment: Mr. H. advises Henry's not venturing with us in the carriage to-morrow; if it were spring, he says, it would be a different thing. One would rather this had not been. He seems to think his going out to-day rather imprudent, though acknowledging at the same time that he is better than he was in the morning.

Fanny has had a letter full of commissions from Goodnestone; we shall be busy about them and her own matters, I dare say, from twelve to four. Nothing, I trust, will keep us from Keppel Street.

This day has brought a most friendly letter from Mr. Fowle, with a brace of pheasants. I did not know before that Henry had written to him a few days ago to ask for them. We shall live upon pheasants,—no bad life!

I send you five one-pound notes, for fear you should be distressed for little money. Lizzy's work is charmingly done; shall you put it to your chintz? A sheet came in this moment; 1st and 3rd vols. are now at 144; 2nd at 48. I am sure you will like particulars. We are not to have the trouble of returning the sheets to Mr. Murray any longer; the printer's boys bring and carry.

I hope Mary continues to get well fast, and I send my love to little Herbert. You will tell me more of Martha's plans, of course, when you write again. Remember me most kindly to everybody, and Miss Benn besides.

Yours very affectionately,
J. AUSTEN.

I have been listening to dreadful insanity. It is Mr. Haden's firm belief that a person not musical is fit for every sort of wickedness. I ventured to assert a little on the other side, but wished the cause in abler hands.

Miss AUSTEN, Chawton.

LXX.

HANS PLACE, Sunday (Nov. 26).

MY DEAREST,—The parcel arrived safely, and I am much obliged to you for your trouble. It cost 2*s.* 10*d.*, but as there is a certain saving of 2*s.* 4½*d.* on the other side, I am sure it is well worth doing. I send four pair of silk stockings, but I do not want them washed at present. In the three neckhandkerchiefs I include the one sent down before. These things, perhaps, Edwd. may be able to bring, but even if he is not, I am extremely pleased with his returning to you from Steventon. It is much better, far preferable.

I did mention the P. R. in my note to Mr. Murray; it brought me a fine compliment in return. Whether it has done any other good I do not know, but Henry thought it worth trying.

The printers continue to supply me very well. I am advanced in Vol. III. to my arra-root, upon which peculiar style of spelling there is a modest query in the margin. I will not forget Anna's arrowroot. I hope you have told Martha of my first resolution of letting nobody know that I might dedicate, etc., for fear of being obliged to do it, and that she is thoroughly convinced of my being influenced now by nothing but the most mercenary motives. I have paid nine shillings on her account to Miss Palmer; there was no more owing.

Well, we were very busy all yesterday; from half-past eleven till four in the streets, working almost entirely for other people, driving from place to place after a parcel for Sandling, which we could never find, and encountering the miseries of Grafton House to get a purple frock for Eleanor Bridges. We got to Keppel St., however, which was all I cared for; and though we could stay only a quarter of an hour, Fanny's calling gave great pleasure, and her sensibility still greater, for she was very much affected at the sight of the children. Poor little F. looked heavy. We saw the whole party.

Aunt Harriet hopes Cassy will not forget to make a pincushion for Mrs. Kelly, as she has spoken of its being promised her several times. I hope we shall see Aunt H. and the dear little girls here on Thursday.

So much for the morning. Then came the dinner and Mr. Haden, who brought good manners and clever conversation. From seven to eight the harp; at eight Mrs. L. and Miss E. arrived, and for the rest of the evening the drawing-room was thus arranged: on the sofa side the two ladies, Henry, and myself making the best of it; on the opposite side Fanny and Mr. Haden, in two chairs (I believe, at least, they had two chairs), talking together uninterruptedly. Fancy the scene! And what is to be fancied next? Why, that Mr. H. dines here again to-morrow. To-day we are to have Mr. Barlow. Mr. H. is reading "Mansfield Park" for the first time, and prefers it to P. and P.

A hare and four rabbits from Gm. yesterday, so that we are stocked for nearly a week. Poor Farmer Andrews! I am very sorry for him, and sincerely wish his recovery.

A better account of the sugar than I could have expected. I should like to help you break some more. I am glad you cannot wake early; I am sure you must have been under great arrears of rest.

Fanny and I have been to B. Chapel, and walked back with Maria Cuthbert. We have been very little plagued with visitors this last week. I remember only Miss Herries, the aunt, but I am in terror for to-day, a fine bright Sunday; plenty of mortar, and nothing to do.

Henry gets out in his garden every day, but at present his inclination for doing more seems over, nor has he now any plan for leaving London before Dec. 18, when he thinks of going to Oxford for a few days; to-day, indeed, his feelings are for continuing where he is through the next two months.

One knows the uncertainty of all this; but should it be so, we must think the best, and hope the best, and do the best; and my idea in that case is, that when he goes to Oxford I should go home, and have nearly a week of you before you take my place. This is only a silent project, you know, to be gladly given up if better things occur. Henry calls himself stronger every day, and Mr. H. keeps on approving his pulse, which seems generally better than ever, but still they will not let him be well. Perhaps when Fanny is gone he will be allowed to recover faster.

I am not disappointed: I never thought the little girl at Wyards very pretty, but she will have a fine complexion and curly hair, and pass for a beauty. We are glad the mamma's cold has not been worse, and send her our love and good wishes by every convenient opportunity. Sweet, amiable Frank! why does he have a cold too? Like Captain Mirvan to Mr. Duval,[33] "I wish it well over with him."

Fanny has heard all that I have said to you about herself and Mr. H. Thank you very much for the sight of dearest Charles's letter to yourself. How pleasantly and how naturally he writes! and how perfect a picture of his disposition and feelings his style conveys! Poor dear fellow! Not a present!

I have a great mind to send him all the twelve copies which were to have been dispersed among my near connections, beginning with the P. R.[34] and ending with Countess Morley. Adieu.

Yours affectionately,
J. AUSTEN.

Give my love to Cassy and Mary Jane. Caroline will be gone when this reaches you. Miss AUSTEN.

---

[33] Characters in Miss Burney's "Evelina."
[34] Prince Regent.

LXXI.

HANS PLACE, Saturday (Dec. 2).

MY DEAR CASSANDRA,—Henry came back yesterday, and might have returned the day before if he had known as much in time. I had the pleasure of hearing from Mr. T. on Wednesday night that Mr. Seymour thought there was not the least occasion for his absenting himself any longer.

I had also the comfort of a few lines on Wednesday morning from Henry himself, just after your letter was gone, giving so good an account of his feelings as made me perfectly easy. He met with the utmost care and attention at Hanwell, spent his two days there very quietly and pleasantly, and being certainly in no respect the worse for going, we may believe that he must be better, as he is quite sure of being himself. To make his return a complete gala, Mr. Haden was secured for dinner. I need not say that our evening was agreeable.

But you seem to be under a mistake as to Mr. H. You call him an apothecary. He is no apothecary; he has never been an apothecary; there is not an apothecary in this neighborhood,—the only inconvenience of the situation, perhaps,—but so it is; we have not a medical man within reach. He is a Haden, nothing but a Haden, a sort of wonderful nondescript creature on two legs, something between a man and an angel, but without the least spice of an apothecary. He is, perhaps, the only person not an apothecary hereabouts. He has never sung to us. He will not sing without a pianoforte accompaniment.

Mr. Meyers gives his three lessons a week, altering his days and his hours, however, just as he chooses, never very punctual, and never giving good measure. I have not Fanny's fondness for masters, and Mr. Meyers does not give me any longing after them. The truth is, I think, that they are all, at least music-masters, made of too much consequence, and allowed to take too many liberties with their scholars' time.

We shall be delighted to see Edward on Monday, only sorry that you must be losing him. A turkey will be equally welcome with himself. He must prepare for his own proper bedchamber here, as Henry moved down to the one below last week; he found the other cold.

I am sorry my mother has been suffering, and am afraid this exquisite weather is too good to agree with her. I enjoy it all over me, from top to toe, from right to left, longitudinally, perpendicularly, diagonally; and I cannot but selfishly hope we are to have it last till Christmas,—nice, unwholesome, unseasonable, relaxing, close, muggy weather.

Oh, thank you very much for your long letter; it did me a great deal of good. Henry accepts your offer of making his nine gallon of mead thankfully. The mistake of the dogs rather vexed him for a moment, but he has not thought of it since. To-day he makes a third attempt at his strengthening plaister, and as I am sure he will now be getting out a great deal, it is to be wished that he may be able to keep it on. He sets off this morning by the Chelsea coach to sign bonds and visit Henrietta St., and I have no doubt will be going every day to Henrietta St.

Fanny and I were very snug by ourselves as soon as we were satisfied about our invalid's being safe at Hanwell. By man[oe]uvring and good luck we foiled all the Malings' attempts upon us. Happily I caught a little cold on Wednesday, the morning we were in town, which we made very useful, and we saw nobody but our precious[35] and Mr. Tilson.

---

[35] Probably a playful allusion to Mr. Haden.

This evening the Malings are allowed to drink tea with us. We are in hopes—that is, we wish—Miss Palmer and the little girls may come this morning. You know, of course, that she could not come on Thursday, and she will not attempt to name any other day.

God bless you. Excuse the shortness of this, but I must finish it now, that I may save you 2*d*. Best love.

Yours affectionately,   J. A.

It strikes me that I have no business to give the P. R. a binding, but we will take counsel upon the question.

I am glad you have put the flounce on your chintz; I am sure it must look particularly well, and it is what I had thought of.

Miss AUSTEN,
Chawton, Alton, Hants.

LXXII.

CHAWTON (Feb. 20, 1816).

MY DEAREST FANNY,—You are inimitable, irresistible. You are the delight of my life. Such letters, such entertaining letters, as you have lately sent! such a description of your queer little heart! such a lovely display of what imagination does! You are worth your weight in gold, or even in the new silver coinage. I cannot express to you what I have felt in reading your history of yourself,—how full of pity and concern, and admiration and amusement I have been! You are the paragon of all that is silly and sensible, commonplace and eccentric, sad and lively, provoking and interesting. Who can keep pace with the fluctuations of your fancy, the capprizios of your taste, the contradictions of your feelings? You are so odd, and all the time so perfectly natural!—so peculiar in yourself, and yet so like everybody else!

It is very, very gratifying to me to know you so intimately. You can hardly think what a pleasure it is to me to have such thorough pictures of your heart. Oh, what a loss it will be when you are married! You are too agreeable in your single state,—too agreeable as a niece. I shall hate you when your delicious play of mind is all settled down into conjugal and maternal affections.

Mr. B—— frightens me. He will have you. I see you at the altar. I have some faith in Mrs. C. Cage's observation, and still more in Lizzy's; and besides, I know it must be so. He must be wishing to attach you. It would be too stupid and too shameful in him to be otherwise; and all the family are seeking your acquaintance.

Do not imagine that I have any real objection; I have rather taken a fancy to him than not, and I like the house for you. I only do not like you should marry anybody. And yet I do wish you to marry very much, because I know you will never be happy till you are; but the loss of a Fanny Knight will be never made up to me. My "affec. niece F. C. B——" will be but a poor substitute. I do not like your being nervous, and so apt to cry,—it is a sign you are not quite well; but I hope Mr. Scud—as you always write his name (your Mr. Scuds amuse me very much)—will do you good.

What a comfort that Cassandra should be so recovered! It was more than we had expected. I can easily believe she was very patient and very good. I always loved Cassandra for her fine dark eyes and sweet temper. I am almost entirely cured of my rheumatism,—just a little pain in my knee now and then, to make me remember what it was, and keep on flannel. Aunt Cassandra nursed me so beautifully.

I enjoy your visit to Goodnestone, it must be a great pleasure to you; you have not seen Fanny Cage in comfort so long. I hope she represents and remonstrates and reasons with you properly. Why should you be living in dread of his marrying somebody else? (Yet how natural!) You did not choose to have him yourself, why not allow him to take comfort where he can? In your conscience you know that he could not bear a companion with a more animated character. You cannot forget how you felt under the idea of its having been possible that he might have dined in Hans Place.

My dearest Fanny, I cannot bear you should be unhappy about him. Think of his principles; think of his father's objection, of want of money, etc., etc. But I am doing no good; no, all that I urge against him will rather make you take his part more,—sweet, perverse Fanny.

And now I will tell you that we like your Henry to the utmost, to the very top of the glass, quite brimful. He is a very pleasing young man. I do not see how he could be mended. He does really bid fair to be everything his father and sister could wish; and William I love very much indeed, and so we do all; he is quite our own William. In short, we are very comfortable together; that is, we can answer for ourselves.

Mrs. Deedes is as welcome as May to all our benevolence to her son; we only lamented that we could not do more, and that the 50*l.* note we slipped into his hand at parting was necessarily the limit of our offering. Good Mrs. Deedes! Scandal and gossip; yes, I dare say you are well stocked, but I am very fond of Mrs. —— for reasons good. Thank you for mentioning her praise of "Emma," etc.

I have contributed the marking to Uncle H.'s shirts, and now they are a complete memorial of the tender regard of many.

Friday.—I had no idea when I began this yesterday of sending it before your brother went back, but I have written away my foolish thoughts at such a rate that I will not keep them many hours longer to stare me in the face.

Much obliged for the quadrilles, which I am grown to think pretty enough, though of course they are very inferior to the cotillons of my own day.

Ben and Anna walked here last Sunday to hear Uncle Henry, and she looked so pretty, it was quite a pleasure to see her, so young and so blooming and so innocent, as if she had never had a wicked thought in her life, which yet one has some reason to suppose she must have had, if we believe the doctrine of original sin. I hope Lizzy will have her play very kindly arranged for her. Henry is generally thought very good-looking, but not so handsome as Edward. I think I prefer his face. Wm. is in excellent looks, has a fine appetite, and seems perfectly well. You will have a great break up at Godmersham in the spring. You must feel their all going. It is very right, however! Poor Miss C.! I shall pity her when she begins to understand herself.

Your objection to the quadrilles delighted me exceedingly. Pretty well, for a lady irrecoverably attached to one person! Sweet Fanny, believe no such thing of yourself, spread no such malicious slander upon your understanding within the precincts of your imagination. Do not speak ill of your sense merely for the gratification of your fancy; yours is sense which deserves more honorable treatment. You are not in love with him; you never have been really in love with him.

Yours very affectionately,
J. Austen.

Miss Knight,
Godmersham Park, Faversham, Kent.

LXXIII.

CHAWTON, Thursday (March 13).

AS to making any adequate return for such a letter as yours, my dearest Fanny, it is absolutely impossible. If I were to labor at it all the rest of my life, and live to the age of Methuselah, I could never accomplish anything so long and so perfect; but I cannot let William go without a few lines of acknowledgment and reply.

I have pretty well done with Mr. ——. By your description, he cannot be in love with you, however he may try at it; and I could not wish the match unless there were a great deal of love on his side. I do not know what to do about Jemima Branfill. What does her dancing away with so much spirit mean? That she does not care for him, or only wishes to appear not to care for him? Who can understand a young lady?

Poor Mrs. C. Milles, that she should die on the wrong day at last, after being about it so long! It was unlucky that the Goodnestone party could not meet you; and I hope her friendly, obliging, social spirit, which delighted in drawing people together, was not conscious of the division and disappointment she was occasioning. I am sorry and surprised that you speak of her as having little to leave, and must feel for Miss Milles, though she is Molly, if a material loss of income is to attend her other loss. Single women have a dreadful propensity for being poor, which is one very strong argument in favor of matrimony; but I need not dwell on such arguments with you, pretty dear.

To you I shall say, as I have often said before, Do not be in a hurry, the right man will come at last; you will in the course of the next two or three years meet with somebody more generally unexceptionable than any one you have yet known, who will love you as warmly as possible, and who will so completely attract you that you will feel you never really loved before.

Do none of the A.'s ever come to balls now? You have never mentioned them as being at any. And what do you hear of the Gripps, or of Fanny and her husband?

Aunt Cassandra walked to Wyards yesterday with Mrs. Digweed. Anna has had a bad cold, and looks pale. She has just weaned Julia.

I have also heard lately from your Aunt Harriot, and cannot understand their plans in parting with Miss S., whom she seems very much to value now that Harriot and Eleanor are both of an age for a governess to be so useful to, especially as, when Caroline was sent to school some years, Miss Bell was still retained, though the others even then were nursery children. They have some good reason, I dare say, though I cannot penetrate it; and till I know what it is I shall invent a bad one, and amuse myself with accounting for the difference of measures by supposing Miss S. to be a superior sort of woman, who has never stooped to recommend herself to the master of the family by flattery, as Miss Bell did.

I will answer your kind questions more than you expect. "Miss Catherine" is put upon the shelf for the present, and I do not know that she will ever come out; but I have a something ready for publication, which may, perhaps, appear about a twelvemonth hence. It is short,— about the length of "Catherine." This is for yourself alone. Neither Mr. Salusbury nor Mr. Wildman is to know of it.

I am got tolerably well again, quite equal to walking about and enjoying the air, and by sitting down and resting a good while between my walks I get exercise enough. I have a scheme, however, for accomplishing more, as the weather grows spring-like. I mean to take to riding the donkey; it will be more independent and less troublesome than the use of the carriage, and I shall be able to go about with Aunt Cassandra in her walks to Alton and Wyards.

I hope you will think Wm. looking well; he was bilious the other day, and At. Cass. supplied him with a dose at his own request. I am sure you would have approved it. Wm. and I are the best of friends. I love him very much. Everything is so natural about him,—his affections, his manners, and his drollery. He entertains and interests us extremely.

Mat. Hammond and A. M. Shaw are people whom I cannot care for in themselves, but I enter into their situation, and am glad they are so happy. If I were the Duchess of Richmond, I should be very miserable about my son's choice.

Our fears increase for poor little Harriot; the latest account is that Sir Ev. Home is confirmed in his opinion of there being water on the brain. I hope Heaven, in its mercy, will take her soon. Her poor father will be quite worn out by his feelings for her; he cannot spare Cassy at present, she is an occupation and a comfort to him.

LXXIV.

CHAWTON, Sunday (March 23).

I AM very much obliged to you, my dearest Fanny, for sending me Mr. W.'s conversation; I had great amusement in reading it, and I hope I am not affronted, and do not think the worse of him for having a brain so very different from mine; but my strongest sensation of all is astonishment at your being able to press him on the subject so perseveringly; and I agree with your papa that it was not fair. When he knows the truth, he will be uncomfortable.

You are the oddest creature! Nervous enough in some respects, but in others perfectly without nerves! Quite unrepulsable, hardened, and impudent. Do not oblige him to read any more. Have mercy on him, tell him the truth, and make him an apology. He and I should not in the least agree, of course, in our ideas of novels and heroines. Pictures of perfection, as you know, make me sick and wicked; but there is some very good sense in what he says, and I particularly respect him for wishing to think well of all young ladies; it shows an amiable and a delicate mind. And he deserves better treatment than to be obliged to read any more of my works.

Do not be surprised at finding Uncle Henry acquainted with my having another ready for publication. I could not say No when he asked me, but he knows nothing more of it. You will not like it, so you need not be impatient. You may perhaps like the heroine, as she is almost too good for me.

Many thanks for your kind care for my health; I certainly have not been well for many weeks, and about a week ago I was very poorly. I have had a good deal of fever at times, and indifferent nights; but I am considerably better now, and am recovering my looks a little, which have been bad enough,—black and white, and every wrong color. I must not depend upon being ever very blooming again. Sickness is a dangerous indulgence at my time of life. Thank you for everything you tell me. I do not feel worthy of it by anything that I can say in return, but I assure you my pleasure in your letters is quite as great as ever, and I am interested and amused just as you could wish me. If there is a Miss Marsden, I perceive whom she will marry.

Evening.—I was languid and dull and very bad company when I wrote the above; I am better now, to my own feelings at least, and wish I may be more agreeable. We are going to have rain, and after that very pleasant genial weather, which will exactly do for me, as my saddle will then be completed, and air and exercise is what I want. Indeed, I shall be very glad when the event at Scarlets is over, the expectation of it keeps us in a worry, your grandmamma especially; she sits brooding over evils which cannot be remedied, and conduct impossible to be understood.

Now the reports from Keppel St. are rather better; little Harriot's headaches are abated, and Sir Evd. is satisfied with the effect of the mercury, and does not despair of a cure. The complaint I find is not considered incurable nowadays, provided the patient be young enough not to have the head hardened. The water in that case may be drawn off by mercury. But though this is a new idea to us, perhaps it may have been long familiar to you through your friend Mr. Scud. I hope his high renown is sustained by driving away William's cough.

Tell Wm. that Triggs is as beautiful and condescending as ever, and was so good as to dine with us to-day, and tell him that I often play at nines and think of him.

The Papillons came back on Friday night, but I have not seen them yet, as I do not venture to church. I cannot hear, however, but that they are the same Mr. P. and his sister they used to be. She has engaged a new maidservant in Mrs. Calker's room, whom she means to make also housekeeper under herself.

Old Philmore was buried yesterday, and I, by way of saying something to Triggs, observed that it had been a very handsome funeral; but his manner of reply made me suppose that it was not generally esteemed so. I can only be sure of one part being very handsome,—Triggs himself, walking behind in his green coat. Mrs. Philmore attended as chief mourner, in bombazine, made very short, and flounced with crape.

Tuesday.—I have had various plans as to this letter, but at last I have determined that Uncle Henry shall forward it from London. I want to see how Canterbury looks in the direction. When once Uncle H. has left us, I shall wish him with you. London has become a hateful place to him, and he is always depressed by the idea of it. I hope he will be in time for your sick. I am sure he must do that part of his duty as excellently as all the rest. He returned yesterday from Steventon, and was with us by breakfast, bringing Edward with him, only that Edwd. stayed to breakfast at Wyards. We had a pleasant family day, for the Altons dined with us, the last visit of the kind probably which she will be able to pay us for many a month.

I hope your own Henry is in France, and that you have heard from him; the passage once over, he will feel all happiness. I took my first ride yesterday, and liked it very much. I went up Mounter's Lane and round by where the new cottages are to be, and found the exercise and everything very pleasant; and I had the advantage of agreeable companions, as At. Cass. and Edward walked by my side. At. Cass. is such an excellent nurse, so assiduous and unwearied! But you know all that already.

Very affectionately yours,
J. AUSTEN.

Miss KNIGHT,
Godmersham Park, Canterbury.

LXXV.

CHAWTON, Sunday (Sept. 8, 1816).

MY DEAREST CASSANDRA,—I have borne the arrival of your letter to-day extremely well; anybody might have thought it was giving me pleasure. I am very glad you find so much to be satisfied with at Cheltenham. While the waters agree, everything else is trifling.

A letter arrived for you from Charles last Thursday. They are all safe and pretty well in Keppel St., the children decidedly better for Broadstairs; and he writes principally to ask when it will be convenient to us to receive Miss P., the little girls, and himself. They would be ready to set off in ten days from the time of his writing, to pay their visits in Hampshire and Berkshire, and he would prefer coming to Chawton first.

I have answered him, and said that we hoped it might suit them to wait till the last week in Septr., as we could not ask them sooner, either on your account or the want of room. I mentioned the 23rd as the probable day of your return. When you have once left Cheltenham, I shall grudge every half-day wasted on the road. If there were but a coach from Hungerford to Chawton! I have desired him to let me hear again soon.

He does not include a maid in the list to be accommodated; but if they bring one, as I suppose they will, we shall have no bed in the house even then for Charles himself,—let alone Henry. But what can we do?

We shall have the Gt. House quite at our command; it is to be cleared of the Papillons' servants in a day or two. They themselves have been hurried off into Essex to take possession,—not of a large estate left them by an uncle, but to scrape together all they can, I suppose, of the effects of a Mrs. Rawstorn, a rich old friend and cousin suddenly deceased, to whom they are joint executors. So there is a happy end of the Kentish Papillons coming here.

No morning service to-day, wherefore I am writing between twelve and one o'clock. Mr. Benn in the afternoon, and likewise more rain again, by the look and the sound of things. You left us in doubt of Mrs. Benn's situation, but she has bespoke her nurse.... The F. A.'s dined with us yesterday, and had fine weather both for coming and going home, which has hardly ever happened to them before. She is still unprovided with a housemaid.

Our day at Alton was very pleasant, venison quite right, children well behaved, and Mr. and Mrs. Digweed taking kindly to our charades and other games. I must also observe, for his mother's satisfaction, that Edward at my suggestion devoted himself very properly to the entertainment of Miss S. Gibson. Nothing was wanting except Mr. Sweeney; but he, alas! had been ordered away to London the day before. We had a beautiful walk home by moonlight.

Thank you, my back has given me scarcely any pain for many days. I have an idea that agitation does it as much harm as fatigue, and that I was ill at the time of your going from the very circumstance of your going. I am nursing myself up now into as beautiful a state as I can, because I hear that Dr. White means to call on me before he leaves the country.

Evening.—Frank and Mary and the children visited us this morning. Mr. and Mrs. Gibson are to come on the 23rd, and there is too much reason to fear they will stay above a week. Little George could tell me where you were gone to, as well as what you were to bring him, when I asked him the other day.

Sir Tho. Miller is dead. I treat you with a dead baronet in almost every letter.

So you have C. Craven among you, as well as the Duke of Orleans and Mr. Pocock. But it mortifies me that you have not added one to the stock of common acquaintance. Do pray meet with somebody belonging to yourself. I am quite weary of your knowing nobody.

Mrs. Digweed parts with both Hannah and old cook: the former will not give up her lover, who is a man of bad character; the latter is guilty only of being unequal to anything.

Miss Terry was to have spent this week with her sister, but as usual it is put off. My amiable friend knows the value of her company. I have not seen Anna since the day you left us; her father and brother visited her most days. Edward and Ben called here on Thursday. Edward was in his way to Selborne. We found him very agreeable. He is come back from France, thinking of the French as one could wish,—disappointed in everything. He did not go beyond Paris.

I have a letter from Mrs. Perigord; she and her mother are in London again. She speaks of France as a scene of general poverty and misery: no money, no trade, nothing to be got but by the innkeepers, and as to her own present prospects she is not much less melancholy than before.I have also a letter from Miss Sharp, quite one of her letters; she has been again obliged to exert herself more than ever, in a more distressing, more harassed state, and has met with another excellent old physician and his wife, with every virtue under heaven, who takes to her and cures her from pure love and benevolence. Dr. and Mrs. Storer are their Mrs. and Miss Palmer—for they are at Bridlington. I am happy to say, however, that the sum of the account is better than usual. Sir William is returned; from Bridlington they go to Chevet, and she is to have a young governess under her.

I enjoyed Edward's company very much, as I said before, and yet I was not sorry when Friday came. It had been a busy week, and I wanted a few days' quiet and exemption from the thought and contrivancy which any sort of company gives. I often wonder how you can find time for what you do, in addition to the care of the house; and how good Mrs. West could have written such books and collected so many hard words, with all her family cares, is still more a matter of astonishment. Composition seems to me impossible with a head full of joints of mutton and doses of rhubarb.

Monday.—Here is a sad morning. I fear you may not have been able to get to the Pump. The two last days were very pleasant. I enjoyed them the more for your sake. But to-day it is really bad enough to make you all cross. I hope Mary will change her lodgings at the fortnight's end; I am sure, if you looked about well, you would find others in some odd corner to suit you better. Mrs. Potter charges for the name of the High St.

Success to the pianoforte! I trust it will drive you away. We hear now that there is to be no honey this year. Bad news for us. We must husband our present stock of mead, and I am sorry to perceive that our twenty gallons is very nearly out. I cannot comprehend how the fourteen gallons could last so long.

We do not much like Mr. Cooper's new sermons. They are fuller of regeneration and conversion than ever, with the addition of his zeal in the cause of the Bible Society.

Martha's love to Mary and Caroline, and she is extremely glad to find they like the pelisse. The Debarys are indeed odious! We are to see my brother to-morrow, but for only one night. I had no idea that he would care for the races without Edward. Remember me to all.

Yours very affectionately,
J. AUSTEN.

Miss AUSTEN, Post-Office, Cheltenham.

Note by Lord Brabourne.

I insert here a letter of Jane Austen's written backwards, addressed to her niece "Cassy," daughter of Captain Charles Austen (afterwards Admiral) when a little girl.

LXXVI.

YM RAED YSSAC,—I hsiw uoy a yppah wen raey. Ruoy xis snisuoc emac ereh yadretsey, dna dah hcae a eceip fo ekac. Siht si elttil Yssac's yadhtrib, dna ehs si eerht sraey dlo. Knarf sah nugeb gninrael Nital ew deef eht Nibor yreve gninrom. Yllas netfo seriuqne retfa uoy. Yllas Mahneb sah tog a wen neerg nwog. Teirrah Thgink semoc yreve yad ot daer ot Tnua Ardnassac. Doog eyb ym raed Yssac.

Tnua Ardnassac sdnes reh tseb evol, dna os ew od lla.

Ruoy etanoitceffa tnua,
ENAJ NETSUA.

NOTWAHC, Naj. 8.

Note by Lord Brabourne.

In January, 1817, she wrote of herself as better and able to walk into Alton, and hoped in the summer she should be able to walk back. In April her father in a note to Mrs. Lefroy says: "I was happy to have a good account of herself written by her own hand, in a letter from your Aunt Jane; but all who love, and that is all who know her, must be anxious on her account." We all know how well grounded that anxiety was, and how soon her relations had to lament over the loss of the dearest and brightest member of their family.

And now I come to the saddest letters of all, those which tell us of the end of that bright life, cut short just at the time when the world might have hoped that unabated intellectual vigor, supplemented by the experience brought by maturer years, would have produced works if possible even more fascinating than those with which she had already embellished the literature of her country. But it was not to be. The fiat had gone forth,—the ties which bound that sweet spirit to earth were to be severed, and a blank left, never to be filled in the family which her loved and loving presence had blessed, and where she had been so well and fondly appreciated. In the early spring of 1817 the unfavorable symptoms increased, and the failure of her health was too visible to be neglected. Still no apprehensions of immediate danger were entertained, and it is probable that when she left Chawton for Winchester in May, she did not recognize the fact that she was bidding a last farewell to "Home." Happy for her if it was so, for there are few things more melancholy than to look upon any beloved place or person with the knowledge that it is for "the last time." In all probability this grief was spared to Jane, for even after her arrival at Winchester she spoke and wrote as if recovery was hopeful; and I fancy that her relations were by no means aware that the end was so near.

Note by Lord Brabourne.

Cassandra's letters tell the tale of the event in words that require no addition from me. They are simple and affecting,—the words of one who had been stricken by a great grief, but whose religion stood her in good stead, and enabled her to bear it with fortitude. The firm and loving bond of union which had ever united the Austen family, naturally intensified their sorrow at the loss of one of their number, and that the one of whom they had been so proud as well as so fond. They laid her within the walls of the old cathedral which she had loved so much, and went sorrowfully back to their homes, with the feeling that nothing could replace to them the treasure they had lost. And most heavily of all must the blow have fallen upon the only sister, the correspondent, the companion, the other self of Jane, who had to return alone to the desolate home, and to the mother to whose comforts the two had hitherto ministered together, but who would henceforward have her alone on whom to rely....

Letters from Miss Cassandra Austen to her niece Miss Knight, after the death of her sister Jane, July 18, 1817.

LXXVII.

WINCHESTER, Sunday.

MY DEAREST FANNY,—Doubly dear to me now for her dear sake whom we have lost. She did love you most sincerely, and never shall I forget the proofs of love you gave her during her illness in writing those kind, amusing letters at a time when I know your feelings would have dictated so different a style. Take the only reward I can give you in the assurance that your benevolent purpose was answered; you did contribute to her enjoyment.

Even your last letter afforded pleasure. I merely cut the seal and gave it to her; she opened it and read it herself, afterwards she gave it to me to read, and then talked to me a little and not uncheerfully of its contents, but there was then a languor about her which prevented her taking the same interest in anything she had been used to do.

Since Tuesday evening, when her complaint returned, there was a visible change, she slept more and much more comfortably; indeed, during the last eight-and-forty hours she was more asleep than awake. Her looks altered and she fell away, but I perceived no material diminution of strength, and though I was then hopeless of a recovery, I had no suspicion how rapidly my loss was approaching.

I have lost a treasure, such a sister, such a friend as never can have been surpassed. She was the sun of my life, the gilder of every pleasure, the soother of every sorrow; I had not a thought concealed from her, and it is as if I had lost a part of myself. I loved her only too well,—not better than she deserved, but I am conscious that my affection for her made me sometimes unjust to and negligent of others; and I can acknowledge, more than as a general principle, the justice of the Hand which has struck this blow.

You know me too well to be at all afraid that I should suffer materially from my feelings; I am perfectly conscious of the extent of my irreparable loss, but I am not at all overpowered and very little indisposed,—nothing but what a short time, with rest and change of air, will remove. I thank God that I was enabled to attend her to the last, and amongst my many causes of self-reproach I have not to add any wilful neglect of her comfort.

She felt herself to be dying about half an hour before she became tranquil and apparently unconscious. During that half-hour was her struggle, poor soul! She said she could not tell us what she suffered, though she complained of little fixed pain. When I asked her if there was anything she wanted, her answer was she wanted nothing but death, and some of her words were: "God grant me patience, pray for me, oh, pray for me!" Her voice was affected, but as long as she spoke she was intelligible.

I hope I do not break your heart, my dearest Fanny, by these particulars; I mean to afford you gratification whilst I am relieving my own feelings. I could not write so to anybody else; indeed you are the only person I have written to at all, excepting your grandmamma,—it was to her, not your Uncle Charles, I wrote on Friday.

Immediately after dinner on Thursday I went into the town to do an errand which your dear aunt was anxious about. I returned about a quarter before six, and found her recovering from faintness and oppression; she got so well as to be able to give me a minute account of her seizure, and when the clock struck six she was talking quietly to me.

I cannot say how soon afterwards she was seized again with the same faintness, which was followed by the sufferings she could not describe; but Mr. Lyford had been sent for, had applied something to give her ease, and she was in a state of quiet insensibility by seven o'clock at the latest. From that time till half-past four, when she ceased to breathe, she scarcely moved a limb, so that we have every reason to think, with gratitude to the Almighty, that her sufferings were over. A slight motion of the head with every breath remained till almost the last. I sat close to her with a pillow in my lap to assist in supporting her head, which was almost off the bed, for six hours; fatigue made me then resign my place to Mrs. J. A. for two hours and a half, when I took it again, and in about an hour more she breathed her last.

I was able to close her eyes myself, and it was a great gratification to me to render her those last services. There was nothing convulsed which gave the idea of pain in her look; on the contrary, but for the continual motion of the head she gave one the idea of a beautiful statue, and even now, in her coffin, there is such a sweet, serene air over her countenance as is quite pleasant to contemplate.

This day, my dearest Fanny, you have had the melancholy intelligence, and I know you suffer severely, but I likewise know that you will apply to the fountain-head for consolation, and that our merciful God is never deaf to such prayers as you will offer.

The last sad ceremony is to take place on Thursday morning; her dear remains are to be deposited in the cathedral. It is a satisfaction to me to think that they are to lie in a building she admired so much; her precious soul, I presume to hope, reposes in a far superior mansion. May mine one day be reunited to it!

Your dear papa, your Uncle Henry, and Frank and Edwd. Austen, instead of his father, will attend. I hope they will none of them suffer lastingly from their pious exertions. The ceremony must be over before ten o'clock, as the cathedral service begins at that hour, so that we shall be at home early in the day, for there will be nothing to keep us here afterwards.

Your Uncle James came to us yesterday, and is gone home to-day. Uncle H. goes to Chawton to-morrow morning; he has given every necessary direction here, and I think his company there will do good. He returns to us again on Tuesday evening.

I did not think to have written a long letter when I began, but I have found the employment draw me on, and I hope I shall have been giving you more pleasure than pain. Remember me kindly to Mrs. J. Bridges (I am so glad she is with you now), and give my best love to Lizzie and all the others.

I am, my dearest Fanny,
Most affectionately yours,
CASS. ELIZ. AUSTEN.

I have said nothing about those at Chawton, because I am sure you hear from your papa.

LXXVIII.

CHAWTON, Tuesday (July 29, 1817).

MY DEAREST FANNY,—I have just read your letter for the third time, and thank you most sincerely for every kind expression to myself, and still more warmly for your praises of her who I believe was better known to you than to any human being besides myself. Nothing of the sort could have been more gratifying to me than the manner in which you write of her; and if the dear angel is conscious of what passes here, and is not above all earthly feelings, she may perhaps receive pleasure in being so mourned. Had she been the survivor, I can fancy her speaking of you in almost the same terms. There are certainly many points of strong resemblance in your characters; in your intimate acquaintance with each other, and your mutual strong affection, you were counterparts.

Thursday was not so dreadful a day to me as you imagined. There was so much necessary to be done that there was no time for additional misery. Everything was conducted with the greatest tranquillity, and but that I was determined I would see the last, and therefore was upon the listen, I should not have known when they left the house. I watched the little mournful procession the length of the street; and when it turned from my sight, and I had lost her forever, even then I was not overpowered, nor so much agitated as I am now in writing of it. Never was human being more sincerely mourned by those who attended her remains than was this dear creature. May the sorrow with which she is parted with on earth be a prognostic of the joy with which she is hailed in heaven!

I continue very tolerably well,—much better than any one could have supposed possible, because I certainly have had considerable fatigue of body as well as anguish of mind for months back; but I really am well, and I hope I am properly grateful to the Almighty for having been so supported. Your grandmamma, too, is much better than when I came home.

I did not think your dear papa appeared unwell, and I understand that he seemed much more comfortable after his return from Winchester than he had done before. I need not tell you that he was a great comfort to me; indeed, I can never say enough of the kindness I have received from him and from every other friend.

I get out of doors a good deal, and am able to employ myself. Of course those employments suit me best which leave me most at leisure to think of her I have lost, and I do think of her in every variety of circumstance,—in our happy hours of confidential intercourse, in the cheerful family party which she so ornamented, in her sick-room, on her death-bed, and as (I hope) an inhabitant of heaven. Oh, if I may one day be reunited to her there! I know the time must come when my mind will be less engrossed by her idea, but I do not like to think of it. If I think of her less as on earth, God grant that I may never cease to reflect on her as inhabiting heaven, and never cease my humble endeavors (when it shall please God) to join her there.

In looking at a few of the precious papers which are now my property I have found some memorandums, amongst which she desires that one of her gold chains may be given to her god-daughter Louisa, and a lock of her hair be set for you. You can need no assurance, my dearest Fanny, that every request of your beloved aunt will be sacred with me. Be so good as to say whether you prefer a brooch or ring. God bless you, my dearest Fanny.

Believe me, most affectionately yours,
CASS. ELIZTH. AUSTEN.

Miss KNIGHT,
Godmersham Park, Canterbury.

THE END.

Juvenilia

VOLUME IN THE FIRST

A Collection of Juvenile Writings

By

Jane Austen

FREDERIC AND ELFRIDA

A Novel

To Miss Lloyd

My Dear Martha,
As a small testimony of the gratitude I feel for your late generosity to me in finishing my muslin Cloak, I beg leave to offer you this little production of your sincere Freind.
The Author

Chapter 1

The Uncle of Elfrida was the Father of Frederic; in other words, they were first cousins by the Father's side.

Being both born in one day & both brought up at one school, it was not wonderfull that they should look on each other with something more than bare politeness. They loved with mutual sincerity, but were both determined not to transgress the rules of Propriety by owning their attachment, either to the object beloved, or to any one else.

They were exceedingly handsome and so much alike, that it was not every one who knew them apart. Nay, even their most intimate freinds had nothing to distinguish them by, but the shape of the face, the colour of the Eye, the length of the Nose, & the difference of the complexion.

Elfrida had an intimate freind to whom, being on a visit to an Aunt, she wrote the following Letter.

To Miss Drummond

Dear Charlotte,
I should be obliged to you, if you would buy me, during your stay with Mrs. Williamson, a new & fashionable Bonnet, to suit the complexion of your

E. Falknor

Charlotte, whose character was a willingness to oblige every one, when she returned into the Country, brought her Freind the wished-for Bonnet, & so ended this little adventure, much to the satisfaction of all parties.

On her return to Crankhumdunberry (of which sweet village her father was Rector), Charlotte was received with the greatest Joy by Frederic & Elfrida, who, after pressing her alternately to their Bosoms, proposed to her to take a walk in a Grove of Poplars which led from the Parsonage to a verdant Lawn enamelled with a variety of variegated flowers & watered by a purling Stream, brought from the Valley of Tempè by a passage under ground.

In this Grove they had scarcely remained above 9 hours, when they were suddenly agreably surprized by hearing a most delightfull voice warble the following stanza.

Song
That Damon was in love with me
   I once thought & beleiv'd
But now that he is not I see,
   I fear I was deceiv'd.

No sooner were the lines finished than they beheld by a turning in the Grove 2 elegant young women leaning on each other's arm, who immediately on perceiving them, took a different path & disappeared from their sight.

Chapter 2

As Elfrida & her companions had seen enough of them to know that they were neither the 2 Miss Greens, nor Mrs. Jackson and her Daughter, they could not help expressing their surprise at their appearance; till at length recollecting, that a new family had lately taken a House not far from the Grove, they hastened home, determined to lose no no time in forming an acquaintance with 2 such amiable & worthy Girls, of which family they rightly imagined them to be a part.

Agreable to such a determination, they went that very evening to pay their respects to Mrs. Fitzroy & her two Daughters. On being shewn into an elegant dressing room, ornamented with festoons of artificial flowers, they were struck with the engaging Exterior & beautifull outside of Jezalinda, the eldest of the young Ladies; but e'er they had been many minutes seated, the Wit & Charms which shone resplendent in the conversation of the amiable Rebecca enchanted them so much, that they all with one accord jumped up and exclaimed:

"Lovely & too charming Fair one, notwithstanding your forbidding Squint, your greazy tresses & your swelling Back, which are more frightfull than imagination can paint or pen describe, I cannot refrain from expressing my raptures, at the engaging Qualities of your Mind, which so amply atone for the Horror with which your first appearance must ever inspire the unwary visitor."

"Your sentiments so nobly expressed on the different excellencies of Indian & English Muslins, & the judicious preference you give the former, have excited in me an admiration of which I can alone give an adequate idea, by assuring you it is nearly equal to what I feel for myself."

Then making a profound Curtesy to the amiable & abashed Rebecca, they left the room & hurried home.

From this period, the intimacy between the Families of Fitzroy, Drummond, and Falknor daily increased, till at length it grew to such a pitch, that they did not scruple to kick one another out of the window on the slightest provocation.

During this happy state of Harmony, the eldest Miss Fitzroy ran off with the Coachman & the amiable Rebecca was asked in marriage by Captain Roger of Buckinghamshire.

Mrs. Fitzroy did not approve of the match on account of the tender years of the young couple, Rebecca being but 36 & Captain Roger little more than 63. To remedy this objection, it was agreed that they should wait a little while till they were a good deal older.

Chapter 3

In the mean time, the parents of Frederic proposed to those of Elfrida an union between them, which being accepted with pleasure, the wedding cloathes were bought & nothing remained to be settled but the naming of the Day.

As to the lovely Charlotte, being importuned with eagerness to pay another visit to her Aunt, she determined to accept the invitation & in consequence of it walked to Mrs. Fitzroy's to take leave of the amiable Rebecca, whom she found surrounded by Patches, Powder, Pomatum, & Paint, with which she was vainly endeavouring to remedy the natural plainness of her face.

"I am come, my amiable Rebecca, to take my leave of you for the fortnight I am destined to spend with my aunt. Beleive me, this separation is painfull to me, but it is as necessary as the labour which now engages you."

"Why to tell you the truth, my Love," replied Rebecca, "I have lately taken it into my head to think (perhaps with little reason) that my complexion is by no means equal to the rest of my face & have therefore taken, as you see, to white & red paint which I would scorn to use on any other occasion, as I hate art."

Charlotte, who perfectly understood the meaning of her freind's speech, was too good-temper'd & obliging to refuse her what she knew she wished—a compliment; and they parted the best freinds in the world.

With a heavy heart & streaming Eyes did she ascend the lovely vehicle which bore her from her freinds & home; but greived as she was, she little thought in what a strange & different manner she should return to it.

On her entrance into the city of London, which was the place of Mrs. Williamson's abode, the postilion, whose stupidity was amazing, declared & declared even without the least shame or Compunction, that having never been informed, he was totally ignorant of what part of the Town he was to drive to.

Charlotte, whose nature we have before intimated was an earnest desire to oblige every one, with the greatest Condescension & Good humour informed him that he was to drive to

Portland Place, which he accordingly did & Charlotte soon found herself in the arms of a fond Aunt.

Scarcely were they seated as usual, in the most affectionate manner in one chair, than the Door suddenly opened & an aged gentleman with a sallow face & old pink Coat, partly by intention & partly thro' weakness was at the feet of the lovely Charlotte, declaring his attachment to her & beseeching her pity in the most moving manner.

Not being able to resolve to make any one miserable, she consented to become his wife; where upon the Gentleman left the room & all was quiet.

Their quiet however continued but a short time, for on a second opening of the door a young & Handsome Gentleman with a new blue coat entered & intreated from the lovely Charlotte, permission to pay to her his addresses.

There was a something in the appearance of the second Stranger, that influenced Charlotte in his favour, to the full as much as the appearance of the first: she could not account for it, but so it was.

Having therefore, agreable to that & the natural turn of her mind to make every one happy, promised to become his Wife the next morning, he took his leave & the two Ladies sat down to Supper on a young Leveret, a brace of Partridges, a leash of Pheasants & a Dozen of Pigeons.

Chapter 4

It was not till the next morning that Charlotte recollected the double engagement she had entered into; but when she did, the reflection of her past folly operated so strongly on her mind, that she resolved to be guilty of a greater, & to that end threw herself into a deep stream which ran thro her Aunt's pleasure Grounds in Portland Place.

She floated to Crankhumdunberry where she was picked up & buried; the following epitaph, composed by Frederic, Elfrida, & Rebecca, was placed on her tomb.

Epitaph
Here lies our friend who having promis-ed
That unto two she would be marri-ed
Threw her sweet Body & her lovely face
Into the Stream that runs thro' Portland Place.

These sweet lines, as pathetic as beautifull, were never read by any one who passed that way, without a shower of tears, which if they should fail of exciting in you, Reader, your mind must be unworthy to peruse them.

Having performed the last sad office to their departed freind, Frederic & Elfrida together with Captain Roger & Rebecca returned to Mrs. Fitzroy's, at whose feet they threw themselves with one accord & addressed her in the following Manner.

"Madam"

"When the sweet Captain Roger first addressed the amiable Rebecca, you alone objected to their union on account of the tender years of the Parties. That plea can be no more, seven days being now expired, together with the lovely Charlotte, since the Captain first spoke to you on the subject."

"Consent then Madam to their union & as a reward, this smelling Bottle which I enclose in my right hand, shall be yours & yours forever; I never will claim it again. But if you refuse to join their hands in 3 days time, this dagger which I enclose in my left shall be steeped in your heart's blood."

"Speak then, Madam, & decide their fate & yours."

Such gentle & sweet persuasion could not fail of having the desired effect. The answer they received, was this.

"My dear young freinds"

"The arguments you have used are too just & too eloquent to be withstood; Rebecca, in 3 days time, you shall be united to the Captain."

This speech, than which nothing could be more satisfactory, was received with Joy by all; & peace being once more restored on all sides, Captain Roger intreated Rebecca to favour them with a Song, in compliance with which request, having first assured them that she had a terrible cold, she sung as follows.

Song
When Corydon went to the fair
 He bought a red ribbon for Bess,
With which she encircled her hair
 made herself look very fess.

Chapter 5

At the end of 3 days Captain Roger and Rebecca were united, and immediately after the Ceremony set off in the Stage Waggon for the Captain's seat in Buckinghamshire.

The parents of Elfrida, alltho' they earnestly wished to see her married to Frederic before they died, yet knowing the delicate frame of her mind could ill bear the least exertion & rightly judging that naming her wedding day would be too great a one, forebore to press her on the subject.

Weeks & Fortnights flew away without gaining the least ground; the Cloathes grew out of fashion & at length Capt. Roger & his Lady arrived, to pay a visit to their Mother & introduce to her their beautifull Daughter of eighteen.

Elfrida, who had found her former acquaintance were growing too old & too ugly to be any longer agreable, was rejoiced to hear of the arrival of so pretty a girl as Eleanor, with whom she determined to form the strictest freindship.

But the Happiness she had expected from an acquaintance with Eleanor, she soon found was not to be received, for she had not only the mortification of finding herself treated by her as little less than an old woman, but had actually the horror of perceiving a growing passion in the Bosom of Frederic for the Daughter of the amiable Rebecca.

The instant she had the first idea of such an attachment, she flew to Frederic & in a manner truly heroick, spluttered out to him her intention of being married the next Day.

To one in his predicament who possessed less personal Courage than Frederic was master of, such a speech would have been Death; but he, not being the least terrified, boldly replied:

"Damme, Elfrida, you may be married tomorrow, but I won't."

This answer distressed her too much for her delicate Constitution. She accordingly fainted & was in such a hurry to have a succession of fainting fits, that she had scarcely patience enough to recover from one before she fell into another.

Tho' in any threatening Danger to his Life or Liberty, Frederic was as bold as brass, yet in other respects his heart was as soft as cotton & immediately on hearing of the dangerous way Elfrida was in, he flew to her & finding her better than he had been taught to expect, was united to her Forever.

Finis

JACK AND ALICE
A Novel

Is respectfully inscribed to Francis William Austen Esq. Midshipman on board
his Majesty's Ship the Perseverance by his obedient humble Servant.
The Author

Chapter 1

Mr. Johnson was once upon a time about 53; in a twelve-month afterwards he was 54, which so much delighted him that he was determined to celebrate his next Birthday by giving a Masquerade to his Children & Freinds. Accordingly on the Day he attained his 55th year, tickets were dispatched to all his Neighbours to that purpose. His acquaintance indeed in that part of the World were not very numerous, as they consisted only of Lady Williams, Mr. & Mrs. Jones, Charles Adams & the 3 Miss Simpsons, who composed the neighbourhood of Pammydiddle & formed the Masquerade.

Before I proceed to give an account of the Evening, it will be proper to describe to my reader the persons and Characters of the party introduced to his acquaintance.

Mr. & Mrs. Jones were both rather tall & very passionate, but were in other respects good tempered, wellbehaved People. Charles Adams was an amiable, accomplished, & bewitching young Man; of so dazzling a Beauty that none but Eagles could look him in the Face.

Miss Simpson was pleasing in her person, in her Manners, & in her Disposition; an unbounded ambition was her only fault. Her second sister Sukey was Envious, Spitefull, & Malicious. Her person was short, fat & disagreable. Cecilia (the youngest) was perfectly handsome, but too affected to be pleasing.

In Lady Williams every virtue met. She was a widow with a handsome Jointure & the remains of a very handsome face. Tho' Benevolent & Candid, she was Generous & sincere; Tho' Pious & Good, she was Religious & amiable, & Tho Elegant & Agreable, she was Polished & Entertaining.

The Johnsons were a family of Love, & though a little addicted to the Bottle & the Dice, had many good Qualities.

Such was the party assembled in the elegant Drawing Room of Johnson Court, amongst which the pleasing figure of a Sultana was the most remarkable of the female Masks. Of the Males, a Mask representing the Sun was the most universally admired. The Beams that darted from his Eyes were like those of that glorious Luminary, tho' infinitely superior. So strong were they that no one dared venture within half a mile of them; he had therefore the best part of the Room to himself, its size not amounting to more than 3 quarters of a mile in length & half a one in breadth. The Gentleman at last finding the feirceness of his beams to be very inconvenient to the concourse, by obliging them to croud together in one corner of the room, half shut his eyes, by which means the Company discovered him to be Charles Adams in his plain green Coat, without any mask at all.

When their astonishment was a little subsided, their attention was attracted by 2 Dominos who advanced in a horrible Passion; they were both very tall, but seemed in other respects to have many good qualities. "These" said the witty Charles, "these are Mr. & Mrs. Jones." and so indeed they were.

No one could imagine who was the Sultana! Till at length, on her addressing a beautifull Flora who was reclining in a studied attitude on a couch, with "Oh Cecilia, I wish I was really what I pretend to be", she was discovered by the never failing genius of Charles Adams to be the elegant but ambitious Caroline Simpson, & the person to whom she addressed herself, he rightly imagined to be her lovely but affected sister Cecilia.

The Company now advanced to a Gaming Table where sat 3 Dominos (each with a bottle in their hand) deeply engaged; but a female in the character of Virtue fled with hasty footsteps from the shocking scene, whilst a little fat woman, representing Envy, sat alternately on the foreheads of the 3 Gamesters. Charles Adams was still as bright as ever; he soon discovered the party at play to be the 3 Johnsons, Envy to be Sukey Simpson & Virtue to be Lady Williams.

The Masks were then all removed & the Company retired to another room, to partake of an elegant & well managed Entertainment, after which, the Bottle being pretty briskly pushed about by the 3 Johnsons, the whole party (not excepting even Virtue) were carried home, Dead Drunk.

Chapter 2

For three months did the Masquerade afford ample subject for conversation to the inhabitants of Pammydiddle; but no character at it was so fully expatiated on as Charles Adams. The singularity of his appearance, the beams which darted from his eyes, the brightness of his Wit, & the whole tout ensemble of his person had subdued the hearts of so many of the young Ladies, that of the six present at the Masquerade but five had returned uncaptivated. Alice Johnson was the unhappy sixth whose heart had not been able to withstand the power of his Charms. But as it may appear strange to my Readers, that so much worth & Excellence as he possessed should have conquered only hers, it will be necessary to inform them that the Miss Simpsons were defended from his Power by Ambition, Envy, & Self-admiration.

Every wish of Caroline was centered in a titled Husband; whilst in Sukey such superior excellence could only raise her Envy not her Love, & Cecilia was too tenderly attached to herself to be pleased with any one besides. As for Lady Williams and Mrs. Jones, the former of them was too sensible to fall in love with one so much her Junior, and the latter, tho' very tall & very passionate, was too fond of her Husband to think of such a thing.

Yet in spite of every endeavour on the part of Miss Johnson to discover any attachment to her in him, the cold & indifferent heart of Charles Adams still, to all appearance, preserved its native freedom; polite to all but partial to none, he still remained the lovely, the lively, but insensible Charles Adams.

One evening, Alice finding herself somewhat heated by wine (no very uncommon case) determined to seek a relief for her disordered Head & Love-sick Heart in the Conversation of the intelligent Lady Williams.

She found her Ladyship at home, as was in general the Case, for she was not fond of going out, & like the great Sir Charles Grandison scorned to deny herself when at Home, as she looked on that fashionable method of shutting out disagreable Visitors, as little less than downright Bigamy.

In spite of the wine she had been drinking, poor Alice was uncommonly out of spirits; she could think of nothing but Charles Adams, she could talk of nothing but him, & in short spoke so openly that Lady Williams soon discovered the unreturned affection she bore him, which excited her Pity & Compassion so strongly that she addressed her in the following Manner.

"I perceive but too plainly, my dear Miss Johnson, that your Heart has not been able to withstand the fascinating Charms of this young Man & I pity you sincerely. Is it a first Love?"

"It is."

"I am still more greived to hear that; I am myself a sad example of the Miseries in general attendant on a first Love & I am determined for the future to avoid the like Misfortune. I wish it may not be too late for you to do the same; if it is not, endeavour, my dear Girl, to secure yourself from so great a Danger. A second attachment is seldom attended with any serious consequences; against that therefore I have nothing to say. Preserve yourself from a first Love & you need not fear a second."

"You mentioned, Madam, something of your having yourself been a sufferer by the misfortune you are so good as to wish me to avoid. Will you favour me with your Life & Adventures?"

"Willingly, my Love."

Chapter 3

"My Father was a gentleman of considerable Fortune in Berkshire; myself & a few more his only Children. I was but six years old when I had the misfortune of losing my Mother, & being at that time young & Tender, my father, instead of sending me to School, procured an able handed Governess to superintend my Education at Home. My Brothers were placed at Schools suitable to their Ages & my Sisters, being all younger than myself, remained still under the Care of their Nurse.

Miss Dickins was an excellent Governess. She instructed me in the Paths of Virtue; under her tuition I daily became more amiable, & might perhaps by this time have nearly attained perfection, had not my worthy Preceptoress been torn from my arms, e'er I had attained my seventeenth year. I never shall forget her last words. "My dear Kitty" she said, "Good night t'ye." I never saw her afterwards", continued Lady Williams, wiping her eyes, "She eloped with the Butler the same night."

"I was invited the following year by a distant relation of my Father's to spend the Winter with her in town. Mrs. Watkins was a Lady of Fashion, Family, & fortune; she was in general esteemed a pretty Woman, but I never thought her very handsome, for my part. She had too high a forehead, Her eyes were too small, & she had too much colour."

"How can that be?" interrupted Miss Johnson, reddening with anger; "Do you think that any one can have too much colour?"

"Indeed I do, & I'll tell you why I do, my dear Alice; when a person has too great a degree of red in their Complexion, it gives their face, in my opinion, too red a look."

"But can a face, my Lady, have too red a look?"

"Certainly, my dear Miss Johnson, & I'll tell you why. When a face has too red a look it does not appear to so much advantage as it would were it paler."

"Pray Ma'am, proceed in your story."

"Well, as I said before, I was invited by this Lady to spend some weeks with her in town. Many Gentlemen thought her Handsome, but in my opinion, Her forehead was too high, her eyes too small, & she had too much colour."

"In that, Madam, as I said before, your Ladyship must have been mistaken. Mrs. Watkins could not have too much colour, since no one can have too much."

"Excuse me, my Love, if I do not agree with you in that particular. Let me explain myself clearly; my idea of the case is this. When a Woman has too great a proportion of red in her Cheeks, she must have too much colour."

"But Madam, I deny that it is possible for any one to have too great a proportion of red in their Cheeks."

"What, my Love, not if they have too much colour?"

Miss Johnson was now out of all patience, the more so, perhaps, as Lady Williams still remained so inflexibly cool. It must be remembered, however, that her Ladyship had in one respect by far the advantage of Alice; I mean in not being drunk, for heated with wine & raised by Passion, she could have little command of her Temper.

The Dispute at length grew so hot on the part of Alice that, "From Words she almost came to Blows", When Mr. Johnson luckily entered, & with some difficulty forced her away from Lady Williams, Mrs. Watkins, & her red cheeks.

Chapter 4

My Readers may perhaps imagine that after such a fracas, no intimacy could longer subsist between the Johnsons and Lady Williams, but in that they are mistaken; for her Ladyship was too sensible to be angry at a conduct which she could not help perceiving to be the natural consequence of inebriety, & Alice had too sincere a respect for Lady Williams, & too great a relish for her Claret, not to make every concession in her power.

A few days after their reconciliation, Lady Williams called on Miss Johnson to propose a walk in a Citron Grove which led from her Ladyship's pigstye to Charles Adams's Horsepond. Alice was too sensible of Lady Williams's kindness in proposing such a walk, & too much pleased with the prospect of seeing at the end of it a Horsepond of Charles's, not to accept it with visible delight. They had not proceeded far before she was roused from the reflection of the happiness she was going to enjoy, by Lady Williams's thus addressing her.

"I have as yet forborn, my dear Alice, to continue the narrative of my Life, from an unwillingness of recalling to your Memory a scene which (since it reflects on you rather disgrace than credit) had better be forgot than remembered."

Alice had already begun to colour up, & was beginning to speak, when her Ladyship, perceiving her displeasure, continued thus.

"I am afraid, my dear Girl, that I have offended you by what I have just said; I assure you I do not mean to distress you by a retrospection of what cannot now be helped; considering all things, I do not think you so much to blame as many People do; for when a person is in Liquor, there is no answering for what they may do."

"Madam, this is not to be borne; I insist—"

"My dear Girl, don't vex yourself about the matter; I assure you I have entirely forgiven every thing respecting it; indeed I was not angry at the time, because as I saw all along, you were nearly dead drunk. I knew you could not help saying the strange things you did. But I see I distress you; so I will change the subject & desire it may never again be mentioned; remember it is all forgot. I will now pursue my story; but I must insist upon not giving you any description of Mrs. Watkins; it would only be reviving old stories & as you never saw her, it can be nothing to you, if her forehead was too high, her eyes were too small, or if she had too much colour."

"Again! Lady Williams: this is too much!"

So provoked was poor Alice at this renewal of the old story, that I know not what might have been the consequence of it, had not their attention been engaged by another object. A lovely young Woman lying apparently in great pain beneath a Citron-tree, was an object too interesting not to attract their notice. Forgetting their own dispute, they both with simpathizing tenderness advanced towards her & accosted her in these terms.

"You seem, fair Nymph, to be labouring under some misfortune which we shall be happy to releive, if you will inform us what it is. Will you favour us with your Life & adventures?"

"Willingly, Ladies, if you will be so kind as to be seated." They took their places & she thus began.

Chapter 5

"I am a native of North Wales & my Father is one of the most capital Taylors in it. Having a numerous family, he was easily prevailed on by a sister of my Mother's, who is a widow in good circumstances & keeps an alehouse in the next Village to ours, to let her take me & breed me up at her own expence. Accordingly, I have lived with her for the last 8 years of my Life, during which time she provided me with some of the first rate Masters, who taught me all the accomplishments requisite for one of my sex and rank. Under their instructions I learned Dancing, Music, Drawing & various Languages, by which means I became more accomplished than any other Taylor's Daughter in Wales. Never was there a happier creature than I was, till within the last half year—but I should have told you before that the principal Estate in our Neighbourhood belongs to Charles Adams, the owner of the brick House, you see yonder."

"Charles Adams!" exclaimed the astonished Alice; "are you acquainted with Charles Adams?"

"To my sorrow, madam, I am. He came about half a year ago to receive the rents of the Estate I have just mentioned. At that time I first saw him; as you seem, ma'am, acquainted with him, I need not describe to you how charming he is. I could not resist his attractions—"

"Ah! who can," said Alice with a deep sigh.

"My aunt, being in terms of the greatest intimacy with his cook, determined, at my request, to try whether she could discover, by means of her freind, if there were any chance of his returning my affection. For this purpose she went one evening to drink tea with Mrs. Susan, who in the course of Conversation mentioned the goodness of her Place & the Goodness of her Master; upon which my Aunt began pumping her with so much dexterity that in a short time Susan owned, that she did not think her Master would ever marry, "for" (said she) "he has often & often declared to me that his wife, whoever she might be, must possess Youth, Beauty, Birth, Wit, Merit, & Money. I have many a time" (she continued) "endeavoured to reason him out of his resolution & to convince him of the improbability of his ever meeting with such a Lady; but my arguments have had no effect, & he continues as firm in his determination as ever." You may imagine, Ladies, my distress on hearing this; for I was fearfull that tho' possessed of Youth, Beauty, Wit & Merit, & tho' the probable Heiress of my Aunt's House & business, he might think me deficient in Rank, & in being so, unworthy of his hand."

"However I was determined to make a bold push & therefore wrote him a very kind letter, offering him with great tenderness my hand & heart. To this I received an angry & peremptory refusal, but thinking it might be rather the effect of his modesty than any thing else, I pressed him again on the subject. But he never answered any more of my Letters & very soon afterwards left the Country. As soon as I heard of his departure, I wrote to him here, informing him that I should shortly do myself the honour of waiting on him at Pammydiddle, to which I received no answer; therefore, choosing to take Silence for Consent, I left Wales, unknown to my Aunt, & arrived here after a tedious Journey this Morning. On enquiring for his House, I was directed thro' this Wood, to the one you there see. With a heart elated by the expected happiness of beholding him, I entered it, & had proceeded thus far in my progress thro' it, when I found myself suddenly seized by the leg & on examining the cause of it, found that I was caught in one of the steel traps so common in gentlemen's grounds."

"Ah! cried Lady Williams, how fortunate we are to meet with you; since we might otherwise perhaps have shared the like misfortune."

"It is indeed happy for you, Ladies, that I should have been a short time before you. I screamed, as you may easily imagine, till the woods resounded again & till one of the inhuman Wretch's servants came to my assistance & released me from my dreadfull prison, but not before one of my legs was entirely broken."

Chapter 6

At this melancholy recital, the fair eyes of Lady Williams were suffused in tears & Alice could not help exclaiming,

"Oh! cruel Charles, to wound the hearts & legs of all the fair."

Lady Williams now interposed, & observed that the young Lady's leg ought to be set without farther delay. After examining the fracture, therefore, she immediately began & performed the operation with great skill, which was the more wonderfull on account of her having never performed such a one before. Lucy then arose from the ground, & finding that she could walk with the greatest ease, accompanied them to Lady Williams's House at her Ladyship's particular request.

The perfect form, the beautifull face, & elegant manners of Lucy so won on the affections of Alice, that when they parted, which was not till after Supper, she assured her that except her Father, Brother, Uncles, Aunts, Cousins & other relations, Lady Williams, Charles Adams, & a few dozen more of particular freinds, she loved her better than almost any other person in the world.

Such a flattering assurance of her regard would justly have given much pleasure to the object of it, had she not plainly perceived that the amiable Alice had partaken too freely of Lady Williams's claret.

Her Ladyship (whose discernment was great) read in the intelligent countenance of Lucy her thoughts on the subject, & as soon as Miss Johnson had taken her leave, thus addressed her.

"When you are more intimately acquainted with my Alice, you will not be surprised, Lucy, to see the dear Creature drink a little too much; for such things happen every day. She has many rare & charming qualities, but Sobriety is not one of them. The whole Family are indeed a sad drunken set. I am sorry to say too that I never knew three such thorough Gamesters as they are, more particularly Alice. But she is a charming girl. I fancy not one of the sweetest tempers in the world; to be sure I have seen her in such passions! However, she is a sweet young Woman. I am sure you'll like her. I scarcely know any one so amiable. — Oh! that you could but have seen her the other Evening! How she raved! & on such a trifle too! She is indeed a most pleasing Girl! I shall always love her!"

"She appears, by your ladyship's account, to have many good qualities", replied Lucy. "Oh! a thousand," answered Lady Williams; "tho' I am very partial to her, and perhaps am blinded, by my affection, to her real defects."

Chapter 7

The next morning brought the three Miss Simpsons to wait on Lady Williams, who received them with the utmost politeness & introduced to their acquaintance Lucy, with whom the eldest was so much pleased that at parting she declared her sole ambition was to have her accompany them the next morning to Bath, whither they were going for some weeks.

"Lucy," said Lady Williams, "is quite at her own disposal & if she chooses to accept so kind an invitation, I hope she will not hesitate from any motives of delicacy on my account. I know not indeed how I shall ever be able to part with her. She never was at Bath & I should think that it would be a most agreable Jaunt to her. Speak, my Love," continued she, turning to Lucy, "what say you to accompanying these Ladies? I shall be miserable without you—t'will be a most pleasant tour to you—I hope you'll go; if you do I am sure t'will be the Death of me—pray be persuaded."

Lucy begged leave to decline the honour of accompanying them, with many expressions of gratitude for the extream politeness of Miss Simpson in inviting her. Miss Simpson appeared much disappointed by her refusal. Lady Williams insisted on her going—declared that she would never forgive her if she did not, and that she should never survive it if she did, & in short, used such persuasive arguments that it was at length resolved she was to go. The Miss Simpsons called for her at ten o'clock the next morning & Lady Williams had soon the satisfaction of receiving from her young freind the pleasing intelligence of their safe arrival in Bath.

It may now be proper to return to the Hero of this Novel, the brother of Alice, of whom I beleive I have scarcely ever had occasion to speak; which may perhaps be partly oweing to his unfortunate propensity to Liquor, which so compleatly deprived him of the use of those faculties Nature had endowed him with, that he never did anything worth mentioning. His Death happened a short time after Lucy's departure & was the natural Consequence of this pernicious practice. By his decease, his sister became the sole inheritress of a very large fortune, which as it gave her fresh Hopes of rendering herself acceptable as a wife to Charles Adams, could not fail of being most pleasing to her—and as the effect was Joyfull, the Cause could scarcely be lamented.

Finding the violence of her attachment to him daily augment, she at length disclosed it to her Father & desired him to propose a union between them to Charles. Her father consented & set out one morning to open the affair to the young Man. Mr. Johnson being a man of few words, his part was soon performed & the answer he received was as follows.

"Sir, I may perhaps be expected to appear pleased at & gratefull for the offer you have made me: but let me tell you that I consider it as an affront. I look upon myself to be, Sir, a perfect Beauty—where would you see a finer figure or a more charming face? Then, sir, I imagine my Manners & Address to be of the most polished kind; there is a certain elegance, a peculiar sweetness in them that I never saw equalled & cannot describe. Partiality aside, I am certainly more accomplished in every Language, every Science, every Art and every thing than any other person in Europe. My temper is even, my virtues innumerable, my self unparalelled. Since such, Sir, is my character, what do you mean by wishing me to marry your Daughter?

Let me give you a short sketch of yourself & of her. I look upon you, Sir, to be a very good sort of Man in the main; a drunken old Dog to be sure, but that's nothing to me. Your daughter sir, is neither sufficiently beautifull, sufficiently amiable, sufficiently witty, nor sufficiently rich for me. I expect nothing more in my wife than my wife will find in me—Perfection. These, sir, are my sentiments & I honour myself for having such. One freind I have, & glory in having but one. She is at present preparing my Dinner, but if you choose to see her, she shall come & she will inform you that these have ever been my sentiments."

Mr. Johnson was satisfied, & expressing himself to be much obliged to Mr. Adams for the characters he had favoured him with of himself & his Daughter, took his leave.

The unfortunate Alice, on receiving from her father the sad account of the ill success his visit had been attended with, could scarcely support the disappointment. She flew to her Bottle & it was soon forgot.

Chapter 8

While these affairs were transacting at Pammydiddle, Lucy was conquering every Heart at Bath. A fortnight's residence there had nearly effaced from her remembrance the captivating form of Charles. The recollection of what her Heart had formerly suffered by his charms & her Leg by his trap, enabled her to forget him with tolerable Ease, which was what she determined to do; & for that purpose dedicated five minutes in every day to the employment of driving him from her remembrance.

Her second Letter to Lady Williams contained the pleasing intelligence of her having accomplished her undertaking to her entire satisfaction; she mentioned in it also an offer of marriage she had received from the Duke of —, an elderly Man of noble fortune whose ill health was the chief inducement of his Journey to Bath.

"I am distressed" (she continued) "to know whether I mean to accept him or not. There are a thousand advantages to be derived from a marriage with the Duke, for besides those more inferior ones of Rank & Fortune, it will procure me a home, which of all other things is what I most desire. Your Ladyship's kind wish of my always remaining with you is noble & generous, but I cannot think of becoming so great a burden on one I so much love & esteem. That one should receive obligations only from those we despise, is a sentiment instilled into my mind by my worthy aunt, in my early years, & cannot in my opinion be too strictly adhered to. The excellent woman of whom I now speak is, I hear, too much incensed by my imprudent departure from Wales, to receive me again. I most earnestly wish to leave the Ladies I am now with. Miss Simpson is indeed (setting aside ambition) very amiable, but her 2d. Sister, the envious & malvolent Sukey, is too disagreable to live with. I have reason to think that the admiration I have met with in the circles of the Great at this Place, has raised her Hatred & Envy; for often has she threatened, &

sometimes endeavoured to cut my throat. Your Ladyship will therefore allow that I am not wrong in wishing to leave Bath, & in wishing to have a home to receive me, when I do. I shall expect with impatience your advice concerning the Duke & am your most obliged &c.
Lucy."

Lady Williams sent her her opinion on the subject in the following Manner.

"Why do you hesitate, my dearest Lucy, a moment with respect to the Duke? I have enquired into his Character & find him to be an unprincipaled, illiterate Man. Never shall my Lucy be united to such a one! He has a princely fortune, which is every day encreasing. How nobly will you spend it!, what credit will you give him in the eyes of all!, How much will he be respected on his Wife's account! But why, my dearest Lucy, why will you not at once decide this affair by returning to me & never leaving me again? Altho' I admire your noble sentiments with respect to obligations, yet, let me beg that they may not prevent your making me happy. It will, to be sure, be a great expence to me, to have you always with me—I shall not be able to support it—but what is that in comparison with the happiness I shall enjoy in your society? 'Twill ruin me I know—you will not therefore surely, withstand these arguments, or refuse to return to yours most affectionately &c. &c.
C. Williams"

Chapter 9

What might have been the effect of her Ladyship's advice, had it ever been received by Lucy, is uncertain, as it reached Bath a few Hours after she had breathed her last. She fell a sacrifice to the Envy & Malice of Sukey, who jealous of her superior charms, took her by poison from an admiring World at the age of seventeen.

Thus fell the amiable & lovely Lucy, whose Life had been marked by no crime, and stained by no blemish but her imprudent departure from her Aunt's, & whose death was sincerely lamented by every one who knew her. Among the most afflicted of her freinds were Lady Williams, Miss Johnson & the Duke; the 2 first of whom had a most sincere regard for her, more particularly Alice, who had spent a whole evening in her company & had never thought of her since. His Grace's affliction may likewise be easily accounted for, since he lost one for whom he had experienced, during the last ten days, a tender affection & sincere regard. He mourned her loss with unshaken constancy for the next fortnight, at the end of which time, he gratified the ambition of Caroline Simpson by raising her to the rank of a Dutchess. Thus was she at length rendered compleatly happy in the gratification of her favourite passion. Her sister, the perfidious Sukey, was likewise shortly after exalted in a manner she truly deserved, & by her actions appeared to have always desired. Her barbarous Murder was discovered, &

in spite of every interceding freind she was speedily raised to the Gallows. The beautifull but affected Cecilia was too sensible of her own superior charms, not to imagine that if Caroline could engage a Duke, she might without censure aspire to the affections of some Prince—and knowing that those of her native Country were cheifly engaged, she left England & I have since heard is at present the favourite Sultana of the great Mogul.

In the mean time, the inhabitants of Pammydiddle were in a state of the greatest astonishment & Wonder, a report being circulated of the intended marriage of Charles Adams. The Lady's name was still a secret. Mr. & Mrs. Jones imagined it to be Miss Johnson; but she knew better; all her fears were centered in his Cook, when to the astonishment of every one, he was publicly united to Lady Williams.

Finis

Chapter 1

"I cannot imagine," said Sir Godfrey to his Lady, "why we continue in such deplorable Lodgings as these, in a paltry Market-town, while we have 3 good Houses of our own situated in some of the finest parts of England, & perfectly ready to receive us!"

"I'm sure, Sir Godfrey," replied Lady Marlow, "it has been much against my inclination that we have staid here so long; or why we should ever have come at all indeed, has been to me a wonder, as none of our Houses have been in the least want of repair."

"Nay, my dear," answered Sir Godfrey, "you are the last person who ought to be displeased with what was always meant as a compliment to you; for you cannot but be sensible of the very great inconvenience your Daughters & I have been put to, during the 2 years we have remained crowded in these Lodgings in order to give you pleasure."

"My dear," replied Lady Marlow, "How can you stand & tell such lies, when you very well know that it was merely to oblige the Girls & you, that I left a most commodious House situated in a most delightfull Country & surrounded by a most agreable Neighbourhood, to live 2 years cramped up in Lodgings three pair of Stairs high, in a smokey & unwholesome town, which has given me a continual fever & almost thrown me into a Consumption."

As, after a few more speeches on both sides, they could not determine which was the most to blame, they prudently laid aside the debate, & having packed up their Cloathes & paid their rent, they set out the next morning with their 2 Daughters for their seat in Sussex.

Sir Godfrey & Lady Marlow were indeed very sensible people & tho' (as in this instance) like many other sensible People, they sometimes did a foolish thing, yet in general their actions were guided by Prudence & regulated by discretion.

After a Journey of two Days & a half they arrived at Marlhurst in good health & high spirits; so overjoyed were they all to inhabit again a place, they had left with mutual regret for two years, that they ordered the bells to be rung & distributed ninepence among the Ringers.

Chapter 2

The news of their arrival being quickly spread throughout the Country, brought them in a few Days visits of congratulation from every family in it.

Amongst the rest came the inhabitants of Willmot Lodge a beautifull Villa not far from Marlhurst. Mr. Willmot was the representative of a very ancient Family & possessed besides his paternal Estate, a considerable share in a Lead mine & a ticket in the Lottery. His Lady was an agreable Woman. Their Children were too numerous to be particularly described; it is sufficient to say that in general they were virtuously inclined & not given to any wicked ways. Their family being too large to accompany them in every visit, they took nine with them alternately. When their Coach stopped at Sir Godfrey's door, the Miss Marlow's Hearts throbbed in the eager expectation of once more beholding a family so dear to them. Emma the youngest (who was more particularly interested in their arrival, being attached to their eldest Son) continued at her Dressing-room window in anxious Hopes of seeing young Edgar descend from the Carriage.

Mr. & Mrs. Willmot with their three eldest Daughters first appeared—Emma began to tremble. Robert, Richard, Ralph, & Rodolphus followed—Emma turned pale. Their two youngest Girls were lifted from the Coach—Emma sunk breathless on a Sopha. A footman came to announce to her the arrival of Company; her heart was too full to contain its afflictions. A confidante was necessary. In Thomas she hoped to experience a faithfull one—for one she must have & Thomas was the only one at Hand. To him she unbosomed herself without restraint & after owning her passion for young Willmot, requested his advice in what manner she should conduct herself in the melancholy Disappointment under which she laboured.

Thomas, who would gladly have been excused from listening to her complaint, begged leave to decline giving any advice concerning it, which much against her will, she was obliged to comply with.

Having dispatched him therefore with many injunctions of secrecy, she descended with a heavy heart into the Parlour, where she found the good Party seated in a social Manner round a blazing fire.

Chapter 3

Emma had continued in the Parlour some time before she could summon up sufficient courage to ask Mrs. Willmot after the rest of her family; & when she did, it was in so low, so faltering a voice that no one knew she spoke. Dejected by the ill success of her first attempt she made no other, till on Mrs. Willmot's desiring one of the little Girls to ring the bell for their Carriage, she stepped across the room & seizing the string said in a resolute manner.

"Mrs. Willmot, you do not stir from this House till you let me know how all the rest of your family do, particularly your eldest son."

They were all greatly surprised by such an unexpected address & the more so, on account of the manner in which it was spoken; but Emma, who would not be again disappointed, requesting an answer, Mrs. Willmot made the following eloquent oration.

"Our children are all extremely well but at present most of them from home. Amy is with my sister Clayton. Sam at Eton. David with his Uncle John. Jem & Will at Winchester. Kitty at Queen's Square. Ned with his Grandmother. Hetty & Patty in a Convent at Brussells. Edgar at college, Peter at Nurse, & all the rest (except the nine here) at home."

It was with difficulty that Emma could refrain from tears on hearing of the absence of Edgar; she remained however tolerably composed till the Willmots were gone when having no check to the overflowings of her greif, she gave free vent to them, & retiring to her own room, continued in tears the remainder of her Life. Finis

Henry and Eliza

A Novel

Is humbly dedicated to Miss Cooper by her obedient Humble Servant.
The Author

As Sir George and Lady Harcourt were superintending the Labours of their Haymakers, rewarding the industry of some by smiles of approbation, & punishing the idleness of others by a cudgel, they perceived lying closely concealed beneath the thick foliage of a Haycock, a beautifull little Girl not more than 3 months old.

Touched with the enchanting Graces of her face & delighted with the infantine tho' sprightly answers she returned to their many questions, they resolved to take her home &, having no Children of their own, to educate her with care & cost.

Being good People themselves, their first & principal care was to incite in her a Love of Virtue & a Hatred of Vice, in which they so well succeeded (Eliza having a natural turn that way herself) that when she grew up, she was the delight of all who knew her.

Beloved by Lady Harcourt, adored by Sir George & admired by all the World, she lived in a continued course of uninterrupted Happiness, till she had attained her eighteenth year, when happening one day to be detected in stealing a banknote of 50£, she was turned out of doors by her inhuman Benefactors. Such a transition, to one who did not possess so noble & exalted a mind as Eliza, would have been Death, but she, happy in the conscious knowledge of her own Excellence, amused herself as she sat beneath a tree with making & singing the following Lines.

Song
Though misfortunes my footsteps may ever attend
   I hope I shall never have need of a Freind
as an innocent Heart I will ever preserve
   and will never from Virtue's dear boundaries swerve.

Having amused herself some hours, with this song & her own pleasing reflections, she arose & took the road to M—, a small market town, of which place her most intimate freind kept the Red Lion.

To this freind she immediately went, to whom having recounted her late misfortune, she communicated her wish of getting into some family in the capacity of Humble Companion.

Mrs. Wilson, who was the most amiable creature on earth, was no sooner acquainted with her Desire, than she sat down in the Bar & wrote the following Letter to the Dutchess of F—, the woman whom of all others she most Esteemed.

To the Dutchess of F—
Receive into your Family, at my request, a young woman of unexceptionable
Character, who is so good as to choose your Society in preference to going to
Service. Hasten, & take her from the arms of your

Sarah Wilson.

The Dutchess, whose freindship for Mrs. Wilson would have carried her any lengths, was overjoyed at such an opportunity of obliging her, & accordingly sate out immediately on the receipt of her letter for the Red Lion, which she reached the same Evening. The Dutchess of F— was about 45 & a half; Her passions were strong, her freindships firm, & her Enmities unconquerable. She was a widow & had only one Daughter, who was on the point of marriage with a young Man of considerable fortune.

The Dutchess no sooner beheld our Heroine than throwing her arms around her neck, she declared herself so much pleased with her, that she was resolved they never more should part. Eliza was delighted with such a protestation of freindship, & after taking a most affecting leave of her dear Mrs. Wilson, accompanied her grace the next morning to her seat in Surry.

With every expression of regard did the Dutchess introduce her to Lady Harriet, who was so much pleased with her appearance that she besought her, to consider her as her Sister, which Eliza with the greatest Condescension promised to do.

Mr. Cecil, the Lover of Lady Harriet, being often with the family was often with Eliza. A mutual Love took place & Cecil having declared his first, prevailed on Eliza to consent to a private union, which was easy to be effected, as the dutchess's chaplain being very much in love with Eliza himself, would, they were certain, do anything to oblige her.

The Dutchess & Lady Harriet being engaged one evening to an assembly, they took the opportunity of their absence & were united by the enamoured Chaplain.

When the Ladies returned, their amazement was great at finding instead of Eliza the following Note.

Madam,
We are married & gone.
Henry & Eliza Cecil

Her Grace, as soon as she had read the letter, which sufficiently explained the whole affair, flew into the most violent passion & after having spent an agreable half hour, in calling them by all the shocking Names her rage could suggest to her, sent out after them 300 armed Men, with orders not to return without their Bodies, dead or alive; intending that if they should be brought to her in the latter condition to have them put to Death in some torturelike manner, after a few years Confinement.

In the mean time, Cecil & Eliza continued their flight to the Continent, which they judged to be more secure than their native Land, from the dreadfull effects of the Dutchess's vengeance which they had so much reason to apprehend.

In France they remained 3 years, during which time they became the parents of two Boys, & at the end of it Eliza became a widow without any thing to support either her or her Children. They had lived since their Marriage at the rate of 18,000£ a year, of which Mr. Cecil's estate being rather less than the twentieth part, they had been able to save but a trifle, having lived to the utmost extent of their Income.

Eliza, being perfectly conscious of the derangement in their affairs, immediately on her Husband's death set sail for England, in a man of War of 55 Guns, which they had built in their more prosperous Days. But no sooner had she stepped on Shore at Dover, with a Child in each hand, than she was seized by the officers of the Dutchess, & conducted by them to a snug little Newgate of their Lady's, which she had erected for the reception of her own private Prisoners.

No sooner had Eliza entered her Dungeon than the first thought which occurred to her, was how to get out of it again.

She went to the Door; but it was locked. She looked at the Window; but it was barred with iron; disappointed in both her expectations, she dispaired of effecting her Escape, when she fortunately perceived in a Corner of her Cell, a small saw & Ladder of ropes. With the saw she instantly went to work & in a few weeks had displaced every Bar but one to which she fastened the Ladder.

A difficulty then occurred which for some time, she knew not how to obviate. Her Children were too small to get down the Ladder by themselves, nor would it be possible for her to take them in her arms when she did. At last she determined to fling down all her Cloathes, of which she had a large Quantity, & then having given them strict Charge not to hurt themselves, threw her Children after them. She herself with ease discended by the Ladder, at the bottom of which she had the pleasure of finding her little boys in perfect Health & fast asleep.

Her wardrobe she now saw a fatal necessity of selling, both for the preservation of her Children & herself. With tears in her eyes, she parted with these last reliques of her former Glory, & with the money she got for them, bought others more usefull, some playthings for Her Boys, and a gold Watch for herself.

But scarcely was she provided with the above-mentioned necessaries, than she began to find herself rather hungry, & had reason to think, by their biting off two of her fingers, that her Children were much in the same situation.

To remedy these unavoidable misfortunes, she determined to return to her old freinds, Sir George & Lady Harcourt, whose generosity she had so often experienced & hoped to experience as often again.

She had about 40 miles to travel before she could reach their hospitable Mansion, of which having walked 30 without stopping, she found herself at the Entrance of a Town, where often in happier times, she had accompanied Sir George & Lady Harcourt to regale themselves with a cold collation at one of the Inns.

The reflections that her adventures since the last time she had partaken of these happy Junketings afforded her, occupied her mind, for some time, as she sat on the steps at the door of a Gentleman's house. As soon as these reflections were ended, she arose & determined to take her station at the very inn she remembered with so much delight, from the Company of which, as they went in & out, she hoped to receive some Charitable Gratuity.

She had but just taken her post at the Inn yard before a Carriage drove out of it, & on turning the Corner at which she was stationed, stopped to give the Postilion an opportunity of admiring the beauty of the prospect. Eliza then advanced to the carriage & was going to request their Charity, when on fixing her Eyes on the Lady, within it, she exclaimed,

"Lady Harcourt!"

To which the lady replied, "Eliza!"

"Yes Madam, it is the wretched Eliza herself."

Sir George, who was also in the Carriage, but too much amazed to speek, was proceeding to demand an explanation from Eliza of the Situation she was then in, when Lady Harcourt in transports of Joy, exclaimed.

"Sir George, Sir George, she is not only Eliza our adopted Daughter, but our real Child."

"Our real Child! What, Lady Harcourt, do you mean? You know you never even was with child. Explain yourself, I beseech you."

"You must remember, Sir George, that when you sailed for America, you left me breeding."

"I do, I do, go on, dear Polly."

"Four months after you were gone, I was delivered of this Girl, but dreading your just resentment at her not proving the Boy you wished, I took her to a Haycock & laid her down. A few weeks afterwards, you returned, & fortunately for me, made no enquiries on the subject. Satisfied within myself of the wellfare of my Child, I soon forgot I had one, insomuch that when we shortly after found her in the very Haycock I had placed her, I had no more idea of her being my own, than you had, & nothing, I will venture to say, would have recalled the circumstance to my remembrance, but my thus accidentally hearing her voice, which now strikes me as being the very counterpart of my own Child's."

"The rational & convincing Account you have given of the whole affair," said Sir George, "leaves no doubt of her being our Daughter & as such I freely forgive the robbery she was guilty of."

A mutual Reconciliation then took place, & Eliza, ascending the Carriage with her two Children, returned to that home from which she had been absent nearly four years.

No sooner was she reinstated in her accustomed power at Harcourt Hall, than she raised an Army, with which she entirely demolished the Dutchess's Newgate, snug as it was, and by that act, gained the Blessings of thousands, & the Applause of her own Heart.

Finis

THE ADVENTURES OF MR. HARLEY

A short, but interesting Tale, is with all imaginable Respect inscribed to Mr. Francis William Austen Midshipman on board his Majesty's Ship the Perseverance by his Obedient Servant.
The Author

Mr. Harley was one of many Children. Destined by his father for the Church & by his Mother for the Sea, desirous of pleasing both, he prevailed on Sir John to obtain for him a Chaplaincy on board a Man of War. He accordingly cut his Hair and sailed.

In half a year he returned & set-off in the Stage Coach for Hogsworth Green, the seat of Emma. His fellow travellers were, A man without a Hat, Another with two, An old maid, & a young Wife.

This last appeared about 17, with fine dark Eyes & an elegant Shape; in short, Mr. Harley soon found out that she was his Emma & recollected he had married her a few weeks before he left England.

Sir William Mountague

Sir William Mountague was the son of Sir Henry Mountague, who was the son of Sir John Mountague, a descendant of Sir Christopher Mountague, whose ancestor was Sir James Mountague, a near relation of Sir Robert Mountague, who inherited the Title and Estate from Sir Frederic Mountague.

Sir William as about 17 when his Father died, and left him a handsome fortune, an ancient House and a Park well stocked with Deer. Sir William had not been long in the possession of this Estate before he fell in Love with the 3 Miss Cliftons of Kilhoobery Park. These young Ladies were all equally young, equally handsome, equally rich and equally admirable—Sir William was equally in Love with them all, and knowing not which to prefer, he left the Country and took Lodgings in a small Village near Dover.

In this retreat, to which he had retired in the hope of finding a shelter from the Pangs of Love, he became enamoured of a young Widow of Quality, who came for a change of air to the same Village, after the death of a Husband, who she had always tenderly loved and now sincerely lamented.

Lady Percival was young, accomplished and lovely. Sir William adored her and she consented to become his Wife. Vehemently pressed by Sir William to name the day in which he might conduct her to the Alter, she at length fixed on the following Monday, which was the first of September.

Sir William was a Shot and could not support the idea of losing such a Day, even for such a Cause. He begged her to delay the Wedding a short time. Lady Percival was enraged and returned to London the next Morning.

Sir William was sorry to lose her, but as he knew that he should have been much more greived by the Loss of the 1st of September, his Sorrow was not without a mixture of Happiness, and his Affliction was considerably lessened by his Joy.

After staying at the Village a few weeks longer, he left it and went to a freind's House in Surry. Mr Brudenell was a sensible Man, and had a beautifull Neice with whom Sir William soon fell in love. But Miss Arundel was cruel; and she preferred a Mr. Stanhope; Sir William shot Mr. Stanhope; the lady had then no reason to refuse him; she accepted him, and they were to be married on the 27th of October.

But on the 25th Sir William received a visit from Emma Stanhope, the sister of the unfortunate Victim of his rage. She begged some recompence, some atonement for the cruel Murder of her Brother. Sir William bade her name her price. She fixed on 14 shillings. Sir

William offered her himself and Fortune. They went to London the next day and were there privately married.

For a fortnight Sir William was compleatly happy, but chancing one day to see a charming young Woman entering a Chariot in Brook Street, he became again most violently in love. On enquiring the name of this fair Unknown, he found that she was the Sister of his old freind Lady Percival, at which he was much rejoiced, as he hoped to have, by his acquaintance with her Ladyship, free access to Miss Wentworth...

MEMIORS OF MR. CLIFFORD

An Unfinished Tale

To Charles John Austen Esqre.

Sir,
Your generous patronage of the unfinished tale I have already taken the Liberty of dedicating to you, encourages me to dedicate to you a second, as unfinished as the first.
I am Sir with every expression of regard for you and yr noble Family, your most obedt &c. &c...
The Author

Mr. Clifford lived at Bath; and having never seen London, set off one Monday morning determined to feast his eyes with a sight of that great Metropolis. He travelled in his Coach and Four, for he was a very rich young Man and kept a great many Carriages of which I do not recollect half. I can only remember that he had a Coach, a Chariot, a Chaise, a Landeau, a Landeaulet, a Phaeton, a Gig, a Whisky, an Italian Chair, a Buggy, a Curricle & a wheelbarrow. He had likewise an amazing fine stud of Horses. To my knowledge he had six Greys, 4 Bays, eight Blacks and a poney.

In his Coach & 4 Bays, Mr. Clifford sate forward about 5 o'clock on Monday Morning the 1st of May for London. He always travelled remarkably expeditiously and contrived therefore to get to Devizes from Bath, which is no less than nineteen miles, the first Day. To be sure he did not Set in till eleven at night and pretty tight work it was, as you may imagine.

However when he was once got to Devizes he was determined to comfort himself with a good hot Supper and therefore ordered a whole Egg to be boiled for him and his Servants. The next morning he pursued his Journey and in the course of 3 days hard labour reached Overton where he was seized with a dangerous fever the Consequence of too violent Exercise.

Five months did our Hero remain in this celebrated City under the care of its no less celebrated Physician, who at length compleatly cured him of his troublesome Desease.

As Mr. Clifford still continued very weak, his first Day's Journey carried him only to Dean Gate where he remained a few Days and found himself much benefited by the change of Air.

In easy Stages he proceeded to Basingstoke. One day Carrying him to Clarkengreen, the next to Worting, the 3d to the bottom of Basingstoke Hill, and the fourth to Mr. Robins's...

THE BEAUTIFULL CASSANDRA

A Novel in Twelve Chapters

Dedicated by permission to Miss Austen.

Madam

You are a Phoenix. Your taste is refined, your Sentiments are noble, & your Virtues innumerable. Your Person is lovely, your Figure, elegant, & your Form, magestic. Your Manners are polished, your Conversation is rational & your appearance singular. If, therefore, the following Tale will afford one moment's amusement to you, every wish will be gratified of Your most obedient humble servant.

The Author

Chapter 1

Cassandra was the Daughter & the only Daughter of a celebrated Millener in Bond Street. Her father was of noble Birth, being the near relation of the Dutchess of —'s Butler.

Chapter 2

When Cassandra had attained her 16th year, she was lovely & amiable, & chancing to fall in love with an elegant Bonnet her Mother had just compleated, bespoke by the Countess of —, she placed it on her gentle Head & walked from her Mother's shop to make her Fortune.

Chapter 3

The first person she met, was the Viscount of —, a young Man, no less celebrated for his Accomplishments & Virtues, than for his Elegance & Beauty. She curtseyed & walked on.

Chapter 4

She then proceeded to a Pastry-cook's, where she devoured six ices, refused to pay for them, knocked down the Pastry Cook & walked away.

Chapter 5

She next ascended a Hackney Coach & ordered it to Hampstead, where she was no sooner arrived than she ordered the Coachman to turn round & drive her back again.

Chapter 6

Being returned to the same spot of the same Street she had set out from, the Coachman demanded his Pay.

Chapter 7

She searched her pockets over again & again; but every search was unsuccessfull. No money could she find. The man grew peremptory. She placed her bonnet on his head & ran away.

Chapter 8

Thro' many a street she then proceeded & met in none the least Adventure, till on turning a Corner of Bloomsbury Square, she met Maria.

Chapter 9

Cassandra started & Maria seemed surprised; they trembled, blushed, turned pale & passed each other in a mutual silence.

Chapter 10

Cassandra was next accosted by her freind the Widow, who squeezing out her little Head thro' her less window, asked her how she did? Cassandra curtseyed & went on.

Chapter 11

A quarter of a mile brought her to her paternal roof in Bond Street, from which she had now been absent nearly 7 hours.

Chapter 12

She entered it & was pressed to her Mother's bosom by that worthy Woman. Cassandra smiled & whispered to herself, "This is a day well spent." Finis

AMELIA WEBSTER

An interesting & well written Tale is dedicated by Permission to Mrs Austen
by Her humble Servant.
The Author

Letter the 1st

To Miss Webster

My Dear Amelia,

You will rejoice to hear of the return of my amiable Brother from abroad. He arrived on thursday, & never did I see a finer form, save that of your sincere freind.

Matilda Hervey

Letter the 2nd

To H. Beverley Esqre.

Dear Beverley,

I arrived here last thursday & met with a hearty reception from my Father, Mother, & Sisters. The latter are both fine Girls—particularly Maud, who I think would suit you as a Wife well enough. What say you to this? She will have two thousand Pounds & as much more as you can get. If you don't marry her you will mortally offend

George Hervey

Letter the 3rd

To Miss Hervey

Dear Maud,

Beleive me, I'm happy to hear of your Brother's arrival. I have a thousand things to tell you, but my paper will only permit me to add that I am yr. affect. Freind

Amelia Webster

Letter the 4th

To Miss S. Hervey

Dear Sally,

I have found a very convenient old hollow oak to put our Letters in; for you know we have long maintained a private Correspondence. It is about a mile from my House & seven from yours. You may perhaps imagine that I might have made choice of a tree which would have divided the Distance more equally. I was sensible of this at the time, but as I considered that the walk would be of benefit to you in your weak & uncertain state of Health, I preferred it to one nearer your House, & am yr. faithfull

Benjamin Bar

Letter the 5th

To Miss Hervey

Dear Maud,

I write now to inform you that I did not stop at your house in my way to Bath last Monday. I have many things to inform you of besides; but my Paper reminds me of concluding; & beleive me yrs. ever &c.

Amelia Webster

Letter the 6th

To Miss Webster

Saturday

Madam,

An humble Admirer now addresses you. I saw you, lovely Fair one, as you passed on Monday last, before our House in your way to Bath. I saw you thro' a telescope, & was so struck by your Charms that from that time to this I have not tasted human food.

George Hervey

Letter the 7th

To Jack

As I was this morning at Breakfast the Newspaper was brought me, & in the list of Marriages I read the following.

"George Hervey Esqre. to Miss Amelia Webster"
"Henry Beverley Esqre. to Miss Hervey"
& "
Benjamin Bar Esqre. to Miss Sarah Hervey".

yours,
Tom

Finis

THE VISIT
A Comedy in 2 Acts

To the Revd. James Austen
Sir,
The following Drama, which I humbly recommend to your Protection & Patronage, tho' inferior to those celebrated Comedies called "The School for Jealousy" & "The Travelled Man", will I hope afford some amusement to so respectable a Curate as yourself; which was the end in veiw when it was first composed by your Humble Servant.
The Author

Dramatis Personae

Men
Sir Arthur Hampton
Lord Fitzgerald
Stanly
Willoughby, Sir Arthur's nephew

Women
Lady Hampton
Miss Fitzgerald
Sophy Hampton
Cloe Willoughby

Location: The scenes are laid in Lord Fitzgerald's House.

Act the First

Scene the first

a Parlour

enter LORD FITZGERALD and STANLY

Stanly: Cousin, your servant.

Fitzgerald: Stanly, good morning to you. I hope you slept well last night.

Stanly: Remarkably well, I thank you.

Fitzgerald: I am afraid you found your Bed too short. It was bought in my Grandmother's time, who was herself a very short woman & made a point of suiting all her Beds to her own length, as she never wished to have any company in the House, on account of an unfortunate impediment in her speech, which she was sensible of being very disagreable to her inmates.

Stanly: Make no more excuses, dear Fitzgerald.

Fitzgerald: I will not distress you by too much civility — I only beg you will consider yourself as much at home as in your Father's house. Remember, "The more free, the more Wellcome."

exit FITZGERALD

Stanly: Amiable Youth!
     "Your virtues, could he imitate
     How happy would be Stanly's fate!"

exit STANLY

Scene the 2d.

STANLY and MISS FITZGERALD, discovered.

Stanly: What Company is it you expect to dine with you to Day, Cousin?

Miss F.: Sir Arthur & Lady Hampton; their Daughter, Nephew & Neice.

Stanly: Miss Hampton & her Cousin are both Handsome, are they not?

Miss F.: Miss Willoughby is extreamly so. Miss Hampton is a fine Girl, but not equal to her.

Stanly: Is not your Brother attached to the Latter?

Miss F.: He admires her, I know, but I beleive nothing more. Indeed I have heard him say that she was the most beautifull, pleasing, & amiable Girl in the world, & that of all others he should prefer her for his Wife. But it never went any farther, I'm certain.

Stanly: And yet my Cousin never says a thing he does not mean.

Miss F.: Never. From his Cradle he has always been a strict adherent to Truth.

Exeunt Severally

End of the First Act.

Act the Second

Scene the first
The Drawing Room

Chairs set round in a row. LORD FITZGERALD, MISS FITZGERALD & STANLY seated.
Enter a Servant.

Servant: Sir Arthur & Lady Hampton. Miss Hampton, Mr. & Miss Willoughby.

Exit SERVANT
Enter the Company.

Miss F.: I hope I have the pleasure of seeing your Ladyship well. Sir Arthur, your servant. Yrs., Mr. Willoughby. Dear Sophy, Dear Cloe, —

They pay their Compliments alternately.
Miss F.: Pray be seated.

They sit

Miss F.: Bless me! there ought to be 8 Chairs & there are but 6. However, if your Ladyship will but take Sir Arthur in your Lap, & Sophy my Brother in hers, I beleive we shall do pretty well.
Lady H.: Oh! with pleasure... .
Sophy: I beg his Lordship would be seated.

Miss F.: I am really shocked at crouding you in such a manner, but my Grandmother (who bought all the furniture of this room) as she had never a very large Party, did not think it necessary to buy more Chairs than were sufficient for her own family and two of her particular freinds.

Sophy: I beg you will make no apologies. Your Brother is very light.

Stanly: *(aside)* What a cherub is Cloe!

Cloe: *(aside)* What a seraph is Stanly!

Enter a Servant.

Servant: Dinner is on table.

They all rise.

Miss F.: Lady Hampton, Miss Hampton, Miss Willoughby.

STANLY hands CLOE; LORD FITZGERALD, SOPHY; WILLOUGHBY, MISS FITZGERALD; and SIR ARTHUR, LADY HAMPTON

Exeunt.

Scene the 2d.

The Dining Parlour

MISS FITZGERALD at top. LORD FITZGERALD at bottom. Company ranged on each side. Servants waiting.

Cloe: I shall trouble Mr. Stanly for a Little of the fried Cow heel & Onion.

Stanly: Oh Madam, there is a secret pleasure in helping so amiable a Lady.

Lady H.: I assure you, my Lord, Sir Arthur never touches wine; but Sophy will toss off a bumper I am sure, to oblige your Lordship.

Lord F.: Elder wine or Mead, Miss Hampton?

Sophy: If it is equal to you, Sir, I should prefer some warm ale with a toast and nutmeg.

Lord F.: Two glasses of warmed ale with a toast and nutmeg.

Miss F.: I am afraid, Mr. Willoughby, you take no care of yourself. I fear you don't meet with any thing to your liking.

Willoughby: Oh! Madam, I can want for nothing while there are red herrings on table.

Lord F.: Sir Arthur, taste that Tripe. I think you will not find it amiss.

Lady H.: Sir Arthur never eats Tripe; tis too savoury for him, you know, my Lord.

Miss F.: Take away the Liver & Crow, & bring in the suet pudding.

a short Pause.

Miss F.: Sir Arthur, shan't I send you a bit of pudding?

Lady H.: Sir Arthur never eats suet pudding, Ma'am. It is too high a Dish for him.

Miss F.: Will no one allow me the honour of helping them? Then John, take away the Pudding, & bring the Wine.

SERVANTS take away the things and bring in the Bottles & Glasses.

Lord F.: I wish we had any Desert to offer you. But my Grandmother in her Lifetime, destroyed the Hothouse in order to build a receptacle for the Turkies with its materials; & we have never been able to raise another tolerable one.

Lady H.: I beg you will make no apologies, my Lord.

Willoughby: Come Girls, let us circulate the Bottle.

Sophy: A very good notion, Cousin; & I will second it with all my Heart. Stanly, you don't drink.

Stanly: Madam, I am drinking draughts of Love from Cloe's eyes.

Sophy: That's poor nourishment truly. Come, drink to her better acquaintance.

MISS FITZGERALD goes to a Closet & brings out a bottle

Miss F.: This, Ladies & Gentlemen, is some of my dear Grandmother's own manufacture. She excelled in Gooseberry Wine. Pray taste it, Lady Hampton

Lady H.: How refreshing it is!

Miss F.: I should think, with your Ladyship's permission, that Sir Arthur might taste a little of it.

Lady H.: Not for Worlds. Sir Arthur never drinks any thing so high.

Lord F.: And now my amiable Sophia, condescend to marry me.

He takes her hand & leads her to the front

Stanly: Oh! Cloe, could I but hope you would make me blessed—

Cloe: I will.

They advance.

Miss F.: Since you, Willoughby, are the only one left, I cannot refuse your earnest solicitations—There is my Hand.

Lady H.: And may you all be Happy!

Finis

The Mystery

An Unfinished Comedy

To the Revd George Austen

Sir,

I humbly solicit your Patronage to the following Comedy, which tho' an unfinished one is, I flatter myself, as complete a Mystery as any of its kind.
I am Sir your most Humble Servant.
The Author

Dramatis Personae

Men:
Colonel Elliott
Sir Edward Spangle
Old Humbug
Yong Humbug, and
Corydon

Women:
Fanny Elliott
Mrs. Humbug, and
Daphne

Act the First

Scene the First
A Garden.

Enter CORYDON.

Cory: But Hush! I am interrupted.

Exit CORYDON.
Enter OLD HUMBUG and his SON, talking.

Old Hum: It is for that reason I wish you to follow my advice. Are you convinced of it's propriety?
Young Hum: I am, Sir, and will certainly manner what you have pointed out to me.
Old Hum: Then let us return to the House.

Exeunt.

Scene the Second
A Parlour in Humbug's House.

MRS. HUMBUG and FANNY, discovered at work.

Mrs. Hum: You understand me, my Love?

Fanny: Perfectly ma'am. Pray continue your narration.

Mrs. Hum: Alas! It is nearly concluded, for I have nothing more to say on the Subject.

Enter DAPHNE.

Daphne: My dear Mrs. Humbug, how d'ye do? Oh! Fanny, t'is all over.

Fanny: It is indeed!

Mrs. Hum: I'm very sorry to hear it.

Fanny: Then t'was to no purpose that I...

Daphne: None upon Earth.

Mrs. Hum: And what is to become of...

Daphne: Oh! That's all settled.

Whispers to MRS. HUMBUG

Fanny: And how is it determined?

Daphne: I'll tell you.

Whispers to FANNY.

Mrs. Hum: And is he to...

Daphne: I'll tell you all I know of the matter.

Whispers MRS. HUMBUG and FANNY.

Fanny: Well! Now I know everything about it, I'll go away.

Mrs. Hum and Daphne: And so will I.

Exeunt.

Scene the Third

The Curtain rises and discovers Sir Edward Spangle reclined in an elegant Attitude on a Sofa, fast asleep.

Enter COLONEL ELLIOTT.

Colonel: My Daughter is not here I see.... There lies Sir Edward.... Shall I tell him the secret?... No, he'll certainly blab it.... But he is asleep and won't hear me.... So I'll e'en venture.

Goes up to SIR EDWARD, whispers to him, and exits.

THE THREE SISTERS

To Edward Austen Esquire

The following unfinished Novel is respectfully inscribed by his obedient humble servant.
The Author

Letter the 1st

Miss Stanhope to Mrs. —

My Dear Fanny,
I am the happiest creature in the World, for I have received an offer of marriage from Mr. Watts. It is the first I have ever had, and I hardly know how to value it enough. How I will triumph over the Duttons! I do not intend to accept it, at least I beleive not, but as I am not quite certain, I gave him an equivocal answer and left him. And now my dear Fanny, I want your Advice whether I should accept his offer or not; but that you may be able to judge of his merits and the situation of affairs, I will give you an account of them. He is quite an old Man, about two and thirty, very plain, so plain that I cannot bear to look at him. He is extremely disagreable and I hate him more than any body else in the world. He has a large fortune and will make great Settlements on me; but then his is very healthy. In short, I do not know what to do. If I refuse him, he as good as told me that he should offer himself to Sophia, and if she refused him, to Georgiana, and I could not bear to have either of them married before me. If I accept him I know I shall be miserable all the rest of my Life, for he is very ill tempered and peevish, extremely jealous, and so stingy that there is no living in the house with him. He told me he should mention the affair to Mama, but I insisted upon it that he did not, for very likely she would make me marry him whether I would or no; however probably he has before now, for he never does anything he is desired to do. I believe I shall have him. It will be such a triumph to be married before Sophy, Georgiana, and the Duttons; And he promised to have a new Carriage on the occasion, but we almost quarrelled about the colour, for I insisted upon its being blue spotted with silver, and he declared it should be a plain Chocolate; and to provoke me more, said it should be just as low as his old one. I won't have him, I declare. He said he should come again tomorrow and take my final answer, so I beleive I must get him while I can. I know the Duttons will envy me and I shall be able to chaperone Sophy and Georgiana to all the Winter Balls. But then, what will be the use of that when very likely he won't let me go myself, for I know he hates dancing, and what he hates himself he has no idea of any other person's liking; and besides he talks a great deal of Women's always staying at home and such stuff. I beleive I shan't have him; I would refuse him at once if I were certain that neither of my

Sisters would accept him, and that if they did not, he would not offer to the Duttons. I cannot run such a risk, so, if he will promise to have the Carriage ordered as I like, I will have him; if not he may ride in it by himself for me. I hope you like my determination; I can think of nothing better; And am your ever Affectionate

Mary Stanhope

Letter the 2nd

From the same to the same

Dear Fanny,

I had but just sealed my last letter to you, when my Mother came up and told me she wanted to speak to me on a very particular subject.

"Ah! I know what you mean; (said I) That old fool Mr. Watts has told you all about it, tho' I bid him not. However you shan't force me to have him if I don't like it."

"I am not going to force you, Child, but only want to know what your resolution is with regard to his Proposals, and to insist upon your making up your mind one way or t'other, that if you don't accept him, Sophy may."

"Indeed (replied I hastily) Sophy need not trouble herself, for I shall certainly marry him myself."

"If that is your resolution (said my Mother) why should you be afraid of my forcing your inclinations?"

"Why, because I have not settled whether I shall have him or not."

"You are the strangest Girl in the World, Mary. What you say one moment, you unsay the next. Do tell me once for all, whether you intend to marry Mr. Watts or not."

"Law! Mama, how can I tell you what I don't know myself?"

"Then I desire you will know, and quickly too, for Mr. Watts says he won't be kept in suspense."

"That depends upon me."

"No it does not, for if you do not give him your final answer tomorrow when he drinks Tea with us, he intends to pay his Addresses to Sophy."

"Then I shall tell all the World that he behaved very ill to me."

"What good will that do? Mr. Watts has been too long abused by all the World to mind it now."

"I wish I had a Father or a Brother, because then they should fight him."

"They would be cunning if they did, for Mr. Watts would run away first; and therefore you must and shall resolve either to accept or refuse him before tomorrow evening."

"But why, if I don't have him, must he offer to my Sisters?"

"Why! because he wishes to be allied to the Family, and because they are as pretty as you are." "But will Sophy marry him, Mama, if he offers to her?"

"Most likely; Why should not she? If, however, she does not choose it, then Georgiana must, for I am determined not to let such an opportunity escape of settling one of my Daughters so advantageously. So make the most of your time, I leave you to settle the Matter with yourself." And then she went away. The only thing I can think of, my dear Fanny, is to ask Sophy and Georgiana whether they would have him were he to make proposals to them, and if they say they would not, I am resolved to refuse him too, for I hate him more than you can imagine. As for the Duttons, if he marries one of them, I shall still have the triumph of having refused him first. So, adeiu my dear Friend.

Yours ever,
M. S.

Letter the 3rd

Miss Geogiana Stanhope to Miss —

Wednesday

My Dear Anne,

Sophy and I have just been practising a little deceit on our eldest Sister, to which we are not perfectly reconciled, and yet the circumstances were such that if any thing will excuse it, they must. Our neighbour Mr. Watts has made proposals to Mary: Proposals which she knew not how to receive, for tho' she has a particular Dislike to him (in which she is not singular), yet she would willingly marry him sooner than risk his offering to Sophy or me, which, in case of a refusal from herself, he told her he should do—for you must know the poor Girl considers our marrying before her as one of the greatest misfortunes that can possibly befall her, and, to prevent it, would willingly ensure herself everlasting Misery by a Marriage with Mr. Watts. An hour ago she came to us to sound our inclinations respecting the affair, which were to determine hers. A little before she came, my Mother had given us an account of it, telling us that she certainly would not let him go farther than our own family for a Wife. "And therefore (said she) if Mary won't have him, Sophy must; and if Sophy won't, Georgiana shall." Poor Georgiana! We neither of us attempted to alter my Mother's resolution, which I am sorry to say is generally more strictly kept, than rationally formed. As soon as she was gone, however, I broke silence to assure Sophy that if Mary should refuse Mr. Watts, I should not expect her to sacrifice her happiness by becoming his Wife from a motive of Generosity to me, which I was afraid her Good nature and sisterly affection might induce her to do. "Let us flatter ourselves (replied She) that Mary will not refuse him. Yet how can I hope that my Sister may accept a man who cannot make her happy."

"*He* cannot it is true but his Fortune, his Name, his House, his Carriage will, and I have no doubt but that Mary will marry him; indeed, why should she not? He is not more than two and thirty, a very proper age for a Man to marry at; He is rather plain to be sure, but then what is Beauty in a Man?—if he has but a genteel figure and a sensible looking Face it is quite sufficient."

"This is all very true, Georgiana, but Mr. Watts's figure is unfortunately extremely vulgar and his Countenance is very heavy."

"And then as to his temper; it has been reckoned bad, but may not the World be deceived in their Judgement of it? There is an open Frankness in his Disposition which

171

becomes a Man. They say he is stingy; We'll call that Prudence. They say he is suspicious. That proceeds from a warmth of Heart always excusable in Youth, and in short, I see no reason why he should not make a very good Husband, or why Mary should not be very happy with him."

Sophy laughed; I continued,

"However whether Mary accepts him or not, I am resolved. My determination is made. I never would marry Mr. Watts, were Beggary the only alternative. So deficient in every respect! Hideous in his person, and without one good Quality to make amends for it. His fortune, to be sure, is good. Yet not so very large! Three thousand a year. What is three thousand a year? It is but six times as much as my Mother's income. It will not tempt me."

"Yet it will be a noble fortune for Mary" said Sophy, laughing again.

"For Mary! Yes indeed, it will give me pleasure to see her in such affluence."

Thus I ran on, to the great Entertainment of my Sister, till Mary came into the room, to appearance in great agitation. She sat down. We made room for her at the fire. She seemed at a loss how to begin, and at last said in some confusion,

"Pray Sophy have you any mind to be married?"

"To be married! None in the least. But why do you ask me? Are you acquainted with any one who means to make me proposals?"

"I—no, how should I? But mayn't I ask a common question?"

"Not a very common one Mary, surely," (said I). She paused, and after some moments silence went on—

"How should you like to marry Mr. Watts, Sophy?"

I winked at Sophy, and replied for her. "Who is there but must rejoice to marry a man of three thousand a year?"

"Very true (she replied), That's very true. So you would have him if he would offer, Georgiana, and would you Sophy?"

Sophy did not like the idea of telling a lie and deceiving her Sister; she prevented the first and saved half her conscience by equivocation.

"I should certainly act just as Georgiana would do."

"Well then," said Mary, with triumph in her Eyes, "I have had an offer from Mr. Watts."

We were of course very much surprised; "Oh! do not accept him," said I, "and then perhaps he may have me."

In short, my scheme took, and Mary is resolved to do that to prevent our supposed happiness, which she would not have done to ensure it in reality. Yet after all, my Heart cannot acquit me and Sophy is even more scrupulous. Quiet our Minds, my dear Anne, by writing and telling us you approve our conduct. Consider it well over. Mary will have real pleasure in being a married Woman, and able to chaperone us, which she certainly shall do, for I think myself bound to contribute as much as possible to her happiness in a State I have made her choose. They will probably have a new Carriage, which will be paradise to her, and if we can prevail on Mr. W. to set up his Phaeton, she will be too happy. These things, however, would be no consolation to Sophy or me for domestic Misery. Remember all this, and do not condemn us.

Friday

Last night, Mr. Watts by appointment drank tea with us. As soon as his Carriage stopped at the Door, Mary went to the Window.

"Would you beleive it, Sophy (said she) the old Fool wants to have his new Chaise just the colour of the old one, and hung as low too. But it shan't—I will carry my point. And if he won't let it be as high as the Duttons', and blue spotted with silver, I won't have him. Yes I will too. Here he comes. I know he'll be rude; I know he'll be ill-tempered and won't say one civil thing to me! nor behave at all like a Lover." She then sat down and Mr. Watts entered.

"Ladies, your most obedient." We paid our Compliments and he seated himself.

"Fine weather, Ladies." Then turning to Mary, "Well, Miss Stanhope, I hope you have at last settled the Matter in your own mind; and will be so good as to let me know whether you will condescend to marry me or not."

"I think, Sir (said Mary) You might have asked in a genteeler way than that. I do not know whether I shall have you if you behave so odd."

"Mary!" (said my Mother). "Well, Mama, if he will be so cross... "

"Hush, hush, Mary, you shall not be rude to Mr. Watts."

"Pray Madam, do not lay any restraint on Miss Stanhope by obliging her to be civil. If she does not choose to accept my hand, I can offer it else where, for as I am by no means guided by a particular preference to you above your Sisters, it is equally the same to me which I marry of the three." Was there ever such a Wretch! Sophy reddened with anger and I felt so spiteful!

"Well then (said Mary in a peevish Accent) I will have you if I must."

"I should have thought, Miss Stanhope, that when such Settlements are offered as I have offered to you, there can be no great violence done to the inclinations in accepting of them." Mary mumbled out something, which I who sat close to her could just distinguish to be "What's the use of a great Jointure, if Men live forever?" And then audibly "Remember the pin-money; two hundred a year."

"A hundred and seventy-five, Madam."

"Two hundred indeed, Sir" said my Mother.

"And Remember, I am to have a new Carriage hung as high as the Duttons', and blue spotted with silver; and I shall expect a new saddle horse, a suit of fine lace, and an infinite number of the most valuable Jewels. Diamonds such as never were seen, and Pearls, Rubies, Emeralds, and Beads out of number. You must set up your Phaeton, which must be cream-coloured with a wreath of silver flowers round it; You must buy 4 of the finest Bays in the Kingdom and you must drive me in it every day. This is not all; You must entirely new furnish your House after my Taste, You must hire two more Footmen to attend me, two Women to wait on me, must always let me do just as I please and make a very good husband."

Here she stopped, I beleive rather out of breath.

"This is all very reasonable, Mr. Watts, for my Daughter to expect."

"And it is very reasonable, Mrs. Stanhope, that your daughter should be disappointed." He was going on, but Mary interrupted him: "You must build me an elegant Greenhouse and stock it with plants. You must let me spend every Winter in Bath, every Spring in Town, Every Summer in taking some Tour, and every Autumn at a Watering Place, and if we are at home the rest of the year (Sophy and I laughed) You must do nothing but give Balls and Masquerades. You must build a room on purpose and a Theatre to act Plays in. The first Play we have shall be Which is the Man, and I will do Lady Bell Bloomer."

"And pray, Miss Stanhope (said Mr. Watts), What am I to expect from you in return for all this."

"Expect? Why, you may expect to have me pleased."

"It would be odd if I did not. Your expectations, Madam, are too high for me, and I must apply to Miss Sophy, who perhaps may not have raised her's so much."

"You are mistaken, Sir, in supposing so, (said Sophy) for tho' they may not be exactly in the same Line, yet my expectations are to the full as high as my Sister's; for I expect my Husband to be good-tempered and Chearful; to consult my Happiness in all his Actions, and to love me with Constancy and Sincerity."

Mr. Watts stared. "These are very odd Ideas, truly, young Lady. You had better discard them before you marry, or you will be obliged to do it afterwards."

My Mother, in the meantime, was lecturing Mary, who was sensible that she had gone too far, and when Mr. Watts was just turning towards me in order, I beleive, to address me, she spoke to him in a voice half humble, half sulky.

"You are mistaken, Mr. Watts, if you think I was in earnest when I said I expected so much. However I must have a new Chaise."

"Yes, Sir, you must allow that Mary has a right to expect that."

"Mrs. Stanhope, I mean and have always meant to have a new one on my Marriage. But it shall be the colour of my present one."

"I think, Mr. Watts, you should pay my Girl the compliment of consulting her Taste on such Matters."

Mr. Watts would not agree to this, and for some time insisted upon its being a Chocolate colour, while Mary was as eager for having it blue with silver Spots. At length, however, Sophy proposed that to please Mr. W. it should be a dark brown, and to please Mary it should be hung rather high and have a silver Border. This was at length agreed to, tho' reluctantly on both sides, as each had intended to carry their point entire. We then proceeded to other Matters, and it was settled that they should be married as soon as the Writings could be completed. Mary was very eager for a Special Licence and Mr. Watts talked of Banns. A common Licence was at last agreed on. Mary is to have all the Family Jewels, which are very inconsiderable, I beleive, and Mr. W. promised to buy her a Saddle horse; but in return, she is not to expect to go to Town or any other public place for these three Years. She is to have neither Greenhouse, Theatre, or Phaeton; to be contented with one Maid without an additional Footman. It engrossed the whole Evening to settle these affairs; Mr. W. supped with us and did not go till twelve. As soon as he was gone, Mary exclaimed "Thank Heaven! he's off at last; how I do hate him!" It was in vain that Mama represented to her the impropriety she was guilty of, in disliking him who was to be her Husband, for she persisted in declaring her aversion to him and hoping she might never see him again. What a Wedding will this be! Adeiu, my dear Anne.

Your faithfully Sincere, Georgiana Stanhope

Letter the 4th

From the same to the same

Saturday

Dear Anne,

Mary, eager to have every one know of her approaching Wedding, and more particularly desirous of triumphing, as she called it, over the Duttons, desired us to walk with her this Morning to Stoneham. As we had nothing else to do, we readily agreed, and had as pleasant a walk as we could have with Mary, whose conversation entirely consisted in abusing the Man she is so soon to marry, and in longing for a blue Chaise spotted with Silver. When we reached the Duttons, we found the two Girls in the dressing-room with a very handsome Young Man, who was of course introduced to us. He is the son of Sir Henry Brudenell of Leicestershire. Mr. Brudenell is the handsomest Man I ever saw in my Life; we are all three very much pleased with him. Mary, who from the moment of our reaching the Dressing-room had been swelling with the knowledge of her own importance, and with the Desire of making it known, could not remain long silent on the Subject after we were seated, and soon addressing herself to Kitty, said,

"Don't you think it will be necessary to have all the Jewels new set?"

"Necessary for what?"

"For What! Why, for my appearance."

"I beg your pardon, but I really do not understand you. What Jewels do you speak of, and where is your appearance to be made?"

"At the next Ball, to be sure, after I am married."

You may imagine their Surprise. They were at first incredulous, but on our joining in the Story, they at last beleived it. "And who is it to?" was of course the first Question. Mary pretended Bashfulness, and answered in Confusion, her Eyes cast down, "to Mr. Watts". This also required Confirmation from us, for that anyone who had the Beauty and fortune (tho' small yet a provision) of Mary would willingly marry Mr. Watts, could by them scarcely be credited. The subject being now fairly introduced, and she found herself the object of every one's attention in company, she lost all her confusion and became perfectly unreserved and communicative.

"I wonder you should never have heard of it before, for in general things of this Nature are very well known in the Neighbourhood."

"I assure you", said Jemima, "I never had the least suspicion of such an affair. Has it been in agitation long?"

"Oh! Yes, ever since Wednesday."

They all smiled, particularly Mr. Brudenell.

"You must know Mr. Watts is very much in love with me, so that it is quite a match of affection on his side."

"Not on his only, I suppose", said Kitty.

"Oh! when there is so much Love on one side, there is no occasion for it on the other. However, I do not much dislike him, tho' he is very plain to be sure."

Mr. Brudenell stared, the Miss Duttons laughed and Sophy and I were heartily ashamed of our Sister. She went on.

"We are to have a new Postchaise, and very likely may set up our Phaeton."

This we knew to be false, but the poor Girl was pleased at the idea of persuading the company that such a thing was to be, and I would not deprive her of so harmless an Enjoyment. She continued,

"Mr. Watts is to present me with the family Jewels, which I fancy are very considerable." I could not help whispering Sophy "I fancy not". "These Jewels are what I suppose must be new set before they can be worn. I shall not wear them till the first Ball I go to after my Marriage. If Mrs. Dutton should not go to it, I hope you will let me chaperone you; I shall certainly take Sophy and Georgiana."

"You are very good (said Kitty) and since you are inclined to undertake the Care of young Ladies, I should advise you to prevail on Mrs. Edgecumbe to let you chaprone her six Daughters, which with your two Sisters and ourselves will make your Entree very respectable."

Kitty made us all smile except Mary, who did not understand her Meaning and coolly said that she should not like to chaperone so many. Sophy and I now endeavoured to change the conversation, but succeeded only for a few Minutes, for Mary took care to bring back their attention to her and her approaching Wedding. I was sorry for my Sister's sake to see that Mr. Brudenell seemed to take pleasure in listening to her account of it, and even encouraged her by his Questions and Remarks, for it was evident that his only Aim was to laugh at her. I am afraid he found her very ridiculous. He kept his Countenance extremely well, yet it was easy to see that it was with difficulty he kept it. At length, however, he seemed fatigued and Disgusted with her ridiculous Conversation, as he turned from her to us, and spoke but little to her for about half an hour before we left Stoneham. As soon as we were out of the House, we all joined in praising the Person and Manners of Mr. Brudenell.

We found Mr. Watts at home.

"So, Miss Stanhope (said he) you see I am come a courting in a true Lover like Manner."

"Well you need not have told me that. I knew why you came very well."

Sophy and I then left the room, imagining of course that we must be in the way, if a Scene of Courtship were to begin. We were surprised at being followed almost immediately by Mary.

"And is your Courting so soon over?" said Sophy.

"Courting! (replied Mary) we have been quarrelling. Watts is such a Fool! I hope I shall never see him again."

"I am afraid you will, (said I) as he dines here today. But what has been your dispute?"

"Why, only because I told him that I had seen a Man much handsomer than he was this Morning, he flew into a great Passion and called me a Vixen, so I only stayed to tell him I thought him a Blackguard and came away."

"Short and sweet; (said Sophy) but pray, Mary, how will this be made up?"

"He ought to ask my pardon; but if he did, I would not forgive him."

"His Submission, then, would not be very useful."

When we were dressed we returned to the Parlour where Mama and Mr. Watts were in close Conversation. It seems that he had been complaining to her of her Daughter's behaviour, and she had persuaded him to think no more of it. He therefore met Mary with all his accustomed Civility, and except one touch at the Phaeton and another at the Greenhouse, the Evening went off with great Harmony and Cordiality. Watts is going to Town to hasten the preparations for the Wedding.

I am your affectionate Freind,

G.S.

To Miss Jane Anna Elizabeth Austen

My Dear Neice,

Though you are at this period not many degrees removed from Infancy, Yet trusting that you will in time be older, and that through the care of your excellent Parents, You will one day or another be able to read written hand, I dedicate to You the following Miscellanious Morsels, convinced that if you seriously attend to them, You will derive from them very important Instructions, with regard to your Conduct in Life. If such my hopes should hereafter be realized, never shall I regret the Days and Nights that have been spent in composing these Treatises for your Benefit. I am, my dear Neice Your very Affectionate Aunt.

The Author

June 2d. 1793

A Fragment written to inculcate the practise of Virtue

(Erased from the original manuscript.)

We all know that many are unfortunate in their progress through the world, but we do not know all that are so. To seek them out to study their wants, & to leave them unsupplied is the duty, and ought to be the Business of Man. But few have time, fewer still have inclination, and no one has either the one or the other for such employments. Who amidst those that perspire away their Evenings in crouded assemblies can have leisure to bestow a thought on such as sweat under the fatigue of their daily Labour

A beautiful description of the different effects of sensibility on different minds

I am but just returned from Melissa's Bedside, & in my Life, tho' it has been a pretty long one, & I have during the course of it been at many Bedsides, I never saw so affecting an object as she exhibits. She lies wrapped in a book muslin bedgown, a chambray gauze shift, and a French net nightcap. Sir William is constantly at her bedside. The only repose he takes is on the Sopha in the Drawing room, where for five minutes every fortnight he remains in an imperfect Slumber, starting up every Moment & exclaiming "Oh! Melissa, Ah! Melissa," then sinking down again, raises his left arm and scratches his head. Poor Mrs. Burnaby is beyond measure afflicted. She sighs every now & then, that is about once a week; while the melancholy Charles says every Moment "Melissa how are you?" The lovely Sisters are much to be pitied. Julia is ever lamenting the situation of her friend, while lying behind her pillow & supporting her head. Maria, more mild in her greif, talks of going to Town next week, & Anna is always recurring to the pleasures we once enjoyed when Melissa was well. I am usually at the fire cooking some little delicacy for the unhappy invalid. Perhaps hashing up the remains of an old Duck, toasting some cheese or making a Curry, which are the favourite dishes of our poor friend. In these situations we were this morning surprised by receiving a visit from Dr. Dowkins; "I am come to see Melissa," said he. "How is She?" "Very weak indeed," said the fainting Melissa. "Very weak," replied the punning Doctor, "aye indeed it is more than a very week since you have taken to your bed. How is your appetite?" "Bad, very bad," said Julia. "That is very bad," replied he; "Are her spirits good, Madam?" "So poorly, Sir, that we are obliged to strengthen her with cordials every Minute." "Well then she receives Spirits from your being with her. Does she sleep?" "Scarcely ever." "And Ever Scarcely, I suppose, when she does. Poor thing! Does she think of dieing?" "She has not strength to think at all." "Nay, then she cannot think to have Strength."

The Generous Curate

A moral Tale, setting forth the Advantages of being Generous and a Curate.

In a part little known of the County of Warwick, a very worthy Clergyman lately resided. The income of his living which amounted to about two hundred pound, and the interest of his Wife's fortune which was nothing at all, was entirely sufficient for the Wants and Wishes of a Family who neither wanted or wished for anything beyond what their income afforded them. Mr Williams had been in possession of his living above twenty Years, when this history commences, and his Marriage which had taken place soon after his presentation to it, had made him the father of six very fine Children. The eldest had been placed at the Royal Academy for Seamen at Portsmouth when about thirteen years old, and from thence had been discharged on board of one of the Vessels of a small fleet destined for Newfoundland, where his promising and amiable disposition had procured him many friends among the Natives, and from whence he regularly sent home a large Newfoundland Dog every Month to his family. The second, who was also a Son, had been adopted by a neighbouring Clergyman with the intention of educating him at his own expence, which would have been a very desirable Circumstance had the Gentleman's fortune been equal to his generosity, but as he had nothing to support himself and a very large family but a Curacy of fifty pound a year, Young Williams knew nothing more at the age of 18 than what a twopenny Dame's School in the village could teach him. His Character however was perfectly amiable though his genius might be cramped, and he was addicted to no vice, or ever guilty of any fault beyond what his age and situation rendered perfectly excusable. He had indeed; sometimes been detected in flinging Stones at a Duck or putting brickbats into his Benefactor's bed; but these innocent efforts of wit were considered by that good Man rather as the effects of a lively imagination, than of anything bad in his Nature, and if any punishment were decreed for the offence it was in general no greater than that the Culprit should pick up the Stones or take the brickbats away.

Finis

Ode to Pity

To Miss Austen
The following Ode to Pity is dedicated, from a thorough knowledge of her pitiful Nature, by her obedt humle Servt.
    The Author

> Ever musing I delight to tread
> The Paths of honour and the Myrtle Grove
> Whilst the pale Moon her beams doth shed
> On disappointed Love.
> While Philomel on airy hawthorn Bush
> Sings sweet and Melancholy, And the thrush
> Converses with the Dove.
>
> Gently brawling down the turnpike road,
> Sweetly noisy falls the Silent Stream—
> The Moon emerges from behind a Cloud
> And darts upon the Myrtle Grove her beam.
> Ah! then what Lovely Scenes appear,
> The hut, the Cot, the Grot, and Chapel queer,
> And eke the Abbey too a mouldering heap,
> Cnceal'd by aged pines her head doth rear
> And quite invisible doth take a peep.

June 3d 1793.

Juvenilia
VOLUME IN THE SECOND

A Collection of Juvenile Writings

By
Jane Austen

Transcriber's Note: A few very small changes have been made to this version: Italics have been converted to capitals. The British 'pound' symbol has been converted to 'L'; but in general the author's erratic spelling, punctuation and capitalizations have been retained.

Love And Freindship

TO MADAME LA COMTESSE DE FEUILLIDE

This novel is inscribed by her obliged humble servant

THE AUTHOR.

"Deceived in Freindship and Betrayed in Love."

LETTER the FIRST From ISABEL to LAURA

How often, in answer to my repeated intreaties that you would give my Daughter a regular detail of the Misfortunes and Adventures of your Life, have you said "No, my freind never will I comply with your request till I may be no longer in Danger of again experiencing such dreadful ones."

Surely that time is now at hand. You are this day 55. If a woman may ever be said to be in safety from the determined Perseverance of disagreeable Lovers and the cruel Persecutions of obstinate Fathers, surely it must be at such a time of Life. Isabel

LETTER 2nd LAURA to ISABEL

Altho' I cannot agree with you in supposing that I shall never again be exposed to Misfortunes as unmerited as those I have already experienced, yet to avoid the imputation of Obstinacy or ill-nature, I will gratify the curiosity of your daughter; and may the fortitude with which I have suffered the many afflictions of my past Life, prove to her a useful lesson for the support of those which may befall her in her own. Laura

LETTER 3rd LAURA to MARIANNE

As the Daughter of my most intimate freind I think you entitled to that knowledge of my unhappy story, which your Mother has so often solicited me to give you.

My Father was a native of Ireland and an inhabitant of Wales; my Mother was the natural Daughter of a Scotch Peer by an italian Opera-girl—I was born in Spain and received my Education at a Convent in France.

When I had reached my eighteenth Year I was recalled by my Parents to my paternal roof in Wales. Our mansion was situated in one of the most romantic parts of the Vale of Uske. Tho' my Charms are now considerably softened and somewhat impaired by the Misfortunes I have undergone, I was once beautiful. But lovely as I was the Graces of my Person were the least of my Perfections. Of every accomplishment accustomary to my sex, I was Mistress. When in the

Convent, my progress had always exceeded my instructions, my Acquirements had been wonderfull for my age, and I had shortly surpassed my Masters.

In my Mind, every Virtue that could adorn it was centered; it was the Rendez-vous of every good Quality and of every noble sentiment.

A sensibility too tremblingly alive to every affliction of my Freinds, my Acquaintance and particularly to every affliction of my own, was my only fault, if a fault it could be called. Alas! how altered now! Tho' indeed my own Misfortunes do not make less impression on me than they ever did, yet now I never feel for those of an other. My accomplishments too, begin to fade—I can neither sing so well nor Dance so gracefully as I once did—and I have entirely forgot the MINUET DELA COUR. Adeiu. Laura.

LETTER 4th Laura to MARIANNE

Our neighbourhood was small, for it consisted only of your Mother. She may probably have already told you that being left by her Parents in indigent Circumstances she had retired into Wales on eoconomical motives. There it was our freindship first commenced. Isobel was then one and twenty. Tho' pleasing both in her Person and Manners (between ourselves) she never possessed the hundredth part of my Beauty or Accomplishments. Isabel had seen the World. She had passed 2 Years at one of the first Boarding-schools in London; had spent a fortnight in Bath and had supped one night in Southampton.

"Beware my Laura (she would often say) Beware of the insipid Vanities and idle Dissipations of the Metropolis of England; Beware of the unmeaning Luxuries of Bath and of the stinking fish of Southampton."

"Alas! (exclaimed I) how am I to avoid those evils I shall never be exposed to? What probability is there of my ever tasting the Dissipations of London, the Luxuries of Bath, or the stinking Fish of Southampton? I who am doomed to waste my Days of Youth and Beauty in an humble Cottage in the Vale of Uske." Ah! little did I then think I was ordained so soon to quit that humble Cottage for the Deceitfull Pleasures of the World. Adeiu Laura.

LETTER 5th LAURA to MARIANNE

One Evening in December as my Father, my Mother and myself, were arranged in social converse round our Fireside, we were on a sudden greatly astonished, by hearing a violent knocking on the outward door of our rustic Cot.

My Father started—"What noise is that," (said he.) "It sounds like a loud rapping at the door"—(replied my Mother.) "it does indeed." (cried I.) "I am of your opinion; (said my Father) it certainly does appear to proceed from some uncommon violence exerted against our unoffending door." "Yes (exclaimed I) I cannot help thinking it must be somebody who knocks for admittance."

"That is another point (replied he;) We must not pretend to determine on what motive the person may knock—tho' that someone DOES rap at the door, I am partly convinced."

Here, a 2d tremendous rap interrupted my Father in his speech, and somewhat alarmed my Mother and me.

"Had we better not go and see who it is? (said she) the servants are out." "I think we had." (replied I.) "Certainly, (added my Father) by all means." "Shall we go now?" (said my Mother,) "The sooner the better." (answered he.) "Oh! let no time be lost" (cried I.)

A third more violent Rap than ever again assaulted our ears. "I am certain there is somebody knocking at the Door." (said my Mother.) "I think there must," (replied my Father) "I fancy the servants are returned; (said I) I think I hear Mary going to the Door." "I'm glad of it (cried my Father) for I long to know who it is."

I was right in my conjecture; for Mary instantly entering the Room, informed us that a young Gentleman and his Servant were at the door, who had lossed their way, were very cold and begged leave to warm themselves by our fire.

"Won't you admit them?" (said I.) "You have no objection, my Dear?" (said my Father.) "None in the World." (replied my Mother.)

Mary, without waiting for any further commands immediately left the room and quickly returned introducing the most beauteous and amiable Youth, I had ever beheld. The servant she kept to herself.

My natural sensibility had already been greatly affected by the sufferings of the unfortunate stranger and no sooner did I first behold him, than I felt that on him the happiness or Misery of my future Life must depend. Adeiu Laura.

LETTER 6th LAURA to MARIANNE

The noble Youth informed us that his name was Lindsay—for particular reasons however I shall conceal it under that of Talbot. He told us that he was the son of an English Baronet, that his Mother had been for many years no more and that he had a Sister of the middle size. "My Father (he continued) is a mean and mercenary wretch—it is only to such particular freinds as this Dear Party that I would thus betray his failings. Your Virtues my amiable Polydore (addressing himself to my father) yours Dear Claudia and yours my Charming Laura call on me to repose in you, my confidence." We bowed. "My Father seduced by the false glare of Fortune and the Deluding Pomp of Title, insisted on my giving my hand to Lady Dorothea. No never exclaimed I. Lady Dorothea is lovely and Engaging; I prefer no woman to her; but know Sir, that I scorn to marry her in compliance with your Wishes. No! Never shall it be said that I obliged my Father."

We all admired the noble Manliness of his reply. He continued.

"Sir Edward was surprised; he had perhaps little expected to meet with so spirited an opposition to his will. "Where, Edward in the name of wonder (said he) did you pick up this unmeaning gibberish? You have been studying Novels I suspect." I scorned to answer: it would have been beneath my dignity. I mounted my Horse and followed by my faithful William set forth for my Aunts."

"My Father's house is situated in Bedfordshire, my Aunt's in Middlesex, and tho' I flatter myself with being a tolerable proficient in Geography, I know not how it happened, but I found myself entering this beautifull Vale which I find is in South Wales, when I had expected to have reached my Aunts."

"After having wandered some time on the Banks of the Uske without knowing which way to go, I began to lament my cruel Destiny in the bitterest and most pathetic Manner. It was now perfectly dark, not a single star was there to direct my steps, and I know not what might have befallen me had I not at length discerned thro' the solemn Gloom that surrounded me a distant light, which as I approached it, I discovered to be the chearfull Blaze of your fire. Impelled by the combination of Misfortunes under which I laboured, namely Fear, Cold and Hunger I hesitated not to ask admittance which at length I have gained; and now my Adorable Laura (continued he taking my Hand) when may I hope to receive that reward of all the painfull sufferings I have undergone during the course of my attachment to you, to which I have ever aspired. Oh! when will you reward me with Yourself?"

"This instant, Dear and Amiable Edward." (replied I.). We were immediately united by my Father, who tho' he had never taken orders had been bred to the Church. Adeiu Laura

LETTER 7th LAURA to MARIANNE

We remained but a few days after our Marriage, in the Vale of Uske. After taking an affecting Farewell of my Father, my Mother and my Isabel, I accompanied Edward to his Aunt's in Middlesex. Philippa received us both with every expression of affectionate Love. My arrival was indeed a most agreable surprise to her as she had not only been totally ignorant of my Marriage with her Nephew, but had never even had the slightest idea of there being such a person in the World.

Augusta, the sister of Edward was on a visit to her when we arrived. I found her exactly what her Brother had described her to be—of the middle size. She received me with equal surprise though not with equal Cordiality, as Philippa. There was a disagreable coldness and Forbidding Reserve in her reception of me which was equally distressing and Unexpected. None of that interesting Sensibility or amiable simpathy in her manners and Address to me when we first met which should have distinguished our introduction to each other. Her Language was neither warm, nor affectionate, her expressions of regard were neither animated nor cordial; her arms were not opened to receive me to her Heart, tho' my own were extended to press her to mine.

A short Conversation between Augusta and her Brother, which I accidentally overheard encreased my dislike to her, and convinced me that her Heart was no more formed for the soft ties of Love than for the endearing intercourse of Freindship.

"But do you think that my Father will ever be reconciled to this imprudent connection?" (said Augusta.)

"Augusta (replied the noble Youth) I thought you had a better opinion of me, than to imagine I would so abjectly degrade myself as to consider my Father's Concurrence in any of my affairs, either of Consequence or concern to me. Tell me Augusta with sincerity; did you ever know me consult his inclinations or follow his Advice in the least trifling Particular since the age of fifteen?"

"Edward (replied she) you are surely too diffident in your own praise. Since you were fifteen only! My Dear Brother since you were five years old, I entirely acquit you of ever having willingly contributed to the satisfaction of your Father. But still I am not without apprehensions of your being shortly obliged to degrade yourself in your own eyes by seeking a support for your wife in the Generosity of Sir Edward."

"Never, never Augusta will I so demean myself. (said Edward). Support! What support will Laura want which she can receive from him?"

"Only those very insignificant ones of Victuals and Drink." (answered she.)

"Victuals and Drink! (replied my Husband in a most nobly contemptuous Manner) and dost thou then imagine that there is no other support for an exalted mind (such as is my Laura's) than the mean and indelicate employment of Eating and Drinking?"

"None that I know of, so efficacious." (returned Augusta).

"And did you then never feel the pleasing Pangs of Love, Augusta? (replied my Edward). Does it appear impossible to your vile and corrupted Palate, to exist on Love? Can you not conceive the Luxury of living in every distress that Poverty can inflict, with the object of your tenderest affection?"

"You are too ridiculous (said Augusta) to argue with; perhaps however you may in time be convinced that..."

Here I was prevented from hearing the remainder of her speech, by the appearance of a very Handsome young Woman, who was ushured into the Room at the Door of which I had been listening. On hearing her announced by the Name of "Lady Dorothea," I instantly quitted my Post and followed her into the Parlour, for I well remembered that she was the Lady, proposed as a Wife for my Edward by the Cruel and Unrelenting Baronet.

Altho' Lady Dorothea's visit was nominally to Philippa and Augusta, yet I have some reason to imagine that (acquainted with the Marriage and arrival of Edward) to see me was a principal motive to it.

I soon perceived that tho' Lovely and Elegant in her Person and tho' Easy and Polite in her Address, she was of that inferior order of Beings with regard to Delicate Feeling, tender Sentiments, and refined Sensibility, of which Augusta was one.

She staid but half an hour and neither in the Course of her Visit, confided to me any of her secret thoughts, nor requested me to confide in her, any of Mine. You will easily imagine therefore my Dear Marianne that I could not feel any ardent affection or very sincere Attachment for Lady Dorothea. Adeiu Laura.

LETTER 8th LAURA to MARIANNE, in continuation

Lady Dorothea had not left us long before another visitor as unexpected a one as her Ladyship, was announced. It was Sir Edward, who informed by Augusta of her Brother's marriage, came doubtless to reproach him for having dared to unite himself to me without his Knowledge. But Edward foreseeing his design, approached him with heroic fortitude as soon as he entered the Room, and addressed him in the following Manner.

"Sir Edward, I know the motive of your Journey here—You come with the base Design of reproaching me for having entered into an indissoluble engagement with my Laura without your Consent. But Sir, I glory in the Act—. It is my greatest boast that I have incurred the displeasure of my Father!"

So saying, he took my hand and whilst Sir Edward, Philippa, and Augusta were doubtless reflecting with admiration on his undaunted Bravery, led me from the Parlour to his Father's Carriage which yet remained at the Door and in which we were instantly conveyed from the pursuit of Sir Edward.

The Postilions had at first received orders only to take the London road; as soon as we had sufficiently reflected However, we ordered them to Drive to M——. the seat of Edward's most particular freind, which was but a few miles distant.

At M——. we arrived in a few hours; and on sending in our names were immediately admitted to Sophia, the Wife of Edward's freind. After having been deprived during the course of 3 weeks of a real freind (for such I term your Mother) imagine my transports at beholding one, most truly worthy of the Name. Sophia was rather above the middle size; most elegantly formed. A soft languor spread over her lovely features, but increased their Beauty—. It was the Charectarestic of her Mind—. She was all sensibility and Feeling. We flew into each others arms and after having exchanged vows of mutual Freindship for the rest of our Lives, instantly unfolded to each other the most inward secrets of our Hearts—. We were interrupted in the delightfull Employment by the entrance of Augustus, (Edward's freind) who was just returned from a solitary ramble.

Never did I see such an affecting Scene as was the meeting of Edward and Augustus.

"My Life! my Soul!" (exclaimed the former) "My adorable angel!" (replied the latter) as they flew into each other's arms. It was too pathetic for the feelings of Sophia and myself—We fainted alternately on a sofa. Adeiu Laura.

LETTER the 9th From the same to the same

Towards the close of the day we received the following Letter from Philippa.

"Sir Edward is greatly incensed by your abrupt departure; he has taken back Augusta to Bedfordshire. Much as I wish to enjoy again your charming society, I cannot determine to snatch you from that, of such dear and deserving Freinds—When your Visit to them is terminated, I trust you will return to the arms of your" "Philippa."

We returned a suitable answer to this affectionate Note and after thanking her for her kind invitation assured her that we would certainly avail ourselves of it, whenever we might have no other place to go to. Tho' certainly nothing could to any reasonable Being, have appeared more satisfactory, than so gratefull a reply to her invitation, yet I know not how it was, but she was certainly capricious enough to be displeased with our behaviour and in a few weeks after, either to revenge our Conduct, or releive her own solitude, married a young and illiterate Fortune-hunter. This imprudent step (tho' we were sensible that it would probably deprive us of that fortune which Philippa had ever taught us to expect) could not on our own accounts, excite from our exalted minds a single sigh; yet fearfull lest it might prove a source of endless misery to the deluded Bride, our trembling Sensibility was greatly affected when we were first informed of the Event. The affectionate Entreaties of Augustus and Sophia that we would for ever consider their House as our Home, easily prevailed on us to determine never more to leave them, In the society of my Edward and this Amiable Pair, I passed the happiest moments of my Life; Our time was most delightfully spent, in mutual Protestations of Freindship, and in vows of unalterable Love, in which we were secure from being interrupted, by intruding and disagreable Visitors, as Augustus and Sophia had on their first Entrance in the Neighbourhood, taken due care to inform the surrounding Families, that as their happiness centered wholly in themselves, they wished for no other society. But alas! my Dear Marianne such Happiness as I then enjoyed was too perfect to be lasting. A most severe and unexpected Blow at once destroyed every sensation of Pleasure. Convinced as you must be from what I have already told you concerning Augustus and Sophia, that there never were a happier Couple, I need not I imagine, inform you that their union had been contrary to the inclinations of their Cruel and Mercenery Parents; who had vainly endeavoured with obstinate Perseverance to force them into a Marriage with those whom they had ever abhorred; but with a Heroic Fortitude worthy to be related and admired, they had both, constantly refused to submit to such despotic Power.

After having so nobly disentangled themselves from the shackles of Parental Authority, by a Clandestine Marriage, they were determined never to forfeit the good opinion they had gained in the World, in so doing, by accepting any proposals of reconciliation that might be offered them by their Fathers—to this farther tryal of their noble independance however they never were exposed.

They had been married but a few months when our visit to them commenced during which time they had been amply supported by a considerable sum of money which Augustus had gracefully purloined from his unworthy father's Escritoire, a few days before his union with Sophia.

By our arrival their Expenses were considerably encreased tho' their means for supplying them were then nearly exhausted. But they, Exalted Creatures! scorned to reflect a moment on their pecuniary Distresses and would have blushed at the idea of paying their Debts.—Alas! what was their Reward for such disinterested Behaviour! The beautifull Augustus was arrested and we were all undone. Such perfidious Treachery in the merciless perpetrators of the Deed will shock your gentle nature Dearest Marianne as much as it then affected the Delicate sensibility of Edward, Sophia, your Laura, and of Augustus himself. To compleat such unparalelled Barbarity we were informed that an Execution in the House would shortly take place. Ah! what could we do but what we did! We sighed and fainted on the sofa. Adeiu Laura.

LETTER 10th LAURA in continuation

When we were somewhat recovered from the overpowering Effusions of our grief, Edward desired that we would consider what was the most prudent step to be taken in our unhappy situation while he repaired to his imprisoned freind to lament over his misfortunes. We promised that we would, and he set forwards on his journey to Town. During his absence we faithfully complied with his Desire and after the most mature Deliberation, at length agreed that the best thing we could do was to leave the House; of which we every moment expected the officers of Justice to take possession. We waited therefore with the greatest impatience, for the return of Edward in order to impart to him the result of our Deliberations. But no Edward appeared. In vain did we count the tedious moments of his absence—in vain did we weep—in vain even did we sigh—no Edward returned—. This was too cruel, too unexpected a Blow to our Gentle Sensibility—we could not support it—we could only faint. At length collecting all the Resolution I was Mistress of, I arose and after packing up some necessary apparel for Sophia and myself, I dragged her to a Carriage I had ordered and we instantly set out for London. As the Habitation of Augustus was within twelve miles of Town, it was not long e'er we arrived there, and no sooner had we entered Holboun than letting down one of the Front Glasses I enquired of every decent-looking Person that we passed "If they had seen my Edward?"

But as we drove too rapidly to allow them to answer my repeated Enquiries, I gained little, or indeed, no information concerning him. "Where am I to drive?" said the Postilion. "To Newgate Gentle Youth (replied I), to see Augustus." "Oh! no, no, (exclaimed Sophia) I cannot go to Newgate; I shall not be able to support the sight of my Augustus in so cruel a confinement—my feelings are sufficiently shocked by the RECITAL, of his Distress, but to behold it will overpower my Sensibility." As I perfectly agreed with her in the Justice of her Sentiments the Postilion was instantly directed to return into the Country. You may perhaps have been somewhat surprised my Dearest Marianne, that in the Distress I then endured, destitute of any support, and unprovided with any Habitation, I should never once have remembered my Father and Mother or my paternal Cottage in the Vale of Uske. To account for this seeming forgetfullness I must inform you of a trifling circumstance concerning them which I have as yet never mentioned. The death of my Parents a few weeks after my Departure, is the circumstance I allude to. By their decease I became the lawfull Inheritress of their House and Fortune. But alas! the House had never been their own and their Fortune had only been an Annuity on their own Lives. Such is the Depravity of the World! To your Mother I should have returned with Pleasure, should have been happy to have introduced to her, my charming Sophia and should with Chearfullness have passed the remainder of my Life in their dear Society in the Vale of Uske, had not one obstacle to the execution of so agreable a scheme, intervened; which was the Marriage and Removal of your Mother to a distant part of Ireland. Adeiu Laura.

LETTER 11th LAURA in continuation

"I have a Relation in Scotland (said Sophia to me as we left London) who I am certain would not hesitate in receiving me." "Shall I order the Boy to drive there?" said I—but instantly recollecting myself, exclaimed, "Alas I fear it will be too long a Journey for the Horses." Unwilling however to act only from my own inadequate Knowledge of the Strength and

Abilities of Horses, I consulted the Postilion, who was entirely of my Opinion concerning the Affair. We therefore determined to change Horses at the next Town and to travel Post the remainder of the Journey—. When we arrived at the last Inn we were to stop at, which was but a few miles from the House of Sophia's Relation, unwilling to intrude our Society on him unexpected and unthought of, we wrote a very elegant and well penned Note to him containing an account of our Destitute and melancholy Situation, and of our intention to spend some months with him in Scotland. As soon as we had dispatched this Letter, we immediately prepared to follow it in person and were stepping into the Carriage for that Purpose when our attention was attracted by the Entrance of a coroneted Coach and 4 into the Inn-yard. A Gentleman considerably advanced in years descended from it. At his first Appearance my Sensibility was wonderfully affected and e'er I had gazed at him a 2d time, an instinctive sympathy whispered to my Heart, that he was my Grandfather. Convinced that I could not be mistaken in my conjecture I instantly sprang from the Carriage I had just entered, and following the Venerable Stranger into the Room he had been shewn to, I threw myself on my knees before him and besought him to acknowledge me as his Grand Child. He started, and having attentively examined my features, raised me from the Ground and throwing his Grand-fatherly arms around my Neck, exclaimed, "Acknowledge thee! Yes dear resemblance of my Laurina and Laurina's Daughter, sweet image of my Claudia and my Claudia's Mother, I do acknowledge thee as the Daughter of the one and the Grandaughter of the other." While he was thus tenderly embracing me, Sophia astonished at my precipitate Departure, entered the Room in search of me. No sooner had she caught the eye of the venerable Peer, than he exclaimed with every mark of Astonishment—"Another Grandaughter! Yes, yes, I see you are the Daughter of my Laurina's eldest Girl; your resemblance to the beauteous Matilda sufficiently proclaims it. "Oh!" replied Sophia, "when I first beheld you the instinct of Nature whispered me that we were in some degree related—But whether Grandfathers, or Grandmothers, I could not pretend to determine." He folded her in his arms, and whilst they were tenderly embracing, the Door of the Apartment opened and a most beautifull young Man appeared. On perceiving him Lord St. Clair started and retreating back a few paces, with uplifted Hands, said, "Another Grand-child! What an unexpected Happiness is this! to discover in the space of 3 minutes, as many of my Descendants! This I am certain is Philander the son of my Laurina's 3d girl the amiable Bertha; there wants now but the presence of Gustavus to compleat the Union of my Laurina's Grand-Children."

"And here he is; (said a Gracefull Youth who that instant entered the room) here is the Gustavus you desire to see. I am the son of Agatha your Laurina's 4th and youngest Daughter," "I see you are indeed; replied Lord St. Clair—But tell me (continued he looking fearfully towards the Door) tell me, have I any other Grand-children in the House." "None my Lord." "Then I will provide for you all without farther delay—Here are 4 Banknotes of 50L each— Take them and remember I have done the Duty of a Grandfather." He instantly left the Room and immediately afterwards the House. Adeiu, Laura.

LETTER the 12th LAURA in continuation

You may imagine how greatly we were surprised by the sudden departure of Lord St Clair. "Ignoble Grand-sire!" exclaimed Sophia. "Unworthy Grandfather!" said I, and instantly fainted in each other's arms. How long we remained in this situation I know not; but when we recovered we found ourselves alone, without either Gustavus, Philander, or the Banknotes. As we were deploring our unhappy fate, the Door of the Apartment opened and "Macdonald" was announced. He was Sophia's cousin. The haste with which he came to our releif so soon after the receipt of our Note, spoke so greatly in his favour that I hesitated not to pronounce him at first sight, a tender and simpathetic Freind. Alas! he little deserved the name—for though he told us that he was much concerned at our Misfortunes, yet by his own account it appeared that the perusal of them, had neither drawn from him a single sigh, nor induced him to bestow one curse on our vindictive stars—. He told Sophia that his Daughter depended on her returning with him to Macdonald-Hall, and that as his Cousin's freind he should be happy to see me there also. To Macdonald-Hall, therefore we went, and were received with great kindness by Janetta the Daughter of Macdonald, and the Mistress of the Mansion. Janetta was then only fifteen; naturally well disposed, endowed with a susceptible Heart, and a simpathetic Disposition, she might, had these amiable qualities been properly encouraged, have been an ornament to human Nature; but unfortunately her Father possessed not a soul sufficiently exalted to admire so promising a Disposition, and had endeavoured by every means on his power to prevent it encreasing with her Years. He had actually so far extinguished the natural noble Sensibility of her Heart, as to prevail on her to accept an offer from a young Man of his Recommendation. They were to be married in a few months, and Graham, was in the House when we arrived. WE soon saw through his character. He was just such a Man as one might have expected to be the choice of Macdonald. They said he was Sensible, well-informed, and Agreable; we did not pretend to Judge of such trifles, but as we were convinced he had no soul, that he had never read the sorrows of Werter, and that his Hair bore not the least resemblance to auburn, we were certain that Janetta could feel no affection for him, or at least that she ought to feel none. The very circumstance of his being her father's choice too, was so much in his disfavour, that had he been deserving her, in every other respect yet THAT of itself ought to have been a sufficient reason in the Eyes of Janetta for rejecting him. These considerations we were determined to represent to her in their proper light and doubted not of meeting with the desired success from one naturally so well disposed; whose errors in the affair had only arisen from a want of proper confidence in her own opinion, and a suitable contempt of her father's. We found her indeed all that our warmest wishes could have hoped for; we had no difficulty to convince her that it was impossible she could love Graham, or that it was her Duty to disobey her Father; the only thing at which she rather seemed to hesitate was our assertion that she must be attached to some other Person. For some time, she persevered in declaring that she knew no other young man for whom she had the the smallest Affection; but upon explaining the impossibility of such a thing she said that she beleived she DID LIKE Captain M'Kenrie better than any one she knew besides. This confession satisfied us and after having enumerated the good Qualities of M'Kenrie and assured her that she was violently in love with him, we desired to know whether he had ever in any wise declared his affection to her.

"So far from having ever declared it, I have no reason to imagine that he has ever felt any for me." said Janetta. "That he certainly adores you (replied Sophia) there can be no doubt—. The Attachment must be reciprocal. Did he never gaze on you with admiration—tenderly press your hand—drop an involantary tear—and leave the room abruptly?" "Never (replied she) that I remember—he has always left the room indeed when his visit has been ended, but has never gone away particularly abruptly or without making a bow." Indeed my Love (said I) you must be mistaken—for it is absolutely impossible that he should ever have left you but with Confusion, Despair, and Precipitation. Consider but for a moment Janetta, and you must be convinced how absurd it is to suppose that he could ever make a Bow, or behave like any other Person." Having settled this Point to our satisfaction, the next we took into consideration was, to determine in what manner we should inform M'Kenrie of the favourable Opinion Janetta entertained of him.... We at length agreed to acquaint him with it by an anonymous Letter which Sophia drew up in the following manner.

"Oh! happy Lover of the beautifull Janetta, oh! amiable Possessor of HER Heart whose hand is destined to another, why do you thus delay a confession of your attachment to the amiable Object of it? Oh! consider that a few weeks will at once put an end to every flattering Hope that you may now entertain, by uniting the unfortunate Victim of her father's Cruelty to the execrable and detested Graham."

"Alas! why do you thus so cruelly connive at the projected Misery of her and of yourself by delaying to communicate that scheme which had doubtless long possessed your imagination? A secret Union will at once secure the felicity of both."

The amiable M'Kenrie, whose modesty as he afterwards assured us had been the only reason of his having so long concealed the violence of his affection for Janetta, on receiving this Billet flew on the wings of Love to Macdonald-Hall, and so powerfully pleaded his Attachment to her who inspired it, that after a few more private interveiws, Sophia and I experienced the satisfaction of seeing them depart for Gretna-Green, which they chose for the celebration of their Nuptials, in preference to any other place although it was at a considerable distance from Macdonald-Hall. Adeiu Laura.

LETTER the 13th LAURA in continuation

They had been gone nearly a couple of Hours, before either Macdonald or Graham had entertained any suspicion of the affair. And they might not even then have suspected it, but for the following little Accident. Sophia happening one day to open a private Drawer in Macdonald's Library with one of her own keys, discovered that it was the Place where he kept his Papers of consequence and amongst them some bank notes of considerable amount. This discovery she imparted to me; and having agreed together that it would be a proper treatment of so vile a Wretch as Macdonald to deprive him of money, perhaps dishonestly gained, it was determined that the next time we should either of us happen to go that way, we would take one or more of the Bank notes from the drawer. This well meant Plan we had often successfully put in Execution; but alas! on the very day of Janetta's Escape, as Sophia was majestically removing the 5th Bank-note from the Drawer to her own purse, she was suddenly most impertinently interrupted in her employment by the entrance of Macdonald himself, in a most abrupt and precipitate Manner. Sophia (who though naturally all winning sweetness could when occasions demanded it call forth the Dignity of her sex) instantly put on a most forbidding look, and darting an angry frown on the undaunted culprit, demanded in a haughty tone of voice "Wherefore her retirement was thus insolently broken in on?" The unblushing Macdonald, without even endeavouring to exculpate himself from the crime he was charged with, meanly endeavoured to reproach Sophia with ignobly defrauding him of his money... The dignity of Sophia was wounded; "Wretch (exclaimed she, hastily replacing the Bank-note in the Drawer) how darest thou to accuse me of an Act, of which the bare idea makes me blush?" The base wretch was still unconvinced and continued to upbraid the justly-offended Sophia in such opprobious Language, that at length he so greatly provoked the gentle sweetness of her Nature, as to induce her to revenge herself on him by informing him of Janetta's Elopement, and of the active Part we had both taken in the affair. At this period of their Quarrel I entered the Library and was as you may imagine equally offended as Sophia at the ill-grounded accusations of the malevolent and contemptible Macdonald. "Base Miscreant! (cried I) how canst thou thus undauntedly endeavour to sully the spotless reputation of such bright Excellence? Why dost thou not suspect MY innocence as soon?" "Be satisfied Madam (replied he) I DO suspect it, and therefore must desire that you will both leave this House in less than half an hour."

"We shall go willingly; (answered Sophia) our hearts have long detested thee, and nothing but our freindship for thy Daughter could have induced us to remain so long beneath thy roof."

"Your Freindship for my Daughter has indeed been most powerfully exerted by throwing her into the arms of an unprincipled Fortune-hunter." (replied he)

"Yes, (exclaimed I) amidst every misfortune, it will afford us some consolation to reflect that by this one act of Freindship to Janetta, we have amply discharged every obligation that we have received from her father."

"It must indeed be a most gratefull reflection, to your exalted minds." (said he.)

As soon as we had packed up our wardrobe and valuables, we left Macdonald Hall, and after having walked about a mile and a half we sate down by the side of a clear limpid stream to refresh our exhausted limbs. The place was suited to meditation. A grove of full-grown Elms sheltered us from the East—. A Bed of full-grown Nettles from the West—. Before us ran the murmuring brook and behind us ran the turn-pike road. We were in a mood for contemplation and in a Disposition to enjoy so beautifull a spot. A mutual silence which had for some time reigned between us, was at length broke by my exclaiming—"What a lovely scene! Alas why are not Edward and Augustus here to enjoy its Beauties with us?"

"Ah! my beloved Laura (cried Sophia) for pity's sake forbear recalling to my remembrance the unhappy situation of my imprisoned Husband. Alas, what would I not give to learn the fate of my Augustus! to know if he is still in Newgate, or if he is yet hung. But never shall I be able so far to conquer my tender sensibility as to enquire after him. Oh! do not I beseech you ever let me again hear you repeat his beloved name—. It affects me too deeply—. I cannot bear to hear him mentioned it wounds my feelings."

"Excuse me my Sophia for having thus unwillingly offended you—" replied I—and then changing the conversation, desired her to admire the noble Grandeur of the Elms which sheltered us from the Eastern Zephyr. "Alas! my Laura (returned she) avoid so melancholy a subject, I intreat you. Do not again wound my Sensibility by observations on those elms. They remind me of Augustus. He was like them, tall, magestic—he possessed that noble grandeur which you admire in them."

I was silent, fearfull lest I might any more unwillingly distress her by fixing on any other subject of conversation which might again remind her of Augustus.

"Why do you not speak my Laura? (said she after a short pause) "I cannot support this silence you must not leave me to my own reflections; they ever recur to Augustus."

"What a beautifull sky! (said I) How charmingly is the azure varied by those delicate streaks of white!"

"Oh! my Laura (replied she hastily withdrawing her Eyes from a momentary glance at the sky) do not thus distress me by calling my Attention to an object which so cruelly reminds me of my Augustus's blue sattin waistcoat striped in white! In pity to your unhappy freind avoid a subject so distressing." What could I do? The feelings of Sophia were at that time so exquisite, and the tenderness she felt for Augustus so poignant that I had not power to start any other topic, justly fearing that it might in some unforseen manner again awaken all her sensibility by directing her thoughts to her Husband. Yet to be silent would be cruel; she had intreated me to talk.

From this Dilemma I was most fortunately relieved by an accident truly apropos; it was the lucky overturning of a Gentleman's Phaeton, on the road which ran murmuring behind us. It was a most fortunate accident as it diverted the attention of Sophia from the melancholy reflections which she had been before indulging. We instantly quitted our seats and ran to the rescue of those who but a few moments before had been in so elevated a situation as a fashionably high Phaeton, but who were now laid low and sprawling in the Dust. "What an ample subject for reflection on the uncertain Enjoyments of this World, would not that Phaeton and the Life of Cardinal Wolsey afford a thinking Mind!" said I to Sophia as we were hastening to the field of Action.

She had not time to answer me, for every thought was now engaged by the horrid spectacle before us. Two Gentlemen most elegantly attired but weltering in their blood was what first struck our Eyes—we approached—they were Edward and Augustus—. Yes dearest Marianne they were our Husbands. Sophia shrieked and fainted on the ground—I screamed and instantly ran mad—. We remained thus mutually deprived of our senses, some minutes, and on regaining them were deprived of them again. For an Hour and a Quarter did we continue in this unfortunate situation—Sophia fainting every moment and I running mad as often. At length a groan from the hapless Edward (who alone retained any share of life) restored us to ourselves. Had we indeed before imagined that either of them lived, we should have been more sparing of our Greif—but as we had supposed when we first beheld them that they were no more, we knew that nothing could remain to be done but what we were about. No sooner did we therefore hear my Edward's groan than postponing our lamentations for the present, we hastily ran to the Dear Youth and kneeling on each side of him implored him not to die—. "Laura (said He fixing his now languid Eyes on me) I fear I have been overturned."

I was overjoyed to find him yet sensible.

"Oh! tell me Edward (said I) tell me I beseech you before you die, what has befallen you since that unhappy Day in which Augustus was arrested and we were separated—"

"I will" (said he) and instantly fetching a deep sigh, Expired—. Sophia immediately sank again into a swoon—. MY greif was more audible. My Voice faltered, My Eyes assumed a vacant stare, my face became as pale as Death, and my senses were considerably impaired—.

"Talk not to me of Phaetons (said I, raving in a frantic, incoherent manner)—Give me a violin—. I'll play to him and sooth him in his melancholy Hours—Beware ye gentle Nymphs of Cupid's Thunderbolts, avoid the piercing shafts of Jupiter—Look at that grove of Firs—I see a Leg of Mutton—They told me Edward was not Dead; but they deceived me—they took him for a cucumber—" Thus I continued wildly exclaiming on my Edward's Death—. For two Hours did I rave thus madly and should not then have left off, as I was not in the least fatigued, had not Sophia who was just recovered from her swoon, intreated me to consider that Night was now approaching and that the Damps began to fall. "And whither shall we go (said I) to shelter us from either?" "To that white Cottage." (replied she pointing to a neat Building which rose up amidst the grove of Elms and which I had not before observed—) I agreed and we instantly walked to it—we knocked at the door—it was opened by an old woman; on being requested to afford us a Night's Lodging, she informed us that her House was but small, that she had only two Bedrooms, but that However we should be wellcome to one of them. We were satisfied and followed the good woman into the House where we were greatly cheered by the sight of a comfortable fire—. She was a widow and had only one Daughter, who was then just seventeen—One of the best of ages; but alas! she was very plain and her name was Bridget..... Nothing therfore could be expected from her—she could not be supposed to possess either exalted Ideas, Delicate Feelings or refined Sensibilities—. She was nothing more than a mere good-tempered, civil and obliging young woman; as such we could scarcely dislike here—she was only an Object of Contempt—. Adeiu Laura.

LETTER the 14th LAURA in continuation

Arm yourself my amiable young Frcind with all the philosophy you are Mistress of; summon up all the fortitude you possess, for alas! in the perusal of the following Pages your sensibility will be most severely tried. Ah! what were the misfortunes I had before experienced and which I have already related to you, to the one I am now going to inform you of. The Death of my Father and my Mother and my Husband though almost more than my gentle Nature could support, were trifles in comparison to the misfortune I am now proceeding to relate. The morning after our arrival at the Cottage, Sophia complained of a violent pain in her delicate limbs, accompanied with a disagreable Head-ake She attributed it to a cold caught by her continued faintings in the open air as the Dew was falling the Evening before. This I feared was but too probably the case; since how could it be otherwise accounted for that I should have escaped the same indisposition, but by supposing that the bodily Exertions I had undergone in my repeated fits of frenzy had so effectually circulated and warmed my Blood as to make me proof against the chilling Damps of Night, whereas, Sophia lying totally inactive on the ground must have been exposed to all their severity. I was most seriously alarmed by her illness which trifling as it may appear to you, a certain instinctive sensibility whispered me, would in the End be fatal to her.

Alas! my fears were but too fully justified; she grew gradually worse—and I daily became more alarmed for her. At length she was obliged to confine herself solely to the Bed allotted us by our worthy Landlady—. Her disorder turned to a galloping Consumption and in a few days carried her off. Amidst all my Lamentations for her (and violent you may suppose they were) I yet received some consolation in the reflection of my having paid every attention to her, that could be offered, in her illness. I had wept over her every Day—had bathed her sweet face with my tears and had pressed her fair Hands continually in mine—. "My beloved Laura (said she to me a few Hours before she died) take warning from my unhappy End and avoid the imprudent conduct which had occasioned it... Beware of fainting-fits... Though at the time they may be refreshing and agreable yet beleive me they will in the end, if too often repeated and at improper seasons, prove destructive to your Constitution... My fate will teach you this.. I die a Martyr to my greif for the loss of Augustus.. One fatal swoon has cost me my Life.. Beware of swoons Dear Laura.... A frenzy fit is not one quarter so pernicious; it is an exercise to the Body and if not too violent, is I dare say conducive to Health in its consequences—Run mad as often as you chuse; but do not faint—"

These were the last words she ever addressed to me.. It was her dieing Advice to her afflicted Laura, who has ever most faithfully adhered to it.

After having attended my lamented freind to her Early Grave, I immediately (tho' late at night) left the detested Village in which she died, and near which had expired my Husband and Augustus. I had not walked many yards from it before I was overtaken by a stage-coach, in which I instantly took a place, determined to proceed in it to Edinburgh, where I hoped to find some kind some pitying Freind who would receive and comfort me in my afflictions.

It was so dark when I entered the Coach that I could not distinguish the Number of my Fellow-travellers; I could only perceive that they were many. Regardless however of anything concerning them, I gave myself up to my own sad Reflections. A general silence prevailed— A silence, which was by nothing interrupted but by the loud and repeated snores of one of the Party.

"What an illiterate villain must that man be! (thought I to myself) What a total want of delicate refinement must he have, who can thus shock our senses by such a brutal noise! He must I am certain be capable of every bad action! There is no crime too black for such a Character!" Thus reasoned I within myself, and doubtless such were the reflections of my fellow travellers.

At length, returning Day enabled me to behold the unprincipled Scoundrel who had so violently disturbed my feelings. It was Sir Edward the father of my Deceased Husband. By his side sate Augusta, and on the same seat with me were your Mother and Lady Dorothea. Imagine my surprise at finding myself thus seated amongst my old Acquaintance. Great as was my astonishment, it was yet increased, when on looking out of Windows, I beheld the Husband of Philippa, with Philippa by his side, on the Coachbox and when on looking behind I beheld, Philander and Gustavus in the Basket. "Oh! Heavens, (exclaimed I) is it possible that I should so unexpectedly be surrounded by my nearest Relations and Connections?" These words roused the rest of the Party, and every eye was directed to the corner in which I sat. "Oh! my Isabel (continued I throwing myself across Lady Dorothea into her arms) receive once more to your Bosom the unfortunate Laura. Alas! when we last parted in the Vale of Usk, I was happy in being united to the best of Edwards; I had then a Father and a Mother, and had never known misfortunes—But now deprived of every freind but you—"

"What! (interrupted Augusta) is my Brother dead then? Tell us I intreat you what is become of him?" "Yes, cold and insensible Nymph, (replied I) that luckless swain your Brother, is no more, and you may now glory in being the Heiress of Sir Edward's fortune."

Although I had always despised her from the Day I had overheard her conversation with my Edward, yet in civility I complied with hers and Sir Edward's intreaties that I would inform them of the whole melancholy affair. They were greatly shocked—even the obdurate Heart of Sir Edward and the insensible one of Augusta, were touched with sorrow, by the unhappy tale. At the request of your Mother I related to them every other misfortune which had befallen me since we parted. Of the imprisonment of Augustus and the absence of Edward—of our arrival in Scotland—of our unexpected Meeting with our Grand-father and our cousins—of our visit to Macdonald-Hall—of the singular service we there performed towards Janetta—of her Fathers ingratitude for it.. of his inhuman Behaviour, unaccountable suspicions, and barbarous treatment of us, in obliging us to leave the House.. of our lamentations on the loss of Edward and Augustus and finally of the melancholy Death of my beloved Companion.Pity and surprise were strongly depictured in your Mother's countenance, during the whole of my narration, but I am sorry to say, that to the eternal reproach of her sensibility, the latter infinitely predominated. Nay, faultless as my conduct had certainly been during the whole course of my late misfortunes and adventures, she pretended to find fault with my behaviour in many of the situations in which I had been placed. As I was sensible myself, that I had always behaved in a manner which reflected Honour on my Feelings and Refinement, I paid little attention to what she said, and desired her to satisfy my Curiosity by informing me how she came there, instead of wounding my spotless reputation with unjustifiable Reproaches. As soon as she had complyed with my wishes in this particular and had given me an accurate detail of every thing that had befallen her since our separation (the particulars of which if you are not already acquainted with, your Mother will give you) I applied to Augusta for the same information respecting herself, Sir Edward and Lady Dorothea.She told me that having a considerable taste for the Beauties of Nature, her curiosity to behold the delightful scenes it exhibited in that part of the World had been so much raised by Gilpin's Tour to the Highlands, that she had prevailed on her Father to undertake a Tour to Scotland and had persuaded Lady Dorothea to accompany them. That they had arrived at Edinburgh a few Days before and from thence had made daily Excursions into the Country around in the Stage Coach they were then in, from one of which Excursions they were at that time returning. My next enquiries were concerning Philippa and her Husband, the latter of whom I learned having spent all her fortune, had recourse for subsistence to the talent in which, he had always most excelled, namely, Driving, and that having sold every thing which belonged to them except their Coach, had converted it into a Stage and in order to be removed from any of his former Acquaintance, had driven it to Edinburgh from whence he went to Sterling every other Day. That Philippa still retaining her affection for her ungratefull Husband, had followed him to Scotland and generally accompanied him in his little Excursions to Sterling. "It has only been to throw a little money into their Pockets (continued Augusta) that my Father has always travelled in their Coach to veiw the beauties of the Country since our arrival in Scotland—for it would certainly have been much more agreable to us, to visit the Highlands in a Postchaise than merely to travel from Edinburgh to Sterling and from Sterling to Edinburgh every other Day in a crowded and uncomfortable Stage." I perfectly agreed with her in her sentiments on the affair, and secretly blamed Sir Edward for thus sacrificing his Daughter's Pleasure for the sake of a ridiculous old woman whose folly in marrying so young a man ought to be punished. His Behaviour however was entirely of a peice with his general Character; for what could be expected from a man who possessed not the smallest atom of Sensibility, who scarcely knew the meaning of simpathy, and who actually snored—. Adeiu Laura.

LETTER the 15th LAURA in continuation.

When we arrived at the town where we were to Breakfast, I was determined to speak with Philander and Gustavus, and to that purpose as soon as I left the Carriage, I went to the Basket and tenderly enquired after their Health, expressing my fears of the uneasiness of their situation. At first they seemed rather confused at my appearance dreading no doubt that I might call them to account for the money which our Grandfather had left me and which they had unjustly deprived me of, but finding that I mentioned nothing of the Matter, they desired me to step into the Basket as we might there converse with greater ease. Accordingly I entered and whilst the rest of the party were devouring green tea and buttered toast, we feasted ourselves in a more refined and sentimental Manner by a confidential Conversation. I informed them of every thing which had befallen me during the course of my life, and at my request they related to me every incident of theirs.

"We are the sons as you already know, of the two youngest Daughters which Lord St Clair had by Laurina an italian opera girl. Our mothers could neither of them exactly ascertain who were our Father, though it is generally beleived that Philander, is the son of one Philip Jones a Bricklayer and that my Father was one Gregory Staves a Staymaker of Edinburgh. This is however of little consequence for as our Mothers were certainly never married to either of them it reflects no Dishonour on our Blood, which is of a most ancient and unpolluted kind. Bertha (the Mother of Philander) and Agatha (my own Mother) always lived together. They were neither of them very rich; their united fortunes had originally amounted to nine thousand Pounds, but as they had always lived on the principal of it, when we were fifteen it was diminished to nine Hundred. This nine Hundred they always kept in a Drawer in one of the Tables which stood in our common sitting Parlour, for the convenience of having it always at Hand. Whether it was from this circumstance, of its being easily taken, or from a wish of being independant, or from an excess of sensibility (for which we were always remarkable) I cannot now determine, but certain it is that when we had reached our 15th year, we took the nine Hundred Pounds and ran away. Having obtained this prize we were determined to manage it with eoconomy and not to spend it either with folly or Extravagance. To this purpose we therefore divided it into nine parcels, one of which we devoted to Victuals, the 2d to Drink, the 3d to Housekeeping, the 4th to Carriages, the 5th to Horses, the 6th to Servants, the 7th to Amusements, the 8th to Cloathes and the 9th to Silver Buckles. Having thus arranged our Expences for two months (for we expected to make the nine Hundred Pounds last as long) we hastened to London and had the good luck to spend it in 7 weeks and a Day which was 6 Days sooner than we had intended. As soon as we had thus happily disencumbered ourselves from the weight of so much money, we began to think of returning to our Mothers, but accidentally hearing that they were both starved to Death, we gave over the design and determined to engage ourselves to some strolling Company of Players, as we had always a turn for the Stage. Accordingly we offered our services to one and were accepted; our Company was indeed rather small, as it consisted only of the Manager his wife and ourselves, but there were fewer to pay and the only inconvenience attending it was the Scarcity of Plays which for want of People to fill the Characters, we could perform. We did not mind trifles however—. One of our most admired Performances was MACBETH, in which we were truly great. The Manager always played BANQUO himself, his Wife my LADY MACBETH. I did the THREE WITCHES and Philander acted ALL THE REST. To say the truth this tragedy was not only the Best, but the only Play that we ever performed; and after having acted it all over England, and Wales, we came to Scotland to exhibit it over the remainder of Great Britain. We happened to be quartered in that very Town, where you came and met your Grandfather—. We were in the Inn-yard when his Carriage entered and perceiving by the arms to whom it belonged, and knowing that Lord St Clair was our Grandfather, we agreed to endeavour to get something from him by discovering the Relationship—. You know how well it succeeded—. Having obtained the two Hundred Pounds, we instantly left the Town, leaving our Manager and his Wife to act MACBETH by themselves, and took the road to Sterling, where we spent our little fortune with great ECLAT. We are now returning to Edinburgh in order to get some preferment in the Acting way; and such my Dear Cousin is our History."

I thanked the amiable Youth for his entertaining narration, and after expressing my wishes for their Welfare and Happiness, left them in their little Habitation and returned to my other Freinds who impatiently expected me.

My adventures are now drawing to a close my dearest Marianne; at least for the present.

When we arrived at Edinburgh Sir Edward told me that as the Widow of his son, he desired I would accept from his Hands of four Hundred a year. I graciously promised that I would, but could not help observing that the unsimpathetic Baronet offered it more on account of my being the Widow of Edward than in being the refined and amiable Laura.

I took up my Residence in a Romantic Village in the Highlands of Scotland where I have ever since continued, and where I can uninterrupted by unmeaning Visits, indulge in a melancholy solitude, my unceasing Lamentations for the Death of my Father, my Mother, my Husband and my Freind.

Augusta has been for several years united to Graham the Man of all others most suited to her; she became acquainted with him during her stay in Scotland.

Sir Edward in hopes of gaining an Heir to his Title and Estate, at the same time married Lady Dorothea—. His wishes have been answered.

Philander and Gustavus, after having raised their reputation by their Performances in the Theatrical Line at Edinburgh, removed to Covent Garden, where they still exhibit under the assumed names of LUVIS and QUICK.

Philippa has long paid the Debt of Nature, Her Husband however still continues to drive the Stage-Coach from Edinburgh to Sterling:—Adeiu my Dearest Marianne. Laura.

Finis

June 13th 1790.

Lesley Castle

AN UNFINISHED NOVEL IN LETTERS

To HENRY THOMAS AUSTEN Esqre.

Sir
I am now availing myself of the Liberty you have frequently honoured me with of dedicating one of my Novels to you. That it is unfinished, I greive; yet fear that from me, it will always remain so; that as far as it is carried, it should be so trifling and so unworthy of you, is another concern to your obliged humble Servant
The Author

Messrs Demand and Co—please to pay Jane Austen Spinster the sum of one hundred guineas on account of your Humble Servant.
H. T. Austen
L105. 0. 0.

LETTER the FIRST is from Miss MARGARET LESLEY to Miss CHARLOTTE

LUTTERELL. Lesley Castle Janry 3rd—1792.

My Brother has just left us. "Matilda (said he at parting) you and Margaret will I am certain take all the care of my dear little one, that she might have received from an indulgent, and affectionate and amiable Mother." Tears rolled down his cheeks as he spoke these words— the remembrance of her, who had so wantonly disgraced the Maternal character and so openly violated the conjugal Duties, prevented his adding anything farther; he embraced his sweet Child and after saluting Matilda and Me hastily broke from us and seating himself in his Chaise, pursued the road to Aberdeen. Never was there a better young Man! Ah! how little did he deserve the misfortunes he has experienced in the Marriage state. So good a Husband to so bad a Wife! for you know my dear Charlotte that the Worthless Louisa left him, her Child and reputation a few weeks ago in company with Danvers and dishonour. Never was there a sweeter face, a finer form, or a less amiable Heart than Louisa owned! Her child already possesses the personal Charms of her unhappy Mother! May she inherit from her Father all his mental ones! Lesley is at present but five and twenty, and has already given himself up to melancholy and Despair; what a difference between him and his Father! Sir George is 57 and still remains the

Beau, the flighty stripling, the gay Lad, and sprightly Youngster, that his Son was really about five years back, and that HE has affected to appear ever since my remembrance. While our father is fluttering about the streets of London, gay, dissipated, and Thoughtless at the age of 57, Matilda and I continue secluded from Mankind in our old and Mouldering Castle, which is situated two miles from Perth on a bold projecting Rock, and commands an extensive veiw of the Town and its delightful Environs. But tho' retired from almost all the World, (for we visit no one but the M'Leods, The M'Kenzies, the M'Phersons, the M'Cartneys, the M'Donalds, The M'kinnons, the M'lellans, the M'kays, the Macbeths and the Macduffs) we are neither dull nor unhappy; on the contrary there never were two more lively, more agreable or more witty girls, than we are; not an hour in the Day hangs heavy on our Hands. We read, we work, we walk, and when fatigued with these Employments releive our spirits, either by a lively song, a graceful Dance, or by some smart bon-mot, and witty repartee. We are handsome my dear Charlotte, very handsome and the greatest of our Perfections is, that we are entirely insensible of them ourselves. But why do I thus dwell on myself! Let me rather repeat the praise of our dear little Neice the innocent Louisa, who is at present sweetly smiling in a gentle Nap, as she reposes on the sofa. The dear Creature is just turned of two years old; as handsome as tho' 2 and 20, as sensible as tho' 2 and 30, and as prudent as tho' 2 and 40. To convince you of this, I must inform you that she has a very fine complexion and very pretty features, that she already knows the two first letters in the Alphabet, and that she never tears her frocks—. If I have not now convinced you of her Beauty, Sense and Prudence, I have nothing more to urge in support of my assertion, and you will therefore have no way of deciding the Affair but by coming to Lesley-Castle, and by a personal acquaintance with Louisa, determine for yourself. Ah! my dear Freind, how happy should I be to see you within these venerable Walls! It is now four years since my removal from School has separated me from you; that two such tender Hearts, so closely linked together by the ties of simpathy and Freindship, should be so widely removed from each other, is vastly moving. I live in Perthshire, You in Sussex. We might meet in London, were my Father disposed to carry me there, and were your Mother to be there at the same time. We might meet at Bath, at Tunbridge, or anywhere else indeed, could we but be at the same place together. We have only to hope that such a period may arrive. My Father does not return to us till Autumn; my Brother will leave Scotland in a few Days; he is impatient to travel. Mistaken Youth! He vainly flatters himself that change of Air will heal the Wounds of a broken Heart! You will join with me I am certain my dear Charlotte, in prayers for the recovery of the unhappy Lesley's peace of Mind, which must ever be essential to that of your sincere freind M. Lesley.

LETTER the SECOND From Miss C. LUTTERELL to Miss M. LESLEY in answer.

Glenford Febry 12

I have a thousand excuses to beg for having so long delayed thanking you my dear Peggy for your agreable Letter, which beleive me I should not have deferred doing, had not every moment of my time during the last five weeks been so fully employed in the necessary arrangements for my sisters wedding, as to allow me no time to devote either to you or myself. And now what provokes me more than anything else is that the Match is broke off, and all my Labour thrown away. Imagine how great the Dissapointment must be to me, when you consider that after having laboured both by Night and by Day, in order to get the Wedding dinner ready by the time appointed, after having roasted Beef, Broiled Mutton, and Stewed Soup enough to last the new-married Couple through the Honey-moon, I had the mortification of finding that I had been Roasting, Broiling and Stewing both the Meat and Myself to no purpose. Indeed my dear Freind, I never remember suffering any vexation equal to what I experienced on last Monday when my sister came running to me in the store-room with her face as White as a Whipt syllabub, and told me that Hervey had been thrown from his Horse, had fractured his Scull and was pronounced by his surgeon to be in the most emminent Danger. "Good God! (said I) you dont say so? Why what in the name of Heaven will become of all the Victuals! We shall never be able to eat it while it is good. However, we'll call in the Surgeon to help us. I shall be able to manage the Sir-loin myself, my Mother will eat the soup, and You and the Doctor must finish the rest." Here I was interrupted, by seeing my poor Sister fall down to appearance Lifeless upon one of the Chests, where we keep our Table linen. I immediately called my Mother and the Maids, and at last we brought her to herself again; as soon as ever she was sensible, she expressed a determination of going instantly to Henry, and was so wildly bent on this Scheme, that we had the greatest Difficulty in the World to prevent her putting it in execution; at last however more by Force than Entreaty we prevailed on her to go into her room; we laid her upon the Bed, and she continued for some Hours in the most dreadful Convulsions. My Mother and I continued in the room with her, and when any intervals of tolerable Composure in Eloisa would allow us, we joined in heartfelt lamentations on the dreadful Waste in our provisions which this Event must occasion, and in concerting some plan for getting rid of them. We agreed that the best thing we could do was to begin eating them immediately, and accordingly we ordered up the cold Ham and Fowls, and instantly began our Devouring Plan on them with great Alacrity. We would have persuaded Eloisa to have taken a Wing of a Chicken, but she would not be persuaded. She was however much quieter than she had been; the convulsions she had before suffered having given way to an almost perfect Insensibility. We endeavoured to rouse her by every means in our power, but to no purpose. I talked to her of Henry. "Dear Eloisa (said I) there's no occasion for your crying so much about such a trifle. (for I was willing to make light of it in order to comfort her) I beg you would not mind it—You see it does not vex me in the least; though perhaps I may suffer most from it after all; for I shall not only be obliged to eat up all the Victuals I have dressed already, but must if Henry should recover (which however is not very likely) dress as much for you again; or should he die (as I suppose he will) I shall still have to prepare a Dinner for you whenever you marry any one else. So you see that tho' perhaps for the present it may afflict you to think of Henry's sufferings, Yet I dare say he'll die soon, and then his pain will be over and you will be easy, whereas my Trouble will last much longer for work as hard as I may, I am certain that the pantry cannot be cleared in less than a fortnight." Thus I did all in my power to console her, but without any effect, and at last as I saw that she did not seem to listen to me, I said no more, but leaving her with my Mother I took down the remains of The Ham and Chicken, and sent William to ask how Henry did. He was not expected to live many Hours; he died the same day. We took all possible care to break the melancholy Event to Eloisa in the tenderest manner; yet in spite of every precaution, her sufferings on hearing it were too violent for her reason, and she continued for many hours in a high Delirium. She is still extremely ill, and her Physicians are greatly afraid of her going into a Decline. We are therefore preparing for Bristol, where we mean to be in the course of the next week. And now my dear Margaret let me talk a little of your affairs; and in the first place I must inform you that it is confidently reported, your Father is going to be married; I am very unwilling to beleive so unpleasing a report, and at the same time cannot wholly discredit it. I have written to my freind Susan Fitzgerald, for information concerning it, which as she is at present in Town, she will be very able to give me. I know not who is the Lady. I think your Brother is extremely right in the resolution he has taken of travelling, as it will perhaps contribute to obliterate from his remembrance, those disagreable Events, which have lately so much afflicted him—I am happy to find that tho' secluded from all the World, neither you nor Matilda are dull or unhappy—that you may never know what it is to, be either is the wish of your sincerely affectionate C.L.

P. S. I have this instant received an answer from my freind Susan, which I enclose to you, and on which you will make your own reflections.

The enclosed LETTER

My dear CHARLOTTE You could not have applied for information concerning the report of Sir George Lesleys Marriage, to any one better able to give it you than I am. Sir George is certainly married; I was myself present at the Ceremony, which you will not be surprised at when I subscribe myself your Affectionate Susan Lesley

LETTER the THIRD From Miss MARGARET LESLEY to Miss C. LUTTERELL Lesley

Castle February the 16th

I have made my own reflections on the letter you enclosed to me, my Dear Charlotte and I will now tell you what those reflections were. I reflected that if by this second Marriage Sir George should have a second family, our fortunes must be considerably diminushed—that if his Wife should be of an extravagant turn, she would encourage him to persevere in that gay and Dissipated way of Life to which little encouragement would be necessary, and which has I fear already proved but too detrimental to his health and fortune—that she would now become Mistress of those Jewels which once adorned our Mother, and which Sir George had always promised us—that if they did not come into Perthshire I should not be able to gratify my curiosity of beholding my Mother-in-law and that if they did, Matilda would no longer sit at the head of her Father's table—. These my dear Charlotte were the melancholy reflections which crowded into my imagination after perusing Susan's letter to you, and which instantly occurred to Matilda when she had perused it likewise. The same ideas, the same fears, immediately occupied her Mind, and I know not which reflection distressed her most, whether the probable Diminution of our Fortunes, or her own Consequence. We both wish very much to know whether Lady Lesley is handsome and what is your opinion of her; as you honour her with the appellation of your freind, we flatter ourselves that she must be amiable. My Brother is already in Paris. He intends to quit it in a few Days, and to begin his route to Italy. He writes in a most chearfull manner, says that the air of France has greatly recovered both his Health and Spirits; that he has now entirely ceased to think of Louisa with any degree either of Pity or Affection, that he even feels himself obliged to her for her Elopement, as he thinks it very good fun to be single again. By this, you may perceive that he has entirely regained that chearful Gaiety, and sprightly Wit, for which he was once so remarkable. When he first became acquainted with Louisa which was little more than three years ago, he was one of the most lively, the most agreable young Men of the age—. I beleive you never yet heard the particulars of his first acquaintance with her. It commenced at our cousin Colonel Drummond's; at whose house in Cumberland he spent the Christmas, in which he attained the age of two and twenty. Louisa Burton was the Daughter of a distant Relation of Mrs. Drummond, who dieing a few Months before in extreme poverty, left his only Child then about eighteen to the protection of any of his Relations who would protect her. Mrs. Drummond was the only one who found herself so disposed—Louisa was therefore removed from a miserable Cottage in Yorkshire to an elegant Mansion in Cumberland, and from every pecuniary Distress that Poverty could inflict, to every elegant Enjoyment that Money could purchase—. Louisa was naturally ill-tempered and Cunning; but she had been taught to disguise her real Disposition, under the appearance of insinuating Sweetness, by a father who but too well knew, that to be married, would be the only chance she would have of not being starved, and who flattered himself that with such an extroidinary share of personal beauty, joined to a gentleness of Manners, and an engaging address, she might stand a good chance of pleasing some young Man who might afford to marry a girl without a Shilling. Louisa perfectly entered into her father's schemes and was determined to forward them with all her care and attention. By dint of Perseverance and Application, she had at length so thoroughly disguised her natural disposition under the mask of Innocence, and Softness, as to impose upon every one who had not by a long and constant intimacy with her discovered her real Character. Such was Louisa when the hapless Lesley first beheld her at Drummond-house. His heart which (to use your favourite comparison) was as delicate as sweet and as tender as a Whipt-syllabub, could not resist her attractions. In a very few Days, he was falling in love, shortly after actually fell, and before he had known her a Month, he had married her. My Father was at first highly displeased at so hasty and imprudent a connection; but when he found that they did not mind it, he soon became perfectly reconciled to the match. The Estate near Aberdeen which my brother possesses by the bounty of his great Uncle independant of Sir George, was entirely sufficient to support him and my Sister in Elegance and Ease. For the first twelvemonth, no one could be happier than Lesley, and no one more amiable to appearance than Louisa, and so plausibly did she act and so cautiously behave that tho' Matilda and I often spent several weeks together with them, yet we neither of us had any suspicion of her real Disposition. After the birth of Louisa however, which one would have thought would have strengthened her regard for Lesley, the mask she had so long supported was by degrees thrown aside, and as probably she then thought herself secure in the affection of her Husband (which did indeed appear if possible augmented by the birth of his Child) she seemed to take no pains to prevent that affection from ever diminushing. Our visits therefore to Dunbeath, were now less frequent and by far less agreable than they used to be. Our absence was however never either mentioned or lamented by Louisa who in the society of young Danvers with whom she became acquainted at Aberdeen (he was at one of the Universities there,) felt infinitely happier than in that of Matilda and your freind, tho' there certainly never were pleasanter girls than we are. You know the sad end of all Lesleys connubial happiness; I will not repeat it—. Adeiu my dear Charlotte; although I have not yet mentioned anything of the matter, I hope you will do me the justice to beleive that I THINK and FEEL, a great deal for your Sisters affliction. I do not doubt but that the healthy air of the Bristol downs will intirely remove it, by erasing from her Mind the remembrance of Henry. I am my dear Charlotte yrs ever M. L.

LETTER the FOURTH From Miss C. LUTTERELL to Miss M. LESLEY Bristol

February 27th

My Dear Peggy I have but just received your letter, which being directed to Sussex while I was at Bristol was obliged to be forwarded to me here, and from some unaccountable Delay, has but this instant reached me—. I return you many thanks for the account it contains of

Lesley's acquaintance, Love and Marriage with Louisa, which has not the less entertained me for having often been repeated to me before.

I have the satisfaction of informing you that we have every reason to imagine our pantry is by this time nearly cleared, as we left Particular orders with the servants to eat as hard as they possibly could, and to call in a couple of Chairwomen to assist them. We brought a cold Pigeon pye, a cold turkey, a cold tongue, and half a dozen Jellies with us, which we were lucky enough with the help of our Landlady, her husband, and their three children, to get rid of, in less than two days after our arrival. Poor Eloisa is still so very indifferent both in Health and Spirits, that I very much fear, the air of the Bristol downs, healthy as it is, has not been able to drive poor Henry from her remembrance.

You ask me whether your new Mother in law is handsome and amiable—I will now give you an exact description of her bodily and mental charms. She is short, and extremely well made; is naturally pale, but rouges a good deal; has fine eyes, and fine teeth, as she will take care to let you know as soon as she sees you, and is altogether very pretty. She is remarkably good-tempered when she has her own way, and very lively when she is not out of humour. She is naturally extravagant and not very affected; she never reads anything but the letters she receives from me, and never writes anything but her answers to them. She plays, sings and Dances, but has no taste for either, and excells in none, tho' she says she is passionately fond of all. Perhaps you may flatter me so far as to be surprised that one of whom I speak with so little affection should be my particular freind; but to tell you the truth, our freindship arose rather from Caprice on her side than Esteem on mine. We spent two or three days together with a Lady in Berkshire with whom we both happened to be connected—. During our visit, the Weather being remarkably bad, and our party particularly stupid, she was so good as to conceive a violent partiality for me, which very soon settled in a downright Freindship and ended in an established correspondence. She is probably by this time as tired of me, as I am of her; but as she is too Polite and I am too civil to say so, our letters are still as frequent and affectionate as ever, and our Attachment as firm and sincere as when it first commenced. As she had a great taste for the pleasures of London, and of Brighthelmstone, she will I dare say find some difficulty in prevailing on herself even to satisfy the curiosity I dare say she feels of beholding you, at the expence of quitting those favourite haunts of Dissipation, for the melancholy tho' venerable gloom of the castle you inhabit. Perhaps however if she finds her health impaired by too much amusement, she may acquire fortitude sufficient to undertake a Journey to Scotland in the hope of its Proving at least beneficial to her health, if not conducive to her happiness. Your fears I am sorry to say, concerning your father's extravagance, your own fortunes, your Mothers Jewels and your Sister's consequence, I should suppose are but too well founded. My freind herself has four thousand pounds, and will probably spend nearly as much every year in Dress and Public places, if she can get it—she will certainly not endeavour to reclaim Sir George from the manner of living to which he has been so long accustomed, and there is therefore some reason to fear that you will be very well off, if you get any fortune at all. The Jewels I should imagine too will undoubtedly be hers, and there is too much reason to think that she will preside at her Husbands table in preference to his Daughter. But as so melancholy a subject must necessarily extremely distress you, I will no longer dwell on it—.

Eloisa's indisposition has brought us to Bristol at so unfashionable a season of the year, that we have actually seen but one genteel family since we came. Mr and Mrs Marlowe are very agreable people; the ill health of their little boy occasioned their arrival here; you may imagine that being the only family with whom we can converse, we are of course on a footing of intimacy with them; we see them indeed almost every day, and dined with them yesterday. We spent a very pleasant Day, and had a very good Dinner, tho' to be sure the Veal was terribly underdone, and the Curry had no seasoning. I could not help wishing all dinner-time that I had been at the dressing it—. A brother of Mrs Marlowe, Mr Cleveland is with them at present; he is a good-looking young Man, and seems to have a good deal to say for himself. I tell Eloisa that she should set her cap at him, but she does not at all seem to relish the proposal. I should like to see the girl married and Cleveland has a very good estate. Perhaps you may wonder that I do not consider myself as well as my Sister in my matrimonial Projects; but to tell you the truth I never wish to act a more principal part at a Wedding than the superintending and directing the Dinner, and therefore while I can get any of my acquaintance to marry for me, I shall never think of doing it myself, as I very much suspect that I should not have so much time for dressing my own Wedding-dinner, as for dressing that of my freinds. Yours sincerely C. L.

LETTER the FIFTH Miss MARGARET LESLEY to Miss CHARLOTTE LUTTERELL

Lesley-Castle March 18th

On the same day that I received your last kind letter, Matilda received one from Sir George which was dated from Edinburgh, and informed us that he should do himself the pleasure of introducing Lady Lesley to us on the following evening. This as you may suppose considerably surprised us, particularly as your account of her Ladyship had given us reason to imagine there was little chance of her visiting Scotland at a time that London must be so gay. As it was our business however to be delighted at such a mark of condescension as a visit from Sir George and Lady Lesley, we prepared to return them an answer expressive of the happiness we enjoyed in expectation of such a Blessing, when luckily recollecting that as they were to reach the Castle the next Evening, it would be impossible for my father to receive it before he left Edinburgh, we contented ourselves with leaving them to suppose that we were as happy as we ought to be. At nine in the Evening on the following day, they came, accompanied by one of Lady Lesleys brothers. Her Ladyship perfectly answers the description you sent me of her, except that I do not think her so pretty as you seem to consider her. She has not a bad face, but there is something so extremely unmajestic in her little diminutive figure, as to render her in comparison with the elegant height of Matilda and Myself, an insignificant Dwarf. Her curiosity to see us (which must have been great to bring her more than four hundred miles) being now perfectly gratified, she already begins to mention their return to town, and has desired us to accompany her. We cannot refuse her request since it is seconded by the commands of our Father, and thirded by the entreaties of Mr. Fitzgerald who is certainly one of the most pleasing young Men, I ever beheld. It is not yet determined when we are to go, but when ever we do we shall certainly take our little Louisa with us. Adeiu my dear Charlotte; Matilda unites in best wishes to you, and Eloisa, with yours ever M. L.

LETTER the SIXTH LADY LESLEY to Miss CHARLOTTE LUTTERELL Lesley-Castle

March 20th

We arrived here my sweet Freind about a fortnight ago, and I already heartily repent that I ever left our charming House in Portman-square for such a dismal old weather-beaten Castle as this. You can form no idea sufficiently hideous, of its dungeon-like form. It is actually perched upon a Rock to appearance so totally inaccessible, that I expected to have been pulled up by a rope; and sincerely repented having gratified my curiosity to behold my Daughters at the expence of being obliged to enter their prison in so dangerous and ridiculous a manner. But as soon as I once found myself safely arrived in the inside of this tremendous building, I comforted myself with the hope of having my spirits revived, by the sight of two beautifull girls, such as the Miss Lesleys had been represented to me, at Edinburgh. But here again, I met with nothing but Disappointment and Surprise. Matilda and Margaret Lesley are two great, tall, out of the way, over-grown, girls, just of a proper size to inhabit a Castle almost as large in comparison as themselves. I wish my dear Charlotte that you could but behold these Scotch giants; I am sure they would frighten you out of your wits. They will do very well as foils to myself, so I have invited them to accompany me to London where I hope to be in the course of a fortnight. Besides these two fair Damsels, I found a little humoured Brat here who I beleive is some relation to them, they told me who she was, and gave me a long rigmerole story of her father and a Miss SOMEBODY which I have entirely forgot. I hate scandal and detest Children. I have been plagued ever since I came here with tiresome visits from a parcel of Scotch wretches, with terrible hard-names; they were so civil, gave me so many invitations, and talked of coming again so soon, that I could not help affronting them. I suppose I shall not see them any more, and yet as a family party we are so stupid, that I do not know what to do with myself. These girls have no Music, but Scotch airs, no Drawings but Scotch Mountains, and no Books but Scotch Poems—and I hate everything Scotch. In general I can spend half the Day at my toilett with a great deal of pleasure, but why should I dress here, since there is not a creature in the House whom I have any wish to please. I have just had a conversation with my Brother in which he has greatly offended me, and which as I have nothing more entertaining to send you I will gave you the particulars of. You must know that I have for these 4 or 5 Days past strongly suspected William of entertaining a partiality to my eldest Daughter. I own indeed that had I been inclined to fall in love with any woman, I should not have made choice of Matilda Lesley for the object of my passion; for there is nothing I hate so much as a tall Woman: but however there is no accounting for some men's taste and as William is himself nearly six feet high, it is not wonderful that he should be partial to that height. Now as I have a very great affection for my Brother and should be extremely sorry to see him unhappy, which I suppose he means to be if he cannot marry Matilda, as moreover I know that his circumstances will not allow him to marry any one without a fortune, and that Matilda's is entirely dependant on her Father, who will neither have his own inclination nor my permission to give her anything at present, I thought it would be doing a good-natured action by my Brother to let him know as much, in order that he might choose for himself, whether to conquer his passion, or Love and Despair. Accordingly finding myself this Morning alone with him in one of the horrid old rooms of this Castle, I opened the cause to him in the following Manner.

"Well my dear William what do you think of these girls? for my part, I do not find them so plain as I expected: but perhaps you may think me partial to the Daughters of my Husband and perhaps you are right—They are indeed so very like Sir George that it is natural to think"—

"My Dear Susan (cried he in a tone of the greatest amazement) You do not really think they bear the least resemblance to their Father! He is so very plain!—but I beg your pardon—I had entirely forgotten to whom I was speaking—"

"Oh! pray dont mind me; (replied I) every one knows Sir George is horribly ugly, and I assure you I always thought him a fright."

"You surprise me extremely (answered William) by what you say both with respect to Sir George and his Daughters. You cannot think your Husband so deficient in personal Charms as you speak of, nor can you surely see any resemblance between him and the Miss Lesleys who are in my opinion perfectly unlike him and perfectly Handsome."

"If that is your opinion with regard to the girls it certainly is no proof of their Fathers beauty, for if they are perfectly unlike him and very handsome at the same time, it is natural to suppose that he is very plain."

"By no means, (said he) for what may be pretty in a Woman, may be very unpleasing in a Man."

"But you yourself (replied I) but a few minutes ago allowed him to be very plain."

"Men are no Judges of Beauty in their own Sex." (said he).

"Neither Men nor Women can think Sir George tolerable."

"Well, well, (said he) we will not dispute about HIS Beauty, but your opinion of his DAUGHTERS is surely very singular, for if I understood you right, you said you did not find them so plain as you expected to do!"

"Why, do YOU find them plainer then?" (said I).

"I can scarcely beleive you to be serious (returned he) when you speak of their persons in so extroidinary a Manner. Do not you think the Miss Lesleys are two very handsome young Women?"

"Lord! No! (cried I) I think them terribly plain!"

"Plain! (replied He) My dear Susan, you cannot really think so! Why what single Feature in the face of either of them, can you possibly find fault with?"

"Oh! trust me for that; (replied I). Come I will begin with the eldest—with Matilda. Shall I, William?" (I looked as cunning as I could when I said it, in order to shame him).

"They are so much alike (said he) that I should suppose the faults of one, would be the faults of both."

"Well, then, in the first place; they are both so horribly tall!"

"They are TALLER than you are indeed." (said he with a saucy smile.)

"Nay, (said I), I know nothing of that."

"Well, but (he continued) tho' they may be above the common size, their figures are perfectly elegant; and as to their faces, their Eyes are beautifull."

"I never can think such tremendous, knock-me-down figures in the least degree elegant, and as for their eyes, they are so tall that I never could strain my neck enough to look at them."

"Nay, (replied he) I know not whether you may not be in the right in not attempting it, for perhaps they might dazzle you with their Lustre."

"Oh! Certainly. (said I, with the greatest complacency, for I assure you my dearest Charlotte I was not in the least offended tho' by what followed, one would suppose that William was conscious of having given me just cause to be so, for coming up to me and taking my hand, he said) "You must not look so grave Susan; you will make me fear I have offended you!"

"Offended me! Dear Brother, how came such a thought in your head! (returned I) No really! I assure you that I am not in the least surprised at your being so warm an advocate for the Beauty of these girls."—

"Well, but (interrupted William) remember that we have not yet concluded our dispute concerning them. What fault do you find with their complexion?"

"They are so horridly pale."

"They have always a little colour, and after any exercise it is considerably heightened."

"Yes, but if there should ever happen to be any rain in this part of the world, they will never be able raise more than their common stock—except indeed they amuse themselves with running up and Down these horrid old galleries and Antichambers."

"Well, (replied my Brother in a tone of vexation, and glancing an impertinent look at me) if they HAVE but little colour, at least, it is all their own."

This was too much my dear Charlotte, for I am certain that he had the impudence by that look, of pretending to suspect the reality of mine. But you I am sure will vindicate my character whenever you may hear it so cruelly aspersed, for you can witness how often I have protested against wearing Rouge, and how much I always told you I disliked it. And I assure you that my opinions are still the same.—. Well, not bearing to be so suspected by my Brother, I left the room immediately, and have been ever since in my own Dressing-room writing to you. What a long letter have I made of it! But you must not expect to receive such from me when I get to Town; for it is only at Lesley castle, that one has time to write even to a Charlotte Lutterell.—. I was so much vexed by William's glance, that I could not summon Patience enough, to stay and give him that advice respecting his attachment to Matilda which had first induced me from pure Love to him to begin the conversation; and I am now so thoroughly convinced by it, of his violent passion for her, that I am certain he would never hear reason on the subject, and I shall there fore give myself no more trouble either about him or his favourite. Adeiu my dear girl—Yrs affectionately Susan L.

LETTER the SEVENTH From Miss C. LUTTERELL to Miss M. LESLEY Bristol

The 27th of March

I have received Letters from you and your Mother-in-law within this week which have greatly entertained me, as I find by them that you are both downright jealous of each others Beauty. It is very odd that two pretty Women tho' actually Mother and Daughter cannot be in the same House without falling out about their faces. Do be convinced that you are both perfectly handsome and say no more of the Matter. I suppose this letter must be directed to Portman Square where probably (great as is your affection for Lesley Castle) you will not be sorry to find yourself. In spite of all that people may say about Green fields and the Country I was always of opinion that London and its amusements must be very agreable for a while, and should be very happy could my Mother's income allow her to jockey us into its Public-places, during Winter. I always longed particularly to go to Vaux-hall, to see whether the cold Beef there is cut so thin as it is reported, for I have a sly suspicion that few people understand the art of cutting a slice of cold Beef so well as I do: nay it would be hard if I did not know something of the Matter, for it was a part of my Education that I took by far the most pains with. Mama always found me HER best scholar, tho' when Papa was alive Eloisa was HIS. Never to be sure were there two more different Dispositions in the World. We both loved Reading. SHE preferred Histories, and I Receipts. She loved drawing, Pictures, and I drawing Pullets. No one could sing a better song than she, and no one make a better Pye than I.—And so it has always continued since we have been no longer children. The only difference is that all disputes on the superior excellence of our Employments THEN so frequent are now no more. We have for many years entered into an agreement always to admire each other's works; I never fail listening to HER Music, and she is as constant in eating my pies. Such at least was the case till Henry Hervey made his appearance in Sussex. Before the arrival of his Aunt in our neighbourhood where she established herself you know about a twelvemonth ago, his visits to her had been at stated times, and of equal and settled Duration; but on her removal to the Hall which is within a walk from our House, they became both more frequent and longer. This as you may suppose could not be pleasing to Mrs Diana who is a professed enemy to everything which is not directed by Decorum and Formality, or which bears the least resemblance to Ease and Good-breeding. Nay so great was her aversion to her Nephews behaviour that I have often heard her give such hints of it before his face that had not Henry at such times been engaged in conversation with Eloisa, they must have caught his Attention and have very much distressed him. The alteration in my Sisters behaviour which I have before hinted at, now took place. The Agreement we had entered into of admiring each others productions she no longer seemed to regard, and tho' I constantly applauded even every Country-dance, she played, yet not even a pidgeon-pye of my making could obtain from her a single word of approbation. This was certainly enough to put any one in a Passion; however, I was as cool as a cream-cheese and having formed my plan and concerted a scheme of Revenge, I was determined to let her have her own way and not even to make her a single reproach. My scheme was to treat her as she treated me, and tho' she might even draw my own Picture or play Malbrook (which is the only tune I ever really liked) not to say so much as "Thank you Eloisa;" tho' I had for many years constantly hollowed whenever she played, BRAVO, BRAVISSIMO, ENCORE, DA CAPO, ALLEGRETTO, CON EXPRESSIONE, and POCO PRESTO with many other such outlandish words, all of them as Eloisa told me expressive of my Admiration; and so indeed I suppose they are, as I see some of them in every Page of every Music book, being the sentiments I imagine of the composer. I executed my Plan with great Punctuality. I can not say success, for alas! my silence while she played seemed not in the least to displease her; on the contrary she actually said to me one day "Well Charlotte, I am very glad to find that you have at last left off that ridiculous custom of applauding my Execution on the Harpsichord till you made my head ake, and yourself hoarse. I feel very much obliged to you for keeping your admiration to yourself." I never shall forget the very witty answer I made to this speech. "Eloisa (said I) I beg you would be quite at your Ease with respect to all such fears in future, for be assured that I shall always keep my admiration to myself and my own pursuits and never extend it to yours." This was the only very severe thing I ever said in my Life; not but that I have often felt myself extremely satirical but it was the only time I ever made my feelings public.

I suppose there never were two Young people who had a greater affection for each other than Henry and Eloisa; no, the Love of your Brother for Miss Burton could not be so strong tho' it might be more violent. You may imagine therefore how provoked my Sister must have been to have him play her such a trick. Poor girl! she still laments his Death with undiminished constancy, notwithstanding he has been dead more than six weeks; but some People mind such things more than others. The ill state of Health into which his loss has thrown her makes her so weak, and so unable to support the least exertion, that she has been in tears all this Morning merely from having taken leave of Mrs. Marlowe who with her Husband, Brother and Child are to leave Bristol this morning. I am sorry to have them go because they are the only family with whom we have here any acquaintance, but I never thought of crying; to be sure Eloisa and Mrs Marlowe have always been more together than with me, and have therefore contracted a kind of affection for each other, which does not make Tears so inexcusable in them as they would be in me. The Marlowes are going to Town; Cliveland accompanies them; as neither Eloisa nor I could catch him I hope you or Matilda may have better Luck. I know not when we shall leave Bristol, Eloisa's spirits are so low that she is very averse to moving, and yet is certainly by no means mended by her residence here. A week or two will I hope determine our Measures—in the mean time believe me and etc—and etc—Charlotte Lutterell.

LETTER the EIGHTH Miss LUTTERELL to Mrs MARLOWE Bristol

April 4th

I feel myself greatly obliged to you my dear Emma for such a mark of your affection as I flatter myself was conveyed in the proposal you made me of our Corresponding; I assure you that it will be a great releif to me to write to you and as long as my Health and Spirits will allow me, you will find me a very constant correspondent; I will not say an entertaining one, for you know my situation suffciently not to be ignorant that in me Mirth would be improper and I know my own Heart too well not to be sensible that it would be unnatural. You must not expect news for we see no one with whom we are in the least acquainted, or in whose proceedings we have any Interest. You must not expect scandal for by the same rule we are equally debarred either from hearing or inventing it.—You must expect from me nothing but the melancholy effusions of a broken Heart which is ever reverting to the Happiness it once enjoyed and which ill supports its present wretchedness. The Possibility of being able to write, to speak, to you of my lost Henry will be a luxury to me, and your goodness will not I know refuse to read what it will so much releive my Heart to write. I once thought that to have what is in general called a Freind (I mean one of my own sex to whom I might speak with less reserve than to any other person) independant of my sister would never be an object of my wishes, but how much was I mistaken! Charlotte is too much engrossed by two confidential correspondents of that sort, to supply the place of one to me, and I hope you will not think me girlishly romantic, when I say that to have some kind and compassionate Freind who might listen to my sorrows without endeavouring to console me was what I had for some time wished for, when our acquaintance with you, the intimacy which followed it and the particular affectionate attention you paid me almost from the first, caused me to entertain the flattering Idea of those attentions being improved on a closer acquaintance into a Freindship which, if you were what my wishes formed you would be the greatest Happiness I could be capable of enjoying. To find that such Hopes are realised is a satisfaction indeed, a satisfaction which is now almost the only one I can ever experience.—I feel myself so languid that I am sure were you with me you would oblige me to leave off writing, and I cannot give you a greater proof of my affection for you than by acting, as I know you would wish me to do, whether Absent or Present. I am my dear Emmas sincere freind E. L.

LETTER the NINTH Mrs MARLOWE to Miss LUTTERELL

Grosvenor Street, April 10th

Need I say my dear Eloisa how wellcome your letter was to me I cannot give a greater proof of the pleasure I received from it, or of the Desire I feel that our Correspondence may be regular and frequent than by setting you so good an example as I now do in answering it before the end of the week—. But do not imagine that I claim any merit in being so punctual; on the contrary I assure you, that it is a far greater Gratification to me to write to you, than to spend the Evening either at a Concert or a Ball. Mr Marlowe is so desirous of my appearing at some of the Public places every evening that I do not like to refuse him, but at the same time so much wish to remain at Home, that independant of the Pleasure I experience in devoting any portion of my Time to my Dear Eloisa, yet the Liberty I claim from having a letter to write of spending an Evening at home with my little Boy, you know me well enough to be sensible, will of itself be a sufficient Inducement (if one is necessary) to my maintaining with Pleasure a Correspondence with you. As to the subject of your letters to me, whether grave or merry, if they concern you they must be equally interesting to me; not but that I think the melancholy Indulgence of your own sorrows by repeating them and dwelling on them to me, will only encourage and increase them, and that it will be more prudent in you to avoid so sad a subject; but yet knowing as I do what a soothing and melancholy Pleasure it must afford you, I cannot prevail on myself to deny you so great an Indulgence, and will only insist on your not expecting me to encourage you in it, by my own letters; on the contrary I intend to fill them with such lively Wit and enlivening Humour as shall even provoke a smile in the sweet but sorrowfull countenance of my Eloisa.

In the first place you are to learn that I have met your sisters three freinds Lady Lesley and her Daughters, twice in Public since I have been here. I know you will be impatient to hear my opinion of the Beauty of three Ladies of whom you have heard so much. Now, as you are too ill and too unhappy to be vain, I think I may venture to inform you that I like none of their faces so well as I do your own. Yet they are all handsome—Lady Lesley indeed I have seen before; her Daughters I beleive would in general be said to have a finer face than her Ladyship, and yet what with the charms of a Blooming complexion, a little Affectation and a great deal of small-talk, (in each of which she is superior to the young Ladies) she will I dare say gain herself as many admirers as the more regular features of Matilda, and Margaret. I am sure you will agree with me in saying that they can none of them be of a proper size for real Beauty, when you know that two of them are taller and the other shorter than ourselves. In spite of this Defect (or rather by reason of it) there is something very noble and majestic in the figures of the Miss Lesleys, and something agreably lively in the appearance of their pretty little Mother-in-law. But tho' one may be majestic and the other lively, yet the faces of neither possess that Bewitching sweetness of my Eloisas, which her present languor is so far from diminushing. What would my Husband and Brother say of us, if they knew all the fine things I have been saying to you in this letter. It is very hard that a pretty woman is never to be told she is so by any one of her own sex without that person's being suspected to be either her determined Enemy, or her professed Toad-eater. How much more amiable are women in that particular! One man may say forty civil things to another without our supposing that he is ever paid for it, and provided he does his Duty by our sex, we care not how Polite he is to his own.

Mrs Lutterell will be so good as to accept my compliments, Charlotte, my Love, and Eloisa the best wishes for the recovery of her Health and Spirits that can be offered by her affectionate Freind E. Marlowe.

I am afraid this letter will be but a poor specimen of my Powers in the witty way; and your opinion of them will not be greatly increased when I assure you that I have been as entertaining as I possibly could.

LETTER the TENTH From Miss MARGARET LESLEY to Miss CHARLOTTE LUTTERELL

Portman Square April 13th

MY DEAR CHARLOTTE We left Lesley-Castle on the 28th of last Month, and arrived safely in London after a Journey of seven Days; I had the pleasure of finding your Letter here waiting my Arrival, for which you have my grateful Thanks. Ah! my dear Freind I every day more regret the serene and tranquil Pleasures of the Castle we have left, in exchange for the uncertain and unequal Amusements of this vaunted City. Not that I will pretend to assert that these uncertain and unequal Amusements are in the least Degree unpleasing to me; on the contrary I enjoy them extremely and should enjoy them even more, were I not certain that every appearance I make in Public but rivetts the Chains of those unhappy Beings whose Passion it is impossible not to pity, tho' it is out of my power to return. In short my Dear Charlotte it is my sensibility for the sufferings of so many amiable young Men, my Dislike of the extreme admiration I meet with, and my aversion to being so celebrated both in Public, in Private, in Papers, and in Printshops, that are the reasons why I cannot more fully enjoy, the Amusements so various and pleasing of London. How often have I wished that I possessed as little Personal Beauty as you do; that my figure were as inelegant; my face as unlovely; and my appearance as unpleasing as yours! But ah! what little chance is there of so desirable an Event; I have had the small-pox, and must therefore submit to my unhappy fate.

I am now going to intrust you my dear Charlotte with a secret which has long disturbed the tranquility of my days, and which is of a kind to require the most inviolable Secrecy from you. Last Monday se'night Matilda and I accompanied Lady Lesley to a Rout at the Honourable Mrs Kickabout's; we were escorted by Mr Fitzgerald who is a very amiable young Man in the main, tho' perhaps a little singular in his Taste—He is in love with Matilda—. We had scarcely paid our Compliments to the Lady of the House and curtseyed to half a score different people when my Attention was attracted by the appearance of a Young Man the most lovely of his Sex, who at that moment entered the Room with another Gentleman and Lady. From the first moment I beheld him, I was certain that on him depended the future Happiness of my Life. Imagine my surprise when he was introduced to me by the name of Cleveland—I instantly recognised him as the Brother of Mrs Marlowe, and the acquaintance of my Charlotte at Bristol. Mr and Mrs M. were the gentleman and Lady who accompanied him. (You do not think Mrs Marlowe handsome?) The elegant address of Mr Cleveland, his polished Manners and Delightful Bow, at once confirmed my attachment. He did not speak; but I can imagine everything he would have said, had he opened his Mouth. I can picture to myself the cultivated Understanding, the Noble sentiments, and elegant Language which would have shone so conspicuous in the conversation of Mr Cleveland. The approach of Sir James Gower (one of my too numerous admirers) prevented the Discovery of any such Powers, by putting an end to a Conversation we had never commenced, and by attracting my attention to himself. But oh! how inferior are the accomplishments of Sir James to those of his so greatly envied Rival! Sir James is one of the most frequent of our Visitors, and is almost always of our Parties. We have since often met Mr and Mrs Marlowe but no Cleveland—he is always engaged some where else. Mrs Marlowe fatigues me to Death every time I see her by her tiresome Conversations about you and Eloisa. She is so stupid! I live in the hope of seeing her irrisistable Brother to night, as we are going to Lady Flambeaus, who is I know intimate with the Marlowes. Our party will be Lady Lesley, Matilda, Fitzgerald, Sir James Gower, and myself. We see little of Sir George, who is almost always at the gaming-table. Ah! my poor Fortune where art thou by this time? We see more of Lady L. who always makes her appearance (highly rouged) at Dinner-time. Alas! what Delightful Jewels will she be decked in this evening at Lady Flambeau's! Yet I wonder how she can herself delight in wearing them; surely she must be sensible of the ridiculous impropriety of loading her little diminutive figure with such superfluous ornaments; is it possible that she can not know how greatly superior an elegant simplicity is to the most studied apparel? Would she but Present them to Matilda and me, how greatly should we be obliged to her, How becoming would Diamonds be on our fine majestic figures! And how surprising it is that such an Idea should never have occurred to HER. I am sure if I have reflected in this manner once, I have fifty times. Whenever I see Lady Lesley dressed in them such reflections immediately come across me. My own Mother's Jewels too! But I will say no more on so melancholy a subject—let me entertain you with something more pleasing—Matilda had a letter this morning from Lesley, by which we have the pleasure of finding that he is at Naples has turned Roman-Catholic, obtained one of the Pope's Bulls for annulling his 1st Marriage and has since actually married a Neapolitan Lady of great Rank and Fortune. He tells us moreover that much the same sort of affair has befallen his first wife the worthless Louisa who is likewise at Naples had turned Roman-catholic, and is soon to be married to a Neapolitan Nobleman of great and Distinguished merit. He says, that they are at present very good Freinds, have quite forgiven all past errors and intend in future to be very good Neighbours. He invites Matilda and me to pay him a visit to Italy and to bring him his little Louisa whom both her Mother, Step-mother, and himself are equally desirous of beholding. As to our accepting his invitation, it is at Present very uncertain; Lady Lesley advises us to go without loss of time; Fitzgerald offers to escort us there, but Matilda has some doubts of the Propriety of such a scheme—she owns it would be very agreable. I am certain she likes the Fellow. My Father desires us not to be in a hurry, as perhaps if we wait a few months both he and Lady Lesley will do themselves the pleasure of attending us. Lady Lesley says no, that nothing will ever tempt her to forego the Amusements of Brighthelmstone for a Journey to Italy merely to see our Brother. "No (says the disagreable Woman) I have once in my life been fool enough to travel I dont know how many hundred Miles to see two of the Family, and I found it did not answer, so Deuce take me, if ever I am so foolish again." So says her Ladyship, but Sir George still Perseveres in saying that perhaps in a month or two, they may accompany us. Adeiu my Dear Charlotte Yrs faithful Margaret Lesley.

The History of England

FROM THE REIGN OF HENRY THE 4TH TO THE DEATH OF CHARLES THE 1ST

BY A PARTIAL, PREJUDICED, AND IGNORANT HISTORIAN.

To Miss Austen, eldest daughter of the Rev. George Austen, this work is inscribed with all due respect by THE AUTHOR.

N.B. There will be very few Dates in this History.

HENRY the 4th

Henry the 4th ascended the throne of England much to his own satisfaction in the year 1399, after having prevailed on his cousin and predecessor Richard the 2nd, to resign it to him, and to retire for the rest of his life to Pomfret Castle, where he happened to be murdered. It is to be supposed that Henry was married, since he had certainly four sons, but it is not in my power to inform the Reader who was his wife. Be this as it may, he did not live for ever, but falling ill, his son the Prince of Wales came and took away the crown; whereupon the King made a long speech, for which I must refer the Reader to Shakespear's Plays, and the Prince made a still longer. Things being thus settled between them the King died, and was succeeded by his son Henry who had previously beat Sir William Gascoigne.

HENRY the 5th

This Prince after he succeeded to the throne grew quite reformed and amiable, forsaking all his dissipated companions, and never thrashing Sir William again. During his reign, Lord Cobham was burnt alive, but I forget what for. His Majesty then turned his thoughts to France, where he went and fought the famous Battle of Agincourt. He afterwards married the King's daughter Catherine, a very agreable woman by Shakespear's account. In spite of all this however he died, and was succeeded by his son Henry.

HENRY the 6th

I cannot say much for this Monarch's sense. Nor would I if I could, for he was a Lancastrian. I suppose you know all about the Wars between him and the Duke of York who was of the right side; if you do not, you had better read some other History, for I shall not be very diffuse in this, meaning by it only to vent my spleen AGAINST, and shew my Hatred TO all those people whose parties or principles do not suit with mine, and not to give information. This King married Margaret of Anjou, a Woman whose distresses and misfortunes were so great as almost to make me who hate her, pity her. It was in this reign that Joan of Arc lived and made such a ROW among the English. They should not have burnt her—but they did. There were several Battles between the Yorkists and Lancastrians, in which the former (as they ought) usually conquered. At length they were entirely overcome; The King was murdered—The Queen was sent home—and Edward the 4th ascended the Throne.

EDWARD the 4th

This Monarch was famous only for his Beauty and his Courage, of which the Picture we have here given of him, and his undaunted Behaviour in marrying one Woman while he was engaged to another, are sufficient proofs. His Wife was Elizabeth Woodville, a Widow who, poor Woman! was afterwards confined in a Convent by that Monster of Iniquity and Avarice Henry the 7th. One of Edward's Mistresses was Jane Shore, who has had a play written about her, but it is a tragedy and therefore not worth reading. Having performed all these noble actions, his Majesty died, and was succeeded by his son.

EDWARD the 5th

This unfortunate Prince lived so little a while that nobody had him to draw his picture. He was murdered by his Uncle's Contrivance, whose name was Richard the 3rd.

RICHARD the 3rd

The Character of this Prince has been in general very severely treated by Historians, but as he was a YORK, I am rather inclined to suppose him a very respectable Man. It has indeed been confidently asserted that he killed his two Nephews and his Wife, but it has also been declared that he did not kill his two Nephews, which I am inclined to beleive true; and if this is the case, it may also be affirmed that he did not kill his Wife, for if Perkin Warbeck was really the Duke of York, why might not Lambert Simnel be the Widow of Richard. Whether innocent or guilty, he did not reign long in peace, for Henry Tudor E. of Richmond as great a villain as ever lived, made a great fuss about getting the Crown and having killed the King at the battle of Bosworth, he succeeded to it.

HENRY the 7th

This Monarch soon after his accession married the Princess Elizabeth of York, by which alliance he plainly proved that he thought his own right inferior to hers, tho' he pretended to the contrary. By this Marriage he had two sons and two daughters, the elder of which Daughters was married to the King of Scotland and had the happiness of being grandmother to one of the first Characters in the World. But of HER, I shall have occasion to speak more at large in future. The youngest, Mary, married first the King of France and secondly the D. of Suffolk, by whom she had one daughter, afterwards the Mother of Lady Jane Grey, who tho' inferior to her lovely Cousin the Queen of Scots, was yet an amiable young woman and famous for reading Greek while other people were hunting. It was in the reign of Henry the 7th that Perkin Warbeck and Lambert Simnel before mentioned made their appearance, the former of whom was set in the stocks, took shelter in Beaulieu Abbey, and was beheaded with the Earl of Warwick, and the latter was taken into the Kings kitchen. His Majesty died and was succeeded by his son Henry whose only merit was his not being quite so bad as his daughter Elizabeth.

HENRY the 8th

It would be an affront to my Readers were I to suppose that they were not as well acquainted with the particulars of this King's reign as I am myself. It will therefore be saving THEM the task of reading again what they have read before, and MYSELF the trouble of writing what I do not perfectly recollect, by giving only a slight sketch of the principal Events which marked his reign. Among these may be ranked Cardinal Wolsey's telling the father Abbott of Leicester Abbey that "he was come to lay his bones among them," the reformation in Religion and the King's riding through the streets of London with Anna Bullen. It is however but Justice, and my Duty to declare that this amiable Woman was entirely innocent of the Crimes with which she was accused, and of which her Beauty, her Elegance, and her Sprightliness were sufficient proofs, not to mention her solemn Protestations of Innocence, the weakness of the Charges against her, and the King's Character; all of which add some confirmation, tho' perhaps but slight ones when in comparison with those before alledged in her favour. Tho' I do not profess giving many dates, yet as I think it proper to give some and shall of course make choice of those which it is most necessary for the Reader to know, I think it right to inform him that her letter to the King was dated on the 6th of May. The Crimes and Cruelties of this Prince, were too numerous to be mentioned, (as this history I trust has fully shown;) and nothing can be said in his vindication, but that his abolishing Religious Houses and leaving them to the ruinous depredations of time has been of infinite use to the landscape of England in general, which probably was a principal motive for his doing it, since otherwise why should a Man who was of no Religion himself be at so much trouble to abolish one which had for ages been established in the Kingdom. His Majesty's 5th Wife was the Duke of Norfolk's Neice who, tho' universally acquitted of the crimes for which she was beheaded, has been by many people supposed to have led an abandoned life before her Marriage—of this however I have many doubts, since she was a relation of that noble Duke of Norfolk who was so warm in the Queen of Scotland's cause, and who at last fell a victim to it. The Kings last wife contrived to survive him, but with difficulty effected it. He was succeeded by his only son Edward.

EDWARD the 6th

As this prince was only nine years old at the time of his Father's death, he was considered by many people as too young to govern, and the late King happening to be of the same opinion, his mother's Brother the Duke of Somerset was chosen Protector of the realm during his minority. This Man was on the whole of a very amiable Character, and is somewhat of a favourite with me, tho' I would by no means pretend to affirm that he was equal to those first of Men Robert Earl of Essex, Delamere, or Gilpin. He was beheaded, of which he might with reason have been proud, had he known that such was the death of Mary Queen of Scotland; but as it was impossible that he should be conscious of what had never happened, it does not appear that he felt particularly delighted with the manner of it. After his decease the Duke of

Northumberland had the care of the King and the Kingdom, and performed his trust of both so well that the King died and the Kingdom was left to his daughter in law the Lady Jane Grey, who has been already mentioned as reading Greek. Whether she really understood that language or whether such a study proceeded only from an excess of vanity for which I beleive she was always rather remarkable, is uncertain. Whatever might be the cause, she preserved the same appearance of knowledge, and contempt of what was generally esteemed pleasure, during the whole of her life, for she declared herself displeased with being appointed Queen, and while conducting to the scaffold, she wrote a sentence in Latin and another in Greek on seeing the dead Body of her Husband accidentally passing that way.

MARY

This woman had the good luck of being advanced to the throne of England, in spite of the superior pretensions, Merit, and Beauty of her Cousins Mary Queen of Scotland and Jane Grey. Nor can I pity the Kingdom for the misfortunes they experienced during her Reign, since they fully deserved them, for having allowed her to succeed her Brother—which was a double peice of folly, since they might have foreseen that as she died without children, she would be succeeded by that disgrace to humanity, that pest of society, Elizabeth. Many were the people who fell martyrs to the protestant Religion during her reign; I suppose not fewer than a dozen. She married Philip King of Spain who in her sister's reign was famous for building Armadas. She died without issue, and then the dreadful moment came in which the destroyer of all comfort, the deceitful Betrayer of trust reposed in her, and the Murderess of her Cousin succeeded to the Throne.——

ELIZABETH

It was the peculiar misfortune of this Woman to have bad Ministers——Since wicked as she herself was, she could not have committed such extensive mischeif, had not these vile and abandoned Men connived at, and encouraged her in her Crimes. I know that it has by many people been asserted and beleived that Lord Burleigh, Sir Francis Walsingham, and the rest of those who filled the cheif offices of State were deserving, experienced, and able Ministers. But oh! how blinded such writers and such Readers must be to true Merit, to Merit despised, neglected and defamed, if they can persist in such opinions when they reflect that these men, these boasted men were such scandals to their Country and their sex as to allow and assist their Queen in confining for the space of nineteen years, a WOMAN who if the claims of Relationship and Merit were of no avail, yet as a Queen and as one who condescended to place confidence in her, had every reason to expect assistance and protection; and at length in allowing Elizabeth to bring this amiable Woman to an untimely, unmerited, and scandalous Death. Can any one if he reflects but for a moment on this blot, this everlasting blot upon their understanding and their Character, allow any praise to Lord Burleigh or Sir Francis Walsingham? Oh! what must this bewitching Princess whose only freind was then the Duke of Norfolk, and whose only ones now Mr Whitaker, Mrs Lefroy, Mrs Knight and myself, who was abandoned by her son, confined by her Cousin, abused, reproached and vilified by all, what must not her most noble mind have suffered when informed that Elizabeth had given orders for her Death! Yet she bore it with a most unshaken fortitude, firm in her mind; constant in her Religion; and prepared herself to meet the cruel fate to which she was doomed, with a magnanimity that would alone proceed from conscious Innocence. And yet could you Reader have beleived it possible that some hardened and zealous Protestants have even abused her for that steadfastness in the Catholic Religion which reflected on her so much credit? But this is a striking proof of THEIR narrow souls and prejudiced Judgements who accuse her. She was executed in the Great Hall at Fortheringay Castle (sacred Place!) on Wednesday the 8th of February 1586—to the everlasting Reproach of Elizabeth, her Ministers, and of England in general. It may not be unnecessary before I entirely conclude my account of this ill-fated Queen, to observe that she had been accused of several crimes during the time of her reigning in Scotland, of which I now most seriously do assure my Reader that she was entirely innocent; having never been guilty of anything more than Imprudencies into which she was betrayed by the openness of her Heart, her Youth, and her Education. Having I trust by this assurance entirely done away every Suspicion and every doubt which might have arisen in the Reader's mind, from what other Historians have written of her, I shall proceed to mention the remaining Events that marked Elizabeth's reign. It was about this time that Sir Francis Drake the first English Navigator who sailed round the World, lived, to be the ornament of his Country and his profession. Yet great as he was, and justly celebrated as a sailor, I cannot help foreseeing that he will be equalled in this or the next Century by one who tho' now but young, already promises to answer all the ardent and sanguine expectations of his Relations and Freinds, amongst whom I may class the amiable Lady to whom this work is dedicated, and my no less amiable self.

Though of a different profession, and shining in a different sphere of Life, yet equally conspicuous in the Character of an Earl, as Drake was in that of a Sailor, was Robert Devereux Lord Essex. This unfortunate young Man was not unlike in character to that equally unfortunate one FREDERIC DELAMERE. The simile may be carried still farther, and Elizabeth the torment of Essex may be compared to the Emmeline of Delamere. It would be endless to recount the misfortunes of this noble and gallant Earl. It is sufficient to say that he was beheaded on the 25th of Feb, after having been Lord Lieutenant of Ireland, after having clapped his hand on his sword, and after performing many other services to his Country. Elizabeth did not long survive his loss, and died so miserable that were it not an injury to the memory of Mary I should pity her.

JAMES the 1st

Though this King had some faults, among which and as the most principal, was his allowing his Mother's death, yet considered on the whole I cannot help liking him. He married Anne of Denmark, and had several Children; fortunately for him his eldest son Prince Henry died before his father or he might have experienced the evils which befell his unfortunate Brother.

As I am myself partial to the roman catholic religion, it is with infinite regret that I am obliged to blame the Behaviour of any Member of it: yet Truth being I think very excusable in an Historian, I am necessitated to say that in this reign the roman Catholics of England did not behave like Gentlemen to the protestants. Their Behaviour indeed to the Royal Family and both Houses of Parliament might justly be considered by them as very uncivil, and even Sir Henry Percy tho' certainly the best bred man of the party, had none of that general politeness which is so universally pleasing, as his attentions were entirely confined to Lord Mounteagle.

Sir Walter Raleigh flourished in this and the preceeding reign, and is by many people held in great veneration and respect—But as he was an enemy of the noble Essex, I have nothing to say in praise of him, and must refer all those who may wish to be acquainted with the particulars of his life, to Mr Sheridan's play of the Critic, where they will find many interesting anecdotes as well of him as of his friend Sir Christopher Hatton.—His Majesty was of that amiable disposition which inclines to Freindship, and in such points was possessed of a keener penetration in discovering Merit than many other people. I once heard an excellent Sharade on a Carpet, of which the subject I am now on reminds me, and as I think it may afford my Readers some amusement to FIND IT OUT, I shall here take the liberty of presenting it to them.

SHARADE My first is what my second was to King James the 1st, and you tread on my whole.

The principal favourites of his Majesty were Car, who was afterwards created Earl of Somerset and whose name perhaps may have some share in the above mentioned Sharade, and George Villiers afterwards Duke of Buckingham. On his Majesty's death he was succeeded by his son Charles.

CHARLES the 1st

This amiable Monarch seems born to have suffered misfortunes equal to those of his lovely Grandmother; misfortunes which he could not deserve since he was her descendant. Never certainly were there before so many detestable Characters at one time in England as in this Period of its History; never were amiable men so scarce. The number of them throughout the whole Kingdom amounting only to FIVE, besides the inhabitants of Oxford who were always loyal to their King and faithful to his interests. The names of this noble five who never forgot the duty of the subject, or swerved from their attachment to his Majesty, were as follows—The King himself, ever stedfast in his own support—Archbishop Laud, Earl of Strafford, Viscount Faulkland and Duke of Ormond, who were scarcely less strenuous or zealous in the cause. While the VILLIANS of the time would make too long a list to be written or read; I shall therefore content myself with mentioning the leaders of the Gang. Cromwell, Fairfax, Hampden, and Pym may be considered as the original Causers of all the disturbances, Distresses, and Civil Wars in which England for many years was embroiled. In this reign as well as in that of Elizabeth, I am obliged in spite of my attachment to the Scotch, to consider them as equally guilty with the generality of the English, since they dared to think differently from their Sovereign, to forget the Adoration which as STUARTS it was their Duty to pay them, to rebel against, dethrone and imprison the unfortunate Mary; to oppose, to deceive, and to sell the no less unfortunate Charles. The Events of this Monarch's reign are too numerous for my pen, and indeed the recital of any Events (except what I make myself) is uninteresting to me; my principal reason for undertaking the History of England being to Prove the innocence of the Queen of Scotland, which I flatter myself with having effectually done, and to abuse Elizabeth, tho' I am rather fearful of having fallen short in the latter part of my scheme.—As therefore it is not my intention to give any particular account of the distresses into which this King was involved through the misconduct and Cruelty of his Parliament, I shall satisfy myself with vindicating him from the Reproach of Arbitrary and tyrannical Government with which he has often been charged. This, I feel, is not difficult to be done, for with one argument I am certain of satisfying every sensible and well disposed person whose opinions have been properly guided by a good Education—and this Argument is that he was a STUART.

Finis Saturday Nov: 26th 1791.

A Collection of Letters

To Miss COOPER

COUSIN Conscious of the Charming Character which in every Country, and every Clime in Christendom is Cried, Concerning you, with Caution and Care I Commend to your Charitable Criticism this Clever Collection of Curious Comments, which have been Carefully Culled, Collected and Classed by your Comical Cousin

The Author.

LETTER the FIRST From a MOTHER to her FREIND.

My Children begin now to claim all my attention in different Manner from that in which they have been used to receive it, as they are now arrived at that age when it is necessary for them in some measure to become conversant with the World, My Augusta is 17 and her sister scarcely a twelvemonth younger. I flatter myself that their education has been such as will not disgrace their appearance in the World, and that THEY will not disgrace their Education I have every reason to beleive. Indeed they are sweet Girls—. Sensible yet unaffected— Accomplished yet Easy—. Lively yet Gentle—. As their progress in every thing they have learnt has been always the same, I am willing to forget the difference of age, and to introduce them together into Public. This very Evening is fixed on as their first ENTREE into Life, as we are to drink tea with Mrs Cope and her Daughter. I am glad that we are to meet no one, for my Girls sake, as it would be awkward for them to enter too wide a Circle on the very first day. But we shall proceed by degrees.—Tomorrow Mr Stanly's family will drink tea with us, and perhaps the Miss Phillips's will meet them. On Tuesday we shall pay Morning Visits—On Wednesday we are to dine at Westbrook. On Thursday we have Company at home. On Friday we are to be at a Private Concert at Sir John Wynna's—and on Saturday we expect Miss Dawson to call in the Morning—which will complete my Daughters Introduction into Life. How they will bear so much dissipation I cannot imagine; of their spirits I have no fear, I only dread their health.

    This mighty affair is now happily over, and my Girls are OUT. As the moment approached for our departure, you can have no idea how the sweet Creatures trembled with fear and expectation. Before the Carriage drove to the door, I called them into my dressing-room, and as soon as they were seated thus addressed them. "My dear Girls the moment is now arrived when I am to reap the rewards of all my Anxieties and Labours towards you during your Education. You are this Evening to enter a World in which you will meet with many wonderfull Things; Yet let me warn you against suffering yourselves to be meanly swayed by the Follies and Vices of others, for beleive me my beloved Children that if you do—I shall be very sorry for it." They both assured me that they would ever remember my advice with Gratitude, and follow it with attention; That they were prepared to find a World full of things to amaze and to shock them: but that they trusted their behaviour would never give me reason to repent the Watchful Care with which I had presided over their infancy and formed their Minds—" "With such expectations and such intentions (cried I) I can have nothing to fear from you—and can chearfully conduct you to Mrs Cope's without a fear of your being seduced by her Example, or contaminated by her Follies. Come, then my Children (added I) the Carriage is driving to the door, and I will not a moment delay the happiness you are so impatient to enjoy." When we arrived at Warleigh, poor Augusta could scarcely breathe, while Margaret was all Life and Rapture. "The long-expected Moment is now arrived (said she) and we shall soon be in the World."—In a few Moments we were in Mrs Cope's parlour, where with her daughter she sate ready to receive us. I observed with delight the impression my Children made on them—. They were indeed two sweet, elegant-looking Girls, and tho' somewhat abashed from the peculiarity of their situation, yet there was an ease in their Manners and address which could not fail of pleasing—. Imagine my dear Madam how delighted I must have been in beholding as I did, how attentively they observed every object they saw, how disgusted with some Things, how enchanted with others, how astonished at all! On the whole however they returned in raptures with the World, its Inhabitants, and Manners.

Yrs Ever—A. F.

LETTER the SECOND From a YOUNG LADY crossed in Love to her friend

Why should this last disappointment hang so heavily on my spirits? Why should I feel it more, why should it wound me deeper than those I have experienced before? Can it be that I have a greater affection for Willoughby than I had for his amiable predecessors? Or is it that our feelings become more acute from being often wounded? I must suppose my dear Belle that this is the Case, since I am not conscious of being more sincerely attached to Willoughby than I was to Neville, Fitzowen, or either of the Crawfords, for all of whom I once felt the most lasting affection that ever warmed a Woman's heart. Tell me then dear Belle why I still sigh when I think of the faithless Edward, or why I weep when I behold his Bride, for too surely this is the case—. My Freinds are all alarmed for me; They fear my declining health; they lament my want of spirits; they dread the effects of both. In hopes of releiving my melancholy, by directing my thoughts to other objects, they have invited several of their freinds to spend the Christmas with us. Lady Bridget Darkwood and her sister-in-law, Miss Jane are expected on Friday; and Colonel Seaton's family will be with us next week. This is all most kindly meant by my Uncle and Cousins; but what can the presence of a dozen indefferent people do to me, but weary and distress me—. I will not finish my Letter till some of our Visitors are arrived.

Friday Evening Lady Bridget came this morning, and with her, her sweet sister Miss Jane—. Although I have been acquainted with this charming Woman above fifteen Years, yet I never before observed how lovely she is. She is now about 35, and in spite of sickness, sorrow and Time is more blooming than I ever saw a Girl of 17. I was delighted with her, the moment she entered the house, and she appeared equally pleased with me, attaching herself to me during the remainder of the day. There is something so sweet, so mild in her Countenance, that she seems more than Mortal. Her Conversation is as bewitching as her appearance; I could not help telling her how much she engaged my admiration—. "Oh! Miss Jane (said I)—and stopped from an inability at the moment of expressing myself as I could wish—Oh! Miss Jane—(I repeated)—I could not think of words to suit my feelings—She seemed waiting for my speech—. I was confused—distressed—my thoughts were bewildered—and I could only add—"How do you do?" She saw and felt for my Embarrassment and with admirable presence of mind releived me from it by saying—"My dear Sophia be not uneasy at having exposed yourself—I will turn the Conversation without appearing to notice it. "Oh! how I loved her for her kindness!" Do you ride as much as you used to do?" said she—. "I am advised to ride by my Physician. We have delightful Rides round us, I have a Charming horse, am uncommonly fond of the Amusement, replied I quite recovered from my Confusion, and in short I ride a great deal." "You are in the right my Love," said she. Then repeating the following line which was an extempore and equally adapted to recommend both Riding and Candour—

"Ride where you may, Be Candid where you can," she added," I rode once, but it is many years ago—She spoke this in so low and tremulous a Voice, that I was silent—. Struck with her Manner of speaking I could make no reply. "I have not ridden, continued she fixing her Eyes on my face, since I was married." I was never so surprised—"Married, Ma'am!" I repeated. "You may well wear that look of astonishment, said she, since what I have said must appear improbable to you—Yet nothing is more true than that I once was married."

"Then why are you called Miss Jane?"

"I married, my Sophia without the consent or knowledge of my father the late Admiral Annesley. It was therefore necessary to keep the secret from him and from every one, till some fortunate opportunity might offer of revealing it—. Such an opportunity alas! was but too soon given in the death of my dear Capt. Dashwood—Pardon these tears, continued Miss Jane wiping her Eyes, I owe them to my Husband's memory. He fell my Sophia, while fighting for his Country in America after a most happy Union of seven years—. My Children, two sweet Boys and a Girl, who had constantly resided with my Father and me, passing with him and with every one as the Children of a Brother (tho' I had ever been an only Child) had as yet been the comforts of my Life. But no sooner had I lossed my Henry, than these sweet Creatures fell sick and died—. Conceive dear Sophia what my feelings must have been when as an Aunt I attended my Children to their early Grave—. My Father did not survive them many weeks— He died, poor Good old man, happily ignorant to his last hour of my Marriage.'

"But did not you own it, and assume his name at your husband's death?"

"No; I could not bring myself to do it; more especially when in my Children I lost all inducement for doing it. Lady Bridget, and yourself are the only persons who are in the knowledge of my having ever been either Wife or Mother. As I could not Prevail on myself to take the name of Dashwood (a name which after my Henry's death I could never hear without emotion) and as I was conscious of having no right to that of Annesley, I dropt all thoughts of either, and have made it a point of bearing only my Christian one since my Father's death." She paused—"Oh! my dear Miss Jane (said I) how infinitely am I obliged to you for so entertaining a story! You cannot think how it has diverted me! But have you quite done?"

"I have only to add my dear Sophia, that my Henry's elder Brother dieing about the same time, Lady Bridget became a Widow like myself, and as we had always loved each other in idea from the high Character in which we had ever been spoken of, though we had never met, we determined to live together. We wrote to one another on the same subject by the same post, so exactly did our feeling and our actions coincide! We both eagerly embraced the proposals we gave and received of becoming one family, and have from that time lived together in the greatest affection."

"And is this all? said I, I hope you have not done."

"Indeed I have; and did you ever hear a story more pathetic?"

"I never did—and it is for that reason it pleases me so much, for when one is unhappy nothing is so delightful to one's sensations as to hear of equal misery."

"Ah! but my Sophia why are YOU unhappy?"

"Have you not heard Madam of Willoughby's Marriage?"

"But my love why lament HIS perfidy, when you bore so well that of many young Men before?"

"Ah! Madam, I was used to it then, but when Willoughby broke his Engagements I had not been dissapointed for half a year."

"Poor Girl!" said Miss Jane.

LETTER the THIRD From a YOUNG LADY in distressed Circumstances to her friend
A few days ago I was at a private Ball given by Mr Ashburnham. As my Mother never goes out she entrusted me to the care of Lady Greville who did me the honour of calling for me in her way and of allowing me to sit forwards, which is a favour about which I am very indifferent especially as I know it is considered as confering a great obligation on me "So Miss Maria (said her Ladyship as she saw me advancing to the door of the Carriage) you seem very smart to night—MY poor Girls will appear quite to disadvantage by YOU—I only hope your Mother may not have distressed herself to set YOU off. Have you got a new Gown on?"

"Yes Ma'am." replied I with as much indifference as I could assume.

"Aye, and a fine one too I think—(feeling it, as by her permission I seated myself by her) I dare say it is all very smart—But I must own, for you know I always speak my mind, that I think it was quite a needless piece of expence—Why could not you have worn your old striped one? It is not my way to find fault with People because they are poor, for I always think that they are more to be despised and pitied than blamed for it, especially if they cannot help it, but at the same time I must say that in my opinion your old striped Gown would have been quite fine enough for its Wearer—for to tell you the truth (I always speak my mind) I am very much afraid that one half of the people in the room will not know whether you have a Gown on or not—But I suppose you intend to make your fortune to night—. Well, the sooner the better; and I wish you success."

"Indeed Ma'am I have no such intention—"

"Who ever heard a young Lady own that she was a Fortune-hunter?" Miss Greville laughed but I am sure Ellen felt for me.

"Was your Mother gone to bed before you left her?" said her Ladyship.

"Dear Ma'am, said Ellen it is but nine o'clock."

"True Ellen, but Candles cost money, and Mrs Williams is too wise to be extravagant."

"She was just sitting down to supper Ma'am."

"And what had she got for supper?" "I did not observe." "Bread and Cheese I suppose." "I should never wish for a better supper." said Ellen. "You have never any reason replied her Mother, as a better is always provided for you." Miss Greville laughed excessively, as she constantly does at her Mother's wit.

Such is the humiliating Situation in which I am forced to appear while riding in her Ladyship's Coach—I dare not be impertinent, as my Mother is always admonishing me to be humble and patient if I wish to make my way in the world. She insists on my accepting every invitation of Lady Greville, or you may be certain that I would never enter either her House, or her Coach with the disagreable certainty I always have of being abused for my Poverty while I am in them.—When we arrived at Ashburnham, it was nearly ten o'clock, which was an hour and a half later than we were desired to be there; but Lady Greville is too fashionable (or fancies herself to be so) to be punctual. The Dancing however was not begun as they waited for Miss Greville. I had not been long in the room before I was engaged to dance by Mr Bernard, but just as we were going to stand up, he recollected that his Servant had got his white Gloves, and immediately ran out to fetch them. In the mean time the Dancing began and Lady Greville in passing to another room went exactly before me—She saw me and instantly stopping, said to me though there were several people close to us,

"Hey day, Miss Maria! What cannot you get a partner? Poor Young Lady! I am afraid your new Gown was put on for nothing. But do not despair; perhaps you may get a hop before the Evening is over." So saying, she passed on without hearing my repeated assurance of being engaged, and leaving me very much provoked at being so exposed before every one—Mr Bernard however soon returned and by coming to me the moment he entered the room, and leading me to the Dancers my Character I hope was cleared from the imputation Lady Greville had thrown on it, in the eyes of all the old Ladies who had heard her speech. I soon forgot all my vexations in the pleasure of dancing and of having the most agreable partner in the room. As he is moreover heir to a very large Estate I could see that Lady Greville did not look very well pleased when she found who had been his Choice—She was determined to mortify me, and accordingly when we were sitting down between the dances, she came to me with more than her usual insulting importance attended by Miss Mason and said loud enough to be heard by half the people in the room, "Pray Miss Maria in what way of business was your Grandfather? for Miss Mason and I cannot agree whether he was a Grocer or a Bookbinder." I saw that she wanted to mortify me, and was resolved if I possibly could to Prevent her seeing that her scheme succeeded. "Neither Madam; he was a Wine Merchant." "Aye, I knew he was in some such low way—He broke did not he?" "I beleive not Ma'am." "Did not he abscond?" "I never heard that he did." "At least he died insolvent?" "I was never told so before." "Why, was not your FATHER as poor as a Rat" "I fancy not." "Was not he in the Kings Bench once?" "I never saw him there." She gave me SUCH a look, and turned away in a great passion; while I was half delighted with myself for my impertinence, and half afraid of being thought too saucy. As Lady Greville was extremely angry with me, she took no further notice of me all the Evening, and indeed had I been in favour I should have been equally neglected, as she was got into a Party of great folks and she never speaks to me when she can to anyone else. Miss Greville was with her Mother's party at supper, but Ellen preferred staying with the Bernards and me. We had a very pleasant Dance and as Lady G—slept all the way home, I had a very comfortable ride.

The next day while we were at dinner Lady Greville's Coach stopped at the door, for that is the time of day she generally contrives it should. She sent in a message by the servant to say that "she should not get out but that Miss Maria must come to the Coach-door, as she wanted to speak to her, and that she must make haste and come immediately—" "What an impertinent Message Mama!" said I—"Go Maria—" replied she—Accordingly I went and was obliged to stand there at her Ladyships pleasure though the Wind was extremely high and very cold.

"Why I think Miss Maria you are not quite so smart as you were last night—But I did not come to examine your dress, but to tell you that you may dine with us the day after tomorrow—Not tomorrow, remember, do not come tomorrow, for we expect Lord and Lady Clermont and Sir Thomas Stanley's family—There will be no occasion for your being very fine for I shant send the Carriage—If it rains you may take an umbrella—" I could hardly help laughing at hearing her give me leave to keep myself dry—"And pray remember to be in time, for I shant wait—I hate my Victuals over-done—But you need not come before the time—How does your Mother do? She is at dinner is not she?" "Yes Ma'am we were in the middle of dinner when your Ladyship came." "I am afraid you find it very cold Maria." said Ellen. "Yes, it is an horrible East wind—said her Mother—I assure you I can hardly bear the window down—But you are used to be blown about by the wind Miss Maria and that is what has made your Complexion so rudely and coarse. You young Ladies who cannot often ride in a Carriage never mind what weather you trudge in, or how the wind shews your legs. I would not have my Girls stand out of doors as you do in such a day as this. But some sort of people have no feelings either of cold or Delicacy—Well, remember that we shall expect you on Thursday at 5 o'clock—You must tell your Maid to come for you at night—There will be no Moon—and you will have an horrid walk home—My compts to Your Mother—I am afraid your dinner will be cold—Drive on—" And away she went, leaving me in a great passion with her as she always does.

Maria Williams.

LETTER the FOURTH From a YOUNG LADY rather impertinent to her friend

We dined yesterday with Mr Evelyn where we were introduced to a very agreable looking Girl his Cousin. I was extremely pleased with her appearance, for added to the charms of an engaging face, her manner and voice had something peculiarly interesting in them. So much so, that they inspired me with a great curiosity to know the history of her Life, who were her Parents, where she came from, and what had befallen her, for it was then only known that she was a relation of Mr Evelyn, and that her name was Grenville. In the evening a favourable opportunity offered to me of attempting at least to know what I wished to know, for every one played at Cards but Mrs Evelyn, My Mother, Dr Drayton, Miss Grenville and myself, and as the two former were engaged in a whispering Conversation, and the Doctor fell asleep, we were of necessity obliged to entertain each other. This was what I wished and being determined not to remain in ignorance for want of asking, I began the Conversation in the following Manner.

"Have you been long in Essex Ma'am?"

"I arrived on Tuesday."

"You came from Derbyshire?"

"No, Ma'am! appearing surprised at my question, from Suffolk." You will think this a good dash of mine my dear Mary, but you know that I am not wanting for Impudence when I have any end in veiw. "Are you pleased with the Country Miss Grenville? Do you find it equal to the one you have left?"

"Much superior Ma'am in point of Beauty." She sighed. I longed to know for why.

"But the face of any Country however beautiful said I, can be but a poor consolation for the loss of one's dearest Freinds." She shook her head, as if she felt the truth of what I said. My Curiosity was so much raised, that I was resolved at any rate to satisfy it.

"You regret having left Suffolk then Miss Grenville?" "Indeed I do." "You were born there I suppose?" "Yes Ma'am I was and passed many happy years there—"

"That is a great comfort—said I—I hope Ma'am that you never spent any unhappy one's there."

"Perfect Felicity is not the property of Mortals, and no one has a right to expect uninterrupted Happiness.—Some Misfortunes I have certainly met with."

"WHAT Misfortunes dear Ma'am? replied I, burning with impatience to know every thing. "NONE Ma'am I hope that have been the effect of any wilfull fault in me." "I dare say not Ma'am, and have no doubt but that any sufferings you may have experienced could arise only from the cruelties of Relations or the Errors of Freinds." She sighed—"You seem unhappy my dear Miss Grenville—Is it in my power to soften your Misfortunes?" "YOUR power Ma'am replied she extremely surprised; it is in NO ONES power to make me happy." She pronounced these words in so mournfull and solemn an accent, that for some time I had not courage to reply. I was actually silenced. I recovered myself however in a few moments and looking at her with all the affection I could, "My dear Miss Grenville said I, you appear extremely young—and may probably stand in need of some one's advice whose regard for you, joined to superior Age, perhaps superior Judgement might authorise her to give it. I am that person, and I now challenge you to accept the offer I make you of my Confidence and Freindship, in return to which I shall only ask for yours—"

"You are extremely obliging Ma'am—said she—and I am highly flattered by your attention to me—But I am in no difficulty, no doubt, no uncertainty of situation in which any advice can be wanted. Whenever I am however continued she brightening into a complaisant smile, I shall know where to apply."

I bowed, but felt a good deal mortified by such a repulse; still however I had not given up my point. I found that by the appearance of sentiment and Freindship nothing was to be gained and determined therefore to renew my attacks by Questions and suppositions. "Do you intend staying long in this part of England Miss Grenville?"

"Yes Ma'am, some time I beleive."

"But how will Mr and Mrs Grenville bear your absence?"

"They are neither of them alive Ma'am." This was an answer I did not expect—I was quite silenced, and never felt so awkward in my Life—-.

LETTER the FIFTH From a YOUNG LADY very much in love to her Friend

My Uncle gets more stingy, my Aunt more particular, and I more in love every day. What shall we all be at this rate by the end of the year! I had this morning the happiness of receiving the following Letter from my dear Musgrove.

Sackville St: Janry 7th

It is a month to day since I first beheld my lovely Henrietta, and the sacred anniversary must and shall be kept in a manner becoming the day—by writing to her. Never shall I forget the moment when her Beauties first broke on my sight—No time as you well know can erase it from my Memory. It was at Lady Scudamores. Happy Lady Scudamore to live within a mile of the divine Henrietta! When the lovely Creature first entered the room, oh! what were my sensations? The sight of you was like the sight of a wonderful fine Thing. I started—I gazed at her with admiration—She appeared every moment more Charming, and the unfortunate Musgrove became a captive to your Charms before I had time to look about me. Yes Madam, I had the happiness of adoring you, an happiness for which I cannot be too grateful. "What said he to himself is Musgrove allowed to die for Henrietta? Enviable Mortal! and may he pine for her who is the object of universal admiration, who is adored by a Colonel, and toasted by a Baronet! Adorable Henrietta how beautiful you are! I declare you are quite divine! You are more than Mortal. You are an Angel. You are Venus herself. In short Madam you are the prettiest Girl I ever saw in my Life—and her Beauty is encreased in her Musgroves Eyes, by permitting him to love her and allowing me to hope. And ah! Angelic Miss Henrietta Heaven is my witness how ardently I do hope for the death of your villanous Uncle and his abandoned Wife, since my fair one will not consent to be mine till their decease has placed her in affluence above what my fortune can procure—. Though it is an improvable Estate—. Cruel Henrietta to persist in such a resolution! I am at Present with my sister where I mean to continue till my own house which tho' an excellent one is at Present somewhat out of repair, is ready to receive me. Amiable princess of my Heart farewell—Of that Heart which trembles while it signs itself Your most ardent Admirer and devoted humble servt.

T. Musgrove.

There is a pattern for a Love-letter Matilda! Did you ever read such a master-piece of Writing? Such sense, such sentiment, such purity of Thought, such flow of Language and such unfeigned Love in one sheet? No, never I can answer for it, since a Musgrove is not to be met with by every Girl. Oh! how I long to be with him! I intend to send him the following in answer to his Letter tomorrow.

My dearest Musgrove—. Words cannot express how happy your Letter made me; I thought I should have cried for joy, for I love you better than any body in the World. I think you the most amiable, and the handsomest Man in England, and so to be sure you are. I never read so sweet a Letter in my Life. Do write me another just like it, and tell me you are in love with me in every other line. I quite die to see you. How shall we manage to see one another? for we are so much in love that we cannot live asunder. Oh! my dear Musgrove you cannot think how impatiently I wait for the death of my Uncle and Aunt—If they will not Die soon, I beleive I shall run mad, for I get more in love with you every day of my Life.

How happy your Sister is to enjoy the pleasure of your Company in her house, and how happy every body in London must be because you are there. I hope you will be so kind as to write to me again soon, for I never read such sweet Letters as yours. I am my dearest Musgrove most truly and faithfully yours for ever and ever

Henrietta Halton.

I hope he will like my answer; it is as good a one as I can write though nothing to his; Indeed I had always heard what a dab he was at a Love-letter. I saw him you know for the first time at Lady Scudamores—And when I saw her Ladyship afterwards she asked me how I liked her Cousin Musgrove?

"Why upon my word said I, I think he is a very handsome young Man."

"I am glad you think so replied she, for he is distractedly in love with you."

"Law! Lady Scudamore said I, how can you talk so ridiculously?"

"Nay, t'is very true answered she, I assure you, for he was in love with you from the first moment he beheld you."

"I wish it may be true said I, for that is the only kind of love I would give a farthing for—There is some sense in being in love at first sight."

"Well, I give you Joy of your conquest, replied Lady Scudamore, and I beleive it to have been a very complete one; I am sure it is not a contemptible one, for my Cousin is a charming young fellow, has seen a great deal of the World, and writes the best Love-letters I ever read."

This made me very happy, and I was excessively pleased with my conquest. However, I thought it was proper to give myself a few Airs—so I said to her—

"This is all very pretty Lady Scudamore, but you know that we young Ladies who are Heiresses must not throw ourselves away upon Men who have no fortune at all."

"My dear Miss Halton said she, I am as much convinced of that as you can be, and I do assure you that I should be the last person to encourage your marrying anyone who had not some pretensions to expect a fortune with you. Mr Musgrove is so far from being poor that he has an estate of several hundreds an year which is capable of great Improvement, and an excellent House, though at Present it is not quite in repair."

"If that is the case replied I, I have nothing more to say against him, and if as you say he is an informed young Man and can write a good Love-letter, I am sure I have no reason to find fault with him for admiring me, tho' perhaps I may not marry him for all that Lady Scudamore."

"You are certainly under no obligation to marry him answered her Ladyship, except that which love himself will dictate to you, for if I am not greatly mistaken you are at this very moment unknown to yourself, cherishing a most tender affection for him."

"Law, Lady Scudamore replied I blushing how can you think of such a thing?"

"Because every look, every word betrays it, answered she; Come my dear Henrietta, consider me as a freind, and be sincere with me—Do not you prefer Mr Musgrove to any man of your acquaintance?"

"Pray do not ask me such questions Lady Scudamore, said I turning away my head, for it is not fit for me to answer them."

"Nay my Love replied she, now you confirm my suspicions. But why Henrietta should you be ashamed to own a well-placed Love, or why refuse to confide in me?"

"I am not ashamed to own it; said I taking Courage. I do not refuse to confide in you or blush to say that I do love your cousin Mr Musgrove, that I am sincerely attached to him, for it is no disgrace to love a handsome Man. If he were plain indeed I might have had reason to be ashamed of a passion which must have been mean since the object would have been unworthy. But with such a figure and face, and such beautiful hair as your Cousin has, why should I blush to own that such superior merit has made an impression on me."

"My sweet Girl (said Lady Scudamore embracing me with great affection) what a delicate way of thinking you have in these matters, and what a quick discernment for one of your years! Oh! how I honour you for such Noble Sentiments!"

"Do you Ma'am said I; You are vastly obliging. But pray Lady Scudamore did your Cousin himself tell you of his affection for me I shall like him the better if he did, for what is a Lover without a Confidante?"

"Oh! my Love replied she, you were born for each other. Every word you say more deeply convinces me that your Minds are actuated by the invisible power of simpathy, for your opinions and sentiments so exactly coincide. Nay, the colour of your Hair is not very different. Yes my dear Girl, the poor despairing Musgrove did reveal to me the story of his Love—. Nor was I surprised at it—I know not how it was, but I had a kind of presentiment that he would be in love with you."

"Well, but how did he break it to you?"

"It was not till after supper. We were sitting round the fire together talking on indifferent subjects, though to say the truth the Conversation was cheifly on my side for he was thoughtful and silent, when on a sudden he interrupted me in the midst of something I was saying, by exclaiming in a most Theatrical tone—

Yes I'm in love I feel it now And Henrietta Halton has undone me

"Oh! What a sweet way replied I, of declaring his Passion! To make such a couple of charming lines about me! What a pity it is that they are not in rhime!"

"I am very glad you like it answered she; To be sure there was a great deal of Taste in it. And are you in love with her, Cousin? said I. I am very sorry for it, for unexceptionable as you are in every respect, with a pretty Estate capable of Great improvements, and an excellent House tho' somewhat out of repair, yet who can hope to aspire with success to the adorable Henrietta who has had an offer from a Colonel and been toasted by a Baronet"—"THAT I have—" cried I. Lady Scudamore continued. "Ah dear Cousin replied he, I am so well convinced of the little Chance I can have of winning her who is adored by thousands, that I need no assurances of yours to make me more thoroughly so. Yet surely neither you or the fair Henrietta herself will deny me the exquisite Gratification of dieing for her, of falling a victim to her Charms. And when I am dead"—continued her—

"Oh Lady Scudamore, said I wiping my eyes, that such a sweet Creature should talk of dieing!"

"It is an affecting Circumstance indeed, replied Lady Scudamore." "When I am dead said he, let me be carried and lain at her feet, and perhaps she may not disdain to drop a pitying tear on my poor remains."

"Dear Lady Scudamore interrupted I, say no more on this affecting subject. I cannot bear it."

"Oh! how I admire the sweet sensibility of your Soul, and as I would not for Worlds wound it too deeply, I will be silent."

"Pray go on." said I. She did so.

"And then added he, Ah! Cousin imagine what my transports will be when I feel the dear precious drops trickle on my face! Who would not die to haste such extacy! And when I am interred, may the divine Henrietta bless some happier Youth with her affection, May he be as tenderly attached to her as the hapless Musgrove and while HE crumbles to dust, May they live an example of Felicity in the Conjugal state!"

Did you ever hear any thing so pathetic? What a charming wish, to be lain at my feet when he was dead! Oh! what an exalted mind he must have to be capable of such a wish! Lady Scudamore went on.

"Ah! my dear Cousin replied I to him, such noble behaviour as this, must melt the heart of any woman however obdurate it may naturally be; and could the divine Henrietta but hear your generous wishes for her happiness, all gentle as is her mind, I have not a doubt but that she would pity your affection and endeavour to return it." "Oh! Cousin answered he, do not endeavour to raise my hopes by such flattering assurances. No, I cannot hope to please this angel of a Woman, and the only thing which remains for me to do, is to die." "True Love is ever desponding replied I, but I my dear Tom will give you even greater hopes of conquering this fair one's heart, than I have yet given you, by assuring you that I watched her with the strictest attention during the whole day, and could plainly discover that she cherishes in her bosom though unknown to herself, a most tender affection for you."

"Dear Lady Scudamore cried I, This is more than I ever knew!"

"Did not I say that it was unknown to yourself? I did not, continued I to him, encourage you by saying this at first, that surprise might render the pleasure still Greater." "No Cousin replied he in a languid voice, nothing will convince me that I can have touched the heart of Henrietta Halton, and if you are deceived yourself, do not attempt deceiving me." "In short my Love it was the work of some hours for me to Persuade the poor despairing Youth that you had really a preference for him; but when at last he could no longer deny the force of my arguments, or discredit what I told him, his transports, his Raptures, his Extacies are beyond my power to describe."

"Oh! the dear Creature, cried I, how passionately he loves me! But dear Lady Scudamore did you tell him that I was totally dependant on my Uncle and Aunt?"

"Yes, I told him every thing."

"And what did he say."

"He exclaimed with virulence against Uncles and Aunts; Accused the laws of England for allowing them to Possess their Estates when wanted by their Nephews or Neices, and wished HE were in the House of Commons, that he might reform the Legislature, and rectify all its abuses."

"Oh! the sweet Man! What a spirit he has!" said I.

"He could not flatter himself he added, that the adorable Henrietta would condescend for his sake to resign those Luxuries and that splendor to which she had been used, and accept only in exchange the Comforts and Elegancies which his limited Income could afford her, even supposing that his house were in Readiness to receive her. I told him that it could not be expected that she would; it would be doing her an injustice to suppose her capable of giving up the power she now possesses and so nobly uses of doing such extensive Good to the poorer part of her fellow Creatures, merely for the gratification of you and herself."

"To be sure said I, I AM very Charitable every now and then. And what did Mr Musgrove say to this?"

"He replied that he was under a melancholy necessity of owning the truth of what I said, and that therefore if he should be the happy Creature destined to be the Husband of the Beautiful Henrietta he must bring himself to wait, however impatiently, for the fortunate day, when she might be freed from the power of worthless Relations and able to bestow herself on him."

What a noble Creature he is! Oh! Matilda what a fortunate one I am, who am to be his Wife! My Aunt is calling me to come and make the pies, so adeiu my dear freind, and beleive me yours etc—H. Halton.

Finis.

Scraps

To Miss FANNY CATHERINE AUSTEN

MY Dear Neice As I am prevented by the great distance between Rowling and Steventon from superintending your Education myself, the care of which will probably on that account devolve on your Father and Mother, I think it is my particular Duty to Prevent your feeling as much as possible the want of my personal instructions, by addressing to you on paper my Opinions and Admonitions on the conduct of Young Women, which you will find expressed in the following pages.—I am my dear Neice Your affectionate Aunt The Author.

THE FEMALE PHILOSOPHER
A LETTER

My Dear Louisa Your friend Mr Millar called upon us yesterday in his way to Bath, whither he is going for his health; two of his daughters were with him, but the eldest and the three Boys are with their Mother in Sussex. Though you have often told me that Miss Millar was remarkably handsome, you never mentioned anything of her Sisters' beauty; yet they are certainly extremely pretty. I'll give you their description.—Julia is eighteen; with a countenance in which Modesty, Sense and Dignity are happily blended, she has a form which at once presents you with Grace, Elegance and Symmetry. Charlotte who is just sixteen is shorter than her Sister, and though her figure cannot boast the easy dignity of Julia's, yet it has a pleasing plumpness which is in a different way as estimable. She is fair and her face is expressive sometimes of softness the most bewitching, and at others of Vivacity the most striking. She appears to have infinite Wit and a good humour unalterable; her conversation during the half hour they set with us, was replete with humourous sallies, Bonmots and repartees; while the sensible, the amiable Julia uttered sentiments of Morality worthy of a heart like her own. Mr Millar appeared to answer the character I had always received of him. My Father met him with that look of Love, that social Shake, and cordial kiss which marked his gladness at beholding an old and valued freind from whom thro' various circumstances he had been separated nearly twenty years. Mr Millar observed (and very justly too) that many events had befallen each during that interval of time, which gave occasion to the lovely Julia for making most sensible reflections on the many changes in their situation which so long a period had occasioned, on the advantages of some, and the disadvantages of others. From this subject she made a short digression to the instability of human pleasures and the uncertainty of their duration, which led her to observe that all earthly Joys must be imperfect. She was proceeding to illustrate this doctrine by examples from the Lives of great Men when the Carriage came to the Door and the amiable Moralist with her Father and Sister was obliged to depart; but not without a promise of spending five or six months with us on their return. We of course mentioned you, and I assure you that ample Justice was done to your Merits by all. "Louisa Clarke (said I) is in general a very pleasant Girl, yet sometimes her good humour is clouded by Peevishness, Envy and Spite. She neither wants Understanding or is without some pretensions to Beauty, but these are so very trifling, that the value she sets on her personal charms, and the adoration she expects them to be offered are at once a striking example of her vanity, her pride, and her folly." So said I, and to my opinion everyone added weight by the concurrence of their own. Your affectionate Arabella Smythe.

THE FIRST ACT OF A COMEDY

CHARACTERS

Popgun, Maria, Charles, Pistolletta, Postilion, Hostess, Chorus of ploughboys, Cook, and Strephon Chloe

SCENE—AN INN

ENTER Hostess, Charles, Maria, and Cook.

Hostess to Maria: If the gentry in the Lion should want beds, shew them number 9.

Maria: Yes Mistress.—EXIT Maria

Hostess: (to Cook) If their Honours in the Moon ask for the bill of fare, give it them.

Cook: I wull, I wull. EXIT Cook.

Hostess: (to Charles) If their Ladyships in the Sun ring their Bell—answerit.

Charles: Yes Madam. EXEUNT Severally.

SCENE CHANGES TO THE MOON, and discovers Popgun and Pistoletta.

Pistoletta: Pray papa how far is it to London?

Popgun: My Girl, my Darling, my favourite of all my Children, who art the picture of thy poor Mother who died two months ago, with whom I am going to Town to marry to Strephon, and to whom I mean to bequeath my whole Estate, it wants seven Miles.

SCENE CHANGES TO THE SUN—

ENTER Chloe and a chorus of ploughboys.

Chloe: Where am I? At Hounslow.—Where go I? To London—. What to do? To be married Unto whom? Unto Strephon. Who is he? A Youth. Then I will sing a song.

SONG
I go to Town
And when I come down,
I shall be married to Streephon[36]
And that to me will be fun.
Chorus: Be fun, be fun, be fun, And that to me will be fun.

---

[36] Note the two e's

ENTER Cook

Cook: Here is the bill of fare.

Chloe: (reads) 2 Ducks, a leg of beef, a stinking partridge, and a tart.—I will have the leg of beef and the partridge.

EXIT Cook. And now I will sing another song.

SONG
I am going to have my dinner,
After which I shan't be thinner,
I wish I had here Strephon
For he would carve the partridge if it should be a tough one.
Chorus: Tough one, tough one, tough one For he would carve the partridge if it Should be a tough one.

EXIT Chloe and Chorus.—

SCENE CHANGES TO THE INSIDE OF THE LION.

ENTER Strephon and Postilion.

Streph: You drove me from Staines to this place, from whence I mean to go to Town to marry Chloe. How much is your due?

Post: Eighteen pence.

Streph: Alas, my freind, I have but a bad guinea with which I mean to support myself in Town. But I will pawn to you an undirected Letter that I received from Chloe.

Post: Sir, I accept your offer.

END OF THE FIRST ACT.

**A LETTER from a YOUNG LADY, whose feelings being too strong for
her Judgement led her into the commission of Errors which her Heart disapproved.**

Many have been the cares and vicissitudes of my past life, my beloved Ellinor, and the only consolation I feel for their bitterness is that on a close examination of my conduct, I am convinced that I have strictly deserved them. I murdered my father at a very early period of my Life, I have since murdered my Mother, and I am now going to murder my Sister. I have changed my religion so often that at present I have not an idea of any left. I have been a perjured witness in every public tryal for these last twelve years; and I have forged my own Will. In short there is scarcely a crime that I have not committed—But I am now going to reform. Colonel Martin of the Horse guards has paid his Addresses to me, and we are to be married in a few days. As there is something singular in our Courtship, I will give you an account of it. Colonel Martin is the second son of the late Sir John Martin who died immensely rich, but bequeathing only one hundred thousand pound apeice to his three younger Children, left the bulk of his fortune, about eight Million to the present Sir Thomas. Upon his small pittance the Colonel lived tolerably contented for nearly four months when he took it into his head to determine on getting the whole of his eldest Brother's Estate. A new will was forged and the Colonel produced it in Court—but nobody would swear to it's being the right will except himself, and he had sworn so much that Nobody beleived him. At that moment I happened to be passing by the door of the Court, and was beckoned in by the Judge who told the Colonel that I was a Lady ready to witness anything for the cause of Justice, and advised him to apply to me. In short the Affair was soon adjusted. The Colonel and I swore to its' being the right will, and Sir Thomas has been obliged to resign all his illgotten wealth. The Colonel in gratitude waited on me the next day with an offer of his hand—. I am now going to murder my Sister. Yours Ever, Anna Parker.

A TOUR THROUGH WALES—in a LETTER from a YOUNG LADY—

My Dear Clara I have been so long on the ramble that I have not till now had it in my power to thank you for your Letter—. We left our dear home on last Monday month; and proceeded on our tour through Wales, which is a principality contiguous to England and gives the title to the Prince of Wales. We travelled on horseback by preference. My Mother rode upon our little poney and Fanny and I walked by her side or rather ran, for my Mother is so fond of riding fast that she galloped all the way. You may be sure that we were in a fine perspiration when we came to our place of resting. Fanny has taken a great many Drawings of the Country, which are very beautiful, tho' perhaps not such exact resemblances as might be wished, from their being taken as she ran along. It would astonish you to see all the Shoes we wore out in our Tour. We determined to take a good Stock with us and therefore each took a pair of our own besides those we set off in. However we were obliged to have them both capped and heelpeiced at Carmarthen, and at last when they were quite gone, Mama was so kind as to lend us a pair of blue Sattin Slippers, of which we each took one and hopped home from Hereford delightfully——I am your ever affectionate Elizabeth Johnson.

A TALE.

A Gentleman whose family name I shall conceal, bought a small Cottage in Pembrokeshire about two years ago. This daring Action was suggested to him by his elder Brother who promised to furnish two rooms and a Closet for him, provided he would take a small house near the borders of an extensive Forest, and about three Miles from the Sea. Wilhelminus gladly accepted the offer and continued for some time searching after such a retreat when he was one morning agreably relieved from his suspence by reading this advertisement in a Newspaper. TO BE LETT A Neat Cottage on the borders of an extensive forest and about three Miles from the Sea. It is ready furnished except two rooms and a Closet.

The delighted Wilhelminus posted away immediately to his brother, and shewed him the advertisement. Robertus congratulated him and sent him in his Carriage to take possession of the Cottage. After travelling for three days and six nights without stopping, they arrived at the Forest and following a track which led by it's side down a steep Hill over which ten Rivulets meandered, they reached the Cottage in half an hour. Wilhelminus alighted, and after knocking for some time without receiving any answer or hearing any one stir within, he opened the door which was fastened only by a wooden latch and entered a small room, which he immediately perceived to be one of the two that were unfurnished—From thence he proceeded into a Closet equally bare. A pair of stairs that went out of it led him into a room above, no less destitute, and these apartments he found composed the whole of the House. He was by no means displeased with this discovery, as he had the comfort of reflecting that he should not be obliged to lay out anything on furniture himself—. He returned immediately to his Brother, who took him the next day to every Shop in Town, and bought what ever was requisite to furnish the two rooms and the Closet, In a few days everything was completed, and Wilhelminus returned to take possession of his Cottage. Robertus accompanied him, with his Lady the amiable Cecilia and her two lovely Sisters Arabella and Marina to whom Wilhelminus was tenderly attached, and a large number of Attendants.—An ordinary Genius might probably have been embarrassed, in endeavouring to accomodate so large a party, but Wilhelminus with admirable presence of mind gave orders for the immediate erection of two noble Tents in an open spot in the Forest adjoining to the house. Their Construction was both simple and elegant—A couple of old blankets, each supported by four sticks, gave a striking proof of that taste for architecture and that happy ease in overcoming difficulties which were some of Wilhelminus's most striking Virtues.

Juvenilia

VOLUME IN THE THIRD

A Collection of Juvenile Writings

By
Jane Austen

To Miss Mary Lloyd

The following Novel is by permission Dedicated, by her Obedt. humble Servt.

The Author

Evelyn

In a retired part of the County of Sussex there is a village (for what I know to the Contrary) called Evelyn, perhaps one of the most beautiful Spots in the south of England. A Gentleman passing through it on horseback about twenty years ago, was so entirely of my opinion in this respect, that he put up at the little Alehouse in it and enquired with great earnestness whether there were any house to be lett in the parish. The Landlady, who as well as every one else in Evelyn was remarkably amiable, shook her head at this question, but seemed unwilling to give him any answer. He could not bear this uncertainty—yet knew not to obtain the information he desired. To repeat a question which had already appear'd to make the good woman uneasy was impossible. He turned from her in visible agitation. "What a situation am I in!" said he to himself as he walked to the window and threw up the sash. He found himself revived by the Air, which he felt to a much greater degree when he had opened the window than he had done before. Yet it was but for a moment. The agonizing pain of Doubt and Suspence again weighed down his Spirits. The good woman who had watched in eager silence every turn of his Countenance with that benevolence which characterizes the inhabitants of Evelyn, intreated him to tell her the cause of his uneasiness. "Is there anything, Sir, in my power to do that may releive your Greifs? Tell me in what manner I can sooth them, and beleive me that the freindly balm of Comfort and Assistance shall not be wanting; for indeed, Sir, I have a simpathetic Soul."

"Amiable Woman" (said Mr. Gower, affected almost to tears by this generous offer) "This Greatness of mind in one to whom I am almost a Stranger, serves but to make me the more warmly wish for a house in this sweet village. What would I not give to be your Neighbour, to be blessed with your Acquaintance, and with the farther knowledge of your virtues! Oh! with what pleasure would I form myself by such an example! Tell me then, best of Women, is there no possibility?—I cannot speak—You know my Meaning—."

"Alas! Sir," replied Mrs. Willis, "there is none. Every house in this village, from the sweetness of the Situation, and the purity of the Air, in which neither Misery, Ill health, or Vice are ever wafted, is inhabited. And yet," (after a short pause) "there is a Family, who tho' warmly attached to the spot, yet from a peculiar Generosity of Disposition would perhaps be willing to oblige you with their house." He eagerly caught at this idea, and having gained a direction to the place, he set off immediately on his walk to it. As he approached the House, he was delighted with its situation. It was in the exact centre of a small circular paddock, which was enclosed by a regular paling, and bordered with a plantation of Lombardy poplars, and Spruce firs alternatively placed in three rows. A gravel walk ran through this beautiful Shrubbery, and as the remainder of the paddock was unincumbered with any other Timber, the surface of it perfectly even and smooth, and grazed by four white Cows which were disposed at equal distances from each other, the whole appearance of the place as Mr. Gower entered the Paddock was uncommonly striking. A beautifully-rounded, gravel road without any turn or interruption led immediately to the house. Mr. Gower rang; the Door was soon opened. "Are Mr. and Mrs.

Webb at home?" "My Good Sir, they are," replied the Servant; And leading the way, conducted Mr. Gower upstairs into a very elegant Dressing room, where a Lady rising from her seat, welcomed him with all the Generosity which Mrs. Willis had attributed to the Family.

"Welcome best of Men. Welcome to this House, and to everything it contains. William, tell your Master of the happiness I enjoy—invite him to partake of it. Bring up some Chocolate immediately; Spread a Cloth in the dining Parlour, and carry in the venison pasty. In the mean time let the Gentleman have some sandwiches, and bring in a Basket of Fruit. Send up some Ices and a bason of Soup, and do not forget some Jellies and Cakes." Then turning to Mr. Gower, and taking out her purse, "Accept this, my good Sir. Beleive me you are welcome to everything that is in my power to bestow. I wish my purse were weightier, but Mr. Webb must make up my deficiences. I know he has cash in the house to the amount of an hundred pounds, which he shall bring you immediately." Mr. Gower felt overpowered by her generosity as he put the purse in his pocket, and from the excess of his Gratitude, could scarcely express himself intelligibly when he accepted her offer of the hundred pounds. Mr. Webb soon entered the room, and repeated every protestation of Freindship and Cordiality which his Lady had already made. The Chocolate, the Sandwiches, the Jellies, the Cakes, the Ice, and the Soup soon made their appearance, and Mr. Gower having tasted something of all, and pocketed the rest, was conducted into the dining parlour, where he eat a most excellent Dinner and partook of the most exquisite Wines, while Mr. and Mrs. Webb stood by him still pressing him to eat and drink a little more. "And now my good Sir," said Mr. Webb, when Mr. Gower's repast was concluded, "what else can we do to contribute to your happiness and express the Affection we bear you. Tell us what you wish more to receive, and depend upon our gratitude for the communication of your wishes." "Give me then your house and Grounds; I ask for nothing else." "It is yours," exclaimed both at once; "from this moment it is yours." The Agreement concluded on and the present accepted by Mr. Gower, Mr. Webb rang to have the Carriage ordered, telling William at the same time to call the Young Ladies.

"Best of Men," said Mrs. Webb, "we will not long intrude upon your Time."

"Make no Apologies, dear Madam," replied Mr. Gower, "You are welcome to stay this half hour if you like it."

They both burst forth into raptures of Admiration at his politeness, which they agreed served only to make their Conduct appear more inexcusable in trespassing on his time.

The Young Ladies soon entered the room. The eldest of them was about seventeen, the other, several years younger. Mr. Gower had no sooner fixed his Eyes on Miss Webb than he felt that something more was necessary to his happiness than the house he had just received. Mrs. Webb introduced him to her daughter. "Our dear freind Mr. Gower, my Love—He has been so good as to accept of this house, small as it is, and to promise to keep it for ever." "Give me leave to assure you, Sir," said Miss Webb, "that I am highly sensible ofyour kindness in this respect, which from the shortness of my Father's and Mother's acquaintance with you, is more than usually flattering."

Mr. Gower bowed, "You are too obliging, Ma'am. I assure you that I like the house extremely, and if they would complete their generosity by giving me their eldest daughter in marriage with a handsome portion, I should have nothing more to wish for." This compliment brought a blush into the cheeks of the lovely Miss Webb, who seemed however to refer herself to her father and Mother. They looked delighted at each other. At length Mrs. Webb, breaking silence, said, "We bend under a weight of obligations to you which we can never repay. Take our girl, take our Maria, and on her must the difficult task fall, of endeavouring to make some return to so much Benefiscence." Mr. Webb added, "Her fortune is but ten thousand pounds, which is almost too small a sum to be offered." This objection however being instantly removed by the generosity of Mr. Gower, who declared himself satisfied with the sum mentioned, Mr. and Mrs. Webb, with their youngest daughter took their leave, and on the next day, the nuptials of their eldest with Mr. Gower were celebrated.

This amiable Man now found himself perfectly happy; united to a very lovely and deserving young woman, with an handsome fortune, an elegant house, settled in the village of Evelyn, and by that means enabled to cultivate his acquaintance with Mrs. Willis, could he have a wish ungratified? For some months he found that he could not, till one day as he was walking in the Shrubbery with Maria leaning on his arm, they observed a rose full-blown lying on the gravel; it had fallen from a rose tree which with three others had been planted by Mr. Webb to give a pleasing variety to the walk. These four Rose trees served also to mark the quarters of the Shrubbery, by which means the Traveller might always know how far in his progress round the Paddock he was got. Maria stooped to pick up the beautiful flower, and with all her Family Generosity presented it to her Husband. "My dear Frederic," said she, "pray take this charming rose." "Rose!" exclaimed Mr. Gower. "Oh! Maria, of what does not that remind me! Alas, my poor Sister, how have I neglected you!" The truth was that Mr. Gower was the only son of a very large Family, of which Miss Rose Gower was the thirteenth daughter. This Young Lady whose merits deserved a better fate than she met with, was the darling of her relations. From the clearness of her skin and the Brilliancy of her Eyes, she was fully entitled to all their partial affection. Another circumstance contributed to the general Love they bore her, and that was one of the finest heads of hair in the world. A few Months before her Brother's Marriage, her heart had been engaged by the attentions and charms of a young Man whose high rank and expectations seemed to foretell objections from his Family to a match which would be highly desirable to theirs. Proposals were made on the young Man's part, and proper objections on his Father's. He was desired to return from Carlisle where he was with his beloved Rose, to the family seat in Sussex. He was obliged to comply, and the angry father then finding from his Conversation how determined he was to marry no other woman, sent him for a fortnight to the Isle of Wight under the care of the Family Chaplin, with the hope of overcoming his Constancy by Time and Absence in a foreign Country. They accordingly prepared to bid a long adieu to England. The young Nobleman was not allowed to see his Rosa. They set sail. A storm arose which baffled the arts of the Seamen. The Vessel was wrecked on the coast of Calshot and every Soul on board perished. This sad Event soon reached Carlisle, and the beautiful Rose was affected by it, beyond the power of Expression. It was to soften her afliction by obtaining a picture ofher unfortunate Lover that her brother undertook a Journey into Sussex, where he hoped that his petition would not be rejected, by the severe yet afflicted Father. When he reached Evelyn he was not many miles from—Castle, but the pleasing events which befell him in that place had for a while made him totally forget the object of his Journey and his unhappy Sister. The little incident of the rose however brought everything concerning her to his recollection again, and he bitterly repented his neglect. He returned to the house immediately and agitated by Greif, Apprehension and Shame wrote the following Letter to Rosa.

> *Evelyn*
> *July 14th*

My dearest Sister,

As it is now four months since I left Carlisle, during which period I have not once written to you, You will perhaps unjustly accuse me of Neglect and Forgetfulness. Alas! I blush when I own the truth of your Accusation. Yet if you are still alive, do not think too harshly of me, or suppose that I could for a moment forget the situation of my Rose. Beleive me I will forget you no longer, but will hasten as soon as possible to—Castle if I find by your answer that you are still alive. Maria joins me in every dutiful and affectionate wish, and I am yours sincerely.

> F. Gower.

He waited in the most anxious expectation for an answer to his Letter, which arrived as soon as the great distance from Carlisle would admit of. But alas, it came not from Rosa.

> *Carlisle*
> *July 17th*

Dear Brother,

My Mother has taken the liberty of opening your Letter to poor Rose, as she has been dead these six weeks. Your long absence and continued Silence gave us all great uneasiness and hastened her to the Grave. Your Journey to—Castle therefore may be spared. You do not tell us where you have been since the time of your quitting Carlisle, nor in any way account for your tedious absence, which gives us some surprise. We all unite in Compliments to Maria, and beg to know who she is.

> Yr affectionate Sister,
> M. Gower.

This Letter, by which Mr. Gower was obliged to attribute to his own conduct, his Sister's death, was so violent a shock to his feelings, that in spite of his living at Evelyn where Illness was scarcely ever heard of, he was attacked by a fit of the gout, which confining him to his own room afforded an opportunity to Maria of shining in that favourite character of Sir Charles Grandison's, a nurse. No woman could ever appear more amiable than Maria did under such circumstances, and at last by her unremitting attentions had the pleasure of seeing him gradually recover the use of his feet. It was a blessing by no means lost on him, for he was no sooner in a condition to leave the house, that he mounted his horse, and rode to—Castle, wishing to find whether his Lordship softened by his Son's death, might have been brought to consent to the match, had both he and Rosa been alive. His amiable Maria followed him with her Eyes till she could see him no longer, and then sinking into her chair overwhelmed with Greif, found that in his absence she could enjoy no comfort.

Mr. Gower arrived late in the evening at the castle, which was situated on a woody Eminence commanding a beautiful prospect of the Sea. Mr. Gower did not dislike the situation, tho' it was certainly greatly inferior to that of his own house. There was an irregularity in the fall of the ground, and a profusion of old Timber which appeared to him illsuited to the stile of the Castle, for it being a building of a very ancient date, he thought it required the Paddock of Evelyn lodge to form a Contrast, and enliven the structure. The gloomy appearance of the old Castle frowning on him as he followed it's winding approach, struck him with terror. Nor did he think himself safe, till he was introduced into the Drawing room where the Family were assembled to tea. Mr. Gower was a perfect stranger to every one in the Circle but tho' he was always timid in the Dark and easily terrified when alone, he did not want that more necessary and more noble courage which enabled him without a Blush to enter a large party of superior Rank, whom he had never seen before, and to take his Seat amongst them with perfect Indifference. The name of Gower was not unknown to Lord —. He felt distressed and astonished; Yet rose and received him with all the politeness of a well-bred Man. Lady — who felt a deeper Sorrow at the loss of her Son, than his Lordship's harder heart was capable of, could hardly keep her Seat when she found that he was the Brother of her lamented Henry's Rosa. "My Lord," said Mr. Gower as soon as he was seated, "You are perhaps surprised at receiving a visit from a Man whom you could not have the least expectation of seeing here. But my Sister, my unfortunate Sister, is the real cause of my thus troubling you: That luckless Girl is now no more—and tho' she can receive no pleasure from the intelligence, yet for the satisfaction of her Family I wish to know whether the Death of this unhappy Pair has made an impression on your heart sufficiently strong to obtain that consent to their Marriage which in happier circumstances you would not be persuaded to give Supposing that they now were both alive." His Lordship seemed lossed in astonishment. Lady — could not support the mention of her son, and left the room in tears; the rest of the Family remained attentively listening, almost persuaded that Mr. Gower was distracted. "Mr. Gower," replied his Lordship, "this is a very odd question. It appears to me that you are supposing an impossibility. No one can more sincerely regret the death of my Son than I have always done, and it gives me great concern to know that Miss Gower's was hastened by his. Yet to suppose them alive is destroying at once the Motive for a change in my sentiments concerning the afrair." "My Lord," replied Mr. Gower in anger,"I see that you are a most inflexible Man, and that not even the death of your Son can make you wish his future Life happy. I will no longer detain your Lordship. I see, I plainly see that you are a very vile Man. And now I have the honour of wishing all your Lordships, and Ladyships a good Night." He immediately left the room, forgetting in the heat of his Anger the lateness of the hour, which at any other time would have made him tremble, and leaving the whole Company unanimous in their opinion of his being Mad. When however he had mounted his horse and the great Gates of the Castle had shut him out, he felt an universal tremor through out his whole frame. If we consider his Situation indeed, alone, on horseback, as late in the year as August, and in the day, as nine o'clock, with no light to direct him but that of the Moon almost full, and the Stars which alarmed him by their twinkling, who can refrain from pitying him? No house within a quarter of a mile, and a Gloomy Castle blackened by the deep shade of Walnuts and Pines, behind him. He felt indeed almost distracted with his fears, and shutting his Eyes till he arrived at the Village to prevent his seeing either Gipsies or Ghosts, he rode on a full gallop all the way.

On his return home, he rang the housebell, but no one appeared, a second time he rang, but the door was not opened, a third and a fourth with as little success, when observing the dining parlour window open he leapt in, and persued his way through the house till he reached Maria's Dressing room, where he found all the Servants assembled at tea. Surprized at so very unusual a sight, he fainted, on his recovery he found himself on the Sofa, with his wife's maid kneeling by him, chafing his temples with Hungary water. From her he learned that his beloved Maria had been so much grieved at his departure that she died of a broken heart about 3 hours after his departure.

He then became sufficiently composed to give necessary orders for her funeral which took place the Monday following this being the Saturday. When Mr. Gower had settled the order of the procession he set out himself to Carlisle, to give vent to his sorrow in the bosom of his family. He arrived there in high health and spirits, after a delightful journey of 3 days and a 1/2. What was his surprize on entering the Breakfast parlour to see Rosa, his beloved Rosa, seated on a Sofa; at the sight of him she fainted and would have fallen had not a Grentleman sitting with his back to the door, started up and saved her from sinking to the ground—She very soon came to herself and then introduced this gentleman to her Brother as her Husband a Mr. Davenport.

"But my dearest Rosa," said the astonished Gower, "I thought you were dead and buried." "Why, my dear Frederick," replied Rosa "I wished you to think so, hoping that you would spread the report about the country and it would thus by some means reach —— Castle. By this I hoped some how or other to touch the hearts of its inhabitants. It was not till the day before yesterday that I heard of the death of my beloved Henry which I learned from Mr. Davenport who concluded by offering me his hand. I accepted it with transport, and was married yesterday." Mr. Gower, embraced his sister and shook hands with Mr. Davenport, he then took a stroll into the town. As he passed by a public house he called for a pot of beer, which was brought him immediately by his old friend Mrs. Willis.

Great was his astonishment at seeing Mrs. Willis in Carlisle. But not forgetful of the respect he owed her, he dropped on one knee, and received the frothy cup from her, more grateful to him than Nectar. He instantly made her an offer of his hand and heart, which she graciously condescended to accept, telling him that she was only on a visit to her cousin, who kept the Anchor and should be ready to return to Evelyn, whenever he chose. The next morning they were married and immediately proceeded to Evelyn. When he reached home, he recollected that he had never written to Mr. and Mrs. Webb to inform them of the death of their daughter, which he rightly supposed they knew nothing of, as they never took in any newspapers. He immediately dispatched the following Letter.

Evelyn
Augst 19th 180—

Dearest Madam,

How can words express the poignancy of my feelings! Our Maria, our beloved Maria is no more, she breathed her last, on Saturday the 12th of Augst. I see you now in an agony of grief lamenting not your own, but my loss. Rest satisfied I am happy, possessed of my lovely Sarah what more can I wish for? I remain respectfully

Yours.

F. Gower

Westgate Builgs
Augst 22nd

Generous, Best of Men,

How truly we rejoice to hear of your present welfare and happiness! and how truly grateful are we for your unexampled generosity in writing to condole with us on the late unlucky accident which befel our Maria. I have enclosed a draught on our banker for 30 pounds, which Mr. Webb joins with me in entreating you and the aimiable Sarah to accept.

Your most grateful,

Anne Augusta Webb

Mr. and Mrs. Gower resided many years at Evelyn enjoying perfect happiness the just reward of their virtues. The only alteration which took place at Evelyn was that Mr. and Mrs. Davenport settled there in Mrs. Willis's former abode and were for many years the proprietors of the White Horse Inn.

CATHARINE

(also known as Kitty or The Bower)

To Miss Austen

Madam,

Encouraged by your warm patronage of The beautiful Cassandra, and The History of England, which through your generous support, have obtained a place in every library in the Kingdom, and run through threescore Editions, I take the liberty of begging the same Exertions in favour of the following Novel, which I humbly flatter myself, possesses Merit beyond any already published, or any that will ever in future appear, except such as may proceed from the pen of Your Most Grateful Humble Servt.

The Author

Steventon, August 1792

Catharine had the misfortune, as many heroines have had before her, of losing her parents when she was very young, and of being brought up under the care of a maiden aunt, who while she tenderly loved her, watched over her conduct with so scrutinizing a severity, as to make it very doubtful to many people, and to Catharine amongst the rest, whether she loved her or not. She had frequently been deprived of a real pleasure through this jealousy; been sometimes obliged to relinquish a ball because an officer was to be there, or to dance with a partner of her aunt's introduction in preference to one of her own choice. But her spirits were naturally good, and not easily depressed, and she possessed such a fund of vivacity and good humour as could only be damped by some very serious vexation. Besides these antidotes against every disappointment, and consolations under them, she had another, which afforded her constant relief in all her misfortunes, and that was a fine shady bower, the work of her own infantine labours assisted by those of two young companions who had resided in the same village. To this bower, which terminated a very pleasant and retired walk in her aunt's garden, she always wandered whenever anything disturbed her, and it possessed such a charm over her senses, as constantly to tranquillize her mind and quiet her spirits. Solitude and reflection might perhaps have had the same effect in her bed chamber, yet habit had so strengthened the idea which fancy had first suggested, that such a thought never occurred to Kitty who was firmly persuaded that her bower alone could restore her to herself. Her imagination was warm, and in her friendships, as well as in the whole tenure of her mind, she was enthusiastic. This beloved bower had been the united work of herself and two amiable girls, for whom since her earliest years, she had felt the tenderest regard. They were the daughters of the clergyman of the parish with whose family, while it had continued there, her aunt had been on the most intimate terms, and the little girls tho' separated for the greatest part of the year by the different modes of their education, were constantly together during the holidays of the Miss Wynnes. In those days of happy childhood, now so often regretted by Kitty, this arbour had been formed, and separated perhaps for ever from these dear friends, it encouraged more than any other place the tender and melancholy recollections of hours rendered pleasant by them, at once so sorrowful, yet so soothing!

It was now two years since the death of Mr. Wynne, and the consequent dispersion of his family who had been left by it in great distress. They had been reduced to a state of absolute dependance on some relations, who though very opulent and very nearly connected with them, had with difficulty been prevailed on to contribute anything towards their support. Mrs. Wynne was fortunately spared the knowledge and participation of their distress, by her release from a painful illness a few months before the death of her husband. The eldest daughter had been obliged to accept the offer of one of her cousins to equip her for the East Indies, and the infinitely against her inclinations had been necessitated to embrace the only possibility that was offered to her, of a maintenance. Yet it was one, so opposite to all her ideas of propriety, so contrary to her wishes, so repugnant to her feelings, that she would almost have preferred servitude to it, had choice been allowed her. Her personal attractions had gained her a husband as soon as she had arrived at Bengal, and she had now been married nearly a twelve month. Splendidly yet unhappily married. United to a man of double her own age, whose disposition was not amiable, and whose manners were unpleasing, though his character was respectable. Kitty had heard twice from her friend since her marriage, but her letters were always unsatisfactory, and though she did not openly avow her feelings, yet every line proved her to be unhappy. She spoke with pleasure of nothing, but of those amusements which they had shared together and which could return no more, and seemed to have no happiness in view but that of returning to England again. Her sister had been taken by another relation the Dowager Lady Halifax as a companion to her daughters, and had accompanied her family into Scotland about the same time of Cecilia's leaving England. From Mary therefore Kitty had the power of hearing more frequently, but her letters were scarcely more comfortable. There was not indeed that hopelessness of sorrow in her situation as in her sister's; she was not married, and could yet look forward to a change in her circumstances, but situated for the present without any immediate hope of it, in a family where, tho' all were her relations, she had no friend, she wrote usually in depressed spirits, which her separation from her sister and her sister's marriage had greatly contributed to make so. Divided thus from the two she loved best on Earth, while Cecilia and Mary were still more endeared to her by their loss, everything that brought a remembrance of them was doubly cherished, and the shrubs they had planted, and the keepsakes they had given were rendered sacred.

The living of Chetwynde was now in the possession of a Mr. Dudley, whose family unlike the Wynnes were productive only of vexation and trouble to Mrs. Percival and her niece. Mr. Dudley, who was the younger son of a very noble family, of a family more famed for their pride than their opulence, tenacious of his dignity, and jealous of his rights, was forever quarrelling, if not with Mrs. Percival herself, with her steward and tenants concerning tithes, and with the principal neighbours themselves concerning the respect and parade, he exacted. His wife, an illeducated, untaught woman of ancient family, was proud of that family almost without knowing why, and like him too was haughty and quarrelsome, without considering for what. Their only daughter, who inherited the ignorance, the insolence, and pride of her parents, was from that beauty of which she was unreasonably vain, considered by them as an irresistible creature, and looked up to as the future restorer, by a Splendid Marriage, of the dignity which their reduced situation and Mr. Dudley's being obliged to take orders for a country living had so much lessened. They at once despised the Percivals as people of mean family, and envied them as people of fortune. They were jealous of their being more respected than themselves and while they affected to consider them as of no consequence, were continually seeking to lessen them in the opinion of the neighbourhood by scandalous and malicious reports. Such a family as this, was ill-calculated to console Kitty for the loss of the Wynnes, or to fill up by their society, those occasionally irksome hours which in so retired a situation would sometimes occur for want of a companion. Her aunt was most excessively fond of her, and miserable if she saw her for a moment out of spirits; Yet she lived in such constant apprehension of her marrying imprudently if she were allowed the opportunity of choosing, and was so dissatisfied with her behaviour when she saw her with young men, for it was, from her natural disposition remarkably open and unreserved, that though she frequently wished for her niece's sake, that the neighbourhood were larger, and that she had used herself to mix more with it, yet the recollection of there being young men in almost every family in it, always conquered the wish. The same fears that prevented Mrs. Percival's joining much in the society of her neighbours, led her equally to avoid inviting her relations to spend any time in her house. She had therefore constantly regretted the annual attempt of a distant relation to visit her at Chetwynde, as there was a young man in the family of whom she had heard many traits that alarmed her. This son was however now on his travels, and the repeated solicitations of Kitty, joined to a consciousness of having declined with too little ceremony the frequent overtures of her friends to be admitted, and a real wish to see them herself, easily prevailed on her to press with great earnestness the pleasure of a visit from them during the summer. Mr. and Mrs. Stanley were accordingly to come, and Catharine, in having an object to look forward to, a something to expect that must inevitably relieve the dullness of a constant tête à tête with her aunt, was so delighted, and her spirits so elevated, that for the three or four days immediately preceding their arrival, she could scarcely fix herself to any employment. In this point Mrs. Percival always thought her defective, and frequently complained of a want of steadiness and perseverance in her occupations, which were by no means congenial to the eagerness of Kitty's disposition, and perhaps not often met with in any young person. The tediousness too of her aunt's conversation and the want of agreeable companions greatly increased this desire of change in her employments, for Kitty found herself much sooner tired of reading, working, or drawing, in Mrs. Percival's parlour than in her own arbour, where Mrs. Percival for fear of its being damp never accompanied her.

As her aunt prided herself on the exact propriety and neatness with which everything in her family was conducted, and had no higher satisfaction than that of knowing her house to be always in complete order, as her fortune was good, and her establishment ample, few were the preparations necessary for the reception of her visitors. The day of their arrival so long expected, at length came, and the noise of the coach and as it drove round the sweep, was to

Catharine a more interesting sound, than the music of an Italian opera, which to most heroines is the height of enjoyment. Mr. and Mrs. Stanley were people of large fortune and high fashion. He was a Member of the House of Commons, and they were therefore most agreeably necessitated to reside half the year in Town; where Miss Stanley had been attended by the most capital masters from the time of her being six years old to the last spring, which comprehending a period of twelve years had been dedicated to the acquirement of accomplishments which were now to be displayed and in a few years entirely neglected. She was elegant in her appearance, rather handsome, and naturally not deficient in abilities; but those years which ought to have been spent in the attainment of useful knowledge and mental improvement, had been all bestowed in learning drawing, Italian and music, more especially the latter, and she now united to these accomplishments, an understanding unimproved by reading and a mind totally devoid either of taste or judgement. Her temper was by nature good, but unassisted by reflection, she had neither patience under disappointment, nor could sacrifice her own inclinations to promote the happiness of others. All her ideas were towards the elegance of her appearance, the fashion of her dress, and the admiration she wished them to excite. She professed a love of books without reading, was lively without wit, and generally good humoured without merit. Such was Camilla Stanley; and Catharine, who was prejudiced by her appearance, and who from her solitary situation was ready to like anyone, tho' her understanding and judgement would not otherwise have been easily satisfied, felt almost convinced when she saw her, that Miss Stanley would be the very companion she wanted, and in some degree make amends for the loss of Cecilia and Mary Wynne. She therefore attached herself to Camilla from the first day of her arrival, and from being the only young people in the house, they were by inclination constant companions. Kitty was herself a great reader, tho' perhaps not a very deep one, and felt therefore highly delighted to find that Miss Stanley was equally fond of it. Eager to know that their sentiments as to books were similar, she very soon began questioning her new acquaintance on the subject; but though she was well read in modern history herself, she chose rather to speak first of books of a lighter kind, of books universally read and admired.

"You have read Mrs. Smith's novels, I suppose!" said she to her companion. "Oh! Yes," replied the other, "and I am quite delighted with them. They are the sweetest things in the world." "And which do you prefer of them?" "Oh! dear, I think there is no comparison between them—Emmeline is so much better than any of the others." "Many people think so, I know; but there does not appear so great a disproportion in their merits to me; do you think it is better written?" "Oh! I do not know anything about that—but it is better in every thing. Besides, Ethelinde is so long." "That is a very common objection I believe," said Kitty, "But for my own part, if a book is well written, I always find it too short." "So do I, only I get tired of it before it is finished." "But did not you find the story of Ethelinde very interesting? And the descriptions of Grasmere, are not they beautiful?" "Oh! I missed them all, because I was in such a hurry to know the end of it." Then from an easy transition she added, "We are going to the Lakes this autumn, and I am quite mad with joy; Sir Henry Devereux has promised to go with us, and that will make it so pleasant, you know."

"I dare say it will; but I think it is a pity that Sir Henry's powers of pleasing were not reserved for an occasion where they might be more wanted. However I quite envy you the pleasure of such a scheme."

"Oh! I am quite delighted with the thoughts of it; I can think of nothing else. I assure you I have done nothing for this last month but plan what clothes I should take with me, and I have at last determined to take very few indeed besides my travelling dress, and so I advise you to do, when ever you go; for I intend in case we should fall in with any races, or stop at Matlock or Scarborough, to have some things made for the occasion."

"You intend then to go into Yorkshire?"

"I believe not—indeed I know nothing of the route, for I never trouble myself about such things. I only know that we are to go from Derbyshire to Matlock and Scarborough, but to which of them first, I neither know nor care. I am in hopes of meeting some particular friends of mine at Scarborough. Augusta told me in her last letter that Sir Peter talked of going; but then you know that is so uncertain. I cannot bear Sir Peter, he is such a horrid creature."

"He is, is he?" said Kitty, not knowing what else to say.

"Oh! he is quite shocking." Here the conversation was interrupted, and Kitty was left in a painful uncertainty, as to the particulars of Sir Peter's character; she knew only that he was horrid and shocking, but why, and in what, yet remained to be discovered. She could scarcely resolve what to think of her new acquaintance; she appeared to be shamefully ignorant as to the geography of England, if she had understood her right, and equally devoid of taste and information. Kitty was however unwilling to decide hastily; she was at once desirous of doing Miss Stanley justice, and of having her own wishes in her answered; she determined therefore to suspend all judgement for some time. After supper, the conversation turning on the state of affairs in the political world, Mrs. Percival, who was firmly of opinion that the whole race of mankind were degenerating, said that for her part, everything she believed was going to rack and ruin, all order was destroyed over the face of the World, the House of Commons she heard did not break up sometimes till five in the morning, and depravity never was so general before; concluding with a wish that she might live to see the manners of the people in Queen Elizabeth's reign, restored again. "Well, ma'am," said her niece, "But I hope you do not mean with the times to restore Queen Elizabeth herself."

"Queen Elizabeth," said Mrs. Stanley, who never hazarded a remark on history that was not well founded, "lived to a good old age, and was a very clever woman." "True, ma'am", said Kitty; "But I do not consider either of those circumstances as meritorious in herself, and they are very far from making me wish her return, for if she were to come again with the same abilities and the same good constitution she might do as much mischief and last as long as she did before." Then turning to Camilla who had been sitting very silent for some time, she added, "What do you think of Elizabeth, Miss Stanley? I hope you will not defend her."

"Oh! dear," said Miss Stanley, "I know nothing of politics, and cannot bear to hear them mentioned." Kitty started at this repulse, but made no answer; that Miss Stanley must be ignorant of what she could not distinguish from politics she felt perfectly convinced. She retired to her own room, perplexed in her opinion about her new acquaintance, and fearful of her being very unlike Cecilia and Mary. She arose the next morning to experience a fuller conviction of this, and every future day increased it. She found no variety in her conversation; She received no information from her but in fashions, and no amusement but in her performance on the harpsichord; and after repeated endeavours to find her what she wished, she was obliged to give up the attempt and to consider it as fruitless. There had occasionally appeared a something like humour in Camilla which had inspired her with hopes, that she might at least have a natural genius, tho' not an improved one, but these sparklings of wit happened so seldom, and were so ill-supported that she was at last convinced of their being merely accidental. All her stock of knowledge was exhausted in a very few days, and when Kitty had learnt from her, how large their house in Town was, when the fashionable amusements began, who were the celebrated beauties and who the best milliner, Camilla had nothing further to teach, except the characters of any of her acquaintance as they occurred in conversation, which was done with equal ease and brevity, by saying that the person was either the sweetest creature in the world, and one of whom she was dotingly fond, or horrid, shocking and not fit to be seen.

As Catharine was very desirous of gaining every possible information as to the characters of the Halifax family, and concluded that Miss Stanley must be acquainted with them, as she seemed to be so with every one of any consequence, she took an opportunity as Camilla was one day enumerating all the people of rank that her mother visited, of asking her whether Lady Halifax were among the number.

"Oh! Thank you for reminding me of her; she is the sweetest woman in the world, and one of our most intimate acquaintance, I do not suppose there is a day passes during the six months that we are in Town, but what we see each other in the course of it. And I correspond with all the girls."

"They are then a very pleasant family!" said Kitty. "They ought to be so indeed, to allow of such frequent meetings, or all conversation must be at end."

"Oh! dear, not at all," said Miss Stanley, "for sometimes we do not speak to each other for a month together. We meet perhaps only in public, and then you know we are often not able to get near enough; but in that case we always nod and smile."

"Which does just as well. But I was going to ask you whether you have ever seen a Miss Wynne with them?"

"I know who you mean perfectly—she wears a blue hat. I have frequently seen her in Brook Street, when I have been at Lady Halifax's balls. She gives one every month during the winter. But only think how good it is in her to take care of Miss Wynne, for she is a very distant relation, and so poor that, as Miss Halifax told me, her Mother was obliged to find her in clothes. Is not it shameful?"

"That she should be so poor? It is indeed, with such wealthy connexions as the family have."

"Oh! no; I mean, was not it shameful in Mr. Wynne to leave his children so distressed, when he had actually the living of Chetwynde and two or three curacies, and only four children to provide for. What would he have done if he had had ten, as many people have?"

"He would have given them all a good education and have left them all equally poor."

"Well I do think there never was so lucky a family. Sir George Fitzgibbon you know sent the eldest girl to India entirely at his own expense, where they say she is most nobly married and the happiest creature in the world. Lady Halifax you see has taken care of the youngest and treats her as if she were her daughter; She does not go out into public with her to be sure; but then she is always present when her Ladyship gives her balls, and nothing can be kinder to her than Lady Halifax is; she would have taken her to Cheltenham last year, if there had been room enough at the lodgings, and therefore I do not think that she can have anything to complain of. Then there are the two sons; one of them the Bishop of M— has got into the Army as a Lieutenant I suppose; and the other is extremely well off I know, for I have a notion that somebody puts him to school somewhere in Wales. Perhaps you knew them when they lived here?"

"Very well, we met as often as your family and the Halifaxes do in Town, but as we seldom had any difficulty in getting near enough to speak, we seldom parted with merely a nod and a smile. They were indeed a most charming family, and I believe have scarcely their equals in the world; the neighbours we now have at the Parsonage, appear to more disadvantage in coming after them."

"Oh! horrid wretches! I wonder you can endure them."

"Why, what would you have one do?"

"Oh! Lord, If I were in your place, I should abuse them all day long."

"So I do, but it does no good."

"Well, I declare it is quite a pity that they should be suffered to live. I wish my father would propose knocking all their brains out, some day or other when he is in the House. So abominably proud of their family! And I dare say after all, that there is nothing particular in it."

"Why yes, I believe they have reason to value themselves on it, if any body has; for you know he is Lord Amyatt's brother."

"Oh! I know all that very well, but it is no reason for their being so horrid. I remember I met Miss Dudley last spring with Lady Amyatt at Ranelagh, and she had such a frightful cap on, that I have never been able to bear any of them since. And so you used to think the Wynnes very pleasant?"

"You speak as if their being so were doubtful! Pleasant! Oh! they were every thing that could interest and attach. It is not in my power to do justice to their merits, tho' not to feel them, I think must be impossible. They have unfitted me for any society but their own!"

"Well, that is just what I think of the Miss Halifaxes; by the bye, I must write to Caroline tomorrow, and I do not know what to say to her. The Barlows too are just such other sweet girls; but I wish Augusta's hair was not so dark. I cannot bear Sir Peter—horrid wretch! He is always laid up with the gout, which is exceedingly disagreeable to the family."

"And perhaps not very pleasant to himself. But as to the Wynnes; do you really think them very fortunate?"

"Do I? Why, does not every body? Miss Halifax and Caroline and Maria all say that they are the luckiest creatures in the world. So does Sir George Fitzgibbon and so do every body."

"That is, every body who have themselves conferred an obligation on them. But do you call it lucky, for a girl of genius and feeling to be sent in quest of a husband to Bengal, to be married there to a man of whose disposition she has no opportunity of judging till her judgement is of no use to her, who may be a tyrant, or a fool or both for what she knows to the contrary. Do you call that fortunate?"

"I know nothing of all that; I only know that it was extremely good in Sir George to fit her out and pay her passage, and that she would not have found many who would have done the same."

"I wish she had not found one," said Kitty with great eagerness, "she might then have remained in England and been happy."

"Well, I cannot conceive the hardship of going out in a very agreeable manner with two or three sweet girls for companions, having a delightful voyage to Bengal or Barbadoes or wherever it is, and being married soon after one's arrival to a very charming man immensely rich. I see no hardship in all that."

"Your representation of the affair," said Kitty laughing, "certainly gives a very different idea of it from mine. But supposing all this to be true, still, as it was by no means certain that she would be so fortunate either in her voyage, her companions, or her husband; in being obliged to run the risk of their proving very different, she undoubtedly experienced a great hardship. Besides, to a girl of any delicacy, the voyage in itself, since the object of it is so universally known, is a punishment that needs no other to make it very severe."

"I do not see that at all. She is not the first girl who has gone to the East Indies for a husband, and I declare I should think it very good fun if I were as poor."

"I believe you would think very differently then. But at least you will not defend her sister's situation! Dependant even for her clothes on the bounty of others, who of course do not pity her, as by your own account, they consider her as very fortunate."

"You are extremely nice upon my word; Lady Halifax is a delightful woman, and one of the sweetest tempered creatures in the world; I am sure I have every reason to speak well of her, for we are under most amazing obligations to her. She has frequently chaperoned me when my mother has been indisposed, and last spring she lent me her own horse three times, which was a prodigious favour, for it is the most beautiful creature that ever was seen, and I am the only person she ever lent it to."

"And then," continued she, "the Miss Halifaxes are quite delightful. Maria is one of the cleverest girls that ever were known—draws in oils, and plays anything by sight. She promised me one of her drawings before I left Town, but I entirely forgot to ask her for it. I would give anything to have one."

"But was not it very odd," said Kitty, "that the Bishop should send Charles Wynne to sea, when he must have had a much better chance of providing for him in the Church, which was the profession that Charles liked best, and the one for which his father had intended him? The Bishop I know had often promised Mr. Wynne a living, and as he never gave him one, I think it was incumbent on him to transfer the promise to his son."

"I believe you think he ought to have resigned his Bishopric to him; you seem determined to be dissatisfied with every thing that has been done for them."

"Well," said Kitty, "this is a subject on which we shall never agree, and therefore it will be useless to continue it farther, or to mention it again." She then left the room, and running out of the house was soon in her dear bower where she could indulge in peace all her affectionate anger against the relations of the Wynnes, which was greatly heightened by finding from Camilla that they were in general considered as having acted particularly well by them. She amused herself for some time in abusing, and hating them all, with great spirit, and when this tribute to her regard for the Wynnes, was paid, and the bower began to have its usual influence over her spirits, she contributed towards settling them, by taking out a book, for she had always one about her, and reading. She had been so employed for nearly an hour, when Camilla came running towards her with great eagerness, and apparently great pleasure. "Oh! my dear Catharine," said she, half out of breath, "I have such delightful news for you. But you shall guess what it is. We are all the happiest creatures in the world; would you believe it, the Dudleys have sent us an invitation to a ball at their own house. What charming people they are! I had no idea of there being so much sense in the whole family. I declare I quite dote upon them. And it happens so fortunately too, for I expect a new cap from Town tomorrow which will just do for a ball—gold net. It will be a most angelic thing—every body will be longing for the pattern." The expectation of a ball was indeed very agreeable intelligence to Kitty, who fond of dancing and seldom able to enjoy it, had reason to feel even greater pleasure in it than her friend; for to her, it was now no novelty. Camilla's delight however was by no means inferior to Kitty's, and she rather expressed the most of the two. The cap came and every other preparation was soon completed; while these were in agitation the days passed gaily away, but when directions were no longer necessary, taste could no longer be displayed, the difficulties no longer overcome, the short period that intervened before the day of the ball hung heavily on their hands, and every hour was too long. The very few times that Kitty had ever enjoyed the amusement of dancing was an excuse for her impatience, and an apology for the idleness it occasioned to a mind naturally very active; but her friend without such a plea was infinitely worse than herself. She could do nothing but wander from the house to the garden, and from the garden to the avenue, wondering when Thursday would come, which she might easily have ascertained, and counting the hours as they passed which served only to lengthen them.

They retired to their rooms in high spirits on Wednesday night, but Kitty awoke the next morning with a violent toothache. It was in vain that she endeavoured at first to deceive herself; her feelings were witnesses too acute of its reality; with as little success did she try to sleep it off, for the pain she suffered prevented her closing her eyes. She then summoned her maid and with the assistance of the housekeeper, every remedy that the receipt book or the head of the latter contained, was tried, but ineffectually; for though for a short time relieved by them, the pain still returned. She was now obliged to give up the endeavour, and to reconcile herself not only to the pain of a toothache, but to the loss of a ball; and though she had with so much eagerness looked forward to the day of its arrival, had received such pleasure in the necessary preparations, and promised herself so much delight in it, yet she was not so totally void of philosophy as many girls of her age might have been in her situation. She considered that there were misfortunes of a much greater magnitude than the loss of a ball, experienced every day by some part of mortality, and that the time might come when she would herself look back with wonder and perhaps with envy on her having known no greater vexation. By such reflections as these, she soon reasoned herself into as much resignation and patience as the pain she suffered, would allow of, which after all was the greatest misfortune of the two, and told the sad story when she entered the breakfast room, with tolerable composure. Mrs. Percival more grieved for her toothache than her disappointment, as she feared that it would not be possible to prevent her dancing with a Man if she went, was eager to try everything that had already been applied to alleviate the pain, while at the same time she declared it was impossible for her to leave the house. Miss Stanley who joined to her concern for her friend, felt a mixture of dread lest her mother's proposal that they should all remain at home, might be accepted, was very violent in her sorrow on the occasion, and though her apprehensions on the subject were soon quieted by Kitty's protesting that sooner than allow any one to stay with her, she would herself go, she continued to lament it with such unceasing vehemence as at last drove Kitty to her own room. Her fears for herself being now entirely dissipated left her more than ever at leisure to pity and persecute her friend who the safe when in her own room, was frequently removing from it to some other in hopes of being more free from pain, and then had no opportunity of escaping her.

"To be sure, there never was anything so shocking," said Camilla; "To come on such a day too! For one would not have minded it you know had it been at any other time. But it always is so. I never was at a ball in my life, but what something happened to prevent somebody from going! I wish there were no such things a teeth in the world; they are nothing but plagues to one, and I dare say that people might easily invent something to eat with instead of them; poor thing! what pain you are in! I declare it is quite shocking to look at you. But you won't have it out, will you! For Heaven's sake don't; for there is nothing I dread so much. I declare I have rather undergo the greatest tortures in the world than have a tooth drawn. Well! how patiently you do bear it! how can you be so quiet! Lord, if I were in your place I should make such a fuss, there would be no bearing me. I should torment you to death."

"So you do, as it is," thought Kitty.

"For my own part, Catharine" said Mrs. Percival "I have not a doubt but that you caught this toothache by sitting so much in that arbour, for it is always damp. I know it has ruined your constitution entirely; and indeed I do not believe it has been of much service to mine; I sat down in it last May to rest myself, and I have never been quite well since. I shall order John to pull it all down I assure you."

"I know you will not do that, ma'am," said Kitty, "as you must be convinced how unhappy it would make me."

"You talk very ridiculously, child; it is all whim and nonsense. Why cannot you fancy this room an arbour!"

"Had this room been built by Cecilia and Mary, I should have valued it equally, ma'am, for it is not merely the name of an arbour, which charms me."

"Why indeed, Mrs. Percival," said Mrs. Stanley, "I must think that Catharine's affection for her bower is the effect of a sensibility that does her credit. I love to see a friendship between young persons and always consider it as a sure mark of an amiable affectionate disposition. I have from Camilla's infancy taught her to think the same, and have taken great pains to introduce her to young people of her own age who were likely to be worthy of her regard. Nothing forms the taste more than sensible and elegant letters. Lady Halifax thinks just like me. Camilla corresponds with her daughters, and I believe I may venture to say that they are none of them the worse for it."

These ideas were too modern to suit Mrs. Percival who considered a correspondence between girls as productive of no good, and as the frequent origin of imprudence and error by the effect of pernicious advice and bad example. She could not therefore refrain from saying that for her part, she had lived fifty years in the world without having ever had a correspondent, and did not find herself at all the less respectable for it. Mrs. Stanley could say nothing in answer to this, but her daughter who was less governed by propriety, said in her thoughtless way, "But who knows what you might have been, ma'am, if you had had a correspondent; perhaps it would have made you quite a different creature. I declare I would not be without those I have for all the world. It is the greatest delight of my life, and you cannot think how much their letters have formed my taste as Mama says, for I hear from them generally every week."

"You received a letter from Augusta Barlow to day, did not you, my love" said her mother. "She writes remarkably well I know."

"Oh! Yes ma'am, the most delightful letter you ever heard of. She sends me a long account of the new Regency walking dress Lady Susan has given her, and it is so beautiful that I am quite dying with envy for it."

"Well, I am prodigiously happy to hear such pleasing news of my young friend; I have a high regard for Augusta, and most sincerely partake in the general joy on the occasion. But does she say nothing else? it seemed to be a long letter. Are they to be at Scarborough?"

"Oh! Lord, she never once mentions it, now I recollect it; and I entirely forgot to ask her when I wrote last. She says nothing indeed except about the Regency." "She must write well" thought Kitty, "to make a long letter upon a bonnet and pelisse." She then left the room tired of listening to a conversation which tho' it might have diverted her had she been well, served only to fatigue and depress her, while in pain. Happy was it for her, when the hour of dressing came, for Camilla satisfied with being surrounded by her mother and half the maids in the house did not want her assistance, and was too agreeably employed to want her society. She remained therefore alone in the parlour, till joined by Mr. Stanley and her aunt, who however after a few enquiries, allowed her to continue undisturbed and began their usual conversation on politics. This was a subject on which they could never agree, for Mr. Stanley who considered himself as perfectly qualified by his seat in the House, to decide on it without hesitation, resolutely maintained that the Kingdom had not for ages been in so flourishing and prosperous a state, and Mrs. Percival with equal warmth, tho' perhaps less argument, as vehemently asserted that the whole nation would speedily be ruined, and everything as she expressed herself be at sixes and sevens. It was not however unamusing to Kitty to listen to the dispute, especially as she began then to be more free from pain, and without taking any share in it herself, she found it very entertaining to observe the eagerness with which they both defended their opinions, and could not help thinking that Mr. Stanley would not feel more disappointed if her aunt's expectations were fulfilled, than her Aunt would be mortified by their failure. After waiting a considerable time Mrs. Stanley and her daughter appeared, and Camilla in high spirits, and perfect good humour with her own looks, was more violent than ever in her lamentations over her friend as she practised her Scotch steps about the room. At length they departed, and Kitty better able to amuse herself than she had been the whole day before, wrote a long account of her misfortunes to Mary Wynne.

When her letter was concluded she had an opportunity of witnessing the truth of that assertion which says that sorrows are lightened by communication, for her toothache was then so much relieved that she began to entertain an idea of following her friends to Mr. Dudley's. They had been gone an hour, and as every thing relative to her dress was in complete readiness, she considered that in another hour since there was so little a way to go, she might be there. They were gone in Mr. Stanley's carriage and therefore she might follow in her aunt's. As the plan seemed so very easy to be executed, and promising so much pleasure, it was after a few minutes deliberation finally adopted, and running up stairs, she rang in great haste for her maid. The bustle and hurry which then ensued for nearly an hour was at last happily concluded by her finding herself very well dressed and in high beauty. Anne was then dispatched in the same haste to order the carriage, while her mistress was putting on her gloves, and arranging the folds of her dress. In a few minutes she heard the carriage drive up to the door, and tho' at first surprised at the expedition with which it had been got ready, she concluded after a little reflection that the men had received some hint of her intentions beforehand, and was hastening out of the room, when Anne came running into it in the greatest hurry and agitation, exclaiming "Lord, ma'am! Here's a gentleman in a chaise and four come, and I cannot for the life conceive who it is! I happened to be crossing the hall when the carriage drove up, and I knew nobody would be in the way to let him in but Tom, and he looks so awkward you know, ma'am, now his hair is just done up, that I was not willing the gentleman should see him, and so I went to the door myself. And he is one of the handsomest young men you would wish to see; I was almost ashamed of being seen in my apron, ma'am, but however he is vastly handsome and did not seem to mind it at all. And he asked me whether the family were at home; and so I said everybody was gone out but you, ma'am, for I would not deny you because I was sure you would like to see him. And then he asked me whether Mr. and Mrs. Stanley were not here, and so I said yes, and then—"

"Good Heavens!" said Kitty, "what can all this mean! And who can it possibly be! Did you never see him before! And did not he tell you his name!"

"No, ma'am, he never said anything about it. So then I asked him to walk into the parlour, and he was prodigious agreeable, and—"

"Whoever he is," said her mistress, "he has made a great impression upon you, Nanny. But where did he come from? and what does he want here?"

"Oh! Ma'am, I was going to tell you, that I fancy his business is with you; for he asked me whether you were at leisure to see anybody, and desired I would give his compliments to you, and say he should be very happy to wait on you. However I thought he had better not come up into your dressing room, especially as everything is in such a litter, so I told him if he would be so obliging as to stay in the parlour, I would run up stairs and tell you he was come, and I dared to say that you would wait upon him. Lord, ma'am, I'd lay anything that he is come to ask you to dance with him tonight, and has got his chaise ready to take you to Mr. Dudley's."

Kitty could not help laughing at this idea, and only wished it might be true, as it was very likely that she would be too late for any other partner. "But what, in the name of wonder, can he have to say to me! Perhaps he is come to rob the house. He comes in style at least; and it will be some consolation for our losses to be robbed by a gentleman in a chaise and four. What livery has his servants?"

"Why that is the most wonderful thing about him, ma'am, for he has not a single servant with him, and came with hack horses; but he is as handsome as a Prince for all that, and has quite the look of one. Do, dear ma'am, go down, for I am sure you will be delighted with him."

"Well, I believe I must go; but it is very odd! What can he have to say to me." Then giving one look at herself in the glass, she walked with great impatience, tho' trembling all the while from not knowing what to expect, down stairs, and after pausing a moment at the door to gather courage for opening it, she resolutely entered the room. The stranger, whose appearance did not disgrace the account she had received of it from her maid, rose up on her entrance, and laying aside the newspaper he had been reading, advanced towards her with an air of the most perfect ease and vivacity, and said to her, "It is certainly a very awkward circumstance to be thus obliged to introduce myself, but I trust that the necessity of the case will plead my excuse, and prevent your being prejudiced by it against me. Your name, I need not ask, ma'am—Miss Percival is too well known to me by description to need any information of that."

Kitty, who had been expecting him to tell his own name, instead of hers, and who from having been little in company, and never before in such a situation, felt herself unable to ask it, tho' she had been planning her speech all the way down stairs, was so confused and distressed by this unexpected address that she could only return a slight curtsy to it, and accepted the chair he reached her, without knowing what she did. The gentleman then continued. "You are, I dare say, surprised to see me returned from France so soon, and nothing indeed but business could have brought me to England; a very melancholy affair has now occasioned it, and I was unwilling to leave it without paying my respects to the family in Devonshire whom I have so long wished to be acquainted with." Kitty, who felt much more surprised at his supposing her to be so, than at seeing a person in England, whose having ever left it was perfectly unknown to her, still continued silent from wonder and perplexity, and her visitor still continued to talk.

"You will suppose, madam, that I was not the less desirous of waiting on you, from your having Mr. and Mrs. Stanley with you. I hope they are well? And Mrs. Percival, how does she do?" Then without waiting for an answer he gaily added, "But my dear Miss Percival, you are going out I am sure; and I am detaining you from your appointment. How can I ever expect to be forgiven for such injustice! Yet how can I, so circumstanced, forbear to offend! You seem dressed for a ball! But this is the land of gaiety I know; I have for many years been desirous of visiting it. You have dances I suppose at least every week. But where are the rest of your party gone, and what kind angel in compassion to me, has excluded you from it?"

"Perhaps sir," said Kitty extremely confused by his manner of speaking to her, and highly displeased with the freedom of his conversation towards one who had never seen him before and did not now know his name, "Perhaps sir, you are acquainted with Mr. and Mrs. Stanley; and your business may be with them?"

"You do me too much honour, ma'am," replied he laughing, "in supposing me to be acquainted with Mr. and Mrs. Stanley; I merely know them by sight; very distant relations; only my father and mother. Nothing more I assure you."

"Gracious Heaven!" said Kitty, "Are you Mr. Stanley then? I beg a thousand pardons. Though really upon recollection I do not know for what—for you never told me your name."

"I beg your pardon. I made a very fine speech when you entered the room, all about introducing myself; I assure you it was very great for me." "The speech had certainly great merit," said Kitty smiling; "I thought so at the time; but since you never mentioned your name in it, as an introductory one it might have been better."

There was such an air of good humour and gaiety in Stanley, that Kitty, tho' perhaps not authorized to address him with so much familiarity on so short an acquaintance, could not forbear indulging the natural unreserve and vivacity of her own disposition, in speaking to him, as he spoke to her. She was intimately acquainted too with his family who were her relations, and she chose to consider herself entitled by the connexion to forget how little a while they had known each other. "Mr. and Mrs. Stanley and your sister are extremely well," said she, "and will I dare say be very much surprised to see you. But I am sorry to hear that your return to England has been occasioned by an unpleasant circumstance."

"Oh, don't talk of it," said he, "it is a most confounded shocking affair, and makes me miserable to think of it; But where are my father and mother, and your aunt gone! Oh! Do you know that I met the prettiest little waiting maid in the world, when I came here; she let me into the house; I took her for you at first."

"You did me a great deal of honour, and give me more credit for good nature than I deserve, for I never go to the door when any one comes."

"Nay do not be angry; I mean no offence. But tell me, where are you going to so smart? Your carriage is just coming round."

"I am going to a dance at a neighbour's, where your family and my aunt are already gone."

"Gone, without you! what's the meaning of that? But I suppose you are like myself, rather long in dressing."

"I must have been so indeed, if that were the case for they have been gone nearly these two hours; The reason however was not what you suppose. I was prevented going by a pain—"

"By a pain!" interrupted Stanley, "Oh! heavens, that is dreadful indeed! No matter where the pain was. But my dear Miss Percival, what do you say to my accompanying you! And suppose you were to dance with me too? I think it would be very pleasant."

"I can have no objection to either I am sure," said Kitty laughing to find how near the truth her maid's conjecture had been; "on the contrary I shall be highly honoured by both, and I can answer for your being extremely welcome to the family who give the ball."

"Oh! hang them; who cares for that; they cannot turn me out of the house. But I am afraid I shall cut a sad figure among all your Devonshire beaux in this dusty, travelling apparel, and I have not wherewithal to change it. You can procure me some powder perhaps, and I must get a pair of shoes from one of the men, for I was in such a devil of a hurry to leave Lyons that

I had not time to have anything pack'd up but some linen." Kitty very readily undertook to procure for him everything he wanted, and telling the footman to show him into Mr. Stanley's dressing room, gave Nanny orders to send in some powder and pomatum, which orders Nanny chose to execute in person. As Stanley's preparations in dressing were confined to such very trifling articles, Kitty of course expected him in about ten minutes; but she found that it had not been merely a boast of vanity in saying that he was dilatory in that respect, as he kept her waiting for him above half an hour, so that the clock had struck ten before he entered the room and the rest of the party had gone by eight.

"Well," said he as he came in, "have not I been very quick! I never hurried so much in my life before."

"In that case you certainly have," replied Kitty, "for all merit you know is comparative."

"Oh! I knew you would be delighted with me for making so much haste. But come, the carriage is ready; so, do not keep me waiting." And so saying he took her by the hand, and led her out of the room.

"Why, my dear Cousin," said he when they were seated, "this will be a most agreeable surprise to everybody to see you enter the room with such a smart young fellow as I am. I hope your aunt won't be alarmed."

"To tell you the truth," replied Kitty, "I think the best way to prevent it, will be to send for her, or your mother before we go into the room, especially as you are a perfect stranger, and must of course be introduced to Mr. and Mrs. Dudley."

"Oh! Nonsense," said he; "I did not expect you to stand upon such ceremony; Our acquaintance with each other renders all such prudery, ridiculous; Besides, if we go in together, we shall be the whole talk of the country."

"To me" replied Kitty, "that would certainly be a most powerful inducement; but I scarcely know whether my aunt would consider it as such. Women at her time of life, have odd ideas of propriety you know."

"Which is the very thing that you ought to break them of; and why should you object to entering a room with me where all our relations are, when you have done me the honour to admit me without any chaperone into your carriage? Do not you think your aunt will be as much offended with you for one, as for the other of these mighty crimes?"

"Why really" said Catharine, "I do not know but that she may; however, it is no reason that I should offend against decorum a second time, because I have already done it once."

"On the contrary, that is the very reason which makes it impossible for you to prevent it, since you cannot offend for the first time again."

"You are very ridiculous," said she laughing, "but I am afraid your arguments divert me too much to convince me."

"At least they will convince you that I am very agreeable, which after all, is the happiest conviction for me, and as to the affair of propriety we will let that rest till we arrive at our journey's end. This is a monthly ball I suppose. Nothing but dancing here."

"I thought I had told you that it was given by a Mr. and Mrs. Dudley."

"Oh! aye so you did; but why should not Mr. Dudley give one every month! By the bye who is that man? Everybody gives balls now I think; I believe I must give one myself soon. Well, but how do you like my father and mother? And poor little Camilla too, has not she plagued you to death with the Halifaxes" Here the carriage fortunately stopped at Mr. Dudley's, and Stanley was too much engaged in handing her out of it, to wait for an answer, or to remember that what he had said required one. They entered the small vestibule which Mr. Dudley had raised to the dignity of a hall, and Kitty immediately desired the footman who was leading the way upstairs, to inform either Mrs. Percival, or Mrs. Stanley of her arrival, and beg them to come to her, but Stanley unused to any contradiction and impatient to be amongst them, would neither allow her to wait, or listen to what she said, and forcibly seizing her arm within his, overpowered her voice with the rapidity of his own, and Kitty half angry, and half laughing was obliged to go with him up stairs, and could even with difficulty prevail on him to relinquish her hand before they entered the room.

Mrs. Percival was at that very moment engaged in conversation with a lady at the upper end of the room, to whom she had been giving a long account of her niece's unlucky disappointment, and the dreadful pain that she had with so much fortitude, endured the whole day. "I left her however," said she, "thank heaven, a little better, and I hope she has been able to amuse herself with a book, poor thing! for she must otherwise be very dull. She is probably in bed by this time, which while she is so poorly, is the best place for her you know, ma'am." The lady was going to give her assent to this opinion, when the noise of voices on the stairs, and the footman's opening the door as if for the entrance of company, attracted the attention of every body in the room; and as it was in one of those intervals between the dances when every one seemed glad to sit down, Mrs. Percival had a most unfortunate opportunity of seeing her niece whom she had supposed in bed, or amusing herself as the height of gaiety with a book, enter the room most elegantly dressed, with a smile on her countenance, and a glow of mingled cheerfulness and confusion on her cheeks, attended by a young man uncommonly handsome, and who without any of her confusion, appeared to have all her vivacity. Mrs. Percival, colouring with anger and astonishment, rose from her seat, and Kitty walked eagerly towards her, impatient to account for what she saw appeared wonderful to every body, and extremely offensive to her, while Camilla on seeing her brother ran instantly towards him, and very soon explained who he was by her words and actions. Mr. Stanley, who so fondly doted on his son, that the pleasure of seeing him again after an absence of three months prevented his feeling for the time any anger against him for returning to England without his knowledge, received him with equal surprise and delight; and soon comprehending the cause of his journey, forbore any further conversation with him, as he was eager to see his mother, and it was necessary that he should be introduced to Mr. Dudley's family. This introduction to any one but Stanley would have been highly unpleasant, for they considered their dignity injured by his coming uninvited to their house, and received him with more than their usual haughtiness. But Stanley who with a vivacity of temper seldom subdued, and a contempt of censure not to be overcome, possessed an opinion of his own consequence, and a perseverance in his own schemes which were not to be damped by the conduct of others, appeared not to perceive it. The civilities therefore which they coldly offered, he received with a gaiety and ease peculiar to himself, and then attended by his father and sister walked into another room where his mother was playing at cards, to experience another meeting, and undergo a repetition of pleasure, surprise and explanations. While these were passing, Camilla eager to communicate all she felt to some one who would attend to her, returned to Catharine, and seating herself by her, immediately began, "Well, did you ever know anything so delightful as this! But it always is so; I never go to a ball in my life but what something or other happens unexpectedly that is quite charming!"

"A ball" replied Kitty, "seems to be a most eventful thing to you."

"Oh! Lord, it is indeed. But only think of my brother's returning so suddenly. And how shocking a thing it is that has brought him over! I never heard anything so dreadful!"

"What is it pray that has occasioned his leaving France! I am sorry to find that it is a melancholy event."

"Oh! it is beyond anything you can conceive! His favourite hunter who was turned out in the park on his going abroad, somehow or other fell ill. No, I believe it was an accident, but however it was something or other, or else it was something else, and so they sent an express immediately to Lyons where my brother was, for they knew that he valued this mare more than anything else in the world besides; an So my brother set off directly for England, and without packing up another coat; I am quite angry with him about it; it was so shocking you know to come away without a change of clothes."

"Why indeed," said Kitty, "it seems to have been a very shocking affair from beginning to end."

"Oh! it is beyond anything you can conceive! I would rather have had anything happen than that he should have lost that mare."

"Except his coming away without another coat."

"Oh! yes, that has vexed me more than you can imagine. Well, and so Edward got to Brampton just as the poor thing was dead; but as he could not bear to remain there then, he came off directly to Chetwynde on purpose to see us. I hope he may not go abroad again."

"Do you think he will not?"

"Oh! dear, to be sure he must, but I wish he may not with all my heart. You cannot think how fond I am of him! By the bye are not you in love with him yourself?"

"To be sure I am," replied Kitty laughing, "I am in love with every handsome man I see."

"That is just like me. I am always in love with every handsome man in the world."

"There you outdo me," replied Catharine, "for I am only in love with those I do see." Mrs. Percival who was sitting on the other side of her, and who began now to distinguish the words, Love and handsome man, turned hastily towards them and said, "What are you talking of, Catharine!" To which Catharine immediately answered with the simple artifice of a child, "Nothing, ma'am." She had already received a very severe lecture from her aunt on the imprudence of her behaviour during the whole evening; She blamed her for coming to the ball, for coming in the same carriage with Edward Stanley, and still more for entering the room with him. For the last-mentioned offence Catharine knew not what apology to give, and tho' she longed in answer to the second to say that she had not thought it would be civil to make Mr. Stanley walk, she dared not so to trifle with her aunt, who would have been but the more offended by it. The first accusation however she considered as very unreasonable, as she thought herself perfectly justified in coming. This conversation continued till Edward Stanley entering the room came instantly towards her, and telling her that every one waited for her to begin the next dance led her to the top of the room, for Kitty, impatient to escape from so unpleasant a companion, without the least hesitation, or one civil scruple at being so distinguished, immediately gave him her hand, and joyfully left her seat. This conduct however was highly resented by several young ladies present, and among the rest by Miss Stanley whose regard for her brother tho' excessive, and whose affection for Kitty tho' prodigious, were not proof against such an injury to her importance and her peace. Edward had however only consulted his own inclinations in desiring Miss Percival to begin the dance, nor had he any reason to know that it was either wished or expected by anyone else in the party. As an heiress she was certainly of consequence, but her birth gave her no other claim to it, for her father had been a merchant. It was this very circumstance which rendered this unfortunate affair so offensive to Camilla, for tho' she would sometimes boast in the pride of her heart, and her eagerness to be admired that she did not know who her grandfather had been, and was as ignorant of everything relative to genealogy as to astronomy, (and she might have added, geography) yet she was really proud of her family and connexions, and easily offended if they were treated with neglect. "I should not have minded it," said she to her mother, "if she had been anybody else's daughter; but to see her pretend to be above me, when her father was only a tradesman, is too bad! It is such an affront to our whole family! I declare I think Papa ought to interfere in it, but he never cares about anything but politics. If I were Mr. Pitt or the Lord Chancellor, he would take care I should not be insulted, but he never thinks about me; And it is so provoking that Edward should let her stand there. I wish with all my heart that he had never come to England! I hope she may fall down and break her neck, or sprain her ankle." Mrs. Stanley perfectly agreed with her daughter concerning the affair, and tho' with less violence, expressed almost equal resentment at the indignity. Kitty in the meantime remained insensible of having given any one offence, and therefore unable either to offer an apology, or make a reparation; her whole attention was occupied by the happiness she enjoyed in dancing with the most elegant young man in the room, and every one else was equally unregarded. The evening indeed to her, passed off delightfully; he was her partner during the greatest part of it, and the united attractions that he possessed of person, address and vivacity, had easily gained that preference from Kitty which they seldom fail of obtaining from every one. She was too happy to care either for her aunt's ill humour which she could not help remarking, or for the alteration in Camilla's behaviour which forced itself at last on her observations. Her spirits were elevated above the influence of displeasure in any one, and she was equally indifferent as to the cause of Camilla's, or the continuance of her aunt's. Though Mr. Stanley could never be really offended by any imprudence or folly in his son that had given him the pleasure of seeing him, he was yet perfectly convinced that Edward ought not to remain in England, and was resolved to hasten his leaving it as soon as possible; but when he talked to Edward about it, he found him much less disposed towards returning to France, than to accompany them in their projected tour, which he assured his father would be infinitely more pleasant to him, and that as to the affair of travelling he considered it of no importance, and what might be pursued at any little odd time, when he had nothing better to do. He advanced these objections in a manner which plainly showed that he had scarcely a doubt of their being complied with, and appeared to consider his father's arguments in opposition to them, as merely given with a view to keep up his authority, and such as he should find little difficulty in combating. He concluded at last by saying, as the chaise in which they returned together from Mr. Dudley's reached Mrs. Percival's, "Well sir, we will settle this point some other time, and fortunately it is of so little consequence, that an immediate discussion of it is unnecessary." He then got out of the chaise and entered the house without waiting for his father's reply.

It was not till their return that Kitty could account for that coldness in Camilla's behaviour to her, which had been so pointed as to render it impossible to be entirely unnoticed. When however they were seated in the coach with the two other ladies, Miss Stanley's indignation was no longer to be suppressed from breaking out into words, and found the following vent.

"Well, I must say this, that I never was at a stupider ball in my life! But it always is so; I am always disappointed in them for some reason or other. I wish there were no such things."

"I am sorry, Miss Stanley," said Mrs. Percival drawing herself up, "that you have not been amused; every thing was meant for the best I am sure, and it is a poor encouragement for your Mama to take you to another if you are so hard to be satisfied."

"I do not know what you mean, ma'am, about Mama's taking me to another. You know I am come out."

"Oh! dear Mrs. Percival," said Mrs. Stanley, "you must not believe everything that my lively Camilla says, for her spirits are prodigiously high sometimes, and she frequently speaks without thinking. I am sure it is impossible for any one to have been at a more elegant or agreeable dance, and so she wishes to express herself I am certain."

"To be sure I do," said Camilla very sulkily, "only I must say that it is not very pleasant to have any body behave so rude to one as to be quite shocking! I am sure I am not at all offended, and should not care if all the world were to stand above me, but still it is extremely abominable, and what I cannot put up with. It is not that I mind it in the least, for I had just as soon stand at the bottom as at the top all night long, if it was not so very disagreeable—. But to have a person come in the middle of the evening and take everybody's place is what I am not used to, and tho' I do not care a pin about it myself, I assure you I shall not easily forgive or forget it."

This speech which perfectly explained the whole affair to Kitty, was shortly followed on her side by a very submissive apology, for she had too much good sense to be proud of her family, and too much good nature to live at variance with any one. The excuses she made, were delivered with so much real concern for the offence, and such unaffected sweetness, that it was almost impossible for Camilla to retain that anger which had occasioned them; She felt indeed most highly gratified to find that no insult had been intended and that Catharine was very far from forgetting the difference in their birth for which she could now only pity her, and her good humour being restored with the same ease in which it had been affected, she spoke with the highest delight of the evening, and declared that she had never before been at so pleasant a ball. The same endeavours that had procured the forgiveness of Miss Stanley ensured to her the cordiality of her mother, and nothing was wanting but Mrs. Percival's good humour to render the happiness of the others complete; but she, offended with Camilla for her affected superiority, still more so with her brother for coming to Chetwynde, and dissatisfied with the whole evening, continued silent and gloomy and was a restraint on the vivacity of her companions. She eagerly seized the very first opportunity which the next morning offered to her of speaking to Mr. Stanley on the subject of his son's return, and after having expressed her opinion of its being a very silly affair that he came at all, concluded with desiring him to inform Mr. Edward Stanley that it was a rule with her never to admit a young man into her house as a visitor for any length of time.

"I do not speak, sir," she continued, "out of any disrespect to you, but I could not answer it to myself to allow of his stay; there is no knowing what might be the consequence of it, if he were to continue here, for girls nowadays will always give a handsome young man the preference before any other, tho' for why, I never could discover, for what after all is youth and beauty! It is but a poor substitute for real worth and merit; Believe me Cousin that, what ever people may say to the contrary, there is certainly nothing like virtue for making us what we ought to be, and as to a young man's being young and handsome and having an agreeable person, it is nothing at all to the purpose for he had much better be respectable. I always did think so, and I always shall, and therefore you will oblige me very much by desiring your son to leave Chetrynde, or I cannot be answerable for what may happen between him and my niece. You will be surprised to hear me say it," she continued, lowering her voice, "But truth will out, and I must own that Kitty is one of the most impudent girls that ever existed. I assure you sir, that I have seen her sit and laugh and whisper with a young man whom she has not seen above half a dozen times. Her behaviour indeed is scandalous, and therefore I beg you will send your son away immediately, or everything will be at sixes and sevens."

Mr. Stanley, who from one part of her speech had scarcely known to what length her insinuations of Kitty's impudence were meant to extend, now endeavoured to quiet her fears on the occasion, by assuring her, that on every account he meant to allow only of his son's continuing that day with them, and that she might depend on his being more earnest in the affair from a wish of obliging her. He added also that he knew Edward to be very desirous himself of returning to France, as he wisely considered all time lost that did not forward the plans in which he was at present engaged, tho' he was but too well convinced of the contrary himself. His assurance in some degree quieted Mrs. Percival, and left her tolerably relieved of her cares and alarms, and better disposed to behave with civility towards his son during the short remainder of his stay at Chetwynde. Mr. Stanley went immediately to Edward, to whom he repeated the conversation that had passed between Mrs. Percival and himself, and strongly pointed out the necessity of his leaving Chetwynde the next day, since his world was already engaged for it. His son however appeared struck only by the ridiculous apprehensions of Mrs. Percival; and highly delighted at having occasioned them himself, seemed engrossed alone in thinking how he might increase them, without attending to any other part of his father's conversation. Mr. Stanley could get no determinate answer from him, and tho' he still hoped for the best, they parted almost in anger on his side.

His son though by no means disposed to marry, or any otherwise attached to Miss Percival than as a good natured lively girl who seemed pleased with him, took infinite pleasure in alarming the jealous fears of her aunt by his attentions to her, without considering what effect they might have on the lady herself. He would always sit by her when she was in the room, appear dissatisfied if she left it, and was the first to enquire whether she meant soon to return. He was delighted with her drawings, and enchanted with her performance on the harpsichord; Everything that she said, appeared to interest him; his conversation was addressed to her alone, and she seemed to be the sole object of his attention. That such efforts should succeed with one so tremblingly alive to every alarm of the kind as Mrs. Percival, is by no means unnatural, and that they should have equal influence with her niece whose imagination was lively, and whose disposition romantic, who was already extremely pleased with him, and of course desirous that he might be so with her, is as little to be wondered at. Every moment as it added to the conviction of his liking her, made him still more pleasing, and strengthened in her mind a wish of knowing him better. As for Mrs. Percival, she was in tortures the whole day; Nothing that she had ever felt before on a similar occasion was to be compared to the sensations which then distracted her; her fears had never been so strongly, or indeed so reasonably excited.—Her dislike of Stanley, her anger at her niece, her impatience to have them separated conquered every idea of propriety and good breeding, and though he had never mentioned any intention of leaving them the next day, she could not help asking him after dinner, in her eagerness to have him gone, at what time he meant to set out.

"Oh! Ma'am," replied he, "if I am off by twelve at night, you may think yourself lucky; and if I am not, you can only blame yourself for having left so much as the hour of my departure to my own disposal." Mrs. Percival coloured very highly at this speech, and without addressing herself to any one in particular, immediately began a long harangue on the shocking behaviour of modern young men, and the wonderful alteration that had taken place in them, since her time, which she illustrated with many Instructive anecdotes of the decorum and modesty which had marked the characters of those whom she had known, when she had been young. This however did not prevent his walking in the garden with her niece, without any other companion for nearly an hour in the course of the evening. They had left the room for that purpose with Camilla at a time when Mrs. Percival had been out of it, nor was it for some time after her return to it, that she could discover where they were. Camilla had taken two or three turns with them in the walk which led to the arbour, but soon growing tired of listening to a conversation in which she was seldom invited to join, and from its turning occasionally on books, very little able to do it, she left them together in the arbour, to wander alone to some other part of the garden, to eat the fruit, and examine Mrs. Percival's greenhouse. Her absence was so far from being regretted, that it was scarcely noticed by them, and they continued conversing together on almost every subject, for Stanley seldom dwelt long on any, and had something to say on all, till they were interrupted by her aunt.

Kitty was by this time perfectly convinced that both in natural abilities, and acquired information, Edward Stanley was infinitely superior to his sister. Her desire of knowing that he was so, had induced her to take every opportunity of turning the conversation on history and they were very soon engaged in an historical dispute, for which no one was more calculated than Stanley who was so far from being really of any party, that he had scarcely a fixed opinion on the subject. He could therefore always take either side, and always argue with temper. In his indifference on all such topics he was very unlike his companion, whose judgement being guided by her feelings which were eager and warm, was easily decided, and though it was not always infallible, she defended it with a spirit and enthusiasm which marked her own reliance on it. They had continued therefore for sometime conversing in this manner on the character of Richard the Third, which he was warmly defending when he suddenly seized hold of her hand, and exclaiming with great emotion, "Upon my honour you are entirely mistaken," pressed it passionately to his lips, and ran out of the arbour. Astonished at this behaviour, for which she was wholly unable to account, she continued for a few moments motionless on the seat where he had left her, and was then on the point of following him up the narrow walk through which he had passed, when on looking up the one that lay immediately before the arbour, she saw her aunt walking towards her with more than her usual quickness. This explained at once the reason for his leaving her, but his leaving her in such manner was rendered still more inexplicable by it. She felt a considerable degree of confusion at having been seen by her in such a place with Edward, and at having that part of his conduct, for which she could not herself account, witnessed by one to whom all gallantry was odious. She remained therefore confused, distressed and irresolute, and suffered her aunt to approach her, without leaving the arbour.

Mrs. Percival's looks were by no means calculated to animate the spirits of her niece, who in silence awaited her accusation, and in silence meditated her defence. After a few moments suspense, for Mrs. Percival was too much fatigued to speak immediately, she began with great anger and asperity, the following harangue. "Well; this is beyond anything I could have supposed. Profligate as I knew you to be, I was not prepared for such a sight. This is beyond any thing you ever did before; beyond any thing I ever heard of in my life! Such impudence, I never witnessed before in such a girl! And this is the reward for all the cares I have taken in your education; for all my troubles and anxieties; and Heaven knows how many they have been! All I wished for, was to breed you up virtuously; I never wanted you to play upon the harpsicord, or draw better than any one else; but I had hoped to see you respectable and good; to see you able and willing to give an example of modesty and virtue to the young people here abouts. I bought you Blair's Sermons, and Coelebs' In Search of a Wife, I gave you the key to my own library, and borrowed a great many good books of my neighbours for you, all to this purpose. But I might have spared myself the trouble. Oh! Catharine, you are an abandoned creature, and I do not know what will become of you. I am glad however," she continued softening into some degree of mildness, "to see that you have some shame for what you have done, and if you are really sorry for it, and your future life is a life of penitence and reformation perhaps you may be forgiven. But I plainly see that every thing is going to sixes and sevens and all order will soon be at an end throughout the Kingdom." "Not however, ma'am, the sooner, I hope, from any conduct of mine," said Catharine in a tone of great humility, "for upon my honour I have done nothing this evening that can contribute to overthrow the establishment of the kingdom."

"You are mistaken, child," replied she "the welfare of every nation depends upon the virtue of its individuals, and any one who offends in so gross a manner against decorum and propriety is certainly hastening its ruin. You have been giving a bad example to the world, and the world is but too well disposed to receive such."

"Pardon me, madam," said her niece; "but I can have given an example only to you, for you alone have seen the offence. Upon my word however there is no danger to fear from what I have done; Mr. Stanley's behaviour has given me as much surprise, as it has done to you, and I can only suppose that it was the effect of his high spirits, authorized in his Opinion by our relationship. But do you consider, madam, that it is growing very late! Indeed you had better return to the house." This speech as she well knew, would be unanswerable with her aunt, who instantly rose, and hurried away under so many apprehensions for her own health, as banished for the time all anxiety about her niece, who walked quietly by her side, revolving within her own mind the occurrence that had given her aunt so much alarm. "I am astonished at my own imprudence," said Mrs. Percival; "How could I be so forgetful as to sit down out of doors at such a time of night! I shall certainly have a return of my rheumatism after it. I begin to feel very chill already. I must have caught a dreadful cold by this time. I am sure of being lain-up all the winter after it." Then reckoning with her fingers, "Let me see; This is July; the cold weather will soon be coming in—August—September—October—November—December—January—February—March—April. Very likely I may not be tolerable again before May. I must and will have that arbour pulled down—it will be the death of me; who knows now, but what I may never recover. Such things have happened. My particular friend Miss Sarah Hutchinson's death was occasioned by nothing more. She stayed out late one evening in April, and got wet through for it rained very hard, and never changed her clothes when she came home. It is unknown how many people have died in consequence of catching cold! I do not believe there is a disorder in the world except the smallpox which does not spring from it." It was in vain that Kitty endeavoured to convince her that her fears on the occasion were groundless; that it was not yet late enough to catch cold, and that even if it were, she might hope to escape any other complaint, and to recover in less than ten months. Mrs. Percival only replied that she hoped she knew more of ill health than to be convinced in such a point by a girl who had always been perfectly well, and hurried up stairs leaving Kitty to make her apologies to Mr. and Mrs. Stanley for going to bed. Tho' Mrs. Percival seemed perfectly satisfied with the goodness of the apology herself, yet Kitty felt somewhat embarrassed to find that the only one she could offer to their visitors was that her aunt had perhaps caught cold, for Mrs. Percival charged her to make light of it, for fear of alarming them. Mr. and Mrs. Stanley however who well knew that their cousin was easily terrified on that score, received the account of it with very little surprise, and all proper concern.

Edward and his sister soon came in, and Kitty had no difficulty in gaining an explanation of his conduct from him, for he was too warm on the subject himself, and too eager to learn its success, to refrain from making immediate enquiries about it; and she could not help feeling both surprised and offended at the ease and indifference with which he owned that all his intentions had been to frighten her aunt by pretending an affection for her, a design so very incompatible with that partiality which she had at one time been almost convinced of his feeling for her. It is true that she had not yet seen enough of him to be actually in love with him, yet she felt greatly disappointed that so handsome, so elegant, so lively a young man should be so perfectly free from any such sentiment as to make it his principal sport. There was a novelty in his character which to her was extremely pleasing; his person was uncommonly fine, his spirits and vivacity suited to her own, and his manners at once so animated and insinuating, that she thought it must be impossible for him to be otherwise than amiable, and was ready to give him credit for being perfectly so. He knew the powers of them himself; to them he had often been indebted for his father's forgiveness of faults which had he been awkward and inelegant would have appeared very serious; to them, even more than to his person or his fortune, he owed the regard which almost every one was disposed to feel for him, and which young women in particular were inclined to entertain.

Their influence was acknowledged on the present occasion by Kitty, whose anger they entirely dispelled, and whose cheerfulness they had power not only to restore, but to raise. The evening passed off as agreeably as the one that had preceeded it; they continued talking to each other, during the chief part of it, and such was the power of his address, and the brilliancy of his eyes, that when they parted for the night, tho' Catharine had but a few hours before totally given up the idea, yet she felt almost convinced again that he was really in love with her. She reflected on their past conversation, and tho' it had been on various and indifferent subjects, and she could not exactly recollect any speech on his side expressive of such a partiality, she was still however nearly certain of its being so; But fearful of being vain enough to suppose such a thing without sufficient reason, she resolved to suspend her final determination on it, till the next day, and more especially till their parting which she thought would infallibly explain his regard if any he had. The more she had seen of him, the more inclined was she to like him, and the more desirous that he should like her. She was convinced of his being naturally very clever and very well disposed, and that his thoughtlessness and negligence, which tho' they appeared to her as very becoming in him, she was aware would by many people be considered as defects in his character, merely proceeded from a vivacity always pleasing in young men, and were far from testifying a weak or vacant understanding. Having settled this point within herself, and being perfectly convinced by her own arguments of its truth, she went to bed in high spirits; determined to study his character, and watch his behaviour still more the next day.

She got up with the same good resolutions and would probably have put them in execution, had not Anne informed her as soon as she entered the room that Mr. Edward Stanley was already gone. At first she refused to credit the information, but when her maid assured her that he had ordered a carriage the evening before to be there at seven o'clock in the morning and that she herself had actually seen him depart in it a little after eight, she could no longer deny her belief to it. "And this," thought she to herself blushing with anger at her own folly, "this is the affection for me of which I was so certain. Oh! what a silly thing is woman! How vain, how unreasonable! To suppose that a young man would be seriously attached in the course of four and twenty hours, to a girl who has nothing to recommend her but a good pair of eyes! And he is really gone! Gone perhaps without bestowing a thought on me! Oh! why was not I up by eight o'clock! But it is a proper punishment for my laziness and folly, and I am heartily glad of it. I deserve it all, and ten times more for such insufferable vanity. It will at least be of service to me in that respect; it will teach me in future not to think every body is in love with me. Yet I should like to have seen him before he went, for perhaps it may be many years before we meet again. By his manner of leaving us however, he seems to have been perfectly indifferent about it. How very odd, that he should go without giving us notice of it, or taking leave of any one! But it is just like a young man, governed by the whim of the moment, or actuated merely by the love of doing anything odd! Unaccountable beings indeed! And young women are equally ridiculous! I shall soon begin to think like my aunt that everything is going to sixes and sevens, and that the whole race of mankind are degenerating." She was just dressed, and on the point of leaving her room to make her personal enquires after Mrs. Percival, when Miss Stanley knocked at her door, and on her being admitted began in her usual strain a long harangue upon her father's being so shocking as to make Edward go at all, and upon Edward's being so horrid as to leave them at such an hour in the morning. "You have no idea," said she, "how surprised I was, when he came into my room to bid me good bye."

"Have you seen him then, this morning?" said Kitty.

"Oh yes! And I was so sleepy that I could not open my eyes. And so he said, 'Camilla, goodbye to you for I am going away. I have not time to take leave of any body else, and I dare not trust myself to see Kitty, for then you know I should never get away.'"

"Nonsense," said Kitty; "he did not say that, or he was in joke if he did."

"Oh! no I assure you he was as much in earnest as he ever was in his life; he was too much out of spirits to joke then. And he desired me when we all met at breakfast to give his compliments to your aunt, and his love to you, for you was a nice girl he said and he only wished it were in his power to be more with you. You were just the girl to suit him, because you were so lively and good-natured, and he wished with all his heart that you might not be married before he came back, for there was nothing he liked better than being here. Oh! You have no idea what fine things he said about you, till at last I fell asleep and he went away. But he certainly is in love with you. I am sure he is. I have thought so a great while I assure you."

"How can you be so ridiculous?" said Kitty smiling with pleasure; "I do not believe him to be so easily affected. But he did desire his love to me then? And wished I might not be married before his return? And said I was a nice girl, did he?"

"Oh! dear, yes, and I assure you it is the greatest praise in his opinion, that he can bestow on any body; I can hardly ever persuade him to call me one, tho' I beg him sometimes for an hour together."

"And do you really think that he was sorry to go."

"Oh! you can have no idea how wretched it made him. He would not have gone this month, if my father had not insisted on it; Edward told me so himself yesterday. He said that he wished with all his heart he had never promised to go abroad, for that he repented it more and more every day; that it interfered with all his other schemes, and that since Papa had spoke to him about it, he was more unwilling to leave Chetwynde than ever."

"Did he really say all this? And why would your father insist upon his going?" "His leaving England interfered with all his other plans, and his conversation with Mr. Stanley had made him still more averse to it." "What can this mean!" "Why that he is excessively in love with you to be sure; what other plans can he have? And I suppose my father said that if he had not been going abroad, he should have wished him to marry you immediately. But I must go and see your aunt's plants. There is one of them that I quite dote on—and two or three more besides."

"Can Camilla's explanation be true?" said Catharine to herself, when her friend had left the room. "And after all my doubts and uncertainties, can Stanley really be averse to leaving England for my sake only? 'His plans interrupted.' And what indeed can his plans be, but towards marriage. Yet so soon to be in love with me! But it is the effect perhaps only of the warmth of heart which to me is the highest recommendation in any one. A heart disposed to love—and such under the appearance of so much gaiety and inattention, is Stanley's. Oh! how much does it endear him to me! But he is gone—gone perhaps for years—obliged to tear himself from what he most loves, his happiness is sacrificed to the vanity of his father! In what anguish he must have left the house! Unable to see me, or to bid me adieu, while I, senseless wretch, was daring to sleep. This, then explained his leaving us at such a time of day. He could not trust himself to see me. Charming young man! How much must you have suffered! I knew that it was impossible for one so elegant, and so well bred, to leave any family in such a manner, but for a motive like this unanswerable." Satisfied, beyond the power of change, of this, she went in high spirits to her aunt's apartment, without giving a moment's recollection on the vanity of young women, or the unaccountable conduct of young men.

Kitty continued in this state of satisfaction during the remainder of the Stanleys' visit—who took their leave with many pressing invitations to visit them in London, when as Camilla said, she might have an opportunity of becoming acquainted with that sweet girl Augusta Halifax. Or rather (thought Kitty,) of seeing my dear Mary Wynne again. Mrs. Percival in answer to Mrs. Stanley's invitation replied that she looked upon London as the hot house of vice where virtue had long been banished from society and wickedness of every description was daily gaining ground—that Kitty was of herself sufficiently inclined to give way to and indulge in vicious inclinations, and therefore was the last girl in the world to be trusted in London, as she would be totally unable to withstand temptation.

After the departure of the Stanleys, Kitty returned to her usual occupations, but alas! they had lost their power of pleasing. Her bower alone retained its interest in her feelings, and perhaps that was owing to the particular remembrance it brought to her mind of Edward Stanley.

The summer passed away unmarked by any incident worth narrating, or any pleasure to Catharine save one, which arose from the receipt of a letter from her friend Cecilia now Mrs. Lascelles, announcing the speedy return of herself and husband to England.

A correspondence productive indeed of little pleasure to either party had been established between Camilla and Catharine. The latter had now lost the only satisfaction she had ever received from the letters of Miss Stanley, as that young lady having informed her friend of the departure of her brother to Lyons now never mentioned his name—her letters seldom contained any intelligence except a description of some new article of dress, an enumeration of various engagements, a panegyric on Augusta Halifax and perhaps a little abuse of the unfortunate Sir Peter.

The Grove, for so was the mansion of Mrs. Percival at Chetwynde denominated, was situated within five miles from Exeter, but though that lady possessed a carriage and horses of her own, it was seldom that Catharine could prevail on her to visit that town for the purpose of shopping, on account of the many officers perpetually quartered there and who infested the principal streets. A company of strolling players on their way from some neighbouring races having opened a temporary theatre there, Mrs. Percival was prevailed on by her niece to indulge her by attending the performance once during their stay. Mrs. Percival insisted on paying Miss Dudley the compliment of inviting her to join the party, when a new difficulty arose, from the necessity of having some gentleman to attend them.

Lady Susan

By

Jane Austen

I

LADY SUSAN VERNON TO MR. VERNON

Langford, Dec.

MY DEAR BROTHER,—I can no longer refuse myself the pleasure of profiting by your kind invitation when we last parted of spending some weeks with you at Churchhill, and, therefore, if quite convenient to you and Mrs. Vernon to receive me at present, I shall hope within a few days to be introduced to a sister whom I have so long desired to be acquainted with. My kind friends here are most affectionately urgent with me to prolong my stay, but their hospitable and cheerful dispositions lead them too much into society for my present situation and state of mind; and I impatiently look forward to the hour when I shall be admitted into your delightful retirement.

I long to be made known to your dear little children, in whose hearts I shall be very eager to secure an interest I shall soon have need for all my fortitude, as I am on the point of separation from my own daughter. The long illness of her dear father prevented my paying her that attention which duty and affection equally dictated, and I have too much reason to fear that the governess to whose care I consigned her was unequal to the charge. I have therefore resolved on placing her at one of the best private schools in town, where I shall have an opportunity of leaving her myself in my way to you. I am determined, you see, not to be denied admittance at Churchhill. It would indeed give me most painful sensations to know that it were not in your power to receive me.

Your most obliged and affectionate sister,

S. VERNON.

II

LADY SUSAN VERNON TO MRS. JOHNSON

Langford.

You were mistaken, my dear Alicia, in supposing me fixed at this place for the rest of the winter: it grieves me to say how greatly you were mistaken, for I have seldom spent three months more agreeably than those which have just flown away. At present, nothing goes smoothly; the females of the family are united against me. You foretold how it would be when I first came to Langford, and Mainwaring is so uncommonly pleasing that I was not without apprehensions for myself. I remember saying to myself, as I drove to the house, "I like this man, pray Heaven no harm come of it!" But I was determined to be discreet, to bear in mind my being only four months a widow, and to be as quiet as possible: and I have been so, my dear creature; I have admitted no one's attentions but Mainwaring's. I have avoided all general flirtation whatever; I have distinguished no creature besides, of all the numbers resorting hither, except Sir James Martin, on whom I bestowed a little notice, in order to detach him from Miss Mainwaring; but, if the world could know my motive THERE they would honour me. I have been called an unkind mother, but it was the sacred impulse of maternal affection, it was the advantage of my daughter that led me on; and if that daughter were not the greatest simpleton on earth, I might have been rewarded for my exertions as I ought.

Sir James did make proposals to me for Frederica; but Frederica, who was born to be the torment of my life, chose to set herself so violently against the match that I thought it better to lay aside the scheme for the present. I have more than once repented that I did not marry him myself; and were he but one degree less contemptibly weak I certainly should: but I must own myself rather romantic in that respect, and that riches only will not satisfy me. The event of all this is very provoking: Sir James is gone, Maria highly incensed, and Mrs. Mainwaring insupportably jealous; so jealous, in short, and so enraged against me, that, in the fury of her temper, I should not be surprized at her appealing to her guardian, if she had the liberty of addressing him: but there your husband stands my friend; and the kindest, most amiable action of his life was his throwing her off for ever on her marriage. Keep up his resentment, therefore, I charge you. We are now in a sad state; no house was ever more altered; the whole party are at war, and Mainwaring scarcely dares speak to me. It is time for me to be gone; I have therefore determined on leaving them, and shall spend, I hope, a comfortable day with you in town within this week. If I am as little in favour with Mr. Johnson as ever, you must come to me at 10 Wigmore street; but I hope this may not be the case, for as Mr. Johnson, with all his faults, is a man to whom that great word "respectable" is always given, and I am known to be so intimate with his wife, his slighting me has an awkward look.

I take London in my way to that insupportable spot, a country village; for I am really going to Churchhill. Forgive me, my dear friend, it is my last resource. Were there another place in England open to me I would prefer it. Charles Vernon is my aversion; and I am afraid of his wife. At Churchhill, however, I must remain till I have something better in view. My young lady accompanies me to town, where I shall deposit her under the care of Miss Summers, in Wigmore street, till she becomes a little more reasonable. She will made good connections there, as the girls are all of the best families. The price is immense, and much beyond what I can ever attempt to pay.

Adieu, I will send you a line as soon as I arrive in town.

Yours ever,

S. VERNON.

MRS. VERNON TO LADY DE COURCY

Churchhill.

My dear Mother,—I am very sorry to tell you that it will not be in our power to keep our promise of spending our Christmas with you; and we are prevented that happiness by a circumstance which is not likely to make us any amends. Lady Susan, in a letter to her brother-in-law, has declared her intention of visiting us almost immediately; and as such a visit is in all probability merely an affair of convenience, it is impossible to conjecture its length. I was by no means prepared for such an event, nor can I now account for her ladyship's conduct; Langford appeared so exactly the place for her in every respect, as well from the elegant and expensive style of living there, as from her particular attachment to Mr. Mainwaring, that I was very far from expecting so speedy a distinction, though I always imagined from her increasing friendship for us since her husband's death that we should, at some future period, be obliged to receive her. Mr. Vernon, I think, was a great deal too kind to her when he was in Staffordshire; her behaviour to him, independent of her general character, has been so inexcusably artful and ungenerous since our marriage was first in agitation that no one less amiable and mild than himself could have overlooked it all; and though, as his brother's widow, and in narrow circumstances, it was proper to render her pecuniary assistance, I cannot help thinking his pressing invitation to her to visit us at Churchhill perfectly unnecessary. Disposed, however, as he always is to think the best of everyone, her display of grief, and professions of regret, and general resolutions of prudence, were sufficient to soften his heart and make him really confide in her sincerity; but, as for myself, I am still unconvinced, and plausibly as her ladyship has now written, I cannot make up my mind till I better understand her real meaning in coming to us. You may guess, therefore, my dear madam, with what feelings I look forward to her arrival. She will have occasion for all those attractive powers for which she is celebrated to gain any share of my regard; and I shall certainly endeavour to guard myself against their influence, if not accompanied by something more substantial. She expresses a most eager desire of being acquainted with me, and makes very gracious mention of my children but I am not quite weak enough to suppose a woman who has behaved with inattention, if not with unkindness, to her own child, should be attached to any of mine. Miss Vernon is to be placed at a school in London before her mother comes to us which I am glad of, for her sake and my own. It must be to her advantage to be separated from her mother, and a girl of sixteen who has received so wretched an education, could not be a very desirable companion here. Reginald has long wished, I know, to see the captivating Lady Susan, and we shall depend on his joining our party soon. I am glad to hear that my father continues so well; and am, with best love, &c.,

CATHERINE VERNON.

MR. DE COURCY TO MRS. VERNON

Parklands.

My dear Sister,—I congratulate you and Mr. Vernon on being about to receive into your family the most accomplished coquette in England. As a very distinguished flirt I have always been taught to consider her, but it has lately fallen in my way to hear some particulars of her conduct at Langford: which prove that she does not confine herself to that sort of honest flirtation which satisfies most people, but aspires to the more delicious gratification of making a whole family miserable. By her behaviour to Mr. Mainwaring she gave jealousy and wretchedness to his wife, and by her attentions to a young man previously attached to Mr. Mainwaring's sister deprived an amiable girl of her lover.

I learnt all this from Mr. Smith, now in this neighbourhood (I have dined with him, at Hurst and Wilford), who is just come from Langford where he was a fortnight with her ladyship, and who is therefore well qualified to make the communication.

What a woman she must be! I long to see her, and shall certainly accept your kind invitation, that I may form some idea of those bewitching powers which can do so much— engaging at the same time, and in the same house, the affections of two men, who were neither of them at liberty to bestow them—and all this without the charm of youth! I am glad to find Miss Vernon does not accompany her mother to Churchhill, as she has not even manners to recommend her; and, according to Mr. Smith's account, is equally dull and proud. Where pride and stupidity unite there can be no dissimulation worthy notice, and Miss Vernon shall be consigned to unrelenting contempt; but by all that I can gather Lady Susan possesses a degree of captivating deceit which it must be pleasing to witness and detect. I shall be with you very soon, and am ever,

Your affectionate brother,

R. DE COURCY.

$$\mathcal{Y}$$

LADY SUSAN VERNON TO MRS. JOHNSON

Churchhill.

I received your note, my dear Alicia, just before I left town, and rejoice to be assured that Mr. Johnson suspected nothing of your engagement the evening before. It is undoubtedly better to deceive him entirely, and since he will be stubborn he must be tricked. I arrived here in safety, and have no reason to complain of my reception from Mr. Vernon; but I confess myself not equally satisfied with the behaviour of his lady. She is perfectly well-bred, indeed, and has the air of a woman of fashion, but her manners are not such as can persuade me of her being prepossessed in my favour. I wanted her to be delighted at seeing me. I was as amiable as possible on the occasion, but all in vain. She does not like me. To be sure when we consider that I DID take some pains to prevent my brother-in-law's marrying her, this want of cordiality is not very surprizing, and yet it shows an illiberal and vindictive spirit to resent a project which influenced me six years ago, and which never succeeded at last.

I am sometimes disposed to repent that I did not let Charles buy Vernon Castle, when we were obliged to sell it; but it was a trying circumstance, especially as the sale took place exactly at the time of his marriage; and everybody ought to respect the delicacy of those feelings which could not endure that my husband's dignity should be lessened by his younger brother's having possession of the family estate. Could matters have been so arranged as to prevent the necessity of our leaving the castle, could we have lived with Charles and kept him single, I should have been very far from persuading my husband to dispose of it elsewhere; but Charles was on the point of marrying Miss De Courcy, and the event has justified me. Here are children in abundance, and what benefit could have accrued to me from his purchasing Vernon? My having prevented it may perhaps have given his wife an unfavourable impression, but where there is a disposition to dislike, a motive will never be wanting; and as to money matters it has not withheld him from being very useful to me. I really have a regard for him, he is so easily imposed upon! The house is a good one, the furniture fashionable, and everything announces plenty and elegance. Charles is very rich I am sure; when a man has once got his name in a banking-house he rolls in money; but they do not know what to do with it, keep very little company, and never go to London but on business. We shall be as stupid as possible. I mean to win my sister-in-law's heart through the children; I know all their names already, and am going to attach myself with the greatest sensibility to one in particular, a young Frederic, whom I take on my lap and sigh over for his dear uncle's sake.

Poor Mainwaring! I need not tell you how much I miss him, how perpetually he is in my thoughts. I found a dismal letter from him on my arrival here, full of complaints of his wife and sister, and lamentations on the cruelty of his fate. I passed off the letter as his wife's, to the Vernons, and when I write to him it must be under cover to you.

Ever yours, S. VERNON.

MRS. VERNON TO MR. DE COURCY

Churchhill.

Well, my dear Reginald, I have seen this dangerous creature, and must give you some description of her, though I hope you will soon be able to form your own judgment. She is really excessively pretty; however you may choose to question the allurements of a lady no longer young, I must, for my own part, declare that I have seldom seen so lovely a woman as Lady Susan. She is delicately fair, with fine grey eyes and dark eyelashes; and from her appearance one would not suppose her more than five and twenty, though she must in fact be ten years older, I was certainly not disposed to admire her, though always hearing she was beautiful; but I cannot help feeling that she possesses an uncommon union of symmetry, brilliancy, and grace. Her address to me was so gentle, frank, and even affectionate, that, if I had not known how much she has always disliked me for marrying Mr. Vernon, and that we had never met before, I should have imagined her an attached friend. One is apt, I believe, to connect assurance of manner with coquetry, and to expect that an impudent address will naturally attend an impudent mind; at least I was myself prepared for an improper degree of confidence in Lady Susan; but her countenance is absolutely sweet, and her voice and manner winningly mild. I am sorry it is so, for what is this but deceit? Unfortunately, one knows her too well. She is clever and agreeable, has all that knowledge of the world which makes conversation easy, and talks very well, with a happy command of language, which is too often used, I believe, to make black appear white. She has already almost persuaded me of her being warmly attached to her daughter, though I have been so long convinced to the contrary. She speaks of her with so much tenderness and anxiety, lamenting so bitterly the neglect of her education, which she represents however as wholly unavoidable, that I am forced to recollect how many successive springs her ladyship spent in town, while her daughter was left in Staffordshire to the care of servants, or a governess very little better, to prevent my believing what she says.

If her manners have so great an influence on my resentful heart, you may judge how much more strongly they operate on Mr. Vernon's generous temper. I wish I could be as well satisfied as he is, that it was really her choice to leave Langford for Churchhill; and if she had not stayed there for months before she discovered that her friend's manner of living did not suit her situation or feelings, I might have believed that concern for the loss of such a husband as Mr. Vernon, to whom her own behaviour was far from unexceptionable, might for a time make her wish for retirement. But I cannot forget the length of her visit to the Mainwarings, and when I reflect on the different mode of life which she led with them from that to which she must now submit, I can only suppose that the wish of establishing her reputation by following though late the path of propriety, occasioned her removal from a family where she must in reality have been particularly happy. Your friend Mr. Smith's story, however, cannot be quite correct, as she corresponds regularly with Mrs. Mainwaring. At any rate it must be exaggerated. It is scarcely possible that two men should be so grossly deceived by her at once.

Yours, &c.,
CATHERINE VERNON

LADY SUSAN VERNON TO MRS. JOHNSON
Churchhill.

My dear Alicia,—You are very good in taking notice of Frederica, and I am grateful for it as a mark of your friendship; but as I cannot have any doubt of the warmth of your affection, I am far from exacting so heavy a sacrifice. She is a stupid girl, and has nothing to recommend her. I would not, therefore, on my account, have you encumber one moment of your precious time by sending for her to Edward Street, especially as every visit is so much deducted from the grand affair of education, which I really wish to have attended to while she remains at Miss Summers's. I want her to play and sing with some portion of taste and a good deal of assurance, as she has my hand and arm and a tolerable voice. I was so much indulged in my infant years that I was never obliged to attend to anything, and consequently am without the accomplishments which are now necessary to finish a pretty woman. Not that I am an advocate for the prevailing fashion of acquiring a perfect knowledge of all languages, arts, and sciences. It is throwing time away to be mistress of French, Italian, and German: music, singing, and drawing, &c., will gain a woman some applause, but will not add one lover to her list—grace and manner, after all, are of the greatest importance. I do not mean, therefore, that Frederica's acquirements should be more than superficial, and I flatter myself that she will not remain long enough at school to understand anything thoroughly. I hope to see her the wife of Sir James within a twelvemonth. You know on what I ground my hope, and it is certainly a good foundation, for school must be very humiliating to a girl of Frederica's age. And, by-the-by, you had better not invite her any more on that account, as I wish her to find her situation as unpleasant as possible. I am sure of Sir James at any time, and could make him renew his application by a line. I shall trouble you meanwhile to prevent his forming any other attachment when he comes to town. Ask him to your house occasionally, and talk to him of Frederica, that he may not forget her. Upon the whole, I commend my own conduct in this affair extremely, and regard it as a very happy instance of circumspection and tenderness. Some mothers would have insisted on their daughter's accepting so good an offer on the first overture; but I could not reconcile it to myself to force Frederica into a marriage from which her heart revolted, and instead of adopting so harsh a measure merely propose to make it her own choice, by rendering her thoroughly uncomfortable till she does accept him—but enough of this tiresome girl. You may well wonder how I contrive to pass my time here, and for the first week it was insufferably dull. Now, however, we begin to mend, our party is enlarged by Mrs. Vernon's brother, a handsome young man, who promises me some amusement. There is something about him which rather interests me, a sort of sauciness and familiarity which I shall teach him to correct. He is lively, and seems clever, and when I have inspired him with greater respect for me than his sister's kind offices have implanted, he may be an agreeable flirt. There is exquisite pleasure in subduing an insolent spirit, in making a person predetermined to dislike acknowledge one's superiority. I have disconcerted him already by my calm reserve, and it shall be my endeavour to humble the pride of these self important De Courcys still lower, to convince Mrs. Vernon that her sisterly cautions have been bestowed in vain, and to persuade Reginald that she has scandalously belied me. This project will serve at least to amuse me, and prevent my feeling so acutely this dreadful separation from you and all whom I love.

Yours ever,

S. VERNON.

MRS. VERNON TO LADY DE COURCY

Churchhill.

My dear Mother,—You must not expect Reginald back again for some time. He desires me to tell you that the present open weather induces him to accept Mr. Vernon's invitation to prolong his stay in Sussex, that they may have some hunting together. He means to send for his horses immediately, and it is impossible to say when you may see him in Kent. I will not disguise my sentiments on this change from you, my dear mother, though I think you had better not communicate them to my father, whose excessive anxiety about Reginald would subject him to an alarm which might seriously affect his health and spirits. Lady Susan has certainly contrived, in the space of a fortnight, to make my brother like her. In short, I am persuaded that his continuing here beyond the time originally fixed for his return is occasioned as much by a degree of fascination towards her, as by the wish of hunting with Mr. Vernon, and of course I cannot receive that pleasure from the length of his visit which my brother's company would otherwise give me. I am, indeed, provoked at the artifice of this unprincipled woman; what stronger proof of her dangerous abilities can be given than this perversion of Reginald's judgment, which when he entered the house was so decidedly against her! In his last letter he actually gave me some particulars of her behaviour at Langford, such as he received from a gentleman who knew her perfectly well, which, if true, must raise abhorrence against her, and which Reginald himself was entirely disposed to credit. His opinion of her, I am sure, was as low as of any woman in England; and when he first came it was evident that he considered her as one entitled neither to delicacy nor respect, and that he felt she would be delighted with the attentions of any man inclined to flirt with her. Her behaviour, I confess, has been calculated to do away with such an idea; I have not detected the smallest impropriety in it—nothing of vanity, of pretension, of levity; and she is altogether so attractive that I should not wonder at his being delighted with her, had he known nothing of her previous to this personal acquaintance; but, against reason, against conviction, to be so well pleased with her, as I am sure he is, does really astonish me. His admiration was at first very strong, but no more than was natural, and I did not wonder at his being much struck by the gentleness and delicacy of her manners; but when he has mentioned her of late it has been in terms of more extraordinary praise; and yesterday he actually said that he could not be surprised at any effect produced on the heart of man by such loveliness and such abilities; and when I lamented, in reply, the badness of her disposition, he observed that whatever might have been her errors they were to be imputed to her neglected education and early marriage, and that she was altogether a wonderful woman. This tendency to excuse her conduct or to forget it, in the warmth of admiration, vexes me; and if I did not know that Reginald is too much at home at Churchhill to need an invitation for lengthening his visit, I should regret Mr. Vernon's giving him any. Lady Susan's intentions are of course those of absolute coquetry, or a desire of universal admiration; I cannot for a moment imagine that she has anything more serious in view; but it mortifies me to see a young man of Reginald's sense duped by her at all.

I am, &c.,

CATHERINE VERNON.

IX

MRS. JOHNSON TO LADY S. VERNON

Edward Street.

My dearest Friend,—I congratulate you on Mr. De Courcy's arrival, and I advise you by all means to marry him; his father's estate is, we know, considerable, and I believe certainly entailed. Sir Reginald is very infirm, and not likely to stand in your way long. I hear the young man well spoken of; and though no one can really deserve you, my dearest Susan, Mr. De Courcy may be worth having. Mainwaring will storm of course, but you easily pacify him; besides, the most scrupulous point of honour could not require you to wait for HIS emancipation. I have seen Sir James; he came to town for a few days last week, and called several times in Edward Street. I talked to him about you and your daughter, and he is so far from having forgotten you, that I am sure he would marry either of you with pleasure. I gave him hopes of Frederica's relenting, and told him a great deal of her improvements. I scolded him for making love to Maria Mainwaring; he protested that he had been only in joke, and we both laughed heartily at her disappointment; and, in short, were very agreeable. He is as silly as ever.

Yours faithfully,

ALICIA.

✗

LADY SUSAN VERNON TO MRS. JOHNSON

Churchhill.

I am much obliged to you, my dear Friend, for your advice respecting Mr. De Courcy, which I know was given with the full conviction of its expediency, though I am not quite determined on following it. I cannot easily resolve on anything so serious as marriage; especially as I am not at present in want of money, and might perhaps, till the old gentleman's death, be very little benefited by the match. It is true that I am vain enough to believe it within my reach. I have made him sensible of my power, and can now enjoy the pleasure of triumphing over a mind prepared to dislike me, and prejudiced against all my past actions. His sister, too, is, I hope, convinced how little the ungenerous representations of anyone to the disadvantage of another will avail when opposed by the immediate influence of intellect and manner. I see plainly that she is uneasy at my progress in the good opinion of her brother, and conclude that nothing will be wanting on her part to counteract me; but having once made him doubt the justice of her opinion of me, I think I may defy her. It has been delightful to me to watch his advances towards intimacy, especially to observe his altered manner in consequence of my repressing by the cool dignity of my deportment his insolent approach to direct familiarity. My conduct has been equally guarded from the first, and I never behaved less like a coquette in the whole course of my life, though perhaps my desire of dominion was never more decided. I have subdued him entirely by sentiment and serious conversation, and made him, I may venture to say, at least half in love with me, without the semblance of the most commonplace flirtation. Mrs. Vernon's consciousness of deserving every sort of revenge that it can be in my power to inflict for her ill-offices could alone enable her to perceive that I am actuated by any design in behaviour so gentle and unpretending. Let her think and act as she chooses, however. I have never yet found that the advice of a sister could prevent a young man's being in love if he chose. We are advancing now to some kind of confidence, and in short are likely to be engaged in a sort of platonic friendship. On my side you may be sure of its never being more, for if I were not attached to another person as much as I can be to anyone, I should make a point of not bestowing my affection on a man who had dared to think so meanly of me. Reginald has a good figure and is not unworthy the praise you have heard given him, but is still greatly inferior to our friend at Langford. He is less polished, less insinuating than Mainwaring, and is comparatively deficient in the power of saying those delightful things which put one in good humour with oneself and all the world. He is quite agreeable enough, however, to afford me amusement, and to make many of those hours pass very pleasantly which would otherwise be spent in endeavouring to overcome my sister-in-law's reserve, and listening to the insipid talk of her husband. Your account of Sir James is most satisfactory, and I mean to give Miss Frederica a hint of my intentions very soon.

Yours, &c.,
S. VERNON.

❧

MRS. VERNON TO LADY DE COURCY

Churchhill

I really grow quite uneasy, my dearest mother, about Reginald, from witnessing the very rapid increase of Lady Susan's influence. They are now on terms of the most particular friendship, frequently engaged in long conversations together; and she has contrived by the most artful coquetry to subdue his judgment to her own purposes. It is impossible to see the intimacy between them so very soon established without some alarm, though I can hardly suppose that Lady Susan's plans extend to marriage. I wish you could get Reginald home again on any plausible pretence; he is not at all disposed to leave us, and I have given him as many hints of my father's precarious state of health as common decency will allow me to do in my own house. Her power over him must now be boundless, as she has entirely effaced all his former ill-opinion, and persuaded him not merely to forget but to justify her conduct. Mr. Smith's account of her proceedings at Langford, where he accused her of having made Mr. Mainwaring and a young man engaged to Miss Mainwaring distractedly in love with her, which Reginald firmly believed when he came here, is now, he is persuaded, only a scandalous invention. He has told me so with a warmth of manner which spoke his regret at having believed the contrary himself. How sincerely do I grieve that she ever entered this house! I always looked forward to her coming with uneasiness; but very far was it from originating in anxiety for Reginald. I expected a most disagreeable companion for myself, but could not imagine that my brother would be in the smallest danger of being captivated by a woman with whose principles he was so well acquainted, and whose character he so heartily despised. If you can get him away it will be a good thing.

Yours, &c.,
CATHERINE VERNON

SIR REGINALD DE COURCY TO HIS SON

Parklands.

I know that young men in general do not admit of any enquiry even from their nearest relations into affairs of the heart, but I hope, my dear Reginald, that you will be superior to such as allow nothing for a father's anxiety, and think themselves privileged to refuse him their confidence and slight his advice. You must be sensible that as an only son, and the representative of an ancient family, your conduct in life is most interesting to your connections; and in the very important concern of marriage especially, there is everything at stake—your own happiness, that of your parents, and the credit of your name. I do not suppose that you would deliberately form an absolute engagement of that nature without acquainting your mother and myself, or at least, without being convinced that we should approve of your choice; but I cannot help fearing that you may be drawn in, by the lady who has lately attached you, to a marriage which the whole of your family, far and near, must highly reprobate. Lady Susan's age is itself a material objection, but her want of character is one so much more serious, that the difference of even twelve years becomes in comparison of small amount. Were you not blinded by a sort of fascination, it would be ridiculous in me to repeat the instances of great misconduct on her side so very generally known.

Her neglect of her husband, her encouragement of other men, her extravagance and dissipation, were so gross and notorious that no one could be ignorant of them at the time, nor can now have forgotten them. To our family she has always been represented in softened colours by the benevolence of Mr. Charles Vernon, and yet, in spite of his generous endeavours to excuse her, we know that she did, from the most selfish motives, take all possible pains to prevent his marriage with Catherine.

My years and increasing infirmities make me very desirous of seeing you settled in the world. To the fortune of a wife, the goodness of my own will make me indifferent, but her family and character must be equally unexceptionable. When your choice is fixed so that no objection can be made to it, then I can promise you a ready and cheerful consent; but it is my duty to oppose a match which deep art only could render possible, and must in the end make wretched. It is possible her behaviour may arise only from vanity, or the wish of gaining the admiration of a man whom she must imagine to be particularly prejudiced against her; but it is more likely that she should aim at something further. She is poor, and may naturally seek an alliance which must be advantageous to herself; you know your own rights, and that it is out of my power to prevent your inheriting the family estate. My ability of distressing you during my life would be a species of revenge to which I could hardly stoop under any circumstances.

I honestly tell you my sentiments and intentions: I do not wish to work on your fears, but on your sense and affection. It would destroy every comfort of my life to know that you were married to Lady Susan Vernon; it would be the death of that honest pride with which I have hitherto considered my son; I should blush to see him, to hear of him, to think of him. I may perhaps do no good but that of relieving my own mind by this letter, but I felt it my duty to tell you that your partiality for Lady Susan is no secret to your friends, and to warn you against her. I should be glad to hear your reasons for disbelieving Mr. Smith's intelligence; you had no doubt of its authenticity a month ago. If you can give me your assurance of having no design beyond enjoying the conversation of a clever woman for a short period, and of yielding admiration only to her beauty and abilities, without being blinded by them to her faults, you will restore me to happiness; but, if you cannot do this, explain to me, at least, what has occasioned so great an alteration in your opinion of her.

I am, &c., &c,
REGINALD DE COURCY

XVIII

LADY DE COURCY TO MRS. VERNON

Parklands.

My dear Catherine,—Unluckily I was confined to my room when your last letter came, by a cold which affected my eyes so much as to prevent my reading it myself, so I could not refuse your father when he offered to read it to me, by which means he became acquainted, to my great vexation, with all your fears about your brother. I had intended to write to Reginald myself as soon as my eyes would let me, to point out, as well as I could, the danger of an intimate acquaintance, with so artful a woman as Lady Susan, to a young man of his age, and high expectations. I meant, moreover, to have reminded him of our being quite alone now, and very much in need of him to keep up our spirits these long winter evenings. Whether it would have done any good can never be settled now, but I am excessively vexed that Sir Reginald should know anything of a matter which we foresaw would make him so uneasy. He caught all your fears the moment he had read your letter, and I am sure he has not had the business out of his head since. He wrote by the same post to Reginald a long letter full of it all, and particularly asking an explanation of what he may have heard from Lady Susan to contradict the late shocking reports. His answer came this morning, which I shall enclose to you, as I think you will like to see it. I wish it was more satisfactory; but it seems written with such a determination to think well of Lady Susan, that his assurances as to marriage, &c., do not set my heart at ease. I say all I can, however, to satisfy your father, and he is certainly less uneasy since Reginald's letter. How provoking it is, my dear Catherine, that this unwelcome guest of yours should not only prevent our meeting this Christmas, but be the occasion of so much vexation and trouble! Kiss the dear children for me.

Your affectionate mother,
C. DE COURCY.

MR. DE COURCY TO SIR REGINALD

Churchhill.

My dear Sir,—I have this moment received your letter, which has given me more astonishment than I ever felt before. I am to thank my sister, I suppose, for having represented me in such a light as to injure me in your opinion, and give you all this alarm. I know not why she should choose to make herself and her family uneasy by apprehending an event which no one but herself, I can affirm, would ever have thought possible. To impute such a design to Lady Susan would be taking from her every claim to that excellent understanding which her bitterest enemies have never denied her; and equally low must sink my pretensions to common sense if I am suspected of matrimonial views in my behaviour to her. Our difference of age must be an insuperable objection, and I entreat you, my dear father, to quiet your mind, and no longer harbour a suspicion which cannot be more injurious to your own peace than to our understandings. I can have no other view in remaining with Lady Susan, than to enjoy for a short time (as you have yourself expressed it) the conversation of a woman of high intellectual powers. If Mrs. Vernon would allow something to my affection for herself and her husband in the length of my visit, she would do more justice to us all; but my sister is unhappily prejudiced beyond the hope of conviction against Lady Susan. From an attachment to her husband, which in itself does honour to both, she cannot forgive the endeavours at preventing their union, which have been attributed to selfishness in Lady Susan; but in this case, as well as in many others, the world has most grossly injured that lady, by supposing the worst where the motives of her conduct have been doubtful. Lady Susan had heard something so materially to the disadvantage of my sister as to persuade her that the happiness of Mr. Vernon, to whom she was always much attached, would be wholly destroyed by the marriage. And this circumstance, while it explains the true motives of Lady Susan's conduct, and removes all the blame which has been so lavished on her, may also convince us how little the general report of anyone ought to be credited; since no character, however upright, can escape the malevolence of slander. If my sister, in the security of retirement, with as little opportunity as inclination to do evil, could not avoid censure, we must not rashly condemn those who, living in the world and surrounded with temptations, should be accused of errors which they are known to have the power of committing.

I blame myself severely for having so easily believed the slanderous tales invented by Charles Smith to the prejudice of Lady Susan, as I am now convinced how greatly they have traduced her. As to Mrs. Mainwaring's jealousy it was totally his own invention, and his account of her attaching Miss Mainwaring's lover was scarcely better founded. Sir James Martin had been drawn in by that young lady to pay her some attention; and as he is a man of fortune, it was easy to see HER views extended to marriage. It is well known that Miss M. is absolutely on the catch for a husband, and no one therefore can pity her for losing, by the superior attractions of another woman, the chance of being able to make a worthy man completely wretched. Lady Susan was far from intending such a conquest, and on finding how warmly Miss Mainwaring resented her lover's defection, determined, in spite of Mr. and Mrs. Mainwaring's most urgent entreaties, to leave the family. I have reason to imagine she did receive serious proposals from Sir James, but her removing to Langford immediately on the discovery of his attachment, must acquit her on that article with any mind of common candour. You will, I am sure, my dear Sir, feel the truth of this, and will hereby learn to do justice to the character of a very injured woman. I know that Lady Susan in coming to Churchhill was governed only by the most honourable and amiable intentions; her prudence and economy are exemplary, her regard for Mr. Vernon equal even to HIS deserts; and her wish of obtaining my sister's good opinion merits a better return than it has received. As a mother she is unexceptionable; her solid affection for her child is shown by placing her in hands where her education will be properly attended to; but because she has not the blind and weak partiality of most mothers, she is accused of wanting maternal tenderness. Every person of sense, however, will know how to value and commend her well-directed affection, and will join me in wishing that Frederica Vernon may prove more worthy than she has yet done of her mother's tender care. I have now, my dear father, written my real sentiments of Lady Susan; you will know from this letter how highly I admire her abilities, and esteem her character; but if you are not equally convinced by my full and solemn assurance that your fears have been most idly created, you will deeply mortify and distress me.

I am, &c., &c.,

R. DE COURCY.

26

MRS. VERNON TO LADY DE COURCY

Churchhill

My dear Mother,—I return you Reginald's letter, and rejoice with all my heart that my father is made easy by it: tell him so, with my congratulations; but, between ourselves, I must own it has only convinced ME of my brother's having no PRESENT intention of marrying Lady Susan, not that he is in no danger of doing so three months hence. He gives a very plausible account of her behaviour at Langford; I wish it may be true, but his intelligence must come from herself, and I am less disposed to believe it than to lament the degree of intimacy subsisting between them, implied by the discussion of such a subject. I am sorry to have incurred his displeasure, but can expect nothing better while he is so very eager in Lady Susan's justification. He is very severe against me indeed, and yet I hope I have not been hasty in my judgment of her. Poor woman! though I have reasons enough for my dislike, I cannot help pitying her at present, as she is in real distress, and with too much cause. She had this morning a letter from the lady with whom she has placed her daughter, to request that Miss Vernon might be immediately removed, as she had been detected in an attempt to run away. Why, or whither she intended to go, does not appear; but, as her situation seems to have been unexceptionable, it is a sad thing, and of course highly distressing to Lady Susan. Frederica must be as much as sixteen, and ought to know better; but from what her mother insinuates, I am afraid she is a perverse girl. She has been sadly neglected, however, and her mother ought to remember it. Mr. Vernon set off for London as soon as she had determined what should be done. He is, if possible, to prevail on Miss Summers to let Frederica continue with her; and if he cannot succeed, to bring her to Churchhill for the present, till some other situation can be found for her. Her ladyship is comforting herself meanwhile by strolling along the shrubbery with Reginald, calling forth all his tender feelings, I suppose, on this distressing occasion. She has been talking a great deal about it to me. She talks vastly well; I am afraid of being ungenerous, or I should say, TOO well to feel so very deeply; but I will not look for her faults; she may be Reginald's wife! Heaven forbid it! but why should I be quicker-sighted than anyone else? Mr. Vernon declares that he never saw deeper distress than hers, on the receipt of the letter; and is his judgment inferior to mine? She was very unwilling that Frederica should be allowed to come to Churchhill, and justly enough, as it seems a sort of reward to behaviour deserving very differently; but it was impossible to take her anywhere else, and she is not to remain here long. "It will be absolutely necessary," said she, "as you, my dear sister, must be sensible, to treat my daughter with some severity while she is here; a most painful necessity, but I will ENDEAVOUR to submit to it. I am afraid I have often been too indulgent, but my poor Frederica's temper could never bear opposition well: you must support and encourage me; you must urge the necessity of reproof if you see me too lenient." All this sounds very reasonable. Reginald is so incensed against the poor silly girl. Surely it is not to Lady Susan's credit that he should be so bitter against her daughter; his idea of her must be drawn from the mother's description. Well, whatever may be his fate, we have the comfort of knowing that we have done our utmost to save him. We must commit the event to a higher power.

Yours ever, &c.,
CATHERINE VERNON.

XVII

LADY SUSAN TO MRS. JOHNSON
Churchhill.

Never, my dearest Alicia, was I so provoked in my life as by a letter this morning from Miss Summers. That horrid girl of mine has been trying to run away. I had not a notion of her being such a little devil before, she seemed to have all the Vernon milkiness; but on receiving the letter in which I declared my intention about Sir James, she actually attempted to elope; at least, I cannot otherwise account for her doing it. She meant, I suppose, to go to the Clarkes in Staffordshire, for she has no other acquaintances. But she shall be punished, she shall have him. I have sent Charles to town to make matters up if he can, for I do not by any means want her here. If Miss Summers will not keep her, you must find me out another school, unless we can get her married immediately. Miss S. writes word that she could not get the young lady to assign any cause for her extraordinary conduct, which confirms me in my own previous explanation of it. Frederica is too shy, I think, and too much in awe of me to tell tales, but if the mildness of her uncle should get anything out of her, I am not afraid. I trust I shall be able to make my story as good as hers. If I am vain of anything, it is of my eloquence. Consideration and esteem as surely follow command of language as admiration waits on beauty, and here I have opportunity enough for the exercise of my talent, as the chief of my time is spent in conversation.

Reginald is never easy unless we are by ourselves, and when the weather is tolerable, we pace the shrubbery for hours together. I like him on the whole very well; he is clever and has a good deal to say, but he is sometimes impertinent and troublesome. There is a sort of ridiculous delicacy about him which requires the fullest explanation of whatever he may have heard to my disadvantage, and is never satisfied till he thinks he has ascertained the beginning and end of everything. This is one sort of love, but I confess it does not particularly recommend itself to me. I infinitely prefer the tender and liberal spirit of Mainwaring, which, impressed with the deepest conviction of my merit, is satisfied that whatever I do must be right; and look with a degree of contempt on the inquisitive and doubtful fancies of that heart which seems always debating on the reasonableness of its emotions. Mainwaring is indeed, beyond all compare, superior to Reginald—superior in everything but the power of being with me! Poor fellow! he is much distracted by jealousy, which I am not sorry for, as I know no better support of love. He has been teazing me to allow of his coming into this country, and lodging somewhere near INCOG.; but I forbade everything of the kind. Those women are inexcusable who forget what is due to themselves, and the opinion of the world.

Yours ever, S. VERNON.

XVIII

MRS. VERNON TO LADY DE COURCY

Churchhill.

My dear Mother,—Mr. Vernon returned on Thursday night, bringing his niece with him. Lady Susan had received a line from him by that day's post, informing her that Miss Summers had absolutely refused to allow of Miss Vernon's continuance in her academy; we were therefore prepared for her arrival, and expected them impatiently the whole evening. They came while we were at tea, and I never saw any creature look so frightened as Frederica when she entered the room. Lady Susan, who had been shedding tears before, and showing great agitation at the idea of the meeting, received her with perfect self-command, and without betraying the least tenderness of spirit. She hardly spoke to her, and on Frederica's bursting into tears as soon as we were seated, took her out of the room, and did not return for some time. When she did, her eyes looked very red and she was as much agitated as before. We saw no more of her daughter. Poor Reginald was beyond measure concerned to see his fair friend in such distress, and watched her with so much tender solicitude, that I, who occasionally caught her observing his countenance with exultation, was quite out of patience. This pathetic representation lasted the whole evening, and so ostentatious and artful a display has entirely convinced me that she did in fact feel nothing. I am more angry with her than ever since I have seen her daughter; the poor girl looks so unhappy that my heart aches for her. Lady Susan is surely too severe, for Frederica does not seem to have the sort of temper to make severity necessary. She looks perfectly timid, dejected, and penitent. She is very pretty, though not so handsome as her mother, nor at all like her. Her complexion is delicate, but neither so fair nor so blooming as Lady Susan's, and she has quite the Vernon cast of countenance, the oval face and mild dark eyes, and there is peculiar sweetness in her look when she speaks either to her uncle or me, for as we behave kindly to her we have of course engaged her gratitude.

Her mother has insinuated that her temper is intractable, but I never saw a face less indicative of any evil disposition than hers; and from what I can see of the behaviour of each to the other, the invariable severity of Lady Susan and the silent dejection of Frederica, I am led to believe as heretofore that the former has no real love for her daughter, and has never done her justice or treated her affectionately. I have not been able to have any conversation with my niece; she is shy, and I think I can see that some pains are taken to prevent her being much with me. Nothing satisfactory transpires as to her reason for running away. Her kind-hearted uncle, you may be sure, was too fearful of distressing her to ask many questions as they travelled. I wish it had been possible for me to fetch her instead of him. I think I should have discovered the truth in the course of a thirty-mile journey. The small pianoforte has been removed within these few days, at Lady Susan's request, into her dressing-room, and Frederica spends great part of the day there, practising as it is called; but I seldom hear any noise when I pass that way; what she does with herself there I do not know. There are plenty of books, but it is not every girl who has been running wild the first fifteen years of her life, that can or will read. Poor creature! the prospect from her window is not very instructive, for that room overlooks the lawn, you know, with the shrubbery on one side, where she may see her mother walking for an hour together in earnest conversation with Reginald. A girl of Frederica's age must be childish indeed, if such things do not strike her. Is it not inexcusable to give such an example to a daughter? Yet Reginald still thinks Lady Susan the best of mothers, and still condemns Frederica as a worthless girl! He is convinced that her attempt to run away proceeded from no, justifiable cause, and had no provocation. I am sure I cannot say that it HAD, but while Miss Summers declares that Miss Vernon showed no signs of obstinacy or perverseness during her whole stay in Wigmore Street, till she was detected in this scheme, I cannot so readily credit what Lady Susan has made him, and wants to make me believe, that it was merely an impatience of restraint and a desire of escaping from the tuition of masters which brought on the plan of an elopement. O Reginald, how is your judgment enslaved! He scarcely dares even allow her to be handsome, and when I speak of her beauty, replies only that her eyes have no brilliancy! Sometimes he is sure she is deficient in understanding, and at others that her temper only is in fault. In short, when a person is always to deceive, it is impossible to be consistent. Lady Susan finds it necessary that Frederica should be to blame, and probably has sometimes judged it expedient to excuse her of ill-nature and sometimes to lament her want of sense. Reginald is only repeating after her ladyship.

I remain, &c., &c.,

CATHERINE VERNON.

XVIII

FROM THE SAME TO THE SAME

Churchhill.

My dear Mother,—I am very glad to find that my description of Frederica Vernon has interested you, for I do believe her truly deserving of your regard; and when I have communicated a notion which has recently struck me, your kind impressions in her favour will, I am sure, be heightened. I cannot help fancying that she is growing partial to my brother. I so very often see her eyes fixed on his face with a remarkable expression of pensive admiration. He is certainly very handsome; and yet more, there is an openness in his manner that must be highly prepossessing, and I am sure she feels it so. Thoughtful and pensive in general, her countenance always brightens into a smile when Reginald says anything amusing; and, let the subject be ever so serious that he may be conversing on, I am much mistaken if a syllable of his uttering escapes her. I want to make him sensible of all this, for we know the power of gratitude on such a heart as his; and could Frederica's artless affection detach him from her mother, we might bless the day which brought her to Churchhill. I think, my dear mother, you would not disapprove of her as a daughter. She is extremely young, to be sure, has had a wretched education, and a dreadful example of levity in her mother; but yet I can pronounce her disposition to be excellent, and her natural abilities very good. Though totally without accomplishments, she is by no means so ignorant as one might expect to find her, being fond of books and spending the chief of her time in reading. Her mother leaves her more to herself than she did, and I have her with me as much as possible, and have taken great pains to overcome her timidity. We are very good friends, and though she never opens her lips before her mother, she talks enough when alone with me to make it clear that, if properly treated by Lady Susan, she would always appear to much greater advantage. There cannot be a more gentle, affectionate heart; or more obliging manners, when acting without restraint; and her little cousins are all very fond of her.

Your affectionate daughter,

C. VERNON

XIX

LADY SUSAN TO MRS. JOHNSON

Churchhill.

You will be eager, I know, to hear something further of Frederica, and perhaps may think me negligent for not writing before. She arrived with her uncle last Thursday fortnight, when, of course, I lost no time in demanding the cause of her behaviour; and soon found myself to have been perfectly right in attributing it to my own letter. The prospect of it frightened her so thoroughly, that, with a mixture of true girlish perverseness and folly, she resolved on getting out of the house and proceeding directly by the stage to her friends, the Clarkes; and had really got as far as the length of two streets in her journey when she was fortunately missed, pursued, and overtaken. Such was the first distinguished exploit of Miss Frederica Vernon; and, if we consider that it was achieved at the tender age of sixteen, we shall have room for the most flattering prognostics of her future renown. I am excessively provoked, however, at the parade of propriety which prevented Miss Summers from keeping the girl; and it seems so extraordinary a piece of nicety, considering my daughter's family connections, that I can only suppose the lady to be governed by the fear of never getting her money. Be that as it may, however, Frederica is returned on my hands; and, having nothing else to employ her, is busy in pursuing the plan of romance begun at Langford. She is actually falling in love with Reginald De Courcy! To disobey her mother by refusing an unexceptionable offer is not enough; her affections must also be given without her mother's approbation. I never saw a girl of her age bid fairer to be the sport of mankind. Her feelings are tolerably acute, and she is so charmingly artless in their display as to afford the most reasonable hope of her being ridiculous, and despised by every man who sees her.

Artlessness will never do in love matters; and that girl is born a simpleton who has it either by nature or affectation. I am not yet certain that Reginald sees what she is about, nor is it of much consequence. She is now an object of indifference to him, and she would be one of contempt were he to understand her emotions. Her beauty is much admired by the Vernons, but it has no effect on him. She is in high favour with her aunt altogether, because she is so little like myself, of course. She is exactly the companion for Mrs. Vernon, who dearly loves to be firm, and to have all the sense and all the wit of the conversation to herself: Frederica will never eclipse her. When she first came I was at some pains to prevent her seeing much of her aunt; but I have relaxed, as I believe I may depend on her observing the rules I have laid down for their discourse. But do not imagine that with all this lenity I have for a moment given up my plan of her marriage. No; I am unalterably fixed on this point, though I have not yet quite decided on the manner of bringing it about. I should not chuse to have the business brought on here, and canvassed by the wise heads of Mr. and Mrs. Vernon; and I cannot just now afford to go to town. Miss Frederica must therefore wait a little.

Yours ever,

S. VERNON.

❧

MRS. VERNON TO LADY DE COURCY

Churchhill

We have a very unexpected guest with us at present, my dear Mother: he arrived yesterday. I heard a carriage at the door, as I was sitting with my children while they dined; and supposing I should be wanted, left the nursery soon afterwards, and was half-way downstairs, when Frederica, as pale as ashes, came running up, and rushed by me into her own room. I instantly followed, and asked her what was the matter. "Oh!" said she, "he is come—Sir James is come, and what shall I do?" This was no explanation; I begged her to tell me what she meant. At that moment we were interrupted by a knock at the door: it was Reginald, who came, by Lady Susan's direction, to call Frederica down. "It is Mr. De Courcy!" said she, colouring violently. "Mamma has sent for me; I must go." We all three went down together; and I saw my brother examining the terrified face of Frederica with surprize. In the breakfast-room we found Lady Susan, and a young man of gentlemanlike appearance, whom she introduced by the name of Sir James Martin—the very person, as you may remember, whom it was said she had been at pains to detach from Miss Mainwaring; but the conquest, it seems, was not designed for herself, or she has since transferred it to her daughter; for Sir James is now desperately in love with Frederica, and with full encouragement from mamma. The poor girl, however, I am sure, dislikes him; and though his person and address are very well, he appears, both to Mr. Vernon and me, a very weak young man. Frederica looked so shy, so confused, when we entered the room, that I felt for her exceedingly. Lady Susan behaved with great attention to her visitor; and yet I thought I could perceive that she had no particular pleasure in seeing him. Sir James talked a great deal, and made many civil excuses to me for the liberty he had taken in coming to Churchhill—mixing more frequent laughter with his discourse than the subject required—said many things over and over again, and told Lady Susan three times that he had seen Mrs. Johnson a few evenings before. He now and then addressed Frederica, but more frequently her mother. The poor girl sat all this time without opening her lips—her eyes cast down, and her colour varying every instant; while Reginald observed all that passed in perfect silence. At length Lady Susan, weary, I believe, of her situation, proposed walking; and we left the two gentlemen together, to put on our pelisses. As we went upstairs Lady Susan begged permission to attend me for a few moments in my dressing-room, as she was anxious to speak with me in private. I led her thither accordingly, and as soon as the door was closed, she said: "I was never more surprized in my life than by Sir James's arrival, and the suddenness of it requires some apology to you, my dear sister; though to ME, as a mother, it is highly flattering. He is so extremely attached to my daughter that he could not exist longer without seeing her. Sir James is a young man of an amiable disposition and excellent character; a little too much of the rattle, perhaps, but a year or two will rectify THAT: and he is in other respects so very eligible a match for Frederica, that I have always observed his attachment with the greatest pleasure; and am persuaded that you and my brother will give the alliance your hearty approbation. I have never before mentioned the likelihood of its taking place to anyone, because I thought that whilst Frederica continued at school it had better not be known to exist; but now, as I am convinced that Frederica is too old ever to submit to school confinement, and have, therefore, begun to consider her union with Sir James as not very distant, I had intended within a few days to acquaint yourself and Mr. Vernon with the whole business. I am sure, my dear sister, you will excuse my remaining silent so long, and agree with me that such circumstances, while they continue from any cause in suspense, cannot be too cautiously concealed. When you have the happiness of bestowing your sweet little Catherine, some years hence, on a man who in connection and character is alike unexceptionable, you will know what I feel now; though, thank Heaven, you cannot have all my reasons for rejoicing in such an event. Catherine will be amply provided for, and not, like my Frederica, indebted to a fortunate establishment for the comforts of life." She concluded by demanding my congratulations. I gave them somewhat awkwardly, I believe; for, in fact, the sudden disclosure of so important a matter took from me the power of speaking with any clearness. She thanked me, however, most affectionately, for my kind concern in the welfare of herself and daughter; and then said: "I am not apt to deal in professions, my dear Mrs. Vernon, and I never had the convenient talent of affecting sensations foreign to my heart; and therefore I trust you will believe me when I declare, that much as I had heard in your praise before I knew you, I had no idea that I should ever love you as I now do; and I must further say that your friendship towards me is more particularly gratifying because I have reason to believe that some attempts were made to prejudice you against me. I only wish that they, whoever they are, to whom I am indebted for such kind intentions, could see the terms on which we now are together, and understand the real affection we feel for each other; but I will not detain you any longer. God bless you, for your goodness to me and my girl, and continue to you all your present happiness." What can one say of such a woman, my dear mother? Such earnestness such solemnity of expression! and yet I cannot help suspecting the truth of everything she says. As for Reginald, I believe he does not know what to make of the matter. When Sir James came, he appeared all astonishment and perplexity; the folly of the young man and the confusion of Frederica entirely engrossed him; and though a little private discourse with Lady Susan has since had its effect, he is still hurt, I am sure, at her allowing of such a man's attentions to her daughter. Sir James invited himself with great composure to remain here a few days—hoped we would not think it odd, was aware of its being very impertinent, but he took the liberty of a relation; and concluded by wishing, with a laugh, that he might be really one very soon. Even Lady Susan seemed a little disconcerted by this forwardness; in her heart I am persuaded she sincerely wished him gone. But something must be done for this poor girl, if her feelings are such as both I and her uncle believe them to be. She must not be sacrificed to policy or ambition, and she must not be left to suffer from the dread of it. The girl whose heart can distinguish Reginald De Courcy, deserves, however he may slight her, a better fate than to be Sir James Martin's wife. As soon as I can get her alone, I will discover the real truth; but she seems to wish to avoid me. I hope this does not proceed from anything wrong, and that I shall not find out I have thought too well of her. Her behaviour to Sir James certainly speaks the greatest consciousness and embarrassment, but I see nothing in it more like encouragement. Adieu, my dear mother.

Yours, &c.,

C. VERNON.

✺✺✺

MISS VERNON TO MR DE COURCY

Sir,—I hope you will excuse this liberty; I am forced upon it by the greatest distress, or I should be ashamed to trouble you. I am very miserable about Sir James Martin, and have no other way in the world of helping myself but by writing to you, for I am forbidden even speaking to my uncle and aunt on the subject; and this being the case, I am afraid my applying to you will appear no better than equivocation, and as if I attended to the letter and not the spirit of mamma's commands. But if you do not take my part and persuade her to break it off, I shall be half distracted, for I cannot bear him. No human being but YOU could have any chance of prevailing with her. If you will, therefore, have the unspeakably great kindness of taking my part with her, and persuading her to send Sir James away, I shall be more obliged to you than it is possible for me to express. I always disliked him from the first: it is not a sudden fancy, I assure you, sir; I always thought him silly and impertinent and disagreeable, and now he is grown worse than ever. I would rather work for my bread than marry him. I do not know how to apologize enough for this letter; I know it is taking so great a liberty. I am aware how dreadfully angry it will make mamma, but I remember the risk.

I am, Sir, your most humble servant,

F. S. V.

❧❧❧❧

LADY SUSAN TO MRS. JOHNSON

Churchhill.

This is insufferable! My dearest friend, I was never so enraged before, and must relieve myself by writing to you, who I know will enter into all my feelings. Who should come on Tuesday but Sir James Martin! Guess my astonishment, and vexation—for, as you well know, I never wished him to be seen at Churchhill. What a pity that you should not have known his intentions! Not content with coming, he actually invited himself to remain here a few days. I could have poisoned him! I made the best of it, however, and told my story with great success to Mrs. Vernon, who, whatever might be her real sentiments, said nothing in opposition to mine. I made a point also of Frederica's behaving civilly to Sir James, and gave her to understand that I was absolutely determined on her marrying him. She said something of her misery, but that was all. I have for some time been more particularly resolved on the match from seeing the rapid increase of her affection for Reginald, and from not feeling secure that a knowledge of such affection might not in the end awaken a return. Contemptible as a regard founded only on compassion must make them both in my eyes, I felt by no means assured that such might not be the consequence. It is true that Reginald had not in any degree grown cool towards me; but yet he has lately mentioned Frederica spontaneously and unnecessarily, and once said something in praise of her person. HE was all astonishment at the appearance of my visitor, and at first observed Sir James with an attention which I was pleased to see not unmixed with jealousy; but unluckily it was impossible for me really to torment him, as Sir James, though extremely gallant to me, very soon made the whole party understand that his heart was devoted to my daughter. I had no great difficulty in convincing De Courcy, when we were alone, that I was perfectly justified, all things considered, in desiring the match; and the whole business seemed most comfortably arranged. They could none of them help perceiving that Sir James was no Solomon; but I had positively forbidden Frederica complaining to Charles Vernon or his wife, and they had therefore no pretence for interference; though my impertinent sister, I believe, wanted only opportunity for doing so. Everything, however, was going on calmly and quietly; and, though I counted the hours of Sir James's stay, my mind was entirely satisfied with the posture of affairs. Guess, then, what I must feel at the sudden disturbance of all my schemes; and that, too, from a quarter where I had least reason to expect it. Reginald came this morning into my dressing-room with a very unusual solemnity of countenance, and after some preface informed me in so many words that he wished to reason with me on the impropriety and unkindness of allowing Sir James Martin to address my daughter contrary to her inclinations. I was all amazement. When I found that he was not to be laughed out of his design, I calmly begged an explanation, and desired to know by what he was impelled, and by whom commissioned, to reprimand me. He then told me, mixing in his speech a few insolent compliments and ill-timed expressions of tenderness, to which I listened with perfect indifference, that my daughter had acquainted him with some circumstances concerning herself, Sir James, and me which had given him great uneasiness. In short, I found that she had in the first place actually written to him to request his interference, and that, on receiving her letter, he had conversed with her on the subject of it, in order to understand the particulars, and to assure himself of her real wishes. I have not a doubt but that the girl took this opportunity of making downright love to him. I am convinced of it by the manner in which he spoke of her. Much good may such love do him! I shall ever despise the man who can be gratified by the passion which he never wished to inspire, nor solicited the avowal of. I shall always detest them both. He can have no true regard for me, or he would not have listened to her; and SHE, with her little rebellious heart and indelicate feelings, to throw herself into the protection of a young man with whom she has scarcely ever exchanged two words before! I am equally confounded at HER impudence and HIS credulity. How dared he believe what she told him in my disfavour! Ought he not to have felt assured that I must have unanswerable motives for all that I had done? Where was his reliance on my sense and goodness then? Where the resentment which true love would have dictated against the person defaming me—that person, too, a chit, a child, without talent or education, whom he had been always taught to despise? I was calm for some time; but the greatest degree of forbearance may be overcome, and I hope I was afterwards sufficiently keen. He endeavoured, long endeavoured, to soften my resentment; but that woman is a fool indeed who, while insulted by accusation, can be worked on by compliments. At length he left me, as deeply provoked as myself; and he showed his anger more. I was quite cool, but he gave way to the most violent indignation; I may therefore expect it will the sooner subside, and perhaps his may be vanished for ever, while mine will be found still fresh and implacable. He is now shut up in his apartment, whither I heard him go on leaving mine. How unpleasant, one would think, must be his reflections! but some people's feelings are incomprehensible. I have not yet tranquillised myself enough to see Frederica. SHE shall not soon forget the occurrences of this day; she shall find that she has poured forth her tender tale of love in vain, and exposed herself for ever to the contempt of the whole world, and the severest resentment of her injured mother.

Your affectionate

S. VERNON.

MRS. VERNON TO LADY DE COURCY

Churchhill.

Let me congratulate you, my dearest Mother! The affair which has given us so much anxiety is drawing to a happy conclusion. Our prospect is most delightful, and since matters have now taken so favourable a turn, I am quite sorry that I ever imparted my apprehensions to you; for the pleasure of learning that the danger is over is perhaps dearly purchased by all that you have previously suffered. I am so much agitated by delight that I can scarcely hold a pen; but am determined to send you a few short lines by James, that you may have some explanation of what must so greatly astonish you, as that Reginald should be returning to Parklands. I was sitting about half an hour ago with Sir James in the breakfast parlour, when my brother called me out of the room. I instantly saw that something was the matter; his complexion was raised, and he spoke with great emotion; you know his eager manner, my dear mother, when his mind is interested. "Catherine," said he, "I am going home to-day; I am sorry to leave you, but I must go: it is a great while since I have seen my father and mother. I am going to send James forward with my hunters immediately; if you have any letter, therefore, he can take it. I shall not be at home myself till Wednesday or Thursday, as I shall go through London, where I have business; but before I leave you," he continued, speaking in a lower tone, and with still greater energy, "I must warn you of one thing—do not let Frederica Vernon be made unhappy by that Martin. He wants to marry her; her mother promotes the match, but she cannot endure the idea of it. Be assured that I speak from the fullest conviction of the truth of what I say; I know that Frederica is made wretched by Sir James's continuing here. She is a sweet girl, and deserves a better fate. Send him away immediately; he is only a fool: but what her mother can mean, Heaven only knows! Good bye," he added, shaking my hand with earnestness; "I do not know when you will see me again; but remember what I tell you of Frederica; you MUST make it your business to see justice done her. She is an amiable girl, and has a very superior mind to what we have given her credit for." He then left me, and ran upstairs. I would not try to stop him, for I know what his feelings must be. The nature of mine, as I listened to him, I need not attempt to describe; for a minute or two I remained in the same spot, overpowered by wonder of a most agreeable sort indeed; yet it required some consideration to be tranquilly happy. In about ten minutes after my return to the parlour Lady Susan entered the room. I concluded, of course, that she and Reginald had been quarrelling; and looked with anxious curiosity for a confirmation of my belief in her face. Mistress of deceit, however, she appeared perfectly unconcerned, and after chatting on indifferent subjects for a short time, said to me, "I find from Wilson that we are going to lose Mr. De Courcy—is it true that he leaves Churchhill this morning?" I replied that it was. "He told us nothing of all this last night," said she, laughing, "or even this morning at breakfast; but perhaps he did not know it himself. Young men are often hasty in their resolutions, and not more sudden in forming than unsteady in keeping them. I should not be surprised if he were to change his mind at last, and not go." She soon afterwards left the room. I trust, however, my dear mother, that we have no reason to fear an alteration of his present plan; things have gone too far. They must have quarrelled, and about Frederica, too. Her calmness astonishes me. What delight will be yours in seeing him again; in seeing him still worthy your esteem, still capable of forming your happiness! When I next write I shall be able to tell you that Sir James is gone, Lady Susan vanquished, and Frederica at peace. We have much to do, but it shall be done. I am all impatience to hear how this astonishing change was effected. I finish as I began, with the warmest congratulations.

Yours ever, &c.,

CATH. VERNON.

FROM THE SAME TO THE SAME

Churchhill.

Little did I imagine, my dear Mother, when I sent off my last letter, that the delightful perturbation of spirits I was then in would undergo so speedy, so melancholy a reverse. I never can sufficiently regret that I wrote to you at all. Yet who could have foreseen what has happened? My dear mother, every hope which made me so happy only two hours ago has vanished. The quarrel between Lady Susan and Reginald is made up, and we are all as we were before. One point only is gained. Sir James Martin is dismissed. What are we now to look forward to? I am indeed disappointed; Reginald was all but gone, his horse was ordered and all but brought to the door; who would not have felt safe? For half an hour I was in momentary expectation of his departure. After I had sent off my letter to you, I went to Mr. Vernon, and sat with him in his room talking over the whole matter, and then determined to look for Frederica, whom I had not seen since breakfast. I met her on the stairs, and saw that she was crying. "My dear aunt," said she, "he is going—Mr. De Courcy is going, and it is all my fault. I am afraid you will be very angry with me, but indeed I had no idea it would end so." "My love," I replied, "do not think it necessary to apologize to me on that account. I shall feel myself under an obligation to anyone who is the means of sending my brother home, because," recollecting myself, "I know my father wants very much to see him. But what is it you have done to occasion all this?" She blushed deeply as she answered: "I was so unhappy about Sir James that I could not help—I have done something very wrong, I know; but you have not an idea of the misery I have been in: and mamma had ordered me never to speak to you or my uncle about it, and—" "You therefore spoke to my brother to engage his interference," said I, to save her the explanation. "No, but I wrote to him—I did indeed, I got up this morning before it was light, and was two hours about it; and when my letter was done I thought I never should have courage to give it. After breakfast however, as I was going to my room, I met him in the passage, and then, as I knew that everything must depend on that moment, I forced myself to give it. He was so good as to take it immediately. I dared not look at him, and ran away directly. I was in such a fright I could hardly breathe. My dear aunt, you do not know how miserable I have been." "Frederica" said I, "you ought to have told me all your distresses. You would have found in me a friend always ready to assist you. Do you think that your uncle or I should not have espoused your cause as warmly as my brother?" "Indeed, I did not doubt your kindness," said she, colouring again, "but I thought Mr. De Courcy could do anything with my mother; but I was mistaken: they have had a dreadful quarrel about it, and he is going away. Mamma will never forgive me, and I shall be worse off than ever." "No, you shall not," I replied; "in such a point as this your mother's prohibition ought not to have prevented your speaking to me on the subject. She has no right to make you unhappy, and she shall NOT do it. Your applying, however, to Reginald can be productive only of good to all parties. I believe it is best as it is. Depend upon it that you shall not be made unhappy any longer." At that moment how great was my astonishment at seeing Reginald come out of Lady Susan's dressing-room. My heart misgave me instantly. His confusion at seeing me was very evident. Frederica immediately disappeared. "Are you going?" I said; "you will find Mr. Vernon in his own room." "No, Catherine," he replied, "I am not going. Will you let me speak to you a moment?" We went into my room. "I find," he continued, his confusion increasing as he spoke, "that I have been acting with my usual foolish impetuosity. I have entirely misunderstood Lady Susan, and was on the point of leaving the house under a false impression of her conduct. There has been some very great mistake; we have been all mistaken, I fancy. Frederica does not know her mother. Lady Susan means nothing but her good, but she will not make a friend of her. Lady Susan does not always know, therefore, what will make her daughter happy. Besides, I could have no right to interfere. Miss Vernon was mistaken in applying to me. In short, Catherine, everything has gone wrong, but it is now all happily settled. Lady Susan, I believe, wishes to speak to you about it, if you are at leisure." "Certainly," I replied, deeply sighing at the recital of so lame a story. I made no comments, however, for words would have been vain.

Reginald was glad to get away, and I went to Lady Susan, curious, indeed, to hear her account of it. "Did I not tell you," said she with a smile, "that your brother would not leave us after all?" "You did, indeed," replied I very gravely; "but I flattered myself you would be mistaken." "I should not have hazarded such an opinion," returned she, "if it had not at that moment occurred to me that his resolution of going might be occasioned by a conversation in which we had been this morning engaged, and which had ended very much to his dissatisfaction, from our not rightly understanding each other's meaning. This idea struck me at the moment, and I instantly determined that an accidental dispute, in which I might probably be as much to blame as himself, should not deprive you of your brother. If you remember, I left the room almost immediately. I was resolved to lose no time in clearing up those mistakes as far as I could. The case was this—Frederica had set herself violently against marrying Sir James." "And can your ladyship wonder that she should?" cried I with some warmth; "Frederica has an excellent understanding, and Sir James has none." "I am at least very far from regretting it, my dear sister," said she; "on the contrary, I am grateful for so favourable a sign of my daughter's sense. Sir James is certainly below par (his boyish manners make him appear worse); and had Frederica possessed the penetration and the abilities which I could have wished in my daughter, or had I even known her to possess as much as she does, I should not have been anxious for the match." "It is odd that you should alone be ignorant of your daughter's sense!" "Frederica never does justice to herself; her manners are shy and childish, and besides she is afraid of me. During her poor father's life she was a spoilt child; the severity which it has since been necessary for me to show has alienated her affection; neither has she any of that brilliancy of intellect, that genius or vigour of mind which will force itself forward." "Say rather that she has been unfortunate in her education!" "Heaven knows, my dearest Mrs. Vernon, how fully I am aware of that; but I would wish to forget every circumstance that might throw blame on the memory of one whose name is sacred with me." Here she pretended to cry; I was out of patience with her. "But what," said I, "was your ladyship going to tell me about your disagreement with my brother?" "It originated in an action of my daughter's, which equally marks her want of judgment and the unfortunate dread of me I have been mentioning—she wrote to Mr. De Courcy." "I know she did; you had forbidden her speaking to Mr. Vernon or to me on the cause of her distress; what could she do, therefore, but apply to my brother?" "Good God!" she exclaimed, "what an opinion you must have of me! Can you possibly suppose that I was aware of her unhappiness! that it was my object to make my own child miserable, and that I had forbidden her speaking to you on the subject from a fear of your interrupting the diabolical scheme? Do you think me destitute of every honest, every natural feeling? Am I capable of consigning HER to everlasting misery whose welfare it is my first earthly duty to promote? The idea is horrible!" "What, then, was your intention when you insisted on her silence?" "Of what use, my dear sister, could be any application to you, however the affair might stand? Why should I subject you to entreaties which I refused to attend to myself? Neither for your sake nor for hers, nor for my own, could such a thing be desirable. When my own resolution was taken I could not wish for the interference, however friendly, of another person. I was mistaken, it is true, but I believed myself right." "But what was this mistake to which your ladyship so often alludes! from whence arose so astonishing a misconception of your daughter's feelings! Did you not know that she disliked Sir James?" "I knew that he was not absolutely the man she would have chosen, but I was persuaded that her objections to him did not arise from any perception of his deficiency. You must not question me, however, my dear sister, too minutely on this point," continued she, taking me affectionately by the hand; "I honestly own that there is something to conceal. Frederica makes me very unhappy! Her applying to Mr. De Courcy hurt me particularly." "What is it you mean to infer," said I, "by this appearance of mystery? If you think your daughter at all attached to Reginald, her objecting to Sir James could not less deserve to be attended to than if the cause of her objecting had been a consciousness of his folly; and why should your ladyship, at any rate, quarrel with my brother for an interference which, you must know, it is not in his nature to refuse when urged in such a manner?"

"His disposition, you know, is warm, and he came to expostulate with me; his compassion all alive for this ill-used girl, this heroine in distress! We misunderstood each other: he believed me more to blame than I really was; I considered his interference less excusable than I now find it. I have a real regard for him, and was beyond expression mortified to find it, as I thought, so ill bestowed. We were both warm, and of course both to blame. His resolution of leaving Churchhill is consistent with his general eagerness. When I understood his intention, however, and at the same time began to think that we had been perhaps equally mistaken in each other's meaning, I resolved to have an explanation before it was too late. For any member of your family I must always feel a degree of affection, and I own it would have sensibly hurt me if my acquaintance with Mr. De Courcy had ended so gloomily. I have now only to say further, that as I am convinced of Frederica's having a reasonable dislike to Sir James, I shall instantly inform him that he must give up all hope of her. I reproach myself for having, even though innocently, made her unhappy on that score. She shall have all the retribution in my power to make; if she value her own happiness as much as I do, if she judge wisely, and command herself as she ought, she may now be easy. Excuse me, my dearest sister, for thus trespassing on your time, but I owe it to my own character; and after this explanation I trust I am in no danger of sinking in your opinion." I could have said, "Not much, indeed!" but I left her almost in silence. It was the greatest stretch of forbearance I could practise. I could not have stopped myself had I begun. Her assurance! her deceit! but I will not allow myself to dwell on them; they will strike you sufficiently. My heart sickens within me. As soon as I was tolerably composed I returned to the parlour. Sir James's carriage was at the door, and he, merry as usual, soon afterwards took his leave. How easily does her ladyship encourage or dismiss a lover! In spite of this release, Frederica still looks unhappy: still fearful, perhaps, of her mother's anger; and though dreading my brother's departure, jealous, it may be, of his staying. I see how closely she observes him and Lady Susan, poor girl! I have now no hope for her. There is not a chance of her affection being returned. He thinks very differently of her from what he used to do; he does her some justice, but his reconciliation with her mother precludes every dearer hope. Prepare, my dear mother, for the worst! The probability of their marrying is surely heightened! He is more securely hers than ever. When that wretched event takes place, Frederica must belong wholly to us. I am thankful that my last letter will precede this by so little, as every moment that you can be saved from feeling a joy which leads only to disappointment is of consequence.

Yours ever, &c.,
CATHERINE VERNON.

XXV

LADY SUSAN TO MRS. JOHNSON

Churchhill.

I call on you, dear Alicia, for congratulations: I am my own self, gay and triumphant! When I wrote to you the other day I was, in truth, in high irritation, and with ample cause. Nay, I know not whether I ought to be quite tranquil now, for I have had more trouble in restoring peace than I ever intended to submit to—a spirit, too, resulting from a fancied sense of superior integrity, which is peculiarly insolent! I shall not easily forgive him, I assure you. He was actually on the point of leaving Churchhill! I had scarcely concluded my last, when Wilson brought me word of it. I found, therefore, that something must be done; for I did not choose to leave my character at the mercy of a man whose passions are so violent and so revengeful. It would have been trifling with my reputation to allow of his departing with such an impression in my disfavour; in this light, condescension was necessary. I sent Wilson to say that I desired to speak with him before he went; he came immediately. The angry emotions which had marked every feature when we last parted were partially subdued. He seemed astonished at the summons, and looked as if half wishing and half fearing to be softened by what I might say. If my countenance expressed

299

what I aimed at, it was composed and dignified; and yet, with a degree of pensiveness which might convince him that I was not quite happy. "I beg your pardon, sir, for the liberty I have taken in sending for you," said I; "but as I have just learnt your intention of leaving this place to-day, I feel it my duty to entreat that you will not on my account shorten your visit here even an hour. I am perfectly aware that after what has passed between us it would ill suit the feelings of either to remain longer in the same house: so very great, so total a change from the intimacy of friendship must render any future intercourse the severest punishment; and your resolution of quitting Churchhill is undoubtedly in unison with our situation, and with those lively feelings which I know you to possess. But, at the same time, it is not for me to suffer such a sacrifice as it must be to leave relations to whom you are so much attached, and are so dear. My remaining here cannot give that pleasure to Mr. and Mrs. Vernon which your society must; and my visit has already perhaps been too long. My removal, therefore, which must, at any rate, take place soon, may, with perfect convenience, be hastened; and I make it my particular request that I may not in any way be instrumental in separating a family so affectionately attached to each other. Where I go is of no consequence to anyone; of very little to myself; but you are of importance to all your connections." Here I concluded, and I hope you will be satisfied with my speech. Its effect on Reginald justifies some portion of vanity, for it was no less favourable than instantaneous. Oh, how delightful it was to watch the variations of his countenance while I spoke! to see the struggle between returning tenderness and the remains of displeasure. There is something agreeable in feelings so easily worked on; not that I envy him their possession, nor would, for the world, have such myself; but they are very convenient when one wishes to influence the passions of another. And yet this Reginald, whom a very few words from me softened at once into the utmost submission, and rendered more tractable, more attached, more devoted than ever, would have left me in the first angry swelling of his proud heart without deigning to seek an explanation. Humbled as he now is, I cannot forgive him such an instance of pride, and am doubtful whether I ought not to punish him by dismissing him at once after this reconciliation, or by marrying and teazing him for ever. But these measures are each too violent to be adopted without some deliberation; at present my thoughts are fluctuating between various schemes. I have many things to compass: I must punish Frederica, and pretty severely too, for her application to Reginald; I must punish him for receiving it so favourably, and for the rest of his conduct. I must torment my sister-in-law for the insolent triumph of her look and manner since Sir James has been dismissed; for, in reconciling Reginald to me, I was not able to save that ill-fated young man; and I must make myself amends for the humiliation to which I have stooped within these few days. To effect all this I have various plans. I have also an idea of being soon in town; and whatever may be my determination as to the rest, I shall probably put THAT project in execution; for London will be always the fairest field of action, however my views may be directed; and at any rate I shall there be rewarded by your society, and a little dissipation, for a ten weeks' penance at Churchhill. I believe I owe it to my character to complete the match between my daughter and Sir James after having so long intended it. Let me know your opinion on this point. Flexibility of mind, a disposition easily biassed by others, is an attribute which you know I am not very desirous of obtaining; nor has Frederica any claim to the indulgence of her notions at the expense of her mother's inclinations. Her idle love for

Reginald, too! It is surely my duty to discourage such romantic nonsense. All things considered, therefore, it seems incumbent on me to take her to town and marry her immediately to Sir James. When my own will is effected contrary to his, I shall have some credit in being on good terms with Reginald, which at present, in fact, I have not; for though he is still in my power, I have given up the very article by which our quarrel was produced, and at best the honour of victory is doubtful. Send me your opinion on all these matters, my dear Alicia, and let me know whether you can get lodgings to suit me within a short distance of you.

Your most attached

S. VERNON.

MRS. JOHNSON TO LADY SUSAN

Edward Street.

I am gratified by your reference, and this is my advice: that you come to town yourself, without loss of time, but that you leave Frederica behind. It would surely be much more to the purpose to get yourself well established by marrying Mr. De Courcy, than to irritate him and the rest of his family by making her marry Sir James. You should think more of yourself and less of your daughter. She is not of a disposition to do you credit in the world, and seems precisely in her proper place at Churchhill, with the Vernons. But you are fitted for society, and it is shameful to have you exiled from it. Leave Frederica, therefore, to punish herself for the plague she has given you, by indulging that romantic tender-heartedness which will always ensure her misery enough, and come to London as soon as you can. I have another reason for urging this: Mainwaring came to town last week, and has contrived, in spite of Mr. Johnson, to make opportunities of seeing me. He is absolutely miserable about you, and jealous to such a degree of De Courcy that it would be highly unadvisable for them to meet at present. And yet, if you do not allow him to see you here, I cannot answer for his not committing some great imprudence—such as going to Churchhill, for instance, which would be dreadful! Besides, if you take my advice, and resolve to marry De Courcy, it will be indispensably necessary to you to get Mainwaring out of the way; and you only can have influence enough to send him back to his wife. I have still another motive for your coming: Mr. Johnson leaves London next Tuesday; he is going for his health to Bath, where, if the waters are favourable to his constitution and my wishes, he will be laid up with the gout many weeks. During his absence we shall be able to chuse our own society, and to have true enjoyment. I would ask you to Edward Street, but that once he forced from me a kind of promise never to invite you to my house; nothing but my being in the utmost distress for money should have extorted it from me. I can get you, however, a nice drawing-room apartment in Upper Seymour Street, and we may be always together there or here; for I consider my promise to Mr. Johnson as comprehending only (at least in his absence) your not sleeping in the house. Poor Mainwaring gives me such histories of his wife's jealousy. Silly woman to expect constancy from so charming a man! but she always was silly—intolerably so in marrying him at all, she the heiress of a large fortune and he without a shilling: one title, I know, she might have had, besides baronets. Her folly in forming the connection was so great that, though Mr. Johnson was her guardian, and I do not in general share HIS feelings, I never can forgive her.

Adieu. Yours ever,

ALICIA.

❦

MRS. VERNON TO LADY DE COURCY

Churchhill.

This letter, my dear Mother, will be brought you by Reginald. His long visit is about to be concluded at last, but I fear the separation takes place too late to do us any good. She is going to London to see her particular friend, Mrs. Johnson. It was at first her intention that Frederica should accompany her, for the benefit of masters, but we overruled her there. Frederica was wretched in the idea of going, and I could not bear to have her at the mercy of her mother; not all the masters in London could compensate for the ruin of her comfort. I should have feared, too, for her health, and for everything but her principles—there I believe she is not to be injured by her mother, or her mother's friends; but with those friends she must have mixed (a very bad set, I doubt not), or have been left in total solitude, and I can hardly tell which would have been worse for her. If she is with her mother, moreover, she must, alas! in all probability be with Reginald, and that would be the greatest evil of all. Here we shall in time be in peace, and our regular employments, our books and conversations, with exercise, the children, and every domestic pleasure in my power to procure her, will, I trust, gradually overcome this youthful attachment. I should not have a doubt of it were she slighted for any other woman in the world than her own mother. How long Lady Susan will be in town, or whether she returns here again, I know not. I could not be cordial in my invitation, but if she chuses to come no want of cordiality on my part will keep her away. I could not help asking Reginald if he intended being in London this winter, as soon as I found her ladyship's steps would be bent thither; and though he professed himself quite undetermined, there was something in his look and voice as he spoke which contradicted his words. I have done with lamentation; I look upon the event as so far decided that I resign myself to it in despair. If he leaves you soon for London everything will be concluded.

Your affectionate, &c.,

C. VERNON.

XXVIII

MRS. JOHNSON TO LADY SUSAN

Edward Street.

My dearest Friend,—I write in the greatest distress; the most unfortunate event has just taken place. Mr. Johnson has hit on the most effectual manner of plaguing us all. He had heard, I imagine, by some means or other, that you were soon to be in London, and immediately contrived to have such an attack of the gout as must at least delay his journey to Bath, if not wholly prevent it. I am persuaded the gout is brought on or kept off at pleasure; it was the same when I wanted to join the Hamiltons to the Lakes; and three years ago, when I had a fancy for Bath, nothing could induce him to have a gouty symptom.

I am pleased to find that my letter had so much effect on you, and that De Courcy is certainly your own. Let me hear from you as soon as you arrive, and in particular tell me what you mean to do with Mainwaring. It is impossible to say when I shall be able to come to you; my confinement must be great. It is such an abominable trick to be ill here instead of at Bath that I can scarcely command myself at all. At Bath his old aunts would have nursed him, but here it all falls upon me; and he bears pain with such patience that I have not the common excuse for losing my temper.

Yours ever,
ALICIA.

XXIX

LADY SUSAN VERNON TO MRS. JOHNSON

Upper Seymour Street.

My dear Alicia,—There needed not this last fit of the gout to make me detest Mr. Johnson, but now the extent of my aversion is not to be estimated. To have you confined as nurse in his apartment! My dear Alicia, of what a mistake were you guilty in marrying a man of his age! just old enough to be formal, ungovernable, and to have the gout; too old to be agreeable, too young to die. I arrived last night about five, had scarcely swallowed my dinner when Mainwaring made his appearance. I will not dissemble what real pleasure his sight afforded me, nor how strongly I felt the contrast between his person and manners and those of Reginald, to the infinite disadvantage of the latter. For an hour or two I was even staggered in my resolution of marrying him, and though this was too idle and nonsensical an idea to remain long on my mind, I do not feel very eager for the conclusion of my marriage, nor look forward with much impatience to the time when Reginald, according to our agreement, is to be in town. I shall probably put off his arrival under some pretence or other. He must not come till Mainwaring is gone. I am still doubtful at times as to marrying; if the old man would die I might not hesitate, but a state of dependance on the caprice of Sir Reginald will not suit the freedom of my spirit; and if I resolve to wait for that event, I shall have excuse enough at present in having been scarcely ten months a widow. I have not given Mainwaring any hint of my intention, or allowed him to consider my acquaintance with Reginald as more than the commonest flirtation, and he is tolerably appeased. Adieu, till we meet; I am enchanted with my lodgings.

Yours ever,

S. VERNON.

LADY SUSAN VERNON TO MR. DE COURCY

Upper Seymour Street.

I have received your letter, and though I do not attempt to conceal that I am gratified by your impatience for the hour of meeting, I yet feel myself under the necessity of delaying that hour beyond the time originally fixed. Do not think me unkind for such an exercise of my power, nor accuse me of instability without first hearing my reasons. In the course of my journey from Churchhill I had ample leisure for reflection on the present state of our affairs, and every review has served to convince me that they require a delicacy and cautiousness of conduct to which we have hitherto been too little attentive. We have been hurried on by our feelings to a degree of precipitation which ill accords with the claims of our friends or the opinion of the world. We have been unguarded in forming this hasty engagement, but we must not complete the imprudence by ratifying it while there is so much reason to fear the connection would be opposed by those friends on whom you depend. It is not for us to blame any expectations on your father's side of your marrying to advantage; where possessions are so extensive as those of your family, the wish of increasing them, if not strictly reasonable, is too common to excite surprize or resentment. He has a right to require; a woman of fortune in his daughter-in-law, and I am sometimes quarrelling with myself for suffering you to form a connection so imprudent; but the influence of reason is often acknowledged too late by those who feel like me. I have now been but a few months a widow, and, however little indebted to my husband's memory for any happiness derived from him during a union of some years, I cannot forget that the indelicacy of so early a second marriage must subject me to the censure of the world, and incur, what would be still more insupportable, the displeasure of Mr. Vernon. I might perhaps harden myself in time against the injustice of general reproach, but the loss of HIS valued esteem I am, as you well know, ill-fitted to endure; and when to this may be added the consciousness of having injured you with your family, how am I to support myself? With feelings so poignant as mine, the conviction of having divided the son from his parents would make me, even with you, the most miserable of beings. It will surely, therefore, be advisable to delay our union—to delay it till appearances are more promising—till affairs have taken a more favourable turn. To assist us in such a resolution I feel that absence will be necessary. We must not meet. Cruel as this sentence may appear, the necessity of pronouncing it, which can alone reconcile it to myself, will be evident to you when you have considered our situation in the light in which I have found myself imperiously obliged to place it. You may be—you must be—well assured that nothing but the strongest conviction of duty could induce me to wound my own feelings by urging a lengthened separation, and of insensibility to yours you will hardly suspect me. Again, therefore, I say that we ought not, we must not, yet meet. By a removal for some months from each other we shall tranquillise the sisterly fears of Mrs. Vernon, who, accustomed herself to the enjoyment of riches, considers fortune as necessary everywhere, and whose sensibilities are not of a nature to comprehend ours. Let me hear from you soon—very soon. Tell me that you submit to my arguments, and do not reproach me for using such. I cannot bear reproaches: my spirits are not so high as to need being repressed. I must endeavour to seek amusement, and fortunately many of my friends are in town; amongst them the Mainwarings; you know how sincerely I regard both husband and wife.

I am, very faithfully yours,

S. VERNON

LADY SUSAN TO MRS. JOHNSON

Upper Seymour Street.

My dear Friend,—That tormenting creature, Reginald, is here. My letter, which was intended to keep him longer in the country, has hastened him to town. Much as I wish him away, however, I cannot help being pleased with such a proof of attachment. He is devoted to me, heart and soul. He will carry this note himself, which is to serve as an introduction to you, with whom he longs to be acquainted. Allow him to spend the evening with you, that I may be in no danger of his returning here. I have told him that I am not quite well, and must be alone; and should he call again there might be confusion, for it is impossible to be sure of servants. Keep him, therefore, I entreat you, in Edward Street. You will not find him a heavy companion, and I allow you to flirt with him as much as you like. At the same time, do not forget my real interest; say all that you can to convince him that I shall be quite wretched if he remains here; you know my reasons—propriety, and so forth. I would urge them more myself, but that I am impatient to be rid of him, as Mainwaring comes within half an hour. Adieu!

S VERNON

MRS. JOHNSON TO LADY SUSAN

Edward Street.

My dear Creature,—I am in agonies, and know not what to do. Mr. De Courcy arrived just when he should not. Mrs. Mainwaring had that instant entered the house, and forced herself into her guardian's presence, though I did not know a syllable of it till afterwards, for I was out when both she and Reginald came, or I should have sent him away at all events; but she was shut up with Mr. Johnson, while he waited in the drawing-room for me. She arrived yesterday in pursuit of her husband, but perhaps you know this already from himself. She came to this house to entreat my husband's interference, and before I could be aware of it, everything that you could wish to be concealed was known to him, and unluckily she had wormed out of Mainwaring's servant that he had visited you every day since your being in town, and had just watched him to your door herself! What could I do! Facts are such horrid things! All is by this time known to De Courcy, who is now alone with Mr. Johnson. Do not accuse me; indeed, it was impossible to prevent it. Mr. Johnson has for some time suspected De Courcy of intending to marry you, and would speak with him alone as soon as he knew him to be in the house. That detestable Mrs. Mainwaring, who, for your comfort, has fretted herself thinner and uglier than ever, is still here, and they have been all closeted together. What can be done? At any rate, I hope he will plague his wife more than ever. With anxious wishes, Yours faithfully,

ALICIA.

LADY SUSAN TO MRS. JOHNSON

Upper Seymour Street.

This eclaircissement is rather provoking. How unlucky that you should have been from home! I thought myself sure of you at seven! I am undismayed however. Do not torment yourself with fears on my account; depend on it, I can make my story good with Reginald. Mainwaring is just gone; he brought me the news of his wife's arrival. Silly woman, what does she expect by such manoeuvres? Yet I wish she had stayed quietly at Langford. Reginald will be a little enraged at first, but by to-morrow's dinner, everything will be well again.

Adieu!

S. V.

MR. DE COURCY TO LADY SUSAN

—Hotel

I write only to bid you farewell, the spell is removed; I see you as you are. Since we parted yesterday, I have received from indisputable authority such a history of you as must bring the most mortifying conviction of the imposition I have been under, and the absolute necessity of an immediate and eternal separation from you. You cannot doubt to what I allude. Langford! Langford! that word will be sufficient. I received my information in Mr. Johnson's house, from Mrs. Mainwaring herself. You know how I have loved you; you can intimately judge of my present feelings, but I am not so weak as to find indulgence in describing them to a woman who will glory in having excited their anguish, but whose affection they have never been able to gain.

R. DE COURCY.

LADY SUSAN TO MR. DE COURCY

Upper Seymour Street.

I will not attempt to describe my astonishment in reading the note this moment received from you. I am bewildered in my endeavours to form some rational conjecture of what Mrs. Mainwaring can have told you to occasion so extraordinary a change in your sentiments. Have I not explained everything to you with respect to myself which could bear a doubtful meaning, and which the ill-nature of the world had interpreted to my discredit? What can you now have heard to stagger your esteem for me? Have I ever had a concealment from you? Reginald, you agitate me beyond expression, I cannot suppose that the old story of Mrs. Mainwaring's jealousy can be revived again, or at least be LISTENED to again. Come to me immediately, and explain what is at present absolutely incomprehensible. Believe me the single word of Langford is not of such potent intelligence as to supersede the necessity of more. If we ARE to part, it will at least be handsome to take your personal leave—but I have little heart to jest; in truth, I am serious enough; for to be sunk, though but for an hour, in your esteem is a humiliation to which I know not how to submit. I shall count every minute till your arrival.

S. V.

MR. DE COURCY TO LADY SUSAN

——Hotel.

Why would you write to me? Why do you require particulars? But, since it must be so, I am obliged to declare that all the accounts of your misconduct during the life, and since the death of Mr. Vernon, which had reached me, in common with the world in general, and gained my entire belief before I saw you, but which you, by the exertion of your perverted abilities, had made me resolved to disallow, have been unanswerably proved to me; nay more, I am assured that a connection, of which I had never before entertained a thought, has for some time existed, and still continues to exist, between you and the man whose family you robbed of its peace in return for the hospitality with which you were received into it; that you have corresponded with him ever since your leaving Langford; not with his wife, but with him, and that he now visits you every day. Can you, dare you deny it? and all this at the time when I was an encouraged, an accepted lover! From what have I not escaped! I have only to be grateful. Far from me be all complaint, every sigh of regret. My own folly had endangered me, my preservation I owe to the kindness, the integrity of another; but the unfortunate Mrs. Mainwaring, whose agonies while she related the past seemed to threaten her reason, how is SHE to be consoled! After such a discovery as this, you will scarcely affect further wonder at my meaning in bidding you adieu. My understanding is at length restored, and teaches no less to abhor the artifices which had subdued me than to despise myself for the weakness on which their strength was founded.

R. DE COURCY.

LADY SUSAN TO MR. DE COURCY

Upper Seymour Street.

I am satisfied, and will trouble you no more when these few lines are dismissed. The engagement which you were eager to form a fortnight ago is no longer compatible with your views, and I rejoice to find that the prudent advice of your parents has not been given in vain. Your restoration to peace will, I doubt not, speedily follow this act of filial obedience, and I flatter myself with the hope of surviving my share in this disappointment.

S. V.

MRS. JOHNSON TO LADY SUSAN VERNON

Edward Street

I am grieved, though I cannot be astonished at your rupture with Mr. De Courcy; he has just informed Mr. Johnson of it by letter. He leaves London, he says, to-day. Be assured that I partake in all your feelings, and do not be angry if I say that our intercourse, even by letter, must soon be given up. It makes me miserable; but Mr. Johnson vows that if I persist in the connection, he will settle in the country for the rest of his life, and you know it is impossible to submit to such an extremity while any other alternative remains. You have heard of course that the Mainwarings are to part, and I am afraid Mrs. M. will come home to us again; but she is still so fond of her husband, and frets so much about him, that perhaps she may not live long. Miss Mainwaring is just come to town to be with her aunt, and they say that she declares she will have Sir James Martin before she leaves London again. If I were you, I would certainly get him myself. I had almost forgot to give you my opinion of Mr. De Courcy; I am really delighted with him; he is full as handsome, I think, as Mainwaring, and with such an open, good-humoured countenance, that one cannot help loving him at first sight. Mr. Johnson and he are the greatest friends in the world. Adieu, my dearest Susan, I wish matters did not go so perversely. That unlucky visit to Langford! but I dare say you did all for the best, and there is no defying destiny.

Your sincerely attached

ALICIA.

LADY SUSAN TO MRS. JOHNSON

Upper Seymour Street.

My dear Alicia,—I yield to the necessity which parts us. Under circumstances you could not act otherwise. Our friendship cannot be impaired by it, and in happier times, when your situation is as independent as mine, it will unite us again in the same intimacy as ever. For this I shall impatiently wait, and meanwhile can safely assure you that I never was more at ease, or better satisfied with myself and everything about me than at the present hour. Your husband I abhor, Reginald I despise, and I am secure of never seeing either again. Have I not reason to rejoice? Mainwaring is more devoted to me than ever; and were we at liberty, I doubt if I could resist even matrimony offered by HIM. This event, if his wife live with you, it may be in your power to hasten. The violence of her feelings, which must wear her out, may be easily kept in irritation. I rely on your friendship for this. I am now satisfied that I never could have brought myself to marry Reginald, and am equally determined that Frederica never shall. To-morrow, I shall fetch her from Churchhill, and let Maria Mainwaring tremble for the consequence. Frederica shall be Sir James's wife before she quits my house, and she may whimper, and the Vernons may storm, I regard them not. I am tired of submitting my will to the caprices of others; of resigning my own judgment in deference to those to whom I owe no duty, and for whom I feel no respect. I have given up too much, have been too easily worked on, but Frederica shall now feel the difference. Adieu, dearest of friends; may the next gouty attack be more favourable! and may you always regard me as unalterably yours,

S. VERNON

LADY DE COURCY TO MRS. VERNON

My dear Catherine,—I have charming news for you, and if I had not sent off my letter this morning you might have been spared the vexation of knowing of Reginald's being gone to London, for he is returned. Reginald is returned, not to ask our consent to his marrying Lady Susan, but to tell us they are parted for ever. He has been only an hour in the house, and I have not been able to learn particulars, for he is so very low that I have not the heart to ask questions, but I hope we shall soon know all. This is the most joyful hour he has ever given us since the day of his birth. Nothing is wanting but to have you here, and it is our particular wish and entreaty that you would come to us as soon as you can. You have owed us a visit many long weeks; I hope nothing will make it inconvenient to Mr. Vernon; and pray bring all my grand-children; and your dear niece is included, of course; I long to see her. It has been a sad, heavy winter hitherto, without Reginald, and seeing nobody from Churchhill. I never found the season so dreary before; but this happy meeting will make us young again. Frederica runs much in my thoughts, and when Reginald has recovered his usual good spirits (as I trust he soon will) we will try to rob him of his heart once more, and I am full of hopes of seeing their hands joined at no great distance.

Your affectionate mother,

C. DE COURCY

✕LI

MRS. VERNON TO LADY DE COURCY

Churchhill.

My dear Mother,—Your letter has surprized me beyond measure! Can it be true that they are really separated—and for ever? I should be overjoyed if I dared depend on it, but after all that I have seen how can one be secure. And Reginald really with you! My surprize is the greater because on Wednesday, the very day of his coming to Parklands, we had a most unexpected and unwelcome visit from Lady Susan, looking all cheerfulness and good-humour, and seeming more as if she were to marry him when she got to London than as if parted from him for ever. She stayed nearly two hours, was as affectionate and agreeable as ever, and not a syllable, not a hint was dropped, of any disagreement or coolness between them. I asked her whether she had seen my brother since his arrival in town; not, as you may suppose, with any doubt of the fact, but merely to see how she looked. She immediately answered, without any embarrassment, that he had been kind enough to call on her on Monday; but she believed he had already returned home, which I was very far from crediting. Your kind invitation is accepted by us with pleasure, and on Thursday next we and our little ones will be with you. Pray heaven, Reginald may not be in town again by that time! I wish we could bring dear Frederica too, but I am sorry to say that her mother's errand hither was to fetch her away; and, miserable as it made the poor girl, it was impossible to detain her. I was thoroughly unwilling to let her go, and so was her uncle; and all that could be urged we did urge; but Lady Susan declared that as she was now about to fix herself in London for several months, she could not be easy if her daughter were not with her for masters, &c. Her manner, to be sure, was very kind and proper, and Mr. Vernon believes that Frederica will now be treated with affection. I wish I could think so too. The poor girl's heart was almost broke at taking leave of us. I charged her to write to me very often, and to remember that if she were in any distress we should be always her friends. I took care to see her alone, that I might say all this, and I hope made her a little more comfortable; but I shall not be easy till I can go to town and judge of her situation myself. I wish there were a better prospect than now appears of the match which the conclusion of your letter declares your expectations of. At present, it is not very likely,

Yours ever, &c.,
C. VERNON

Conclusion

This correspondence, by a meeting between some of the parties, and a separation between the others, could not, to the great detriment of the Post Office revenue, be continued any longer. Very little assistance to the State could be derived from the epistolary intercourse of Mrs. Vernon and her niece; for the former soon perceived, by the style of Frederica's letters, that they were written under her mother's inspection! and therefore, deferring all particular enquiry till she could make it personally in London, ceased writing minutely or often. Having learnt enough, in the meanwhile, from her open-hearted brother, of what had passed between him and Lady Susan to sink the latter lower than ever in her opinion, she was proportionably more anxious to get Frederica removed from such a mother, and placed under her own care; and, though with little hope of success, was resolved to leave nothing unattempted that might offer a chance of obtaining her sister-in-law's consent to it. Her anxiety on the subject made her press for an early visit to London; and Mr. Vernon, who, as it must already have appeared, lived only to do whatever he was desired, soon found some accommodating business to call him thither. With a heart full of the matter, Mrs. Vernon waited on Lady Susan shortly after her arrival in town, and was met with such an easy and cheerful affection, as made her almost turn from her with horror. No remembrance of Reginald, no consciousness of guilt, gave one look of embarrassment; she was in excellent spirits, and seemed eager to show at once by ever possible attention to her brother and sister her sense of their kindness, and her pleasure in their society. Frederica was no more altered than Lady Susan; the same restrained manners, the same timid look in the presence of her mother as heretofore, assured her aunt of her situation being uncomfortable, and confirmed her in the plan of altering it. No unkindness, however, on the part of Lady Susan appeared. Persecution on the subject of Sir James was entirely at an end; his name merely mentioned to say that he was not in London; and indeed, in all her conversation, she was solicitous only for the welfare and improvement of her daughter, acknowledging, in terms of grateful delight, that Frederica was now growing every day more and more what a parent could desire. Mrs. Vernon, surprized and incredulous, knew not what to suspect, and, without any change in her own views, only feared greater difficulty in accomplishing them. The first hope of anything better was derived from Lady Susan's asking her whether she thought Frederica looked quite as well as she had done at Churchhill, as she must confess herself to have sometimes an anxious doubt of London's perfectly agreeing with her. Mrs. Vernon, encouraging the doubt, directly proposed her niece's returning with them into the country. Lady Susan was unable to express her sense of such kindness, yet knew not, from a variety of reasons, how to part with her daughter; and as, though her own plans were not yet wholly fixed, she trusted it would ere long be in her power to take Frederica into the country herself, concluded by declining entirely to profit by such unexampled attention. Mrs. Vernon persevered, however, in the offer of it, and though Lady Susan continued to resist, her resistance in the course of a few days seemed somewhat less formidable. The lucky alarm of an influenza decided what might not have been decided quite so soon. Lady Susan's maternal fears were then too much awakened for her to think of anything but Frederica's removal from the risk of infection; above all disorders in the world she most dreaded the influenza for her daughter's constitution!

Frederica returned to Churchhill with her uncle and aunt; and three weeks afterwards, Lady Susan announced her being married to Sir James Martin. Mrs. Vernon was then convinced of what she had only suspected before, that she might have spared herself all the trouble of urging a removal which Lady Susan had doubtless resolved on from the first. Frederica's visit was nominally for six weeks, but her mother, though inviting her to return in one or two affectionate letters, was very ready to oblige the whole party by consenting to a prolongation of her stay, and in the course of two months ceased to write of her absence, and in the course of two or more to write to her at all. Frederica was therefore fixed in the family of her uncle and aunt till such time as Reginald De Courcy could be talked, flattered, and finessed into an affection for her which, allowing leisure for the conquest of his attachment to her mother, for his abjuring all future attachments, and detesting the sex, might be reasonably looked for in the course of a twelvemonth. Three months might have done it in general, but Reginald's feelings were no less lasting than lively. Whether Lady Susan was or was not happy in her second choice, I do not see how it can ever be ascertained; for who would take her assurance of it on either side of the question? The world must judge from probabilities; she had nothing against her but her husband, and her conscience. Sir James may seem to have drawn a harder lot than mere folly merited; I leave him, therefore, to all the pity that anybody can give him. For myself, I confess that I can pity only Miss Mainwaring; who, coming to town, and putting herself to an expense in clothes which impoverished her for two years, on purpose to secure him, was defrauded of her due by a woman ten years older than herself.

The Watsons

BY

Jane Austen

PREFACE

This work was left by its author, a fragment without a name, in so elementary a state as not even to be divided into chapters, and some obscurities and inaccuracies of expression may be observed in it which the author would probably have corrected. The original manuscript is the property of my sister, Miss Austen, by whose permission it is now published. I have called it *The Watsons*, for the sake of having a title by which to designate it. Two questions may be asked concerning it. When was it written? And, why was it never finished? I was unable to answer the first question, so long as I had only the internal evidence of the style to guide me. I felt satisfied, indeed, that it did not belong to that early class of her writings which are mentioned at page 46 of the *Memoir*, but rather bore marks of her more mature style, though it had never been subjected to the filing and polishing process by which she was accustomed to impart a high finish to her published works. At last, on a close inspection of the original manuscript, the water-marks of 1803 and 1804 were found in the paper on which it was written. It is therefore probable that it was composed at Bath, before she ceased to reside there in 1805. This would place the date a few years later than the composition, but earlier than the publication of *Sense and Sensibility*, and *Pride and Prejudice*. To the second question, why was it never finished? I can give no satisfactory answer. I think it will be generally admitted that there is much in it which promised well; that some of the characters are drawn with her wonted vigour, and some with a delicate discrimination peculiarly her own; and that it is rich in her especial power of telling the story, and bringing out the characters by conversation rather than by description. It could not have been broken up for the purpose of using the materials in another fabric; for, with the exception of Mrs. Robert Watson, in whom a resemblance to the future Mrs. Elton is very discernible, it would not be easy to trace much resemblance between this and any of her subsequent works. She must have felt some regret at leaving Tom Musgrave's character incomplete; yet he never appears elsewhere. My own idea is, but it is only a guess, that the author became aware of the evil of having placed her heroine too low, in such a position of poverty and obscurity as, though not necessarily connected with vulgarity, has a sad tendency to degenerate into it; and, therefore, like a singer who has begun on too low a note, she discontinued the strain. It was an error of which she was likely to become more sensible, as she grew older and saw more of Society; certainly she never repeated it by placing the heroine of any subsequent work under circumstances likely to be unfavourable to the refinement of a lady.

J. E. Austen Leigh

CHAPTER I

The first winter assembly in the town of D——, in Surrey, was to be held on Tuesday, October 13th, and it was generally expected to be a very good one. A long list of county families was confidently run over as sure of attending, and sanguine hopes were entertained that the Osbornes themselves would be there. The Edwards' invitation to the Watsons followed, as a matter of course. The Edwards were people of fortune, who lived in the town and kept their coach. The Watsons inhabited a village about three miles distant, were poor and had no close carriage; and ever since there had been balls in the place, the former were accustomed to invite the latter to dress, dine, and sleep at their house on every monthly return throughout the winter. On the present occasion, as only two of Mr. Watson's children were at home, and one was always necessary as companion to himself, for he was sickly and had lost his wife, one only could profit by the kindness of their friends. Miss Emma Watson, who was very recently returned to her family from the care of an aunt who had brought her up, was to make her first public appearance in the neighbourhood; and her eldest sister, whose delight in a ball was not lessened by a ten years' enjoyment, had some merit in cheerfully undertaking to drive her and all her finery in the old chair to D—— on the important morning.

As they splashed along the dirty lane Miss Watson thus instructed and cautioned her inexperienced sister.

"I daresay it will be a very good ball, and among so many officers you will hardly want partners. You will find Mrs. Edwards' maid very willing to help you, and I would advise you to ask Mary Edwards' opinion if you are at all at a loss, for she has a very good taste. If Mr. Edwards does not lose his money at cards you will stay as late as you can wish for; if he does he will hurry you home perhaps—but you are sure of some comfortable soup. I hope you will be in good looks. I should not be surprised if you were to be thought one of the prettiest girls in the room, there is a great deal in novelty. Perhaps Tom Musgrave may take notice of you, but I would advise you by all means not to give him any encouragement. He generally pays attention to every new girl, but he is a great flirt, and never means anything serious."

"I think I have heard you speak of him before," said Emma. "Who is he?"

"A young man of very good fortune, quite independent, and remarkably agreeable, an universal favourite wherever he goes. Most of the girls hereabouts are in love with him, or have been. I believe I am the only one among them that have escaped with a whole heart; and yet I was the first he paid attention to when he came into this country six years ago; and very great attention did he pay me. Some people say that he has never seemed to like any girl so well since, though he is always behaving in a particular way to one or another."

"And how came *your* heart to be the only cold one?" asked Emma, smiling.

"There was a reason for that," replied Miss Watson, changing colour. "I have not been very well used among them, Emma. I hope you will have better luck."

"Dear sister, I beg your pardon, if I have unthinkingly given you pain."

"When we first knew Tom Musgrave," continued Miss Watson, without seeming to hear her, "I was very much attached to a young man of the name of Purvis, a particular friend of Robert's, who used to be with us a great deal. Everybody thought it would have been a match."

A sigh accompanied these words, which Emma respected in silence. But her sister, after a short pause, went on.

"You will naturally ask why it did not take place, and why he is married to another woman, while I am still single. But you must ask him—not me—you must ask Penelope. Yes, Emma,

Penelope was at the bottom of it all. She thinks everything fair for a husband. I trusted her: she set him against me, with a view of gaining him herself, and it ended in his discontinuing his visits, and, soon after, marrying somebody else. Penelope makes light of her conduct, but *I* think such treachery very bad. It has been the ruin of my happiness. I shall never love any man as I loved Purvis. I do not think Tom Musgrave should be named with him in the same day."

"You quite shock me by what you say of Penelope," said Emma. "Could a sister do such a thing? Rivalry, treachery between sisters! I shall be afraid of being acquainted with her. But I hope it was not so; appearances were against her."

"You do not know Penelope. There is nothing she would not do to get married. She would as good as tell you so herself. Do not trust her with any secrets of your own, take warning by me, do not trust her; she has her good qualities, but she has no faith, no honour, no scruples, if she can promote her own advantage. I wish with all my heart she was well married. I declare I had rather have her well married than myself."

"Than yourself! Yes, I can suppose so. A heart wounded like yours can have little inclination for matrimony."

"Not much, indeed—but you know we must marry."

"I could do very well single for my own part."

"A little company, and a pleasant ball now and then, would be enough for me, if one could be young for ever; but my father cannot provide for us, and it is very bad to grow old and be poor and laughed at. I have lost Purvis, it is true; but very few people marry their first loves. I should not refuse a man because he was not Purvis. Not that I can ever quite forgive Penelope."

Emma shook her head in acquiescence.

"Penelope, however, has had her troubles," continued Miss Watson. "She was sadly disappointed in Tom Musgrave, who afterwards transferred his attentions from me to her, and whom she was very fond of, but he never means anything serious, and when he had trifled with her long enough, he began to slight her for Margaret, and poor Penelope was very wretched. And since then she has been trying to make some match at Chichester—she won't tell us with whom, but I believe it is a rich old Dr. Harding, uncle to the friend she goes to see; and she has taken a vast deal of trouble about him, and given up a great deal of time to no purpose as yet. When she went away the other day, she said it should be the last time. I suppose you did not know what her particular business was at Chichester, nor guess at the object which could take her away from Stanton just as you were coming home after so many years' absence."

"No, indeed, I had not the smallest suspicion of it. I considered her engagement to Mrs. Shaw just at that time as very unfortunate for me. I had hoped to find all my sisters at home, to be able to make an immediate friend of each."

"I suspect the Doctor to have had an attack of the asthma, and that she was hurried away on that account. The Shaws are quite on her side—at least I believe so; but she tells me nothing. She professes to keep her own counsel; she says, and truly enough, that 'Too many cooks spoil the broth.'"

"I am sorry for her anxieties," said Emma, "but I do not like her plans or her opinions. I shall be afraid of her. She must have too masculine and bold a temper. To be so bent on marriage—to pursue a man merely for the sake of situation, is a sort of thing that shocks me; I cannot understand it. Poverty is a great evil; but to a woman of education and feeling it ought not, it cannot be, the greatest. I would rather be teacher at a school—and I can think of nothing worse—than marry a man I did not like."

"I would rather do anything than be teacher at a school," said her sister. "*I* have been at school, Emma, and know what a life they lead; *you* never have. I should not like marrying a disagreeable man any more than yourself, but I do not think there *are* many very disagreeable men; I think I could like any good-humoured man with a comfortable income. I suppose my aunt brought you up to be rather refined."

"Indeed, I do not know. My conduct must tell you how I have been brought up. I am no judge of it myself. I cannot compare my aunt's method with any other person's, because I know no other."

"But I can see in a great many things that you are very refined. I have observed it ever since you came home, and I am afraid it will not be for your happiness. Penelope will laugh at you very much."

"That will not be for my happiness, I am sure. If my opinions are wrong I must correct them; if they are above my situation, I must endeavour to conceal them; but I doubt whether ridicule—has Penelope much wit?"

"Yes, she has great spirit, and never cares what she says."

"Margaret is more gentle, I imagine?"

"Yes, especially in company; she is all gentleness and mildness when anybody is by. But she is a little fretful and perverse among ourselves. Poor creature! She is possessed with the notion of Tom Musgrave's being more seriously in love with her than he ever was with anybody else, and is always expecting him to come to the point. This is the second time within this twelvemonth that she has gone to spend a month with Robert and Jane on purpose to egg him on by her absence; but I am sure she is mistaken, and that he will no more follow her to Croydon now than he did last March. He will never marry unless he can marry somebody very great; Miss Osborne, perhaps, or somebody in that style."

"Your account of this Tom Musgrave, Elizabeth, gives me very little inclination for his acquaintance."

"You are afraid of him; I do not wonder at you."

"No, indeed, I dislike and despise him."

"Dislike and despise Tom Musgrave! No, *that* you never can. I defy you not to be delighted with him if he takes notice of you. I hope he will dance with you, and I daresay he will, unless the Osbornes come with a large party, and then he will not speak to anybody else."

"He seems to have most engaging manners!" said Emma. "Well, we shall see how irresistible Mr. Tom Musgrave and I find each other. I suppose I shall know him as soon as I enter the ball-room: he *must* carry some of his charms in his face."

"You will not find him in the ball-room, I can tell you; you will go early, that Mrs. Edwards may get a good place by the fire, and he never comes till late; if the Osbornes are coming, he will wait in the passage and come in with them. I should like to look in upon you, Emma. If it was but a good day with my father, I would wrap myself up, and James should drive me over as soon as I had made tea for him, and I should be with you by the time the dancing began."

"What! Would you come late at night in this chair?"

"To be sure I would. There, I said you were very refined, and that's an instance of it."

Emma for a moment made no answer. At last she said—

"I wish, Elizabeth, you had not made a point of my going to this ball; I wish you were going instead of me. Your pleasure would be greater than mine. I am a stranger here, and know nobody but the Edwards; my enjoyment, therefore, must be very doubtful. Yours, among all your acquaintances, would be certain. It is not too late to change. Very little apology would be requisite to the Edwards, who must be more glad of your company than of mine; and I should most readily return to my father, and should not be at all afraid to drive this quiet old creature home. Your clothes I would undertake to find means of sending to you."

"My dearest Emma," cried Elizabeth, warmly. "Do you think I would do such a thing? Not for the universe! But I shall never forget your good-nature in proposing it. You must have a sweet temper indeed! I never met anything like it! And would you really give up the ball that I might be able to go to it? Believe me, Emma, I am not so selfish as that comes to. No; though I am nine years older than you are, I would not be the means of keeping you from being seen. You are very pretty, and it would be very hard that you should not have as fair a chance as we have all had to make your fortune. No, Emma; whoever stays at home this winter, it shan't be you. I am sure I should never have forgiven the person who kept me from a ball at nineteen."

Emma expressed her gratitude, and for a few minutes they jogged on in silence. Elizabeth first spoke—

"You will take notice who Mary Edwards dances with?"

"I will remember her partners, if I can; but you know they will be all strangers to me."

"Only observe whether she dances with Captain Hunter more than once—I have my fears in that quarter. Not that her father or mother like officers; but if she does, you know, it is all over with poor Sam. And I have promised to write him word who she dances with."

"Is Sam attached to Miss Edwards?"

"Did not you know *that*?"

"How should I know it? How should I know in Shropshire what is passing of that nature in Surrey? It is not likely that circumstances of such delicacy should have made any part of the scanty communication which passed between you and me for the last fourteen years."

"I wonder I never mentioned it when I wrote. Since you have been at home, I have been so busy with my poor father, and our great wash, that I have had no leisure to tell you anything; but, indeed, I concluded you knew it all. He has been very much in love with her these two years, and it is a great disappointment to him that he cannot always get away to our balls; but Mr. Curtis won't often spare him, and just now it is a sickly time at Guildford."

"Do you suppose Miss Edwards inclined to like him?"

"I am afraid not; you know, she is an only child, and will have at least ten thousand pounds."

"But, still, she may like our brother."

"Oh, no! The Edwards look much higher. Her father and mother would never consent to it. Sam is only a surgeon, you know. Sometimes I think she does like him. But Mary Edwards is rather prim and reserved; I do not always know what she would be at."

"Unless Sam feels on sure grounds with the lady herself, it seems a pity to me that he should be encouraged to think of her at all."

"A young man must think of somebody," said Elizabeth; "and why should not he be as lucky as Robert, who has got a good wife and six thousand pounds?"

"We must not all expect to be individually lucky," replied Emma. "The luck of one member of a family is luck to all."

"Mine is all to come, I am sure," said Elizabeth, giving another sigh to the remembrance of Purvis. "I have been unlucky enough, and I cannot say much for you, as my aunt married again so foolishly. Well, you will have a good ball, I daresay. The next turning will bring us to the turnpike; you may see the church-tower over the hedge, and the 'White Hart' is close by it. I shall long to know what you think of Tom Musgrave."

Such were the last audible sounds of Miss Watson's voice, before they passed through the turnpike-gate and entered on the pitching of the town, the jumbling and noise of which made further conversation most thoroughly undesirable. The old mare trotted heavily on, wanting no direction of the reins to take a right turning; and making only one blunder, in proposing to stop at the milliner's, before she drew up towards Mr. Edwards' door. Mr. Edwards lived in the best house in the street, and the best in the place; if Mr. Tomlinson, the banker, might be indulged in calling his newly-erected house at the end of the town, with a shrubbery and sweep, in the country.

Mr. Edwards' house was higher than most of its neighbours, with four windows on each side the door; the windows guarded by posts and chains, and the door approached by a flight of stone steps.

"Here we are," said Elizabeth, as the carriage ceased moving, "safely arrived; and by the market clock we have been only five-and-thirty minutes coming; which, I think, is doing pretty well, though it would be nothing for Penelope. Is not it a nice town? The Edwards have a noble house, you see, and they live quite in style. The door will be opened by a man in livery, with a powdered head, I can tell you."

CHAPTER II

Emma had seen the Edwards only one morning at Stanton; they were therefore all but strangers to her, and though her spirits were by no means insensible to the expected joys of the evening, she felt a little uncomfortable in the thought of all that was to precede them. Her conversation with Elizabeth, too, giving her some very unpleasant feelings with respect to her own family, had made her more open to disagreeable impressions from any other cause, and increased her sense of the awkwardness of rushing into intimacy on so slight an acquaintance.

There was nothing in the manner of Mrs. and Miss Edwards to give immediate change to these ideas. The mother, though a very friendly woman, had a reserved air and a great deal of formal civility; and the daughter, a genteel-looking girl of twenty-two, with her hair in papers, seemed very naturally to have caught something of the style of her mother, who had brought her up. Emma was soon left to know what they could be, by Elizabeth being obliged to hurry away; and some very languid remarks on the probable brilliancy of the ball were all that broke, at intervals, a silence of half-an-hour before they were joined by the master of the house. Mr. Edwards had a much easier and more communicative air than the ladies of the family; he was fresh from the street, and he came ready to tell whatever might interest. After a cordial reception of Emma, he turned to his daughter with—

"Well, Mary, I bring you good news: the Osbornes will certainly be at the ball to-night. Horses for two carriages are ordered from the 'White Hart' to be at Osborne Castle by nine."

"I am glad of it," observed Mrs. Edwards, "because their coming gives a credit to our assembly. The Osbornes being known to have been at the first ball, will dispose a great many people to attend the second. It is more than they deserve, for, in fact, they add nothing to the pleasure of the evening; they come so late and go so early; but great people have always their charm."

Mr. Edwards proceeded to relate many other little articles of news which his morning's lounge had supplied him with, and they chatted with greater briskness till Mrs. Edwards' moment for dressing arrived, and the young ladies were carefully recommended to lose no time. Emma was shown to a very comfortable apartment, and as soon as Mrs. Edwards' civilities could leave her to herself, the happy occupation, the first bliss of a ball, began. The girls, dressing in some measure together, grew unavoidably better acquainted. Emma found in Miss Edwards the show of good sense, a modest unpretending mind, and a great wish of obliging; and when they returned to the parlour where Mrs. Edwards was sitting, respectably attired in one of the two satin gowns which went through the winter, and a new cap from the milliner's, they entered it with much easier feelings and more natural smiles than they had taken away. Their dress was now to be examined: Mrs. Edwards acknowledged herself too old-fashioned to approve of every modern extravagance, however sanctioned; and though complacently viewing her daughter's good looks, would give but a qualified admiration; and Mr. Edwards, not less satisfied with Mary, paid some compliments of good-humoured gallantry to Emma at her expense.

The discussion led to more intimate remarks, and Miss Edwards gently asked Emma if she was not often reckoned very like her youngest brother. Emma thought she could perceive a faint blush accompany the question, and there seemed something still more suspicious in the manner in which Mr. Edwards took up the subject.

"You are paying Miss Emma no great compliment, I think, Mary," said he hastily. "Mr. Sam Watson is a very good sort of young man, and I daresay a very clever surgeon; but his complexion has been rather too much exposed to all weathers to make a likeness to him very flattering."

Mary apologised, in some confusion—

"She had not thought a strong likeness at all incompatible with very different degrees of beauty. There might be resemblance in countenance, and the complexion, and even the features, be very unlike."

"I know nothing of my brother's beauty," said Emma, "for I have not seen him since he was seven years old; but my father reckons us alike."

"Mr. Watson!" cried Mr. Edwards, "well, you astonish me. There is not the least likeness in the world; your brother's eyes are grey, yours are brown; he has a long face, and a wide mouth. My dear, do *you* perceive the least resemblance?"

"Not the least; Miss Emma Watson puts me very much in mind of her eldest sister, and sometimes I see a look of Miss Penelope, and once or twice there has been a glance of Mr. Robert; but I cannot perceive any likeness to Mr. Samuel."

"I see the likeness between her and Miss Watson," replied Mr. Edwards, "very strongly, but I am not sensible of the others. I do not much think she is like any of the family *but* Miss Watson; but I am very sure there is no resemblance between her and Sam."

This matter was settled, and they went to dinner.

"Your father, Miss Emma, is one of my oldest friends," said Mr. Edwards, as he helped her to wine, when they were drawn round the fire to enjoy their dessert. "We must drink to his better health. It is a great concern to me, I assure you, that he should be such an invalid. I know nobody who likes a game of cards, in a social way, better than he does, and very few people who play a fairer rubber. It is a thousand pities that he should be so deprived of the pleasure. For now, we have a quiet little whist club, that meets three times a week at the 'White Hart'; and if he could but have his health, how much he would enjoy it!"

"I daresay he would, sir; and I wish, with all my heart, he were equal to it."

"Your club would be better fitted for an invalid," said Mrs. Edwards, "if you did not keep it up so late." This was an old grievance.

"So late, my dear! What are you talking of?" cried her husband with sturdy pleasantry. "We are always at home before midnight. They would laugh at Osborne Castle to hear you call *that* late. They are but just rising from dinner at midnight."

"That is nothing to the purpose," retorted the lady calmly. "The Osbornes are to be no rule for us. You had better meet every night and break up two hours sooner."

So far the subject was very often carried; but Mr. and Mrs. Edwards were so wise as never to pass that point; and Mr. Edwards now turned to something else. He had lived long enough in the idleness of a town to become a little of a gossip, and having some anxiety to know more of the circumstances of his young guest than had yet reached him, he began with—

"I think, Miss Emma, I remember your aunt very well, about thirty years ago; I am pretty sure I danced with her in the old rooms at Bath the year before I married. She was a very fine woman then, but like other people, I suppose, she is grown somewhat older since that time. I hope she is likely to be happy in her second choice."

"I hope so; I believe so, sir," said Emma, in some agitation.

"Mr. Turner had not been dead a great while, I think?"

"About two years, sir."

"I forget what her name is now."

"O'Brien."

"Irish! Ah, I remember; and she is gone to settle in Ireland. I do not wonder that you should not wish to go with her into *that* country, Miss Emma; but it must be a great deprivation to her, poor lady! after bringing you up like a child of her own."

"I was not so ungrateful, sir," said Emma, warmly, "as to wish to be anywhere but with her. It did not suit Captain O'Brien that I should be of the party."

"Captain!" repeated Mrs. Edwards. "The gentleman is in the army, then?"

"Yes, ma'am."

"Aye, there is nothing like your officers for captivating the ladies, young or old. There is no resisting a cockade, my dear."

"I hope there is," said Mrs. Edwards gravely, with a quick glance at her daughter; and Emma had just recovered from her own perturbation in time to see a blush on Miss Edwards' cheek; and, in remembering what Elizabeth had said of Captain Hunter, to wonder and waver between his influence and her brother's.

"Elderly ladies should be careful how they make a second choice," observed Mr. Edwards.

"Carefulness and discretion should not be confined to elderly ladies, or to a second choice," added his wife. "They are quite as necessary to young ladies in their first."

"Rather more so, my dear," replied he; "because young ladies are likely to feel the effects of it longer. When an old lady plays the fool, it is not in the course of nature that she should suffer from it many years."

Emma drew her hand across her eyes; and Mrs. Edwards, in perceiving it, changed the subject to one of less anxiety to all.

With nothing to do but to expect the hour of setting off, the afternoon was long to the two young ladies; and though Miss Edwards was rather discomposed at the very early hour which her mother always fixed for going, that early hour itself was watched for with some eagerness. The entrance of the tea-things at seven o'clock was some relief; and, luckily, Mr. and Mrs. Edwards always drank a dish extraordinary and ate an additional muffin when they were going to sit up late, which lengthened the ceremony almost to the wished-for moment.

At a little before eight o'clock the Tomlinsons' carriage was heard to go by, which was the constant signal for Mrs. Edwards to order hers to the door; and in a very few minutes the party were transported from the quiet and warmth of a snug parlour to the bustle, noise, and draughts of air of a broad entrance passage of an inn. Mrs. Edwards, carefully guarding her own dress, while she attended to the proper security of her young charges' shoulders and throats, led the way up the wide staircase, while no sound of a ball, but the first scrape of one violin, blessed the ears of her followers; and Miss Edwards, on hazarding the anxious enquiry of whether there were many people come yet, was told by the waiter, as she knew she should be, that Mr. Tomlinson's family were in the room.

In passing along a short gallery to the assembly room, brilliant in lights before them, they were accosted by a young man in a morning dress and boots, who was standing in the doorway of a bedchamber apparently on purpose to see them go by.

"Ah! Mrs. Edwards, how do you do? How do you do, Miss Edwards?" he cried, with an easy air. "You are determined to be in good time, I see, as usual. The candles are but this moment lit."

"I like to get a good seat by the fire, you know, Mr. Musgrave," replied Mrs. Edwards.

"I am this moment going to dress," said he. "I am waiting for my stupid fellow. We shall have a famous ball. The Osbornes are certainly coming; you may depend upon *that*, for I was with Lord Osborne this morning."

The party passed on. Mrs. Edwards' satin gown swept along the clean floor of the ball-room to the fireplace at the upper end, where one party only were formally seated, while three or four officers were lounging together, passing in and out from the adjoining card-room. A very stiff meeting between these near neighbours ensued, and as soon as they were all duly placed again, Emma, in a low whisper, which became the solemn scene, said to Miss Edwards—

"The gentleman we passed in the passage was Mr. Musgrave, then; he is reckoned remarkably agreeable, I understand?"

Miss Edwards answered hesitatingly: "Yes, he is very much liked by many people; but we are not very intimate."

"He is rich, is not he?"

"He has about eight or nine hundred a year, I believe. He came into possession of it when he was very young, and my father and mother think it has given him rather an unsettled turn. He is no favourite with them."

The cold and empty appearance of the room, and the demure air of the small cluster of females at one end of it, began soon to give way. The inspiriting sound of other carriages was heard, and continual accessions of portly chaperones, and strings of smartly dressed girls, were received, with now and then a fresh gentleman straggler, who, if not enough in love to station himself near any fair creature, seemed glad to escape into the card-room.

Among the increasing number of military men, one now made his way to Miss Edwards with an air of *empressement* which decidedly said to her companion: "I am Captain Hunter"; and Emma, who could not but watch her at such a moment, saw her looking rather distressed, but by no means displeased, and heard an engagement formed for the two first dances, which made her think her brother Sam's a hopeless case.

Emma, in the meanwhile, was not unobserved or unadmired herself. A new face, and a very pretty one, could not be slighted. Her name was whispered from one party to another, and no sooner had the signal been given by the orchestra's striking up a favourite air, which seemed to call the young to their duty, and people the centre of the room, than she found herself engaged to dance with a brother officer, introduced by Captain Hunter.

Emma Watson was not more than of the middle height, well made and plump, with an air of healthy vigour. Her skin was very brown, but clear, smooth, and glowing; which, with a lively eye, a sweet smile, and an open countenance, gave beauty to attract, and expression to make that beauty improve on acquaintance. Having no reason to be dissatisfied with her partner, the evening began very pleasantly to her, and her feelings perfectly coincided with the reiterated observation of others, that it was an excellent ball. The two first dances were not quite over when the returning sound of carriages, after a long interruption, called general notice—"the Osbornes are coming!" was repeated round the room. After some minutes of extraordinary bustle without, and watchful curiosity within, the important party, preceded by the attentive master of the inn to open a door which was never shut, made their appearance. They consisted of Lady Osborne; her son, Lord Osborne; her daughter, Miss Osborne; Miss Carr, her daughter's friend; Mr. Howard, formerly tutor to Lord Osborne, now clergyman of the parish in which the castle stood; Mrs. Blake, a widow sister, who lived with him; her son, a fine boy of ten years old; and Mr. Tom Musgrave, who probably, imprisoned within his own room, had been listening in bitter impatience to the sound of music for the last half-hour. In their progress up the room they paused almost immediately behind Emma to receive the compliments of some acquaintance, and she heard Lady Osborne observe that they had made a point of coming early for the gratification of Mrs. Blake's little boy, who was uncommonly fond of dancing. Emma looked at them all as they passed, but chiefly and with most interest on Tom Musgrave, who was certainly a genteel, good-looking young man. Of the females, Lady Osborne had by much the finest person; though nearly fifty, she was very handsome, and had all the dignity of rank.

Lord Osborne was a very fine young man; but there was an air of coldness, of carelessness, even of awkwardness about him, which seemed to speak him out of his element in a ball-room. He came, in fact, only because it was judged expedient for him to please the borough; he was not fond of women's company, and he never danced. Mr. Howard was an agreeable-looking man, a little more than thirty.

At the conclusion of the two dances, Emma found herself, she knew not how, seated amongst the Osbornes' set; and she was immediately struck with the fine countenance and animated gestures of the little boy, as he was standing before his mother, considering when they should begin.

"You will not be surprised at Charles's impatience," said Mrs. Blake, a lively, pleasant-looking little woman of five- or six-and-thirty, to a lady who was standing near her, "when you know what a partner he is to have. Miss Osborne has been so very kind as to promise to dance the two first dances with him."

"Oh, yes! we have been engaged this week," cried the boy, "and we are to dance down every couple."

On the other side of Emma, Miss Osborne, Miss Carr, and a party of young men were standing engaged in a very lively consultation; and soon afterwards she saw the smartest officer of the set walking off to the orchestra to order the dance, while Miss Osborne, passing before her to her little expecting partner, hastily said: "Charles, I beg your pardon for not keeping my engagement, but I am going to dance these two dances with Colonel Beresford. I know you will excuse me, and I will certainly dance with you after tea"; and without staying for an answer, she turned again to Miss Carr, and in another minute was led by Colonel Beresford to begin the set. If the poor little boy's face had in its happiness been interesting to Emma, it was infinitely more so under this sudden reverse; he stood the picture of disappointment with crimsoned cheeks, quivering lips, and eyes bent on the floor. His mother, stifling her own mortification, tried to soothe him with the prospect of Miss Osborne's second promise; but, though he contrived to utter with an effort of boyish bravery, "Oh, I do not mind it!" it was very evident by the unceasing agitation of his features that he minded it as much as ever.

Emma did not think or reflect; she felt and acted. "I shall be very happy to dance with you, sir, if you like it," said she, holding out her hand with the most unaffected good-humour. The boy, in one moment restored to all his first delight, looked joyfully at his mother; and stepping forwards with an honest, simple "Thank you, ma'am," was instantly ready to attend his new acquaintance. The thankfulness of Mrs. Blake was more diffuse; with a look most expressive of unexpected pleasure and lively gratitude, she turned to her neighbour with repeated and fervent acknowledgments of so great and condescending a kindness to her boy. Emma, with perfect truth, assured her that she could not be giving greater pleasure than she felt herself; and Charles, being provided with his gloves and charged to keep them on, they joined the set which was now rapidly forming, with nearly equal complacency. It was a partnership which could not be noticed without surprise. It gained her a broad stare from Miss Osborne and Miss Carr, as they passed her in the dance. "Upon my word, Charles, you are in luck," said the former, as she turned him; "you have got a better partner than me"; to which the happy Charles answered "Yes."

Tom Musgrave, who was dancing with Miss Carr, gave her many inquisitive glances; and after a time Lord Osborne himself came, and under pretence of talking to Charles, stood to look at his partner. Though rather distressed by such observation, Emma could not repent what she had done, so happy had it made both the boy and his mother; the latter of whom was continually making opportunities of addressing her with the warmest civility. Her little partner she found, though bent chiefly on dancing, was not unwilling to speak, when her questions or remarks gave him anything to say; and she learnt, by a sort of inevitable enquiry, that he had two brothers and a sister, that they and their mamma all lived with his uncle at Wickstead, that his uncle taught him Latin, that he was very fond of riding, and had a horse of his own given him by Lord Osborne; and that he had been out once already with Lord Osborne's hounds.

At the end of these dances, Emma found they were to drink tea; Miss Edwards gave her a caution to be at hand, in a manner which convinced her of Mrs. Edwards' holding it very important to have them both close to her when she moved into the tea-room; and Emma was accordingly on the alert to gain her proper station.

It was always the pleasure of the company to have a little bustle and crowd when they adjourned for refreshment. The tea-room was a small room within the card-room; and in passing through the latter, where the passage was straitened by tables, Mrs. Edwards and her party were for a few moments hemmed in. It happened close by Lady Osborne's casino table; Mr. Howard, who belonged to it, spoke to his nephew; and Emma, on perceiving herself the object of attention both to Lady Osborne and him, had just turned away her eyes in time to avoid seeming to hear her young companion exclaim delightedly aloud: "Oh, uncle! do look at my partner, she is so pretty!" As they were immediately in motion again, however, Charles was hurried off without being able to receive his uncle's suffrage. On entering the tea-room, in which two long tables were prepared, Lord Osborne was to be seen quite alone at the end of one, as if retreating as far as he could from the ball, to enjoy his own thoughts and gape without restraint. Charles instantly pointed him out to Emma. "There's Lord Osborne; let you and I go and sit by him."

"No, no," said Emma laughing, "you must sit with my friends."

Charles was now free enough to hazard a few questions in his turn. "What o'clock was it?"

"Eleven."

"Eleven! and I am not at all sleepy. Mamma said I should be asleep before ten. Do you think Miss Osborne will keep her word with me when tea is over?"

"Oh, yes; I suppose so," though she felt that she had no better reason to give than that Miss Osborne had *not* kept it before.

"When shall you come to Osborne Castle?"

"Never, probably. I am not acquainted with the family."

"But you may come to Wickstead and see mamma, and she can take you to the castle. There is a monstrous curious stuffed fox there, and a badger; anybody would think they were alive. It is a pity you should not see them."

On rising from tea there was again a scramble for the pleasure of being first out of the room, which happened to be increased by one or two of the card-parties having just broken up, and the players being disposed to move exactly the different way. Among these was Mr. Howard, his sister leaning on his arm; and no sooner were they within reach of Emma, than Mrs. Blake, calling her notice by a friendly touch, said: "Your goodness to Charles, my dear Miss Watson, brings all his family upon you. Give me leave to introduce my brother." Emma curtsied, the gentleman bowed, made a hasty request for the honour of her hand in the two next dances, to which as hasty an affirmative was given, and they were immediately impelled in opposite directions. Emma was very well pleased with the circumstance; there was a quietly cheerful, gentlemanlike air in Mr. Howard, which suited her; and in a few minutes afterwards the value of her engagement increased when, as she was sitting in the card-room, somewhat screened by a door, she heard Lord Osborne, who was lounging on a vacant table near her, call Tom Musgrave towards him and say: "Why do not you dance with that beautiful Emma Watson? I want you to dance with her, and I will come and stand by you."

"I was determined on it this very moment, my lord; I'll be introduced and dance with her directly."

"Aye, do; and if you find she does not want much talking to, you may introduce me by-and-by."

"Very well, my lord; if she is like her sisters, she will only want to be listened to. I will go this moment. I shall find her in the tea-room. That stiff old Mrs. Edwards has never done tea."

Away he went, Lord Osborne after him; and Emma lost no time in hurrying from her corner exactly the other way, forgetting in her haste that she left Mrs. Edwards behind.

"We had quite lost you," said Mrs. Edwards, who followed in less than five minutes. "If you prefer this room to the other, there is no reason why you should not be here; but we had better all be together."

Emma was saved the trouble of apologising, by their being joined at the moment by Tom Musgrave, who, requesting Mrs. Edwards aloud to do him the honour of presenting him to Miss Emma Watson, left that good lady without any choice in the business, but that of testifying by the coldness of her manner that she did it unwillingly. The honour of dancing with her was solicited without loss of time; and Emma, however she might like to be thought a beautiful girl by lord or commoner, was so little disposed to favour Tom Musgrave himself, that she had considerable satisfaction in avowing her previous engagement. He was evidently surprised and discomposed. The style of her last partner had probably led him to believe her not overpowered with applications.

"My little friend, Charles Blake," he cried, "must not expect to engross you the whole evening. We can never suffer this. It is against the rules of the assembly, and I am sure it will never be patronised by our good friend here, Mrs. Edwards; she is by much too nice a judge of decorum to give her licence to such a dangerous particularity——"

"I am not going to dance with Master Blake, sir!"

The gentleman, a little disconcerted, could only hope he might be fortunate another time; and seeming unwilling to leave her, though his friend, Lord Osborne, was waiting in the doorway for the result, as Emma with some amusement perceived, he began to make civil enquiries after her family.

"How comes it that we have not the pleasure of seeing your sisters here this evening? Our assemblies have been used to be so well treated by them that we do not know how to take this neglect."

"My eldest sister is the only one at home, and she could not leave my father."

"Miss Watson the only one at home! You astonish me! It seems but the day before yesterday that I saw them all three in the town. But I am afraid I have been a very sad neighbour of late. I hear dreadful complaints of my negligence wherever I go, and I confess it is a shameful length of time since I was at Stanton. But I shall *now* endeavour to make myself amends for the past."

Emma's calm curtsey in reply must have struck him as very unlike the encouraging warmth he had been used to receive from her sisters; and gave him probably the novel sensation of doubting his own influence, and of wishing for more attention than she bestowed. The dancing now recommenced. Miss Carr being impatient to *call*, everybody was required to stand up; and Tom Musgrave's curiosity was appeased on seeing Mr. Howard come forward and claim Emma's hand.

"That will do as well for me," was Lord Osborne's remark, when his friend carried him the news, and he was continually at Howard's elbow during the two dances.

The frequency of his appearance there was the only unpleasant part of the engagement, the only objection she could make to Mr. Howard. In himself, she thought him as agreeable as he looked; though chatting on the commonest topics, he had a sensible, unaffected way of expressing himself, which made whatever he said worth hearing, and she only regretted that he had not been able to make his pupil's manners as unexceptionable as his own. The two dances seemed very short, and she had her partner's authority for considering them so. At their conclusion, the Osbornes and their train were all on the move.

"We are off at last," said his lordship to Tom. "How much longer do you stay in this heavenly place?—till sunrise?"

"No, faith! my lord; I have had quite enough of it, I assure you. I shall not show myself here again when I have had the honour of attending Lady Osborne to her carriage. I shall retreat in as much secrecy as possible to the most remote corner of the house, where I shall order a barrel of oysters, and be famously snug."

"Let me see you soon at the castle, and bring me word how she looks by daylight."

Emma and Mrs. Blake parted as old acquaintance; and Charles shook her by the hand and wished her good-bye at least a dozen times. From Miss Osborne and Miss Carr she received something like a jerking curtsey as they passed her; even Lady Osborne gave her a look of complacency, and his lordship actually came back after the others were out of the room, to "beg her pardon," and look in the window-seat behind her for the gloves which were visibly compressed in his hand. As Tom Musgrave was seen no more, we may suppose his plan to have succeeded, and imagine him mortifying with his barrel of oysters in dreary solitude, or gladly assisting the landlady in her bar to make fresh negus for the happy dancers above. Emma could not help missing the party by whom she had been, though in some respects unpleasantly, distinguished; and the two dances which followed and concluded the ball were rather flat in comparison with the others. Mr. Edwards having played with good luck, they were some of the last in the room.

"Here we are back again, I declare," said Emma sorrowfully, as she walked into the dining-room, where the table was prepared, and the neat upper maid was lighting the candles.

"My dear Miss Edwards, how soon it is at an end! I wish it could all come over again."

A great deal of kind pleasure was expressed in her having enjoyed the evening so much; and Mr. Edwards was as warm as herself in the praise of the fulness, brilliancy, and spirit of the meeting; though as he had been fixed the whole time at the same table in the same room, with only one change of chairs, it might have seemed a matter scarcely perceived; but he had won four rubbers out of five, and everything went well. His daughter felt the advantage of this gratified state of mind in the course of the remarks and retrospections which now ensued over the welcome soup.

"How came you not to dance with either of the Mr. Tomlinsons, Mary?" said her mother.

"I was always engaged when they asked me."

"I thought you were to have stood up with Mr. James the two last dances; Mrs. Tomlinson told me he was gone to ask you, and I had heard you say two minutes before that you were *not* engaged?"

"Yes, but there was a mistake; I had misunderstood. I did not know I was engaged. I thought it had been for the two dances after, if we stayed so long; but Captain Hunter assured me it was for those very two."

"So you ended with Captain Hunter, Mary, did you?" said her father. "And whom did you begin with?"

"Captain Hunter," was repeated in a very humble tone.

"Hum! That is being constant, however. But who else did you dance with?"

"Mr. Norton and Mr. Styles."

"And who are they?"

"Mr. Norton is a cousin of Captain Hunter's."

"And who is Mr. Styles?"

"One of his particular friends."

"All in the same regiment," added Mrs. Edwards. "Mary was surrounded by redcoats all the evening. I should have been better pleased to see her dancing with some of our old neighbours, I confess."

"Yes, yes; we must not neglect our old neighbours. But if these soldiers are quicker than other people in a ball-room, what are young ladies to do?"

"I think there is no occasion for their engaging themselves so many dances beforehand, Mr. Edwards."

"No, perhaps not; but I remember, my dear, when you and I did the same."

Mrs. Edwards said no more, and Mary breathed again. A good deal of good-humoured pleasantry followed, and Emma went to bed in charming spirits, her head full of Osbornes, Blakes, and Howards.

CHAPTER III

The next morning brought a great many visitors. It was the way of the place always to call on Mrs. Edwards the morning after a ball, and this neighbourly inclination was increased in the present instance by a general spirit of curiosity on Emma's account, as everybody wanted to look again at the girl who had been admired the night before by Lord Osborne. Many were the eyes, and various the degrees of approbation, with which she was examined. Some saw no fault, and some no beauty. With some, her brown skin was the annihilation of every grace, and others could never be persuaded that she was half so handsome as Elizabeth Watson had been ten years ago. The morning passed quickly away in discussing the merits of the ball with all this succession of company, and Emma was at once astonished by finding it two o'clock, and considering that she had heard nothing of her father's chair. After this discovery she had walked twice to the window to examine the street, and was on the point of asking leave to ring the bell and make enquiries, when the light sound of a carriage driving up to the door set her heart at ease. She stepped again to the window, but instead of the convenient though very un-smart family equipage, perceived a neat curricle. Mr. Musgrave was shortly afterwards announced, and Mrs. Edwards put on her very stiffest look at the sound. Not at all dismayed, however, by her chilling air, he paid his compliments to each of the ladies with no unbecoming ease, and continuing to address Emma, presented her a note, which "he had the honour of bringing from her sister, but to which, he must observe, a verbal postscript from himself would be requisite."

The note, which Emma was beginning to read rather before Mrs. Edwards had entreated her to use no ceremony, contained a few lines from Elizabeth importing that their father, in consequence of being unusually well, had taken the sudden resolution of attending the visitation that day; and that as his road lay quite wide from D——, it was impossible for her to come home till the following morning; unless the Edwards would send her, which was hardly to be expected, or she could meet with any chance conveyance, or did not mind walking so far. She had scarcely run her eye through the whole, before she found herself obliged to listen to Tom Musgrave's further account.

"I received that note from the fair hands of Miss Watson only ten minutes ago," said he; "I met her in the village of Stanton, whither my good stars prompted me to run my horses' heads. She was at that moment in quest of a person to employ on the errand, and I was fortunate enough to convince her that she could not find a more willing or speedy messenger than myself. Remember, I say nothing of my disinterestedness. My reward is to be the indulgence of conveying you to Stanton in my curricle. Though they are not written down, I bring your sister's orders for the same."

Emma felt distressed; she did not like the proposal—she did not wish to be on terms of intimacy with the proposer: and yet, fearful of encroaching on the Edwards, as well as wishing to go home herself, she was at a loss how entirely to decline what he offered. Mrs. Edwards continued silent, either not understanding the case, or waiting to see how the young lady's inclination lay. Emma thanked him, but professed herself very unwilling to give him so much trouble. The trouble was of course, honour, pleasure, delight—what had he or his horses to do? Still she hesitated—she believed she must beg leave to decline his assistance; she was rather afraid of the sort of carriage. The distance was not beyond a walk. Mrs. Edwards was silent no longer. She enquired into the particulars, and then said, "We shall be extremely happy, Miss Emma, if you can give us the pleasure of your company till to-morrow; but if you cannot conveniently do so, our carriage is quite at your service, and Mary will be pleased with the opportunity of seeing your sister."

This was precisely what Emma longed for, and she accepted the offer most thankfully; acknowledging that as Elizabeth was entirely alone, it was her wish to return home to dinner. The plan was warmly opposed by their visitor.

"I cannot suffer it, indeed. I must not be deprived of the happiness of escorting you. I assure you there is not a possibility of fear with my horses. You might guide them yourself. Your sisters all know how quiet they are; they have none of them the smallest scruple intrusting themselves with me, even on a racecourse. Believe me," added he, lowering his voice, "*you* are quite safe—the danger is only *mine*."

Emma was not more disposed to oblige him for all this.

"And as for Mrs. Edwards' carriage being used the day after the ball, it is a thing out of all rule, I assure you—never heard of before. The old coachman will look as black as his horses— won't he, Miss Edwards?"

No notice was taken. The ladies were silently firm, and the gentleman found himself obliged to submit.

"What a famous ball we had last night," he cried, after a short pause. "How long did you keep it up after the Osbornes and I went away?"

"We had two dances more."

"It is making it too much of a fatigue, I think, to stay so late. I suppose your set was not a very full one?"

"Yes, quite as full as ever, except the Osbornes. There seemed no vacancy anywhere; and everybody danced with uncommon spirit to the very last."

Emma said this, though against her conscience.

"Indeed! Perhaps I might have looked in upon you again, if I had been aware of as much; for I am rather fond of dancing than not. Miss Osborne is a charming girl, is not she?"

"I do not think her handsome," replied Emma, to whom all this was chiefly addressed.

"Perhaps she is not critically handsome, but her manners are delightful. And Fanny Carr is a most interesting little creature. You can imagine nothing more naïve or *piquante*; and what do you think of Lord Osborne, Miss Watson?"

"He would be handsome even though he were *not* a lord, and perhaps better himself pleased in a right place."

"Upon my word, you are severe upon my friend! I assure you Lord Osborne is a very good fellow."

"I do not dispute his virtues, but I do not like his careless air."

"If it were not a breach of confidence," replied Tom, with an important look, "perhaps I might be able to win a more favourable opinion of poor Osborne."

Emma gave him no encouragement, and he was obliged to keep his friend's secret. He was also obliged to put an end to his visit, for Mrs. Edwards having ordered her carriage, there was no time to be lost on Emma's side in preparing for it. Miss Edwards accompanied her home; but as it was dinner hour at Stanton, stayed with them only a few minutes.

"Now, my dear Emma," said Miss Watson, as soon as they were alone, "you must talk to me all the rest of the day without stopping, or I shall not be satisfied; but, first of all, Nanny shall bring in the dinner. Poor thing! You will not dine as you did yesterday, for we have nothing but some fried beef. How nice Mary Edwards looks in her new pelisse! And now tell me how you like them all, and what I am to say to Sam. I have begun my letter; Jack Stokes is to call for it to-morrow, for his uncle is going within a mile of Guildford next day."

Nanny brought in the dinner.

"We will wait upon ourselves," continued Elizabeth, "and then we shall lose no time. And so you would not come home with Tom Musgrave?"

"No, you had said so much against him that I could not wish either for the obligation or the intimacy which the use of his carriage must have created. I should not even have liked the appearance of it."

"You did very right, though I wonder at your forbearance, and I do not think I could have done it myself. He seemed so eager to fetch you that I could not say no, though it rather went against me to be throwing you together, so well as I knew his tricks; but I did long to see you, and it was a clever way of getting you home. Besides, it won't do to be too nice. Nobody could have thought of the Edwards letting you have their coach, after the horses being out so late. But what am I to say to Sam?"

"If you are guided by me you will not encourage him to think of Miss Edwards. The father is decidedly against him, the mother shows him no favour, and I doubt his having any interest with Mary. She danced twice with Captain Hunter, and I think shows him in general as much encouragement as is consistent with her disposition and the circumstances she is placed in. She once mentioned Sam, and certainly with a little confusion; but that was perhaps merely owing to the consciousness of his liking her, which may very probably have come to her knowledge.

"Oh! dear, yes. She has heard enough of *that* from us all! Poor Sam! he is out of luck as well as other people. For the life of me, Emma, I cannot help feeling for those that are crossed in love. Well, now begin and give me an account of everything as it happened."

Emma obeyed her, and Elizabeth listened with very little interruption till she heard of Mr. Howard as a partner.

"Dance with Mr. Howard. Good heavens! You don't say so! Why, he is quite one of the great and grand ones. Did you not find him very high?"

"His manners are of a kind to give me much more ease and confidence than Tom Musgrave's."

"Well, go on. I should have been frightened out of my wits to have had anything to do with the Osbornes' set."

Emma concluded her narration.

"And so you really did not dance with Tom Musgrave at all, but you must have liked him—you must have been struck with him altogether?"

"I do *not* like him, Elizabeth. I allow his person and air to be good; and that his manners to a certain point—his address rather—is pleasing. But I see nothing else to admire in him. On the contrary, he seems very vain, very conceited, absurdly anxious for distinction, and absolutely contemptible in some of the measures he takes for being so. There is a ridiculousness about him that entertains me; but his company gives me no other agreeable emotion."

"My dearest Emma! You are like nobody else in the world. It is well Margaret is not by. You do not offend *me*, though I hardly know how to believe you; but Margaret would never forgive such words."

"I wish Margaret could have heard him profess his ignorance of her being out of the country; he declared it seemed only two days since he had seen her."

"Aye, that is just like him; and yet this is the man she *will* fancy so desperately in love with her. He is no favourite of mine, as you well know, Emma; but you must think him agreeable. Can you lay your hand on your heart and say you do not?"

"Indeed I can, both hands; and spread them to their widest extent."

"I should like to know the man you *do* think agreeable."

"His name is Howard."

"Howard! Dear me, I cannot think of him but as playing cards with Lady Osborne, and looking proud. I must own, however, that it is a relief to me to find you can speak as you do of Tom Musgrave. My heart did misgive me that you would like him too well. You talked so stoutly beforehand, that I was sadly afraid your brag would be punished. I only hope it will last, and that he will not come on to pay you much attention. It is a hard thing for a woman to stand against the flattering ways of a man when he is bent upon pleasing her."

As their quietly sociable little meal concluded, Miss Watson could not help observing how comfortably it had passed.

"It is so delightful to me," said she, "to have things going on in peace and good-humour. Nobody can tell how much I hate quarrelling. Now, though we have had nothing but fried beef, how good it has all seemed. I wish everybody were as easily satisfied as you; but poor Margaret is very snappish, and Penelope owns she would rather have quarrelling going on than nothing at all."

Mr. Watson returned in the evening not the worse for the exertion of the day and, consequently, pleased with what he had done, and glad to talk of it over his own fireside. Emma had not foreseen any interest to herself in the occurrences of a visitation; but when she heard Mr. Howard spoken of as the preacher, and as having given them an excellent sermon, she could not help listening with a quicker ear.

"I do not know when I have heard a discourse more to my mind," continued Mr. Watson, "or one better delivered. He reads extremely well, with great propriety, and in a very impressive manner; and at the same time without any theatrical grimace or violence. I own I do not like much action in the pulpit; I do not like the studied air and artificial inflexions of voice which your very popular and most admired preachers generally have. A simple delivery is much better calculated to inspire devotion, and shows a much better taste. Mr. Howard read like a scholar and a gentleman."

"And what had you for dinner, sir?" said his eldest daughter.

He related the dishes, and told what he had ate himself.

"Upon the whole," he added, "I have had a very comfortable day. My old friends were quite surprised to see me amongst them, and I must say that everybody paid me great attention, and seemed to feel for me as an invalid. They would make me sit near the fire; and as the partridges were pretty high, Dr. Richards would have them sent away to the other end of the table, 'that they might not offend Mr. Watson,' which I thought very kind of him. But what pleased me as much as anything was Mr. Howard's attention. There is a pretty steep flight of steps up to the room we dine in, which do not agree with my gouty foot, and Mr. Howard walked by me from the bottom to the top, and would make me take his arm. It struck me as very becoming in so young a man, but I am sure I had no claim to expect it, for I never saw him before in my life. By the by, he enquired after one of my daughters, but I do not know which. I suppose you know among yourselves."

CHAPTER IV

On the third day after the ball, as Nanny at five minutes before three, was beginning to bustle into the parlour with the tray and knife case, she was suddenly called to the front door by the sound of as smart a rap as the end of a riding whip could give; and though charged by Miss Watson to let nobody in, returned in half a minute with a look of awkward dismay to hold the parlour door open for Lord Osborne and Tom Musgrave. The surprise of the young ladies may be imagined. No visitors would have been welcome at such a moment, but such visitors as these—such an one as Lord Osborne at least, a nobleman and a stranger, was really distressing.

He looked a little embarrassed himself, as, on being introduced by his easy voluble friend, he muttered something of doing himself the honour of waiting upon Mr. Watson. Though Emma could not but take the compliment of the visit to herself, she was very far from enjoying it. She felt all the inconsistency of such an acquaintance with the very humble style in which they were obliged to live; and having in her aunt's family been used to many of the elegancies of life, was fully sensible of all that must be open to the ridicule of richer people in her present home. Of the pain of such feelings, Elizabeth knew very little. Her simple mind or juster reason saved her from such mortification; and though shrinking under a general sense of inferiority, she felt no particular shame. Mr. Watson, as the gentlemen had already heard from Nanny, was not well enough to be down stairs. With much concern they took their seats; Lord Osborne near Emma, and the convenient Mr. Musgrave, in high spirits at his own importance, on the other side of the fireplace with Elizabeth. *He* was at no loss for words; but when Lord Osborne had hoped that Emma had not caught cold at the ball, he had nothing more to say for some time, and could only gratify his eye by occasional glances at his fair companion. Emma was not inclined to give herself much trouble for his entertainment; and after hard labour of mind, he produced the remark of its being a very fine day; and followed it up with the question of "Have you been walking this morning?"

"No, my lord, we thought it too dirty."

"You should wear half-boots." After another pause: "Nothing sets off a neat ankle more than a half-boot; nankeen, goloshed with black, looks very well. Do not you like half-boots?"

"Yes; but unless they are so stout as to injure their beauty, they are not fit for country walking."

"Ladies should ride in dirty weather. Do you ride?"

"No, my lord."

"I wonder every lady does not; a woman never looks better than on horseback."

"But every woman may not have the inclination or the means."

"If they knew how much it became them, they would all have the inclination; and I fancy, Miss Watson, when once they had the inclination, the means would soon follow."

"Your lordship thinks we always have our own way. *That* is a point on which ladies and gentlemen have long disagreed; but without pretending to decide it, I may say that there are some circumstances which even *women* cannot control. Female economy will do a great deal, my lord; but it cannot turn a small income into a large one."

Lord Osborne was silenced. Her manner had been neither sententious nor sarcastic, but there was a something in its mild seriousness, as well as in the words themselves, which made his lordship think; and when he addressed her again, it was with a degree of considerable propriety totally unlike the half-awkward, half-fearless style of his former remarks. It was a new thing with him to wish to please a woman; it was the first time that he had ever felt what was due to a woman in Emma's situation; but as he was wanting neither in sense nor a good disposition, he did not feel it without effect.

"You have not been long in this country, I understand," said he in the tone of a gentleman. "I hope you are pleased with it."

He was rewarded by a gracious answer and a more liberal full view of her face than she had yet bestowed. Unused to exert himself, and happy in contemplating her, he then sat in silence for some minutes longer, while Tom Musgrave was chattering to Elizabeth, till they were interrupted by Nanny's approach, who, half-opening the door and putting in her head, said—

"Please, ma'am, master wants to know why he be'nt to have his dinner?"

The gentlemen, who had hitherto disregarded every symptom, however positive, of the nearness of that meal, now jumped up with apologies; while Elizabeth called briskly after Nanny to take up the fowls.

"I am sorry it happens so," she added, turning good-humouredly towards Musgrave, "but you know what early hours we keep."

Tom had nothing to say for himself, he knew it very well; and such honest simplicity, such shameless truth, rather bewildered him. Lord Osborne's parting compliments took some time, his inclination for speech seeming to increase with the shortness of the term for indulgence. He recommended exercise in defiance of dirt; spoke again in praise of half-boots; begged that his sister might be allowed to send Emma the name of her shoemaker; and concluded with saying: "My hounds will be hunting this country next week. I believe they will throw off at Stanton Wood on Wednesday at nine o'clock. I mention this in hopes of your being drawn out to see what's going on. If the morning's tolerable, pray do us the honour of giving us your good wishes in person."

The sisters looked on each other with astonishment when their visitors had withdrawn.

"Here's an unaccountable honour!" cried Elizabeth at last. "Who would have thought of Lord Osborne's coming to Stanton? He is very handsome; but Tom Musgrave looks all to nothing the smartest and most fashionable man of the two. I am glad he did not say anything to me; I would not have had to talk to such a great man for the world. Tom was very agreeable, was not he? But did you hear him ask where Miss Penelope and Miss Margaret were, when he first came in? It put me out of patience. I am glad Nanny had not laid the cloth, however, it would have looked so awkward; just the tray did not signify."

To say that Emma was not flattered by Lord Osborne's visit, would be to assert a very unlikely thing, and describe a very odd young lady; but the gratification was by no means unalloyed; his coming was a sort of notice which might please her vanity, but did not suit her pride; and she would rather have known that he wished the visit without presuming to make it, than have seen him at Stanton.

Among other unsatisfactory feelings, it once occurred to her to wonder why Mr. Howard had not taken the same privilege of coming, and accompanied his lordship; but she was willing to suppose that he had either known nothing about it, or had declined any share in a measure which carried quite as much impertinence in form as good breeding. Mr. Watson was very far from being delighted when he heard what had passed; a little peevish under immediate pain, and ill-disposed to be pleased, he only replied—

"Pooh! Pooh! what occasion could there be for Lord Osborne's coming? I have lived here fourteen years without being noticed by any of the family. It is some fooling of that idle fellow, Tom Musgrave. I cannot return the visit. I would not if I could." And when Tom Musgrave was met with again, he was commissioned with a message of excuse to Osborne Castle on the too sufficient plea of Mr. Watson's infirm state of health.

CHAPTER V

A week or ten days rolled quietly away after this visit before any new bustle arose to interrupt, even for half a day, the tranquil and affectionate intercourse of the two sisters, whose mutual regard was increasing with the intimate knowledge of each other which such intercourse produced. The first circumstance to break in on their security was the receipt of a letter from Croydon, to announce the speedy return of Margaret, and a visit of two or three days from Mr. and Mrs. Robert Watson, who undertook to bring her home, and wished to see their sister Emma.

It was an expectation to fill the thoughts of the sisters at Stanton and to busy the hours of one of them at least; for, as Jane had been a woman of fortune, the preparations for her entertainment were considerable; and as Elizabeth had at all times more goodwill than method in her guidance of the house, she could make no change without a bustle. An absence of fourteen years had made all her brothers and sisters strangers to Emma, but in her expectation of Margaret there was more than the awkwardness of such an alienation; she had heard things which made her dread her return; and the day which brought the party to Stanton, seemed to her the probable conclusion of almost all that had been comfortable in the house.

Robert Watson was an attorney at Croydon in a good way of business, very well satisfied with himself for the same, and for having married the only daughter of the attorney to whom he had been clerk, with a fortune of six thousand pounds. Mrs. Robert was not less pleased with herself for having had that six thousand pounds, and for being now in possession of a very smart house in Croydon, where she gave genteel parties and wore fine clothes. In her person there was nothing remarkable; her manners were pert and conceited. Margaret was not without beauty; she had a slight, pretty figure, and rather wanted countenance than good features; but the sharp and anxious expression on her face made her beauty in general little felt. On meeting her long-absent sister, as on every occasion of show, her manner was all affection and her voice all gentleness; continual smiles and a very slow articulation being her constant resource when determined on pleasing.

She was now "so delighted to see dear, dear Emma," that she could hardly speak a word in a minute.

"I am sure we shall be great friends," she observed with much sentiment as they were sitting together. Emma scarcely knew how to answer such a proposition, and the manner in which it was spoken she could not attempt to equal. Mrs. Robert Watson eyed her with much familiar curiosity and triumphant compassion; the loss of her aunt's fortune was uppermost in her mind at the moment of meeting, and she could not but feel how much better it was to be the daughter of a gentleman of property in Croydon than the niece of an old woman who threw herself away on an Irish captain. Robert was carelessly kind, as became a prosperous man and a brother; more intent on settling with the post-boy, inveighing against the exorbitant advance in posting, and pondering over a doubtful half-crown, than on welcoming a sister who was no longer likely to have any property for him to get the direction of.

"Your road through the village is infamous, Elizabeth," said he; "worse than ever it was. By heaven! I would indict it if I lived near you. Who is the surveyor now?"

There was a little niece at Croydon to be fondly enquired after by the kind-hearted Elizabeth, who regretted very much her not being of the party.

"You are very good," replied her mother, "and I assure you it went very hard with Augusta to have us come away without her. I was forced to say we were only going to church, and promise to come back for her directly. But you know it would not do to bring her without her maid, and I am as particular as ever in having her properly attended to."

"Sweet little darling," cried Margaret. "It quite broke my heart to leave her."

"Then why was you in such a hurry to run away from her?" cried Mrs. Robert. "You are a sad, shabby girl. I have been quarrelling with you all the way we came, have not I? Such a visit as this I never heard of! You know how glad we are to have any of you with us, if it be for months together; and I am sorry (with a witty smile) we have not been able to make Croydon agreeable this autumn."

"My dearest Jane, do not overpower me with your raillery. You know what inducements I had to bring me home. Spare me, I entreat you. I am no match for your arch sallies."

"Well, I only beg you will not set your neighbours against the place. Perhaps Emma may be tempted to go back with us and stay till Christmas, if you don't put in your word."

Emma was greatly obliged. "I assure you we have very good society at Croydon. I do not much attend the balls, they are rather too mixed; but our parties are very select and good. I had seven tables last week in my drawing-room.

"Are you fond of the country? How do you like Stanton?"

"Very much," replied Emma, who thought a comprehensive answer most to the purpose. She saw that her sister-in-law despised her immediately. Mrs. Robert Watson was indeed wondering what sort of a home Emma could possibly have been used to in Shropshire, and setting it down as certain that the aunt could never have had six thousand pounds.

"How charming Emma is," whispered Margaret to Mrs. Robert in her most languishing tone. Emma was quite distressed by such behaviour, and she did not like it better when she heard Margaret, five minutes afterwards, say to Elizabeth in a sharp, quick accent, totally unlike the first: "Have you heard from Pen since she went to Chichester? I had a letter the other day. I don't find she is likely to make anything of it. I fancy she'll come back 'Miss Penelope,' as she went."

Such she feared would be Margaret's common voice when the novelty of her own appearance was over; the tone of artificial sensibility was not recommended by the idea. The ladies were invited upstairs to prepare for dinner.

"I hope you will find things tolerably comfortable, Jane," said Elizabeth, as she opened the door of the spare bedchamber.

"My good creature," replied she, "use no ceremony with me, I entreat you. I am one of those who always take things as they find them. I hope I can put up with a small apartment for two or three nights without making a piece of work. I always wish to be treated quite *en famille* when I come to see you. And now I do hope you have not been getting a great dinner for us. Remember, we never eat suppers."

"I suppose," said Margaret rather quickly to Emma, "you and I are to be together; Elizabeth always takes care to have a room to herself."

"No. Elizabeth gives me half hers."

"Oh!" in a softened voice, and rather mortified to find that she was not ill-used.

"I am sorry I am not to have the pleasure of your company, especially as it makes me nervous to be much alone."

Emma was the first of the females in the parlour again; on entering it, she found her brother alone.

"So, Emma," said he, "you are quite a stranger at home. It must seem odd enough for you to be here. A pretty piece of work your Aunt Turner has made of it! By heaven! A woman should never be trusted with money. I always said she ought to have settled something on you, as soon as her husband died."

"But that would have been trusting *me* with money," replied Emma; "and I am a woman, too."

"It might have been secured to your future use, without your having any power over it now. What a blow it must have been upon you! To find yourself, instead of heiress of eight thousand pounds or nine thousand pounds, sent back a weight upon your family, without a sixpence. I hope the old woman will smart for it."

"Do not speak disrespectfully of her; she was very good to me, and if she has made an imprudent choice, she will suffer more from it herself than I can possibly do."

"I do not mean to distress you, but you know everybody must think her an old fool. I thought Turner had been reckoned an extraordinarily sensible, clever man. How the devil came he to make such a will?"

"My uncle's sense is not at all impeached in my opinion by his attachment to my aunt. She had been an excellent wife to him. The most liberal and enlightened minds are always the most confiding. The event has been unfortunate, but my uncle's memory is, if possible, endeared to me by such a proof of tender respect for my aunt."

"That's odd sort of talking. He might have provided decently for his widow, without leaving everything that he had to dispose of, or any part of it, at her mercy."

"My aunt may have erred," said Emma warmly; "she *has* erred, but my uncle's conduct was faultless; I was her own niece, and he left to her the power of providing for me."

"But unluckily she has left the pleasure of providing for you to your father, and without the power. That's the long and short of the business. After keeping you at a distance from your family for such a length of time as must do away with all natural affection among us, and breeding you up (I suppose) in a superior style, you are returned upon their hands without a sixpence."

"You know," replied Emma, struggling with her tears, "my uncle's melancholy state of health. He was a greater invalid than my father. He could not leave home."

"I do not mean to make you cry," said Robert, rather softened; and after a short silence, by way of changing the subject, he added: "I am just come from my father's room; he seems very indifferent. It will be a sad break up if he dies. Pity you can none of you get married! You must come to Croydon as well as the rest, and see what you can do there. I believe if Margaret had had a thousand or fifteen hundred pounds, there was a young man who would have thought of her."

Emma was glad when they were joined by the others; it was better to look at her sister-in-law's finery than listen to Robert, who had equally irritated and grieved her. Mrs. Robert, exactly as smart as she had been at her own party, came in with apologies for her dress.

"I would not make you wait," said she, "so I put on the first thing I met with. I am afraid I am a sad figure. My dear Mr. W—— (addressing her husband), you have not put fresh powder in your hair."

"No, I do not intend it. I think there is powder enough in my hair for my wife and sisters."

"Indeed, you ought to make some alteration in your dress before dinner when you are out visiting, though you do not at home."

"Nonsense."

"It is very odd you do not like to do what other gentlemen do. Mr. Marshall and Mr. Hemming change their dress every day of their lives before dinner. And what was the use of my putting up your last new coat, if you are never to wear it?"

"Do be satisfied with being fine yourself and leave your husband alone."

To put an end to this altercation and soften the evident vexation of her sister-in-law, Emma (though in no spirits to make nonsense easy) began to admire her gown. It produced immediate complacency.

"Do you like it?" she said. "I am very happy. It has been excessively admired, but sometimes I think the pattern too large. I shall wear one to-morrow which I think you will prefer to this. Have you seen the one I gave Margaret?"

Dinner came, and except when Mrs. Robert looked at her husband's head, she continued gay and flippant; chiding Elizabeth for the profusion on the table, and absolutely protesting against the entrance of the roast turkey, which formed the only exception to "you see your dinner." "I do beg and entreat that no turkey may be seen to-day. I am really frightened out of my wits with the number of dishes we have already. Let us have no turkey, I beseech you."

"My dear," replied Elizabeth, "the turkey is roasted, and it may just as well come in as stay in the kitchen. Besides, if it is cut, I am in hopes my father may be tempted to eat a bit, for it is rather a favourite dish."

"You may have it in, then, my dear; but I assure you I shan't touch it."

Mr. Watson had not been well enough to join the party at dinner, but was prevailed on to come down and drink tea with them.

"I wish he may be able to have a game of cards to-night," said Elizabeth to Mrs. Robert, after seeing her father comfortably seated in his arm-chair.

"Not on my account, my dear, I beg. You know I am no card-player. I think a snug chat infinitely better. I always say cards are very well sometimes to break a formal circle, but one never wants them among friends."

"I was thinking of its being something to amuse my father," said Elizabeth, "if it was not disagreeable to you. He says his head won't bear whist, but perhaps if we make a round game he may be tempted to sit down with us."

"By all means, my dear creature; I am quite at your service, only do not oblige me to choose the game, that's all. Speculation is the only round game at Croydon now, but I can play anything. When there is only one or two of you at home, you must be quite at a loss to amuse him. Why do not you get him to play at cribbage? Margaret and I have played at cribbage most nights that we have not been engaged."

A sound like a distant carriage was at this moment caught; everybody listened; it became more decided; it certainly drew nearer. It was an unusual sound for Stanton at any time of the day, for the village was on no very public road, and contained no gentleman's family but the rector's. The wheels rapidly approached, in two minutes the general expectation was answered; they stopped beyond a doubt at the garden-gate of the parsonage. Who could it be? It was certainly a post-chaise. Penelope was the only creature to be thought of: she might perhaps have met with some unexpected opportunity of returning. A pause of suspense ensued. Steps were distinguished along the paved footway, which led under the window of the house to the front door, and then within the passage. They were the steps of a man. It could not be Penelope. It must be Samuel. The door opened, and displayed Tom Musgrave in the wrap of a traveller. He had been in London and was now on his way home, and he had come half a mile out of his road to call for ten minutes at Stanton. He loved to take people by surprise with sudden visits at extraordinary seasons and, in the present instance, he had the additional motive of being able to tell the Miss Watsons, whom he depended on finding sitting quietly employed after tea, that he was going home to an eight o'clock dinner.

As it happened, he did not give more surprise than he received, when, instead of being shown into the usual little sitting-room, the door of the best parlour (a foot larger each way than the other) was thrown open, and he beheld a circle of smart people, whom he could not immediately recognise, arranged with all the honours of visiting round the fire; and Miss Watson seated at the best Pembroke table, with the best tea-things before her.

He stood a few seconds in silent amazement. "Musgrave," ejaculated Margaret, in a tender voice. He recollected himself, and came forward, delighted to find such a circle of friends, and blessing his good fortune for the unlooked-for indulgence. He shook hands with Robert, bowed and smiled to the ladies, and did everything very prettily; but as to any particularity of address or emotion towards Margaret, Emma, who closely observed him, perceived nothing that did not justify Elizabeth's opinion; though Margaret's modest smiles imported that she meant to take the visit to herself. He was persuaded without much difficulty to throw off his great coat and drink tea with them. For "whether he dined at eight or nine," as he observed, "was a matter of very little consequence"; and without seeming to seek, he did not turn away from the chair close by Margaret, which she was assiduous in providing him. She had thus secured him from her sisters, but it was not immediately in her power to preserve him from her brother's claims; for as he came avowedly from London, and had left it only four hours ago, the last current report as to public news, and the general opinion of the day, must be understood before Robert could let his attention be yielded to the less rational and important demands of the women.[Pg 90 At last, however, he was at liberty to hear Margaret's soft address, as she spoke her fears of his having had a most terrible cold, dark, dreadful journey.

"Indeed, you should not have set out so late."

"I could not be earlier," he replied. "I was detained chatting at the 'Bedford' by a friend. All hours are alike to me. How long have you been in the country, Miss Margaret?"

"We only came this morning; my kind brother and sister brought me home this very morning. 'Tis singular—is not it?"

"You were gone a great while, were not you? A fortnight, I suppose?"

"*You* may call a *fortnight* a great while, Mr. Musgrave," said Mrs. Robert, sharply; "but *we* think a *month* very little. I assure you we bring her home at the end of a month much against our will."

"A month! Have you really been gone a month? 'Tis amazing how time flies."

"You may imagine," said Margaret, in a sort of whisper, "what are my sensations in finding myself once more at Stanton; you know what a sad visitor I make. And I was so excessively impatient to see Emma; I dreaded the meeting, and at the same time longed for it. Do you not comprehend the sort of feeling?"

"Not at all," cried he, aloud. "I could never dread a meeting with Miss Emma Watson, or any of her sisters."

It was lucky that he added that finish.

"Were you speaking of me?" said Emma, who had caught her own name.

"Not absolutely," he answered; "but I was thinking of you, as many at a greater distance are probably doing at this moment. Fine open weather, Miss Emma—charming season for hunting."

"Emma is delightful, is not she?" whispered Margaret; "I have found her more than answer my warmest hopes. Did you ever see anything more perfectly beautiful? I think even *you* must be a convert to a brown complexion."

He hesitated. Margaret was fair herself, and he did not particularly want to compliment her; but Miss Osborne and Miss Carr were likewise fair, and his devotion to them carried the day.

"Your sister's complexion," said he, at last, "is as fine as a dark complexion can be; but I still profess my preference of a white skin. You have seen Miss Osborne? She is my model for a truly feminine complexion, and she is very fair."

"Is she fairer than me?"

Tom made no reply. "Upon my honour, ladies," said he, giving a glance over his own person, "I am highly indebted to your condescension for admitting me in such dishabille into your drawing-room. I really did not consider how unfit I was to be here, or I hope I should have kept my distance. Lady Osborne would tell me that I was growing as careless as her son if she saw me in this condition."

The ladies were not wanting in civil returns, and Robert Watson, stealing a view of his own head in an opposite glass, said with equal civility—

"You cannot be more in dishabille than myself. We got here so late that I had not time even to put a little fresh powder into my hair."

Emma could not help entering into what she supposed her sister-in-law's feelings at the moment.

When the tea-things were removed, Tom began to talk of his carriage; but the old card-table being set out, and the fish and counters, with a tolerably clean pack brought forward from the buffet by Miss Watson, the general voice was so urgent with him to join their party, that he agreed to allow himself another quarter of an hour. Even Emma was pleased that he would stay, for she was beginning to feel that a family party might be the worst of all parties; and the others were delighted.

"What's the game?" cried he, as they stood round the table.

"Speculation, I believe," said Elizabeth. "My sister recommends it, and I fancy we all like it. I know *you* do, Tom."

"It is the only round game played at Croydon now," said Mrs. Robert; "we never think of any other. I am glad it is a favourite with you."

"Oh! *me*," said Tom. "Whatever you decide on will be a favourite with *me*. I have had some pleasant hours at speculation in my time; but I have not been in the way of it for a long while. Vingt-un is the game at Osborne Castle. I have played nothing but vingt-un of late. You would be astonished to hear the noise we make there—the fine old lofty drawing-room rings again. Lady Osborne sometimes declares she cannot hear herself speak. Lord Osborne enjoys it famously, and he makes the best dealer without exception that I ever beheld—such quickness and spirit; he lets nobody dream over their cards. I wish you could see him overdraw himself on both his own cards. It is worth anything in the world!"

"Dear me!" cried Margaret, "why should not we play vingt-un? I think it is a much better game than speculation. I cannot say I am very fond of speculation."

Mrs. Robert offered not another word in support of the game. She was quite vanquished, and the fashions of Osborne Castle carried it over the fashions of Croydon.

"Do you see much of the parsonage family at the castle, Mr. Musgrave?" said Emma, as they were taking their seats.

"Oh, yes; they are almost always there. Mrs. Blake is a nice, little, good-humoured woman; she and I are sworn friends; and Howard's a very gentlemanlike sort of fellow. You are not forgotten, I assure you, by any of the party. I fancy you must have a little cheek-glowing now and then, Miss Emma. Were not you rather warm last Saturday about nine or ten o'clock in the evening? I will tell you how it was—I see you are dying to know. Says Howard to Lord Osborne——"

At this interesting moment he was called on by the others to regulate the game and determine some disputable point; and his attention was so totally engaged in the business, and afterwards by the course of the game, as never to revert to what he had been saying before; and Emma, though suffering a good deal from curiosity, dared not remind him.

He proved a very useful addition at their table. Without him it would have been a party of such very near relations as could have felt little interest, and perhaps maintained little complaisance, but his presence gave variety and secured good manners. He was, in fact, excellently qualified to shine at a round game, and few situations made him appear to greater advantage. He played with spirit, and had a great deal to say; and though no wit himself, could sometimes make use of the wit of an absent friend, and had a lively way of retailing a commonplace, or saying a mere nothing, that had great effect at a card-table. The ways and good jokes of Osborne Castle were now added to his ordinary means of entertainment. He repeated the smart sayings of one lady, detailed the oversights of another, and indulged them even with a copy of Lord Osborne's overdrawing himself on both cards.

The clock struck nine while he was thus agreeably occupied; and when Nanny came in with her master's basin of gruel, he had the pleasure of observing to Mr. Watson that he should leave him at supper while he went home to dinner himself. The carriage was ordered to the door, and no entreaties for his staying longer could now avail; for he well knew that if he stayed he would have to sit down to supper in less than ten minutes, which to a man whose heart has been long fixed on calling his next meal a dinner, was quite insupportable. On finding him determined to go, Margaret began to wink and nod at Elizabeth to ask him to dinner the following day; and Elizabeth at last, not able to resist hints which her own hospitable social temper more than half seconded, gave the invitation: "Would he give Robert the meeting, they would be very happy?"

"With the greatest pleasure," was his first reply. In a moment afterwards: "That is, if I can possibly get here in time; but I shoot with Lord Osborne, and therefore must not engage. You will not think of me unless you see me." And so he departed, delighted in the uncertainty in which he had left it.

Margaret, in the joy of her heart, under circumstances which she chose to consider as peculiarly propitious, would willingly have made a confidante of Emma, when they were alone for a short time the next morning, and had proceeded so far as to say: "The young man who was here last night, my dear Emma, and returns to-day, is more interesting to me than perhaps you may be aware"; but Emma, pretending to understand nothing extraordinary in the words, made some very inapplicable reply, and, jumping up, ran away from a subject which was odious to her. As Margaret would not allow a doubt to be repeated of Musgrave's coming to dinner, preparations were made for his entertainment much exceeding what had been deemed necessary the day before; and taking the office of superintendence entirely from her sister, she was half the morning in the kitchen herself, directing and scolding.

After a great deal of indifferent cooking and anxious suspense, however, they were obliged to sit down without their guest. Tom Musgrave never came; and Margaret was at no pains to conceal her vexation under the disappointment, or repress the peevishness of her temper. The peace of the party for the remainder of that day and the whole of the next, which comprised the length of Robert and Jane's visit, was continually invaded by her fretful displeasure and querulous attacks. Elizabeth was the usual object of both. Margaret had just respect enough for her brother's and sister's opinion to behave properly by *them*, but Elizabeth and the maids could never do right; and Emma, whom she seemed no longer to think about, found the continuance of the gentle voice beyond calculation short. Eager to be as little among them as possible, Emma was delighted with the alternative of sitting above with her father, and warmly entreated to be his constant companion each evening; and as Elizabeth loved company of any kind too well not to prefer being below at all risks; as she had rather talk of Croydon with Jane, with every interruption of Margaret's perverseness, than sit with only her father, who frequently could not endure talking at all, the affair was so settled, as soon as she could be persuaded to believe it no sacrifice on her sister's part. To Emma, the change was most acceptable and delightful. Her father, if ill, required little more than gentleness and silence; and being a man of sense and education, was, if able to converse, a welcome companion. In *his* chamber, Emma was at peace from the dreadful mortifications of unequal society and family discord, and from the immediate endurance of hard-hearted prosperity, low-minded conceit, and wrong-headed folly engrafted on an untoward disposition. She still suffered from them in the contemplation of their existence, in memory and in prospect, but for the moment she ceased to be tortured by their effects. She was at leisure; she could read and think, though her situation was hardly such as to make reflection very soothing. The evils arising from the loss of her uncle were neither trifling nor likely to lessen; and when thought had been freely indulged, in contrasting the past and the present, the employment of mind and dissipation of unpleasant ideas, which only reading could produce, made her thankfully return to a book.

CHAPTER VI

The change in Emma's home society and style of life, in consequence of the death of one friend and the imprudence of another, had indeed been striking. From being the first object of hope and solicitude to an uncle who had formed her mind with the care of a parent, and of tenderness to an aunt whose amiable temper had delighted to give her every indulgence; from being the life and spirit of a house where all had been comfort and elegance, and the expected heiress of an easy independence, she was become of importance to no one—a burden on those whose affections she could not expect, an addition in a house already overstocked, surrounded by inferior minds, with little chance of domestic comfort, and as little hope of future support. It was well for her that she was naturally cheerful, for the change had been such as might have plunged weak spirits in despondence.

She was very much pressed by Robert and Jane to return with them to Croydon, and had some difficulty in getting a refusal accepted, as they thought too highly of their own kindness and situation to suppose the offer could appear in less advantageous light to anybody else. Elizabeth gave them her interest, though evidently against her own, in privately urging Emma to go.

"You do not know what you refuse, Emma," said she, "nor what you have to bear at home. I would advise you by all means to accept the invitation; there is always something lively going on at Croydon. You will be in company almost every day, and Robert and Jane will be very kind to you. As for me, I shall be no worse off without you than I have been used to be; but poor Margaret's disagreeable ways are new to *you*, and they would vex you more than you think for, if you stay at home."

Emma was, of course, uninfluenced, except to greater esteem for Elizabeth by such representations; and the visitors departed without her.

On the following day, as Emma and Elizabeth were in the best parlour, setting the sofa before the fire for their father to lie on, for a little change, they heard a carriage stopping at the garden gate; and a minute or two later Nanny showed in Mrs. Blake and her little boy, closely followed by Mr. Howard.

Charles was carrying a beautiful bunch of greenhouse flowers and, on seeing Emma, he ran eagerly forward, saying—

"I have brought you these flowers, ma'am, because you were so good as to dance with me. Lord Osborne gave me anything I liked for you, and cut some for you himself."

Emma blushed as she smiled and curtsied, and blushed again as she advanced to receive her other visitors and present her sister to them.

They had often observed Elizabeth at balls, and had considered her handsome, but they had never before spoken to her, and were at once favourably impressed by her unaffected good-humour and pleasant manner. Before long they were conversing with almost as little formality as though they had been old friends. On questioning Emma, Mrs. Blake easily drew from her some account of her former life and, on learning her aunt's name, recollected having heard it mentioned by friends in a manner entirely agreeable to Emma's feelings.

Presently Mr. Watson came into the room, and although he was a good deal surprised at finding himself in company, as Mr. Howard at once came forward with a show of friendliness, he had not time to lose his temper.

He was a man of considerable information, and finding the present society entirely congenial to him, contributed not a little to the pleasure of the visit, even going so far as to show Charles a volume of coloured prints; and before taking leave, Mr. Howard had persuaded him to join him, with his three daughters, at dinner, on the following Thursday, promising to send the carriage for them, and assuring him of his return at an early hour.

On Margaret's coming in from the village, where she had gone on an errand, she was all amazement on learning the arrangement; and displeased her father by enquiring if Mr. Musgrave and Lord Osborne were to be present.

"Mr. Howard expressly said they were to be by themselves," he replied, with the importance of an invalid. "He took particular care to assure me that I should suffer as little fatigue as possible."

He was therefore by no means too well pleased when, on the appointed evening, shortly after they had assembled in the drawing-room at Wickstead, Lord Osborne and Mr. Musgrave were ushered in; and before any explanation could be vouchsafed him, dinner was announced.

Turning to Lord Osborne, Mr. Howard said—

"As I cannot very well, my lord, ask Mr. Watson to hand in his daughter, I must ask him to conduct Mrs. Blake; and I will lead with Miss Watson if you will be good enough to give your arm to Miss Emma Watson; while Mr. Musgrave takes in Miss Margaret."

This arrangement was agreeable to all, except Mr. Musgrave, who, had he been of greater sensibility, would have been embarrassed by Margaret's manner towards him; and, as it was, felt not a little irritated by her determination to consider his escort as a *personal compliment*, rather than as *inevitable* on his part.

He had long since tired of his fancy for her, which indeed had always been of the slightest; and now in his determination to free himself from her, did not hesitate to go beyond the limits of propriety, openly disregarding her, and entering into conversation with everyone else in preference to her. Greatly mortified, she would have sunk under this neglect but for the kindness of Mrs. Blake, who addressed her as often as possible; and even Lord Osborne, vaguely aware that there was something wanting in ease, observed to her across the table that the roads were monstrous wet when it rained.

In the meantime, his lordship had not been enjoying himself either, to any great extent; for Emma, having perceived a volume on the drawing-room table with which she was familiar, on finding herself placed beside her host at the dinner table, fell to discussing it with him with much sense and spirit; and from this proceeded to contrast her favourite authors and the merits of their respective works. As Lord Osborne had as little knowledge of literature as well might be, he was compelled, despite the kindly efforts of his host, to sit more or less in silence, trying to look as if he had not less in his head than might reasonably be expected.

Elizabeth was only too glad to share her partner with her sister, as she did not very well know what to say to him; and she enjoyed listening to their conversation, the more so as they repeatedly explained to her the situation, or the point, in question. Moreover, she could not help hoping that another future, far different to what she had feared for her young sister, might possibly be in store for her.

With dessert, Charles arrived on the scene, which created a diversion in Lord Osborne's favour, as he came to place himself between the latter and his dear Miss Emma Watson, and both joined in the endeavour to entertain him.

On the ladies withdrawing, Lord Osborne turned to Mr. Watson and said—

"You have a very beautiful daughter, sir," but he received in reply such a chilling bow that he could find nothing more to say; and Tom Musgrave nearly choked himself over his wine in the effort to control his merriment at his friend's discomfiture. Mr. Howard then placed himself at the other side of Mr. Watson, and speedily restored him to good-humour by discussing the late visitation with him.

They were not long in returning to the drawing-room for tea; and shortly after, Mrs. Blake and Mr. Watson began to play the new game of écarté, proposing to one another with a pleasant air; whilst the others, seating themselves round the larger table, started vingt-un.

They had scarcely commenced, however, when a carriage drove up to the door, and Miss Osborne and Miss Carr were shown in.

"Oh, Mr. Howard! how could you have used us so?" cried Miss Osborne archly. "I protest we are vastly offended with you!—to give a party and leave us out!"

Miss Carr joined in, in the same strain. She had never heard of anything so perfidious—it was really beyond everything she had ever known in all her life!

Mr. Howard received them with the quiet courtesy that was habitual to him; and when he deemed it possible to make his voice heard, expressed his sense of the honour they had done him; but observed that one family was scarcely a party, adding that Lord Osborne and Mr. Musgrave had been good enough to invite themselves.

Lord Osborne remained silent, looking rather ashamed; but Mr. Tom Musgrave protested vigorously that if Howard were such a sly dog, plotting to cut them out like this, they were bound to look after themselves!

The Miss Watsons and their father having been presented, and tea declined, and Miss Carr, having, further, declared that there was nothing she so doted on as vingt-un, the game was once more started.

Miss Osborne at once took possession of the chair at Mr. Howard's right hand, which had previously been occupied by Emma; and just as he was about to request the latter to accept the one at his left, he found it already secured by Miss Carr. Lord Osborne, therefore, shared Emma with Charles; and Tom Musgrave devoted himself assiduously to Miss Carr. Presently he was heard endeavouring to persuade her to accept him as her cavalier at the next meet. Unfortunately this reminded Charles of the stuffed fox, and again he implored Emma to come and see it, adding—

"Lord Osborne will now ask you himself, ma'am—will you not, Lord Osborne?"

Before he could reply, Emma had hastily excused herself; but Miss Carr, leaning forward, said impertinently—

"It is a pity you should not see the castle, Miss Watson; it is thrown open to the public every Wednesday—all except the private apartments."

Emma coloured and made no reply; but Lord Osborne quite shocked his sister and her friend by saying—

"Lady Osborne will wait on Miss Watson."

Miss Osborne stared at her brother, but there was something in his face that compelled her to lower her eyes. Never before had he so asserted himself, and she had not deemed him capable of it.

At the conclusion of the game, Mr. Watson asked to return home—declining to wait for supper—and took leave with his daughters.

Mr. Howard conducted them to the carriage, and as Emma curtsied in passing him, held out his hand to her, and retaining hers for a moment, thanked her in a low tone for the honour she had done him in coming.

CHAPTER VII

During the drive back, Mr. Watson was in very good humour, speaking several times of the civility and attention he had received from Mr. Howard and his sister; and praising Charles, to whom he had taken a considerable fancy.

"As for Lord Osborne," he continued, "though I do not think very much of him, he is at least preferable to that fellow Musgrave, whom I have never thought a gentleman."

This was cruelly mortifying to Margaret, who was nevertheless forced to constrain her feelings in the presence of her father; but on their return home, as he went directly to his room, she gave way to her agitation—quite shocking Emma by the violence of her passion, as well as by a wholly unexpected attack on her own conduct.

Elizabeth endeavoured in vain to interpose, but Margaret would not be stayed; and Emma stood motionless under a shower of angry accusations. She was running after Lord Osborne—her intentions were plain to everyone, and she would only have herself despised! Lord Osborne would never *look at her*!

Mr. Musgrave saw through her! No doubt he was in Miss Osborne's confidence, and knew she was coming—*that* was why he had been so wanting in civility to herself!—he did not want the Osbornes to think he was mixed up with them—but Lord Osborne would never think of her, except to insult her!

At this, Emma, in silent indignation, took up her candlestick and retired to her room.

When she had gone, Elizabeth spoke more seriously to her sister than ever she had done in her life before; and as Margaret at first refused to listen to reason, threatened to appeal to her father should there be any repetition of the scene. Completely overcome, Margaret then burst into tears, and shortly after permitted Elizabeth to lead her upstairs.

A few days later, Lady Osborne and her daughter called on the Miss Watsons. Miss Osborne, supported by her friend Miss Carr, had endeavoured to dissuade her mother from taking this step; but Lady Osborne, seeing that her son's feelings were more deeply engaged than ever she had previously known them to be, was too clever not to be assured that opposition would only serve to fan his flame; and, moreover, she did not choose that he should visit with people whom she would not acknowledge.

She was showed by Nanny into the parlour, and though it was not such a room as she was accustomed to be received in, everything was in order; and Elizabeth, who had become more refined from her intercourse with Emma, received her with greater dignity than she had expected. As for Emma herself, she was not less elegant in her simple house frock than in her ball-dress, and the Osbornes were compelled to acknowledge her beauty. It was not such a marriage as Lady Osborne could possibly countenance for her son; but nevertheless she found herself drawn towards Emma; and placing herself near to her, directed the greater part of her conversation to her; while Margaret sat somewhat aside, white and silent, only able to join in the conversation when directly addressed.

"I understand from Mrs. Blake," said Lady Osborne, "that you have been brought up by a relative at some distance?"

"By my aunt, Mrs. Turner, now Mrs. O'Brien."

"And where has she gone to live?"

"In the South of Ireland, ma'am, where Captain O'Brien has a small property."

"Captain O'Brien? There was an officer of that name in the Royal ——s, my brother's regiment."

"That was his regiment, but he resigned his commission many years ago."

"I am afraid it could scarcely have been a prudent marriage."

Seeing tears gathering in Emma's eyes, Lady Osborne hastened to change the conversation by speaking of other officers in the same regiment; and on mentioning a Colonel Norwood, was interested to hear that he had been a friend of the late Mr. Turner, with whom he had frequently dined.

"It is a pity your aunt did not marry him instead," she observed.

"But he is dead, ma'am. He left me this brooch I am wearing and also a legacy of fifty pounds."

"I did not know you had fifty pounds, Emma," said Elizabeth, surprised. Miss Osborne looked her disdain, but Lady Osborne said kindly—

"It will be very useful to Miss Emma for her trousseau, in a few years; well, do not be in too great a hurry to marry, my dear."

Emma blushed, and Lady Osborne, believing that it was on account of her son, grew more reserved for a few moments. Determined, however, to have fuller proof, she presently mentioned him by name, and was gratified to observe that Emma received it without any embarrassment.

"Perhaps there is someone else," she thought to herself.

But on sharing this surmise with Miss Osborne, during the drive home, she was surprised to find that her daughter received it with so little favour.

Elizabeth and Emma shortly returned the visit, but Lady Osborne was not at home.

Soon after this event, Lord Osborne sent game for Mr. Watson; Mr. Howard was not less civil with a present of fruit; and Mr. Musgrave, not to be out of the fashion, called with a basket of fish. Poor Mr. Watson was considerably surprised at finding himself become so popular all at once; but when he questioned Emma on the subject, received surprisingly little information in her reply.

In the meantime, Margaret's health was occasioning not a little anxiety to her sisters. She seemed to have no interest in anything, had quite lost her appetite, and went listlessly about the house; before long she was confined to her room with a feverish attack.

Elizabeth and Emma were assiduous in their care of her, and were presently rewarded, not only by her being restored to some measure of health, but also by her being rendered less irritable towards them, from a sense of gratitude for their sympathy.

Just as she was beginning to come down stairs again, the Osbornes issued invitations for a ball; and the Miss Watsons were among the first to receive a card.

Elizabeth had no idea but that they should go with the Edwards, and was considerably put out when she found that not only were they not going, but that Mrs. Edwards was offended at having been ignored, when the Watsons (on whom she had always looked down) had been included.

Mary Edwards was absent at the moment, but, on learning what had transpired, with great good sense pointed out to her mother that as they had never before been taken notice of by the Osbornes, they had now no cause for mortification, generously adding that such beauty as Emma's could not but be distinguished.

Nevertheless there is no young lady who can hear of a ball without desiring to go to it; and the matter occasioned not a little stir in the small country town, where any subject for gossip was eagerly seized upon. Tom Musgrave, hearing of it, reported it at the Castle as a good joke, believing the Osbornes would be gratified by learning of the disappointment they had unwittingly occasioned.

It had quite a different effect, however, on Lady Osborne, who at once despatched an invitation to Mary Edwards, together with a kind note in which she said she understood that she was a friend of the Miss Watsons, and that it would give her much pleasure if she would accompany them to the dance.

All was now happily settled, as Mrs. Blake had arranged to meet them in the cloakroom at the Castle and act as chaperon.

Miss Osborne, though in some awe of her mother, had done all in her power to prevent her inviting Emma.

"You are encouraging Osborne in every way," she said, "to make this disgraceful marriage—to ask Emma Watson to this house will be to throw her into his arms."

"I think differently," replied Lady Osborne coldly, "and I do not choose that Osborne should give a dance in the Assembly Rooms, which was what he had intended doing."

"It would have been far better, ma'am. You could then have refused to attend."

"I have not the slightest intention of ever inflicting such a slight upon my son."

"It would have put Miss Watson in her place. She will now be more forward and impertinent than ever."

"I find her neither forward nor impertinent."

"You do not know her, ma'am; there is a sort of independence in her which I find insupportable."

"I believe I am the better judge—and it is not a question of *her* conduct, but of *mine*."

Miss Osborne, finding nothing to reply, curtsied and left the room.

CHAPTER VIII

During the interval which elapsed, Lord Osborne and Mr. Howard both discovered various pretexts for calling at the Rectory; Mr. Watson's health, for one thing, causing them no inconsiderable anxiety; and on different occasions when the latter was riding by chance in the neighbourhood of Stanton, and had met Emma out walking with Elizabeth, in view of all the perils of a singularly quiet neighbourhood, had believed it incumbent on him to escort her the whole way home, leading his horse by the bridle.

Nor is it to be supposed that Mr. Musgrave permitted himself to be relegated to the background, where a new and pretty woman was concerned; even had she not possessed the additional importance, in his eyes, of having aroused Lord Osborne from his habitual apathy. He addressed himself to her without loss of time, confident of success, and wholly incapable of believing that her indifference was genuine.

But Emma's contempt for him, as can well be imagined, only served to aggravate the mortification from which poor Margaret was constrained to suffer; and she could not be prevailed upon to go to the Osbornes' dance, although her father had expressed his willingness to remain, for once, by himself.

On the night of the ball, Emma and Elizabeth were received with every attention by Lord Osborne, who met them in the hall; and Lady Osborne both curtsied and held out her hand; but Miss Osborne contented herself with a very short curtsey; while Miss Carr found herself obliged to become so engrossed in Colonel Beresford that she could not see them at all.

Lord Osborne was to open the ball with the Countess of X——, but he engaged Emma for the next two dances; and Mr. Howard secured her for the first two, and led her aside.

"This is just your second dance, is it not?"

"Oh, no! I have been out a year."

"Preposterous! A year's licence for breaking hearts in."

"Hearts so easily broken would be scarcely worth considering."

"Do not you, then, preserve them in a glass case?"

"I never preserve what I do not value."

"So young and so untender!"

"'So young, my lord, and true!'"

"I did not know young ladies were students of Shakespeare."

"No doubt they are more intelligent at breaking hearts, and preserving them in a glass case!"

Miss Osborne, who was near to her at the moment, turned and looked at her in cold surprise, then passed on; but Emma's face was at once so arch and sweet that Mr. Howard was wholly charmed, and bending slightly over her, took a white rose from his coat and begged her to honour him by wearing it. Then as the violins were playing, and several couples leaving the room, they followed in their wake.

As Emma entered the ball-room, all eyes were fixed on her—it passed from mouth to mouth that she was the prettiest woman in the room, and she was speedily acclaimed the *belle*.

Gentlemen flocked round her, begging for introductions; and Tom Musgrave was foremost in presenting himself; but Emma felt so keenly all the misery he had caused her sister, that she declined to give him an engagement for any dance, and without affording him any semblance of excuse.

Never before had he received such treatment at the hands of any lady, and least of all had he expected it from a Miss Watson.

Highly incensed, and with a view to covering his discomfiture, he approached Miss Carr, and solicited her; but as she had witnessed what had transpired, and would have been the last to accept a rejected suitor, he was promptly dismissed, and retired to the card-room vowing vengeance.

Meanwhile, Elizabeth and Mary Edwards had no lack of partners, as they knew several of the officers present; and Lord Osborne had made a point of introducing other gentlemen to them. Both were in good looks, especially Elizabeth, who was accounted by several to be almost as handsome as her sister.

In the course of the evening the Boulangeries were danced. This had been arranged by Miss Osborne and Miss Carr, with a special view to mortifying Emma; but to their disappointment, it transpired that she was not only conversant with the several figures, but was also accustomed to innovations; and on Lord Osborne requesting her to direct a new movement, conducted it with a simple confidence which proved her to be no novice.

Had Elizabeth been her mother, she could not have taken a greater pride in her performance; and Charles was in ecstasies as she selected him for her cavalier.

Lady Osborne, who had come in with Mrs. Blake to watch the dance, entirely approved her conduct, fully recognizing that she acted in this manner, not only that she might keep her promise to Charles of giving him a dance, but also in order to avoid Lord Osborne, who made not the slightest effort to conceal his admiration of her. Her eyes then fell on her own daughter, and it seemed to her that never had she seen her less in looks. Near to her was Miss Carr, and she could not but note the ill-humour of her countenance. The next moment she was almost startled by its sudden change of expression as she leaned forward to speak to her son, and as she did so her designs on him were betrayed.

In point of fortune and connection there was nothing to be urged; but in that moment Lady Osborne felt that if she were asked to choose between her and Emma Watson for a daughter-in-law, she would be constrained to give her suffrage to the latter—and again her eyes wandered to her.

She was now dancing with Mr. Howard, in a temporary exchange of partners, and it was very evident that he was quite absorbed in her.

At this moment, Miss Osborne passed near to her mother, and her excessive pallor showed beneath her rouge.

Presently Colonel Beresford and his partner paused within a few steps of her, without observing her, and she could not help hearing part of their conversation.

"Osborne must be monstrous hard hit when he gives a dance."

"But you are all in love with this beautiful girl—are not you?—Look at Mr. Howard!—and she is not insensible to his merit!"

"He has no chance against Lord Osborne. No young lady could refuse a title!"

"Why such strictures! Do not you then allow anything for our hearts?"

"Zounds, Madam; I have more respect for your wits! I should form but a mean opinion of any woman's understanding who would reject Lord Osborne for his former tutor!"

Then they passed on; but in the short space that Lady Osborne had stood there, it seemed to her that all the comedy and tragedy of the ball had been revealed to her; no longer could she find any enjoyment in it; and, sick at heart, she would have left the room only for the observation it would have occasioned.

As Lady X—— had been obliged to return home early, Lord Osborne, having danced twice with Emma, took her in to supper. Mr. Howard then danced twice with her. He had admired her very much from the first; and now was in a fair way to be very much in love with her. Casting prudence to the winds, he drew her into the greenhouse and, in accents which betrayed his emotion, endeavoured to thank her for having given him the happiest evening of his life, begging her to favour him by returning him the rose he had presented to her.

Emma was unable to meet the ardour of his eyes, and with fingers which slightly trembled, she removed it from her dress.

He placed it in his breast and, raising her hand, pressed it to his lips.

"I believe this is our dance, Mr. Howard," Miss Osborne's cold voice broke in on them, and nothing could well have been less opportune. Mr. Howard, however, appeared entirely unembarrassed, and, bowing and smiling, gave her his arm—seeing that Colonel Beresford was claiming Emma; and the latter saw him no more. For almost immediately afterwards, Miss Edwards came to beg her to come home, as she had promised her father to return early; and as Lady X—— had already gone, there could be no impropriety in their doing so.

Lord Osborne attended them to the carriage, but Emma was almost wholly silent, and he was deeply mortified by her reserve.

CHAPTER IX

The next day Mr. Watson was taken seriously ill; and though he lingered for some weeks, his daughters were almost completely cut off from all social intercourse.

Towards Christmas he died.

Everything was overshadowed by the sense of loss; but Emma found that she could be still more lonely, when, on receipt of a kind letter from Mrs. Blake, she learned that she had taken a house in London, in order to put Charles to school; and that Mr. Howard had been called to Cumberland to the bedside of a relative who had had a stroke.

The Osbornes had gone abroad.

The clergyman who had been doing duty for Mr. Watson, had been appointed to the parish; but with great consideration had begged them not to move till the following March; so that they might have sufficient leisure to dispose of their furniture, and to make their arrangements.

Penelope had returned for some time, and Emma had learned to dread the sound of her sharp voice. She and Margaret quarrelled perpetually. There seemed never to be any peace in the house. Her ill-humour was aggravated by her friends, the Shaws, having secured a situation for her as assistant teacher in a private seminary; for not only was she averse to this position, but she felt, even more keenly, that it was a tacit acknowledgment of the fatal obduracy of the heart, she had wasted so much time in endeavouring to subdue.

Margaret had got an engagement as companion to a delicate girl.

Emma's case was the hardest. She was to find her home with Robert and Jane, who openly discussed her prospects of making a good match. In vain she pleaded her desire to take a situation, like her sisters. Robert would not hear of it. She had already received ill-treatment enough from her family, he affirmed, and he would do his best to give her a good chance. Even Elizabeth joined her voice to her brother's.

"You do not know what you would suffer as governess or companion. Your beauty would be for ever making you enemies."

Emma could say no more while her brother was present, but when she found herself alone with Elizabeth, she besought her to aid her in getting a post where she might earn her bread independently.

"My position with Robert and Jane would not be tolerable," she pleaded.

"Do not stand in your own light, dear Emma," Elizabeth replied; "your position would be much worse with strangers. Robert and Jane will both be kind to you if you do not offend them. They were not too well pleased by your refusing to go with them in October; and now that Lord Osborne has admired you, they are all for having you. Believe me, it will be the best thing for you."

"Anyway, I shall stay here until March."

"Yes—Robert has consented to that—and as Penelope and Margaret are to go to their situations in February, we can have a little time in peace to ourselves."

To Elizabeth alone did there come any prospect of happiness.

Mr. Purvis, now a widower, had been engaged by Mr. Howard to do duty for him; and, on learning that Miss Watson was as handsome as ever, considered it to be his duty to call as soon as circumstances permitted.

His earlier feelings for her were very soon revived, and although he could not immediately enter into an engagement with her, on account of his recent bereavement, it was quite evident to all that the old relations between them would be happily restored.

In the meantime it was arranged that Elizabeth should go to his aunt as companion.

His marriage had not been happy, which is scarcely to be wondered at, seeing that he had entered somewhat hastily into it in order to assuage his feelings of disappointment; and as his wife shortly afterwards fell into ill-health, matters had been scarcely brightened by the peevish temper of an invalid.

The more Emma saw of him, the better was she pleased with him. He was good-looking and gentlemanlike, with unaffected manners, and a pleasant countenance. She could not but feel confident that Elizabeth would be happy at his side.

Towards the end of February, Mr. Howard returned, and lost no time in riding over to Stanton. Unfortunately, however, as he drew near to the Rectory gate, he met Tom Musgrave coming out of it, and was instantly hailed by that gentleman.

"Upon my word, Howard, I thought you had taken root in Cumberland. Oh, a sad break up here!—monstrous pleasant girls as ever I met! Miss Emma is going to Croydon with her brother, and I hear is shortly to be married to an old flame. Oh, a famous little flirt, I can assure you!"

So saying, and waving his hand, he took himself off, laughing heartily at his own ingenuity.

In consequence therefore of this unwelcome intelligence, Mr. Howard merely called at the door; and, ignoring Nanny's information that the ladies were in, rode gloomily away.

Emma had watched his approach from an upper window, and blushed and blushed again.

She was pausing before coming down, in the endeavour to quell the beating of her heart, when to her surprise she heard the clattering of his horse's hoofs; and, running back to the window, saw him vanishing round the corner.

At first she was all disappointment, and did not know what to think. Tears gathered thickly in her eyes, and fell on her black dress. But presently she considered that he might perhaps think it right to call at first without coming in, on account of her father's death, and that he would come again.

But he never came again, and about a week later she was carried away to Croydon by her brother, who had returned for her.

CHAPTER X

Emma had now entered on a new chapter of her life, and one which she could not but regard with pain and misgiving. Being in mourning, however, she was for the present saved from any special distress; and she at once found an object for her affection in little Augusta, a very pretty child, with much more natural refinement than either her father or mother. As her health was indifferent, Emma was the more drawn to her, and devoted all the time to her that she could spare from Jane's constant demands on her needle.

All this time she had never seen her brother Sam, as he had been seriously ill when the others had been called to the bedside of their father. During this period he had been attended by Mr. Curtis with the solicitude of a relative; and, on his recovering sufficiently to be removed, he had sent him to Bath at his own charge.

Towards the end of March, he gave him a few days' leave to go and see his brother and sisters at Croydon.

On the day previous to that on which he was expected, as Emma was sitting alone in the drawing-room, the door opened and a young gentleman, with a very open, attractive countenance, entered the room unannounced.

He bowed on seeing her, apologising for his intrusion, and she rose and curtsied—when suddenly he called out——

"As sure as anything, it is little Emma!" and came over to her with both hands stretched out.

"Oh, Sam! Can it be really you?"

"Were not you, then, expecting me?"

"Not until to-morrow. How came you a day sooner?"

"I met Tom Musgrave in Guildford, and he drove me over in his curricle. He will be staying here for a couple of days, and is coming this evening to wait on you and Jane—but let me look at you properly! You have got your nice little brown face still, I see; and I dare say you have that fine little vixenish temper that you used to have—I vow you gave me a famous slap the last time I had the honour of seeing you!"

"No doubt it was the price of you, sir! and I shall give you another, if you do not be careful!"

Before very long, Jane came into the room and affected a great start of surprise on seeing Sam and Emma sitting on the sofa together.

"Good Lord, Sam!" she cried. "I thought you must be one of Emma's lovers come after her!"

"Has she so many as all that?—I protest I must look into this!" he replied, laughing; then seeing a shade on Emma's face, he easily turned the conversation by enquiring for Robert, and begging that little Augusta might be sent for.

In the course of the evening, Tom Musgrave arrived, and was received with great cordiality by Robert and Jane.

After the usual enquiries and civilities, he threw himself back in the easiest chair in the room, and beamed round at them, saying—

"I vow and declare there are no friends like old friends. Oh, it's monstrous dull since you and the Osbornes left—positively I have half a mind to go after Osborne!"

"Is not he soon coming back?" asked Robert.

"Faith, there's no sign of it! Howard has joined them at Rome. He is very likely to be engaged to Miss Osborne."

Emma was sitting beyond the candles, so that he could not see her face; but by her very stillness he was satisfied that he had wounded her.

"I think it is Miss Carr that he is after," said Jane in an important tone, as though she were intimate.

"Oh, Fanny Carr is all for me! She won't look at anyone else, I can assure you, when I am by!"

"Take care, Tom!" said Sam, laughing. "Out of sight, out of mind! She will have forgotten you months ago, I wager!"

"Why do not you join Lord Osborne?" enquired Jane.

Now, as this was precisely what Tom Musgrave had been straining every nerve to accomplish—giving hints to his lordship of unimaginable breadth, which so far had been entirely ignored—he was by no means too well pleased by the question; and delighted Sam, who saw through him perfectly, by reeling off a string of excuses, each less convincing than the last.

"Does Miss Carr never stay with her own people?" enquired Robert.

"She has been at Castle Carr all winter," said Sam carelessly. "She will be going up to Berkeley Square next month with Lord and Lady Carr."

Tom Musgrave stared at him.

"How came you to know this?" he asked in a sulky tone.

"Lord Montague told me."

"Lord Montague? How came you to meet with him?"

"I was called in to attend him when Mr. Curtis was away. I had supposed he would consider a surgeon's assistant as little superior to his valet; but he was very civil, and chatted away—told me he had seen my sisters at the Osbornes' dance, and was so obliging as to add they were prodigious pretty! Emma, do not be listening!"

Jane was as surprised as Musgrave, but shrewd enough not to betray it; and, seeing the clouded look on his face, suggested a game of cards.

Robert hesitated a little, but, as Tom caught eagerly at the suggestion, she produced a pack; and, Emma declining to play, whist was selected.

CHAPTER XI

Sam was so little satisfied with Augusta's health that he insisted on her being taken to the sea; and a client of Robert's at once offered to lend him his house, which was in a sheltered bay on the South Coast, for six months. As Jane was unable to go into company, she demurred a good deal less than she might otherwise have done; and, like most wives, was not averse to suffering the mild anguish of a temporary separation from her husband.

Sam himself took charge of them on the journey, as Robert was engaged on an important case; and he had the satisfaction of assuring himself that the climate was suited to his little patient.

She and Emma were delighted with the change, and as the weather was unusually mild, they rambled about the greater part of the day.

It was with sincere regret that Emma parted from Sam; she had found in him a true friend, and one who comprehended the possible evils of her situation with much greater distinctness than had been the case with Elizabeth. They all escorted him to the mail coach at A———, and Emma was constrained to wonder if it were to be for ever her lot to be parted from all to whom she had become attached; while little Augusta, holding her young uncle's hands, danced round with him on the publick road, to the indignation of her mother and the amusement of the other passengers.

At Emma's request, the child's nurse had been dismissed on their leaving Croydon; Emma now taking Augusta under her sole charge, to the great advantage of the little girl, who had been considerably tried by the vagaries of an uncertain temper and an injudicious arrangement of her meals.

As her health rapidly improved, Emma commenced some simple lessons with her, which included instruction in drawing, for which she showed some aptitude. In the course of a few weeks she had copied a little picture so neatly, that Jane enclosed it in a letter to her father, who was so pleased that he sent her down a box of water-colours. This was a great boon to the child during the broken weather, which set in for a short time.

As Jane was really fond of her little daughter, she could not but feel grateful to Emma for her care of her; but she had been not a little offended at finding her indifferent to the petty gossip of Croydon, which occupied half her own time, and had always been willingly listened to by both Elizabeth and Margaret. At once jealous of her, and yet considering her to be wanting in fashion, she was nevertheless gratified by the pretty manners she was instilling into Augusta.

Emma was teaching her to curtsey before leaving the room; but, as she was of a very lively disposition, she would often run out into the hall before she could remember to do so. They would then hear her stopping short, and saying to herself, "Oh, I forgot!" when she would come running back to make her curtsey. It was all done so prettily, they could not but be delighted with her.

It had been apparent from the first that Jane had derived but little pleasure from the excursions by the sea, or through the country lanes, which delighted Emma and Augusta so much; preferring rather to drive in the pony chaise, which had been left for their use, into the neighbouring town of A———. It was not, however, until the early days of June that Emma began to notice how many hours she was spending there; and presently Jane informed her that a former school friend, a Mrs. Burton, now a widow, had taken rooms in the hotel there, and that she spent the most of her time with her, playing cards. She also confessed that this lady was no favourite of Robert's. This was very unwelcome news to Emma, who knew her brother to be very far from particular.

"I assure you, Emma," Jane continued earnestly, "it is all prejudice; Jemima Burton is of quite superior style, and very well off. You could hardly meet with anyone more agreeable; and she is all anxiety to know you. I hope you will come with me to-morrow—she will not be having company—we shall be quite by ourselves."

Emma was considerably embarrassed.

"I could not leave Augusta," she said.

"Oh! The maids here will take every care of her—she will not be wanting for anything. I cannot very well go without you, when she has made such a point of it."

On the following afternoon, therefore, Emma was constrained to drive with her sister-in-law into A———, and they were shown into the common sitting-room of the hotel, where they were warmly received by a vulgar, over-dressed woman.

"Now, I call this kind," she exclaimed. "And so this is the young lady Lord Osborne admired!"

This was said in such a loud voice that everyone in the room turned and stared at Emma; so that, in spite of her efforts to maintain her countenance, she grew crimson.

"Introduce me, madam, I beg," said a thin, unpleasant-looking man, thrusting himself boldly forward; "I know his Lordship well, and am proud to make the acquaintance of any friend of his."

"Allow me to have the pleasure of introducing Captain Conway, Miss Watson."

Emma's curtsey was of the slightest. They were then joined by two or three other men, all of them desiring to be presented, and each more objectionable than the last.

With a quiet courage which surprised Emma herself, she said—

"I am in mourning for my father and do not desire introductions. I understood, ma'am, that we were to be received by you in your own rooms."

Jane stared at her sister-in-law; but Mrs. Burton at once gave in; and, waving them all aside, declared that they were sad fellows, and that none of them need think to be introduced. With that she led the way to her apartments; but, to Emma's surprise, they were closely followed by Captain Conway.

"Oh! he is my cousin," she said with bold assurance; but Emma was convinced that this was a falsehood; the more so that the gentleman in question laughed immoderately, and repeated the assertion several times over.

He placed himself at her side and, fixing his glass in his eye, ogled her in a manner she had never before been subjected to in the whole course of her life; whilst he did his utmost to draw her into conversation. But she would neither answer him, nor raise her eyes from the ground.

Jane grew uncomfortable and, in order to conceal it and to regain confidence, began to speak in a much louder voice than was her wont. In this she was ably assisted by her friend— one would have thought that there were at least a dozen women in the room.

At first, Emma was too agitated to pay any attention to what they were saying—she was even too confused to arrange her thoughts; but presently, as she grew more composed, the contrast of her past life with her present position came home to her with such poignancy, that she could scarcely contain her tears. Were it possible, she thought, that her aunt could have seen her in such company, what would not have been her feelings?

Presently, however, her attention was caught by Jane saying—

"Thursday, then; you will both come and have a dish of tea with me on Thursday evening; and we can start a quiet rubber of whist."

During the drive home, Jane was in more ill-humour than Emma could have conceived possible.

"Good heavens! Emma," she said. "How can you give yourself such airs? Your head is completely turned by Lord Osborne having admired you! I could not have imagined anyone could have been so silly!"

Emma remained silent.

"I assure you I am very much offended at the way you have been treating my friends. Mrs. Burton has more style than you; and Captain Conway is quite the gentleman. I never saw anyone of more fashion—and such attentions he paid you! Mrs. Burton told me he was wild to know you; and anyone could see how he was struck with you. Good Lord! Emma, what more do you want—a *Captain!*—and *second cousin* to the *Marquis of H——!*—Mrs. Burton told me so!—Why do not you answer?"

"I cannot permit his attentions."

"You cannot permit his attentions!—did anyone ever hear the like! Well, let me tell you, Miss Emma, you *must* permit them—You should be only too thankful he should *wish* to pay them, when you are just nothing!—you are all of you beggars!"

Emma covered her face with her hands.

"There, Emma—I did not mean to make you cry."

*   *   *   *   *   *

On the evening on which Mrs. Burton and Captain Conway were expected, Augusta was laid up with a feverish cold, and Emma steadily refused to leave her bedside. Jane was at first angry, but, seeing the child's flushed cheeks, was obliged to give way and send for the apothecary, who prescribed a soothing draught.

A few days later, however, Captain Conway called again, and as on this occasion Emma happened to be in the drawing-room with her sister, she was obliged to submit to his company; but she remained almost as silent as before, and would scarcely raise her eyes.

On his departure, Jane again turned on her and vowed that she would soon bring her to her senses by writing to Robert.

"He will send you such a message as you will be bound to obey," she said. "We have done all that could be thought of to fix one of you, and now when there is a chance of your getting settled you are all for throwing it away! You put me quite out of patience with you!"

Robert answered the letter in person; and, to Jane's amazement, declared positively that he was not going to have Emma thrown away on any half-pay officer; and that he had so much information against Captain Conway, he would hunt him out of the neighbourhood.

On the following morning, however, when he drove into A——, he found that that gentleman, having caught sight of him on the stage coach the previous afternoon, had hastily cleared out, taking Mrs. Burton along with him.

It then transpired that the two had been in collusion; and that Mrs. Burton, believing Emma to be the heiress of her aunt, had introduced Captain Conway to her, on the understanding that she was to receive a substantial sum on the consummation of his marriage with her.

Jane was deeply mortified at having allowed herself to be mixed up with such people; and it was in a very chastened frame of mind that Robert left her, on his return to Croydon, promising to come back in August for a fortnight's holiday.

CHAPTER XII

Mr. Howard had been but a short time with the Osbornes when he was obliged to confess that he had made a mistake in coming.

A man of singular charm of manner, eminently gifted for social success, he had as little vanity as well might be; and his devotion to literature engendered in him a sort of absent-mindedness which rendered him unconscious of things which were sufficiently obvious to others.

He could scarcely himself have said what now opened his eyes in some measure to the nature of Miss Osborne's regard for him; for never before had it occurred to him that she entertained anything beyond an ordinary friendship—the very fact of her occasional efforts to flirt with him only confirming his confidence in her indifference and merely contributing to his amusement.

He had been but little pleased by her incursion into his dinner party; but had attributed it to her lack of variety in a dull neighbourhood and to the influence of Miss Carr, of whom he entertained but a slight opinion. The jealousy of Emma, which she had betrayed at the ball, he believed to be entirely owing to her brother's admiration of her—the connection being such as she could scarcely be expected to advocate.

The knowledge of her feelings occasioned him so much regret, that he would fain have left Italy then and there; but in view of the urgent invitations he had received from Lady Osborne and her son, this was scarcely possible. For the moment at least, he must remain where he was.

He began at once, however, to cast about for some excuse to shorten his stay; and presently urged his desire to prosecute his travels in Spain and Portugal. He had long desired to journey there, and there was now no impediment to his doing so, as his cousin, whose bedside he had attended, had bequeathed him a large fortune, independently of the handsome property to which he had succeeded as heir-presumptive; but, to his surprise, Lady Osborne withstood him, with flushed cheeks and tears in her eyes.

"Do not desert us the moment you have come," she said; "Osborne has seemed so much more composed since you joined us—I never before knew him to be so disquieted as he has been. I cannot but admire Miss Watson's conduct—had she chosen to accept him, nothing could have prevented the marriage. I had scarcely realised how serious his passion was until the night of the ball—after she had left us. He was quite in despair."

"I understand she is shortly to be married."

"Have you told Osborne?"

"No. He has not mentioned her name to me."

"Am I at liberty to tell him?"

"Certainly, madam; what object could be served in concealing it? Osborne could scarcely conceive the idea of rushing home to present a pistol at her lover's head!"

Later on in the evening, Lord Osborne entered the private sitting-room of his late tutor, and said abruptly—

"My mother has informed me of Miss Watson's engagement. To whom is she to be married?"

"That I cannot tell you."

"How came you to know?"

"Musgrave told me.'

"*Musgrave!* I would place monstrous little faith in anything he said!"

"He was certainly never *my* friend, but I understood him to be *yours*," replied Mr. Howard, coldly.

"What can a man do in that delectable neighbourhood?—He helps one to get through the time. I dare swear he made the whole thing up!" So saying, Lord Osborne swung out of the room.

He had not been long gone when there was a timid knock, and Miss Osborne entered with a book in her hand.

Mr. Howard rose and placed a chair for her; but did not sit down himself.

"I came to ask you if you would be so very good as to help me with this passage in Dante's *Inferno*," she said.

He read it at once without any hesitation, as the portion indicated presented no special difficulty that he could see; and he was constrained to wonder wherefore she had selected it— the truth being that she had opened the volume at random.

"I have just heard from Lady Osborne that Miss Watson is about to be married."

In spite of himself, he was obliged to smile.

"I regret that I have nothing to add to this thunderbolt!"

"You are quite sure that she is to be married?"

He was aware that she was watching him narrowly, and both his face and voice were entirely under control as he replied—

"I see no reason to doubt Mr. Musgrave's statement. He was just coming from the Rectory, and I know he was intimate with them."

"He was altogether mad with her for refusing to dance with him at our ball—Fanny Carr told me so."

Mr. Howard looked startled for a moment; and she proceeded—

"Fanny thought it showed a great want of breeding on her part to be so insolent to a guest of ours—she is not in a position to be disdainful of anyone—I should never think of calling her a lady."

She received no answer to this.

"Oh, I know you were vastly in love with her—I was quite expecting to have to congratulate you!"—with an attempt at archness.

Mr. Howard contented himself with bowing.

"I thought her rather handsome myself; but several gentlemen said to me that they did not at all think her anything out of the common."

This again was received in silence; and Julia Osborne, considerably mortified, and perfectly aware of Lady Osborne's displeasure, should she learn of her adventure, thought it best to retire to her room.

A few days later they were joined by Lord Edward Sothern, to whom Miss Osborne turned her attentions, and with much greater prospect of ultimate success.

This, however, was not at all what she desired; but to inflict some gentle damage on an unimpressive heart, which she should presently be called upon to repair. In vain was the snare laid; and she was shortly engaged in a flirtation which obliged Lady Osborne to compel her to accept the proposal which speedily followed, and was urged with insistence.

Julia Osborne was not a little incensed at the turn affairs had taken; and believing Mr. Howard to be the cause of all the mischief, felt that she had been barbarously used. Her resentment grew with reflection; and for a time nothing could appease her, although it was incumbent on her to dissemble her feelings. All this, however, had the salutary effect of estranging her from the first object of her affections; and by degrees the good-humour and attentions of her lover reconciled her to the hardship of her fate.

CHAPTER XIII

As the period for which the Osbornes had engaged a suite of apartments (in an old palace) had drawn to a close, they proceeded with their guests by easy stages to Florence.

Mr. Howard was now Lady Osborne's constant companion, as they rambled about amongst the old churches, and through the galleries, so rich in the masterpieces of the world. He was much more attached to her than to any member of the family, always finding in her a congenial companion. She was an amiable, intelligent, elegant woman, greatly superior to her son and daughter, as well by nature as cultivation.

Her beauty was wonderfully preserved; her fair hair untouched by time; her eyes undimmed; and a bright colour glowing in her cheeks as she walked along under the perfect blue of the Italian sky. As they turned down the "Way of the Beautiful Ladies," he could not but acknowledge how well she fulfilled the tradition.

"You are very silent, Arthur," she said.

He looked at her with a smile in his eyes, and made some brief answer.

Never before had she addressed him by his christian name, and he was at once gratified by a friendship which was sincere enough to desire the intimacy; and disappointed that the music of his name had not sounded for him on the lips of another, whose image he was as yet unable to banish from his heart.

As though divining something of the trend of his thought, she began to speak of Emma; continuing—

"I thought her a perfect lady—I could find no want of breeding in her. Modest, yet confident, as one used to Society; refined, yet without affectation. When I think of the difference between her and the other members of her family, whom I have noticed at the Assembly balls, I am forced to the conclusion that her father must have married very much beneath him. It must be trying for her, when she has been brought up so differently, to be obliged to live with them now."

"She seems to be attached to her eldest sister."

"*She* impressed me much more favourably than her other sisters, whose conduct has attracted my attention on different occasions—she is too simple to be accused of vulgarity."

They walked along in silence for a brief space; and then Lady Osborne continued—

"Is it not very much to be deplored that men so seldom ask for anything beyond youth and beauty?—so seldom consider merit, or suitability? How often have not men disregarded every indication of personal qualities that would have assured their happiness, and turned aside after the first pretty face that came in their way? It is a sort of blindness—an absence of penetration—which must bring ultimate regret. Do you remember the Sacristan, in Santa Croce, telling us of the priceless frescoes of Giotto that lay hidden under the whitewash on the walls of the Chapel of the Bardi della Liberta? It made me think of how often so much lies hidden from us by an even slighter veil—a gossamer so slender that we may afterwards come to wonder what obstacle it could have presented to us!"

Her companion looked at her in wonder, not unmixed with sorrow, though the appeal in her voice held no meaning for him; and he was constrained to walk along in silence at her side.

Later on, as she sat beneath Botticelli's *Fortitude*, with her hand on her parasol, the likeness between them struck him with almost a sense of dismay. Her bright colour had faded, and there was a look of weariness and lassitude on her face. As in the picture, it was the face of one who had suffered, and would yet again suffer, before she had laid her head on the quiet pillow of her grave.

*   *   *   *   *   *

Towards the end of May, the Osbornes returned to London to prepare for Miss Osborne's wedding, whilst Mr. Howard went on his way to Spain.

CHAPTER XIV

The Watsons returned to Croydon in October; and a few weeks later, Mrs. Watson, finding the resignation of second mourning eminently becoming, sent out invitations for a party.

Emma was very sensible of the want of propriety in having company within a year of her father's death; but Robert welcomed the arrangement, as he was anxious to show attention to some new and important clients.

About a week before the entertainment was to take place, Lord Osborne called. He was shown into the drawing-room where Emma was working at her embroidery; while Jane sat near her, making out a list of the dishes that would be necessary for the supper.

It was with a sinking heart that Emma rose and curtsied to him. She had hoped that he had forgotten her; and his persistence in once more following her could only serve to aggravate the difficulty of her position. Jane was not a little agitated at finding herself, for the first time in her life, in the society of a man of his position; and was also a good deal disconcerted by having thrown her second best tippet round her shoulders, when her *best* would have been so much more suitable to such an important occasion.

As Emma remained silent, she believed it to be incumbent on her to express her sense of the honour he had done them in calling, enquiring with immense affability for Lady Osborne and Lady Edward Sothern.

Emma then enquired for Mrs. Blake and Charles, and learned that the latter was head of his class at school, and was grown a monstrous fine fellow. Lord Osborne then added that Mr. Howard was not yet returned from Spain.

"How do you like Croydon, Miss Watson?" he continued. "I always thought it famously dull myself."

"There are some pleasant walks towards the country," she began, when she was hastily interrupted by Jane.

"Oh! I assure you, Lord Osborne, there is an immense deal of fashion in Croydon! Many of the families live in the first style—and as for sociability, there are few places to equal it! When not in mourning, we are in company nearly every evening!"

Lord Osborne looked not a little astonished; then, after a short pause, turning to Emma, said—

"I am glad to hear you are taking exercise. Do not you now wear half-boots?"

Emma began to laugh; and believing he must have said something witty, he joined in very heartily.

At this moment, Robert entered the room. He had not expected to find Lord Osborne there; but Emma was gratified by the quiet manner in which he received him. Taking the conversation into his own hands, he discussed the harvest; the French; the incapacity of the Government (that unfailing source of gratification to those who govern not); and a new play, which a friend of his had seen in London. Emma had never before heard him talk so well; and yet she was aware that there was something wanting in cordiality; but Lord Osborne was apparently very well satisfied to be spared the fatigue of exercising his brain.

Jane, however, listened with ill-concealed impatience; and when, at length, Robert paused, she lost no time in striking in, and began—

"We are arranging to have a little company, my lord——"

But Robert was quite equal to playing the husband; and the instant displeasure of his eye froze the invitation which was hovering on her lips.

"Mr. Musgrave mentioned something of the sort to me," replied Lord Osborne, colouring slightly. "I should be very much honoured, madam, if you would be so good as to include me."

The request was made with a sort of simple shyness that made it impossible to be refused; but as Robert returned to the drawing-room, after seeing him out, his face was clouded.

"I am sure you are too sensible, Emma," he said, "to desire to have Lord Osborne dangling after you. It will not be possible for him to marry you. It will only occasion spiteful gossip; and perhaps prevent your getting fixed."

"I assure you, Robert," replied Emma, blushing, "that not for anything in the world would I encourage him—I sincerely hope that he will not continue to call." With that, she left the room.

Jane had been watching her, with shrewd eyes, in silence.

"I declare I never met a girl like her!" she exclaimed. "I am as certain as anything that she is not wanting to have him! But mark my words, Robert, Lord Osborne is in earnest! He is not for flirting at all. And, unless she is a born fool, Emma will be 'my lady'!"

*   *   *   *   *   *

On the night of the party, Augusta was allowed to remain up for half-an-hour; Sam had got leave to join them; and Lord Osborne and Mr. Musgrave were amongst the first arrivals.

After the usual civilities, Lord Osborne sat down by Emma; and as the guests began to arrive in quick succession, and were not long in being informed by Jane as to his quality, inquisitive glances were constantly directed towards them. Seeing this, Emma presently excused herself, and went to sit by a lady to whom she had been previously introduced; but in a few moments he had followed her. She then presented him to the lady, who was only too pleased to form the acquaintance; and moved on to speak to a pretty girl who was sitting somewhat apart, and who appeared to know as few people as Emma herself. But again he came after her; and although she did her best to engage the two in conversation, the former was so shy, and the latter so dull, that it appeared to her as though they had simultaneously embarked on a game as to which should limit their observations to the fewest words of one syllable. In response to an imploring eye, Sam came over, and she introduced them; and shortly afterwards they were joined by little Augusta. Lord Osborne was at once attracted by the pretty child; and, lifting her up on his knee, presented her with his silver comfit-box. It was soon time for her to retire, and Emma took her, herself, up to her room, remaining with her until Sam was sent in search of her.

As she was coming down stairs, with her hand on his arm, she paused and said earnestly—

"Sam—cannot you help me?"

He remained silent, and she continued: "You can have no conception how I have been suffering from Jane's boasting—and now that Lord Osborne has come, it will be worse than ever! Could not you persuade Robert to forbid him the house?"

"Are you quite sure, Emma, that you know your own heart? Should he be sent away, can you be certain that you will not be regretting it?"

"Quite sure and quite certain!" she replied, smiling.

"Is there anyone else, then, that you care for?"

She blushed deeply, and tears gathered in her eyes.

"There—my love!" he said, gently. "I should not have asked you."

When they re-entered the drawing-room, Lord Osborne was at once at her side. The card-table was being set, and he was anxious to arrange a party for whist, which should include Emma and himself.

Robert, however, interposed by coming forward and requesting his sister to be so kind as to sit beside old Lady Brown, and show her how to play speculation. "Did I hear you say 'whist,' my lord?—this way, if you will be good enough."

At supper, Lord Osborne found himself separated by the length of the room from the object of his admiration; and when he endeavoured to engage her afterwards as his partner, Sam had already secured her for another table.

Jane was perfectly aware of the manoeuvres of her husband and brother, and was not a little entertained by them. "It will only serve to inflame Lord Osborne," she thought to herself. "They could not be playing her cards better!"

*　　*　　*　　*　　*　　*

Sam was obliged to leave them on the following day; but, before going, he urged Robert to put a stop to Lord Osborne calling.

"It is not so simple as you think, Sam," replied his brother. "I shall certainly not give him any encouragement—still less, allow Emma to be thrown at his head. But Jane will have it that he is violently in love with Emma, and quite determined to marry her. If such should be the case, I would not be justified in standing in her way—it would be a very fine match for her."

"I assure you she does not desire it."

"Emma is a good girl—I am perfectly satisfied with her conduct; but, of course, if Lord Osborne intends to ask her, everything will be quite different—she will not think of him in the same way. She is now afraid of being made to appear foolish."

With this, Sam had perforce to be satisfied; and he was at least confident that Robert would secure his sister from any impertinence.

CHAPTER XV

Mrs. Robert Watson having announced her emancipation from the trammels of woe, invitations poured in, fast and thick, in all of which Emma was specially included.

It was fine, bright weather, with the pleasantest frost; and Emma was able to take out Augusta nearly every morning for a walk. To her dismay, however, she found herself frequently joined by Lord Osborne, who had taken rooms in a neighbouring inn; and she appealed in vain to her sister to accompany them, or to take charge of the child herself.

Matters were brought to a head by Jane, who deliberately informed Lord Osborne one morning when he called, of the direction in which Emma had gone. She herself had sent her some little distance beyond the town, in order to enquire for an old servant who was ill. The result was, that as Emma was turning but the first corner on her return home, she came face to face with Lord Osborne.

She replied to his greeting as coldly as might be; and was endeavouring to proceed on her way, when she was brought to a standstill by his informing her that Mrs. Watson had been so good as to indicate to him where he might find her. "She was particularly kind," he said. "I am very much obliged to her—the more so that I have been missing you for so many mornings."

Emma's eyes had been fixed on the ground, but she now suddenly raised them. His face was slightly flushed, and his whole manner betrayed confidence.

Pale with anger, and holding Augusta's hand tightly, she confronted him.

"Lord Osborne, I am alone and unprotected," she said. "You must surely see that your attentions only cause me distress. Be good enough to let me proceed on my way, without accompanying me."

"Mrs. Watson has given me her permission to escort you home."

"My sister-in-law has no conception of her duty to me."

"Believe me, Miss Watson, my intentions are entirely honourable. You have no reason to treat me with such coldness. My whole desire is to make you my wife—if you will honour me by accepting me."

Emma curtsied.

"I cannot possibly accept you, my lord—I beseech you to accept this answer as final—I can never be your wife!—but, believe me, I am deeply sensible to the honour you have done me."

"What reason can you have for refusing me? Do not be so hasty! You do not perhaps know me well enough. I will wait—I will be patient—if you will only give me one word of hope!"

"My lord, I cannot!"

"You cannot?—why cannot you?"

Emma remained silent, but she was walking onward, the while he kept at her side.

"Miss Emma! why do not you speak?"

She could find no reply.

"I know I am a dull fellow—but I love you so much! There is not anything I would not do for you! Could not you care for me a little?"

"No, my lord."

"If you were only married to me, you would care for me!—you could not but care for me if we were married—I would love you so much!"

Emma wept.

"Why do you make my aunt cry? Why do not you go away?" asked little Augusta, looking over at him reproachfully.

"It needs a child to point out my obvious duty," he said bitterly; and, turning back, he strode away.

Augusta remained silent for several minutes, and then said—

"Is not a lord nicer than a gentleman?"

Emma was obliged to smile.

"Shall not you marry him after a while?" she continued.

"Would *you* like to marry him, Augusta?"

"No," replied the child, after a little hesitation; "it always seems a long time when he is there."

On their return home, Jane herself opened the door and, fixing her eyes on Emma, said—

"Has Lord Osborne asked you?"

Emma admitted it.

"Well, you have accepted him?"

"No."

"You have *not* accepted him! Good heavens! Emma!—do you tell me you have *refused* him?—refused *Lord Osborne*!"

"Yes."

"Wicked, ungrateful girl! How have you the face to stand there and tell me such a thing? Are you mad, Emma? What bewitched you to refuse him?"

Emma remained silent.

"Speak, wretched girl! How dared you to refuse him?"

Emma looked at her haughtily.

"I shall speak to my brother," she replied coldly.

"It is your brother who will speak to *you*—Minx! Do not look at me like that! You are insufferable with your airs—and you *just nothing*! Owing every stick on your back to your brother and to me!"

Jane had completely lost all self-control; and little Augusta, terrified, clung to Emma, crying bitterly.

At this moment, Robert came into the hall.

"Here is Emma gone and refused Lord Osborne!" cried his wife.

"Do you consider the servants to be stone deaf!" he demanded angrily. "Come with me into my study, Emma. Go with your mother, Augusta."

Crossing the hall, he opened the door of his room for Emma to enter, and, following her in, closed and locked it.

"What is the meaning of all this?"

Emma was too agitated to reply.

"Is it true that you have refused Lord Osborne?"

"Yes, Robert."

"And why have you refused him?" Emma strove to answer, but no words came.

"I insist on your answering me. Why have you refused him?—you must have some reason."

"I do not love him."

"As far as I am aware, it is not the custom for a nice girl to love a man before he asks her. It will come in time. Listen to me, Emma. I was anything but pleased when Lord Osborne followed you here, but he has shown that his intentions are wholly honourable. Shortly after our party he called on me to obtain my permission to offer himself to you, as soon as he deemed that he might do so with reasonable hope of success. This morning he acquainted your sister with his design in following you. You have nothing to complain of with regard to his conduct; he is a handsome man; and his position is far above that you have any right to expect."

Emma remained silent, with her eyes on the ground and her cheeks burning.

"I stand to you in the light of a father," continued Robert; "I have a right to your obedience; and if you have any natural feelings you will be glad to make me some return for all I have done for you—and I am ready to do much more—by showing some willingness to comply with what I judge to be best for you. I am not saying that I might not have preferred that you had married a man in a simpler rank; but as you are so difficult to suit, I could not run the risk of dismissing him. Our aunt was no friend to you, breeding you up in a different way to us all, making you discontented; and you should be grateful to Lord Osborne for overlooking so much and being willing to marry you. Promise me, Emma, that there will be no more nonsense, if he should be so good as to forgive you for the insult you have done him, and should come forward again."

"I cannot promise. I can never marry him."

"You *can*, and *will* marry him! Obstinate girl! What are you aiming at? Would you prefer to attract the attentions of a royal prince?"

Robert had no sooner uttered these words than he would gladly have recalled them—shrinking from the flash of his sister's eyes. The next moment she had swept past him, unlocked the door, and was gone.

Half-an-hour later she had left the house, and was on her way to Sam at Guildford.

CHAPTER XVI

Early in January Mr. Howard returned from Spain. Had he been able to follow his own inclinations, he would have gone straight to Cumberland in order to look after his property, and confer with his agent on some matters of importance; but he received such an urgent summons from Lady Osborne that he did not like to disregard it, and went down into Surrey.

As he entered the beautiful drawing-room of the Castle, where everything was so familiar to him, and Lady Osborne, so entirely in keeping with her surroundings, came forward to greet him, with a slight flush upon her face, he could not but feel how good it was to be once more at home.

They sat together by the wide hearth, and it seemed to him that in the soft light of the candles she might well pass for ten years less than her age, but as a matter of fact a stranger might well have taken her for but little older than himself; in her beauty there was something so soft and fair.

They had been chatting of one thing and another—principally of Lady Edward Sothern, and the wedding—when suddenly it occurred to him that he had not enquired for Lord Osborne, and, to his amazement, learned that he was in Paris.

"Upon my word I do not understand him," he said, rising to his feet, and leaning against the mantelpiece. "When we were in Italy he was for ever playing the *rôle* of lonely exile, and pining for his native land!"

He looked down at Lady Osborne, and she coloured.

"I was particularly anxious to speak to you about him," she replied. "It is on account of his disappointment with Miss Watson. She has definitely refused him."

"But what could have induced him to ask her when she is the betrothed of another?"

"It was all a mistake—Mr. Musgrave confesses to having been misinformed. She continues to live with her brother and sister at Croydon—vulgar impossible people!—though Osborne insists that they have a child who is a perfect little lady!—I cannot understand these Watsons!"

On the plea of his disordered dress, Mr. Howard soon after retired, but, as he crossed the room it was as though something of its beauty had faded. It no longer held the same spell for him. Something of disquiet had wakened in him. An instinct, not unakin to a sense of shrinking, had possessed him—almost as though there were a pitfall at his feet.

As he entered his old apartment, he was again conscious of uneasiness. It had been freshly decorated, and re-furnished, and there was an air of luxury which somehow repelled him, giving him a feeling of oppression. He went over to the casement, and throwing it wide open, regardless of frost and snow, looked out into the quiet night, with its myriad of stars.

On the following day he set out to call on some old parishioners, and had not gone very far on his way when he encountered Tom Musgrave riding along.

"If ever I met such a fellow as you are, Howard! We all thought you'd been eaten by cannibals!"

"Sorry to disappoint you!—but there are no cannibals in Spain!"

"Well, crocodiles!—it's all one!—and here's Osborne gone off to Paris, clean out of his wits over Miss Watson!"

"How came you to make such a mistake with regard to Miss Watson?"

"Faith! I don't know that there was any mistake! Her people are wild with her for not having Osborne—but there seems to be some other fellow in the background—someone she had met at her aunt's—and she seems fully determined to have her own way. She has, absolutely, left them at Croydon, and gone to stay with her younger brother, where there will be nobody to look after her from morning to night!"

This story unfortunately received confirmation during the morning; and on the following day, when he rode over to the Rectory to see Purvis, it received a still more disquieting aspect. Emma had been seen in the company of a Captain Conway at A——, a man who was said to be highly connected, though of this there was no certain proof—but who, on the other hand, was well known to be a profligate. Heavy at heart he returned to the Castle.

As he sat with Lady Osborne over the fire that night, she told him more of her history than ever he had previously known.

He had always deplored the inferiority of her son and daughter to their mother, but hitherto it had never occurred to him that she had been conscious of it herself.

"I have known but little happiness in my life," she said. "My father, Lord Foulke, was a gambler; and, in view of the increasing difficulty of living, my mother believed it to be her duty to marry off all her daughters as soon as they came out. I was the third of five girls, and married when scarcely sixteen—no more than a child. I could not endure Lord Osborne—my every instinct revolted against him—but though I implored my father and mother, with tears, to spare me, they would not listen to me. No one may know the misery of my married life. When I was about twenty-three, however, my husband died, leaving me with two young children—the boy so backward that I believed him for a time to be deficient; but as I spared no effort to develop him he gradually improved. Not long afterwards my father died from an accident. The shock brought a stroke on my mother, depriving her of the power of speech, which she never afterwards recovered, though she lingered on for several years. My brother, despite the remonstrances of the doctor, insisted on her removal to the Dower House, and short as was the drive, she never recovered from it; so that I dared not attempt to bring her here. As it was seldom possible to leave her, I could see but little of my children, for as the Dower House was small, and indifferently built, she could not endure their noise. But never had I loved her so well. Qualities, that I had never before discerned in her, now showed themselves, and we were drawn together as we never had been before. At her death I returned home, to find my daughter almost a stranger to me. Julia was now fourteen, and her pretty manners, which I had believed to be the expression of her affection for me, had merely served as a mask to her serious defects of character. Perhaps unjustly, I dismissed her governess, believing her to be blamed, and endeavoured myself to correct them, but I had come too late, and it only served to estrange her the further. Osborne, on the other hand, has always held for me the simple affection of his childhood, and his faults are rather of a negative than of a positive character, but he cares for little beyond hunting and fishing—we have almost nothing in common. Until you came, Arthur, I had scarcely known what it was to have a companion."

There was a slight falter in her voice as she uttered the last words, and she looked at her visitor wistfully.

His eyes, half veiled by their lashes, were fixed on the glowing embers, and he remained silent. Once again Emma's soft hand trembled in his own, and he was conscious of the beating of her heart. Why had he not taken her into his arms, then and there, to shelter in his breast for ever?

"Arthur, you are not listening to me!"

There was a note of reproach in the gentle voice at his side.

"I assure you, Lady Osborne, that I am deeply concerned and distressed to hear of all that you have suffered. Perhaps in view of my office it is scarcely orthodox for me to say how very unfair it has all seemed—but from the point of view of a simple human being, it is impossible to think otherwise."

Nothing could have been kinder than the tone in which he pronounced these words; but that she had expected something altogether different was quite evident by the expression of disappointment which overspread her countenance, as she shrank into the shadow.

After a moment's silence he continued:

"The want of sympathy between parents and children is only too common, but there must have been a total absence of all natural feeling on the part of your brother, with regard to Lady Foulke, when he could act in such a manner towards her. The counterpart of it, however, I witnessed at the bedside of my cousin. His son, as you know, broke his neck in the hunting field, as his father lay dying. I was deputed to tell him, and did so in fear and trembling as to the possible effect it might have on him, but he just looked round at me and said: 'And a good thing, too!' Although I had been aware that the relations between them were very unfortunate, I had not believed it possible that there could be such an estrangement between father and son."

After a pause Mr. Howard then announced that he had written to his agent to expect him on the following Saturday.

"Oh, surely not!" exclaimed his hostess, leaning forward in expostulation. "Cumberland will be quite intolerable in this weather—I have heard that the cold there is beyond everything!"

"I have yet to learn that I am in a galloping consumption. I assure you there is no country more delightful and wonderful than Cumberland in the grasp of winter!"

"I am well aware a Northman will swear *anything* with respect to his country!"

"Madam! I protest!"

"Oh, protest away! you are all of you alike! I had hoped that you might have been prevailed upon to remain with us until Easter—in which case Osborne would have come back at once."

"Do not you think he had much better remain where he is? In the gay world of Paris he will have everything to distract him, and may possibly find someone to replace Miss Watson?"

"I do not think so."

"Surely you do not believe that Osborne will remain inconsolable for ever?"

There was a gleam of humour in his dark eyes as he turned them towards her. In all his intimate knowledge of his former pupil, it had certainly never occurred to him that he possessed a heart of untold depths!

"No. What I believe is, that he will revert to his former indifference towards women, and never marry at all."

"That would be very much to be deplored."

"I am not so sure of that. He is scarcely fitted to attract a superior mind, and you could not expect me to welcome an inferior one, or to view, without pain, an unwilling bride forced into his arms."

A day or two later Lady Osborne stood beneath the portico, to wish her guest "God-speed."

"Remember I shall be counting on you for an invitation!" she said, smiling.

He bowed low.

"I shall have to secure a fair chatelaine, madam, in order to receive you worthily!"
How little did he realize that his idle words were as a naked sword in her breast.

CHAPTER XVII

Sam was walking along the High Street of Guildford just as the coach drove up to the stage; and, for the moment, thinking less of anything in the world than of Emma, when, to his amazement, she suddenly appeared on the platform. Hastening forward, he lifted her down; but seeing she could scarcely maintain her composure, forbore to question her, and, drawing her hand within his arm, he led her home.

He now lived entirely with Mr. Curtis at his residence, in a quiet suburban road, not far off: a large, red-brick house, standing in its own grounds, and furnished with all the comfort and suitability of wealth and refinement. As soon as they were seated by a comfortable fire in the library, Emma, in a few words, informed her brother of all that had happened. He was much moved by the recital, but deeply gratified that she had come to him at once—indeed his satisfaction at having her would have been without bounds, had it not been for his indignation at the conduct of Robert and Jane, and the shock he had sustained at finding Emma travelling by herself.

Presently Mr. Curtis, who had been out, returned to the house, and entered the room. Sam at once introduced his sister, and while sparing her feelings as much as possible, made him acquainted with a sufficient account of what had occurred, to let him see that it was impossible for Emma to return to Croydon. He then announced his intention of at once seeking for suitable lodgings for his sister and himself, but Mr. Curtis steadily refused to countenance such an arrangement, insisting that as he already regarded Sam as a son, he had some justification in venturing to hope that Miss Emma might come to look on him as her father, and in the meantime his house was as truly at her service. Emma thanked him charmingly, but begged for permission to look for a situation, as governess, or companion. On perceiving, however, the mortification she was occasioning, both to Sam and Mr. Curtis, she was soon obliged to give way.

Before very long her box was forwarded from Croydon, and both Robert and Jane wrote more suitably than might have been expected, expressing considerable regret that she had left them.

Emma was now more at ease than she had been since her quiet time with Elizabeth, although she daily missed little Augusta; but her health had been injured by all she had gone through. Her cheek, once rounded with perfect health, was now thin and worn, and to Sam's dismay she did not appear to be regaining her vitality as the weeks went by. In view of her half-confession to him, he feared she was suffering from a secret sorrow, and he and Mr. Curtis spared no effort to restore her.

Towards the end of February Elizabeth's marriage was arranged, and Mrs. John Purvis, with whom she had been residing, and from whose house the wedding was to take place, kindly invited the whole family, including Augusta. Emma's embarrassment at meeting Robert and Jane was considerably lessened by this arrangement, and she and the child were inseparable during the few days they spent together. Penelope and Margaret had obtained leave to be present, and both appeared improved by having been provided with occupation, other than hunting for husbands. Mary Edwards had also been invited, and Emma was now able to satisfy herself that she was not wholly indifferent to Sam.

Elizabeth looked very sweet and handsome in her white bonnet and shawl, and the bridegroom distinguished himself not a little by forgetting neither cheque nor ring.

The sisters had been truly happy to have met together again, and their parting was much less sorrowful than before, both bride and bridegroom insisting that Emma should come to them in April to make her home with them.

Poor Sam protested with no little warmth against this arrangement, but Elizabeth was not his elder sister for nothing.

"Cannot you have some sense, Sam!" she said. "Emma is quite too pretty, and has already been too much talked about, to be left alone with a pair of old bachelors!—the two of you out the half of the time! Oh! I know she can take care of herself better than could have been thought possible—she has told me all about Captain Conway—but she should not be left in such a position—her home is with her sister!"

CHAPTER XVIII

Unfortunately, Emma contracted a chill during the long drive back from the wedding, and in spite of, or perhaps, rather as a result of the various remedies with which she was treated, she was still very far from strong when Sam took her over to Wickstead, and left her in the care of Elizabeth.

With what mingled feelings did not Emma view once more the scene where she had spent one of the happiest evenings of her life. Once again, in fancy, she was received by Mr. Howard with all that particularity which had assured her that the entertainment had been arranged with a sole view to enjoying her society. Once again as she entered the dining-parlour, she saw herself at his side, and heard the raillery of his voice as he combated her cherished opinions— from no personal conviction as she had been well aware, but in order to draw her into friendly combat. In the evening afterwards, perhaps she alone had been conscious of his vexation at Miss Osborne's intrusion; and she had also divined his intention of retaining her as his neighbour at cards. The moment of parting was also present with her.

But more to her than all these memories was that of the fateful moment at the ball, when he had begged her to return him the rose he had given to her. Even now it so moved her that she endeavoured to refrain from dwelling on it. Yet how had she been so vain, so foolish, as to have mistaken an ordinary flirtation of a man of the world, for an emotion of a deeper character? For there could no longer be any doubt in her mind with respect to him. He had simply been amusing himself, he had had no intentions with regard to her. Nor had he in any way stepped beyond the limits of convention—blame rested solely with herself. Her former experience of life, slight as it had been, should have taught her that all men of breeding and fashion are more or less adepts at flirting—unless indeed they are scarcely to be tolerated.

Sweet and unselfish as was Emma's nature, the perfect happiness of Elizabeth and Henry Purvis, in a setting so pregnant of another—where every article of furniture seemed to speak of that other—could not but make her sensible of a feeling of bereavement; nor could she withhold her wayward fancy from depicting herself, and that other, as playing the part of her sister and brother-in-law, in their daily life.

Lord Osborne had rejoined his regiment, but Lady Osborne, to the surprise of all, continued to remain on at the Castle, instead of going up to the family town house. Tom Musgrave was as much to the fore as ever, and as busily occupied in impressing his own importance wherever he went, and Mary Edwards drove over at once to welcome Emma. Happening by accident to mention Sam, she gave Emma the opportunity of telling her that Mr. Curtis had formally declared him his heir, for which she was rewarded by a quick blush.

A ball was to take place shortly at the Assembly Rooms, and the Edwards were anxious that Emma should come to them for it, but as can readily be supposed it was almost the last entertainment she would have cared to attend. Elizabeth, however, relieved her from all embarrassment by saying that she did not desire her to go out at night till she was recovered from a cough which had troubled her for some time.

It was not till the end of the month that she took her to a party, given by Mrs. Stephenson, of Ashley Park. Emma had no sooner entered the drawing-room, and before ever her eyes had rested on his tall figure, than she was aware of the presence of Mr. Howard.

Following Elizabeth, she was slightly screened by her, and although they passed within no great distance of him, as he appeared to be looking the other way, she was able to persuade herself, for a short time, that he had not observed her. But it was impossible she should long continue in this belief. The moments were as hours to her, when, presently, as he was conducting a lady into the room beyond, he was obliged to come quite close to her, and recognition was inevitable. He merely bowed and passed on.

Emma had never sought to disguise her feelings from herself, but how deeply her heart was engaged she had not realised until that moment, when she felt that it must break.

A minute or two later Mr. Howard grew aware of a sudden commotion, and then heard it said that a lady had fainted.

Instinctively he knew that it was Emma—and almost immediately, he knew not how, had reached her side. Motioning everyone away, he raised her in his arms, and carried her out to the hall, where there was a couch, but just before he laid her down she opened her eyes, and there was no mistaking the look of deep joy which flashed into them, as she saw him bending over her.

"Emma—my dearest Emma!"

He could say no more, as they were instantly joined by Mrs. Stephenson and Elizabeth; other guests—some impelled by solicitude, and some by curiosity—quickly following.

These, however, were quietly got rid of by their hostess, who at the same time directed the servants to bring restoratives, and soon Emma was able to sit up. She remained so pale and shaken, however, that Mrs. Stephenson begged her to remain all night; but this was steadily opposed by Elizabeth, who was anxious to bring her back with her, and as Emma herself joined in begging to return, the carriage was sent for.

At this moment Henry, who had just heard of Emma's indisposition, came hurrying up, and assisted in conveying her home.

On the following morning Mr. Howard rode over to Wickstead, and, meeting Emma in the shrubbery, declared his passion.

She could not speak, but she laid her trembling hands in his.

CHAPTER XIX

The engagement created not a little stir, and many and various were the comments.

Mr. Curtis composed a pretty speech, for the edification of his patients, to the effect that had he been some forty years younger, when he had had the honour of meeting with Miss Emma, his bachelorhood would have been seriously imperilled.

It is said that when this was reported to Mr. Howard, he vowed he would have imperilled it still further for him.

Mrs. Blake was rejoiced at the news, but it must be confessed that it would be scarcely prudent to record the observations of Charles, who thirsted for his uncle's blood for fully three days after.

Jane still protested that Emma was a fool to have refused a title.

Augusta enquired if she might not be married on the same day?

Lady Edward Sothern's comment was perhaps characteristic—

"There must be something singularly wanting in Arthur Howard to marry a woman of the lower orders."

In a remote room of the Castle Lady Osborne sat, with her head bowed on her hands. No one could have condemned her more severely than she condemned herself. Having missed all hope of romance in her youth, she had endeavoured to secure some measure of it when it was no longer reasonable to expect it; and now she felt that her punishment was almost greater than she well might bear—standing alone, as the slow years went by.

*　　*　　*　　*　　*　　*

Emma's wedding morning shone fair, and people flocked from far and near to see her married.

Lady Osborne lent her her own veil, placing it herself on her head.

Penelope and Margaret could not get leave so soon again, but the bride was attended by Charles and Augusta, carrying baskets of flowers; and it was easy to discern that the former, with the charming fickleness of his sex, had wholly transferred his allegiance from the elder to the younger lady.

As Emma came down from the altar on her husband's arm, she looked all loveliness, but the eyes of different among the congregation strayed from her fresh young beauty to the face of Lady Osborne, and rested there. To the mind of more than one there was something, they knew not what, that seemed to elevate it beyond all they could have believed possible.

Sam and Mary Edwards, now happily betrothed (as Mr. and Mrs. Edwards were unable any longer to urge anything against the alliance) were amongst the company, and received the congratulations of all. It had been arranged that they were to live on with Mr. Curtis, as the old gentleman declared that he could not be deserted in his advancing years.

Shortly after Emma's marriage, Captain O'Brien died, and his widow, surviving him but a short time, Emma found herself the recipient of a legacy of twelve thousand pounds. With her husband's cordial approval, she shared it equally with her sisters; and Penelope lost no time in investing hers in a husband.

But Margaret had suffered so deeply through Tom Musgrave, that in spite of anything Robert and Jane could urge, she insisted on keeping her situation. It was only on the death of the young girl, some years later, to whom she had been acting as companion, that she married a naval officer, whom she had frequently met at her house, and to whom she had become attached, finding with him a much greater measure of happiness than could ever have been her lot had she become the wife of one so worthless as Tom Musgrave.

This gentleman, not long after, fell a prey to a vixen, who lost but little time in reducing him, and on his endeavouring to console himself with strong waters, secured the keys of the cellar, and retained them with a firm hand.

As the Rector of the living, on Mr. Howard's property, shortly resigned it, on account of ill-health, he undertook it himself, appointing Henry Purvis his curate, at a much handsomer figure than he would have received as incumbent, and installing him in the rectory, with its excellent gardens and farm. Emma and Elizabeth's happiness was complete, now that they were settled so near to each other, and as the years went by, there were many merry games between the children of the Rectory and those of the Manor.

Lady Osborne was a frequent visitor at the Howards', some saying that she was fonder of their young people than of her own grandchildren, but this was scarcely the case, as the latter added, in no little degree, to the happiness of her life. Perhaps it might have been nearer the mark had they divined that in Emma she had found the companionship that she had always missed in her own daughter.

She also became very fond of Mrs. Blake, whom Lord Osborne, to the surprise of everyone, married a couple of years later.

If he did not entertain for her the same degree of love that Emma had awakened in him, he was very sincerely attached to her, making an excellent step-father to her children.

Charles entered the Royal Navy.

As he and Augusta spend the greater part of their holidays together at the Howards', and do not find matter for heated argument above seven times in the week, it is confidently believed by several that they will ultimately embark on the more serious argument of life, with all its possibilities for sweetness, or disaster.

FINIS

Sanditon

by

Jane Austen

Sanditon was the last work which Jane Austen wrote, and was unfinished at the time of her death on 18 July, 1817.

Chapter 1

A gentleman and a lady travelling from Tunbridge towards that part of the Sussex coast which lies between Hastings and Eastbourne, being induced by business to quit the high road and attempt a very rough lane, were overturned in toiling up its long ascent, half rock, half sand. The accident happened just beyond the only gentleman's house near the lane—a house which their driver, on being first required to take that direction, had conceived to be necessarily their object and had with most unwilling looks been constrained to pass by. He had grumbled and shaken his shoulders and pitied and cut his horses so sharply that he might have been open to the suspicion of overturning them on purpose (especially as the carriage was not his master's own) if the road had not indisputably become worse than before, as soon as the premises of the said house were left behind—expressing with a most portentous countenance that, beyond it, no wheels but cart wheels could safely proceed. The severity of the fall was broken by their slow pace and the narrowness of the lane; and the gentleman having scrambled out and helped out his companion, they neither of them at first felt more than shaken and bruised. But the gentleman had, in the course of the extrication, sprained his foot—and soon becoming sensible of it, was obliged in a few moments to cut short both his remonstrances to the driver and his congratulations to his wife and himself—and sit down on the bank, unable to stand.

"There is something wrong here," said he, putting his hand to his ankle. "But never mind, my dear—" looking up at her with a smile, "it could not have happened, you know, in a better place—Good out of evil. The very thing perhaps to be wished for. We shall soon get relief. *There,* I fancy, lies my cure—" pointing to the neat-looking end of a cottage, which was seen romantically situated among wood on a high eminence at some little distance—"Does not *that* promise to be the very place?"

His wife fervently hoped it was; but stood, terrified and anxious, neither able to do or suggest anything, and receiving her first real comfort from the sight of several persons now coming to their assistance. The accident had been discerned from a hayfield adjoining the house they had passed. And the persons who approached were a well-looking, hale, gentlemanlike man, of middle age, the proprietor of the place, who happened to be among his haymakers at the time, and three or four of the ablest of them summoned to attend their master—to say nothing of all the rest of the field—men, women and children, not very far off.

Mr. Heywood, such was the name of the said proprietor, advanced with a very civil salutation, much concern for the accident, some surprise at anybody's attempting that road in a carriage, and ready offers of assistance. His courtesies were received with good breeding and gratitude, and while one or two of the men lent their help to the driver in getting the carriage upright again, the traveller said, "You are extremely obliging, sir, and I take you at your word. The injury to my leg is, I dare say, very trifling. But it is always best in these cases, you know, to have a surgeon's opinion without loss of time; and as the road does not seem in a favourable state for my getting up to his house myself, I will thank you to send off one of these good people for the surgeon."

"The surgeon, sir!" exclaimed Mr. Heywood. "I am afraid you will find no surgeon at hand here, but I dare say we shall do very well without him."

"Nay sir, if *he* is not in the way, his partner will do just as well, or rather better. I would rather see his partner. Indeed I would prefer the attendance of his partner. One of these good people can be with him in three minutes, I am sure. I need not ask whether I see the house," (looking towards the cottage) "for excepting your own, we have passed none in this place which can be the abode of a gentleman."

Mr. Heywood looked very much astonished, and replied: "What, sir! Are you expecting to find a surgeon in that cottage? We have neither surgeon nor partner in the parish, I assure you."

"Excuse me, sir," replied the other. "I am sorry to have the appearance of contradicting you, but from the extent of the parish or some other cause you may not be aware of the fact. Stay. Can I be mistaken in the place? Am I not in Willingden? Is not this Willingden?"

"Yes, sir, this is certainly Willingden."

"Then, sir, I can bring proof of your having a surgeon in the parish, whether you may know it or not. Here, sir," (taking out his pocket book) "if you will do me the favor of casting your eye over these advertisements which I cut out myself from the *Morning Post* and the *Kentish Gazette*, only yesterday morning in London, I think you will be convinced that I am not speaking at random. You will find in it an advertisement of the dissolution of a partnership in the medical line in your own parish—extensive business, undeniable character respectable references wishing to form a separate establishment. You will find it at full length, sir,"— offering the two little oblong extracts.

"Sir," said Mr. Heywood with a good humoured smile, "if you were to show me all the newspapers that are printed in one week throughout the kingdom, you would not persuade me of there being a surgeon in Willingden," said Mr. Heywood with a good-humoured smile. "Having lived here ever since I was born, man and boy fifty-seven years, I think I must have known of such a person. At least I may venture to say that he has not much business. To be sure, if gentlemen were to be often attempting this lane in post-chaises, it might not be a bad speculation for a surgeon to get a house at the top of the hill. But as to that cottage, I can assure you, sir, that it is in fact, in spite of its spruce air at this distance, as indifferent a double tenement as any in the parish, and that my shepherd lives at one end and three old women at the other."

He took the pieces of paper as he spoke, and, having looked them over, added, "I believe I can explain it, sir. Your mistake *is* in the place. There are two Willingdens in this country. And your advertisement refers to the other, which is Great Willingden or Willingden Abbots, and lies seven miles off on the other side of Battle—quite down in the Weald. And *we, sir,*" he added, speaking rather proudly, "are not in the Weald."

"Not *down* in the weald, I am sure," replied the traveller pleasantly. "It took us half an hour to climb your hill. Well, I dare say it is as you say and I have made an abominably stupid blunder—all done in a moment. The advertisements did not catch my eye till the last half hour of our being in town—when everything was in the hurry and confusion which always attend a short stay there. One is never able to complete anything in the way of business, you know, till the carriage is at the door. And, accordingly satisfying myself with a brief inquiry, and finding we were actually to pass within a mile or two of a *Willingden,* I sought no farther...My dear," (to his wife) "I am very sorry to have brought you into this scrape. But do not be alarmed about my leg. It gives me no pain while I am quiet. And as soon as these good people have succeeded in setting the carriage to rights and turning the horses round, the best thing we can do will be to measure back our steps into the turnpike road and proceed to Hailsham, and so home, without attempting anything farther. Two hours take us home from Hailsham. And once at home, we have our remedy at hand, you know. A little of our own bracing sea air will soon set me on my feet again. Depend upon it, my dear, it is exactly a case for the sea. Saline air and immersion will be the very thing. My sensations tell me so already."

In a most friendly manner Mr. Heywood here interposed, entreating them not to think of proceeding till the ankle had been examined and some refreshment taken, and very cordially pressing them to make use of his house for both purposes.

"We are always well stocked," said he, "with all the common remedies for sprains and bruises. And I will answer for the pleasure it will give my wife and daughters to be of service to you in every way in their power."

A twinge or two, in trying to move his foot, disposed the traveller to think rather more than he had done at first of the benefit of immediate assistance; and consulting his wife in the few words of "Well, my dear, I believe it will be better for us," he turned again to Mr. Heywood, and said: "Before we accept your hospitality sir, and in order to do away with any unfavourable impression which the sort of wild-goose chase you find me in may have given rise to, allow me to tell you who we are. My name is Parker, Mr. Parker of Sanditon; this lady, my wife, Mrs. Parker. We are on our road home from London. My name perhaps, though I am by no means the first of my family holding landed property in the parish of Sanditon, may be unknown at this distance from the coast. But Sanditon itself—everybody has heard of Sanditon. The favourite for a young and rising bathing-place, certainly the favourite spot of all that are to be found along the coast of Sussex—the most favoured by nature, and promising to be the most chosen by man."

"Yes, I have heard of Sanditon," replied Mr. Heywood. "Every five years, one hears of some new place or other starting up by the sea and growing the fashion. How they can half of them be filled is the wonder! *Where* people can be found with money and time to go to them! Bad things for a country—sure to raise the price of provisions and make the poor good for nothing—as I dare say you find, sir."

"Not at all, sir, not at all," cried Mr. Parker eagerly. "Quite the contrary, I assure you. A common idea, but a mistaken one. It may apply to your large, overgrown places like Brighton or Worthing or Eastbourne but *not* to a small village like Sanditon, precluded by its size from experiencing any of the evils of civilization. While the growth of the place, the buildings, the nursery grounds, the demand for everything and the sure resort of the very best company whose regular, steady, private families of thorough gentility and character who are a blessing everywhere, excited the industry of the poor and diffuse comfort and improvement among them of every sort. No sir, I assure you, Sanditon is not a place—"

"I do not mean to take exception to any place in particular," answered Mr. Heywood. "I only think our coast is too full of them altogether. But had we not better try to get you—"

"Our coast too full!" repeated Mr. Parker. "On that point perhaps we may not totally disagree. At least there are *enough.* Our coast is abundant enough. It demands no more. Everybody's taste and everybody's finances may be suited. And those good people who are trying to add to the number are, in my opinion, excessively absurd and must soon find themselves the dupes of their own fallacious calculations. Such a place as Sanditon, sir, I may say was wanted, was called for. Nature had marked it out, had spoken in most intelligible characters. The finest, purest sea breeze on the coast—acknowledged to be so—excellent bathing—fine hard sand—deep water ten yards from the shore—no mud—no weeds—no slimy rocks. Never was there a place more palpably designed by nature for the resort of the invalid— the very spot which thousands seemed in need of! The most desirable distance from London! One complete, measured mile nearer than Eastbourne. Only conceive, sir, the advantage of saving a whole mile in a long journey. But Brinshore, sir, which I dare say you have in your eye—the attempts of two or three speculating people about Brinshore this last year to raise that paltry hamlet lying as it does between a stagnant marsh, a bleak moor and the constant effluvia of a ridge of putrefying seaweed—can end in nothing but their own disappointment. What in the name of common sense is to *recommend* Brinshore? A most insalubrious air—roads proverbially detestable—water brackish beyond example—impossible to get a good dish of tea within three miles of the place. And as for the soil it is so cold and ungrateful that it can hardly be made to yield a cabbage. Depend upon it, sir, that this is a most faithful Brinshore—not in the smallest degree exaggerated—and if you have heard it differently spoken of—"

"Sir, I never heard it spoken of in my life before," said Mr. Heywood. "I did not know there was such a place in the world."

"You did not! There, my dear," turning with exultation to his wife, "you see how it is. So much for the celebrity of Brinshore! This gentleman did not know there was such a place in the world. Why, in truth, sir, I fancy we may apply to Brinshore that line of the poet Cowper in his description of the religious cottager, as opposed to Voltaire—*She,* never heard of half a mile from home."

"With all my heart, sir, apply any verses you like to it. But I want to see something applied to your leg. And I am sure by your lady's countenance that she is quite of my opinion and thinks it a pity to lose any more time. And here come my girls to speak for themselves and their mother." (Two or three genteel-looking young women, followed by as many maid servants, were now seen issuing from the house.) "I began to wonder the bustle should not have reached *them.* A thing of this kind soon makes a stir in a lonely place like ours. Now, sir, let us see how you can be best conveyed into the house."

The young ladies approached and said everything that was proper to recommend their father's offers, and in an unaffected manner calculated to make the strangers easy. And, as Mrs. Parker was exceedingly anxious for relief, and her husband by this time not much less disposed for it, a very few civil scruples were enough; especially as the carriage, being now set up, was discovered to have received such injury on the fallen side as to be unfit for present use. Mr. Parker was therefore carried into the house and his carriage wheeled off to a vacant barn.

Chapter 2

The acquaintance, thus oddly begun, was neither short nor unimportant. For a whole fortnight the travellers were fixed at Willingden, Mr. Parker's sprain proving too serious for him to move sooner. He had fallen into very good hands. The Heywoods were a thoroughly respectable family and every possible attention was paid, in the kindest and most unpretending manner, to both husband and wife. *He* was waited on and nursed, and *she* cheered and comforted with unremitting kindness; and as every office of hospitality and friendliness was received as it ought, as there was not more good will on one side than gratitude on the other, nor any deficiency of generally pleasant manners in either, they grew to like each other, in the course of that fortnight, exceedingly well.

Mr. Parker's character and history were soon unfolded. All that he understood of himself, he readily told, for he was very open-hearted; and where he might be himself in the dark, his conversation was still giving information, to such of the Heywoods as could observe. By such he was perceived to be an enthusiast on the subject of Sanditon, a complete enthusiast. Sanditon—the success of Sanditon as a small, fashionable bathing place, was the object for which he seemed to live. A very few years ago, it had been a quiet village of no pretensions, but some natural advantages in its position and some accidental circumstances having suggested to himself, and the other principal landholder, the probability of its becoming a profitable speculation, they had engaged in it, and planned and built, and praised and puffed, and raised it to something of young renown; and Mr. Parker could now think of very little besides.

The facts which, in more direct communication, he laid before them were that he was about five and thirty, had been married—very happily married—seven years, and had four sweet children at home; that he was of a respectable family and easy, though not large, fortune; no profession—succeeding as eldest son to the property which two or three generations had been holding and accumulating before him—that he had two brothers and two sisters, all single and all independent—the eldest of the two former indeed, by collateral inheritance, quite as well provided for as himself.

His object in quitting the high road to hunt for an advertising surgeon was also plainly stated. It had not proceeded from any intention of spraining his ankle or doing himself any other injury for the good of such surgeon, nor (as Mr. Heywood had been apt to suppose) from any design of entering into partnership with him. It was merely in consequence of a wish to establish some medical man at Sanditon, which the nature of the advertisement induced him to expect to accomplish in Willingden. He was convinced that the advantage of a medical man at hand would very materially promote the rise and prosperity of the place, would in fact tend to bring a prodigious influx—nothing else was wanting. He had *strong* reason to believe that *one* family had been deterred last year from trying Sanditon on that account and probably very many more—and his own sisters, who were sad invalids and whom he was very anxious to get to Sanditon this summer, could hardly be expected to hazard themselves in a place where they could not have immediate medical advice.

Upon the whole, Mr. Parker was evidently an amiable family man, fond of wife, children, brothers and sisters, and generally kind-hearted; liberal, gentlemanlike, easy to please; of a sanguine turn of mind, with more imagination than judgement. And Mrs. Parker was as evidently a gentle, amiable, sweet-tempered woman, the properest wife in the world for a man of strong understanding but not of a capacity to supply the cooler reflection which her own husband sometimes needed; and so entirely waiting to be guided on every occasion that whether he was risking his fortune or spraining his ankle, she remained equally useless.

Sanditon was a second wife and four children to him, hardly less dear, and certainly more engrossing. He could talk of it forever. It had indeed the highest claims; not only those of birthplace, property and home; it was his mine, his lottery, his speculation and his hobby horse; his occupation, his hope and his futurity. He was extremely desirous of drawing his good friends at Willingden thither; and his endeavours in the cause were as grateful and disinterested as they were warm.

He wanted to secure the promise of a visit, to get as many of the family as his own house would contain, to follow him to Sanditon as soon as possible; and, healthy as they all undeniably were, foresaw that every one of them would be benefited by the sea. He held it indeed as certain that no person could be really well, no person (however upheld for the present by fortuitous aids of exercise and spirits in a semblance of health) could be really in a state of secure and permanent health without spending at least six weeks by the sea every year. The sea air and sea bathing together were nearly infallible, one or the other of them being a match for every disorder of the stomach, the lungs or the blood. They were anti-spasmodic, anti-pulmonary, anti-septic, anti-billious and anti-rheumatic. Nobody could catch cold by the sea; nobody wanted appetite by the sea; nobody wanted spirits; nobody wanted strength. Sea air was healing, softening, relaxing fortifying and bracing seemingly just as was wanted sometimes one, sometimes the other. If the sea breeze failed, the sea-bath was the certain corrective; and where bathing disagreed, the sea air alone was evidently designed by nature for the cure.

His eloquence, however, could not prevail. Mr. and Mrs. Heywood never left home. Marrying early and having a very numerous family, their movements had long been limited to one small circle; and they were older in habits than in age. Excepting two journeys to London in the year to receive his dividends, Mr. Heywood went no farther than his feet or his well-tried old horse could carry him; and Mrs. Heywood's adventurings were only now and then to visit her neighbours in the old coach which had been new when they married and fresh-lined on their eldest son's coming of age ten years ago. They had a very pretty property; enough, had their family been of reasonable limits, to have allowed them a very gentlemanlike share of luxuries and change; enough for them to have indulged in a new carriage and better roads, an occasional month at Tunbridge Wells, and symptoms of the gout and a winter at Bath. But the maintenance, education and fitting out of fourteen children demanded a very quiet, settled, careful course of life, and obliged them to be stationary and healthy at Willingden.

What prudence had at first enjoined was now rendered pleasant by habit. They never left home and they had gratification in saying so. But very far from wishing their children to do the same, they were glad to promote *their* getting out into the world as much as possible. *They* stayed at home that their children *might* get out; and, while making that home extremely comfortable, welcomed every change from it which could give useful connections or respectable acquaintance to sons or daughters. When Mr. and Mrs. Parker, therefore, ceased from soliciting a family visit and bounded their views to carrying back one daughter with them, no difficulties were started. It was general pleasure and consent.

Their invitation was to Miss Charlotte Heywood, a very pleasing young woman of two and twenty, the eldest of the daughters at home and the one who, under her mother's directions, had been particularly useful and obliging to them; who had attended them most and knew them best. Charlotte was to go, with excellent health, to bathe and be better if she could; to receive every possible pleasure which Sanditon could be made to supply by the gratitude of those she went with; and to buy new parasols, new gloves and new brooches for her sisters and herself at the library, which Mr. Parker was anxiously wishing to support.

All that Mr. Heywood himself could be persuaded to promise was that he would send everyone to Sanditon who asked his advice, and that nothing should ever induce him (as far as the future could be answered for) to spend even five shilling at Brinshore.

Chapter 3

Every neighbourhood should have a great lady. The great lady of Sanditon was Lady Denham; and in their journey from Willingden to the coast, Mr. Parker gave Charlotte a more detailed account of her than had been called for before. She had been necessarily often mentioned at Willingden for being his colleague in speculation. Sanditon itself could not be talked of long without the introduction of Lady Denham. That she was a very rich old lady, who had buried two husbands, who knew the value of money, and was very much looked up to and had a poor cousin living with her, were facts already known; but some further particulars of her history and her character served to lighten the tediousness of a long hill, or a heavy bit of road, and to give the visiting young lady a suitable knowledge of the person with whom she might now expect to be daily associating.

Lady Denham had been a rich Miss Brereton, born to wealth but not to education. Her first husband had been a Mr. Hollis, a man of considerable property in the country, of which a large share of the parish of Sanditon, with manor and mansion house, made a part. He had been an elderly man when she married him, her own age about thirty. Her motives for such a match could be little understood at the distance of forty years, but she had so well nursed and pleased Mr. Hollis that at his death he left her everything—all his estates, and all at her disposal. After a widowhood of some years, she had been induced to marry again. The late Sir Harry Denham, of Denham Park in the neighbourhood of Sanditon, had succeeded in removing her and her large income to his own domains, but he could not succeed in the views of permanently enriching his family which were attributed to him. She had been too wary to put anything out of her own power and when, on Sir Harry's decease, she returned again to her own house at Sanditon, she was said to have made this boast to a friend: "that though she had *got* nothing but her title from the family, still she had *given* nothing for it."

For the title, it was to be supposed, she had married; and Mr. Parker acknowledged there being just such a degree of value for it apparent now, as to give her conduct that natural explanation. "There is at times," said he, "a little self-importance but it is not offensive and there are moments, there are points, when her love of money is carried greatly too far. But she is a good-natured woman, a very good-natured woman—a very obliging, friendly neighbour; a cheerful, independent, valuable character and her faults may be entirely imputed to her want of education. She has good natural sense, but quite uncultivated. She has a fine active mind as well as a fine healthy frame for a woman of seventy, and enters into the improvement of Sanditon with a spirit truly admirable. Though now and then, a littleness *will* appear. She cannot look forward quite as I would have her and takes alarm at a trifling present expense without considering what returns it *will* make her in a year or two. That is—awe think *differently,* we now and then see things *differently,* Miss Heywood. Those who tell their own story, you know, must be listened to with caution. When you see us in contact, you will judge for yourself."

Lady Denham was indeed a great lady beyond the common wants of society, for she had many thousands a year to bequeath, and three distinct sets of people to be courted by: her own relations, who might very reasonably wish for her original thirty thousand pounds among them; the legal heirs of Mr. Hollis, who must hope to be more indebted to *her* sense of justice than he had allowed them to be to *his;* and those members of the Denham family whom her second husband had hoped to make a good bargain for. By all of these, or by branches of them, she had no doubt been long, and still continued to be, well attacked; and of these three divisions, Mr. Parker did not hesitate to say that Mr. Hollis's kindred were the *least* in favour and Sir Harry Denham's the *most.* The former, he believed, had done themselves irremediable harm by expressions of very unwise and unjustifiable resentment at the time of Mr. Hollis's death; the latter had the advantage of being the remnant of a connection which she certainly valued, of having been known to her from their childhood and of being always at hand to preserve their interest by reasonable attention. Sir Edward, the present baronet, nephew to Sir Harry, resided constantly at Denham Park; and Mr. Parker had little doubt that he and his sister, Miss Denham, who lived with him, would be principally remembered in her will. He sincerely hoped it. Miss Denham had a very small provision; and her brother was a poor man for his rank in society.

"He is a warm friend to Sanditon," said Mr. Parker, "and his hand would be as liberal as his heart, had he the power. He would be a noble coadjutor! As it is, he does what he can and is running up a tasteful little cottage *ornèe,* on a strip of waste ground Lady Denham has granted him, which I have no doubt we shall have many a candidate for, before the end even of *this* season."

Till within the last twelvemonth, Mr. Parker had considered Sir Edward as standing without a rival, as having the fairest chance of succeeding to the greater part of all that she had to give; but there were now another person's claims to be taken into account, those of the young female relation whom Lady Denham had been induced to receive into her family. After having always protested against any such addition, and long and often enjoyed the repeated defeats she had given to every attempt of her relations to introduce this young lady or that young lady as a companion at Sanditon House, she had brought back with her from London last Michaelmas a Miss Brereton, who bid fair by her merits to vie in favour with Sir Edward and to secure for herself and her family that share of the accumulated property which they had certainly the best right to inherit.

Mr. Parker spoke warmly of Clara Brereton, and the interest of his story increased very much with the introduction of such a character. Charlotte listened with more than amusement now; it was solicitude and enjoyment, as she heard her described to be lovely, amiable, gentle, unassuming, conducting herself uniformly with great good sense, and evidently gaining by her innate worth on, the affections of her patroness. Beauty, sweetness, poverty and dependence do not want the imagination of a man to operate upon; with due exceptions, woman feels for woman very promptly and compassionately. He gave the particulars which had led to Clara's admission at Sanditon as no bad exemplification of that mixture of character, that union of littleness with kindness with good sense with even liberality which he saw in Lady Denham.

After having avoided London for many years, principally on account of these very cousins who were continually writing, inviting and tormenting her, and whom she was determined to keep at a distance, she had been obliged to go there last Michaelmas with the certainty of being detained at least a fortnight. She had gone to a hotel, living by her own account as prudently as possible to defy the reputed expensiveness of such a home, and at the end of three days calling for her bill that she might judge of her state. Its amount was such as determined her on staying not another hour in the house, and she was preparing in all the anger and perturbation of her belief in very gross imposition *there*, and her ignorance of where to go for better usage, to leave the hotel at all hazards, when the cousins, the politic and lucky cousins, who seemed always to have a spy on her, introduced themselves at this important moment, and learning her situation, persuaded her to accept such a home for the rest of her stay as their humbler house in a very inferior part of London could offer.

She went; was delighted with her welcome and the hospitality and attention she received from everybody—found her good cousins the Breretons beyond her expectation worthy people—and finally was impelled by a personal knowledge of their narrow income and pecuniary difficulties to invite one of the girls of the family to pass the winter with her. The invitation was to *one*, for six months—with the probability of another being then to take her place—but in *selecting* the one, Lady Denham had shown the good part of her character. For, passing by the actual *daughters* of the house, she had chosen Clara, a niece—more helpless and more pitiable of course than any—a dependent on poverty—an additional burden on an encumbered circle—and one who had been so low in every worldly view as, with all her natural endowments and powers, to have been preparing for a situation little better than a nursery maid.

Clara had returned with her—and by her good sense and merit had now, to all appearance, secured a very strong hold in Lady Denham's regard. The six months had long been over—and not a syllable was breathed of any change or exchange. She was a general favourite. The influence of her steady conduct and mild, gentle temper was felt by everybody. The prejudices which had met her at first, in some quarters, were all dissipated. She was felt to be worthy of trust, to be the very companion who would guide and soften Lady Denham, who would enlarge her mind and open her hand. She was as thoroughly amiable as she was lovely—and since having had the advantage of their Sanditon breezes, that loveliness was complete.

Chapter 4

"And whose very snug-looking place is this?" said Charlotte as, in a sheltered dip within two miles of the sea, they passed close by a moderate-sized house, well fenced and planted, and rich in the garden, orchard and meadows which are the best embellishments of such a dwelling. "It seems to have as many comforts about it as Willingden."

"Ah," said Mr. Parker. "This is my old house, the house of my forefathers, the house where I and all my brothers and sisters were born and bred, and where my own three eldest children were born; where Mrs. Parker and I lived till within the last two years, till our new house was finished. I am glad you are pleased with it. It is an honest old place; and Hillier keeps it in very good order. I have given it up, you know, to the man who occupies the chief of my land. He gets a better house by it, and I, a rather better situation! One other hill brings us to Sanditon—modern Sanditon—a beautiful spot. Our ancestors, you know, always built in a hole. Here were we, pent down in this little contracted nook, without air or view, only one mile and three quarters from the noblest expanse of ocean between the South Foreland and Land's End, and without the smallest advantage from it. You will not think I have made a bad exchange when we reach Trafalgar House—which by the bye, I almost wish I had not named Trafalgar—for Waterloo is more the thing now. However, Waterloo is in reserve; and if we have encouragement enough this year for a little crescent to be ventured on, as I trust we shall, then we shall be able to call it Waterloo Crescent—and the name joined to the form of the building, which always takes, will give us the command of lodgers. In a good season we should have more applications than we could attend to."

"It was always a very comfortable house," said Mrs. Parker, looking at it through the back window with something like the fondness of regret. "And such a nice garden such an excellent garden."

"Yes, my love, but *that* we may be said to carry with us. *It* supplies us, as before, with all the fruit and vegetables we want. And we have, in fact, all the comfort of an excellent kitchen garden without the constant eyesore of its formalities or the yearly nuisance of its decaying vegetation. Who can endure a cabbage bed in October?"

"Oh dear, yes. We are quite as well off for garden stuff as ever we were; for if it is forgot to be brought at any time, we can always buy what we want at Sanditon House. The gardener there is glad enough to supply us. But it was a nice place for the children to run about in. So shady in summer!"

"My dear, we shall have shade enough on the hill, and more than enough in the course of a very few years. The growth of my plantations is a general astonishment. In the meanwhile we have the canvas awning which gives us the most complete comfort within doors. And you can get a parasol at Whitby's for little Mary at any time, or a large bonnet at Jebb's. And as for the boys, I must say I would rather *them* run about in the sunshine than not. I am sure we agree, my dear, in wishing our boys to be as hardy as possible."

"Yes indeed, I am sure we do. And I will get Mary a little parasol, which will make her as proud as can be. How grave she will walk about with it and fancy herself quite a little woman. Oh, I have not the smallest doubt of our being a great deal better off where we are now. If we any of us want to bathe, we have not a quarter of a mile to go. But you know," (still looking back), "one loves to look at an old friend at a place where one has been happy. The Hilliers did not seem to feel the storms last winter at all. I remember seeing Mrs. Hillier after one of those dreadful nights, when *we* had been literally rocked in our bed, and she did not seem at all aware of the wind being anything more than common."

"Yes, yes, that's likely enough. *We* have all the grandeur of the storm with less real danger because the wind, meeting with nothing to oppose or confine it around our house, simply rages and passes on; while down in this gutter, nothing is known of the state of the air below the tops of the trees; and the inhabitants may be taken totally unawares by one of those dreadful currents, which do more mischief in a valley when they *do* arise than an open country ever experiences in the heaviest gale. But, my dear love, as to gardenstuff, you were saying that any accidental omission is supplied in a moment by Lady Denham's gardener. But it occurs to me that we ought to go elsewhere upon such occasions, and that old Stringer and his son have a higher claim. I encouraged him to set up, you know, and am afraid he does not do very well. That is, there has not been time enough yet. He *will* do very well beyond a doubt. But at first it is uphill work, and therefore we must give him what help we can. When any vegetables or fruit happen to be wanted—and it will not be amiss to have them often wanted, to have something or other forgotten most days—just to have a nominal supply, you know, that poor old Andrew may not lose his daily job—but in fact to buy the chief of our consumption from the Stringers."

"Very well, my love, that can be easily done. And cook will be satisfied, which will be a great comfort, for she is always complaining of old Andrew now and says he never brings her what she wants. There now the old house is quite left behind. What is it your brother Sidney says about its being a hospital?"

"Oh, my dear Mary, merely a joke of his. He pretends to advise me to make a hospital of it. He pretends to laugh at my improvements. Sidney says anything, you know. He has always said what he chose, of and to us all. Most families have such a member among them, I believe, Miss Heywood. There is someone in most families privileged by superior abilities or spirits to say anything. In ours, it is Sidney, who is a very clever young man and with great powers of pleasing. He lives too much in the world to be settled; that is his only fault. He is here and there and everywhere. I wish we may get him to Sanditon. I should like to have you acquainted with him. And it would be a fine thing for the place! Such a young man as Sidney, with his neat equipage and fashionable air. You and I, Mary, know what effect it might have. Many a respectable family, many a careful mother, many a pretty daughter might it secure us to the prejudice of Eastbourne and Hastings."

They were now approaching the church and the real village of Sanditon, which stood at the foot of the hill they were afterwards to ascend—a hill whose side was covered with the woods and enclosures of Sanditon House and whose height ended in an open down where the new buildings might soon be looked for. A branch only, of the valley, winding more obliquely towards the sea, gave a passage to an inconsiderable stream, and formed at its mouth a third habitable division in a small cluster of fishermen's houses.

The original village contained little more than cottages; but the spirit of the day had been caught, as Mr. Parker observed with delight to Charlotte, and two or three of the best of them were smartened up with a white curtain and "Lodgings to let," and farther on, in the little green court of an old farm house, two females in elegant white were actually to be seen with their books and camp stools; and in turning the corner of the baker's shop, the sound of a harp might be heard through the upper casement.

Such sights and sounds were highly blissful to Mr. Parker. Not that he had any personal concern in the success of the village itself; for considering it as too remote from the beach, he had done nothing there; but it was a most valuable proof of the increasing fashion of the place altogether. If the *village* could attract, the hill might be nearly full. He anticipated an amazing season. At the same time last year (late in July) there had not been a single lodger in the village! Nor did he remember any during the whole summer, excepting one family of children who came from London for sea air after the whooping cough, and whose mother would not let them be nearer the shore for fear of their tumbling in.

"Civilization, civilization indeed!" cried Mr. Parker, delighted. "Look, my dear Mary, look at William Heeley's windows. Blue shoes, and nankin boots! Who would have expected such a sight at a shoemaker's in old Sanditon! This is new within the month. There was no blue shoe when we passed this way a month ago. Glorious indeed! Well, I think I *have* done something in my day. Now, for our hill, our health-breathing hill."

In ascending, they passed the lodge gates of Sanditon House and saw the top of the house itself among its groves. It was the last building of former days in that line of the parish. A little higher up, the modern began; and in crossing the down, a Prospect House, a Bellevue Cottage and a Denham Place were to be looked at by Charlotte with the calmness of amused curiosity, and by Mr. Parker with the eager eye which hoped to see scarcely any empty houses. More bills at the windows than he had calculated on—and a smaller show of company on the hill— fewer carriages, fewer walkers. He had fancied it just the time of day for them to be all returning from their airings to dinner; but the sands and the Terrace always attracted some—and the tide must be flowing about half-tide now.

He longed to be on the sands, the cliffs, at his own house, and everywhere out of his house at once. His spirits rose with the very sight of the sea and he could almost feel his ankle getting stronger already. Trafalgar House, on the most elevated spot on the down, was a light, elegant building, standing in a small lawn with a very young plantation round it, about a hundred yards from the brow of a steep but not very lofty cliff—and the nearest to it of every building, excepting one short row of smart-looking houses called the Terrace, with a broad walk in front, aspiring to be the Mall of the place. In this row were the best milliner's shop and the library— a little detached from it, the hotel and billiard room. Here began the descent to the beach and to the bathing machines. And this was therefore the favourite spot for beauty and fashion.

At Trafalgar House, rising at a little distance behind the Terrace, the travellers were safely set down; and all was happiness and joy between Papa and Mama and their children; while Charlotte, having received possession of her apartment, found amusement enough in standing at her ample Venetian window and looking over the miscellaneous foreground of unfinished buildings, waving linen and tops of houses, to the sea, dancing and sparkling in sunshine and freshness.

Chapter 5

When they met before dinner, Mr. Parker was looking over letters.

"Not a line from Sidney!" said he. "He is an idle fellow. I sent him an account of my accident from Willingden and thought he would have vouchsafed me an answer. But perhaps it implies that he is coming himself. I trust it may. But here is a letter from one of my sisters. *They* never fail me. Women are the only correspondents to be depended on. Now, Mary," smiling at his wife, "before I open it, what shall we guess as to the state of health of those it comes from or rather what would Sidney say if he were here? Sidney is a saucy fellow, Miss Heywood. And you must know, he will have it there is a good deal of imagination in my two sisters' complaints. But it really is not so, or very little. They have wretched health, as you have heard us say frequently, and are subject to a variety of very serious disorders. Indeed, I do not believe they know what a day's health is. And at the same time, they are such excellent useful women and have so much energy of character that where any good is to be done, they force themselves on exertions which, to those who do not thoroughly know them, have an extraordinary appearance. But there is really no affectation about them, you know. They have only weaker constitutions and stronger minds than are often met with, either separate or together. And our youngest brother, who lives with them and who is not much above twenty, I am sorry to say is almost as great an invalid as themselves. He is so delicate that he can engage in no profession. Sidney laughs at him. But it really is no joke, though Sidney often makes me laugh at them all in spite of myself. Now, if he were here, I know he would be offering odds that either Susan, Diana or Arthur would appear by this letter to have been at the point of death within the last month."

Having run his eye over the letter, he shook his head and began: "No chance of seeing them at Sanditon I am sorry to say. A very indifferent account of them indeed. Seriously, a very indifferent account. Mary, you will be quite sorry to hear how ill they have been and are. Miss Heywood, if you will give me leave, I will read Diana's letter aloud. I like to have my friends acquainted with each other and I am afraid this is the only sort of acquaintance I shall have the means of accomplishing between you. And I can have no scruple on Diana's account; for her letters show her exactly as she is, the most active, friendly, warm-hearted being in existence, and therefore must give a good impression."

He read: "My dear Tom, we were all much grieved at your accident, and if you had not described yourself as fallen into such very good hands, I should have been with you at all hazards the day after the receipt of your letter, though it found me suffering under a more severe attack than usual of my old grievance, spasmodic bile, and hardly able to crawl from my bed to the sofa. But how were you treated? Send me more Particulars in your next. If indeed a simple sprain, as you denominate it, nothing would have been so judicious as friction, friction by the hand alone, supposing it could be applied *instantly*. Two years ago I happened to be calling on Mrs. Sheldon when her coachman sprained his foot as he was cleaning the carriage and could hardly limp into the house, but by the immediate use of friction alone steadily persevered in (and I rubbed his ankle with my own hand for six hours without intermission) he was well in three days. Many thanks, my dear Tom, for the kindness with respect to us, which had so large a share in bringing on your accident. But pray never run into peril again in looking for an apothecary on our account, for had you the most experienced man in his line settled at Sanditon, it would be no recommendation to us. We have entirely done with the whole medical tribe. We have consulted physician after physician in vain, till we are quite convinced that they can do nothing for us and that we must trust to our own knowledge of our own wretched constitutions for any relief. But if you think it advisable for the interest of the *place*, to get a medical man there, I will undertake the commission with pleasure, and have no doubt of succeeding. I could soon put the necessary irons in the fire. As for getting to Sanditon myself, it is quite an impossibility. I grieve to say that I dare not attempt it, but my feelings tell me too plainly that, in my present state, the sea air would probably be the death of me. And neither of my dear companions will leave me or I would promote their going down to you for a fortnight. But in truth, I doubt whether Susan's nerves would be equal to the effort. She has been suffering much from the headache, and six leeches a day for ten days together relieved her so little that we thought it right to change our measures, and being convinced on examination that much of the evil lay in her gum, I persuaded her to attack the disorder there. She has accordingly had three teeth drawn, and is decidedly better, but her nerves are a good deal deranged. She can only speak in a whisper and fainted away twice this morning on poor Arthur's trying to suppress a cough. He, I am happy to say, is tolerably well though more languid than I like and I fear for his liver. I have heard nothing of Sidney since your being together in town, but conclude his scheme to the Isle of Wight has not taken place or we should have seen him in his way. Most sincerely do we wish you a good season at Sanditon, and though we cannot contribute to your

Beau Monde in person, we are doing our utmost to send you company worth having and think we may safely reckon on securing you two large families, one a rich West Indian from Surrey, the other a most respectable Girls Boarding School, or Academy, from Camberwell. I will not tell you how many people I have employed in the business—Wheel within wheel—but success more than repays. Yours most affectionately."

"Well," said Mr. Parker, as he finished. "Though I dare say Sidney might find something extremely entertaining in this letter and make us laugh for half an hour together, I declare *I*, by myself, can see nothing in it but what is either very pitiable or very creditable. With all their sufferings, you perceive how much they are occupied in promoting the good of others! So anxious for Sanditon! Two large families one for Prospect House probably, the other for Number two Denham place or the end house of the Terrace, with extra beds at the hotel. I told you my sister were excellent women, Miss Heywood."

"And I am sure they must be very extraordinary ones," said Charlotte. "I am astonished at the cheerful style of the letter, considering the state in which both sisters appear to be. Three teeth drawn at once—frightful! Your sister Diana seems almost as ill as possible, but those three teeth of your sister Susan's are more distressing than all the rest."

"Oh, they are so used to the operation—to every operation—and have such fortitude!"

"Your sisters know what they are about, I dare say, but their measures seem to touch on extremes. I feel that in any illness *I* should be so anxious for professional advice, so very little venturesome for myself or anybody I loved! But then, *we* have been so healthy a family that I can be no judge of what the habit of self-doctoring may do."

"Why to own the truth," said Mrs. Parker, "I do think the Miss Parkers carry it too far sometimes. And so do you, my love, you know. You often think they would be better if they would leave themselves more alone and especially Arthur. I know you think it a great pity they should give *him* such a turn for being ill."

"Well, well, my dear Mary, I grant you, it *is* unfortunate for poor Arthur that at his time of life he should be encouraged to give way to indisposition. It *is* bad that he should be fancying himself too sickly for any profession and sit down at one and twenty, on the interest of his own little fortune, without any idea of attempting to improve it or of engaging in any occupation that may be of use to himself or others. But let us talk of pleasanter things. These two large families are just what we wanted. But here is something at hand pleasanter still—Morgan with his 'Dinner on table.'"

Chapter 6

The party were very soon moving after dinner. Mr. Parker could not be satisfied without an early visit to the library and the library subscription book; and Charlotte was glad to see as much and as quickly as possible where all was new. They were out in the very quietest part of a watering-place day, when the important business of dinner or of sitting after dinner was going on in almost every inhabited lodging. Here and there might be seen a solitary elderly man, who was forced to move early and walk for health; but in general, it was a thorough pause of company, it was emptiness and tranquillity on the Terrace, the cliffs and the sands.

The shops were deserted. The straw hats and pendant lace seemed left to their fate both within the house and without, and Mrs. Whitby at the library was sitting in her inner room, reading one of her own novels for want of employment. The list of subscribers was but commonplace. The Lady Denham, Miss Brereton, Mr. and Mrs. Parker, Sir Edward Denham and Miss Denham, whose names might be said to lead off the season, were followed by nothing better than: Mrs. Mathews, Miss Mathews, Miss E. Mathews, Miss H. Mathews; Dr. and Mrs. Brown; Mr. Richard Pratt; Lieutenant Smith R.N.; Captain Little Limehouse; Mrs. Jane Fisher, Miss Fisher, Miss Scroggs; Reverend Mr. Hanking; Mr. Beard, Solicitor, Grays Inn; Mrs. Davis and Miss Merryweather.

Mr. Parker could not but feel that the list was not only without distinction but less numerous than he had hoped. It was but July, however, and August and September were the months. And besides, the promised large families from Surrey and Camberwell were an ever-ready consolation.

Mrs. Whitby came forward without delay from her literary recess, delighted to see Mr. Parker, whose manners recommended him to everybody, and they were fully occupied in their various civilities and communications, while Charlotte, having added her name to the list as the first offering to the success of the season, was busy in some immediate purchases for the further good of everybody, as soon as Miss Whitby could be hurried down from her toilette, with all her glossy curls and smart trinkets, to wait on her.

The library, of course, afforded everything: all the useless things in the world that could not be done without; and among so many pretty temptations, and with so much good will for Mr. Parker to encourage expenditure, Charlotte began to feel that she must check herself—or rather she reflected that at two and twenty there could be no excuse for her doing otherwise— and that it would not do for her to be spending all her money the very first evening. She took up a book; it happened to be a volume of *Camilla*. She had not *Camilla's* youth, and had no intention of having her distress; so, she turned from the drawers of rings and brooches, repressed further solicitation and paid for what she had bought.

For her particular gratification, they were then to take a turn on the cliff; but as they quitted the library they were met by two ladies whose arrival made an alteration necessary: Lady Denham and Miss Brereton. They had been to Trafalgar House and been directed thence to the library; and though Lady Denham was a great deal too active to regard the walk of a mile as anything requiring rest, and talked of going home again directly, the Parkers knew that to be pressed into their house and obliged to take her tea with them would suit her best; and therefore the stroll on the cliff gave way to an immediate return home.

"No, no," said her Ladyship. "I will not have you hurry your tea on my account. I know you like your tea late. My early hours are not to put my neighbours to inconvenience. No, no, Miss Clara and I will get back to our own tea. We came out with no other thought. We wanted just to see you and make sure of your being really come, but we get back to our own tea."

She went on however towards Trafalgar House and took possession of the drawing room very quietly without seeming to hear a word of Mrs. Parker's orders to the servant, as they entered, to bring tea directly. Charlotte was fully consoled for the loss of her walk by finding herself in company with those whom the conversation of the morning had given her a great curiosity to see. She observed them well. Lady Denham was of middle height, stout, upright and alert in her motions, with a shrewd eye and self-satisfied air but not an unagreeable countenance; and though her manner was rather downright and abrupt, as of a person who valued herself on being free-spoken, there was a good humour and cordiality about her—a civility and readiness to be acquainted with Charlotte herself, and a heartiness of welcome towards her old friends, which was inspiring the good will, she seemed to feel. And as for Miss Brereton, her appearance so completely justified Mr. Parker's praise that Charlotte thought she had never beheld a more lovely or more interesting young woman.

Elegantly tall, regularly handsome, with great delicacy of complexion and soft blue eyes, a sweetly modest and yet naturally graceful address, Charlotte could see in her only the most perfect representation of whatever heroine might be most beautiful and bewitching in all the numerous volumes they had left behind on Mrs. Whitby's shelves. Perhaps it might be partly owing to her having just issued from a circulating library but she could not separate the idea of a complete heroine from Clara Brereton. Her situation with Lady Denham so very much in favour of it! She seemed placed with her on purpose to be ill-used. Such poverty and dependence joined to such beauty and merit seemed to leave no choice in the business.

These feelings were not the result of any spirit of romance in Charlotte herself. No, she was a very sober-minded young lady, sufficiently well-read in novels to supply her imagination with amusement, but not at all unreasonably influenced by them; and while she pleased herself the first five minutes with fancying the persecution which *ought* to be the lot of the interesting Clara, especially in the form of the most barbarous conduct on Lady Denham's side, she found no reluctance to admit from subsequent observation that they appeared to be on very comfortable terms. She could see nothing worse in Lady Denham than the sort of old-fashioned formality of always calling her *Miss Clara;* nor anything objectionable in the degree of observance and attention which Clara paid. On one side it seemed protecting kindness, on the other grateful and affectionate respect.

The conversation turned entirely upon Sanditon, its present number of visitants and the chances of a good season. It was evident that Lady Denham had more anxiety, more fears of loss, than her coadjutor. She wanted to have the place fill faster and seemed to have many harassing apprehensions of the lodgings being in some instances underlet. Miss Diana Parker's two large families were not forgotten.

"Very good, very good," said her Ladyship. "A West Indy family and a school. That sounds well. That will bring money."

"No people spend more freely, I believe, than West Indians," observed Mr. Parker.

"Aye, so I have heard; and because they have full purses fancy themselves equal, may be, to your old country families. But then, they who scatter their money so freely never think of whether they may not be doing mischief by raising the price of things. And I have heard that's very much the case with your West-injines. And if they come among us to raise the price of our necessaries of life, we shall not much thank them, Mr. Parker."

"My dear Madam, they can only raise the price of consumable articles by such an extraordinary demand for them and such a diffusion of money among us as must do us more good than harm. Our butchers and bakers and traders in general cannot get rich without bringing prosperity to *us*. If *they* do not gain, our rents must be insecure; and in proportion to their profit must be ours eventually in the increased value of our houses."

"Oh! well. But I should not like to have butcher's meat raised, though. And I shall keep it down as long as I can. Aye, that young lady smiles, I see. I dare say she thinks me an odd sort of creature; but *she* will come to care about such matters herself in time. Yes, yes, my dear, depend upon it, you will be thinking of the price of butcher's meat in time, though you may not happen to have quite such a servants' hall to feed as I have. And I do believe those are best off that have fewest servants. I am not a woman of parade as all the world knows, and if it was not for what I owe to poor Mr. Hollis's memory, I should never keep up Sanditon House as I do. It is not for my own pleasure. Well, Mr. Parker, and the other is a boarding school, a French boarding school, is it? No harm in that. They'll stay their six weeks. And out of such a number, who knows but some may be consumptive and want asses' milk; and I have two milch asses at this present time. But perhaps the little Misses may hurt the furniture. I hope they will have a good sharp governess to look after them."

Poor Mr. Parker got no more credit from Lady Denham than he had from his sisters for the object which had taken him to Willingden.

"Lord! my dear sir," she cried. "How could you think of such a thing? I am very sorry you met with your accident, but upon my word, you deserved it. Going after a doctor! Why, what should we do with a doctor here? It would be only encouraging our servants and the poor to fancy themselves ill if there was a doctor at hand. Oh! pray, let us have none of the tribe at Sanditon. We go on very well as we are. There is the sea and the downs and my milch asses. And I have told Mrs. Whitby that if anybody inquires for a chamber-horse, they may be supplied at a fair rate—poor Mr. Hollis's chamber-horse as good as new—and what can people want for more? Here have I lived seventy good years in the world and never took physic above twice and never saw the face of a doctor in all my life on my *own* account. And I verily believe if my poor dear Sir Harry had never seen one neither, he would have been alive now. Ten fees, one after another, did the man take who sent *him* out of the world. I beseech you Mr. Parker, no doctors here."

The tea things were brought in.

"Oh, my dear Mrs. Parker—you should not indeed—why would you do so? I was just upon the point of wishing you good evening. But since you are so very neighbourly, I believe Miss Clara and I must stay."

Chapter 7

The popularity of the Parkers brought them some visitors the very next morning; amongst them, Sir Edward Denham and his sister who, having been at Sanditon House, drove on to pay their compliments; and the duty of letter writing being accomplished, Charlotte was settled with Mrs. Parker in the drawing room in time to see them all. The Denhams were the only ones to excite particular attention. Charlotte was glad to complete her knowledge of the family by an introduction to them; and found them, the better half at least—for while single, the *gentleman* may sometimes be thought the better half of the pair—not unworthy of notice. Miss Denham was a fine young woman, but cold and reserved, giving the idea of one who felt her consequence with pride and her poverty with discontent, and who was immediately gnawed by the want of a handsomer equipage than the simple gig in which they travelled, and which their groom was leading about still in her sight. Sir Edward was much her superior in air and manner—certainly handsome, but yet more to be remarked for his very good address and wish of paying attention and giving pleasure. He came into the room remarkably well, talked much—and very much to Charlotte, by whom he chanced to be placed—and she soon perceived that he had a fine countenance, a most pleasing gentleness of voice and a great deal of conversation. She liked him. Sober-minded as she was, she thought him agreeable and did not quarrel with the suspicion of his finding her equally so, which *would* arise from his evidently disregarding his sister's motion to go, and persisting in his station and his discourse. I make no apologies for my heroine's vanity. If there are young ladies in the world at her time of life more dull of fancy and more careless of pleasing, I know them not and never wish to know them.

At last, from the low French windows of the drawing room which commanded the road and all the paths across the down, Charlotte and Sir Edward as they sat could not but observe Lady Denham and Miss Brereton walking by—and there was instantly a slight change in Sir Edward's countenance—with an anxious glance after them as they proceeded—followed by an early proposal to his sister—not merely for moving, but for walking on together to the Terrace—which altogether gave a hasty turn to Charlotte's fancy, cured her of her half-hour's fever, and placed her in a more capable state of judging, when Sir Edward was gone, of *how* agreeable he had actually been. "Perhaps there was a good deal in his air and address; and his title did him no harm."

She was very soon in his company again. The first object of the Parkers, when their house was cleared of morning visitors, was to get out themselves. The Terrace was the attraction to all. Everybody who walked must begin with the Terrace; and there, seated on one of the two green benches by the gravel walk, they found the united Denham party; but though united in the gross, very distinctly divided again—the two superior ladies being at one end of the bench, and Sir Edward and Miss Brereton at the other. Charlotte's first glance told her that Sir Edward's air was that of a lover. There could be no doubt of his devotion to Clara. How Clara received it was less obvious, but she was inclined to think not very favourably; for though sitting thus apart with him (which probably she might not have been able to prevent) her air was calm and grave.

That the young lady at the other end of the bench was doing penance was indubitable. The difference in Miss Denham's countenance, the change from Miss Denham sitting in cold grandeur in Mrs. Parker's drawing room, to be kept from silence by the efforts of others, to Miss Denham at Lady Denham's elbow, listening and talking with smiling attention or solicitous eagerness, was very striking—and very amusing—or very melancholy, just as satire or morality might prevail. Miss Denham's character was pretty well decided with Charlotte. Sir Edward's required longer observation. He surprised her by quitting Clara immediately on their all joining and agreeing to walk, and by addressing his attentions entirely to herself.

Stationing himself close by her, he seemed to mean to detach her as much as possible from the rest of the party and to give her the whole of his conversation. He began, in a tone of great taste and feeling, to talk of the sea and the sea shore; and ran with energy through all the usual phrases employed in praise of their sublimity and descriptive of the *undescribable* emotions they excite in the mind of sensibility. The terrific grandeur of the ocean in a storm, its glass surface in a calm, its gulls and its samphire and the deep fathoms of its abysses, its quick vicissitudes, its direful deceptions, its mariners tempting it in sunshine and overwhelmed by the sudden tempest, all were eagerly and fluently touched—rather commonplace perhaps, but doing very well from the lips of a handsome Sir Edward—and she could not but think him a man of feeling—till he began to stagger her by the number of his quotations and the bewilderment of some of his sentences.

"Do you remember," said he, "Scott's beautiful lines on the sea? Oh! what a description they convey! They are never out of my thoughts when I walk here. That man who can read them unmoved must have the nerves of an assassin! Heaven defend me from meeting such a man unarmed."

"What description do you mean?" said Charlotte. "I remember none at this moment, of the sea, in either of Scott's poems."

"Do you not indeed? Nor can I exactly recall the beginning at this moment. But you cannot have forgotten his description of woman—

'Oh! Woman in our hours of ease—'

"Delicious! Delicious! Had he written nothing more, he would have been immortal. And then again, that unequalled, unrivalled address to parental affection—

'Some feelings are to mortals given
With less of earth in them than heaven' etc.

"But while we are on the subject of poetry, what think you, Miss Heywood, of Burns's lines to his Mary? Oh! there is pathos to madden one! If ever there was a man who *felt,* it was Burns. Montgomery has all the fire of poetry, Wordsworth has the true soul of it, Campbell in his pleasures of hope has touched the extreme of our sensations—'Like angel's visits, few and far between.' Can you conceive anything more subduing, more melting, more fraught with the deep sublime than that line? But Burns—I confess my sense of his pre-eminence, Miss Heywood. If Scott *has* a fault, it is the want of passion. Tender, elegant, descriptive but *tame*. The man who cannot do justice to the attributes of woman is my contempt. Sometimes indeed a flash of feeling seems to irradiate him, as in the lines we were speaking of—'Oh. Woman in our hours of ease'—. But Burns is always on fire. His soul was the altar in which lovely woman sat enshrined, his spirit truly breathed the immortal incense which is her due."

"I have read several of Burns's poems with great delight," said Charlotte as soon as she had time to speak. "But I am not poetic enough to separate a man's poetry entirely from his character; and poor Burns's known irregularities greatly interrupt my enjoyment of his lines. I have difficulty in depending on the *truth* of his feelings as a lover. I have not faith in the *sincerity* of the affections of a man of his description. He felt and he wrote and he forgot."

"Oh! no, no," exclaimed Sir Edward in an ecstasy. "He was all ardour and truth! His genius and his susceptibilities might lead him into some aberrations but who is perfect? It were hyper-criticism, it were pseudo-philosophy to expect from the soul of high-toned genius the grovellings of a common mind. The coruscations of talent, elicited by impassioned feeling in the breast of man, are perhaps incompatible with some of the prosaic decencies of life; nor can you, loveliest Miss Heywood," speaking with an air of deep sentiment, "nor can any woman be a fair judge of what a man may be propelled to say, write or do by the sovereign impulses of illimitable ardour."

This was very fine, but if Charlotte understood it at all, not very moral; and being moreover by no means pleased with his extraordinary style of compliment, she gravely answered, "I really know nothing of the matter. This is a charming day. The wind, I fancy, must be southerly."

"Happy, happy wind, to engage Miss Heywood's thoughts!"

She began to think him downright silly. His choosing to walk with her, she had learnt to understand. It was done to pique Miss Brereton. She had read it, in an anxious glance or two on his side; but why he should talk so much nonsense, unless he could do no better, was unintelligible. He seemed very sentimental, very full of some feeling or other, and very much addicted to all the newest-fashioned hard words, had not a very clear brain, she presumed, and talked a good deal by rote. The future might explain him further. But when there was a proposition for going into the library, she felt that she had had quite enough of Sir Edward for one morning and very gladly accepted Lady Denham's invitation of remaining on the Terrace with her.

The others all left them, Sir Edward with looks of very gallant despair in tearing himself away, and they united their agreeableness—that is, Lady Denham, like a true great lady, talked and talked only of her own concerns, and Charlotte listened, amused in considering the contrast between her two companions. Certainly there was no strain of doubtful sentiment nor any phrase of difficult interpretation in Lady Denham's discourse. Taking hold of Charlotte's arm with the ease of one who felt that any notice from her was an honour, and communicative from the influence of the same conscious importance or a natural love of talking, she immediately said in a tone of great satisfaction and with a look of arch sagacity, "Miss Esther wants me to invite her and her brother to spend a week with me at Sanditon House, as I did last summer. But I shan't. She has been trying to get round me every way with her praise of this and her praise of that; but I saw what she was about. I saw through it all. I am not very easily taken in, my dear."

Charlotte could think of nothing more harmless to be said than the simple enquiry of "Sir Edward and Miss Denham?"

"Yes, my dear. *My young folks,* as I call them sometimes, for I take them very much by the hand. I had them with me last summer, about this time, for a week; from Monday to Monday; and very delighted and thankful they were. For they are very good young people, my dear. I would not have you think that I *only* notice them for poor dear Sir Harry's sake. No, no; they are very deserving themselves or, trust me, they would not be so much in my company. I am not the woman to help anybody blindfold. I always take care to know what I am about and who I have to deal with before I stir a finger. I do not think I was ever over-reached in my life. And that is a good deal for a woman to say that has been married twice. Poor dear Sir Harry, between ourselves, thought at first to have got more. But, with a bit of a sigh, he is gone, and we must not find fault with the dead. Nobody could live happier together than us and he was a very honourable man, quite the gentleman of ancient family. And when he died, I gave Sir Edward his gold watch."

She said this with a look at her companion which implied its right to produce a great impression; and seeing no rapturous astonishment in Charlotte's countenance, added quickly, "He did not bequeath it to his nephew, my dear. It was no bequest. It was not in the will. He only told me, and *that* but once, that he should wish his nephew to have his watch; but it need not have been binding if I had not chose it."

"Very kind indeed! Very handsome!" said Charlotte, absolutely forced to affect admiration.

"Yes, my dear, and it is not the *only* kind thing I have done by him. I have been a very liberal friend to Sir Edward. And poor young man, he needs it bad enough. For though I am *only* the *dowager,* my dear, and he is the *heir,* things do not stand between us in the way they commonly do between those two parties. Not a shilling do I receive from the Denham estate. Sir Edward has no payments to make *me.* He don't stand uppermost, believe me. It is *I* that help *him.*"

"Indeed! He is a very fine young man, particularly elegant in his address."

This was said chiefly for the sake of saying something, but Charlotte directly saw that it was laying her open to suspicion by Lady Denham's giving a shrewd glance at her and replying, "Yes, yes, he is very well to look at. And it is to be hoped that some lady of large fortune will think so, for Sir Edward *must* marry for money. He and I often talk that matter over. A handsome young fellow like him will go smirking and smiling about and paying girls compliments, but he knows he *must* marry for money. And Sir Edward is a very steady young man in the main and has got very good notions.

"Sir Edward Denham," said Charlotte, "with such personal advantages may be almost sure of getting a woman of fortune, if he chooses it."

This glorious sentiment seemed quite to remove suspicion.

"Aye my dear, that's very sensibly said," cried Lady Denham. "And if we could but get a young heiress to Sanditon! But heiresses are monstrous scarce! I do not think we have had an heiress here or even a co-heiress since Sanditon has been a public place. Families come after families but, as far as I can learn, it is not one in a hundred of them that have any real property, landed or funded. An income perhaps, but no property. Clergymen maybe, or lawyers from town, or half-pay officers, or widows with only a jointure. And what good can such people do anybody?—except just as they take our empty houses and, between ourselves, I think they are great fools for not staying at home. Now if we could get a young heiress to be sent here for her health and if she was ordered to drink asses' milk I could supply her and, as soon as she got well, have her fall in love with Sir Edward!"

"That would be very fortunate indeed."

"And Miss Esther must marry somebody of fortune too. She must get a rich husband. Ah, young ladies that have no money are very much to be pitied! But," after a short pause, "if Miss Esther thinks to talk me into inviting them to come and stay at Sanditon House, she will find herself mistaken. Matters are altered with me since last summer, you know. I have Miss Clara with me now which makes a great difference."

She spoke this so seriously that Charlotte instantly saw in it the evidence of real penetration and prepared for some fuller remarks; but it was followed only by, "I have no fancy for having my house as full as an hotel. I should not choose to have my two housemaids' time taken up all the morning in dusting out bed-rooms. They have Miss Clara's room to put to rights as well as my own every day. If they had hard places, they would want higher wages."

For objections of this nature, Charlotte was not prepared. She found it so impossible even to affect sympathy that she could say nothing. Lady Denham soon added, with great glee, "And besides all this, my dear, am I to be filling my house to the prejudice of Sanditon? If people want to be by the sea, why don't they take lodgings? Here are a great many empty houses—three on this very Terrace—no fewer than three lodging papers staring me in the face at this very moment, Numbers three, four and eight. Eight, the corner house, may be too large for them, but either of the two others are nice little snug houses, very fit for a young gentleman and his sister. And so, my dear, the next time Miss Esther begins talking about the dampness of Denham park and the good bathing always does her, I shall advise them to come and take one of these lodgings for a fortnight. Don't you think that will be very fair? Charity begins at home, you know."

Charlotte's feelings were divided between amusement and indignation—but indignation had the larger and the increasing share. She kept her countenance and she kept a civil silence. She could not carry her forbearance farther; but without attempting to listen longer, and only conscious that Lady Denham was still talking on in the same way, allowed her thoughts to form themselves into such a meditation as this:

"She is thoroughly mean. I had not expected anything so bad. Mr. Parker spoke too mildly of her. His judgement is evidently not to be trusted. His own good nature misleads him. He is too kind-hearted to see clearly. I must judge for myself. And their very *connection* prejudices him. He has persuaded her to engage in the same speculation, and because their object in that line is the same, he fancies she feels like him in others. But she is very, very mean. I can see no good in her. Poor Miss Brereton! And she makes everybody mean about her. This poor Sir Edward and his sister—how far nature meant them to be respectable I cannot tell—but they are *obliged* to be mean in their servility to her. And I am mean, too, in giving her my attention with the appearance of coinciding with her. Thus it is, when rich people are sordid."

Chapter 8

The two ladies continued walking together till rejoined by the others, who, as they issued from the library, were followed by a young Whitby running off with five volumes under his arm to Sir Edward's gig; and Sir Edward, approaching Charlotte, said, "You may perceive what has been our occupation. My sister wanted my counsel in the selection of some books. We have many leisure hours and read a great deal. I am no indiscriminate novel reader. The mere trash of the common circulating library I hold in the highest contempt. You will never hear me advocating those puerile emanations which detail nothing but discordant principles incapable of amalgamation, or those vapid tissues of ordinary occurrences, from which no useful deductions can be drawn. In vain may we put them into a literary alembic; we distil nothing which can add to science. You understand me, I am sure?"

"I am not quite certain that I do. But if you will describe the sort of novels which you *do* approve, I dare say it will give me a clearer idea."

"Most willingly, fair questioner. The novels which I approve are such as display human nature with grandeur; such as show her in the sublimities of intense feeling; such as exhibit the progress of strong passion from the first germ of incipient susceptibility to the utmost energies of reason half-dethroned—where we see the strong spark of woman's captivations elicit such fire in the soul of man as leads him—though at the risk of some aberration—from the strict line of primitive obligations to hazard all, dare all, achieve all to obtain her. Such are the works which I peruse with delight and, I hope I may say, with amelioration. They hold forth the most splendid portraitures of high conceptions, unbounded views, illimitable ardour, indomitable decision. And even when the event is mainly anti-prosperous to the high-toned machinations of the prime character, the potent, pervading hero of the story, it leaves us full of generous emotions for him; our hearts are paralysed. T'were pseudo-philosophy to assert that we do not feel more enwrapped by the brilliancy of his career than by the tranquil and morbid virtues of any opposing character. Our approbation of the latter is but eleemosynary. These are the novels which enlarge the primitive capabilities of the heart; and which it cannot impugn the sense or be any dereliction of the character of the most anti-puerile man, to be conversant with."

"If I understand you aright," said Charlotte, "our taste in novels is not at all the same."

And here they were obliged to part, Miss Denham being much too tired of them all to stay any longer.

The truth was that Sir Edward, whom circumstances had confined very much to one spot, had read more sentimental novels than agreed with him. His fancy had been early caught by all the impassioned and most exceptionable parts of Richardson's, and such authors as had since appeared to tread in Richardson's steps, so far as man's determined pursuit of woman in defiance of every opposition of feeling and convenience was concerned, had since occupied the greater part of his literary hours, and formed his character. With a perversity of judgement which must be attributed to his not having by nature a very strong head, the graces, the spirit, the sagacity and the perseverance of the villain of the story out-weighed all his absurdities and all his atrocities with Sir Edward. With him such conduct was genius, fire and feeling. It interested and inflamed him. And he was always more anxious for its success, and mourned over its discomfitures with more tenderness, than could ever have been contemplated by the authors.

Though he owed many of his ideas to this sort of reading, it would be unjust to say that he read nothing else or that his language was not formed on a more general knowledge of modern literature. He read all the essays, letters, tours and criticisms of the day; and with the same ill-luck which made him derive only false principles from lessons of morality, and incentives to vice from the history of its overthrow, he gathered only hard words and involved sentences from the style of our most approved writers.

Sir Edward's great object in life was to be seductive. With such personal advantages as he knew himself to possess, and such talents as he did also give himself credit for, he regarded it as his duty. He felt that he was formed to be a dangerous man, quite in the line of the Lovelaces. The very name of Sir Edward, he thought, carried some degree of fascination with it. To be generally gallant and assiduous about the fair, to make fine speeches to every pretty girl, was but the inferior part of the character he had to play. Miss Heywood, or any other young woman with any pretensions to beauty, he was entitled (according to his own view of society) to approach with high compliment and rhapsody on the slightest acquaintance. But it was Clara alone on whom he had serious designs; it was Clara whom he meant to seduce.

Her seduction was quite determined on. Her situation in every way called for it. She was his rival in Lady Denham's favour; she was young, lovely and dependent. He had very early seen the necessity of the case, and had now been long trying with cautious assiduity to make an impression on her heart and to undermine her principles. Clara saw through him and had not the least intention of being seduced; but she bore with him patiently enough to confirm the sort of attachment which her personal charms had raised. A greater degree of discouragement indeed would not have affected Sir Edward. He was armed against the highest pitch of disdain or aversion. If she could not be won by affection, he must carry her off. He knew his business. Already had he had many musings on the subject. If he *were* constrained so to act, he must naturally wish to strike out something new, to exceed those who had gone before him; and he felt a strong curiosity to ascertain whether the neighbourhood of Timbuctoo might not afford some solitary house adapted for Clara's reception. But the expense, alas! of measures in that masterly style was ill-suited to his purse; and prudence obliged him to prefer the quietest sort of ruin and disgrace for the object of his affections to the more renowned.

Chapter 9

One day, soon after Charlotte's arrival at Sanditon, she had the pleasure of seeing, just as she ascended from the sands to the Terrace, a gentleman's carriage with post horses standing at the door of the hotel, as very lately arrived and by the quantity of luggage being taken off, bringing, it might be hoped, some respectable family determined on a long residence.

Delighted to have such good news for Mr. and Mrs. Parker, who had both gone home some time before, she proceeded to Trafalgar House with as much alacrity as could remain after having contended for the last two hours with a very fine wind blowing directly on shore. But she had not reached the little lawn when she saw a lady walking nimbly behind her at no great distance; and convinced that it could be no acquaintance of her own, she resolved to hurry on and get into the house if possible before her. But the stranger's pace did not allow this to be accomplished. Charlotte was on the steps and had rung, but the door was not opened, when the other crossed the lawn—and when the servant appeared, they were just equally ready for entering the house.

The ease of the lady, her "How do you do, Morgan?" and Morgan's looks on seeing her, were a moment's astonishment; but another moment brought Mr. Parker into the hall to welcome the sister he had seen from the drawing room; and Charlotte was soon introduced to Miss Diana Parker. There was a great deal of surprise but still more pleasure in seeing her. Nothing could be kinder than her reception from both husband and wife. How did she come? And with whom? And they were so glad to find her equal to the journey! And that she was to belong to *them* was taken as a thing of course.

Miss Diana Parker was about four and thirty, of middling height and slender; delicate looking rather than sickly; with an agreeable face and a very animated eye; her manners resembling her brother's in their ease and frankness, though with more decision and less mildness in her tone. She began an account of herself without delay. Thanking them for their invitation but "*that* was quite out of the question for, they were all three come and meant to get into lodgings and make some stay."

"All three come! What! Susan and Arthur! Susan able to come too! This is better and better."

"Yes, we are actually all come. Quite unavoidable. Nothing else to be done. You shall hear all about it. But my dear Mary, send for the children, I long to see them."

"And how has Susan born the journey? And how is Arthur? And why do we not see him here with you?"

"Susan has born it wonderfully. She had not a wink of sleep either the night before we set out or last night at Chichester, and as this is not so common with her as with *me*, I have had a thousand fears for her. But she has kept up wonderfully—no hysterics of consequence till we came within sight of poor old Sanditon and the attack was not very violent—nearly over by the time we reached your hotel so that we got her out of the carriage extremely well, with only Mr. Woodcock's assistance. And when I left her she was directing the disposal of the luggage and helping old Sam uncord the trunks. She desired her best love with a thousand regrets at being so poor a creature that she could not come with me. And as for poor Arthur, he would not have been unwilling himself, but there is so much wind that I did not think he could safely venture for I am *sure* there is lumbago hanging about him; and so I helped him on with his great coat and sent him off to the Terrace to take us lodgings. Miss Heywood must have seen our carriage standing at the hotel. I knew Miss Heywood the moment I saw her before me on the down. My dear Tom, I am so glad to see you walk so well. Let me feel your ankle. That's right; all right and clean. The play of your sinews a *very* little affected, barely perceptible. Well, now for the explanation of my being here. I told you in my letter of the two considerable families I was hoping to secure for you, the West Indians and the seminary."

Here Mr. Parker drew his chair still nearer to his sister and took her hand again most affectionately as he answered, "Yes, yes, how active and how kind you have been!"

"The West Indians," she continued, "whom I look upon as the *most* desirable of the two, as the best of the good, prove to be a Mrs. Griffiths and her family. I know them only through others. You must have heard me mention Miss Capper, the particular friend of *my* very particular friend Fanny Noyce. Now, Miss Capper is extremely intimate with a Mrs. Darling, who is on terms of constant correspondence with Mrs. Griffiths herself. Only a *short* chain, you see, between us, and not a link wanting. Mrs. Griffiths meant to go to the sea for her young people's benefit, had fixed on the coast of Sussex, but was undecided as to the where, wanted something private, and wrote to ask the opinion of her friend, Mrs. Darling. Miss Capper happened to be staying with Mrs. Darling when Mrs. Griffiths' letter arrived and was consulted on the question. *She* wrote the same day to Fanny Noyce and mentioned it to her; and Fanny, all alive for *us*, instantly took up her pen and forwarded the circumstance to me, except as to *names*—which have but lately transpired. There was but *one* thing for *me* to do. I answered Fanny's letter by the same post and pressed for the recommendation of Sanditon. Fanny had feared your having no house large enough to receive such a family. But I seem to be spinning out my story to an endless length. You see how it was all managed. I had the pleasure of hearing soon afterwards, by the same simple link of connection, that Sanditon *had been* recommended by Mrs. Darling, and that the West Indians were very much disposed to go thither. This was the state of the case when I wrote to you. But two days ago—yes, the day before yesterday—I heard again from Fanny Noyce, saying that *she* had heard from Miss Capper, who by a letter from Mrs. Darling understood that Mrs. Griffiths had expressed herself in a letter to Mrs. Darling more doubtingly on the subject of Sanditon. Am I clear? I would be anything rather than not clear."

"Oh, perfectly, perfectly. Well?"

"The reason of this hesitation was her having no connections in the place, and no means of ascertaining that she should have good accommodations on arriving there; and she was particularly careful and scrupulous on all those matters, more on account of a certain Miss

Lambe, a young lady—probably a niece—under her care, than on her own account, or her daughters'. Miss Lambe has an immense fortune, richer than all the rest, and very delicate health. One sees clearly enough by all this the *sort* of woman Mrs. Griffiths must be: as helpless and indolent as wealth and a hot climate are apt to make us. But we are not born to equal energy. What was to be done? I had a few moments' indecision, whether to offer to write to you, or to Mrs. Whitby, to secure them a house; but neither pleased me. I hate to employ others when I am equal to act myself; and my conscience told me that this was an occasion which called for me. Here was a family of helpless invalids whom I might essentially serve. I sounded Susan. The same thought had occurred to her. Arthur made no difficulties. Our plan was arranged immediately, we were off yesterday morning at six, left Chichester at the same hour today, and here we are."

"Excellent! Excellent!" cried Mr. Parker. "Diana, you are unequalled in serving your friends and doing good to all the world. I know nobody like you. Mary, my love, is not she a wonderful creature? Well, and now, what house do you design to engage for them? What is the size of their family?"

"I do not at all know," replied his sister, "have not the least idea, never heard any particulars; but I am very sure that the largest house at Sanditon cannot be *too* large. They are more likely to want a second. I shall take only one, however, and that but for a week certain. Miss Heywood, I astonish you. You hardly know what to make of me. I see by your looks that you are not used to such quick measures."

The words "Unaccountable officiousness!—Activity run mad!" had just passed through Charlotte's mind, but a civil answer was easy.

"I dare say I do look surprised," said she, "because these are very great exertions, and I know what invalids both you and your sister are.

"Invalids indeed. I trust there are not three people in England who have so sad a right to that appellation! But my dear Miss Heywood, we are sent into this world to be as extensively useful as possible, and where some degree of strength of mind is given, it is not a feeble body which will excuse us or incline us to excuse ourselves. The world is pretty much divided between the weak of mind and the strong; between those who can act and those who cannot; and it is the bounden duty of the capable to let no opportunity of being useful escape them. My sister's complaints and mine are happily not often of a nature to threaten existence *immediately*. And as long as we *can* exert ourselves to be of use to others, I am convinced that the body is the better for the refreshment the mind receives in doing its duty. While I have been travelling with this object in view, I have been perfectly well."

The entrance of the children ended this little panegyric on her own disposition; and after having noticed and caressed them all, she prepared to go.

"Cannot you dine with us? Is not it possible to prevail on you to dine with us?" was then the cry. And that being absolutely negatived, it was, "And when shall we see you again? And how can we be of use to you?" And Mr. Parker warmly offered his assistance in taking the house for Mrs. Griffiths.

"I will come to you the moment I have dined," said he, "and we will go about together."

But this was immediately declined.

"No, my dear Tom, upon no account in the world shall you stir a step on any business of mine. Your ankle wants rest. I see by the position of your foot that you have used it too much already. No, I shall go about my house-taking directly. Our dinner is not ordered till six; and by that time I hope to have completed it. It is now only half past four. As to seeing *me* again today, I cannot answer for it. The others will be at the hotel all the evening and delighted to see you at any time; but as soon as I get back I shall hear what Arthur has done about our own lodgings, and probably the moment dinner is over shall be out again on business relative to them, for we hope to get into some lodgings or other and be settled after breakfast tomorrow. I have not much confidence in poor Arthur's skill for lodging-taking, but he seemed to like the commission."

"I think you are doing too much," said Mr. Parker. "You will knock yourself up. You should not move again after dinner."

"No, indeed you should not," cried his wife, "for dinner is such a mere *name* with you all that it can do you no good. I know what your appetites are."

"My appetite is very much mended, I assure you, lately. I have been taking some bitters of my own decocting, which have done wonders. Susan never eats, I grant you; and just at present I shall want nothing. I never eat for about a week after a journey. But as for Arthur, he is only too much disposed for food. We are often obliged to check him."

"But you have not told me anything of the *other* family coming to Sanditon," said Mr. Parker as he walked with her to the door of the house. "The Camberwell Seminary. Have we a good chance of *them?"*

"Oh, certain. Quite certain. I had forgotten them for the moment. But I had a letter three days ago from my friend Mrs. Charles Dupuis, which assured me of Camberwell. Camberwell will be here to a certainty, and very soon. *That* good woman—I do not know her name—not being so wealthy and independent as Mrs. Griffiths, can travel and choose for herself. I will tell you how I got at *her*. Mrs. Charles Dupuis lives almost next door to a lady, who has a relation lately settled at Clapham, who actually attends the seminary and gives lessons on eloquence and Belles Lettres to some of the girls. I got this man a hare from one of Sidney's friends; and he recommended Sanditon. Without *my* appearing however, Mrs. Charles Dupuis managed it all."

Chapter 10

It was not a week since Miss Diana Parker had been told by her feelings, that the sea air would probably, in her present state, be the death of her; and now she was at Sanditon, intending to make some stay and without appearing to have the slightest recollection of having written or felt any such thing. It was impossible for Charlotte not to suspect a good deal of fancy in such an extraordinary state of health. Disorders and recoveries so very much out of the common way seemed more like the amusement of eager minds in want of employment, than of actual afflictions and relief. The Parkers were, no doubt, a family of imagination and quick feelings, and while the eldest brother found vent for his superfluity of sensation as a projector, the sisters were perhaps driven to dissipate theirs in the invention of odd complaints.

The *whole* of their mental vivacity was evidently not so employed; part was laid out in a zeal for being useful. It would seem that they must either be very busy for the good of others or else extremely ill themselves. Some natural delicacy of constitution in fact, with an unfortunate turn for medicine, especially quack medicine, had given them an early tendency at various times, to various disorders; the rest of their sufferings was from fancy, the love of distinction and the love of the wonderful. They had charitable hearts and many amiable feelings; but a spirit of restless activity, and the glory of doing more than anybody else, had their share in every exertion of benevolence; and there was vanity in all they did, as well as in all they endured.

Mr. and Mrs. Parker spent a great part of the evening at the hotel; but Charlotte had only two or three views of Miss Diana posting over the down after a house for this lady whom she had never seen, and who had never employed her. She was not made acquainted with the others till the following day, when, being removed into lodgings and all the party continuing quite well, their brother and sister and herself were entreated to drink tea with them.

They were in one of the Terrace houses; and she found them arranged for the evening in a small neat drawing room, with a beautiful view of the sea if they had chosen it; but though it had been a very fair English summer day, not only was there no open window, but the sofa and the table, and the establishment in general was all at the other end of the room by a brisk fire. Miss Parker, whom, remembering the three teeth drawn in one day, Charlotte approached with a peculiar degree of respectful compassion, was not very unlike her sister in person or manner, though more thin and worn by illness and medicine, more relaxed in air and more subdued in voice. She talked, however, the whole evening as incessantly as Diana; and excepting that she sat with salts in her hand, took drops two or three times from one out of several phials already at home on the mantelpiece, and made a great many odd faces and contortions, Charlotte could perceive no symptoms of illness which she, in the boldness of her own good health, would not have undertaken to cure by putting out the fire, opening the window and disposing of the drops and the salts by means of one or the other. She had had considerable curiosity to see Mr. Arthur Parker; and having fancied him a very puny, delicate-looking young man, materially the smallest of a not very robust family, was astonished to find him quite as tall as his brother, and a great deal stouter, broad made and lusty, and with no other look of an invalid than a sodden complexion.

Diana was evidently the chief of the family, principal mover and actor. She had been on her feet the whole morning, on Mrs. Griffiths' business or their own, and was still the most alert of the three. Susan had only superintended their final removal from the hotel, bringing two heavy boxes herself, and Arthur had found the air so cold that he had merely walked from one house to the other as nimbly as he could, and boasted much of sitting by the fire till he had cooked up a very good one. Diana, whose exercise had been too domestic to admit of calculation but who, by her own account, had not once sat down during the space of seven hours, confessed herself a little tired. She had been too successful, however, for much fatigue; for not only had she, by walking and talking down a thousand difficulties, at last secured a proper house at eight guineas per week for Mrs. Griffiths; she had also opened so many treaties with cooks, housemaids, washerwomen and bathing women, that Mrs. Griffiths would have little more to do on her arrival than to wave her hand and collect them around her for choice. Her concluding effort in the cause, had been a few polite lines of information to Mrs. Griffiths herself, time not allowing for the circuitous train of intelligence which had been hitherto kept up; and she was now regaling in the delight of opening the first trenches of an acquaintance with such a powerful discharge of unexpected obligation.

Mr. and Mrs. Parker and Charlotte had seen two post chaises crossing the down to the hotel as they were setting off, a joyful sight and full of speculation. The Miss Parkers and Arthur had also seen something; they could distinguish from their window that there *was* an arrival at the hotel, but not its amount. Their visitors answered for two hack chaises. Could it be the Camberwell Seminary? No, no. Had there been a third carriage, perhaps it might; but it was very generally agreed that two hack chaises could never contain a seminary. Mr. Parker was confident of another new family.

When they were all finally seated, after some removals to look at the sea and the hotel, Charlotte's place was by Arthur, who was sitting next to the fire with a degree of enjoyment which gave a good deal of merit to his civility in wishing her to take his chair. There was nothing dubious in her manner of declining it and he sat down again with much satisfaction. She drew back her chair to have all the advantage of his person as a screen, and was very thankful for every inch of back and shoulders beyond her preconceived idea. Arthur was heavy in eye as well as figure, but by no means indisposed to talk; and while the other four were chiefly engaged together, he evidently felt it no penance to have a fine young woman next to him, requiring in common politeness some attention—as his brother, who felt the decided want of some motive for action, some powerful object of animation for him, observed with considerable pleasure.

Such was the influence of youth and bloom that he began even to make a sort of apology for having a fire. "We should not have had one at home," said he, "but the sea air is always damp. I am not afraid of anything so much as damp."

"I am so fortunate," said Charlotte, "as never to know whether the air is damp or dry. It has always some property that is wholesome and invigorating to me."

"I like the air too, as well as anybody can," replied Arthur. "I am very fond of standing at an open window when there is no wind. But, unluckily, a damp air does not like *me*. It gives me the rheumatism. You are not rheumatic, I suppose?"

"Not at all."

"That's a great blessing. But perhaps you are nervous?"

"No, I believe not. I have no idea that I am."

"I am very nervous. To say the truth, nerves are the worst part of my complaints in *my* opinion. My sisters think me bilious, but I doubt it."

"You are quite in the right to doubt it as long as you possibly can, I am sure."

"If I were bilious," he continued, "you know, wine would disagree with me, but it always does me good. The more wine I drink in moderation the better I am. I am always best of an evening. If you had seen me today before dinner, you would have thought me a very poor creature."

Charlotte could believe it. She kept her countenance, however, and said, "As far as I can understand what nervous complaints are, I have a great idea of the efficacy of air and exercise for them—daily, regular exercise—and I should recommend rather more of it to *you* than I suspect you are in the habit of taking."

"Oh, I am very fond of exercise myself," he replied, "and I mean to walk a great deal while I am here, if the weather is temperate. I shall be out every morning before breakfast and take several turns upon the Terrace, and you will often see me at Trafalgar House."

"But you do not call a walk to Trafalgar House much exercise?"

"Not as to mere distance, but the hill is so steep! Walking up that hill, in the middle of the day, would throw me into such a perspiration! You would see me all in a bath by the time I got there! I am very subject to perspiration, and there cannot be a surer sign of nervousness."

They were now advancing so deep in physics, that Charlotte viewed the entrance of the servant with the tea things as a very fortunate interruption. It produced a great and immediate change. The young man's attentions were instantly lost. He took his own cocoa from the tray, which seemed provided with almost as many teapots as there were persons in company, Miss Parker drinking one sort of herb tea, and Miss Diana another and turning completely to the fire, sat coddling and cooking it to his own satisfaction and toasting some slices of bread, brought up ready-prepared in the toast rack—and till it was all done, she heard nothing of his voice but the murmuring of a few broken sentences of self-approbation and success.

When his toils were over, however, he moved back his chair into as gallant a line as ever, and proved that he had not been working only for himself by his earnest invitation to her to take both cocoa and toast. She was already helped to tea, which surprised him, so totally self-engrossed had he been.

"I thought I should have been in time," said he, "but cocoa takes a great deal of boiling."

"I am much obliged to you," replied Charlotte. "But I *prefer* tea."

"Then I will help myself," said he. "A large dish of rather weak cocoa every evening agrees with me better than anything."

It struck her, however, as he poured out this rather weak cocoa, that it came forth in a very fine, dark-coloured stream; and at the same moment, his sisters both crying out, "Oh, Arthur, you get your cocoa stronger and stronger every evening," with Arthur's somewhat conscious reply of *'Tis* rather stronger than it should be tonight,"—convinced her that Arthur was by no means so fond of being starved as they could desire, or as he felt proper himself. He was certainly very happy to turn the conversation on dry toast and hear no more of his sisters.

"I hope you will eat some of this toast," said he. "I reckon myself a very good toaster. I never burn my toasts, I never put them too near the fire at first. And yet, you see, there is not a corner but what is well browned. I hope you like dry toast."

"With a reasonable quantity of butter spread over it, very much," said Charlotte, "but not otherwise.

"No more do I," said he, exceedingly pleased. "We think quite alike there. So far from dry toast being wholesome, I think it a very bad thing for the stomach. Without a little butter to soften it, it hurts the coats of the stomach. I am sure it does. I will have the pleasure of spreading some for you directly, and afterwards I will spread some for myself. Very bad indeed for the coats of the stomach, but there is no convincing *some* people. It irritates and acts like a nutmeg grater."

He could not get command of the butter, however, without a struggle; his sisters accusing him of eating a great deal too much and declaring he was not to be trusted, and he maintaining that he only ate enough to secure the coats of his stomach, and besides, he only wanted it now for Miss Heywood.

Such a plea must prevail. He got the butter and spread away for her with an accuracy of judgement which at least delighted himself. But when her toast was done and he took his own in hand, Charlotte could hardly contain herself as she saw him watching his sisters while he scrupulously scraped off almost as much butter as he put on, and then seizing an odd moment for adding a great dab just before it went into his mouth. Certainly, Mr. Arthur Parker's enjoyments in invalidism were very different from his sisters—by no means so spiritualised. A good deal of earthy dross hung about him. Charlotte could not but suspect him of adopting that line of life principally for the indulgence of an indolent temper, and to be determined on having no disorders but such as called for warm rooms and good nourishment.

In one particular, however, she soon found that he had caught something from *them*. "What!" said he. "Do you venture upon two dishes of strong green tea in one evening? What nerves you must have! How I envy you. Now, if I were to swallow only one such dish, what do you think its effect would be upon me?"

"Keep you awake perhaps all night," replied Charlotte, meaning to overthrow his attempts at surprise, by the grandeur of her own conceptions.

"Oh, if that were all!" he exclaimed. "No. It acts on me like poison and would entirely take away the use of my right side before I had swallowed it five minutes. It sounds almost incredible, but it has happened to me so often that I cannot doubt it. The use of my right side is entirely taken away for several hours!"

"It sounds rather odd to be sure," answered Charlotte coolly, "but I dare say it would be proved to be the simplest thing in the world by those who have studied right sides and green tea scientifically and thoroughly understand all the possibilities of their action on each other."

Soon after tea, a letter was brought to Miss Diana Parker from the hotel.

"From Mrs. Charles Dupuis," said she, "some private hand."

And, having read a few lines, exclaimed aloud, "Well, this is very extraordinary! Very extraordinary indeed! That both should have the same name. Two Mrs. Griffiths! This is a letter of recommendation and introduction to me of the lady from Camberwell and *her* name happens to be Griffiths too."

A few more lines, however, and the colour rushed into her cheeks and with much perturbation, she added, "The oddest thing that ever was! A Miss Lambe too! A young West Indian of large fortune. But it *cannot* be the same. Impossible that it should be the same."

She read the letter aloud for comfort. It was merely to introduce the bearer, Mrs. Griffiths from Camberwell, and the three young ladies under her care, to Miss Diana Parker's notice. Mrs. Griffiths, being a stranger at Sanditon, was anxious for a respectable introduction; and Mrs. Charles Dupuis, therefore, at the instance of the intermediate friend, provided her with this letter, knowing that she could not do her dear Diana a greater kindness than by giving her the means of being useful. "Mrs. Griffiths' chief solicitude would be for the accommodation and comfort of one of the young ladies under her care, a Miss Lambe, a young West Indian of large fortune in delicate health."

It was very strange! Very remarkable! Very extraordinary! But they were all agreed in determining it to be *impossible* that there should not be two families; such a totally distinct set of people as were concerned in the reports of each made that matter quite certain. There *must* be two families. Impossible to be otherwise. "Impossible" and "Impossible" were repeated over and over again with great fervour. An accidental resemblance of names and circumstances, however striking at first, involved nothing really incredible; and so it was settled.

Miss Diana herself derived an immediate advantage to counter-balance her perplexity. She must put her shawl over her shoulders and be running about again. Tired as she was, she must instantly repair to the hotel to investigate the truth and offer her services.

Chapter 11

It would not do. Not all that the whole Parker race could say among themselves could produce a happier *catastrophé* than that the family from Surrey and the family from Camberwell were one and the same. The rich West Indians and the young ladies' seminary had all entered Sanditon in those two hack chaises. The Mrs. Griffiths who, in her friend Mrs. Darling's hands, had wavered as to coming and been unequal to the journey, was the very same Mrs. Griffiths whose plans were at the same period (under another representation) perfectly decided, and who was without fears or difficulties.

All that had the appearance of incongruity in the reports of the two might very fairly be placed to the account of the vanity, the ignorance, or the blunders of the many engaged in the cause by the vigilance and caution of Miss Diana Parker. *Her* intimate friends must be officious like herself; and the subject had supplied letters and extracts and messages enough to make everything appear what it was not. Miss Diana probably felt a little awkward on being first obliged to admit her mistake. A long journey from Hampshire taken for nothing, a brother disappointed, an expensive house on her hands for a week must have been some of her immediate reflections; and much worse than all the rest must have been the sensation of being less clear-sighted and infallible than she had believed herself.

No part of it, however, seemed to trouble her for long. There were so many to share in the shame and the blame that probably, when she had divided out their proper portions to Mrs. Darling, Miss Capper, Fanny Noyce, Mrs. Charles Dupuis and Mrs. Charles Dupuis's neighbour, there might be a mere trifle of reproach remaining for herself. At any rate, she was seen all the following morning walking about after lodgings with Mrs. Griffiths as alert as ever.

Mrs. Griffiths was a very well-behaved, genteel kind of woman, who supported herself by receiving such great girls and young ladies as wanted either masters for finishing their education or a home for beginning their displays. She had several more under her care than the three who were now come to Sanditon, but the others all happened to be absent. Of these three, and indeed of all, Miss Lambe was beyond comparison the most important and precious, as she paid in proportion to her fortune. She was about seventeen, half mulatto, chilly and tender, had a maid of her own, was to have the best room in the lodgings, and was always of the first consequence in every plan of Mrs. Griffiths.

The other girls, two Miss Beauforts, were just such young ladies as may be met with, in at least one family out of three, throughout the kingdom. They had tolerable complections, showy figures, an upright decided carriage and an assured look; they were very accomplished and very ignorant, their time being divided between such pursuits as might attract admiration, and those labours and expedients of dexterous ingenuity by which they could dress in a style much beyond what they ought to have afforded; they were some of the first in every change of fashion. And the object of all was to captivate some man of much better fortune than their own.

Mrs. Griffiths had preferred a small, retired place like Sanditon on Miss Lambe's account; and the Miss Beauforts, though naturally preferring anything to smallness and retirement, having in the course of the spring been involved in the inevitable expense of six new dresses each for a three-days visit, were constrained to be satisfied with Sanditon also till their circumstances were retrieved. There, with the hire of a harp for one and the purchase of some drawing paper for the other, and all the finery they could already command, they meant to be very economical, very elegant and very secluded; with the hope, on Miss Beaufort's side, of praise and celebrity from all who walked within the sound of her instrument, and on Miss Letitia's, of curiosity and rapture in all who came near her while she sketched; and to both, the consolation of meaning to be the most stylish girls in the place. The particular introduction of Mrs. Griffiths to Miss Diana Parker secured them immediately an acquaintance with the Trafalgar House family and with the Denhams; and the Miss Beauforts were soon satisfied with "the circle in which they moved in Sanditon," to use a proper phrase, for everybody must now "move in a circle" to the prevalence of which rotatory motion is perhaps to be attributed the giddiness and false steps of many.

Lady Denham had other motives for calling on Mrs. Griffiths besides attention to the Parkers. In Miss Lambe, here was the very young lady, sickly and rich, whom she had been asking for; and she made the acquaintance for Sir Edward's sake and the sake of her milch asses. How it might answer with regard to the baronet, remained to be proved, but as to the animals, she soon found that all her calculations of profit would be vain. Mrs. Griffiths would not allow Miss Lambe to have the smallest symptom of a decline or any complaint which asses' milk could possibly relieve. Miss Lambe was "under the constant care of an experienced physician," and his prescriptions must be their rule. And except in favour of some tonic pills, which a cousin of her own had a property in, Mrs. Griffiths never deviated from the strict medicinal page.

The corner house of the Terrace was the one in which Miss Diana Parker had the pleasure of settling her new friends; and considering that it commanded in front the favourite lounge of all the visitors at Sanditon, and on one side whatever might be going on at the hotel, there could not have been a more favourable spot for the seclusion of the Miss Beauforts. And accordingly, long before they had suited themselves with an instrument or with drawing paper, they had, by the frequence of their appearance at the low windows upstairs, in order to close the blinds, or open the blinds, to arrange a flower pot on the balcony, or look at nothing through a telescope, attracted many an eye upwards and made many a gazer gaze again.

A little novelty has a great effect in so small a place. The Miss Beauforts, who would have been nothing at Brighton, could not move here without notice. And even Mr. Arthur Parker, though little disposed for supernumerary exertion, always quitted the Terrace in his way to his brother's by this corner house, for the sake of a glimpse of the Miss Beauforts, though it was half a quarter of a mile round about and added two steps to the ascent of the hill.

Chapter 12

Charlotte had been ten days at Sanditon without seeing Sanditon House, every attempt at calling on Lady Denham having been defeated by meeting with her beforehand. But now it was to be more resolutely undertaken, at a more early hour, that nothing might be neglected of attention to Lady Denham or amusement to Charlotte.

"And if you should find a favourable opening, my love," said Mr. Parker, who did not mean to go with them, "I think you had better mention the poor Mullins's situation and sound her Ladyship as to a subscription for them. I am not fond of charitable subscriptions in a place of this kind—it is a sort of tax upon all that come—yet as their distress is very great and I almost promised the poor woman yesterday to get something done for her, I believe we must set a subscription on foot, and, therefore, the sooner the better; and Lady Denham's name at the head of the list will be a very necessary beginning. You will not dislike speaking to her about it, Mary?"

"I will do whatever you wish me," replied his wife, "but you would do it so much better yourself. I shall not know what to say."

"My dear Mary," he cried. "It is impossible you can be really at a loss. Nothing can be more simple. You have only to state the present afflicted situation of the family, their earnest application to me, and my being willing to promote a little subscription for their relief, provided it meet with her approbation."

"The easiest thing in the world," cried Miss Diana Parker, who happened to be calling on them at the moment. "All said and done in less time than you have been talking of it now. And while you are on the subject of subscriptions, Mary, I will thank you to mention a very melancholy case to Lady Denham which has been represented to me in the most affecting terms. There is a poor woman in Worcestershire, whom some friends of mine are exceedingly interested about, and I have undertaken to collect whatever I can for her. If you would mention the circumstance to Lady Denham! Lady Denham *can* give, if she is properly attacked. And I look upon her to be the sort of person who, when once she is prevailed on to undraw her purse, would as readily give ten guineas as five. And therefore, if you find her in a giving mood, you might as well speak in favour of another charity which I and a few more have very much at heart—the establishment of a Charitable Repository at Burton on Trent. And then there is the family of the poor man who was hung last assizes at York, though we really *have* raised the sum we wanted for putting them all out, yet if you *can* get a guinea from her on their behalf, it may as well be done."

"My dear Diana!" exclaimed Mrs. Parker, "I could no more mention these things to Lady Denham than I could fly."

"Where's the difficulty? I wish I could go with you myself. But in five minutes I must be at Mrs. Griffiths', to encourage Miss Lambe in taking her first dip. She is so frightened, poor thing, that I promised to come and keep up her spirits, and go in the machine with her if she wished it. And as soon as that is over, I must hurry home, for Susan is to have leeches at one o clock which will be a three hours' business. Therefore I really have not a moment to spare. Besides that, between ourselves, I ought to be in bed myself at this present time, for I am hardly able to stand; and when the leeches have done, I dare say we shall both go to our rooms for the rest of the day."

"I am sorry to hear it, indeed. But if this is the case I hope Arthur will come to us."

"If Arthur takes my advice, he will go to bed too, for if he stays up by himself he will certainly eat and drink more than he ought. But you see, Mary, how impossible it is for me to go with you to Lady Denham's."

"Upon second thoughts, Mary," said her husband. "I will not trouble you to speak about the Mullinses. I will take an opportunity of seeing Lady Denham myself. I know how little it suits you to be pressing matters upon a mind at all unwilling."

His application thus withdrawn, his sister could say no more in support of hers, which was his object, as he felt all their impropriety, and all the certainty of their ill effect upon his own better claim. Mrs. Parker was delighted at this release and set off very happy with her friend and her little girl on this walk to Sanditon House.

It was a close, misty morning and, when they reached the brow of the hill, they could not for some time make out what sort of carriage it was which they saw coming up. It appeared at different moments to be everything from a gig to a phaeton, from one horse to four; and just as they were concluding in favour of a tandem, little Mary's young eyes distinguished the coachman and she eagerly called out, "It is Uncle Sidney, Mama, it is indeed." And so it proved.

Mr. Sidney Parker, driving his servant in a very neat carriage, was soon opposite to them, and they all stopped for a few minutes. The manners of the Parkers were always pleasant among themselves; and it was a very friendly meeting between Sidney and his sister-in-law, who was most kindly taking it for granted that he was on his way to Trafalgar House. This he declined, however. He was "just come from Eastbourne proposing to spend two or three days, as it might happen, at Sanditon" but the hotel must be his quarters. He was expecting to be joined there by a friend or two.

The rest was common enquiries and remarks, with kind notice of little Mary, and a very well-bred bow and proper address to Miss Heywood on her being named to him. And they parted to meet again within a few hours. Sidney Parker was about seven or eight and twenty, very good-looking, with a decided air of ease and fashion and a lively countenance. This adventure afforded agreeable discussion for some time. Mrs. Parker entered into all her husband's joy on the occasion and exulted in the credit which Sidney's arrival would give to the place.

The road to Sanditon House was a broad, handsome, planted approach between fields, leading at the end of a quarter of a mile through second gates into grounds which, though not extensive, had all the beauty and respectability which an abundance of very fine timber could give. These entrance gates were so much in a corner of the grounds or paddock, so near to one of its boundaries, that an outside fence was at first almost pressing on the road, till an angle *here* and a curve *there* threw them to a better distance. The fence was a proper park paling in excellent condition, with clusters of fine elms or rows of old thorns following its line almost everywhere.

Almost must be stipulated, for there were vacant spaces, and through one of these, Charlotte, as soon as they entered the enclosure, caught a glimpse over the pales of something white and womanish in the field on the other side. It was something which immediately brought Miss Brereton into her head; and stepping to the pales, she saw indeed and very decidedly, in spite of the mist, Miss Brereton seated not far before her at the foot of the bank, which sloped down from the outside of the paling, and which a narrow path seemed to skirt along—Miss Brereton seated, apparently very composedly—and Sir Edward Denham by her side.

They were sitting so near each other and appeared so closely engaged in gentle conversation that Charlotte instantly felt she had nothing to do but to step back again and say not a word. Privacy was certainly their object. It could not but strike her rather unfavourably with regard to Clara; but hers was a situation which must not be judged with severity.

She was glad to perceive that nothing had been discerned by Mrs. Parker. If Charlotte had not been considerably the taller of the two, Miss Brereton's white ribbons might not have fallen within the ken of *her* more observant eyes. Among other points of moralising reflection which the sight of this tête-à-tête produced, Charlotte could not but think of the extreme difficulty which secret lovers must have in finding a proper spot for their stolen interviews. Here perhaps they had thought themselves so perfectly secure from observation; the whole field open before them, a steep bank and pales never crossed by the foot of man at their back, and a great thickness of air to aid them as well! Yet here she had seen them. They were really ill-used.

The house was large and handsome. Two servants appeared to admit them and everything had a suitable air of property and order, Lady Denham valued herself upon her liberal establishment and had great enjoyment in the order and importance of her style of living. They were shown into the usual sitting room, well proportioned and well furnished, though it was furniture rather originally good and extremely well kept than new or showy. And as Lady Denham was not there, Charlotte had leisure to look about her and to be told by Mrs. Parker that the whole-length portrait of a stately gentleman which, placed over the mantelpiece, caught the eye immediately, was the picture of Sir Henry Denham; and that one among many miniatures in another part of the room, little conspicuous, represented Mr. Hollis, poor Mr. Hollis! It was impossible not to feel him hardly used: to be obliged to stand back in his own house and see the best place by the fire constantly occupied by Sir Harry Denham.

Novels by Jane Austen

Sense and Sensibility

Marianne Dashwood wears her heart on her sleeve, and when she falls in love with the dashing but unsuitable John Willoughby she ignores her sister Elinor's warning that her impulsive behavior leaves her open to gossip and innuendo. Meanwhile Elinor, always sensitive to social convention, is struggling to conceal her own romantic disappointment, even from those closest to her. Through their parallel experience of love—and its threatened loss—the sisters learn that sense must mix with sensibility if they are to find personal happiness in a society where status and money govern the rules of love.

Pride and Prejudice

Since its immediate success in 1813, *Pride and Prejudice* has remained one of the most popular novels in the English language. Jane Austen called this brilliant work "her own darling child" and its vivacious heroine, Elizabeth Bennet, "as delightful a creature as ever appeared in print." The romantic clash between the opinionated Elizabeth and her proud beau, Mr. Darcy, is a splendid performance of civilized sparring. And Jane Austen's radiant wit sparkles as her characters dance a delicate quadrille of flirtation and intrigue, making this book the most superb comedy of manners of Regency England.

Mansfield Park

The novel tells the story of Fanny Price, starting when her overburdened family sends her at age ten to live in the household of her wealthy aunt and uncle and following her development into early adulthood. From early on critical interpretation has been diverse, differing particularly over the character of the heroine, Austen's views about theatrical performance and the centrality or otherwise of ordination and religion, and on the question of slavery.

Emma

Emma Woodhouse is one of Austen's most captivating and vivid characters. Beautiful, spoilt, vain and irrepressibly witty, Emma organizes the lives of the inhabitants of her sleepy little village and plays matchmaker with devastating effect.

Northanger Abbey

The story's unlikely heroine is Catherine Morland, a remarkably innocent seventeen-year-old woman from a country parsonage. While spending a few weeks in Bath with a family friend, Catherine meets and falls in love with Henry Tilney, who invites her to visit his family estate, Northanger Abbey. Once there, Catherine, a great reader of Gothic thrillers, lets the shadowy atmosphere of the old mansion fill her mind with terrible suspicions. What is the mystery surrounding the death of Henry's mother? Is the family concealing a terrible secret within the elegant rooms of the Abbey? Can she trust Henry, or is he part of an evil conspiracy? Catherine finds dreadful portents in the most prosaic events, until Henry persuades her to see the peril in confusing life with art.

Persuasion

Twenty-seven-year old Anne Elliot is Austen's most adult heroine. Eight years before the story proper begins, she is happily betrothed to a naval officer, Frederick Wentworth, but she precipitously breaks off the engagement when persuaded by her friend Lady Russell that such a match is unworthy. The breakup produces in Anne a deep and long-lasting regret. When later Wentworth returns from sea a rich and successful captain, he finds Anne's family on the brink of financial ruin and his own sister a tenant in Kellynch Hall, the Elliot estate. All the tension of the novel revolves around one question: Will Anne and Wentworth be reunited in their love?

www.ingramcontent.com/pod-product-compliance
Lightning Source LLC
Chambersburg PA
CBHW080912190726
48294CB00009B/2063